rise of INK and SMOKE

PAM GODWIN
NEW YORK TIMES BESTSELLING AUTHOR

Copyright © 2026 by Pam Godwin
All rights reserved.
Interior Designer: Pam Godwin
Cover Artist: Pam Godwin
Editor: Fairest Reviews Editing

This is a work of fiction. Names, characters, places, and incidents are the product of the author's imagination or are used fictitiously, and any resemblance to actual persons, living or dead, events, or locales is entirely coincidental.
No part of this book may be reproduced in any form, except for the inclusion of brief quotations in a review or article, without written permission from the author.

Visit my website at pamgodwin.com

This is a spin-off of the **FROZEN FATE** trilogy.

The books must be read in order.
Hills of Shivers and Shadows #1
Cage of Ice and Echoes #2
Heart of Frost and Scars #3
Rise of Ink and Smoke - Spin-off

Content Warning

"You smell different when you're awake."
~ Eddie B, Whistler Canada

wolfson
PROLOGUE

One year ago

I sit in the hollow silence of my prison. No windows to the outside world. No lights to ruin the ambiance of hopelessness. No mouth-breathers to invade my hell.

Just me and my voyeuristic companion.

"Hello, Regret." I can't see a dirty godsdamn thing beyond the reach of my hand, but... "I know you're there."

Silent and cold, Regret stares back.

"Admiring my banging good looks again?" I stroke my full beard. "Four months in this cage, and I'm still a sexy beast. Jealous?"

No answer. Of course not. Regret doesn't speak. It seeps. Slithers around my rib cage. Crawls inside my lungs. It's the dark abyss squeezing my balls with clammy tentacles and yawning in my face, unimpressed.

"Serious question. Why are you so clingy? Got nothing better to do than lurk in the damn corner like a bad habit?"

Regret swells, filling my empty spaces.

I have a lot of those.

"I feel you smothering." I chuckle bitterly. "Breathing down my neck. Rubbing up inside me like a dirty dick. I get it. I fucked up. Is that what you want to hear?"

A chill pebbles my skin.

I shove off the musty mattress, needing movement. And a smoke.

Titties would be good, too. A couple of supple pillows to rest my weary head. Can't remember the last time I felt up a girl.

Never sounds accurate.

The room stinks of sweat and stale breath, of time stretching too thin, of Regret festering in my bowels.

I should be dead.

To think, if I hadn't thrown myself off that cliff, I wouldn't be trapped in a concrete room without basic necessities like smokes and titties.

Instead, I did the damn thing. I stretched out my arms like Caucasian Jesus, died for mythical reasons, and resurrected downstream, right into the manicured hands of Dr. Try-Hard.

Yeah. My captor is a medical doctor. Good for me. He mended the arrow wound in my arm, dragged me from the brink of death, and locked me in this tomb.

The best part? He has an unhealthy hard-on for the psycho who raised me. Like, he wants to *be* Denver Strakh.

As if.

Dr. Limp Dick is a cheap imitation. A dollar-store Dahmer. I've been here for four months, and he hasn't tried to rape me or eat me.

Why not?

Why keep me alive if not to fuck my heavenly body ten ways to Sabbath?

I inhale deeply and regret it immediately.

The damp air, ripe with mildew, carries a sharp bite of antiseptic.

Bleach.

Urine.

Blood.

Unthinkable fluids live in these walls.

How many people have died here? How many bodies have rotted down the drain?

I curl my fingers, pressing them to my nose. It's fine. I'm fine. I just need to think.

The facts are these. If I hadn't jumped, I'd be dead. I

would've starved with Frankie and my brothers. Or we would've crashed the plane and burned alive.

But I wouldn't have died alone.

Now you will. Regret fists my stomach. *You'll die a virgin. Caged. Forgotten. Alone.*

"What do you want from me? An apology?" My jaw tightens. "Want me to fall on my knees and beg for forgiveness? It won't change anything. They're dead. Everyone I love is dead, and I'm not. I wasn't supposed to make it out. Not without them."

My insides clench as Regret strengthens its hold.

"You love this, don't you? Watching me tear myself apart. Watching me drown in my mistakes."

Regret leans in, waiting.

"I know. You won't let me forget her. Or them. Or the last thing I said…"

I definitely tried to kill her. She's dead anyway. We all are.

The echo of my words scrapes through my skull like rusted iron.

"No." I grip my head. "That was a lie."

A cruel, desperate lie. One I needed Leo to believe.

I would never hurt Frankie. When I fired that gun on the cliff, I aimed wide, knowing I wouldn't hit her.

What if she believes the lie? What if she thinks you tried to kill her?

"She's smarter than that. She knows I only said it so Leo would put a hot one in my chest. But the moron didn't pull the trigger."

So I jumped.

And instantly regretted it.

I tried to break the fall, repositioned to absorb the impact, and narrowly avoided a jutting rock. I landed like a fucking baller. I mean, the river was brutal, but I survived. Obviously.

And now you're trapped. Regret drapes a phantom arm over my shoulders. *With me. Keeping me here. Feeding me.*

"I can't escape."

Don't pretend you want to escape me. The whisper retreats into the shadows. *When you're ready to talk again, I'll be here.*

I rake my fingers down my face, digging into my beard and filthy skin. I need to focus. I need to get the fuck out of here.

But where the hell is *here*?

The doctor flew me to this place. I was drugged out of my mind and half-dead as he hauled me from his plane to this outbuilding. But as consciousness flickered in and out, I saw...

Trees.

Real, breathing, towering trees. A whole line of them.

It was just a glimpse. A trippy, high-as-fuck peek at an evergreen forest against the snow-covered mountains.

Spruce trees, I think. Or hemlock. Thick at the base, their trunks partially buried under snowdrift, with dark green needles weighed down by heavy icicles that glistened like frozen dicks in the weak winter sunlight.

Maybe I imagined it.

I lived in the Arctic for twenty-three years. Or am I twenty-four now? Sure. Let's go with that. In my twenty-four years on this planet, I've never seen a tree outside of books and movies. I've never stepped beyond the hills of shivers and shadows.

Hoss is the only place I know.

But if I'm right and trees really do exist on the other side of these walls...

Toto, I don't think we're in Hoss anymore.

I'm below the tree line.

I escaped the Arctic Circle.

Except I'm not free.

Leaning against the wall, I consider masturbating to pass the time, but even that has lost its appeal.

Talking to Regret is even less stimulating.

Moments drift without count. No clocks. No sunlight. Just the occasional scratch of metal against concrete when the old man remembers to feed me.

The doctor has only visited twice, but the old man comes often. He never speaks. Never makes eye contact. His only job is to shove food and water through the bars and retreat before my eyes adjust to the brief light.

So I wait.

And pace.

Ten steps east to west. Twelve steps north to south.

Like I know which way is up.

I don't.

This sucks.

When the door opens again, daylight slashes my retinas like hot, serrated razors. I rear back, hissing and squeezing my eyes shut against the assault. The pain is immediate, a deep stab straight through my brain.

Every time with this shit.

Months in the pitch black has turned me into a damn mole person. If I had claws, I'd dig my way to freedom instead of sitting in a cold, damp corner, stinking like a grave.

Footsteps. Slow. Measured. The scuff of polished leather against dirt-covered cement. I don't need to see to know who it is. He smells like jet fuel and mental hospitals.

Not the old man.

The doctor.

The door swings shut, followed by the soft buzz of an overhead light.

Gods forbid he leaves that on when he's not here.

"Wolfson." His voice is silk dragged over steel, delicate with a slur of fang. "How are you feeling?"

"Like a million bucks. It's amazing what a pitch-black spa retreat can do for the skin." I crack my eyelids open just enough to see a blurry figure dressed in threads far too impractical for this shithole. "Can we talk about how fabulous the decor is? I especially love the total darkness. Gives it a torture dungeon vibe while conserving electricity. Five stars."

The doctor smiles like he's indulging a child.

I have that effect on people.

"You always have something clever to say." He approaches the bars that separate us, his fine wool coat brushing the grime-covered steel.

"Gotta have hobbies. Some people knit. Others kidnap and murder. I provide clever commentary for the latter. Did you know that of the nine people I've met in my life—"

"Nine?"

"Well, there was Denver, Leo, and Kody." I tick them off on my fingers. "My mother, Frankie, and two other women Denver kidnapped. That's seven plus you and the old man. Anyway, I've met nine people, and three of them were psychos. Thirty-three percent, man. What a fucked-up world we live in."

"How do you define psycho?"

"Rapists, pedophiles, kidnappers, murderers... Shall I keep going?"

His fingers twitch at his side as if holding back the urge to...

Touch me? Hit me? Prove he's all the things I not-so-subtly called him?

He hasn't hurt me yet, not directly. But that doesn't mean he won't.

I sigh into the silence. "If you could point me to the suggestion box—"

"You're not in the position to offer suggestions."

"Hear me out." I make a sweeping motion around me. "Candles. Just a few here and there. Ambient light would really add to the Gothic charm."

"So you can set yourself on fire?"

"Ew, no. Do I look suicidal?"

"You jumped off a cliff."

"That was a one-time performance. I never do anything—or *anyone*—twice. Try to keep up, Doc."

"You haven't asked why you're here."

"Figured you needed time to rehearse your villain monologue. Seems like your thing."

He hums, his blue eyes swirling with insanity. "Do you know what the heart does when deprived of light?"

"Gives up?"

"It adapts, beats slower, and conserves energy. But eventually, it weakens. It forgets how to be strong."

"Are you writing a self-help book?" I snap my fingers. "*The Kidnapper's Guide to Cardiology.* Might be a bestseller."

"You amuse me." His smile flattens.

"That makes one of us."

He reaches into his coat and removes a small, metallic object. The overhead light catches the piercing glint of it.

A scalpel.

My mouth dries, but I keep my expression bored.

"Is this when we start the fun part?" I roll my neck. "Because if you're planning on taking a kidney, I should warn you. I drink too much for mine to be valuable."

"I don't need your organs." He turns the scalpel between his fingers, thoughtful.

"Cool, cool. Because I'm kind of attached to them, and they're attached to me. We have a special bond."

"I need information on your family."

My pulse spikes. He sees it, his eyes darting to my throat.

"They're dead," I say carefully.

"You don't know that."

If he wants to torture me, this is how to do it.

He found me a few miles downstream from Hoss. He could've easily flown over our lost cabin in the hills and spotted Leo, Kody, and Frankie.

Is that where he goes when he's not here? Does he hurt them with that scalpel?

No.

Fuck that.

Holding onto any hope that they survived would put me at his mercy. I know this and still can't stop myself from asking, "Are they alive?"

"Answer my questions, and I'll answer yours."

"What questions?"

"Denver raised three boys, but only one is his biological son. Who is it?"

This is news to me, but something tells me he already knows.

"I could answer." I wet my lips. "But I'd hate to ruin your dramatic reveal."

"How generous of you. However, I prefer my revelations to be slow and dripping." His gaze sharpens. "Like blood from an open wound."

"Ah. So this is when you show off your wicked scalpel skills. Got it. Totally unnecessary, by the way. Not to mention, unhinged and—"

"Put your wrists in the shackles."

I glance at the handcuffs hanging on the bars between us, my pulse hammering. "If I don't?"

"I'll feed your brothers to the wolves in pieces."

"See, that's just rude." My voice shakes, but I force my expression into emptiness.

They're not alive. They're not alive. The twat is bluffing.

"Shackles, Wolfson."

"Proof of life, Doc." I cross my arms. "I need to see that all three are breathing and safe before I let you have your way with me."

Good thing he can't provide that proof because I'm not going anywhere near those cuffs.

He removes his phone, taps the screen, and angles it toward

me.

The air flees my lungs as I scan the online news article.

The fuck?

My heart stops and restarts.

I can't believe what I'm seeing.

No.

Fucking.

Way.

How is this possible?

"They're safe." He pockets the phone. "For now."

The threat pounds in my ears, shaking me to the core.

This changes everything.

I hesitate long enough to lose feeling in my face.

Are you there, God? It's me, your favorite atheist. Just want to say I'm sorry. I take back everything I said about you fucking goats and eating aborted babies. And all the other things, too. Sorry, sorry, it's just that... I need a teeny little favor. Get me out of this, and I'll tattoo your face on my chest. I swear on your Pepsi-with-the-wild-cherry Mother Mary. Please?

Silence.

Yeah.

That's the problem with talking to things that aren't real.

Slowly, I extend my arms and slip my wrists into the cold metal restraints. The cuffs snap shut, tight and unyielding. I suppress a shudder.

"Good boy." The doctor unlocks the gate and steps into the cage, slipping off his coat.

That's not good.

The chains allow me to turn, and I do, facing him head-on.

His fingers trail along my forearm, deceptively gentle. Then he rips open my shirt and presses the scalpel to my bare stomach.

I clench. Everywhere.

"Now," he murmurs, "let's begin."

Hours pass.

Eternal, excruciating hours.

My body twists and writhes, a pathetic attempt to escape the agony.

It doesn't work. It never does. Pain isn't escapable. It's the world I live in, the reality that defines every nerve, every vein, until I'm nothing but suffering incarnate.

wolfson

I see his lips moving, the crazy bitch, but whatever he says is lost to me. Doesn't matter. Words are for mortals. Pain is for gods. And right now, I am Lord of All That Hurts.

My skull pounds, reminding me I'm still alive when every rational part of me begs for death. Each cut sends another bolt of white-hot lightning through me, igniting fresh waves of torment and blurring my vision.

How fucked up is it that I ache for Hoss right now, for those years when Denver came into my room and fucked me raw in the name of fatherly love? Good times.

A few hours with Dr. Hack-'n'-Slash, and it already feels like a lifetime in hell.

I focus on his face, memorizing the details I will one day carve away with a blade.

My jaw locks, teeth grinding against the scream clawing in my throat. Tears slip past my control, burning hot trails down my cheeks, but I don't care. Let them fall. Let him think I'm broken. Let him think he's won.

My back bows, muscles seizing and locking, every inch of me on fire. It's impossible to force myself to relax. I can't loosen an inch of this iron-clad tension, but I try. Not for him. For me. For the moment when this ends, and I still have enough strength left to breathe and plot and survive.

When he finally pockets the scalpel and frees me from the shackles, I slump to the floor.

He knows I can't attack him. Each inhale stretches the cuts across my torso, slick with blood and gaping open. Each exhale is an assault from within, my body demanding me to surrender.

I won't.

I'll live just to remember this. Every second. Every slice. Every flicker of sadistic pleasure in his eyes.

When the time comes, I'll make him feel this pain.

All of it.

Tenfold.

Slowly.

"We'll talk again soon." He stands, wiping bloody hands on my ripped, discarded shirt. My only shirt.

"Can't wait."

The overhead light clicks off, and the door shuts, plunging me into darkness. Outside, the lock gives a final clunk.

He's gone.

Regret slithers across the floor, pausing to sniff my wounds.

I release a breath, and it feels like I'm forcing air from a punctured lung.

My heart is a raging monster in my chest, stomping so violently I can feel it in my gums. It's not fear. It's not rage. It's worse. It's more dangerous and crushing.

Hope.

They're alive.

Leo. Kody. Frankie.

They didn't just survive.

They escaped Hoss.

The doctor showed me more news stories on his phone, torturing me with videos of them, grainy and low-resolution, but I saw their faces.

I felt them.

A rush of static hits my bloodstream, spasming my fingers. I wanted so badly to reach through the screen and touch them.

They survived the Arctic. Frankie and my brothers are free.

Except they're not my brothers.

The truth came in pieces. Little incisions of information carved between swipes of the scalpel.

Leo is my cousin.

Kody is my uncle.

Denver, the man who raised us, the devil we all feared, is Leo's father and my uncle.

And my sperm donor?

I almost laugh, but the sound catches in my throat, too sharp to swallow. My lips might've curled into a grin if my face wasn't so wrecked with pain.

My father is Frankie's husband.

The cheating, two-pump-chump billionaire Monty Novak is my damn father.

I press my tongue against my teeth, biting down hard enough to taste iron.

Montgomery Strakh. That's his real name.

My father.

I wouldn't believe it if the doctor hadn't played the audio clips of my family discussing it in private. I heard their voices, their validations of our DNA.

It's too much. Too fucking much.

I want to roar. I want to laugh. I want to tear the truth out of my skin like shrapnel because what the fuck does it even mean? I spent my whole life not knowing who fathered me. How fitting that I learned the truth while being cut open during my own autopsy?

I let out a breathless, shuddering, maniacal laugh, my torso shaking and weeping blood. The pain lances through me, but it's distant now, nothing compared to the torture of my thoughts.

The doctor told me everything he knew about my family, and I told him nothing.

I won't be able to keep my silence next time. And there *will* be a next time. Many, many more.

He has terrible plans for my family and me. Delusional, mad-clown, chainsaw-massacre plans.

I don't know what to do with this information. I don't know how to save them.

"They escaped," I whisper. "They survived."

Now I must do the same.

jag

PROLOGUE

3500 miles away

The screen shatters in my grip, glass and pixels dying under my fist. I've already wiped the drives, but it's not enough. I have to make sure there's nothing left. No scraps. No fragments. No breadcrumbs for them to follow.

The laptop hits the floor, a final blow from my boot reducing it to a mangled corpse of circuits and plastic.

Controlled destruction.

Precision in violence.

The walls of my studio apartment close in, the air thick with the scent of sweat and burned hardware.

I should've seen this coming. I track everyone. I watch from the shadows, pulling their strings. I'm the ghost in their machines, the virus in their networks, the spider in their dark webs they don't even know they fear.

Yet somehow, they found me.

A miscalculation. A hairline fracture in my impenetrable firewalls.

I grin, seething.

They think they're omnipotent, but they have no idea what

jag

they've done. They stirred the waters and released the Kraken. They should've let the sleeping beast lie.

The law thinks it has me in its sights. I see them lurking outside, the unmarked cars and pathetic attempts at surveillance.

They think I don't know, don't see them, don't feel them breathing.

They don't know me at all.

They think I'm just another criminal, a hacker playing games.

I don't play games. I play god, and I'm vengeful as fuck.

They've been sniffing around my accounts, tracking the money trails, trying to pin something on me. Fraud. Cyberterrorism. Murder by proxy. Oh, they'd love to slap those labels on me and drag me into a courtroom.

The law is nothing but a crippled institution run by the weak to corral the strong. They want to put me behind bars? I'll burn their prisons to the ground.

I rip the cords from the wall, dragging my rig to the center of the room. The servers hum their last breaths as I take a sledgehammer to them. The sound is deafening, like breaking bones, like punching a reset button I never wanted to press.

Adios, California.

Time to go.

I grab the duffel bag already packed with cash, fake IDs, and burner phones. The .45 tucked against the fabric is more than a weapon. It's my promise to finish this with blood.

I'm ready. I've been ready.

Everything I need is in my head. Names, faces, crimes—the people I've been watching, tracking, and planning to erase from existence. I was careful. Methodical. But I got too close. Touched a nerve. And now they're hunting me.

I hunted them first.

Come for me, bitches.

They won't find me where I'm going.

Sitka, Alaska.

I own a small, unassuming tattoo shop there. A shell business I've been using to clean money and make my digital sins look pure and legal. It was meant to be a safe house, a place to disappear if the walls caved in.

Time to cash in on that contingency plan.

They think I'm running. Cowards run.

I vanish. Slip between the cracks. Become the thing they fear most. The thing that doesn't die.

As I stride toward the door, I take one last look at the carnage I'm leaving behind. Scattered wires. Destroyed machines. The gutted remains of an empire I built from nothing.

I'll rebuild.

Then I'll make them bleed. I'll engrave my vengeance into their bones. I'll burn their world to the ground and laugh as they choke on the ashes.

I grip the door handle, and my gaze lands on a photograph. The one I intended to shred.

It lies on the desk, the edges curled and the glossy finish dulled with time. My head pounds as I reach for it, unable to part with it.

With *her*.

My pretty little bird.

She shouldn't have this hold on me.

But she does.

She makes me feel. Reckless, terrible goddamn feelings. Feelings I don't have room for.

I hate her for that.

I want to hurt her for it.

Beat her.

Bind her.

Fuck her.

My jaw flexes as I shove the photo into my pocket, crumpling it in my grip. I should leave it. I should burn it along with the rest.

But I'm not done with her.

wolfson
ONE

Present day

The apartment at the rear of Kody's distillery smells like old wood and liquor. Since no one stays here, I sneak in on my breaks from the tattoo shop to nap or drink. Usually both.

In the back closet, I dig through Kody's favorite stash until my fingers wrap around the cool glass of a top-shelf vodka bottle.

The burn in my gut isn't from thirst. It's from everything else.

Everything I don't talk about.

Alcohol dulls the throb in the back of my skull. It makes memories feel like someone else's nightmares, distant enough I can pretend they aren't mine.

The more I drink, the easier it is to convince myself I'm just a guy killing time in a quiet room, not a man trying to slay the ghosts of hands that took, voices that taunted, and pain that never leaves.

I uncork the bottle and steal a long swallow, letting the heat sear a path down my throat. A few more gulps, and the buzz starts to kick in.

Just as I sink into a dope mellow, the apartment door bangs

open.

Fuck.

I come here to escape people, and that includes my nagging, overprotective family.

Ducking behind the closet door, I peer through the crack. My pulse thumps as I hold my breath, forcing my limbs to be still.

Monty and Kody stumble in with Frankie caught between them. Her red hair spills over Monty's arm as he clasps her nape and pulls her into a kiss.

Kody watches, his black eyes unreadable, but there's possession in the hands that encircle her waist as he hauls her against his grinding hips.

The air shifts, sizzling with raw, primal panting.

Fucking great.

I exhale slowly, pressing my back against the wooden panels, keeping my breath even.

Frankie moans softly, a whisper of sound amid the rustle of fabric, the scrape of belts unbuckling, and the wet sucking of mouths on skin.

Shut your eyes, pervert. Stop creeping on your dad and his—

Yep, that's his boner.

Right next to Kody's.

If they start sword-fighting, I'm out of here.

The room becomes an explosion of sensation. Low murmurs, the creak of the mattress, hushed gasps, and...

Now they're fucking.

My fingers tighten around the bottle. I can't ignore the cruel twist of envy and resentment knifing inside me. And something else. Not lust. Not exactly. It feels like yearning, the kind that digs deep and refuses to let go.

I spent twenty-four years with a pedophile and ten months with a homicidal surgeon.

Frankie killed Denver, and six months ago, I slaughtered the doctor. I cut him into bite-sized pieces and fed him to the wolves.

Now I'm free. Free to fuck and fall in love and be happy. But I don't know how to do any of those things.

I don't know how to move forward.

Shifting, I rest my temple against the doorframe and close my eyes.

wolfson

My body knows pain. It knows touches that end in bruises, broken bones, and stitches.

The contrast between what's happening in the next room and what I've lived through is suffocating. While they're shamelessly nude and groping one another, I can't take off my shirt in front of another person.

I despise the scars crisscrossing my torso. Some from Denver. Most from the doctor. My family doesn't know the worst of it. I don't tell them. What's the point? Monty already looks at me like he failed. Maybe he did. I don't need to remind him.

The bed groans, signaling Kody's climactic finish. As he retreats to the bathroom, Frankie and my dad continue to go at it.

Give her a break, old man.

Looks like he's killing her. Pounding her flesh. Sucking her face. Splitting her in half.

Should he be doing that while she's pregnant? She's not showing yet, but still. His stamina is both impressive and deeply disturbing.

And Kody? The creeper stands in the doorway of the bathroom, watching them with hooded eyes. Probably filing away her moans so he can savor them later like a feral, sex-starved Lycan.

Finally, they finish and stagger off to the bathroom. Water runs. Clothes are collected and donned. Amid it all, Frankie's melodic laughter makes me smile.

Until a deep grunt cuts through the space. Kody's voice, low and knowing.

I peer out just as Monty's head snaps toward the closet.

Of course, Kody knows I'm here. He has supernatural hearing, a souvenir he kept from our Arctic nightmare.

Without another word, he and Frankie slip out of the apartment.

"Come out, Wolf." Monty shrugs on his suit jacket and lowers to the bed.

I've never been shy about shit that makes other people uncomfortable. Sex. Death. The cringe in between. So I push open the door and step into the dim light.

He looks... *Off.* Sex-mussed black hair, silver at the temples. Expensive suit, slightly wrinkled. Blue eyes softer than usual. He's a handsome fucker. Like father, like son. But right now, he's chewing on the inside of his cheek, looking a little uncomfortable.

I can help with that.

"Relax, Dad. That wasn't the first time you raw-dogged my childhood trauma. I've seen you grunting and groaning in every position all over the island. Your technique isn't terrible, but if you want a performance review—"

"I don't." He shoots me a look, but there's no bite behind it. Just exhaustion.

"Don't act like you don't love an audience."

"Not from my son." He rubs a hand down his face. "We need to establish some boundaries."

"And miss out on this father-son bonding? We need a road trip. You, me, some hookers with hearts of gold. Think of the memories we'd make together."

His eyes go hollow, flashing with darkness and…

Shame.

What did I say?

Oh.

Right.

He cheated on Frankie once, while she was a prisoner at Hoss, and he's never forgiven himself. His hand clenches into a fist, jaw flexing like I just took a swing at him.

Well, shit.

"Kidding, obviously. I was going for inappropriate, not whatever the hell just happened to your face." I push out a laugh, too quick, too forced. "I mean, you wouldn't last five minutes in a car with me. Too much personality. You'd kill me before we hit the first motel."

"I would never hurt you, Wolf." His eyes laser into mine. "*Never.*"

"I know. *Jesus tits.* Lighten up." I cross the room and drop into the armchair facing him.

He's trying. I'll give him that. Since I met him, he's been making an effort. Trying to be my father. But there's too much distance between us, filled with twenty-four years of trauma and regret.

"So…" He rests his elbows on spread knees. "How's the tattoo shop?"

"Declan talks a lot. He's a great mentor, but there's no off switch. I could strap him to a wind turbine and power half of

Alaska."

"Talking with people can be exhausting."

"I don't mind the talking. It's the listening. I have selective hearing. It selects *fuck this conversation* every time."

He nods, waiting, probably wondering if this is one of those conversations.

I drag my nails along the arm of the chair, letting the tension stretch before I break it. "He said the other owner of the shop is in town. For good."

I've never met the elusive Jag Rath, but his name carries some serious street cred. People talk about him like he's the godfather of Sitka.

It's just cheap fear porn.

Everyone knows Monty Novak is the richest man in Alaska. He owns the whole damn state.

But the mention of Jag sparks something in Monty's eyes. Interest. Concern.

"Jag is the sole owner of your tattoo shop," he says. "He bought it anonymously many years ago and let everyone believe Declan was the owner."

"You know Jag?"

"I know of him."

Monty knows everything about everyone who comes and goes in this town, but he doesn't offer more.

"Come on. Tell me." I nudge his leg with my boot. "Is he actually scary, or is he compensating for a small dick?"

"Wolf." He sighs.

"Just trying to get a solid dick-to-danger ratio."

"You are..." He sighs again.

"I'm your flesh and blood. Like herpes, but worse."

"You're *mine*."

A surge of emotion singes my throat.

I shrug it off. "Cool."

"Look, I know you're trying to find your own way, and I respect that. But Jag Rath isn't someone you want to be involved with."

"Okay, daddy."

His brows furrow.

"I can handle myself." I stand, grabbing the vodka bottle from the closet.

"That's not the point."

"Then what is?"

"Your mental health."

I go still. "What about it?"

"I don't know how to be what you need. I wasn't there for you before. I can't change that. But I'm here now, and I need to know... What do you need from me?"

My chest constricts.

How long have I dreamed of hearing those words from a parent who cared enough to ask?

Never.

I never dared to dream of such a thing.

What am I supposed to say to him?

I could be honest. Just peel back my ribs, let the nightmares crawl out, and traumatize him until he's eating trauma for every meal. But I don't know how to bleed without making a mess.

So I do what I always do.

I smirk. "A million dollars, a private jet, and a harem of horny women."

He doesn't laugh. He just watches me with too-perceptive eyes.

"I don't know." I shift on my feet. "I guess... Just... Don't give up."

"Never."

"I'm gonna dip." I tip the bottle in a mock salute and turn toward the door.

He watches me go, his gaze burning between my shoulder blades. He wants to say more. Wants to tell me he cares. Maybe even that he loves me.

But he doesn't.

And that's fine.

Because I already know.

wolfson
TWO

The moment I step out onto the quiet street, I light a smoke. As the first drag hits my lungs, I shudder with relief. Nicotine threads through my veins, sanding down the toothy edges of my thoughts.

The vodka helps, too.

I take a long pull from the bottle and turn the corner, nearly stepping on a homeless man.

He sleeps in the doorway of a jewelry store, the windows dark. Closed for the night.

One eye slits open, his expression slack. Resigned.

As I dig through my pockets for money, his gaze narrows on my bottle of vodka.

"You think you need this more than I do?" I lean down. "I sold my soul to the devil for a woman, and I just watched my dad and my brother pull a train on that woman. But that's a regular Saturday. The unspeakable things I experienced in an outbuilding last year would break your mind."

He flashes a toothless grin and reaches for the bottle.

"Okay, fine." I release my grip. "You win."

He tucks it under his arm, and I continue along the sidewalk.

The small port town hums with the low murmurs of

conversations, the occasional growl of a passing engine, and the buzz of streetlights.

For twenty-four years, my world was the Arctic. Harsh. Unrelenting. A place where silence wasn't peace but survival.

Civilization is strange. Some aspects were easy to adopt. Warm meals don't taste like freeze-dried fear, and the wolves here wear sweaters, walk on leashes, and don't try to eat me.

But other things hit me out of nowhere.

Crowds. The sheer number of people, the way they move and crash their voices together in an overwhelming storm of noise, it's maddening. Terrifying.

Traffic lights and car horns spike my pulse, too. Enclosed spaces like tight hallways and packed rooms squeeze me like a coffin.

Then there are the unexpected things that sneak up. The scent of freshly cut wood reminds me of firewood back home. The twinkle of stars over the island reminds me of the vastness of the hills. Snow collecting in my hair reminds me of those long polar nights.

Nostalgia. It creeps in and knocks the wind out of me.

Pulling a beanie from my back pocket, I shove it on my head.

I like nights like this. When all is quiet, Sitka reminds me of the solitude in the Arctic, but... *Not.* Amid the glow of passing headlights and random greetings from strangers, I'm learning how to exist in a world that isn't trying to kill me at every turn.

Burrowing into my leather jacket, I tuck my hands into the pockets and head toward the tattoo shop, eager to start some new sketches. Maybe Sleeping Beauty in an opium den with bruises under her eyes and a needle in her hand. Or Cinderella's stepsisters holding knives and cutting off their toes to fit into a bloody slipper.

Nothing like a moonlit stroll straight into a dark and twisted fairy tale.

Then, like magic, she appears.

A princess.

A real-life, honest-to-gods princess in a wedding gown runs full speed down the street like she just fled a castle and a life she never wanted.

Layers of white satin billow around her in a shimmering cloud. The harbor lights catch on beads and sequins, making her sparkle like a magical godsdamn fantasy.

wolfson

Warm. For the first time in my life, I feel warm *everywhere.*

The wind plucks long hair from her bejeweled clips, whipping the gilded strands into a glorious tangle. Her huge, pale eyes brim with fear and determination, locking onto the darkness ahead as if she's chasing, or being chased by, something only she can see.

I stop in my tracks, utterly spellbound.

My first thought? She's a runaway bride. My second? She's the closest thing to a real Disney princess I've ever seen. My third? I have to follow her.

She moves fast, but I keep pace. My boots echo against the pavement as I trail behind her, curiosity pulling me forward. She doesn't glance back once, doesn't hesitate or falter. She's on a mission.

On the next block, I realize where she's leading me.

To the tattoo shop.

She throws open the door and vanishes inside. Cautiously, I follow, stepping over the threshold just in time to see her tearing through the place in a fury. She upends chairs, shoves aside furniture, her frantic hands searching, searching...

For what?

I don't have to wonder for long.

She dives behind the sofa and pops back up, holding a damn rifle.

"The fuck?" I've worked here for six months and didn't know that was there. "How did you find that?"

"I lived with the son of a bitch half my life." Her breath comes hard and fast, her entire body coiled. "I know where he keeps his weapons."

"I'm sorry. Who?"

"Me." A man steps out from the back room.

I don't know him. But I know of him.

Jag Rath.

The mysterious owner of the shop. The man I've only heard about in passing, a shadow daddy wrapped in urban legend.

He stands in the doorway, staring down the barrel of a rifle held by the princess in the wedding gown.

The guy is ridiculously good-looking in a cruel, rugged way. Makes me wonder if he's always been jaded or if life whittled him into this hard, unbreakable marble.

His light brown hair is thick, textured, and perfectly unkempt. Stubble frames a strong jaw. And his jeans... Hell, his denim fits him just right. He's broad, imposing, late thirties or early forties, and carries the aura of a man who has seen too much.

His gaze slides between the gun and the woman holding it. No fear. No surprise.

"Dove." His timbre is deep and growly. Dangerous.

So that's her name.

Dove.

It fits.

She doesn't lower the gun. If anything, her grip tightens.

"I'll kill you." Breath shudders out of her, and her voice cuts like a blade.

She means it. Every syllable drips with conviction and something deeper than anger.

Betrayal.

Heartbreak.

Reminds me of Frankie the day she watched the video of her husband—*my father*—banging another woman.

I step forward before my brain catches up with my body.

"This is awkward." I lean against the wall, arms crossed. "I usually prefer a little foreplay before the bleeding starts."

She angles her head just enough for me to see the fury blazing in those syrupy, honey-colored eyes. But I also see the hurt buried beneath it. And now I really want to know what the hell is going on.

"You must be Wolfson." Jag gives me a slow, violating perusal.

"Shut up, you fuck." She shuffles closer to him. "Look at me!"

"It's always about you, isn't it?" he drawls. "Poor little Dove."

"I loved him!" she shouts, her voice breaking. Then, softer, quieter, almost to herself, "I loved him. Why did you have to fuck him?"

Oh.

Oh.

This just got interesting.

Jag's expression doesn't change. He closes the distance, ignoring the gun she still aims at his chest.

"Go back to California, Dove." His tone is bored. "This isn't your scene."

wolfson

"I have nothing to return to." Her grip on the rifle trembles, her entire frame shaking. "You took him from me."

"He's a grown-ass man, capable of making his own choices."

Her lip quivers, and for the first time, her finger falters on the trigger.

Whatever this is, it's gutting her from the inside out.

"Look, I don't know who *he* is." I edge forward, prepared to disarm her. "But maybe shooting people isn't the best way to work through this?"

Jag lets out a humorless laugh. "Stay out of this, kid."

"Not a kid." I scowl. "Just the poor bastard who stumbled in on your public therapy session. Feel free to keep unraveling, though. Especially if it leads to a public hate-fuck."

Dove chokes. "We're not—"

"I can be persuaded." A mean smile tugs at Jag's mouth. "Now that you're single again…"

"Go to hell!" she shouts.

His features harden, and a beat of silence stretches between them, stiff and suffocating. I can't decide if he wants to kick her out or rip off her gown.

"Stop looking at me like that." She lifts the gun higher.

"Like this?" His gaze lowers down her body, giving her the same perusal he gave me.

"Stop," she spits. "You're my brother."

My eyebrows shoot up.

Wait.

What?

"And I thought my family was fucked up." I blink.

"*Step*brother." Jag's amber-gold eyes aren't warm like honey or whiskey. They're cold and threatening, like a predator watching from the tree line, deciding whether to pounce.

"We grew up together, you sick fuck." She lowers the gun, her shoulders collapsing as whatever this is sinks into her bones. "You were my guardian."

I hover at her side, completely enthralled, waiting to see if they'll unpack their shit or let it simmer.

"So that's it?" She flings out a hand. "You passed me off like I'm someone else's problem. Didn't even have the decency to tell me yourself."

Jag says nothing.

She nods as if expecting that. "Gavin decided an hour before our wedding to tell me he was in love with you. Imagine my surprise when he said your name. I didn't even know he knew you!" Betrayal blotches her pretty face. "Did you pay him to marry me? Tell me the truth."

My brain spins to keep up. Gavin? The fiancé? In love with Jag? I glance between them, searching for clarification. This is some toxic, kinky family drama, and I'm here for it.

"Gavin and I had a fling." Jag lifts a shoulder. "It was short and meaningless."

He says this after she confesses that Gavin is in love with him?

Harsh.

"You fucked your sister's fiancé." I raise an eyebrow at Jag. "Then fled town and skipped out on her wedding? Bruh. That's weak."

"Sorry, who are you?" Dove turns to me, giving me her full attention.

"I'm Wolf, official member of Team Dove." I grin in the glow of her honeyed glare. "You're doing great, princess."

She furrows her brows.

Jag's face remains indifferent, but a shadow flashes in his eyes. Annoyance? Homicidal rage? Hard to tell. I file it away for later.

"You're not telling me everything." She scowls at Jag. "Gavin said you paid him to date me. To marry me. He needed the money, so he agreed, but all this time, he's been in love with *you.*"

"Gavin's feelings aren't my problem."

"You're a real piece of shit."

"Yet here you are, following me to Alaska like a lost puppy."

That does it. Fury detonates in her eyes as she grips the gun tighter. "You always do this! You fuck my boyfriends. And my girlfriends. You ruin lives and walk away like nothing happened. The only person you care about is yourself!"

Rage steams off her as she trains the gun and starts to squeeze the trigger.

That's my cue.

I launch forward, grabbing her before she does something she'll regret.

She's small and fragile compared to my brothers whom I

fought my entire life. Taking her down is easy. Too easy. My arms wrap around her, and for a brief second, I register the warmth of her body and the velvety satin of her dress pressing against my skin. She smells soft and dreamlike.

My fingers dig into her arms, pinning her. She thrashes, seething, snarling, her fury vibrating against me.

This isn't what I expected tonight, but hell if I let her throw her life away.

I shouldn't be thinking about how beautiful she is, but I am. I'm obsessed with the beauty mark on her collarbone, the adorable little dot just begging to be kissed. She's all sequins, satin, and rage, a fairy tale princess turned warrior, and I don't want to let go.

She wrenches free, twisting from my grasp, and bolts for the door.

Jag shifts to go after her.

"Not a chance." I step into his path.

"Move."

"You're not going near her." My low tone delivers a steady command. Primal. Feral. *Do not fuck with me.*

That old familiar feeling rushes through me, swelling and heating, like I'm standing in the Arctic again, face-to-face with a bear, knowing there's no room for fear, only instinct.

My muscles coil, every inch of me alert and ready. I've fought for my life so many times, and I'll do it again.

Jag opens his mouth, but whatever he sees in my eyes makes his jaw snap shut.

That surprises me.

Most people don't take me seriously. They see the punk clothes, makeup, and theatrics. They don't know what lurks beneath the facade.

There's a wild animal inside me. An unpredictable, unflinching killer who spent hours cutting up a man and didn't feel a thing.

But Jag sees me. He looks past the fake smile and sees what others miss.

His eyes widen just a fraction, and he takes a slow step back. He's bigger and stronger but smart enough to recognize a madman when he sees one.

I don't break my stance. I don't blink. I just watch him back off, feeling the savagery inside me settle. For now.

Then I turn and chase after the princess for a second time tonight.

love

THREE

I yank on the stupid wedding gown, tripping over the ripped hem as I dart out of the tattoo shop. A hateful gust of cold air slaps my face, and I suck in a breath, missing the California sun.

I need to return to the pier.

When I flew into Sitka this afternoon, I walked thirty minutes from the airport to the harbor, hauling my backpack in this dress.

The bag contains everything I own.

Exhaustion forced me to hide it under the pier while I searched for Jag.

I need that bag. I need a place to sleep. And a meal. Beyond that, I'll figure it out.

I don't have money. Definitely not enough to travel back to Anaheim. Not that I have anything left there. I hate Gavin almost as much as I hate my brother.

My fingers strangle the rifle's strap on my shoulder. I didn't realize I was still holding it until now, but I don't loosen my grip.

It's the only thing protecting me. The only thing keeping people away. I don't trust anyone. Gavin was an exception, a mistake I'll never make again.

My pulse rattles as I hurry along the vacant streets, seeking the shadows. Most businesses are closed for the night, the windows and doors draped in darkness. Except for the occasional bar and liquor store, it's a ghost town. Too quiet. The slap of my footfalls could be heard in Canada. Or wherever Jag is lurking.

Up ahead, a man leans against the corner of a building, a cigarette lighting up his features in ember-red pulses.

Luminous eyes study me through a curtain of heavy lashes. Unnerving. Striking. Too unreal.

Black hair curls from beneath his beanie, his face both chiseled and soft, demonic and angelic, intimidating and beautiful on a level that wrings my stomach. He's so tall and lean, all careless grace and rebellion encased in black leather.

I recognize him instantly.

He followed me to the tattoo shop. Now he's here.

Still following me.

Jag knew his name. *Wolfson.* Does that mean he's a regular customer at the shop? Or an employee? Is he covered in ink under all that leather?

Why do I care?

"Not every day I see a bride running down the street with a rifle." His lips curve as he exhales smoke. "What's the verdict? Will there be a honeymoon or a homicide?"

I duck my head and keep walking.

He pushes off the wall, flicking his cigarette into the gutter. His boots silently hit the pavement as he falls into step behind me.

"I get it." His deep baritone rumbles with amusement. "The gown and gun combo makes you mysterious. Tragic, even."

I keep my gaze forward. *Ignore him.* Maybe he'll go away.

"Not much of a talker, huh?" His voice chases me like a shadow, full of unbothered charm. "Maybe you don't trust me. That'd be a shame. I'm full of great bad ideas."

I clutch the rifle harder, not sparing him a glance.

When I reach the harbor, I step off the sidewalk and slide down the embankment, careful not to slip on the rocks.

Crouching under the pier, I grope through the darkness until my fingers brush against the worn canvas of my backpack.

Relief washes over me. No one stole it.

I haul it up, sling it over my shoulder, and turn back toward

love

the street, where Wolfson stands above me.

The moonlight hits him just right, and for a moment, I'm taken aback.

He's so fucking beautiful but in every way that feels wrong. Like a broken angel with nowhere left to fall.

His black leather jacket molds to his physique, the edges decorated with metal spikes and chains. More black covers his long, muscular legs. A beanie slouches over his shaggy black hair, framing his features in shadows. His sculpted cheekbones reflect the light like cut glass.

Women in California spend hours contouring and injecting their faces to achieve the perfect, angular look he wears so naturally.

Lucky bastard.

Everything about him is both deliberate and careless. His tattered band tee, half-hidden beneath the leather. The heavy boots that seem built for running or wrecking things. The rings stacked on his fingers like stolen trophies. He radiates a strange, untamed energy that warns of trouble while begging for a closer look.

His vibe is a contradiction. Aloof yet all-consuming. A ghost with a heartbeat. A drifter hardened by life and wearing his ruin like an art form.

"Where to now?" His eyes—too blue, too *wolfish*—bore into mine. "Back to the airport?"

I push past with no destination other than away from this unsettling man.

"You sat on a plane in that dress?" He falls into step beside me, side-eying my ridiculous appearance. "Wore it all the way from California? That's commitment, Cinderella."

Cinderella?

I shoot him a questioning glower.

"There are two types. The one who flees the ball and the one who runs from her wedding. In both versions, she loses her slipper." He angles down as if trying to see my feet. "We know which Cinderella you are."

With a huff, I kick at the filthy, shredded skirt and pick up my pace.

I didn't lose a fucking slipper. But when Gavin confessed his betrayal this morning, I lost my ability to think straight. In a fit of rage, I booked the first flight to Sitka, maxed out my credit card to buy the ticket, and had fifteen minutes to pack a bag and catch the plane.

Maybe I could've changed clothes on the way, but fuck me, I savored the thought of confronting Jag in this dress.

Too bad I lost the nerve to paint the white satin in his blood.

But I haven't given up on my revenge. I'm not leaving this frigid hellhole until Jag pays for what he's done.

"So you don't talk to strangers." Wolfson strolls along at my side. "I respect that."

"Why are you following me?" I stop walking, cutting him a razored glare.

"You're the darkest, most vengeful Disney princess I've ever met." An infuriating grin transforms his gorgeous face.

"You meet a lot of Disney princesses?"

"No. I've waited my whole life for you."

I scoff, turn, and keep walking.

"All right, I'll bite." He trails behind, his voice all lazy curiosity. "What's the plan?"

I walk faster, scanning the dark streets, looking for a way to lose him.

"I know you're good at running. I can tell you've been doing it for years." He lights up another cigarette. "But eventually, Princess Bride, you'll have to stop."

Something twists in my chest. I don't like that he sees me. That he's reading between the lines of my silence.

"And when you do..." He bends closer, his growl dark and silken. "You'll need someone. Might as well be me."

My throat locks up.

No. I don't need anyone. Not now. Not ever.

"Not in this lifetime, Wolfson." I yank the rifle's strap higher on my shoulder and resume walking, refusing to acknowledge how deep his words land.

"My friends call me Wolf."

"I'm not your friend." I turn sharply down a side street, my heart hammering.

I need to lose him.

The alleyways are empty and unlit, the buildings looming with places to hide.

At the next corner, I race ahead, zigzag around multiple turns, and duck behind a dumpster, pressing myself into the shadows, listening.

Nothing.

Good. Maybe he's gone.

After several minutes of silence, I creep forward, my breath shallow.

The alley holds still, the path clear. As I turn to check the other direction, a hand snatches my wrist, yanking me backward.

My body collides with solid muscle, the scent of mint and cruelty filling my nose.

Jag.

"Running back to me already, Little Bird?" His fingers bite into my skin. "That was fast."

My breath halts. The air around us thins, the world shrinking. Blood pulses in my ears, frantic and rushing.

"Let go." I wrench away, lifting the rifle between us, the barrel aimed at his chest.

"You won't shoot me." He gives me those eyes. The melty, amber-gold bedroom eyes that enthrall everyone.

But not me. Not anymore.

I don't lower the gun.

"You won't. You never could." He slowly extends an arm, reaching for the weapon. "I'm all you have."

A chill snakes down my spine, and my muscles lock.

He moves too fast. One second, he's in front of me. The next, he's knocking the rifle from my grip. The impact numbs my hands as the weapon clatters to the pavement.

I rear back, but he's faster, his arm banding around my waist, his strength overwhelming. He lifts me off the ground, dragging me backward.

"Let me go!" I thrash and kick, bucking against his chest.

"Never." His lips brush against my ear, a menacing growl. "You belong to me."

Panic explodes. I claw at his arms, twisting, struggling, but his grip only tightens.

A sharp whistle cleaves the night air.

He whirls, his clutch faltering for half a second.

I slam my elbow into his ribs, and he grunts, his hold loosening. I drop to the ground and scramble for the rifle.

Just as my fingers close around it, he rips it away and springs to his feet. Panting, I roll onto my back and meet his soulless gaze. He stares back, aiming the gun at my face.

I'm fucked.

He used to love me, I think. When we were kids, when our parents died, he protected me like it was his purpose in life. Then everything changed. *He* changed.

He became this.

I let my head rest on the pavement and force my muscles to relax. Our eye contact hangs, throbbing with history and pain. So much pain it's hard to hold his gaze. But if he's going to kill me, I want him to look into my eyes as he does it.

His finger twitches on the trigger.

My lungs shrivel.

As I wait for my death, a shadow lunges from the darkness. Fast and silent, the silhouette crashes into Jag with a force of pure violence.

They hit the cement with a sickening thud, the impact echoing through the night like a gunshot. In a blur of limbs, they explode into a brutal, unrelenting brawl.

I don't realize it's Wolf until I see the glint of his eyes. He moves like a feral animal, his hand locking around Jag's throat, forcing him to the asphalt as his other hand holds a smoldering cigarette to Jag's bulging eye.

Stunned, my breath lodges in my throat. I've never seen anyone move like that. Not even Jag. Wolf's control is absolute, his fury ice-cold and calculated.

Jag seethes, his nails buried in Wolf's forearm, but Wolf doesn't lift that threatening ember. One twitch and Jag will lose his eyesight.

Gone is Wolf's playful smirk. In its place gleams something far colder, a face that doesn't belong in civilization.

"If you hurt her again, I'll break things that aren't meant to break." He bares his teeth, his features devoid of humanity.

He straddles Jag's chest as Jag widens unblinking eyes. If he blinks, his lashes will surely catch fire.

Jag might be stronger, but holy fuck, Wolf is ruthless. He's a maniac that Jag doesn't know how to fight.

The rifle lies beside them, and I grab it, removing the magazine, emptying the chamber, and tossing it out of reach. Since he knows I won't shoot him, no sense waving it around like a useless threat.

Jag manages to free an arm and reaches for the knife in his

love

boot.

But Wolf is faster. He grabs Jag's wrist and slams it against the pavement, the force so vicious I hear the bones crack.

Jag grunts, his head jerking back in pain.

"I warned you." Wolf clucks his tongue, returning the cigarette to Jag's eye. "You should've run when you had the chance."

For a horrifying moment, I think he intends to kill Jag. The way his fingers flex around Jag's throat, the smoke curling from that cig with pure, deadly intent, he's seconds away from finishing this.

I don't know if I want to stop him.

Jag has taken everything from me. He's hunted me, bullied me, stolen everyone I cared about, and twisted my life until every choice became a knot he tightened around my throat.

But as I watch Wolf strangle him, a different fear creeps up my spine.

Wolf isn't doing this for revenge.

He's doing it because this is who he is.

Jag's face turns red, but Wolf doesn't relent, his arm straining, making Jag suffer. When I take a step forward, Wolf finally relaxes his grip just enough for Jag to suck air.

"Say the word, Buttercup." Wolf lifts heartless eyes to mine. "Mercy or death?"

"Mercy."

"Remember this, Stepbro. She's far more forgiving than I am." Wolf rolls to his feet and shifts closer to me. "Don't make me regret letting you keep that pretty eyeball."

Jag slowly pushes himself up, clutching his broken wrist. Murder simmers in his eyes. His lips curl back, and a pained breath hisses past his teeth.

"You think this is over? You just made the biggest mistake of your life, freak."

Wolf doesn't react. Not outwardly. But the tension crackles between them, an unspoken war waging in the silence. Two predators staring each other down, locked in a standoff.

"You work for my shop?" Jag scoops up the rifle. "Guess what happens when you try to kill your boss."

"You're still breathing." A twitch bounces in the corner of Wolf's eye. "I went easy on you."

"Consider yourself unemployed." He turns to me with vitriol in his tone. "He isn't your hero, Dove. He's just another hungry wolf in the dark. Wolves don't save. They hunt."

"Walk away, Jag." My blood runs cold. "Before I change my mind."

I only need to say the word, and Wolf will kill him. I have no doubt.

Nodding slowly, Jag takes a measured step backward.

"Enjoy your victory. It won't last." He pivots and strolls into the shadows, leaving behind the promise of retribution.

Wolf remains unmoving, watching his retreat. Only when Jag fully disappears does he roll his shoulders and shake off the fight.

"Told you." He brushes blood off his knuckles and meets my eyes. "You need me."

love
FOUR

I run.

Where to? Hell if I know. This town's too small to outrun that fight.

Too small to outrun Wolf.

I don't trust him. He's ruthless and unpredictable. A savage beneath the lazy grin.

But he saved me.

And he lost his job in the process.

That complicates things.

Salty ocean air clings to my skin, mixing with a sheen of moisture. Am I sweating?

No, wait. It's drizzling.

Within minutes, a whispering mist slicks the streets in shimmering reflections of amber and blue, curling around the buildings like smoke.

The world feels hushed, blurred at the edges, and Jag is out there. Watching. Waiting. The thought unsettles me, careening my heart against my ribs.

He won't let this go. Not after tonight.

My stomach twists with hunger, but I can't eat until I find a job.

Should be easy. Every town has a mechanic shop.

Dragging my ruined dress through puddles, I jog past a bank, church, school, bakery, another church, multiple gift shops, chiropractor's office, another bank, another church, on and on until...

There!

The sign above the garage is faded, the letters curling from years of rain and wind. The place is locked up, the bay doors drawn shut.

Around back, there's a patch of grass, dry beneath an awning and hidden from the streetlights. A private place to bunker down for the night.

But first, I need out of this wet dress.

As I move toward the awning, the crunch of boots behind me sends a fresh spike of irritation up my spine. I don't have to look to know it's him.

"Ignoring me won't make me disappear," Wolf drawls.

While he's shockingly violent, he hasn't given me a reason to think he would aim that violence at me. The opposite, in fact. It's weird.

Men have not been kind to me, but I get the feeling that men haven't been kind to Wolf either.

I drop my bag under the awning and tug at the back of my bodice, my fingers slipping over the ties. They won't budge, and after a few minutes, my arms ache from the effort.

Goddammit.

"What are you doing?" His voice is closer.

"Changing." I turn my back to him. "Unlace it."

For once, silence.

I peer over my shoulder and find his mouth open and his brows raised. Finally, something that shuts him up.

"No," he growls.

"I can't reach."

"You're not stripping outside in public."

"There's no one here."

"There's me."

"Then don't look."

He scans the ground, my bag, and the awning, realizing my intention. "You can't sleep here."

"Says who?"

"Me."

love

"I don't have a choice."

"You do." He shifts to face me, his blue eyes burning into mine. "My broth...errr...uncle has an unused apartment at the distillery."

"Your brother? Or your uncle?"

"Both-ish."

"No thanks."

"What's the problem?"

"I don't like options that involve you or males you know. Go away."

"But *your* brother is an option?" He drifts closer, charging the air with his overbearing maleness. "You want to wake with a knife to your throat?"

I know he's right, but accepting his help feels reckless. I'd rather take my chances with Jag. Better the enemy I know than the one I don't.

"I have a better idea." He shrugs out of his jacket and drapes it over my shoulders. "Come to the island with me."

Heady notes of vanilla vodka, weathered leather soaked by rain, and a trace of tobacco overwhelm my senses. Wolf's scent. Masculine and dangerous, like a motorcycle ride through a thunderstorm.

I frown. "What island?"

"My father's." He motions toward the harbor. "Just across Sitka Sound."

"I don't know you."

"My father is Monty Novak. Google him." He studies his chewed fingernails. "Go ahead. I'll wait."

I pull out my phone, and the search results punch the breath from my lungs.

Monty Novak. The richest man in Alaska. His name is everywhere—business articles, interviews, photos of him standing beside world leaders and celebrities.

"This is *your* dad?" I lob a dubious look at Wolf.

"The captain of his yacht will confirm it."

"And this captain will take us to your dad's private island?"

"You'll be safe there."

"I don't need you to keep me safe."

"I know. You handled yourself like a shield maiden back there." Raindrops cling to his lashes, softening his eyes. "I was just there to make sure you didn't have to do it alone."

"Why?" Heat flares up my spine.

"She wants a reason," he mumbles to himself. "Right. Okay. I need to earn your trust. Let's see..." He paces in the rain, shoulders hunched in his black T-shirt. "Being alone sucks. That's the reason."

His expression contorts, revealing raw, unexpected vulnerability that pinches my chest. I expect him to leave it at that, but he doesn't.

"For twenty-four years, I was held captive by a psychopath in the Arctic Circle." He rubs a hand down his shirt as if massaging wounds beneath the fabric. "I've only been in civilization for six months."

His words penetrate my chest and punch the air from my throat. He says it so plainly, like it's just a fact of life, like it doesn't crack open the world beneath him.

"You're lying."

"Look up my brothers. Leonid and Kodiak. Same last name as mine. Strakh."

I hesitate before searching, and sure enough, their names flood the screen.

Kidnapped as children. Raised in isolation. Stranded until starvation and near death. Escaped on a plane after teaching themselves how to fly it.

A lifetime of horror buried under sensationalized headlines. It's all there. Including a heavily-reported missing persons case. Frankie Novak, wife of billionaire Monty Novak, was found alive one year ago when she escaped with the Strakh men.

I remember this story, but the details are fuzzy. Wolf's involvement doesn't ring any bells as I search on variations of his name. *Wolf, Wolfson Strakh...*

"Your name isn't mentioned in any of this." I glance up at him.

"Because I didn't exist." His lips flatten. "Not in records. No birth certificate. Not until my father aided in my escape six months ago and forged the documents to make me a legal citizen."

I study his face for deception, but there's nothing there except invisible bruises. The kind I know too well.

He's risking something by telling me this. I can feel it.

"My father can validate everything when we get to the

island."

I believe him. It's strange, but the truth shimmers in his eyes, and his jaw tenses like he's waiting for me to call him a liar again.

"Why do you want to help me?" I swallow.

"Because you need it."

He bends his knees, leaning in. Too close, his presence devours the space between us, making my pulse spike. This push and pull is suffocating and addictive. I don't trust him. I don't even like him. But I believe him when he says I'd be safer with him than sleeping in the dirt behind some mechanic shop.

I take a breath and exhale slowly. "Fine."

"Bullets *and* brains."

He grabs my backpack. Before I can protest, he takes my hand in his and tugs me down the street toward the harbor.

I try to pull free, but his fingers squeeze, keeping me from slipping away without hurting me. He moves with purpose as if this was already decided. I let him lead me, but unease coils in my stomach.

He lights a cigarette with his free hand, the glow illuminating his striking features.

The moment his lips wrap around the filter, I yank my hand from his, pluck the cigarette from his mouth, and take a drag.

"You don't strike me as a thief." His brows lift.

"You don't strike me as a rich boy." I exhale smoke into the night.

"You have no idea what I am, princess."

No truer words, and that's what scares me.

Doubt follows me down the pier, hitting on all cylinders as we approach the waiting yacht. The water laps against the dock, crooning a dark warning.

Am I making a fatal mistake?

I glance back toward the town. Jag will find me. He'll try to break me. More than he already has.

And Wolf just lost his job for me.

"How many islands are in Sitka?" I ask.

"Eleven-hundred-ish, but no one knows for sure."

More importantly, Jag won't know. If he figures out I left on a yacht, he'll have to search over a thousand unknown islands to find me.

I love those odds.

"I'll get your job back," I say reluctantly.

It's the least I can do.

"No. I will get my job back." His finger dives toward my nose. "You will stay away from him."

He boards the yacht, and I dig in my heels.

"Now what?" He pauses, pivoting to face me, hands on his hips.

"You can't expect me to just jump on a boat with a stranger."

"Well, now, that's exactly what I expect. Except I'm not a stranger. You know some of my innermost secrets."

"Some?"

"I can't dump my load all in one go. You gotta earn it, Gunslinger."

"Where's that captain you promised?"

"Kai!" he yells and gives me a patient smile.

Within seconds, a tall man in a suit emerges from the helm.

"Aye, aye, Captain Kai." Wolf waves him forward. "Where's my family?"

"They returned to the island on Kodiak's yacht. I was instructed to wait for you." The captain casts a quizzical look at my wedding gown and backpack. "Good evening, ma'am. Are congratulations in order?"

"Not yet," Wolf says cryptically. "Who do you work for, Kai?"

"Monty Novak, sir."

"And who is my father?"

"Sir?"

"Just answer the question. For whatever reason, the princess trusts the word of a complete stranger over mine, her one and only soul mate."

"Wise decision, ma'am." Kai winks at me and quickly clears his throat when Wolf levels him with a look. "Monty Novak sired this uncivilized creature. With much regret, I suspect."

"You're a gem." Wolf pats Kai's cheek. "Now go pretend you're Jack Sparrow and try not to crash us." To me, he holds out a hand. "Decision time, Annie Oakley."

Stalling, I stare at those long fingers.

If I turn back now, I'll never know what he's really hiding or what he sees in me that makes him so sure I'm worth helping.

This isn't about trusting him. It's about trusting myself to handle whatever comes next.

Safe has never given me a leg up. Maybe a risky ride into the unknown will.

Lifting my chin, I shoulder past him and board the yacht like my nerves aren't unfurling in rapid heartbeats.

Wolf leads me to the railing, the cold wind whipping my hair around my face. He openly stares at me from inches away, poking at my silence as if trying to pry me open. It only makes me want to close tighter.

"You always this moody, or is this just your honeymoon glow?" he asks.

"You always this annoying, or is this just my bad luck?"

"Nah, you caught me on a good night."

"Look, I just need a place to stay until I get my feet under me."

"So it's like that?"

"What else is it like?"

"So many possibilities, the most logical being that you're a princess, and I'm Prince Charming."

"You really don't know how normal people interact, do you?"

"Fuck normal. You're dressed for an epic adventure, and I'm at your side with a sword in my..." He looks down.

"Don't say it."

"Boot?" He lifts a pant leg, revealing the handle of a knife, before kicking the hem back in place. "Our fairy tale has already begun."

He leans on the railing beside me, cigarette dangling from his lips and a smirk ghosting his mouth like it's his default setting.

What a weirdo.

Possibly insane.

But no.

No, that's not it at all.

There's too much calculation in his sarcasm, too much intelligence in those ice-blue eyes. Maybe the whole nice-with-a-knife thing works on other people, but I'm well-versed in sugar-coated hostility. He's hiding something.

If what he said is true, if he spent his life in a psychopath's prison, then whatever he's showing me is only the surface.

A performance.

A deflection.

Under the cocky grin and flippant remarks, there's depth. Pain. Maybe rage. I don't know why that realization disturbs me more than his violence earlier. Maybe because it makes me want to understand him. To see what's behind that chaos-colored mask.

That's a problem.

I don't need more trouble in my life. I'm already neck-deep in it. I don't need a wild, beautiful, emotionally unstable man with a tragic past and a dangerous smile.

Too late now.

I'm on his yacht, moving through dark water toward an island I've never seen, with a stranger I should've refused.

The lights of Sitka grow dim behind us, swallowed by fog and sea. The island waits somewhere ahead, shadowed and ominous. Whatever's coming, I've already made my choice.

"You scare me," I admit, staring across the water. "But not for the reasons you probably think. Not in a bad way. More like…"

"Like?"

"Like someone who learned to survive by pretending they're bulletproof."

"Hm." He draws on the cigarette and sighs through the exhale. "What gave me away?"

"Smiling through your teeth. Grudges dressed as jokes. Acting like you know what you're doing, even when you don't. Rehearsed confidence. You carry yourself like someone who's been shot too many times to worry about the next bullet."

The haunted look in his eyes doesn't match the smile he gives me. "When I saw you run down the street like you fled a castle, I thought… Holy hellfire and heartbreak, I've stepped into a dark fairy tale. Your dress moved as if caught in a dream, flowing behind you as you ran. But it wasn't marital bliss that trailed you. It was sorrow. You looked like you were halfway to forever before the world yanked it out from under you. Doesn't help that you're insanely beautiful. Makes it that much harder to look away."

He should talk. The man oozes perfect genes from every pore.

"All I could think was…" He rests his forearms on the railing, shaking his head. "She shouldn't be real. Fairy tales aren't real. Not for people like me. But here you are. You're real. And being part of your story, even if just a small, insignificant part, has sent

love

me to a dimension of utter joy." He straightens. "We're here."

My breath hitches at his declaration. Then it hitches again as I take in the view.

The island rises out of the water, silent, hidden, and entirely otherworldly. Soaring evergreens blanket every inch, their canopies so thick they knit the sky shut.

In Anaheim, everything is sun-bleached and buzzing, with an overabundance of strip malls, traffic, and baking concrete.

Here, moisture and mystery saturate the air, swollen with the scent of pine, damp earth, and cold moss.

The gentle purr of the yacht feels intrusive as if it shouldn't be here.

Half-hidden in the trees, a stone mansion emerges from the shadows. Massive and still, it glows with the warmth of golden light that pulses behind tall windows.

The estate doesn't stand atop the island. It's cradled by it. Like the forest grew around it and decided to keep it.

The beauty here is rich and wild, much like the man at my side. The sort of beauty that comes with a warning, a trick of the light that lures unsuspecting souls and traps them forever.

I clutch the railing, my insides tumbling in free fall.

A dark fairy tale, indeed.

love

FIVE

Curiosity wars with misgiving as I follow Wolf into the mansion. The skirt of my once-white gown drags across the pristine floors like a dishwater mop.

The warm jacket lifts from my shoulders, and he hangs it in the entryway. Since he doesn't remove his boots, I keep mine.

And gape.

This isn't a house. It's a goddamn lifestyle flex. Stunning beams, massive glass windows, and high ceilings that feel like a cathedral if it were designed by a billionaire lumberjack with an inclination for moody art.

Fire dances in a stone hearth, licking the air with orange tongues. The living room, foyer, and rooms beyond are all designer shapes and rich-people textures. Pretty sure that twelve-person sectional would swallow me whole, and honestly, I wouldn't fight it.

Wolf doesn't give me enough time to admire each room properly as he pulls me along. His devil-may-care pushiness is both maddening and magnetic.

We climb a grand staircase. Real wood, thick and strong. Iron railing, cold under my fingertips. The air grows warmer as we ascend, more intimate.

love

Where is he taking me? A guest bedroom? I really need out of this heavy, wet dress.

He leads me down a hallway lined with closed doors and stops before one that's ajar. Glancing back at me with a mischievous smile, he swings it open and grabs my hand.

My muscles freeze.

He hauls me inside.

The smell hits first. Skin. Sweat. Sleep. And something deeper. Something feral.

Sex.

Then my eyes adjust to the darkness.

A massive bed squats in the center of the room. Like comically massive. Custom made.

The sheets are tangled in knots like they've been twisted and kicked and grabbed at. What makes my blood pressure detonate are the human-shaped lumps.

There are people in the bed. Multiple.

How many? Two? Three? Four?

I stumble back, my heels hitting the doorframe.

"Wolf," I whisper. "What the actual hell?"

Someone stirs. A huge, imposing, chiseled-from-pure-intimidation figure rises from the bed.

Black, bottomless eyes glare out of a face that doesn't smile. And he's naked. Just standing there in all his terrifying glory like a war god who doesn't need armor.

"Go back to bed, pet." Wolf waves him off, calm as ever.

Pet? That mountain of a man?

The fuck?

"Pssst, Frankie." Wolf paws through the bedding, searching.

A smaller form pops up and slips from beneath the sheets. A woman. Her movements are soft and elegant as she whispers to Wolf, too low for me to hear. She's naked, too, her silhouette barely lit by the hallway light.

As she walks past him, he stops her and offers a robe. She takes it, sliding it on like she's done this a thousand times.

Then she notices me.

Her eyes bulge, round and startling green, as she gasps. "Wolf! Did you get married?"

Chaos.

The bed explodes with motion. Sheets fly. Bodies scramble.

A second man stumbles out. Then a third. A fourth?

No.

Definitely three men.

All of them knee-weakenly gorgeous.

All of them naked.

Given the suffocating reek of sex and testosterone, I can only assume they just shared that tiny redhead like a hedonistic fever dream.

Lucky girl.

Meanwhile, I hover half in the hall, half in the room, gaping like an idiot in my rain-soaked wedding gown.

Boxers and pajama pants materialize, and within seconds, all the dicks are covered.

Wolf flicks on the light and pushes me back into the room. "Okay, so... This is Dove."

Everyone stares.

"She's not my wife," he adds quickly. "She ran away from her wedding. Long story. She needs a place to crash. I'm putting her in the guest house, but I wanted you to know so you don't freak out."

They are definitely freaking out.

The terrifying one—dark eyes, darker mood—doesn't say a word. He just grunts and glares, arms folded across a chest full of scars, radiating *nope*.

Wolf follows my gaze. "That's my brother, Kody. Technically, my uncle. He's harmless. Unless you touch his *woman*," he says in an ape-man voice.

"You make a beautiful bride." The woman offers me a small, sleepy smile. "Probably not what you want to hear. You look like you had a day and lived to fight another. You okay?"

She looks younger than me. Impossibly delicate. Almost childlike. With the most direct, soul-piercing eye contact I've ever experienced.

Uncomfortable, I look away, colliding with the mismatched eyes of a Viking. He leans against the wall, scratching the scar on his abdomen. His pants hang so low I can see Valhalla. Zero shame, this guy.

"You dragged a runaway bride into our lair." He tsks. "Bold."

"I'll go." I back away and bump into Wolf's chest.

"Apologize, bonehead." Frankie pinches the underside of the Viking's bulging bicep, making him hiss.

Love

"That's Leo," Wolf says at my ear. "Don't engage." Then he adds, "He's my least favorite brother. Technically, my cousin."

"I'm Monty." The older one offers a hand, squints at his extended fingers with a wrinkled nose, and yanks his hand away before I can touch it.

Guess we know where those fingers have been. Inside someone, but who? If they're all related...

"I'm Wolf's father." Monty Novak stands tall and regal, wrapping a sheet around his waist like a royal robe. "This is... Unexpected."

"Now you know." Wolf nudges me. "Ask them whatever you want, whatever will make you feel comfortable enough to stay."

So that's why he dragged me in here and woke them? He wants me to feel comfortable?

He wasn't lying about his relationship to the richest man in Alaska and the captives mentioned in the news articles. I only need to look at the four men to see the family resemblance. Not just their appearances but their demeanors.

Wolf isn't the only one hiding a feral, predatory side.

I have so many questions, but I don't want to ask anything right now. Thanks to my reclusive nature, I burn with anxiety and awkwardness in regular situations. This is so far beyond my comfort zone, I can't feel my tongue.

Kody studies me, his voice a deep, grave-cold vibration. "Are you in danger?"

I hear the question he doesn't ask.

Did you bring danger to our home?

"Not tonight." Wolf gives him a look. "We'll talk tomorrow."

"Nice to meet you, Dove." The redhead steps through the chaos like she's used to it. "I'm Frankie. You're safe here, okay?"

I nod slowly, not sure if that's true or if I'm in the middle of some exclusive Alaskan sex cult.

"Do you need anything?" Frankie asks. "Clothes? Girl stuff? Food?"

"Cherry-berry." Wolf tugs a strand of her hair. "I got this."

"Yeah." She smiles and presses a kiss to his sternum. "You do."

"All right. Show's over." Wolf claps his hands and pulls me into the hall. "Back to bed, you crazy kids. Don't make it weird."

"You made it weird," Leo calls after us.

Back down the stairs, we go, my hand still in his. The silence settles again, broken only by the creak of the house and the hum of appliances.

We hit the kitchen. It's warm, glowing with soft light. He opens the fridge as if this is the most normal thing in the world.

"What was that?" I tug on my dress, unsure what to do.

"My family." He pulls out leftovers, stacking the containers on the huge island.

"In one bed?"

"They've been through hell, and fourgies are their therapy. It's how they keep it together."

"Trauma bonding with benefits?"

"Foursome is the dreamsome. I'm not part of that." He gestures at a door off the kitchen. "There's a bathroom if you want to change. Do you need something to wear?"

"I have clothes."

And questions.

So many questions.

When I don't move, he guides me into the small guest bathroom and spins me away. Then a tug jerks me back. And another. And another.

He's unlacing my bodice.

I clutch the material as it loosens and droops, relief flooding through me.

"Shout if you need anything." He steps out, shutting the door behind him.

I change into a camisole and cotton pajama pants and emerge with the gown bundled in my arms.

"I'll have that dry cleaned." He takes it from me and hangs it in a mudroom off the kitchen.

"Throw it away."

"You might change your mind."

"I won't."

He slides a dish in front of me. Salmon, rice pilaf, and green beans with almonds. The scent of hot food sends my stomach into somersaults.

"Eat." He makes his own plate.

"You brought me to an island full of naked people." I lower onto a stool.

"You needed a place to stay."

I stare at him. At the rain hitting the windows. At the

firelight flickering from the other room. And I wonder, not for the first time, what the hell I got myself into.

And why I'm not in a hurry to leave.

He hands me a fork, plops down beside me, and watches me eat like I'm the most interesting part of his night.

The food is too hot, but my stomach doesn't care. I chew slowly, unconcerned with the dense silence churning between us.

Eventually, he sets down his fork and pulls off his beanie, shaking out a luxurious mop of inky curls. While I was in the bathroom, he removed his boots, socks, and rings and washed the dark makeup from his eyes.

"Spill it, Angel Wings." His stare draws me in.

"What?"

"Whatever you're thinking."

"It's none of my business."

"Cute. Let's pretend you didn't meet the family at a full-frontal welcome party. Nothing says hello like surprise nudity." He shudders dramatically. "Good luck un-seeing Kody's third leg."

"I didn't look." My face heats.

"Denial's a lovely color on you. I may not be caught up on all the social norms, but I know what you saw—" he directs a finger toward the second floor "—isn't a paint-by-numbers situation."

Since he met me in the trigger-happy-bridezilla phase of my life, we've established I'm not the standard type.

"Okay. Fine." I push away my finished plate and twist on the stool to face him. "You refer to Leo and Kody as your brothers, but they're not?"

"We were raised in the Arctic as brothers."

"Raised by a psychopath. The news reports said he's dead. Who was he?"

"He was a Strakh. Monty and Kody's brother. Leo's father. And—"

"Your uncle."

"Right. But we didn't know our DNA lineage until we escaped." A dark shadow flashes across his face. "Doesn't matter what those tests say."

"They're still your brothers."

"Yeah. Until I push them off a cliff." He winces. "Bad joke.

Delete, delete."

"Monty wasn't in the Arctic with you?"

"No. We didn't meet him until we escaped. And before you ask... The men in my family aren't fucking one another. Legally, Frankie is married to my dad. But she's also married to Leo and Kody in every other sense of the word. They share her. Standard foursome rules apply. Guys can't make eye contact. Guys can't make bodily contact. High fives are acceptable."

"You're kidding."

"Yeah. I'm kidding. There's definitely contact. You know... One in the pink? Two in the stink? Please, tell me you get it so I can shut up."

"I get it."

"Praise Jesus."

As I let that sink in, a million other questions bubble up. The sharing thing doesn't faze me. Jag has always been openly bisexual with an aversion to monogamy.

The men I just met are imposing, domineering, testosterone-fueled alphas. Like Jag. Except they're committed in a conjugal relationship with one woman.

A woman who seemed entirely too comfortable prancing around naked in front of Wolf.

"What is your relationship with Frankie?" The question is out before I can stop it.

"She's like a sister to me. Sometimes a mother. Other times, a best friend."

"But you've had sex with her."

"What Frankie and I shared..." His focus falters, looking through me, not at me. "It was more intimate than sex."

My mind sifts through situations that fit that description, and I take a dark turn fast.

Held captive by a psychopath in the Arctic Circle.
Only been in civilization for six months.
I didn't exist.
They've been through hell.

He stares at his empty plate. "If you stick around, maybe I'll tell you the story someday."

"Thank you. For dinner. And a place to stay. For all of it." *Even though it's weird as hell.*

"I know it's a lot, but you're safe here."

God, that word again.

love

Safe.

Everyone throws it around like it means something. I've never heard a word more fragile. People promise it, whisper it, swear by it, and still, the worst things happen anyway.

I lean back and examine him. He's barefoot, lean but muscled, with those wild blue eyes that never seem to settle. His damp hair curls at the ends, and there's a smear of charcoal under one eye like he forgot to wipe off his makeup completely.

He's lethally beautiful.

Beautiful men have always been trouble for me. They make promises with their eyes, seduce with their tongues, and vanish before morning. Or worse, they stay and destroy me slowly.

"You ever sleep with them?" I tip my chin toward the staircase.

"Used to. In the Arctic. Not anymore."

"Why not?"

"I snore. They voted me out."

"What's the real answer?"

"They found something I haven't."

The way he says it—shoulders relaxed, gaze level, as if he isn't standing outside the circle with his nose pressed to the glass—he wants the world to think nothing can touch him.

It's all bullshit.

"Come on." He grabs our empty plates. "I'll show you the guest house."

dove
SIX

My nerves regroup as we step outside. Rain drizzles in misty sheets, and the cold wind pushes against us with salty breath.

Wolf grabs a flashlight and leads us along a paved path, the beam cutting through the dark.

Tucked beneath the evergreens, the guest house comes into view, close enough to the mansion to feel like part of the compound. The cozy two-story cottage matches its stone counterpart with accented wood, glass, and soft amber light.

He unlocks the door and flicks on a lamp.

It's warm. Lived-in. Not overly fancy like the main house, but comfortable with a leather couch, open kitchen, and fire crackling in the wood stove.

Shouldering my backpack, I step inside and toe off my boots.

"The locks around here are solid." Wolf shows me the keypad on the door and gives me the passcode. "The bedrooms are up there." He motions toward the staircase. "Separate bathrooms, in case you're worried about accidental defilement."

"What about *intentional* defilement?"

"Say that again, but slower." His eyes darken.

"That wasn't an invitation."

"Could've sworn I heard the mating call of a dove." He

Love

arches a brow. "What? Didn't say I would accept it."

"The answer is no."

"What was the question?"

I brush past him and take the stairs two at a time. Peeking into each doorway, I choose the room less lived-in and drop my bag on the bed.

When I spin back around, I come face-to-chest with the intoxicating scent of leather and tobacco. My nose bounces off a hard pectoral, and I swallow a gasp.

Christ, he's overwhelming, taking up space, and sucking all the oxygen.

What does he want?

Shit, did I pick the wrong room?

"You're not sleeping here, right?" I crane my neck to meet his eyes.

"You want me to?"

"No," I say too fast.

"Keep flirting with me, and I'll have you back in that wedding dress and wearing *my* ring."

"I'm *not* flirting."

"Careful, Runaway. Mixed signals are my kink."

"You've lost your mind."

"Says the woman who ran from her wedding to an island of naked strangers."

"Get out." I push him toward the door as if it's my room, not his.

"Still don't trust me?" He lets me manhandle him into the hall, his grin lopsided and eyes sparkling. Clearly enjoying the hell out of this.

"I don't trust anyone."

"Join the club. We meet on Tuesdays."

I start to close the door in his face, but his expression stalls my hand, and I catch the door mid-swing.

A beat of silence pulses between us, our gazes locked. Too loud and intimate.

"For what it's worth..." He grips the doorframe overhead, inadvertently flexing his forearms. "I haven't lied to you."

He's underselling it.

From the moment I met him, he protected me, lost his job for me, fed me, gave me a place to sleep, and shared personal details about his life.

I've given nothing in return. No answers. No trust. No repayment. The least I could do is fuck him into a mindless coma. It wouldn't be a hardship. Just thinking about riding his sexy body ignites a greedy little throb between my legs.

But that's not why he's helping me.

Being alone sucks. That's the reason.

Wouldn't kill me to give him something.

"I'm a mechanic." I release my hold on the door. "I used to have my own garage. Specialized in vintage engines, mostly."

"Yeah?"

"Yeah. But the garage burned to the ground. I lost everything. Then I met Gavin, and he was going to help me rebuild after the wedding. Turns out, he's so broke that he took a bribe to marry me. I can't go back to California. I have nothing there. Nothing worth salvaging."

He studies me quietly, all sarcasm gone.

"I need a job," I say. "I need to earn and save and start over somewhere."

"You can work here."

"Doing what? Fixing all the cars on your private island?"

"No." He laughs. "I meant in town. You can ride with me and look for work when I go to the tattoo shop tomorrow to get my apprenticeship back."

"Okay." My shoulders relax. "I'll do that."

"We should swap numbers."

I grab my phone from my backpack, ignoring the missed messages from Jag and Gavin.

Once our numbers are stored, Wolf reaches for the door and pauses with his hand on the knob. "There's food in the fridge downstairs. Bathroom's stocked. If you need anything, I'm right next door."

"Thanks."

He gives me a long look. Not flirtatious. Not even overly curious. Just... Present. Like he sees me. "You're not okay."

"I will be."

"The island blocks cell signals and scrambles outgoing data. Jag can't track you here. Even if he did, the island is more heavily guarded than Area 51. No one can abduct you. Not even little green men." He shrugs. "After what we survived, my family doesn't fuck around."

love

"Good to know."

He nods once and closes the door behind him.

I crawl onto the soft, oversized bed, covers pulled tight, and melt into the scent of Wolf all around me. That shouldn't comfort me, goddammit. But it does.

Sleep doesn't come.

My mind spins, replaying Gavin's betrayal on a loop. His confession. The one-year whirlwind of dates and promises and polished lies. The horrified look on his face when I packed my bag and left.

He thought I'd still marry him. Like love meant I had to forgive him.

I did love him. That much is true.

But I'm not heartbroken.

I'm fucking furious.

Furious at him.

Furious at myself for letting it happen again. For trusting the wrong people. For thinking this time would be different.

My phone lights up on the nightstand, a steady pulse in the dark, the notifications on silent.

I know who it is.

Jag and Gavin.

Fuck them both to hell.

I roll onto my side, yanking the blanket over my shoulder like it can block out their energy.

It doesn't help. The light flashes again.

I don't want to look.

I really, really don't want to look.

But if I don't answer, it'll only make Jag more unhinged.

I reach over, grab the phone, and unlock the screen.

47 unread messages.

Gavin:
Please talk to me.
I messed up. I know that. But you're overreacting.
It's over with him. Completely done.
I love you. Doesn't that mean anything?
Don't throw everything away because of a mistake.
You're being cruel.
I'm not the enemy.

You left me.
You don't get to disappear.
You're being dramatic. Come home.
Answer me.
Don't make me come find you.

I clench my jaw. That last one chafes my ass.
Don't make me come find you?
Like I'm the problem. Like I'm the one who broke him.
I scroll past the rest without reading, knowing the rhythm. The shift from apology to guilt-tripping to threats.
Classic Gavin.
Petulant man-child.
Expelling a breath, I block his number and switch to the messages from Jag.
My scalp chills before I open them. Just seeing his name on the screen feels like a death threat, like he's staring into my soul and watching me squirm.
Ridiculous. I trade out my phones regularly in case he installs sneaky tracker shit.
Same number. New phone. Location data off.
He can't see me.
I open the chat.

Jag:
You think you can run? With him?
He can't protect you.
I fucking raised you. You owe me. Every breath in your lungs is mine.
You don't get to disappear. Not from me.
Does he know what kind of dirty little stray he dragged onto his yacht?
Get back here. Now.
You're not thinking straight.
You're acting like a cheap whore with a new leash.
If you fuck him, I'll make him regret ever touching what's mine.
I'm serious, Dove. Come back now. Or I'll come get you.
You think an island can keep me out?
I built your fucking firewall. I am your firewall.
Don't make me break it down.
I'm not playing anymore.

love

I've killed for you before.
Don't make me do it again.

I sit up, clutching the phone, hands shaking.
He knows I left on the yacht.
He knows I'm with Wolf.
Of course, he does.
But he doesn't know where I am.
Eleven-hundred islands.
And that?
That realization sparks not only fear but a sense of power I've never felt before.
For the first time in my life, Jag can't see me.
He's losing his mind behind the screen because the cameras he planted, the trackers, the tricks, none of them work here.
He's blind. And that terrifies him.
I toss the phone face-down on the nightstand and press the heels of my hands to my eyes. My heart pounds like a jackhammer trying to drill its way out of my chest.
I'm so tempted to text back, *How's your hand?* Just to push his buttons. To remind him that I'm not afraid to fight back.
But I don't.
What if that one text pinpoints my location? What if he traces it? What if he already has?
By now, he's done a deep dive into Wolf's digital footprint. Wolf said he didn't exist until six months ago, but his birth records, social media activity, hospitalizations, employment info at the tattoo shop—all of that will be used to track me down.
Not to mention, his billionaire father. Won't be hard to determine which island Monty Novak owns.
I clench my fists and curl up beneath the blankets.
What scares me more than Jag is the stranger who pulled me out of the storm and dragged me onto his island of Alaskan gods. The stranger with ocean eyes and lickable lips.
Wolf talks about death like he spent a lifetime flirting with it. The same guy who made sure I had food, a place to sleep, and a door that locks.
He hasn't tried anything.
Hasn't pushed.
But he could.

The part of me that's terrified of being touched again is still imagining his hands on me.

I hate that.

I hate how drawn I am to a man I don't know, can't trust, shouldn't even want.

But there's something about him. Something broken and brave. Something so deliciously wild. It calls to the worst parts of me. The reckless, self-destructive parts that scream for chaos when what I need is silence.

I close my eyes and grit my teeth.

No.

Nope.

Not again.

I didn't run from one manipulative asshole to fall into the arms of another pretty disaster. I don't care how captivating his eyes are. Or how solid his chest felt under that worn black shirt.

I need to get a job.

I need to get revenge on Jag.

I need to build a new life somewhere far, far away, where no one knows my name, where I can be more than the girl my brother tried to break.

Maybe, if I'm lucky, I'll forget what it feels like to want someone who could shatter me all over again.

I toss and turn and pull the blanket over my head, shutting out my past, my thoughts, and my attraction to toxic men.

I won't respond to Gavin or Jag.

For now, that's the only power I have.

wolfson
SEVEN

I wake slowly, immediately assaulted by plaguing questions.

Why do vegans hate plants so much if they're all about protecting nature? Is it the same reason they pretend to enjoy kale? Who hurt them?

And if civilization is so advanced, why is toilet paper still the best we've come up with?

Why are some people still insisting we all came from one incestuous family? First with Adam and Eve. Then with Noah. The God of the Bible made incest necessary for human existence to continue, and I'm really struggling with that.

Am I supposed to just get over my childhood trauma because the tyrant of heaven is pro-incest?

Nope. Nuh-uh. His Holiness can fuck right off with that.

I groan.

Overthinking should come after coffee, not before pants.

Opening my eyes, I find Leo beside me, propped on one elbow and staring intently. His gold eye glints with mischief, and his blue eye just looks lazy and dumb.

"Sweet icy goatballs." I shove his face away. "Ignoring personal boundaries is *my* thing, you creep. Get your own thing."

"Morning to you, too, Sleeping Beauty." He flops to his back and drums his fingers on his chest. "Thought you'd want to know your bride is on the dock. Looks like she's making a run for it."

"What?" I jackknife to a sitting position, pulse racing.

"Seems your little runaway is eager to run away from you." He stretches and yawns. "Can't say I blame her."

"Dammit." I scramble out of bed, hot panic surging through my system.

"Relax." He follows me into the bathroom and leans against the doorway while I piss. "It's not like she has keys to the yachts. Apparently, she prefers yacht-jacking to asking for things."

I keep my back to him and strip off my shirt, hiding the scars that mar my chest and abdomen. Stepping quickly into the shower, I angle myself so he can't see the damaged skin. "She's not a thief."

"You sure about that?"

She stole my cigarette last night. Not the same as hot-wiring a yacht.

I lather up in record time, anxious to find out how much hell she's managed to raise without me.

"She was up before the rest of us, sneaking around the yachts as if hoping to find a key." Leo chuckles at my back. "The woman on the dock looks nothing like the bride you brought home last night."

I pause mid-rinse, still shielding my scars from his gaze. "Explain."

"Nah." He crosses his arms. "You gotta see this for yourself. I will say... The reboot is way more your style."

"Stop being a cryptic bitch and tell me everything."

"Where's the fun in that?"

I grab the handheld showerhead and aim it over my shoulder, directly at his infuriating face.

Water drenches his beard, his braids, and the entire front of his body. He throws back his head and roars with laughter, widening his mouth, sticking out his tongue, and shaking his face in the spray like a wild dog.

Turning off the water, I reach for a towel. "You can put lipstick on a yeti, and he'll still piss in snowbanks and eat your cat."

That only makes the yeti laugh harder.

"Get out, you idiot."

"Fine, fine." He backs away, still grinning obnoxiously. "But you owe us a conversation. I'm not leaving without it."

"I need some privacy first."

"Since when?" He fixes me with an intense glare, and just like that, Playful Leo has left the chat. "I know about the scars."

Fuck.

Fuck him, fuck the scars, and fuck the demon who cut them into me.

"Not today, Sunshine." I shoulder past him and pull open the closet, grabbing clothes that match my mood.

A pair of electric blue jeans patterned with purple lightning bolts, a loose white shirt with ragged edges, and a glittery black cardigan that swallows me whole.

"Dove's stepbrother is Jag Rath." I tug on knee-high rain boots painted with daisies, knowing they'll withstand the soggy misery of Sitka. "I broke his wrist last night. On purpose."

"Start from the beginning." He perches on the bed.

While brushing my teeth and finger-raking my hair, I tell him everything. The confrontation in the tattoo parlor, the brawl in the alley, and every nibble of information I pried from Dove.

"She's not big on words." I shove on my beanie. "One of my favorite things about her. But I need to understand her relationship with Jag if I'm gonna figure out how the hell to help."

"Sounds like she doesn't want your help."

"Yeah, she's doing that stubborn *I can fix it myself* routine. Full-blown mechanic girl energy. She'll come around."

"Before or after her stepbrother comes around and hurts her?"

"He'll have to go through me." I shrug on my leather jacket and head out the door. "In the meantime, double up on Frankie's security."

"Already done."

He follows me back to the main house, and I dash into the kitchen, stuffing two apples and a handful of granola bars into my pockets.

Frankie stands at the island, coffee mug in one hand and phone in the other. Dressed in her scrubs with her fiery red hair tied back in a high ponytail, she looks like she's ready to tackle the world. Or stitch up its wounds.

She glances up, eyebrows raised in question. Then her gaze

flicks to Leo behind me. "Why are you wet?"

"Why aren't you?" Grinning like a berserker, he crosses the kitchen in two long strides, lifts her off her feet, and smashes her against his soaked clothes.

With a shriek, she pounds her fists against his back, which only encourages him to grind her face into his wet shirt.

Ah, yes. Nothing says *I love you* like waterboarding your soul mate before breakfast.

I leave them to their foreplay and sprint out the door toward the dock.

The scent of damp earth and brine awakens my lungs as I hurry down the winding path. A thin veil of fog drapes over the water, evaporating slowly as the morning sun climbs higher.

And there she is, standing boldly against the backdrop of a glittering sea and hazy mountains.

Dove's silhouette is fragile yet fiercely resilient. The kind of fragile that fools people right before she punches them in the throat.

She's built like poetry and barbed wire. Delicate enough to catch the light. Sharp enough to leave me bleeding.

But Leo wasn't exaggerating.

Her hair is no longer blonde. Bright electric blue strands shine vividly in the sunlight, twisted into two messy buns atop her head.

Now *that* is a choice.

One I wholeheartedly approve.

She notices me, her gaze defiant and challenging. Same unforgettable expression I remember. Except now her face is adorned with metal. Septum, lip, and eyebrow piercings, and numerous studs line her ears.

Yesterday, she was every bit the traditional princess in her white wedding gown.

Today, she radiates a delicious, sexy-as-fuck, cyberpunk superpower. Bold. Untouchable. Rare. The sort of rare that doesn't want to be kept.

Makes me want to keep her even more.

My pulse quickens. My skin heats, and my boxers feel too damn tight.

I pause longer than necessary, drinking in how the sunlight kisses her cheeks, how the breeze teases the blue strands that frame her face.

She wears an oversized bomber jacket with a patch that says NO GODS NO MASTERS. The crop top underneath is printed with an anatomical heart made of gears and wires. Her high-waisted cargo pants cinch at the ankles with buckles, and green neon cords lace her combat boots.

Hot. Every single inch of her.

She touches her chin to her shoulder, watching me with a death glare. Then she turns away.

Playing hard to get. I'm down.

I approach carefully, curiosity burning. "When did you decide to join the rebellion?"

She ignores me, her gaze directed stubbornly out at sea.

"Don't leave me hanging." I sidestep into her line of vision, tipping my head. "That blue? That glare? You're either going to break my heart or my nose. Either way, I'm here for it."

She still refuses to acknowledge me.

"You know..." I lean in, putting my face in hers. "Silence only makes me more persistent. And I can be incredibly persuasive."

I reach into my pocket and hold up an apple in offering.

She stares into my eyes. "Did you poison it?"

"Depends. Do you consider charm a slow-acting drug?"

"Can't you take a hint?" She snatches the apple.

"I don't do subtle, Princess Leia. I do obsession and revenge." Stepping back, I dig out the other apple and bite into it. "Why the wedding-day disguise?"

"Gavin's family." She rotates the fruit, examining it. "Conservative assholes. They didn't exactly jump for joy about him marrying a mechanic with piercings and blue hair. He asked me to tone it down for the day." Her voice tightens. "I agreed. Cleaned up. Looked normal. I hated myself for it."

I believe her. Of all the things she packed in that one bag, she made sure it included her hair dye and body jewelry.

Makes me wonder where else she's pierced.

"Normal is boring. This..." I gesture at her with my apple. "This is badass. Not that you don't make a gorgeous princess bride. But the real you is extraordinary."

Her gaze holds mine, a flash of vulnerability, there and gone.

"Stop flattering me or there will be blood." She turns back to the ocean and bites into her apple. "I thought we were leaving."

I draw my lips between my teeth, trying not to smile. I can't help it. Her fucking attitude... Christ, she makes me so damn hard.

We board the yacht in silence. She keeps her distance at the stern, her gaze locked on the horizon.

I let her be, gripping the wheel, mind spinning with questions I know she won't answer.

When we dock, she leaps onto the pier and vanishes into the crowd without a word or a backward glance.

I follow at a distance, shadowing her movements as she weaves around clusters of locals and tourists with graceful confidence.

A few blocks later, she disappears into the auto mechanic shop she found last night.

Safe. For now.

wolfson
EIGHT

Forcing myself to give Dove space, I head to the tattoo parlor. My pulse quickens at the familiarity of the route, the buildings and signs all etched into my memory from countless days wandering aimlessly.

The shop comes into view, a dark brick-fronted building tucked between a bookstore and café. My designs clutter the window display, sketches I poured myself into when I thought maybe this place could be home.

I step inside, and the door chimes.

Declan looks up, eyes going wide.

This guy.

His mullet has zero fucks to give this morning, and he's holding his signature coffee mug with the faded quote, DO OR DO NOT, THERE IS NO TRY.

If there were an art school for scarecrows, he would be the mascot. He's like seven feet tall and a hundred pounds dripping wet with glasses that refuse to stay on his nose. Probably because he never stops moving.

"Dude." He throws his hands up like I'm holding a gun and glances nervously at the security camera in the corner. "I was given strict instructions. You can't be here."

"You gonna call the cops on me?" I stroll in without hesitation.

"Well, no, man, of course not, but like... Jag was super clear, okay?"

He saunters to the coffee machine and refills his mug. He drinks coffee like a tweaker about to launch into space, twitchy and hyper-focused on everything and nothing at the same time.

"What did Jag say?" I rest my forearms on the counter.

"He said if you showed up, I'm supposed to tell you to leave. Like, no drama, no scene. Just *get lost* in the friendliest way possible. But between you and me? You should be running this place. I'm supposed to be your mentor, but you're a natural, man. People come in all the time asking for you. You got regulars. Your own damn fan club. I had this chick last week—two face tattoos—asked if you died. I mean, it was the only day you took off in six months. I told her no, that you were just being mysterious."

"Where's Jag?"

"Out of town. Left this morning. Honestly, I don't even know if he has a home. Sometimes he crashes here, in the back, on that disgusting cot that probably has more DNA samples than a crime lab. I hear he's got like a million secret girlfriends or maybe even a few boyfriends. Did you know that? It wouldn't surprise me. He's so secretive and brooding and honestly kinda terrifying. Anyway, he's not here now, said something about going out of town. Didn't say where. Typical Jag, right? Sometimes, I don't see him for weeks. He just kinda appeared one day about a year ago. Before that, he was a ghost. Anonymous owner. Paid the bills. Didn't exist. Then boom! He's here, watching everything, barely talking, just hovering like a hungry gargoyle. And this morning when I saw him, he had a bandage on his hand."

Humans are eighty percent water. But not Declan. He's one-hundred percent wind.

"Did he tell you what happened?" I ask.

"No. I think he punched a mirror or someone's face." He pushes his glasses up his nose. "You'd think he'd wear it like a trophy, but he was acting like he wanted to bite me because I noticed."

"You sure he's gone?"

"Positive. He packed up and left when I got here at seven. Took that creepy duffel bag he always carries. The one that probably has a murder weapon or a severed head in it. I didn't ask. I never ask."

I push off the counter, scanning the space. My chair. My tools. Everything is still there.

"So," I say, "you hiring?"

He snorts. "Technically, we're always hiring because we're the only tattoo shop in Sitka, and we're always understaffed. I'm running solo here. Could really use the help. But you're banned. So like… You're banned but beloved? A legendary outlaw-type deal."

"That's fine. I'm not here to beg. I'm here to work."

"Wolf—"

"Tell the camera I broke in. That way, you're off the hook. I'll take the back corner. Won't touch clients unless they ask."

He stares at me, torn between excitement and panic. "Jag's gonna kill me."

"Not if I kill him first." I flash a grin. "Worst he can do is fire me again."

"You're trouble."

"You say that like it's not my entire brand."

"Fine. Back corner still has your crap in it. But if he finds out I let you in—"

"I'm an outlaw, remember? Just doing outlaw things."

I settle into my corner, surrounded by the aroma of ink, antiseptic, and fake leather. My little kingdom of creativity.

Everything is where I left it. My chair. My station. The worn stool I kick more times than I sit on. Even my rusty old lamp with the sticker that says DON'T TOUCH ME, I BITE.

Running my fingers along the edge of the workbench, I admire my machines. All lined up like soldiers waiting to be picked for battle. I spend hours here. Days. Nearly every day for the past six months.

Tattooing is the only time my brain shuts up. Dragging ink under someone's skin feels like a holy ritual. Meditation with needles. Primal and permanent.

But even in my happy place, my mind won't stop drifting to Dove.

I pull out my phone and start a chat.

Me:
I'm at work. Technically trespassing. Stepbro skipped town.
So did you get the job or what?
I brought snacks.
I'm out of apples. The fruit, not the tech company. Unless you want me to steal you a laptop. I'm flexible.

Ten minutes pass.

Me: Are you ghosting me already? That's cold, mechanic girl.
Bluebird: Stop

Stop sending messages? Or stop being so damn charming? I grin.

Me: Rude. But fair.

I set the phone down and crack my knuckles.

Time to sketch a new Disney princess. I'm thinking blue hair, grease-streaked cheekbones, boots too heavy to run in, and gilded eyes that know how to dismantle a man's heart with a socket wrench.

I pull a sketchpad from under the table and start roughing her out in graphite. Gloves with the fingers cut off. Welding goggles slung around her neck like jewelry. A clockwork dove tattoo on her thigh that she inked herself with stolen parts and a homemade rig.

If she's gonna haunt my thoughts, I might as well make her immortal.

NINE

I push open the door to the mechanic shop, the squeak of rusted hinges protesting my arrival.

The familiar scent of motor oil, gasoline, and worn tires fills my senses. Tools scatter across benches. Grease-covered rags drape over car parts. An air compressor hums softly in the corner.

Feels like home.

Two middle-aged men pause their work and stare at me, eyes wide, brows lifted, surprise painted on their sweat-slicked faces.

One leans against the hood of a battered Ford truck, a socket wrench hanging from his hand. If I had to guess, he's the boss. He's tall and broad, with thick black hair pulled into a low ponytail, and deep-set dark eyes that don't miss a thing.

His features are strong and weathered, his expression impassive beneath a smear of engine grease. Inuit, no doubt, and someone used to commanding the room without speaking much.

The other man steps up behind him, wiping his fingers on a rag. He's younger, maybe mid-forties, with ruddy cheeks, a beer belly under his flannel, and short-cropped sandy blond hair. His eyes narrow with skeptical amusement, like he's seen enough of me to think he knows everything.

"You lost, sweetheart?" the Inuit man asks, his voice dripping with interest.

Not the kind of interest I'm hoping for.

My jaw hardens, but I keep my face neutral. "Are you the manager? I'm here for a job. Name's Dove Rath."

They exchange bewildered glances before the younger man chuckles.

"Honey," the Inuit man says, attempting patience. "We aren't hiring. Haven't hired anyone in years."

"I see that." I direct my eyes around the cluttered shop. "Looks like you need a new hand—or two—around here."

The younger man snorts. "Listen, girl—"

"I'm thirty-two and could teach you a thing or twelve about fixing cars."

"That so?" Curiosity flickers in the younger man's expression. "I'm Chester. This here's my brother-in-law, Taaq. He's the owner. No offense, miss, but we don't get girls just walking in here, outta nowhere, claiming to out-wrench two guys who've been doing this since before you got your hands greasy."

"Test me." I stand tall, lifting my chin and reining in my temper. "Carburetors, transmissions, brakes, electrical... Take your pick."

Chester raises an eyebrow at Taaq, an unspoken challenge passing between them.

My heart quickens in the pause. I can't miss this chance. This isn't just about a job. It's about proving I belong and being as competent as any man. Something I've had to do again and again since I grew boobs.

"All right, Dove." Taaq grins wickedly. "See that '69 Camaro over there?"

I glance toward the corner where a dusty Camaro sits, clearly abandoned, its hood propped open as if it's been screaming for attention for decades.

"You got it." I stride toward it, a rush of adrenaline pulsing through me.

"That thing hasn't run in years." Taaq chuckles. "If you can get it started, maybe we'll reconsider your application."

They'll be begging me to stay by the time I'm finished.

The men trail after me, curious but openly doubtful.

Tossing my jacket on a stack of tires, I bend over the engine

love

and quickly assess the situation. Spark plugs corroded, distributor wires hanging loose, battery hopelessly dead. Typical neglect, nothing I haven't fixed a hundred times.

"Wrench." I reach my hand out expectantly, my tone cutting, betraying my urgency.

Chester grunts but directs me to the toolbox.

I immediately dive in, navigating the tools, replacing spark plugs, adjusting the distributor wires, repairing loose hoses, and tossing aside the dead battery.

"New battery?" I glance over my shoulder, impatient.

Chester silently hands me a fresh one, his skepticism melting into curiosity.

Within minutes, I've reconnected everything, tightened every bolt, and wiped the sweat and grime from my forehead with the back of my hand.

My pulse quickens as I slide into the driver's seat, turning the key in the ignition.

A harsh cough fills the garage, followed by a deep, rumbling roar as the engine catches, humming to life in a resurrection song.

I step out, cock my hip against the door, and wipe my hands on a rag, hiding my surging relief behind a bored expression.

Chester's jaw practically touches the oil-stained floor, and Taaq looks like he's about to piss himself.

"When do I start?" I hang the rag from my back pocket.

Taaq clears his throat awkwardly, exchanging a glance with Chester.

"Cool." I crack my knuckles. "I'll start now."

"Uh—usually..." Taaq blinks rapidly. "We need to figure out—"

"No need." I head toward the next waiting car, my chest swelling with triumph. "Just pay me cash."

"That makes it easy." He steps back, quietly impressed.

As I lift the hood of the next car, I let my eyes scan the corners of the garage, slow and deliberate, looking for security cameras. I know Jag. If he hasn't already hacked the feed, he will soon. And I need to know what he sees and hears.

I spot only one camera mounted near the back corner, a dusty little dome overlooking the main bay. Subtle. Barely operational by the look of it.

"Hey, Taaq." I loosen a bolt and move to the next one. "That camera work?"

"Yeah." He looks up from a clipboard, brows furrowing like the question caught him off guard. "It's old. I only check the footage if something goes missing."

"Fair warning. I like to sing off-key when I'm working alone."

"Oh, it doesn't record audio. Sing your heart out."

I duck back under the hood, pretending to accept the answer with casual indifference.

Jag and I went our separate ways long ago, but we always know each other's locations. He knows mine because he's an unapologetic stalker with deadly hacker skills. And I know when he changes residences because he tells me.

He never texts this information. No digital messages. Nothing that can be tracked. We have a system.

I visit our parents' graves in Anaheim often. He knows that's where I go when I need to feel tethered to something, even if it's pain.

Whenever I find a new plant in their grave dirt, I know he's been there. And he's left a message for me.

A year ago, I found a black willow sapling rooted near the headstones. He always chooses a plant that attracts doves. He's strangely into symbolism like that, probably just to fuck with me.

I dug it up and found a smooth white rock underneath with sharpie-inked words bleeding into the cracks.

Sitka Tattoo.

It's always a rock. Always a new city or phone number.

But of all places, why Sitka?

He must've already owned the shop to launder money or something like that.

Doesn't matter. I'm here now, but this time, I'm not running. I'm not hiding. I'm making damn sure he sees me.

A few hours later, when my new coworkers are distracted—Chester arguing with a parts supplier over the phone and Taaq elbows-deep in a carb rebuild—I turn toward the camera.

Eyes locked on the lens, I hold my middle finger high and mouth, *Fuck you, Jag.*

Then I turn back to work and start singing "You Don't Own Me" by Leslie Gore.

jag
TEN

I sit in the unlit kitchen, surrounded by the scent of stale coffee and looming retaliation. My elbow rests on the table, an ankle propped on my knee, my eyes glued to the blue glow of my phone.

The grainy feed flickers, scattering pixels before the image steadies again.

I've hacked into every camera worth hacking into across Sitka—convenience stores, traffic signals, ATMs, residential security systems. I tapped them all, establishing a network of eyes, never blinking, always searching.

And there she is, my burdensome baby Dove. Working earlier today at the mechanic shop. Her stubborn independence and resourcefulness never cease to amaze me. And piss me off.

I've watched her every step since she started walking. Every stumble, every victory, every quiet moment when she believed herself alone.

She was never alone.

As she crouches to repair a tire on the recording, the two fuckheads who hired her stop what they're doing to stare at her ass.

Add them to the list of dead men walking.

I scowl at my broken wrist, irritation crawling through my veins.

And Wolfson Strakh.

I've been balls-deep in research, digging through every database, every dark corner of the net, finding horrifying secrets about his family. But Wolfson himself? Almost nothing. That's more terrifying than any file I've opened.

Something happened to him. Something sick and unspeakable in an off-grid cabin in the Arctic. A cabin that no one knows how to find.

His family knows.

His bloodline is tied to the old-world Russian mob. The real deal. Soviet-era executioners. Men who ruled from the summits of mass graves.

The Strakh family doesn't just disappear. They hide in plain sight, fortified by fear and an ancient code of conduct that this world could never understand. Scary shit.

Wolfson isn't just dangerous. He's fucking mesmerizing. Ethereal beauty with a predator underneath. Dove is vulnerable to men like him. Broken, beautiful, seductive men. She'll fall. She always does.

Which means I have no choice. He goes on the list. Another problem. Another threat. Another mess to clean up.

This was supposed to be Gavin's responsibility. If he'd kept his mouth shut and his dick in his pants, Dove wouldn't have followed me to Alaska and entangled herself with the Strakhs.

A soft moan rises from the adjoining room, followed by a muffled laugh and a deeper grunt.

Gavin is in there with another man, getting his donut glazed, their groans seeping through the thin walls.

I clench my jaw, annoyance twisting into rage.

He had one fucking job.

But like everyone else, he's a goddamn disappointment. Sex blinds him. Makes him careless. If I've learned anything, it's that the only eyes I can trust are my own.

To think, I studied him for months, sharing his bed while digging through his secrets. He needed a bride and a better financial standing to appease his conservative family, and I saw an opportunity.

When the feds discovered me a year ago, I paid Gavin to watch Dove so I could vanish to Alaska.

jag

Convincing him to marry her was easy.

He hides his sexuality for appearance's sake. Unbeknownst to her, she was to be his cover, and as a bonus, he would make some money to fund that lavish lifestyle he can't afford.

Tricking Dove to take the bait was the challenge.

I knew she would be attracted to him. Every man and woman with a pulse finds Gavin sexy. He's a real Matt Bomer type. Impossible to resist with his chiseled jaw, bedroom-blue eyes, and pretty-boy smile that could sell salvation to a sinner.

She didn't know he's gay to his core. Not until his confession yesterday. He's masculine as hell, physically fit, perfectly groomed, and smells like expensive things.

Hitching her to a gay man was a calculated risk.

I don't want anyone—gay or straight—touching my sister.

Of course, I know she slept with him. I had to coach him through it, step by fucking step, so he could fake his way into her bed. I told him what she likes, how she moves, what makes her unravel. I crafted the whole unholy performance like a director coaching an actor, and he nailed it.

The knowledge that his hands were on her, that his mouth touched her skin... Fuck, it boils my blood. Just picturing his lips on her—his filthy, lying mouth—makes me want to gut him right here and now.

Did I watch them together? Yeah, I fucking did. Through a camera lens, of course.

No one knows her like I do. Every trigger, guarded thought, and freckle on her body—she's etched into my brain like scripture.

I shaped Gavin into her perfect distraction, taught him how to talk to her, move around her, and disarm her with carefully planted charm. I built him like a weapon, tailored to break through her armor.

I did it all for her.

She needs structure and guardrails. She needs protection from our enemies. She needs protection from *me*.

Now I'm back in Cali because no matter how much I trusted Gavin to be her babysitter, trust is always broken.

I shift my weight, tapping impatiently on the phone screen, cycling through dozens of recorded camera feeds.

Inside the mechanic shop, Dove wipes her hands on a rag

and walks to the corner of the garage where the only camera is mounted. She looks directly at the lens, flips off the camera, and mouths, *Fuck you, Jag.*

Real mature.

My good hand twitches to smack all that rebellious metal out of her pretty face. When it comes to her, my resentment battles with my infatuation. She doesn't know the lengths I'll go to keep her locked down.

The grunting from Gavin's room crescendos and quickly fades into whispered conversations. They'll be finished soon, basking in their fragile afterglow.

Weak.

Gavin's indulgence makes him utterly useless.

I remain seated, slipping the phone into my pocket. If I want something done right, it always comes down to me. Dove is mine to watch, and Gavin was a temporary solution.

The bedroom door opens, spilling soft light and whispered laughter into the hallway. Footsteps approach, and Gavin appears in the kitchen doorway, shirtless and flushed, his eyes widening when he spots me sitting in the dark.

"Send your hookup home," I say for his ears only.

His face reddens because he knows he fucked up. After an awkward hesitation, he hurries back into the bedroom.

Murmurs float through the door, followed by rustling clothes and the shuffle of feet.

Moments later, Gavin reappears, ushering a man toward the front door. The stranger leaves without noticing me.

Gavin closes the door, lingering there a minute, visibly bracing himself before turning to face me again.

"I'm sorry," he stammers, marching into the kitchen. "Let me explain."

"You did the one thing I told you not to do."

"I... I..."

"You told her about our arrangement."

"Fuck, Jag. I tried. I did everything you said. But I missed you. You weren't answering my calls. I haven't spoken to you in months. Don't you get it? I'm in love with you."

"Were you in love with me while getting rammed ten minutes ago?"

"I know how it looks." He winces. "It was just a little NSA fun. It meant nothing."

jag

"It's been less than a day since your wedding to my sister was canceled."

"She canceled it! I begged her to stay, but you know how she is. Impossible to control, emotionally withdrawn..." He throws a hand out, gesturing helplessly. "It's like talking to a wall."

Hard to argue. But more than that, she's fiercely self-reliant, crazy smart, and possesses an unbending moral code.

"You fucked up," I say calmly, rising to my full height. I step close enough to smell the sex on his body.

"I'll make it up to you." His lashes lower as he tentatively reaches out, trailing a finger down my chest.

He was a terrible fucking lay, tedious and quick to finish. Every encounter with him was a chore, one I'm happy never to repeat.

I already emptied his bank accounts and took back every penny I gave him. There's just one thing left to do.

His gaze follows the path of his finger, down, down, down to my zipper. Then he gasps. "What happened to your hand?"

"Smashed a mirror."

"I'm sorry. I know you're angry."

"My broken wrist has fuck all to do with you."

"Oh. Okay. Well, let me take your mind off it." He lowers to his knees and rubs the front of my pants.

As if he has any chance in hell of charming the cobra. The only thing that will make me hard right now is his last breath.

With my injured wrist cradled against my chest, I reach into my coat pocket and remove a thin piano wire fixed between two short wooden dowels.

Gavin's focus is so transfixed on freeing my cock, he doesn't track the movement.

In a fluid motion, I sweep behind him, loop the wire around his throat, and pull.

His eyes bulge, realizing too late the cold finality in mine.

He jerks and claws at the garrote, mouth gaping as the wire bites deep.

I anchor one dowel against the counter with my forearm and pull with my good hand, using leverage instead of strength.

His heels scrape the floor in a desperate, violent dance.

"Shhhh." I rest my brow against his as life drains from his eyes.

His body convulses and fights for an eternity before finally falling limp. I hold for ten seconds more.

Silence.

I release the tension, pocket the wire, and carefully lower his body to the floor. No blood. No mess. No fingerprints. Just clean, silent revenge.

Standing over his lifeless form, I feel nothing.

Without another glance, I slip out the back door and disappear into the night. I already took care of the cameras.

I was never here.

Dove waits for me in Alaska, and once again, it's my responsibility to keep her under lock and key.

wolfson
ELEVEN

I lose time again.

It happens a lot. Hunched over my sketchpad with graphite smudges up to my wrist, I get in the zone.

Sometimes it happens in other ways. When I'm thinking about Hoss. When bad memories cloud my vision until my brain breaks. Those are more like blackouts. But I didn't think about Denver today. Or the doctor. Or the scars I keep hidden.

Today is a good day.

So far.

Music thrums low on the speakers. Grunge, old punk, and some Glass Animals thrown in to keep it weird. Just the way I like it. Outside, rain patters lazily against the windows, and I glance up.

Shit. It's already noon.

My phone flashes. One unread message. Not from Dove. Just Kody checking in to make sure I ate something that isn't vodka.

I grab my jacket and head to the deli down the street. The deli guy knows me by now. Probably thinks I'm a freak for never ordering the same thing twice.

Today, it's a Reuben for Declan, turkey pesto for Dove, and roast beef for me.

Back at the shop, I drop Declan's at his station, where he works on a geometric sleeve for a tourist with a sunburn. I bounce before he can give me a dissertation on deli meat.

Hood up and head down, I cut through alleys and side streets, letting the drizzle soak through the edges of my sleeves. Dove's shop isn't far, just a few minutes from the tattoo parlor if I walk like I have somewhere to be, even if she makes it clear I don't.

In the bay with the roll-up door open, she bends over the guts of an engine. Grease smears her forearms, and that somehow makes her look even hotter than this morning.

I stand there, sandwich in hand, watching her for a long, hungry minute. Waiting for her to look up.

She doesn't.

"Brought you lunch." I sidestep into her line of vision.

Nothing. Not even a shift of her eyes.

There's a tall guy next to the tool bench, wearing a name patch that says *Taaq*. He leans against a tool cart with his arms folded and an eyebrow raised.

I nod in his direction, and he nods back. Just two wolves sizing each other up across neutral territory.

"For her." I hold out the sandwich.

He takes it and inspects the wrapping like he's checking for explosives. "She eat meat?"

Fuck, I didn't think of that. She ate salmon last night, so I know she's not vegan.

Feeling suddenly irrationally territorial, I snap, "She didn't gag last night, so either she eats meat or she was being polite."

He grins at that, and I hate how easy his grin looks. Hate it even more when he turns toward her as if I don't exist.

"Hey, Dove," he calls. "Your boyfriend dropped off food."

Her only response is a grunt.

Not even a glance.

I'm suddenly cold despite the muggy shop air. Her frostiness doesn't bother me, but *come on*. A half-second glare in my direction wouldn't kill her.

If she expects me to stand here like a simp until she deigns to give me her attention, she has the wrong guy. But that's the thing. She doesn't expect that. She expects nothing from me. Not my help. Not my protection. Not my sandwich.

Without another word, I leave before I do something

unforgivable like grab her throat and shove my tongue between her pressed lips.

Back at the tattoo shop, I plant myself behind my station and draw until I forget how to feel. The sketchpad fills fast. Faces, shapes, dark fairy tale designs I keep obsessing over. I don't stop until my fingers cramp.

Then the clients start coming in.

First, a girl from Juneau. She wants a black rose on her ribs, and I slay it. Delicate lines. Bold shading. She stares at it in the mirror afterward like I just gave her a mind-blowing orgasm. Then she hangs out, flirting and begging me to go out with her tonight.

Not interested. Even if I didn't have Dove on the brain, I don't date clients.

I don't date anyone.

A local fisherman walks in next. He wants a giant squid wrapped around a lighthouse. Unusual request. Killer design. I freehand the whole thing while he talks about storms and losing his brother to the sea. I don't say much. Just let him talk. I think he's lonely.

I get it, man.

The afternoon drags on with ink and music and fading light. My phone vibrates every few hours. I check it. Nothing from her.

I text again.

Me:
You good?
Brought a sandwich just to watch you pretend I don't exist.
Worth it.
I'll be there when you're finished. I dare you to look at me this time.
Dove?
Okay.

Nothing.
Ghosted.

The setting that shows *Read* is disabled on her phone, so it feels like a double punch.

Declan leaves around eight, flipping the sign to CLOSED on his way out. I clean my station, mop the floors, and restock needles until ten. Everything is neat and controlled. Unlike me.

The rain picks up again, drumming harder, like it's trying to get inside. I slip the sketchbook into my satchel, tug on my beanie, and lock up the shop.

The streets are mostly empty, the kind of quiet that makes my thoughts louder. I take the long way to her shop. I don't want to seem eager, even if I am.

The garage is still lit. I stand in the doorway, watching for a second, smoking a cigarette. I don't know why my pulse is so high. Everyone else went home. It's just Dove in there.

Dove and that unworthy engine she apparently loves more than me.

I flick away the cig and slip into the bay, my rain boots squeaking on the concrete. She lifts her head at the sound.

Finally.

She sees me. Straightens up. Wipes her hands on a rag but doesn't smile. Doesn't say my name.

"You change your phone number?" I tuck my fingers into my pockets.

"Didn't check it."

"All day?"

"Been busy."

She doesn't offer more. Doesn't step toward me. Doesn't look sorry.

"I brought you lunch."

"I saw."

"You done?" I squint at her.

"Give me five."

I wait in the rain.

She comes out five minutes later, wiping grease off her cheek, her bomber jacket zipped halfway up. No purse or umbrella. The rain soaks her blue hair.

We walk in silence, side by side but miles apart. The dull orange glow of streetlights reflects on wet pavement.

She doesn't speak.

I don't ask why.

The harbor appears like it always does, silent, mist-veiled, boats bobbing in their slips. The yacht I share with Leo waits at the far dock, ropes taut against the cleats, haloed in dock lights and sea fog.

Dove follows me down the ramp without question.

I untie the lines and hop aboard first, reaching back to steady her hand as she steps on deck. She doesn't need it, but she takes it anyway.

That's something.

Inside, I fire up the controls and ease us out of the slip. The yacht hums as we glide through the black, rain-slicked bay with only the sound of water curling off the hull and the low rumble of the motor.

She sits in the passenger seat, arms folded, watching the shoreline fade into mist. Her fingers twitch in her lap like she's counting something. Maybe all the things she hasn't said. Maybe all the things she never will.

I don't push. I just steer. Back to the island. Back to more silence and loneliness.

Her phone buzzes in her pocket. She checks it.

Not me.

"Everything okay?" I can't keep the resentment out of my voice. I don't want to fight. I want her to talk to me. Look at me. Be with me.

"Yeah." That's it. One word. Short. Flat. Nothing behind it.

"You mad about something?"

"No." She looks out the window.

"Well, I am." I press my tongue to the roof of my mouth, staring hard through the windshield. The rain makes it easier not to look at her. I feel my heartbeat in my jaw, in the back of my neck, in the way I grip the wheel too tight. "You didn't answer a single text."

"I was working."

"You could've said that."

"I didn't think it mattered."

I flinch.

She might as well have kneed me in the nuts.

When I reach the island, I dock, kill the engine, and sit there. My fingers drum the wheel. She doesn't move to get out.

"I'm not your past." I roll my neck. "I'm not Jag. Or your piece-of-shit ex. Or any of the assholes who made you feel like you have to avoid men to survive. I'm here. I show up."

"I didn't ask you to."

That hits harder than anything she said—or didn't say—all day.

"Yeah." Blood throbs in my ears. "You've made that clear as fuck."

For several minutes, the only sound is the ping of the engine cooling down.

"I know you show up." She exhales and rubs her hands on her thighs. "I don't know what to do with that."

I study her features. She looks exhausted. Haunted.

"You don't have to do anything." I want to touch her, but I don't. "Just let me be near you."

"I'm not good at that."

"Neither am I." Dragging a hand down my face, I bark a humorless laugh. "Holy frozen hell, you have no idea. I've lived the most abnormal, fucked-up life. I'm not here to compare shitty experiences. But if anyone can understand what you're going through, it's me."

A small smile dimples the corner of her mouth and quickly fades. She finally looks at me. Really looks with those honey-warm eyes. "I didn't mean to ignore you."

"Yeah, you did."

I lead her to the guest house, shrouded by a dense mist, the windows fogged and lights low.

Inside, I spot a pizza box on the counter, still warm. Someone dropped it off. Kody, probably. Ever since he took over the distillery and expanded into culinary service, he's been feeding everyone like it's part of his job description.

We kick off our boots and hang our jackets by the door. I toss my sketchbook on the table, and we eat without talking, hunched over our plates, scrolling on our phones like strangers.

"Who's texting you?" Finished eating, I collect our empty plates.

She hesitates, then says, "Jag."

My jaw tightens.

I don't ask for details. She'll just ignore me. But my anger rises fast, pressing under my skin.

"Want a drink?" I ask instead.

"Sure."

I pour two vodkas, one of Kody's latest infusions. Birch and spruce tip. Smoky. Earthy. Tastes like Alaska in a glass. I hand her a tumbler and lean against the counter, sipping from mine.

We stand in silence. The kitchen light hums overhead. Our shadows stretch across the floor, reaching for each other, trying to bridge the gap we don't know how to cross.

"You drew today?" She turns her attention to my sketchbook.

"Yeah."

"Anything good?"

I flip it open, the pages curling from being handled too much, and show her the latest ones.

Dark Disney princesses. Horror-style. Steampunk Belle with mechanical limbs and cracked porcelain skin. A reimagined Sleeping Beauty tangled in IV lines, trapped in an endless lucid dream. Snow White with broken mirror shards embedded in her skin, each one reflecting a different distorted version of her face.

Most of them look like Dove in some twisted way. The graceful shape of her features. The curve of her mouth. Her eyes, always angry or defiant.

"Wow." She stares at the illustrations for a long time, flipping back and forth between them. "You're insanely talented."

"Thanks. It's my take on the classic fairy tale heroines. They're all tough in an unconventional and misunderstood way. They appear self-destructive, but some dark shit has happened to them, and they take matters into their own hands."

Like someone else I know.

Her gaze flicks to mine.

She doesn't move closer. Doesn't touch me. But she gifts me with her eyes. Steady, bright, curious eyes. It's the most intimate thing she's given me.

"Do you have tattoos?" Her gaze skips down my body and quickly returns to my face.

"You wanna check?"

She gives me a bland look.

The truth is I have too many scars. Deep, ugly scars that aren't healed enough to cover with ink. I'm not sure they will ever heal.

"No tattoos." I shrug. "You?"

"None." She tips the glass back, swallows what's left, and sets it down with a soft clink. "I always wanted ink. Know anyone good who works with difficult canvases?"

"Depends." I lean in, making her blink. "I'd love to mark you. But not if you're going to disappear the second it means something."

Her breath catches, and she briefly closes her eyes. "I'm sorry I shut you out today."

"I forgive you."

"Don't forgive me so fast."

"Then be sorry slower."

A soft breath pushes through her nose. If she were another woman, it could've been a laugh.

I finish my drink and rinse our glasses. "Tell me about your new job."

"I can come and go whenever." She rests a hip against the counter beside me. "Work as much or as little as I want. Paid by the job. No pressure."

"That's good, right?"

"I need to work as much as possible."

"I go to Sitka every morning, catching a ride with Kody and Leo, or I take one of their yachts. You're not trapped here. You can commute with me. Or Kai can take you whenever."

She nods.

"I didn't see Jag today." I nod at her phone. "You're talking to him?"

"He texts me. I don't respond."

Good to know the scary stepbrother isn't getting better treatment than me.

I grab my sketchpad and head to the couch.

Shockingly, she curls up beside me, feet tucked under her, keeping her distance, but her eyes stay on mine.

"Jag will be back in Sitka tonight." She draws in a slow breath. "What are you going to do about your job?"

"I'll go in. I'll draw. I'll ink. And I'll leave."

"You know what I mean."

"I'll deal with him." I twist on the couch to face her. "Did he make you this way?"

"What way is that? Cold? Defensive? Distant?"

"You're not cold. You're armored."

"And you?" She tilts her head. "What are you?"

"Charming."

"And humble." Her lips twitch.

I reach for her hand, and she tenses. But she doesn't pull away. My thumb traces the calluses on her fingers, her palm warm and small against mine.

"You didn't have to bring me lunch," she whispers.

"I wanted to."

"Why?"

"Because the thought of you going hungry makes me feel sick."

She looks down at our hands.

Then she stands, walks to the stairs, and, without a backward glance, goes up. The door to her room closes. Not a slam. Just... Final.

I sit there, staring at the dent her body left in the couch cushion.

I've never felt more alone.

Everything inside me vibrates with the urge to chase her. To force her to talk. To ask her why she's always halfway on the run from me.

But I don't.

If I go up there, she'll open the door only to shut it in my face.

I've known her for all of two days. She needs time. I'll give her that.

But when she's ready, I'll be the one waiting at the cliff's edge to catch her.

wolfson
TWELVE

I balance the sketchbook on my thigh, pencil gliding fast and rough across the page. My eyes ache, but sleep isn't an option. Not with my head where it is. Not with the ghosts crawling up the walls.

Dove went to bed hours ago.

The lamp beside the couch casts a warm puddle of light that doesn't touch the corners of the room. I keep my head down and my hands moving.

Shapes, lines, graphite... The image forming tonight is a woman with feathered wings stitched shut and her mouth open like she's screaming, but no sound comes out.

Real subtle, Wolf.

My thoughts keep drifting to places I can't let them go. Back to the river. Back to the doctor. Back to the woman sleeping upstairs. I grit my teeth and keep drawing.

wolfson

Sometime around the Witching Hour, the floorboards creak above me.

I pause.

Another creak.

Footsteps.

I set aside the sketchbook and crane my neck toward the sound.

Dove appears on the stairs, floating down them and into the light like a nocturnal hallucination. Same pajama pants and camisole she wore to bed yesterday. That backpack of hers didn't hold much.

I make a mental note to take her shopping.

Long blue hair falls around her slender arms. Wavy, bright, freshly washed. She looks like a silk trap, all soft and sweet. The kind of soft that makes a man stupid. The kind that makes a man sin.

She doesn't make a sound as she steps into the room. Her eyes don't leave mine as she closes the distance slowly, deliberately. She's made up her mind about something, and I'm the decision.

Without speaking, she slides one leg over me and sinks onto my lap, straddling my hips.

I freeze, hands hovering midair, heart in my throat.

Her thighs clamp around mine. She smells like sleep and feminine soap.

And I'm hard. An instant, full-on chub that she knowingly, painfully traps between our bodies.

"What are you doing?" I ask, voice rough.

Not a twitch in her expression as she reaches for my waistband and starts unbuttoning my pants.

"Wait." I grip her wrist, trying to catch her gaze.

"Stop talking." Eyes on her hands, she yanks down my zipper.

This isn't right. But holy anti-God in fishnets, it feels right.

My breath shortens. I don't know where to put my hands. I keep them frozen at her sides.

She's going through something. We haven't even had a real conversation. She's hurting. This isn't how this should go.

"You don't have to do this," I whisper. "If this is about something else, something you're trying not to feel—"

She covers my mouth with her hand, her breath as steady as

her gaze.

Then she leans back and yanks off her shirt.

My throat goes dry, and my insides turn molten.

Her nipples are pierced. Of course, they fucking are. Two tiny hoops glint in the pink buds of the prettiest tits I've ever seen.

How the hell did I miss those through her top?

Because I was being a gentleman. Because I wasn't looking. I didn't let myself.

"Dove." I choke. "We need to stop."

"I'm not some simpering virgin."

"*I* am. Not the simpering part. The other part."

She blinks. "You're a virgin?"

"Shocking, right?"

"Well, yeah." Her eyebrows climb together. "Jesus. You've really only been in civilization for six months?"

"I haven't lied to you."

"I thought... I don't know. A guy with your looks and confidence would've banged every woman in Sitka by now."

"I haven't. By choice. Mostly."

"Okay. I can work with that." She shifts down my thighs, dragging my pants lower.

I can't move. Can't breathe. I can only stare.

Her tiny waist dips into curvy hips that make my hands ache to grab her there. And her tits... Lord, take me now. They're perfect. High and full and so prettily pierced. She's art. Raw and exquisite and more stunning than anything I could draw.

And I'm an idiot with trembling hands and no idea where to start.

As I reach up to trace the line of her collarbone, she grabs the hem of my shirt and lifts fast.

I forget.

I forget until I see her eyes go wide.

Until the cold air hits my chest. My scars.

"No." I flinch away, scrambling to shove down my shirt. "Don't look at me."

She stills.

I push her off me. Or maybe she slides off on her own. It's an ugly blur as I curl up, elbows on my knees, hands clutching my shirt tight against me.

Fuck, I'm breathing hard.

Too hard.

"Wolf." Her voice sounds broken open.

"Don't," I snap.

She pulls her camisole back over her head, the movement so slow as if she's afraid I'll spook. Then she settles at the far end of the couch, her posture stiff and defensive.

I feel like I'm bleeding inside.

"I wasn't trying to hurt you." She picks at the hem of her shirt, eyes on her hands.

"Yeah, well, doesn't take much."

A heavy blanket of *awwwwwkward* drapes the room.

Congratulations, Wolf. You successfully turned your lifelong fantasy into an emotional crime scene.

If I had a dollar for every time I self-sabotaged, I could buy a space balloon and float into the void.

"I'm not mad at you. I'm mad at me." I force my gaze to hers. "For feeling too much. Too fast. Too stupid."

"Nothing about this is stupid. I'm not good with words. I act on feeling and needed something to anchor me." She pauses, chewing her lip. "I didn't want to be alone. Didn't want to be in my head. And I didn't want to owe you anything. You helped me, and this was... I wanted to thank you. And to feel like I had some control again." She winces. "That sounds terrible. I don't mean it like that. I just... I don't want to depend on anyone. Not even you. Even though I..."

I stare at her sidelong, waiting with held breath.

"Even though I find you impossibly attractive." Her eyes shift to me. Honest. Tired. Raw.

I blink. And blink again.

A shit storm of confusion and lust knots in my gut. And that other thing I don't let myself feel. The one that cartwheels in all cocky and irresponsible.

Hope.

That's the one that infuriates me.

"Why now?" I lift my head, uncurling from my hunched position. "After ignoring me all day, what changed?"

"I thought you wanted me." She doesn't look away.

"I do." The lump in my throat throbs. "But I'm not... I don't know how to be normal."

"I don't want normal." Her voice falls flat.

"You can sit closer." I loosen my death grip on the hem of my shirt. "Just don't ask about what you saw."

She scoots toward me slowly, cautiously, until her thigh brushes mine.

"Closer." I lean back, tucking my shirt into my pants.

After a beat, her hand reaches. Just her fingers on my arm.

We sit like that. Staring straight ahead. Neither of us moves.

Eventually, I pull in a breath and throw myself into the hush. "You ever try to scream, but your throat just locks up? Like you want to claw out the sound, but it won't come?"

"All the time." She turns toward me, holding my gaze.

"Yeah. That."

"I get it." She leans into me, resting her head on my shoulder. "Thank you for stopping me. You would've regretted it."

I huff a bitter breath. "Stopping you is the second most regrettable thing I've ever done."

"And the first?"

"Jumping off an unsurvivable cliff."

"You..." She tilts her head. "Jumped on purpose? To die?"

"To escape."

"I'm glad you didn't die."

We both fall silent again.

The sketchpad sits forgotten on the table. The ghosts continue to hover. But they feel quieter now.

"If you want to give me something..." I shift, bringing my mouth within a kiss from hers. "Tell me the truth about Jag. I need to know if my family's in danger. I need to know what you're running from."

She tenses. I feel it in her shoulders, in the acceleration of her breath.

"I won't use it against you." I touch the soft hair that flutters against her cheek. "But if there's something we need to prepare for..."

"Okay." She straightens and runs her hands along her thighs. "You're right. I'll tell you. Just... Don't interrupt. It's messy."

I nod.

"I was eight when I watched Jag kill a man for the first time."

"And here I thought this would be a slow burn story."

"You're interrupting."

I mime zipping my lips.

"My mom married his dad when I was a baby. David Rath was the only father I knew. Our parents weren't perfect, but they were good people. They loved each other. And they loved us." She flexes her fingers on her knees, her voice hollow. "Until that night."

I hold still, waiting for her to continue.

"Someone broke into our house. Jag pulled me into the kitchen pantry and covered my mouth while our parents were butchered on the other side of the door. I still remember the sound of their bodies hitting the floor."

My eyes stay with hers, my expression stripped of shock and pity. I have no soft edges to offer, just understanding. I've lived through worse and learned that silence says more than sympathy.

"The murderer knew we were hiding in the pantry. I thought we were dead. But the instant that door opened, Jag attacked him with a kitchen knife. Stabbed him over and over and over. There was so much blood. I'll never forget that smell. Or his total lack of emotion. He killed that man and showed no remorse. Nothing." She licks her Medusa piercing. "After that, we ran, and for a while, Jag became my *illegal* guardian."

"Illegal?"

"He was sixteen, barely able to take care of himself, let alone an eight-year-old. We lived on the streets, dodging social workers and cops. He taught me how to lie, how to steal, how to disappear. He saw threats everywhere, and me... I was the little sister he had to feed and protect. A burden. A reminder of the night he lost everything."

"Everything but *you*."

"He wasn't exactly grateful for that."

"Did he hurt you?"

"Not like that." She draws in a long breath. "But he hurt me. Emotionally. He kept me under his thumb. Kept me scared. Trapped. I thought I owed him everything. I thought..."

"You thought what?"

"I'll make some more drinks." She jumps from the couch and darts to the kitchen.

Seconds later, she returns with two glasses and a bottle of vodka. Perching on the coffee table before me, she pours the shots and hands me one.

"Is he dangerous?" I swallow the drink, savoring the smooth burn. "To us? To my family?"

"I was separated from Jag several times over the years, forced into the system, and... People died. When I was ten, I was molested by an older boy in my foster family. That night, the boy was beaten to death in his own bed. When I was eleven, another foster family roughed me up pretty good. Their house burned to the ground with them inside it. At age thirteen, I started down a long road of bad decisions regarding men, those I dated and those who didn't take *no* for an answer. Every male who put his hands on me met an untimely death. I can't prove Jag was behind all the murders, but I know. It was always him. And if he thinks you're interested in me, he'll come after you, too. He's not just smart. He's obsessive."

"He wants you." I breathe out through my nose. "He's jealous and possessive and wants you for himself."

"Is that why he paid one of his lovers to marry me? That's not jealous and possessive, Wolf. It's controlling. Besides, he's my stepbrother."

"*Stepbrother.* You throw that word around like it means something. But that's not how he looked at you last night."

She stiffens.

"He looked at you like he wanted to eat you alive. Consume you. Like the line between rage and desire doesn't exist for him." I lean into her space, elbows on my knees, shot glass dangling from my fingers. "And that thing he said... Now that you're single, he could be persuaded?" I slowly shake my head. "That wasn't a joke, Bluebird. It was a confession wrapped in a dare. He's not thinking like a brother. He's thinking like a man hellbent on owning you. Body and soul."

"You're wrong." She finishes her shot and pours another, avoiding my eyes.

There's more to that response. Something dark and unresolved festers between her and Jag. A secret she's not sharing. But I won't push. Not tonight. I have a graveyard of my own secrets, twenty-four years deep. I'll let her keep hers for now. Fair's fair.

I wait for her to look at me, and when she does, I see the questions scratching their way to the surface. She wants the stories. The juicy bits of the hell I crawled out of. The greatest hits from my personal apocalypse. Maybe if she hears how bad it got for me, she'll feel less alone in her own wreckage. Trauma roulette. Spin the wheel. Spill the damage. Pretend it makes us whole.

That's a game I'm not interested in playing.

"What's Gavin's story?" I set aside my glass.

"He's gay. I didn't know that until an hour before our wedding. God, how can I be so stupid?"

"It's not your fault."

"Yes, it is. Gavin told me he had erectile dysfunction." She holds up a finger and lets it flop like a boneless thing. "The only way he could get off was when he fucked me in the ass in the dark."

"So specific."

"And I was going to marry him because you know what? A nice guy is really fucking hard to find. I convinced myself that a nice guy with a limp dick was better than..."

"An asshole with a hard dick?"

"Being alone."

"Right." I bow my head against hers, letting our brows touch and our breaths mingle. "We're not all terrible. Some of us are fully functional and have ten out of ten Yelp reviews."

"I'm drawn to the worst of the worst."

"You're drawn to *me*." I stare into her hot-honey eyes.

Her breath catches. Barely audible. But I hear it. Feel it.

I pluck the shot glass from her fingers and set it aside. Then I trail the back of my hand along her jaw, soft and slow. Deliberate. My thumb grazes her bottom lip.

"You're dangerous." She doesn't pull away.

"You know I won't hurt you."

Lips parted and pupils wide, she presses her knees against mine as if her body pulls forward while her brain screams retreat. "You're a terrible idea."

"Terrible in all the best ways. That's why you aren't moving."

She doesn't answer. Doesn't need to. Her hands grip the table's edge, fighting the urge to reach for me.

"I've never done this." I set a knuckle under her chin, lifting her mouth to mine. "I've only kissed one woman in my life."

"Frankie?"

"Yes. In a faraway, frozen world, I kissed her. And she kissed me." I shift closer. "It wasn't sexual."

"What was it?" She breathes against my lips.

"Survival."

"And what is this?" Her whisper tastes like vodka.

"This is sexual." I erase the last millimeter. "And so much more."

Our lips meet, and the world folds in on itself. There's nothing else. No past. No ghosts. No nightmares. Just her and her warm mouth, colliding with mine in a crash of hunger and fire.

My hands hover for half a second before I find her waist, my fingers curling against the soft fabric of her top.

She kisses like she wants to forget. Like she's on the edge of a cliff, and I'm the drop.

And me? I kiss her like a virgin on a mission to save the world.

I don't know how to do this, but instinct takes over. My lips move against hers, learning her rhythm, tasting her urgency. She opens to me, and I groan from deep within my being. It spills out, confessing a truth I can't hide. I want her so badly it hurts.

Her hands abandon the table and find my chest, the line of my jaw, the ends of my hair. She tugs me closer, and I can't get enough. She invades my bloodstream.

I tilt my head and deepen the kiss, one hand sliding up her back, finding the curve of her neck. Her pulse pounds under my fingertips, mirroring mine, wild and free.

I pull her onto my lap, and she doesn't resist. Her thighs straddle me again, but this time, it's not chaotic. It's electric. Her breath hitches as I press our lips together, licking, exploring, imprinting.

Her body molds to mine, and merciful gods, she belongs here. This is where she was always meant to end up. My fingers dig into her hips, anchoring her to me as I kiss her like it's the first and last time I'll ever get the chance.

When we finally break apart, it's not for lack of wanting. It's because we have to breathe or die trying.

"Damn." Her forehead rests against mine, chest heaving, and lips swollen.

"You started it."

"Don't stop it."

wolfson
THIRTEEN

The first real kiss of my life doesn't sneak in like a whisper. It rips me open like a knife wound, messy and aching. I've been so starved for this and didn't know how empty I was until now.

Her lips feel warm and hungry, matching me beat for beat. Maybe she's been waiting for this, too. Waiting for a man who missed out on kissing his whole life.

With years of exploration to make up for, I map her mouth like it's the last frontier on Earth, my tongue dipping into every groove, learning the shape of her sighs and the density of her breath.

Straddling my lap, she digs her knees into the sides of my hips, and suddenly, the kiss isn't slow anymore.

Her hands knot in my hair, pulling and demanding. Mine slide under the hem of her tank top, up her back, feeling the curve of her spine, the heat of her skin. She's magnificent.

We shift and grip and press, her thighs clenching around me, my fingers digging into her waist as I wrench her closer, trying to melt us together.

We kiss until our lips are raw. Until my tongue goes numb. Until I know every secret hollow inside her mouth, and her taste permanently fuses with mine. There's nothing gentle about it.

wolfson

Nothing careful. It bruises into memory and sets the benchmark for all that come after.

At some point, I carry her upstairs, our lips locked together. She's light but fierce, clinging to me as if I'll disappear.

I lower her onto her bed and tuck the blankets around her. She's so sensual and precious, and when our lips finally part, our foreheads remain touching.

"I need to talk to my family." I brush the hair from her face.

"At five in the morning?"

"Yeah."

Frankie often works early, and I need to raise the alarms before she heads to the hospital.

Dove's eyes, glazed with sleep, darken with worry. And doubt.

"Hey." I cup her face, my thumb roving her cheek. "You're not alone. Not anymore. I swear to you, whatever this is between us, I'm in. You don't have to trust the world. Just trust me. And sleep. I'll be back before you know it."

She nods, but her hand catches mine as I stand. She doesn't grip, just holds, reminding me she exists.

I press a kiss to her knuckles and slip free. It's not easy. But keeping her safe means staying proactive. So I force my ass out of the room, out of the guest house, and into the pre-dawn morning.

Tugging up my hood, I make my way through the trees. My boots squish against the soft earth still damp from last night's rain. The house looms ahead, the massive stone monster that shouldn't feel like home.

But my brothers live there. And my father. And my Frankie, who's carrying my favorite future sister or brother. Technically, the baby will be my cousin since Monty had a vasectomy.

Who cares? If it's all the same to them, I want to be a big brother and call this island home.

Out back, under the wide awning of the porch, I spot them.

Leo, Kody, and Monty lounge on the outdoor sectional, wrapped in fleece and hoodie layers, hands curled around steaming mugs, staring at the flames flickering from the fire table.

A carafe of coffee waits on the sideboard, surrounded by a butcher block tray stacked with breakfast sandwiches, halved bagels, and foil-wrapped egg burritos. Probably Kody's doing.

The bear with eyes as black as soot is the first to glance my way, lifting his chin in a silent *You good?* gesture.

Oblivious, Leo laughs with a mouthful of food, muffling whatever joke Monty made.

Monty leans back like a king, a mug in one hand, his other resting comfortably on the back of Leo's seat.

They're not touching exactly, but the space between them is nonexistent. Legs brushing. Shoulders bumping. A shared language in every shift of their weight, every glance.

Leo's foot nudges Monty's absently as he reaches for another burrito. Kody tears his in half to share. Like they've done this a hundred times. Maybe they have.

Feels like I'm intruding on something sacred.

"There he is." Leo finally clocks me with a crooked tilt of his mouth. "Were your ears burning?"

"Only the important ones." I sit on the porch steps, not too close but not too far either.

"She settling in okay?" Monty sips his coffee.

"Right now, she's just trying to breathe."

They all share looks, knowing exactly how those first breaths feel after drowning. But underneath their empathy, there's a cautious undercurrent between them. Uncertainty about their new house guest.

"Where's Frankie?" I glance over my shoulder into the dark kitchen.

"Late night at the hospital." Leo chomps on his burrito, talking with his mouth full. "We're letting her sleep."

"No morning sex?" Eyes bulging, I bite my knuckles. "Oh, no."

He flips me off without looking up from his second favorite thing in the world. Food.

They're strange. All three of them. Beautiful and strange. They don't talk about it, what it means to share her, what it feels like, but it's there in every glance, every casual touch. The way Leo leans his head against Monty's shoulder for half a second before reaching for more coffee. The way Kody's knuckles brush Leo's thigh as he grabs a napkin. The way Monty looks at both of them with something between pride and possession.

It's not sexual. But it's intimate. Like a braided rope. Three strands, different colors, different textures, woven so tight I would need a blade to separate them.

Before Monty entered the scene, I was the third in the brotherhood. I still am, but Leo's and Kody's relationship with me is different than their relationship with Monty. Not lesser. Just different.

I watch them for a while. The way they exist together. The quiet rhythm of shared intimacy and loving the same woman without jealousy. It's not about ownership with them. It's about devotion. Like monks at the altar of Frankie Strakh.

A soft wind blows in from the trees. The sky bruises purple. Monty slugs back the dregs of his coffee.

Time to start the conversation I came for. "What have you found on Jag Rath?"

That sobers them instantly.

"I ran his name through my contacts." Monty leans forward, resting his forearms on his knees. "Interpol has a red notice for him under different aliases. Cyberterrorism. Fraud. Murder. He's connected to The Shadow Collection."

"Never heard of it."

"The group sells women out of Texas and California." Disgust flashes across Kody's face. "Your runaway bride wasn't wrong to run."

"We also traced several shell companies in South America back to his IP." Monty sets his mug down. "All funded through offshore accounts. This guy isn't just dirty. He's fucking radioactive."

"Dove said he's left a trail of carnage since she was eight." I exhale slowly. "She and Jag watched someone murder their parents, and he's been controlling her life since. He became her guardian and treated her like a burden. He used her. Scared her." I tell them everything she told me and the bits I pieced together. "She came to Sitka to kill him."

"She had the opportunity when she aimed a gun at him and didn't take it." Monty narrows his eyes. "What's her plan now?"

"Work, save money, and run far away." I rake a hand through my hair, knocking off my hood. "But I'm certain she still has revenge on the mind. He's returning to Sitka tonight."

"How do you know?" Leo asks.

"She got a text from him. He'll come for her. Probably doesn't know she's here yet, but it's only a matter of time."

Monty exchanges a glance with Kody and Leo. It's fast and efficient. A silent agreement. Then he turns back to me.

"Untangle yourself from this," he says in a steel-edged voice. "Send her away."

He's never used that tone on me, and it lands like a scalpel across my chest.

I laugh. Once. A hollow sound scraped straight from the marrow. Then I stand, slowly, because my sudden, protective rage requires unwrapping. "I'm not one of your fuck boys, Monty. I'm not yours to command, and she's not yours to dismiss."

"Out of line!" Leo launches to his feet, finger stabbing the air toward me, fire blazing in his mismatched eyes. "Talk to Monty like that again, and I swear to God—"

"Swear to God what?" I shift closer. "You gonna teach me a lesson, Leo? A lesson on how to let unprotected women die? You're good at that."

It's a low blow. He blames himself for the deaths of the women in Hoss, but it wasn't his fault. Not entirely.

"This isn't about your new friend." His fists flex at his sides, nostrils flaring. "It's about you treating Monty like shit because you can't stand taking orders."

"Oh, fuck you." I study the displeased faces of my family. "Look, I don't need your permission. With or without your support, I'll tear this town apart to keep my girl safe."

"*Your* girl?" Leo's eyes widen, disbelieving. "Come on, Wolf. You barely know her. You can't just dive in headfirst and think that loving her hard enough will fix the cracks inside you."

That does it. I grab the first thing within reach, an empty coffee mug off the sideboard, and hurl it.

Leo ducks, and it explodes against the concrete behind him, shards flying.

Kody stands. No words. Just the quiet scrape of his chair legs, his posture stone-still. The signal. The moment before someone bleeds.

If Frankie were here, she'd shut this shit down with one look. But I handled these pillow humpers for twenty years before she showed up. I don't need a damn chaperone now.

As I plant my legs, bracing for a fight, Monty's cold command whips across the patio.

"Stand down." He looks at Kody, then me, and wraps his

fingers around Leo's hand.

Leo jerks like he'll resist, but Monty rises and puts his lips near Leo's ear.

I don't hear what Monty says, but the fight slowly leaks from Leo's shoulders like steam escaping a cracked pipe. His breathing slows. His glare loses its venom. Then he nods and drops to the couch with Monty at his side.

"All right." Monty trains his ice-blue eyes on me as the air continues to crackle. "Say your piece, Son."

I take a breath. Not a shaky one. An important one. Because everything I'm about to say matters.

"I'm not asking for your approval." I glance between them. My blood. My family. My chaos and my anchors. "When it was Frankie on the line, you threw yourselves into battle for her. Against Denver. Against the Arctic. Against the doctor. Against all odds. You protected her, chose her, when the cost could've been your lives. I didn't question it. I respected the hell out of it. That level of loyalty and love? It's the only thing that's ever made sense to me."

I turn to Leo. "You would've died for her."

To Kody. "You almost did. Twice."

Then to my dad. "You gave up your life, your career, everything in your world to get her back."

They don't argue. They remember.

"That's what this is for me." I tap my chest, slow and hard. "You think I'm reckless and fall too fast. Maybe you're right. But this isn't some crush or passing obsession. It's instinct, bone-deep and loud as a gunshot. My gut, the same one that kept us alive in the hills, tells me she's the one I'm supposed to protect now. Not because she's weak or helpless. But for the first time in my fucked-up life, I look at someone and see a future that doesn't end in loneliness."

They don't move. Don't speak.

"If I ignore this instinct, if I walk away because it's inconvenient or messy or dangerous..." A huff escapes my throat. "I'll regret it every day for the rest of my hellborn life. I have enough ghosts. I'm not adding her to the list." I square my shoulders, my voice calm despite the volcanic heat in my chest. "You don't have to trust her. You just have to trust me. The same way I've always trusted you."

Silence swells around them, no longer angry or hostile. Just heavy. When it settles in their eyes, I see approval. And something deeper.

Pride.

Respect.

For once, I think that means I said it right.

"You want to protect her." Monty straightens. "Then we'll protect her. But understand this. When she brings danger to our door, we'll do what's necessary. All of us. No hesitation. No apologies. We go full Strakh on this."

My mouth dries.

Full Strakh.

I know what that means. I've seen what that means. When they're in, they're *all in*.

"She's under our roof now." Monty shares a look with Leo and Kody. "So we'll protect her like she's one of our own."

"Fine." Leo sits back.

Kody nods and returns to his spot on the couch.

One of our own.

Deep in my chest, an ancient instinct coils. The instinct to kill for her. Or die trying.

"We'll handle the legal and digital side and put a discreet security detail on her." Monty meets my eyes. "How will she respond to that?"

"She won't run." I rub my nape, thinking. "She's different than anyone I've met. She's tough and doesn't want anyone to save her. But she needs us. She needs *me.*"

The patio goes quiet for a stretch before Leo speaks. "If she doesn't want anyone saving her, she won't tolerate a security team."

"She's stubborn." I exhale a breath. "But not irrational. She knows when to accept help."

"Ask her." Kody directs his gaze toward the edge of the trees. "She's been eavesdropping this whole time."

We all turn.

I squint at the shadows between the guest house and the trees. Sure enough, there's a pale glint. A shimmer of blue hair.

"Dove," I call, not harsh, just enough to let her know she's been made.

"I didn't mean to eavesdrop." She steps out of the dark, arms crossed and shoulders tight. "When I heard my name…"

"Come here." I crook a finger.

Carefully, as if stepping into enemy territory, she edges closer. And closer. When she settles on the edge of the porch beside me, still not touching but close enough to share heat, the night air settles, too.

She's one of us now.

For a moment, no one says anything.

Then Leo, predictably, breaks the silence. "So Dove... You want his head, his balls, or his bank accounts first?"

"He doesn't keep anything valuable in his pants." Dove blinks. "I want the only thing he's ever really loved. His control."

Leo's expression slackens, all woolly bigfoot-like with knotty braids twisting around his face.

"We need to understand what kind of criminal we're dealing with." Monty tips his head. "We have money, resources, and a lot of reach, but we need to know what we're fighting."

Dove hesitates, and I give her a small nod.

"Jag's a hacker." She exhales through her nose. "A damn good one. He doesn't just break into systems. He burrows into them. Governments, banks, private security firms, even hospitals. He covers his tracks better than anyone. I don't know why he does it. He never told me."

"He has enemies." Kody leans forward.

She nods. "Some are underground. Violent. I've seen things over the years. Scary men following me and him showing up at the right time to stop the attack. He would chase me from one town to the next then up and disappear for a month. I stopped asking questions. He doesn't like questions."

"He's possessive of you." Leo frowns.

"I don't know why. It's not the hacking. Not the power. It's me. The one thing he thinks he can control. Since our parents died when I was eight, he's been watching me, shaping me, caging me. If I step outside the role he wrote for me, he loses his mind."

"Then we start there." Monty nods, already building a strategy behind his eyes. "We disrupt his control and identify his contacts and enemies."

"I'll lure him." Eagerness charges my blood. "Play with him for a bit."

"You don't know what he will do." Dove's expression

hardens.

"You don't know what *I* will do." I grip her chin.

Rather than pulling away, she leans into my touch.

"In the meantime," I breathe, pressing closer, "you won't go anywhere without armed guards."

"I can't afford that."

"We can," Monty says.

"I appreciate your help, but…" She shifts aways from my touch. "What do you want in return?"

"Nothing."

She makes a sound of disbelief.

"Don't insult us, Sparkplug." I clasp her nape, capturing her gaze. "Accept our protection."

"I don't understand. You're… What? Offering a security team pro bono? Without payment of any kind?"

"Exactly."

She sits with that for a moment, absorbing the repercussions with a pinched expression. "Will they be discreet?"

"You'll hardly notice them."

"Okay."

"Okay?" I arch a brow. "No fight?"

"I would be an idiot to turn down your help."

"Good girl." I kiss her lips and release her.

When I glance at my father and brothers, their predatory eyes watch with curiosity.

I can't control life. I may never control my demons. But keeping Dove safe? That's one fate I'll bend until it screams.

jag
FOURTEEN

The salt-tinged morning air stabs through my hair as I lean against the weathered rail of Sitka Harbor. Fog lifts from the water like a ghost fleeing the sun, revealing sleek yachts and rugged fishing boats.

My eyes lock on a specific vessel as it slices through the waves and docks effortlessly, its polished exterior a gleaming insult against my shit life.

Dove emerges alone.

Sunlight spills over her blue hair as she steps onto the dock, confident and unafraid, heading straight toward me.

She doesn't see me, the wheelhouse of a longliner blocking her view. But I see her, her defiant gait a challenge to my patience as she saunters past.

No sign of Wolfson Strakh. She probably slipped away before he realized he'd been ditched.

I push off from the rail, rest the thumb of my broken wrist in my pocket, and keep a careful distance.

The docks buzz with early morning life, fishermen hauling nets, tourists snapping photos, and children darting between legs. Perfect cover.

Dove moves swiftly, unaware of my gaze drilling into her

back.

My heart pounds, my blood a silent squall beneath the surface. I don't know what I'll do when I get my hands on her. The idea of locking her away and caging her like a feral pet is appealing. Somewhere remote. Somewhere no one can find her.

Movement shifts at the edge of my vision.

Two men trail her, blending expertly, keeping a discreet yet constant distance.

I narrow my eyes.

Not ordinary men. Professionals. Disciplined, alert professionals.

My chest constricts.

Are they here for me? Impossible. No one knows I'm in Alaska.

Realization hits. They're not stalking Dove. They're *protecting* her. Strakh family guards, no doubt.

A dark surge of rage twists through my gut.

Dove is mine. No one has the right to keep her from me.

A few blocks later, she disappears into the mechanic shop. Her coworkers shuffle around inside, visible through grimy windows. The security detail sets up silently around the perimeter, vigilant and lethal.

I clench my jaw, every muscle vibrating with restrained fury. I have to rethink this. She's not unguarded. Not vulnerable. Not anymore. Plans need changing, angles reconsidered.

Turning sharply, I head toward the tattoo shop, my boots heavy against the damp concrete.

The shop sits quiet, closed on Mondays, a sanctuary and hideaway rolled into one. But it's not my real haven. My servers, hacker equipment, and surveillance gear lie hidden in an abandoned shed a few blocks away.

Losing that is as dangerous as losing Dove.

Sliding my key into the lock, I swing open the door to the tattoo shop. The darkness inside feels innocuous.

Until I sense a shift in the shadows, a loose breath betraying another presence.

My hand freezes on the door, and my pulse jumps into an alert rhythm.

"Took you long enough." The voice comes smooth, darkly amused, from a shadowed corner. "I almost started without you."

Wolfson Strakh sits comfortably, a leg crossed over his knee and eyes glittering like arctic ice in the low light. Disarming and casual all at once.

A chill curls up my spine, anticipation threading through the anger. His presence means trouble, maybe even disaster. But if he thinks he has the upper hand, he's gravely mistaken.

"Started what without me?" I shut the door, locking us in the shadows.

"Making the playlist for your funeral. Any last requests?"

"'Don't Fear the Reaper.'"

"Good choice." He leans forward, resting his elbows on his knees. "Leave town. You're not welcome here."

"Is that a threat, Strakh? Or an invitation to play? Either way, I'm not going anywhere."

"You misunderstand." He tilts his head, assessing me. "It's a warning. Dove doesn't want you here. None of us do."

"Dove belongs to *me*." I step closer, thrumming with a sinister thrill of anticipation.

"Belongs to you?" He rises from the chair, controlled grace infused with menace. The faint scent of smoke drifts off him as he closes the distance. "She's not your property, pretty kitty. Touch her again, and I'll rearrange your internal organs. Alphabetically."

"Dove and I have a history that spans a lifetime." Fury ignites my veins. "What do you have? Two days with her? No matter how many thugs your family hires, you can't erase me."

"Yeah, your history's a real fairy tale. Murdered parents, paranoid obsession, pathological stalking, dead bodies... You're every girl's dream psycho."

Heat floods my face and drains to a cold numbness.

Dove confided in him. She shared our pain. Our past. The thought scrapes my chest raw, gouging deeper than a blade. It feels like betrayal, like death, like everything I've fought for is slipping away.

"You might think you own this town, but you don't own me." I straighten. "You don't own Dove. And you don't scare me."

"If you're not scared, you're even more fucked in the head than I thought. Dove hates you. How does it feel knowing she'd rather die than see your face again?"

"She'll come around. She always does." My breath turns ragged, hatred flaring white-hot. "But you? You're just another mistake she'll regret in a long line of mistakes."

He spreads his arms open, palms up in a challenge, silently inviting me to try harder.

This guy. He's not normal.

"Last chance." His mouth quirks into a bored half-smile. "Leave town. Disappear. Or you won't leave here alive."

"You think you're untouchable?" The weight of the gun at my waist makes my fingers twitch, itching to draw. "I'll enjoy proving you wrong."

In a flash, my good hand jerks toward my weapon, but he moves faster, steel glinting from the sleeve of his jacket.

A cold, sharp blade presses against my throat before I can finish drawing.

"Try that again, sugar." He flicks his goddamn tongue against my earlobe. "I'll make sure your blood splashes beautifully."

Adrenaline roars through my veins. Too bad my free hand is broken. Otherwise, I'd grab his dick just to watch his reaction.

I see it clearly, the ruthless violence behind his calm mask. But I sense his confusion, too. He doesn't know whether to gut me or fuck me. I bet he's never been with a man. But he thinks about it. Jacks himself to images of it.

All that untapped curiosity and testosterone make him easy prey. Easy to draw him close, twist him around my finger, and break him down until Dove returns to me.

"You're playing with fire." I swallow against the blade's tip, causing it to nick my skin.

"I live in fire. Now get the hell out of my town."

The blade digs deeper, drawing a thin trickle of blood that warms as it trails down my throat. "Everyone bleeds, Strakh. Even you."

"Oh, sweetheart, I bleed just fine. The difference is I like it."

I move swiftly, jerking back just enough to free myself from the blade's immediate threat, and draw my gun fully this time. I level it directly at his chest, my finger tense against the trigger.

"Go on, Codebreaker." He doesn't flinch or blink. "Let's see what your fingers can do without a keyboard."

I'm not surprised he knows about my criminal activities. With a family like his, stacked with money, muscle, and roots that can be traced back to Soviet nightmares, they probably dug up some juicy, high-profile shit on me. My hacks. My breaches.

jag

My fingerprints in digital blood.

But here's the thing.

He only knows the tip of the iceberg.

Most people think the surface is all there is. The pretty white tip glinting in the sun. A couple of cyber crimes, a few blackmail trails, some corrupted files on a senator's server. That's child's play. That's bait.

The real iceberg is structured like the nine circles of hell.

The upper layer is a breeding ground for script kiddies and amateur hackers. Wannabes trading malware like porn and chasing dopamine highs with ransomware.

The professionals play in the middle layers. Governments. Corporate espionage. Silent wars waged in fiber-optic veins. It's clean, efficient, and mostly anonymous.

But deep beneath it all, where no light touches, is where I live.

The bottom layer.

The abyss.

That's where the monsters dwell. We don't leave digital footprints. We leave ghost stories. We don't crash systems. We dismantle lives, identities, infrastructures, *nations.* Down there, code isn't written. It's etched in bone.

That's where I made my kingdom.

For all of Wolfson's charm and knives and mobbed-up bloodlines, he's never been that deep. He doesn't even know that kind of cold exists.

Not yet.

But he will.

"You're not the first pretty thing I've broken," I murmur.

For a long second, we stare each other down, tension thickening the air, every heartbeat resonating like thunder.

I can squeeze the trigger and end this right now. One bullet and all that wolfish sex appeal would bleed out onto the floor. The Strakhs would retaliate, sure. But not before I disappear. Not before I take Dove and vanish.

But I don't move.

Not because I'm scared. Not because he's faster, though he is. No, something in me just…

Hesitates.

I hate to fucking admit it, but Dove's safe with him. With all of them. The Strakhs won't hurt her. If anything, she'll hurt Wolfson.

That's fine. Let her break his heart like she breaks every damn thing she touches.

But sex?

No.

That's the line.

I can't stomach the thought of her hands in his hair, her legs around his waist. That kind of betrayal would rupture something vital in me.

And yet...

I don't pull the trigger.

There's something about him. Something magnetic. Unholy. The way he moves. The way he smiles like a man who's already tasted my secrets. I hate it. I want to destroy him for it. But deep down, an ugly, buried part of me likes it.

Not that I'll admit that.

So I rewrite the story. Turn it into strategy.

Wolfson comes from money. Filthy, generational, mob-fueled money. His family bleeds power. I can use that.

I'll get close and seduce him with the right words, irresistible glances, and perfect tension. Poor little emo boy won't even know he's being manipulated.

He'll fall.

When I've taken his trust, his access, and his inheritance, I'll take Dove, and we'll disappear again. New city. New names. Same shadows.

That's the long game.

And that's when the front door bursts open, breaking our fragile standoff.

Three figures flood into the tattoo shop, all unmistakably lethal.

Monty, Leonid, and Kodiak Strakh fan out, instantly encircling me. Monty and Leonid hold sleek black pistols, their stances formidable, murderous intent radiating from their eyes. Kodiak aims a damn crossbow at me, his expression predatory.

Hunters. Savages. Murderers.

Just like me.

"Throwing a party?" Leonid's gold and blue eyes glitter with malicious amusement. "Didn't invite us?"

"We would've been here sooner if your shower routine

didn't take an hour." Monty points a smirk at Leo's braids.

"I have a lot of sins to wash off." Leo waggles a brow in return.

I clench my jaw, recognizing each face from exhaustive surveillance and digging. They're killers, ruthless and efficient, as monstrous as the rumors. This isn't a situation I can win through force. But pride keeps me anchored.

"Your town, your rules." Gun steady on Wolfson, I meet Monty's eyes. "Is that it?"

Monty hardens his glare, casually aiming his gun, and damn it all, he looks good doing it. It's the suit. Each tailored thread clings to him like sin, cut to perfection over a body that shouldn't belong to a fifty-year-old man.

Not just any man. A legacy. Old money. Russian mob. How many lives has he ruined with a single phone call?

My stomach twists with admiration and resentment. I hate men like him.

Wish I could say the same about his son.

Wolfson looks like him. Same bone structure, same god-tier DNA, but younger, wilder, and draped in rebellion instead of Armani. While he carries it differently, less polished, more unpredictable, the effect is the same.

No, it's worse. Wolfson's perfect, symmetrical, angelic face could start wars or end them, depending on who's watching.

It's me. I'm watching. And I'm inconveniently aroused.

Hell knows I've dug up everything on the Strakhs, memorizing every photo and studying their habits. None more than Monty's blue-eyed freak of a son. And yet nothing prepares me for standing in the same room with all four of them.

They don't just live in Alaska. They *are* Alaska. Raw, stunning, and carved out of ice. If I'm being honest with myself, I'd let them rip me open if it meant I could crawl inside their minds and understand what makes predators like them breathe. Because there's a terrible, majestic beauty in them. A beauty that seduces.

But I'm not here for that. I'm here to take back what's mine.

"Pull your dogs off my sister." I flex my jaw. "Or I'll start dropping bodies."

Kodiak grunts behind his crossbow.

"We know all about your body count." Leo shifts his weight.

"Then you know I've buried better men in worse places."

"I appreciate the show of support, ladies." Wolfson lowers his blade and strolls forward, positioning himself between me and his murderous family. "But you interrupted a special moment. Jag was about to admit his undying love for me."

"By undying, you mean dead." Leonid directs a pointed look at the gun I still aim at Wolfson.

"He's misunderstood." Wolfson shrugs and winks at me over his shoulder. "Aren't you, baby?"

My brows furrow. How does anyone take him seriously?

"He's a threat," Monty snaps.

"I hear you." Wolfson pinches the bridge of his nose and peers at me. "When it comes to threats, the Strakhs do one thing and one thing only."

"We kill them." Leo bares his teeth.

"Mm-hmm. Yeah." Wolfson nods to himself. "But we all agreed I would take the lead on this."

"No." Monty exchanges a look with the others. "No one agreed to that."

"Let's try something new." Ignoring my gun, Wolfson returns to my side, drapes an arm over my shoulders, and taps his blade on my chest. "Threats can be managed. Let's do some managing."

"We don't negotiate with terrorists," Kodiak snarls.

"True, but he's no ordinary terrorist." Wolfson squeezes my shoulder. "He's mine."

My chest heaves, torn between homicidal impulses and curiosity at his bizarre approach.

Sex is my weapon of choice. Give me five minutes with a man, woman, trans, or non-binary person of any sexual orientation, and I can have them on their back and panting through a release before they realize I've stolen their passwords, drained their bank accounts, and opened their throat.

With Wolfson, it won't just be easy. I'll fucking enjoy it. He's irrationally gorgeous, viciously uncivilized, and sculpted in the image of an archangel from the underworld. I'll savor every glorious inch of him before I take his last breath.

But first, I need to get rid of his family. If I'm reading the room correctly, Wolfson doesn't want them here, either.

I catch his gaze. "You want me to leave town. Your family wants me dead." I look between each armed man. "And I want my sister back. How do we reconcile that?"

"Newsflash. Dove's decisions are non-negotiable. She made her choice, and shocker, it's not you. But here's what I can do." Wolfson swishes the knife in the direction of his workstation. "Let me keep my job here, and I'll let you leave breathing. Simple enough?"

"Absolutely not." Monty scowls.

"And he wonders why we don't let him take the lead." Leonid huffs.

"Yet here we are." Wolfson keeps his eyes locked on mine, gauging my response, before turning back to his family. "Look, Rath Vader isn't going anywhere. We all know that."

"Rath Vader?" I arch a brow.

"Heavy breathing, dramatic entrances, daddy issues... The helmet fits." He returns his attention to the Strakhs. "Killing the dark one just complicates things."

"Or solves them." Leonid steps forward.

"Do we really need another dead psychopath? Yawn. Been there, stabbed that. Let's try this new thing called restraint."

"And risk Dove's safety?" Monty asks.

"Dove's protected. Unlike her brother." Wolfson ruffles my hair. "I always wanted a house pet. I'll feed him and deworm him and buy him a pretty collar. If he bites, I'll put him down. I promise."

I study Wolfson closely, trying to unravel his angle.

He's not sane. Not even close. He's madness dressed in eyeliner and flower-printed rain boots. Unmedicated, unbothered, and somehow still functioning. But put a needle in his hand, and the tragedy becomes alchemy.

Wolfson Strakh can tattoo like no one I've ever seen. A fact I discovered through meticulous research.

An idea forms quickly, driven partly by cruelty, partly by intrigue.

"Fine." I narrow my eyes, catching the interest in his. "I'll take your deal. Under one condition."

"Yes?" He flutters his lashes.

"You give me a tattoo. Today."

Silence hugs the room for an awkward moment before Wolfson bursts out laughing. "For real?"

A chorus of objections resounds from the rational ones as I

nod, confirming my offer.

"Told you." He smiles at his disapproving family. "He wants me under his skin in every sense. I should charge double."

He jokes, but he doesn't see it. He's inviting me in. The second he touches me, *I* will be under *his* skin.

People think it's greed or fear that destroys them. It's not. It's the need to be unique. The sick little ache to be noticed. Recognized. Admired by all. That's the real human weakness. The fatal flaw.

Nothing cracks open a human faster than the sweet sound of their own name.

Wolfson wears that flaw like a badge. He might not realize how tightly he clings to his ego-stroking art and personalized validation, but he will. When it all burns, it won't be blood paving the way to his demise. It'll be that deep hunger for affirmation that he couldn't live without.

I don't have to do much. Just wait. Wait until he falls to his knees, arms reaching, shattered, and shaking.

And I'll be there. No lube. No mercy.

wolfson
FIFTEEN

"Out." I make a shooing motion at my brothers. "You have a distillery to run, planes to fly, and..." I lock eyes with my father. "You have a pint-sized baby mama to irritate."

When Frankie got abducted, Monty dropped the whole CEO gig like a bad habit, ditched his billion-dollar empire, and spent every second tearing the world apart to find her. When he finally got her back, he didn't return to work.

He still wears the suits and owns the global enterprise. But he spends every waking moment orbiting Frankie and my brothers like a control freak. Watching. Managing. Pulling strings no one asked him to touch.

I don't know how they stand it. If he tried that shit with me, I'd fold his pretentious clothes with him in it.

At the mention of Frankie, Monty leans back against the counter, arms folded and jaw clenched. Leo's eyes blaze with the flesh-mauling thoughts of a mountain troll, and Kody's dark stare drills into Jag, aiming to crush him with a single glance.

They can't hide Frankie's existence or their baby growing inside her. They sure as hell can't hide what they would do if someone touched what's theirs. It wouldn't be justice. It would be annihilation.

As the shop bleeds hostility, Jag Rath stands at the center, shoulders back, hands relaxed at his sides as if he isn't the target of their violent thoughts. His smirk mocks us all.

At least the weapons have been sheathed.

"You're going to ink the man who wants you dead?" Monty growls. "Think through this, Son."

"Relax. He's letting me put needles in his skin. Not the other way around. If he twitches, I'll just bleed him a little faster."

They know I can handle myself. I don't need a gun or a blade. I am the weapon. My reflexes, instincts, and total lack of fucks to give... No civilized man can match that.

I wasn't made here. Hoss built me. I'm apex by design. Teeth, fists, and ferocity are my factory settings. Same as my brothers.

Which is why Monty gives a tight nod and steps into Jag's space like he owns the man's air. "Hand over your weapons."

Jag flashes his teeth, bristling with ice and arrogance, but he does it. So do I. Not that it matters. There are enough guns stashed in this place to start a small war.

But that's not the point.

Monty is laying down the rules. If this gets ugly, it stays personal. No steel. No bullets. Just skin, bone, and pain. Because Monty knows, if it comes down to bare hands, I'm walking out. Jag is not.

Even if Jag's wrist wasn't as swollen and black as roadkill, I'd still put him down. But damn. Just looking at the busted thing makes my knuckles ache in sympathy. He should really get it checked out.

Or not. I'm not his babysitter. Let it rot.

Monty leaves first. Leo and Kody follow, casting dark looks at Jag. When the door shuts, I exhale slowly and size up my opponent.

Alone, he's more menacing. All coiled muscle and primal stillness. Everything about him radiates sex. It pisses me off that I feel it.

Lucky for me, I have a thing for women.

Women who dye their hair blue and smell like motor oil.

"Get comfortable." I gesture at the tattoo chair. "Do you know what you want?"

"A leg sleeve."

I go still. "That's..."

"Sixty hours of work. Longer if the design is complex." He cocks his head. "I expect complex."

"Riiiight. But when you said a tattoo…"

"You assumed it would be a single session. That's *your* problem." He reaches for his belt with his good hand, fingers deftly working the buckle. "Start with a thigh piece."

"Intimate." I lean against my workbench, watching him undress without modesty.

"Thought you were a professional." He steps out of his jeans, revealing sculpted thighs dusted with hair.

"I am. Strippers are professional, too. And while you're working them, they're working you. Are you trying to work me, Rath?"

"Maybe you're reading too much into it." He removes his shirt because… *Why?*

"And you're saying nothing while revealing everything."

Jesus in a crop top, his physique is imposing. Broad shoulders, lean waist, rippling muscles, all that shit. Why am I staring? It's just aesthetics. Like admiring a weapon. Doesn't mean I want to fuck the knife.

Still… There's a pull. Feral. Wrong.

Impossible.

I shove it down hard. I'm not into him.

"Do you have a design in mind?" I force my gaze to his.

"I want a biomechanical jaguar. Full-sized." He gestures at the rock-hard muscle from his knee to his hip. "With electrical circuits for veins and its claws gripping an anatomical heart covered in feathers."

"A heart with feathers?" I narrow my eyes.

"You heard me."

"Sounds personal."

"It is." He smiles, cold and secretive.

I nod slowly, understanding too well. The jaguar is his namesake. The feathered heart, obviously Dove's. The circuits, his hacker skills, his need for control.

The whole thing is fucked-up and obsessive, exactly like him. It's also clever, unapologetic, and badass. I hate myself for appreciating his vision.

Without another word, I sketch the design, blending sleek fur into intricate circuit patterns and claws sinking deep into the symbolic heart of a bird. Each line feels like a confession, each stroke a betrayal.

When I present the outline to Jag, his gaze softens with satisfaction, barely perceptible but undeniably there.

"Perfect." He drops onto the chair.

After I prep my station, I don my gloves and straddle the stool, rolling it close to where he sits. Right up to his exposed, muscular thigh.

The room holds its breath as I grab a razor.

Why are my hands shaking? I shave strangers every day.

Resting a palm on his leg for balance, I drag the blade along the curve of his thigh and clear away the fine dusting of hair. The razor glides in slow strokes, and each pass leaves a clean, bare path behind it. His skin is smooth beneath the steel, the muscle taut underneath.

I focus too hard on the task. Maybe because Jag focuses too hard on me. The intensity in his stare makes the back of my neck prickle.

That done, I grab a sharpie and sketch directly onto his skin. No stencil. I rely on instinct and muscle memory.

Hard flesh flexes beneath my pen, sending a jolt through my nerves.

"Higher," he murmurs.

With his black briefs in the way, I stretch the material to the side and add more detail farther up. Muscle leaps under my touch, but I don't look at his face. I can't.

"Higher," he repeats. "I want the piece to wrap over the hip, reaching into the oblique."

I can't move the fabric high enough for what he wants. I pause, about to tell him it won't work unless—

In one fluid motion, he hooks a thumb into the waistband and lowers his underwear, letting it hang around his knees. He's completely exposed, utterly shameless.

Sweet suffering Christ.

I flick my gaze away before I get a good look at his dick.

"Problem?" he asks.

"Only if you start moaning. Cover yourself."

"Are you this shy with all your clients?" He fully removes his underwear and drapes it over himself. "Or just me?"

"You're not the first pervert to drop his pants in my chair."

But he's the sexiest.

Not that I care.

I return to the outline, drawing carefully, aware of my knuckles moving within inches of his groin and my breath brushing the inside of his leg. Every line I sketch is another line I'll have to ink.

It's going to be a long damn day.

"So…" My hand glides up the inside of his leg, the jaguar taking shape in my mind and flowing from my fingers. "Why her?"

He stares ahead for a beat, then down at me. "She's mine."

"That's a diagnosis."

"You think I'm sick?"

"I think you're obsessive. Murderous. Maybe worse."

"Obsessive is just another word for consistent."

"And murderous?"

"You tell me." His hooded copper eyes dip to my mouth. "You chopped up Sitka's beloved heart surgeon without blinking an eye. That wasn't survival. It was pleasure."

I pause, the sharpie frozen above his skin.

How the fuck does he know about the doctor?

"Don't pretend you're the gentler animal." He drags his tongue across his bottom lip. "You think if you play hero to a woman with scars, no one will notice the ones you're trying to hide?"

"You don't know a fucking thing about me." Reflexively, I clench my scarred abdomen.

"I know enough.

"How did Dove get her scars?"

"How did you get yours?"

"Your hacker skills didn't divulge that?"

He sighs.

I return to drawing, pressing harder, making the lines bolder. More jagged. Less art. More confession. "She's not a prize to fight over."

"No," Jag says. "She's a battlefield, and we're the soldiers."

"We're not the same."

"Not when it comes to her. You hold her hand. I hold her by the throat."

"And you think she wants that?"

"She came to Sitka. For *me*."

"To kill you."

"She had multiple opportunities. Yet here I am."

I finish the sketch in silence, swap my gloves for a fresh pair, and grab the machine.

With a quick glance at his nude form, I confirm what I already assumed. This will be his first tattoo.

But I notice something else.

A scar.

Faint, old, but not forgotten by the flesh, it lives just below his rib cage. A thin line, no longer angry but stubborn in its permanence. The width of my thumb. Clean entry. No fraying at the edges. Someone knew how to hold a blade, and they sank it deep.

A kill shot.

Whoever did it meant for him to bleed out.

I've seen stab wounds. Too many. Dozens mar my reflection in the mirror. I know how they age, how they change over time. This one is ancient history.

Who put it there? An ex-lover? A job gone wrong? Dove?

I hope it was her.

The buzz of the machine is the only warning I give him before driving the needle into his knee.

It's an excruciatingly sensitive spot, but his body doesn't flinch. Eyes half-lidded, breathing steady, he takes the pain like it's a cigarette break.

The only sign he feels anything is the way his fingers flex against the chair, slow and rhythmic, syncing with the pulse of the needle.

"You like hurting me," he says after the initial shock of pain passes.

"You deserve worse."

We lock eyes.

The buzz returns.

The ink sinks deeper.

Neither of us speaks for a long time, but I feel his gaze pressing against my skin, stroking, burning, never leaving.

"Watching your artist work?" I don't look up. "Or are you undressing me with your eyes again?"

"I can multitask."

"Yeah, well, keep your fantasies to yourself. You're not my type."

"Sure about that?"

"You're not even your type." I wipe away a bead of ink and angle the machine higher, tracing around the outline of the heart. "She told me you used to scare her."

"I protected her."

"By fucking her fiancé?"

He's quiet a breath too long. Then... "Dove and I survived things together. Things you wouldn't understand."

"Try me."

He shifts, the motion subtle. Not discomfort. Something else. "We were hunted. Homeless. Starving. On the run. I was sixteen. She was eight. I kept her alive."

"Hunted by whom?"

"The police. Social services. The people who murdered our parents. You name it."

"Who murdered your parents?"

"Monsters. That's all you need to know."

"So you went through some shit together. Doesn't explain why you look at her the way you do. Like she's not your stepsister." I grind the needle a little deeper, intentional, watching the skin respond.

He doesn't flinch. "Maybe you should pay attention to how she looks at *me*."

"She seems more interested in disappearing from your life entirely."

"You assume she knows what she feels."

"And you do?"

"I know she needs me. That's never changed."

"You're the reason she sleeps with a knife under her pillow."

This time, he does flinch. "You protect her like you know her."

"I protect her because I recognize a cage when I see one."

"You think I'm her prison." He tilts his head.

"I think that's your plan."

The machine buzzes against his skin as I begin detailing the circuitry veins running along the jaguar's spine.

His eyes remain on my face, studying, curious. Carnal.

"Why didn't you let your vicious brothers kill me?" he asks.

"Dove doesn't want that, and for now, that's enough. But don't mistake my patience for forgiveness."

"I don't think you want me dead, either."

I pause, glancing at his swollen, broken wrist resting on his abdomen. "Nice hand."

Fury ignites in his eyes, reminding me who I'm tattooing.

"Touchy." I wipe the ink away with more force than necessary.

"Speaking of touchy, have you touched my sister?"

"Yes. But that's not what you're asking." I meet his gaze evenly. "You want to know if I'm giving her the ol' in and out."

"Are you?" His voice drops to a guttural rasp.

Ah. There it is. The edge beneath the question. The crack in his tone he tried to bury under a cool, murderous whisper. I struck something vital.

He doesn't care if I'm dangerous. Doesn't care that I have needles in his skin or that I could break his other wrist without blinking.

But the idea that I've been inside her? That I've touched what he thinks belongs to him? That's the wound that bleeds. He's not afraid of death. He's afraid of being replaced. That's his weakness. Not pain. Not blood. *Her.*

I could lie. Feed him every brutal detail he's terrified to hear. Watch the storm roll in behind his eyes and swallow him whole.

I could own him with a few graphic words.

Too easy. Too fast. Better to let him squirm. Let him question. Let that image poison his brain from the inside out. Because if I want to break Jag Rath, I won't do it with fists.

I'll do it with suggestion.

With silence.

With every moment I don't answer, every breath I leave hanging.

Let him wonder if I've claimed the only thing he's ever pretended to love.

Let him choke on it.

wolfson

wolfson

SIXTEEN

As I resume tattooing, the silence pulls like skin over bone, broken only by the hum of the machine.

The intensity vibrating off Jag Rath won't quit. Neither will my questions.

What is he to Dove? More than a stepbrother? Has he touched her? Has she let him? How far have they gone behind closed doors, and how fucking wrong did it feel when they didn't stop?

I want to ask. Hell, I want to demand it.

But I don't. He won't give me the truth.

Besides, it's not just his story to tell. When I hear what happened between them, it must come from Dove. Her voice. Her terms.

I force myself to focus on the tattoo, my steady hands contradicting my turbulent thoughts.

Hours slip by. The needle purrs, and my fingers move closer to Jag's groin, toward the untouched space beneath that sad little drape of underwear we're still pretending is a barrier.

A barrier that does nothing to hide his unmistakable reaction.

Goth Jesus, help me.

He's hard.

Not subtly. Not maybe. This isn't some half-chub he could blame on pressure or friction.

This is full mast.

Salute-the-flag.

Big enough to be a third wheel on date night.

Maybe he gets off on pain. Not unheard of. Some people become glassy-eyed and float when the needle hits.

But this doesn't feel floaty. It feels diabolical. Like I'm being observed, analyzed, and seduced by something that's not supposed to seduce me.

Or is it me? The way I'm leaning between his legs? The way my fingers drag across his inner thigh, anchoring my hand while I work?

My face is close. Closer now. Heat rolls off his body, blending with the scent of ink, blood, skin, and something darker. Spicier.

Desire.

The worst part? I'm not repulsed. I should be. After what Denver did to me, this should trigger the full freak show, complete with a panic attack, explosive violence, and a sobbing manic spiral into lights-out land. But I don't sense any of that looming.

Maybe because Jag doesn't scare me.

He fascinates me.

My heart thuds in my ears, and after a long, internal debate, I slowly lift my head and meet him stare for stare.

You're sporting a hard-on, genius.

He knows. I know. His dick definitely knows. I'm pretty sure it nodded at me.

His smirk is gone. No mockery in his expression. He wears a tight look, controlled and waiting.

He tilts his head as if curious what I'll do with the ten hard inches of *Don't read too much into this* bobbing under my nose.

"How about you tuck that before it starts making eye contact?" I turn off the machine and set it down. "If you need to jerk, you know where the bathroom is."

"You do it." He doesn't look away, daring me.

"Hand jobs are extra."

"Name your price."

Most straight men would laugh off this whole exchange and awkwardly change the subject. But I'm not most men.

I was raised by a psychopath.

The only way to survive Denver Strakh was to learn how to outmaneuver him, to outsmart a pedophile who used love as a weapon and sex as a punishment.

So yeah. I know how to play sick games. Really fucking well.

Holding Jag's unwavering gaze, I remove the gloves and let a wicked, slow-burning grin crawl onto my face.

"When I ruin your life, kitten, I won't use my hands." I lean forward. Not rushed. Not hesitant. I reach for the material draped over his lap with my mouth and slowly, tauntingly, slide it off with my teeth.

His breath hitches, and his dick stands fully erect, flushed, and throbbing against the absence of fabric. For once, he has nothing to say. No quip. No smirk. Just wide, unguarded silence.

He wants this, wants me, more than he wants control.

I bend in. Close. Close enough to feather my breath over the head of his cock. Close enough to make it twitch. To feel the heat coming off him in waves.

He stops breathing, his bedroom eyes in full effect, heavy-lidded and smoldering amber.

Please, his body says. *Please suck me.*

I smirk.

Then I sit back, grab clean gloves, and snap them on with a loud, surgical pop.

"Settle down, sugar." I reach for the machine again. "I agreed to scar your surface layers. Nothing more."

"You're a tease. Didn't see that coming."

"I know what you're doing."

"What am I doing?" A charming grin. "Besides flirting with a beautiful man?"

"Someone without a drop of ink doesn't walk into a tattoo parlor and demand a full-leg sleeve. That's not impulse. It's strategy. You saw an opportunity to spend sixty hours with me. With your dick hanging out. You're not here to mark your territory. You're playing the long game. You want something from me."

"What do I want, Wolfie?"

"You want Dove. But by now, you've learned she has a security detail. What better way to separate her from her guards than to flip the threat and turn me to your side? That's your usual game, right? You don't fight for her. You infiltrate. You get inside her circle, fuck her friends, bogart her lovers, and make them yours. You manipulate them. Bribe them. Turn them into weapons to use against her." I wipe away ink and blood, revealing a shaded jaguar paw. "You're not here for my art. You're here to see if I'm weak enough to fall for your tricks."

"Smarter than I thought." His smile spreads like a blade being unsheathed. "Good. I was starting to get bored."

"Don't get excited." I wipe the blood again and drag the needle across the curve of his thigh, slower this time. "When this tug of war turns on you, and it will, you'll already have my teeth in your throat."

"Promise?"

Rather than taking the bait or acknowledging the heat tightening in my boxers, I concentrate on the tattoo.

"You only have it half right." He watches me like he's several moves ahead on the board. "This *is* about the art. *Your* art. It's also about access."

"To her," I growl.

"To you. Dove's already mine." He lets the words hang, then continues slowly, like he's explaining a truth I'm too stupid to understand. "She surrounds herself with broken things. Strays. Freaks. Tortured souls that are too much trouble to keep. I don't need to pull her away from you. She does that herself."

Stray. Freak. Too much trouble to keep.

That's me.

I have trauma like other people have blood pressure—high, genetic, and emotionally triggered. I have scars I don't remember earning and instincts wired for survival, not connection. I know I'm a risk. A walking warning label. Broken in places I'll never let anyone see.

But hearing him say it so casually makes my chest hurt. He's not poking at a wound. He's shoving his fingers in it and grinning at the twitch.

I don't rise to it. I don't need to, because I'm not just damaged.

I'm dangerous.

And Jag just reminded me why.

He straightens to a sitting position, not caring how close he is or that he's naked or that my needle's in his skin.

"Seduction is part of the play." His voice sinks into intimate darkness. "Her lovers, her friends, they never see it coming. A few smiles, a well-timed confession, and suddenly they're looking at me like I'm the answer to problems they didn't know they had."

"You're such an inspiration. Really." I force my attention back to the tattoo, the whirring machine barely audible over the pounding in my ears.

"You're no different, Strakh. The way your hand shakes when it gets too close to my cock, the way you won't look at me unless you're thinking about killing me or kissing me... That's not hate. That's friction. And friction is how fire starts."

"Is that what you told Gavin before you gift-wrapped him for Dove? How'd that work out again?" I glance up, eyes cold. "Oh, right. She left him at the altar and came hunting you."

"Gavin was a mistake."

"Then by all means, try again. I could use the exercise."

A few minutes later, I finish the final strokes, the vibration of the machine tapering into silence.

"That's all for today." I wipe away the stippling of blood and excess ink and study the raw, reddened skin.

The lower half is fully inked, the claws sinking into a half-shaded anatomical heart, feathers curling along the base, and veins tangled with circuits that trail into clean outlines waiting to be filled. A beast mid-transformation.

It's not finished. But it's already alive.

I hate how good it looks.

I hate what it says about the man beneath it. The obsession. The need to own something fragile and call it love.

When the jaguar is complete, I wonder what he'll ask for next.

I wonder if I'll give it to him.

I wonder if he'll live long enough to finish the entire leg.

I peer up at him, finding his head tipped back, breathing slow, and eyes lowered, hooded, savoring his view.

His view of me.

Adrenaline floods my circulation, and my dick gives a happy little deranged kick.

He doesn't move immediately, his gaze fixed on mine. Unsettling. Then he rises, naked and semi-hard, and steps to the full-length mirror.

The man has no respect for modesty.

I avert my gaze from his tight, chiseled ass and focus on cleaning my workstation.

"Christ." He rests his good hand over his groin, holding his cock out of the way as he examines his new ink in the mirror. "You saw what I am, and you still made it beautiful. You're part of me now, Strakh."

"Yeah, you can cancel my subscription on that."

"She'll see this." He turns his leg left and right, studying it from every angle, his eyes glittering darkly. "And she'll know it was you."

"Stay away from her."

He would have to be nude for Dove to see it, and that will never happen.

Pivoting, he ambles toward me and invades my space. A menacing allure radiates from him, drawing me and repelling me as his voice drops a sinister whisper against my lips. "Make me."

My body screams, *Fuck yes,* as I mutter, "Hard pass."

With an unsettling smile, he dresses slowly, one-handed, holding my gaze hostage until he's fully clothed.

I give the station one last wipe, grab my hoodie, and sling my satchel over my shoulder. No ceremony. No lingering. I'm done bleeding into this room.

"We can resume the leg in two or three weeks." *Or never.* I reach for the door.

"Tomorrow. Same time. We'll start the lower leg. And the day after that. And every day until it's done." He doesn't ask. He decides.

Idiot.

"You have an open wound on your thigh. Not to mention a broken wrist. You need time to heal."

"You heard me."

"Yep. Now hear *me.* If you push it, you'll blow out the lines. Ink will migrate. The whole thing will heal like shit, and you'll be stuck with a smeared jaguar that looks like it lost a bar fight." I let that sink in. "I'm good, Rath, but I'm not God. Let your body catch up before your obsession does."

I turn to leave, but his voice stops me.

"You want to lecture someone about first aid, find a Boy Scout. I'll be here tomorrow." He disappears into the back room, leaving me alone with lingering dread, fascination, and a realization I can't deny.

Jag Rath isn't finished with me, not by a long shot, and I'm not mad about it.

Outside, the sky is in full meltdown. Slick sheets pour down the alley, drowning everything.

My hoodie clings to my shoulders, useless against the cold. I let it soak through, needing it to rinse off the last eight hours. The smell of him. The heat of him. The sickness he's spreading.

As the mechanic shop emerges ahead, Dove's guards spot me immediately. Before I reach the entrance, they step from their parked SUV, eyes scanning the shadows. Ex-military, both of them. Clean cut. Necks as thick as my thigh.

"Evening, Mr. Strakh." Jasper approaches, blinking rain from his eyes.

"Anything?"

"Uneventful, sir."

That tracks. Jag's been glued to my hip all day like a parasite with a hard-on.

"Did she eat?" I ask.

"No, sir. She hasn't left the premises."

"Thanks. I'll take it from here."

They nod and strike off toward their car.

Warmth bleeds into my skin as I slip into the garage bays, breathing in the scent of gasoline, motor oil, and sweat.

Fluorescent lights glow over the central lift. No music. No shouting. No clanking wrenches. Everyone's gone.

Except her.

She doesn't acknowledge me as she rolls past.

On skates.

Old-school quad skates, black leather, red laces. That's not the only thing that's different. She wears striped knee-high socks, mini denim shorts that should be illegal, and a brand-new tool belt slung low on her hips like she's about to throw hands at a 1970s roller derby.

Love the look, but where the hell did it come from? It sure as hell didn't fit in her backpack.

When I left her on the island this morning, she wore the same clothes she wore yesterday. I planned to fix that tonight and take her shopping. Build her a closet full of armor. Stuff that screams *Don't touch me* in five different languages and still makes people stare. Badass shit for a badass girl.

But nope. She beat me to it.

Except...

She hasn't left the premises.

The only explanation? She built a time machine, robbed a punk rock pin-up, and said, *Yeah, this'll do.*

She weaves between car skeletons, skating slowly, effortlessly, one hand dragging along the top of a parked engine.

Blue hair piles atop her head in a messy twist, and a grease-smudged flannel hangs unbuttoned halfway, revealing a thin tank top beneath.

Her hips sway with each lazy glide, and those honey-colored eyes flick toward me for half a heartbeat before sweeping away.

That game again.

I lean against a steel post, arms crossed, letting my breath slow as I watch her move. It's not what she's doing that enraptures me. It's how.

She rolls through oil stains and shadows like a figure skater on ice. Bending over the open hood of a Mustang, she locks those skates in a mechanic's stance, her balance impeccable.

Breathtaking.

She's been doing this for a while. Like it's normal. Like it makes sense.

Maybe it does. When it comes to Dove, strangeness isn't a glitch. It's her signature.

"When did you go shopping?" I push off the post and prowl toward her.

"I didn't."

"Shoplifting, then." I fish out my smokes and light one. "No judgment."

"I'm not a thief." She plucks the ciggy from my mouth, sets it between her lips, and skates backward.

I stay with her, a wolf stalking a bird. "Where'd you get the gear, Rink Rat?"

"It was delivered." She rolls to a stop and kicks a large box at her feet. "Waiting right here this morning."

My pulse detonates.

A quick glance tells me the box contains rockabilly clothes, boots, and cyberpunk accessories. All things I would've chosen for her.

Except I didn't send it.

I can guess who did.

Violent, explosive fire crawls up the back of my neck.

"Who?" Keeping my voice even, I step into her space. "Who sent it?"

She offers a facial shrug.

"Don't lie to me, brat." I lean down, growling against her lips. "Who?"

She pulls herself taller. "Jag."

There it is.

Jag.

That slippery fucking cunt. He knew she needs clothes. Knew she loves skates. Knew exactly how to remind her he's still orbiting her life.

It was supposed to be me.

I was supposed to take her shopping tonight. Fill her closet. Feed her. Protect her. Give her everything.

A tiny black eye blinks in the rafters. A camera pointed straight at me. I feel him watching through that lens, smug and smirking, getting off on the show. Watching me lose. Watching me boil and burn and do nothing.

My hands don't shake. My breath doesn't hitch. But inside, I'm nuclear.

I don't touch her.

I don't look at the box again.

I turn and stride out before I torch the whole fucking garage.

love
SEVENTEEN

I don't hear the door slam behind Wolf. He just leaves. Silently. That's somehow worse.

My throat aches, and I don't know why.

I don't know why he looked at me like that before disappearing.

The look wasn't angry. Not exactly. It was tense and closed off, as if he wanted to say something but decided it would hurt.

Removing my tool belt, I bend to untie the laces and swap the skates for my boots. Then I sit there for a second.

Okay. So maybe he's mad. But not about the skates. That would be stupid.

The skates arrived in that box. The one with the clothes. The new tool belt. The perfume I haven't touched. All of it handpicked by the man who used to braid my hair with bloodstains under his fingernails.

I stare at the skates, black with red laces, just like the pair I left in California. But not the same ones. My old skates had cracks in the wheels and a missing toe stop.

These are brand new.

I didn't ask for them. I didn't ask for any of it. But Jag sent it anyway, like he always does. Strings attached. Mind games sharpened to a razor point. He doesn't care what I wear. He cares what it does to me.

And maybe... What it does to Wolf.

Is that what this is?

Jealousy?

I scoff under my breath and immediately hate myself for it.

Does Wolf even get jealous? Not with me.

Except he looked at me like I betrayed something unspoken between us.

Did I?

Am I supposed to feel guilty? For wearing the shit Jag sent me?

Because I don't.

Or... I do. A little.

But I shouldn't.

Jag stole everything from me. He burned through my life more times than I can count. I left my favorite pair of skates behind when I ran from the last dumpster fire. He owes me this. And I need clothes. It would be dumb to throw them away.

Still...

Maybe I should've said something to Wolf. Warned him. Explained. Is that what normal women do? They... Talk? Confront conflicts? Decode feelings?

I don't know how to do that. I only know how to survive.

But something in me says, *Try.*

Grabbing my jacket, I lock the shop and head out to find him.

I don't have to go far.

Across the street, he huddles beneath an awning, a cigarette glowing at the corner of his mouth, his eyes locked on his phone.

I shove my hands in my coat pockets and close the distance. I hate this part. Talking. People-ing. Being human. I'm terrible at it.

But I'll do it for him.

"Hey." My voice comes out scratchy. Useless.

He looks up. Doesn't speak. Just flicks ash to the pavement.

"You left."

He shrugs. "Didn't want to interrupt your roller disco."

"It's not a disco. I was working."

"Sure." He doesn't smile. Not even a little.

"Look, I didn't..." My pulse skips up my neck. "He sent the

love

box. I didn't ask for it. It's just clothes. And skates. It's not a message or whatever you think it is."

His arctic eyes stay on me as his face shifts into an eerie calm. A quiet, curling fury. Warrior-mode. Beautiful and terrifying.

"Kai will collect the box and bring it to the island." He pockets his phone and empties his expression. "If you want to keep it, fine. If not, we can burn it. Doesn't matter to me."

"Okay." I blink.

"I want to take you somewhere."

"What?"

"I want to show you something." He crushes the cigarette under his heel. "You game?"

I nod, too fast.

"Let's go." He offers his elbow.

"Where are Carl and Jasper?" I loop my arm through his and let him lead me away from the harbor.

"Didn't realize you were on a first-name basis with the security team." He tilts his head, regarding me. "Do you trust them more than me?"

"No." An easy, honest answer. But I have questions. "What do you want, Wolf?"

"Kisses on speed dial."

"You didn't text me today."

He glances at me sideways, that crooked smirk reappearing. "Figured I'd give your phone a break before it filed a restraining order." Then, softer, like he means it... "Didn't think you'd miss me."

"I did." A swallow strangles my whisper. "I missed you. I thought... Did something happen? Did Jag show up?"

"Yeah. I gave him a tattoo."

I slam to a stop, releasing his arm. "You didn't."

"I did. It was fucked up."

"The tattoo?"

"All of it. But I made a deal with him."

"No. No, you don't deal with Jag. You don't negotiate." I grip my hair, knocking the messy bun loose and waving my arms around. "He doesn't play fair. He manipulates and twists your mind until he gets what he wants."

"Hey." He catches my hands and brushes the fallen strands

from my face, the metal from his rings cold against my cheek. "You don't think I know that? I told you I would lure him in and play with him. That's all this is. Do you trust me?"

"Yes, but I don't trust *him*."

"Let's keep moving." He scans our surroundings, his head on a swivel. "I'll tell you about my day."

And he does. As we stroll along the wet streets, he walks through the confrontation with his family at the shop, the negotiation he struck with Jag, and the thigh piece he spent all day inking. The beginning of a long and dangerous leg sleeve.

"What's the design?"

"A jaguar."

Disgust and worry send my heart rate into overdrive. "He'll try to seduce you."

"He already tried."

"And?"

"He's not my type."

"He's everyone's type."

"Including yours?"

"He's my stepbrother." My arms wrap around my midsection before I register the defensive posture.

"What did he do to you?" He bends his knees, putting his face level with mine.

"Exactly what he'll do to *you* if you continue down this path." I spot the pack of smokes peeking from his coat pocket and swipe them, seeking a distraction.

Before I pull one free, he snatches the pack from my hand.

"Clear something up for me." He tucks the cigarettes in his back pocket.

I brace for the question I will never answer.

"Are you a smoker?" He tilts his head. "Or am I a bad influence?"

Relief loosens my breath, and a smile touches his sculpted lips.

He's letting me off the hook. For now.

"Both." I smile back.

love

The cold, damp air sticks to our coats as he leads me around the corner. The next thing I know, we're standing before the fogged glass doors of a local diner, the kind that smells like hash browns and burnt coffee no matter the hour.

"This is what you wanted to show me?" I follow him inside, the dining room half-full of locals hunched over plates and mugs.

"No." He slides into a booth and waves down the server. "First, I want to feed you."

As I start to sit opposite him, he grabs my hand and pulls me down to his side.

"Two mugs of coffee." He wraps an arm around my waist, tugs me until our hips press together, and smiles at the older woman. "Two cheeseburgers, extra pickles, curly fries, and a slice of blueberry pie, warmed. One fork." He angles that sexy grin toward me. "Anything else?"

"Are the pickles negotiable?" I shrug off my jacket.

"Not tonight." He raises a brow, daring me to fight him over it.

No way in hell.

The coffee arrives first, thick and bitter. I drown mine in cream while he takes his black, one hand wrapped around the chipped mug, the other resting casually near the napkin dispenser. He's more relaxed now. The kind of relaxed that comes after a knife fight.

"So." I twist toward him. "Tell me more about your day with Jag."

He leans back, stretching his legs beneath the table. "If you can call that a day. It was more like ten hours of psychological warfare with a side of needlework."

"What did he say to you?"

He shrugs. "Talked about you mostly. About your shared trauma." He twirls a sugar packet between his fingers. "He knows how to weaponize eye contact. The way he stares without blinking, with his mouth all soft and parted just right..." He shakes his head. "He makes everything feel sexual."

"That's part of the act." I sip my coffee, wishing it was spiked. "He makes you feel significant and beautiful. Convinces you that he wants you and no one else in the world. Then he takes everything you offer and uses it to destroy you."

"Is that what he did to you?"

"Worse."

"Did you...?" He rolls his lips together. "Have you and he...?"

"I've never had sex with my stepbrother."

His lashes flicker once, too fast, registering his shock. He looks away. "He said Gavin was a mistake."

"Only because I found out about his betrayal."

"Do you surround yourself with strays and freaks?" His gaze turns inward, avoiding mine. "Broken things like me?"

"That's what he said?" My stomach drops. "Don't listen to that. It's bait."

"I know."

"You're not broken."

"No. Broken is too gentle for what I am." Finally, he gives me his eyes. "I'm cracked all to hell, Birdie. Mangled beyond repair in most places and missing some pieces. What's left is taped together and unraveling in ways that make people flinch and stay away." He leans in, his voice secret-soft. "But I like what I am. Especially when you look at me like you see it. You see me, and you still stay."

Oh, Wolf.

"Jag sees me, too." He smiles without humor. "But without the same effect."

"How so?"

"I watched the way his eyes tracked me today. The way he tensed when I touched the inside of his thigh. He's used to controlling every room he walks into. But when he's in my space, when I have his skin stretched beneath my hands..."

"He doesn't know what to make of you."

"Most people don't." He shrugs.

"That's a good thing."

The food arrives, and the aroma of grease, melted cheese, and warm bread wraps me in instant comfort. I dig in like I haven't eaten in a week, and he matches my pace. The crispy fries are perfectly curled, and the pie oozes blueberries and sugar with every forkful.

We don't talk while we eat. Lots of eye contact, though. And smiling. The food is good, but the company is even better.

When I reach for the bill, he snatches it first and hands over a wad of cash.

"I was going to get it."

"No, you weren't."

"I could have."

"You could, but I take care of my girl. Don't fight me on this again." He stands and fixes me with a look that shuts down my protest.

I accepted clothes from Jag. Denying food from Wolf would only hurt him. So I let it go.

Outside, the fog clings to the streetlamps, and the silence stretches between us again, but this time, it's not heavy. It's charged.

We stop in front of a building tucked between a pharmacy and a warehouse, unmarked except for a security camera above the steel door.

"Ready to see what flashiness looks like when it has unlimited money?" He turns to a keypad beside the entrance and taps in a code. "Welcome to my dad's profligate lifestyle."

The door unlocks with a satisfying click, and he pushes it open. The overhead lights stutter to life as we step inside a windowless garage.

Endless, polished gray floors gleam like lacquered stone under industrial LEDs. The place smells like wax and machine oil and money. Not the kind of money that pays rent on time. The kind that owns cities. The kind that gets handed down and never runs out.

"You've gotta be shitting me." I slow my steps as we walk deeper.

Wolf strolls in like this is normal. As if rows of hypercars and luxury beasts aren't lining the walls like a showroom in Monaco.

Bugatti. Koenigsegg. Ferrari. Rolls. Each one gleams like angels with microfiber wings detailed them. Some are on car lifts, suspended mid-air like sacred artifacts, their guts half-exposed in mechanical ecstasy.

"Leo gets that same look on his face every time he walks in here." Wolf studies me like he's cataloging my reaction.

I move toward a black Lamborghini, the Aventador I used to dream about when I was sixteen and pissed off at the world. I used to keep a poster of it on the bedroom wall in one of my foster homes. Right next to the knife I hid in the vent.

This car is real. More than real. It swallows light like a black hole.

A few feet away sits a Jesko, blood red and just as slick. I want to touch them all.

"These aren't just exotic cars," I murmur. "They're gods."

"Soulless ones." Wolf ambles past them without reverence.

"You don't approve?"

"I prefer riding," he says. "Not posing."

He turns, gesturing for me to follow. We slip between the giants until we reach the back of the garage, where the air feels a little colder. That's when I see it.

A motorcycle.

Not a showpiece. Not one of those custom chrome monstrosities meant to sit on velvet.

This thing's all muscle and grit, matte black with silver accents, built low to the ground, its design stripped down and unforgiving. A beast with two wheels and no leash.

"That's yours?" I raise my brows.

"Yep." He holds up his keys. "Want to see what this island looks like at ninety miles per hour?"

I hesitate. Not because I'm scared. But because I'm not sure what this is.

He's angry. Or was. Still smoldering in that silent, brooding Wolf way. But now he's offering me a ride.

This feels like trust. Or forgiveness. Or maybe just distraction.

Either way, I nod.

"You'll need this." He tosses me a helmet.

"What about you?"

He smirks, swinging his leg over the bike. "I like to feel the wind on my face when I die."

I snort and shove the helmet on. "You're such a drama queen."

"Have you heard the fairy tale about the lion, the bear, and the drag queen?"

I shake my head.

"If you stick around, maybe I'll tell you the story someday." He pats the seat behind him.

He said that the night I met him, and my reaction is still the same. I can't stay. Long-term never works out.

But I'm here now.

I climb on and lock my arms around his waist. He's warm and solid, and dammit, I love the feel of his hard body against mine.

He leans back enough for me to hear him murmur, "Hold on, Trouble."

Then we roar out of the garage like we're escaping something. Or chasing it. Hard to tell with Wolf.

The engine growls beneath us, raw and guttural, as he twists the throttle, and we rocket into the night.

Sitka blurs around us, rows of sleepy storefronts with hand-painted signs and amber windows casting golden pools onto the pavement.

A dog barks from a porch. Wind whistles past my ears as we zip down the main road, fast enough to blur past cameras and the stalker monitoring them.

The scent of cedar and sea brine wraps around me, a balm that isn't cold for once. It's alive. The salty tang from the harbor mixes with the musk of pine and damp earth as we speed past the edge of town, streetlights giving way to shadow.

I tighten my grip on Wolf, surrendering to the impulse to feel him against me.

His body is a furnace. Lean muscle, wild heat, and too much restraint. My chest presses to his back, and I feel everything. Every inhale. Every twitch of his shoulders as he leans into the curves. The strength in his core as he controls the bike like it's an extension of himself.

We're flying now. Past the last of the houses. Past the tree line. Past logic.

He accelerates as the road opens up. Rural, unlined, and kissed by the moon. No headlights in the distance. No brakes. Just us.

The wind tears at my coat and helmet, and I hold on. My thighs cling to the seat. My hands curl against his stomach. The engine's vibration rises through me, slow and hot and steady.

It's obscene, the way I feel. Not just the speed. Not just the risk.

It's him.

This man. This beautiful, battered man wrapped in heat and secrets.

I rest my helmet between his shoulder blades, trying to inhale the scent I've come to crave, the waft of smoke and something primal. Something mine.

A growl rumbles from his chest as I shift against him. I can't

love

tell if it's frustration or pleasure.

His hand leaves the throttle for a second to find my thigh and squeeze. A question.

I answer him by sliding my fingers under the hem of his jacket. Over his shirt. Against the pattern of scars that torment my thoughts.

For twenty-four years, he was held captive by a psychopath in the Arctic Circle. He's only been in civilization for six months.

I'm too scared to ask for the details. Too scared he'll refuse to tell me.

Too scared he'll expect *my* secrets in return.

We ride like that, past the river, past the craggy cliffs where spruce trees bend like old men in the wind. The moon guides us. The world disappears.

And I feel it.

Not fear.

Not guilt.

Not the gnawing ache of survival.

But freedom.

Real, gut-deep, full-throttle freedom.

With him.

love
EIGHTEEN

Wolf pulls off onto a gravel shoulder where the trees fall away, and the sky opens wide. The bike slows, coasting to a halt beneath a stretch of moonlight that spills across a rocky overlook.

I slide off his back, remove the helmet, and plant my boots on the ground, breath fogging in the crisp air.

The view is staggering.

Below us, Sitka glimmers like a constellation curled against the dark curve of the bay. Golden specks of porch lights, streetlamps, and late-night diners flicker against the black velvet ocean. Beyond that, the islands slouch under a shroud of mist.

The harbor, tattoo parlor, mechanic shop—my world is a cluster of lights, shrunken to the size of a snow globe. It's too much and not enough all at once. Beauty edged with mystery.

Like Wolf.

I hear the click of the kickstand and feel his presence behind me. He doesn't say anything, giving me the moment, letting me soak it in, letting it scrape something soft and vulnerable inside me I didn't know was still there.

Then his arms wrap around my waist.

He pulls me gently, insistently, until I'm lifted and straddling him on the bike, facing him, our breath tangling in the cold.

"I don't approve of his gifts." His gravel-deep voice nips across my skin, leaving pleasurable goosebumps. "The skates. The clothes. That wasn't generosity. It was invasion." His hands settle on my hips, hot even through denim. "I'm not mad at you, darling. I'm mad at him for thinking he can buy his way into your thoughts. Into your life. That's not how this works. Not with you. Not with me."

I swallow hard.

"I have more money than I'll ever need. More than I want." He works his jaw. "I don't give a fuck about any of it, except what it can do for you. I want to feed you. Clothe you. Protect you. Not because I think you need a savior. I want the chance to court you like you deserve. To earn you."

"I didn't come to Sitka to start another relationship."

His brow creases, but he doesn't interrupt.

"I'm wreckage. You don't want what I am. I'm the aftermath, not the beginning. And you..." I lift my hand and press it against his chest, right over the place where his heartbeat fights beneath the scars. "You don't trust me to see you without a shirt."

He closes his eyes, pained. My words hurt.

When they open again, they're soft. Liquid blue. "I'll show you mine if you show me yours."

"I don't carry many scars you can see. The few I do?" A wind rushes through the cliffside trees, and I shiver. "I put them there myself."

"Self-harm?"

"Nothing like that."

"Then what?"

"Self-preservation. Stupidity. Maybe both."

The silence returns. Loud. Dense. Mutual. Two crippled creatures sitting in the dark, unable to name what broke them. But knowing.

Knowing.

He stares at me for a long, breathless heartbeat. Our eye contact stretches between seconds, waiting for the world to tilt.

Then he moves.

One hand threads into my hair, gripping tight enough to anchor. The other sweeps around my waist, dragging me flush against him with a strength that speaks of ownership, not apology.

His mouth claims mine.

There's nothing soft about it. No hesitant question. No careful easing in. It's a full-bodied answer to everything I just said, denied, and refused to admit I want.

He kisses like a storm breaking loose. Like I'm his. Like he's never tasted a real meal. Until me.

His lips are rough and sure, parting mine, his hot tongue sliding deep, branding his name on the inside of my mouth. I clutch his jacket, fingernails digging into leather, thighs tightening around his hips as heat floods my chest and pools lower.

He growls into me, a wild animal sound, and shifts beneath me so I feel the full, hard length of his need press up between us. There's no hiding it. He doesn't try. He wants me to feel it. Wants me to understand exactly what I do to him.

When he pulls back, his forehead stays against mine.

"Understand something," he rasps, voice guttural and breath hot. "I don't share. Not space. Not the past. And not you."

My heart hammers against his chest.

"Jag puts his name on boxes. I'll put mine on your heart." His lips brush mine again, softer this time, but no less territorial. No less potent. "Leave your scars all over me, Heartcleaver. Just don't leave me."

He kisses me again, slow and deep and final. A promise sealed with heat and fury.

I kiss him back because I don't want to pretend I don't want him.

Because I'm terrified of losing him.

Not to another girl.

Not to my own destruction.

But to Jag.

Jag doesn't need blades or bullets. He uses charm and seduction, hacking people the way he hacks systems, slipping past firewalls, cloaking himself in manufactured sincerity, and swapping passwords for intimacy.

And Wolf feels too much. He hides it under sarcasm and eccentric clothes, but I see how he takes people into himself. Lets them nest in his ribs. Lets their pain echo in his bones.

That's why I'm afraid.

If Jag worms his way in deep enough, he'll rot everything

love

good in Wolf from the inside out. I know that rot. I lived it, and I don't think Wolf understands how fast it spreads.

So I kiss him like I can root him here, like my mouth on his might be enough to keep him from drifting toward the insidious trap that is Jag Rath.

Pressing closer, I loop my arms around Wolf as if I can shield him from the poison I escaped. Maybe I can plant something real in his chest before Jag gets the chance to strip it hollow.

I kiss him with a warning on my lips. A plea.

He'll devour you, Wolf.

And I don't know if I'll survive watching it happen.

I pull away. Reluctantly. My lips sting. My lungs burn. My pulse hasn't slowed since I climbed onto the bike.

"We should get back," I whisper.

He nods once, jaw flexing. He doesn't want to let go either, but he does. Slowly.

When I strap my helmet back on, he kicks the bike into gear, and we roar away from the cliff's edge, down the winding road.

Sitka rises ahead, sleepy and gold-lit, the harbor blinking in the distance.

But something's off.

I feel it before I see it.

A car. Nondescript. Pale gray or maybe white. Hard to tell in the dark. It lingers at the edge of the tree line, lights off but engine on.

I swear I saw that same vehicle in town earlier, just a shadow behind another car.

But now it's here, pulling onto the road behind us.

It doesn't get close. Doesn't flash lights or rev the engine. It doesn't turn off, either. Just hovers. Creeping. Following.

Jag?

Maybe. Maybe not. But my shoulder blades tighten, and a chill needles across my scalp. I've felt this before. The prelude to something awful.

We hit a straightaway, slicing between blocks. I know this town now, the way the shadows move when something's not right. And that car? It's not right.

I lift my visor and lean forward, mouth to Wolf's ear.

"We're being followed."

His body stiffens.

"Gray sedan," I shout. "Saw it earlier."

He reaches back, smacks my visor closed, and grips my arms around his waist. "Don't let go."

The engine snarls, and we're off, the sudden jolt of speed whipping me backward. He weaves through the quiet town, taking sharp turns, cutting through alleys, blasting past glowing diner windows and shuttered storefronts.

The car follows. Always a few seconds behind. Never too close.

But too present.

"Shit." My arms clench around him. I don't know if I'm holding on or bracing for impact.

He darts left, tires spinning on wet pavement, and I realize where he's headed.

Monty's garage.

He kills the lights a block early, coasting the rest of the way in shadows. At the last second, he ducks into an alley, loops behind a construction site, and zips around the back of the property. The rear garage door looms ahead.

At the gate, he punches in the code.

Gravel sprays as we skid inside. The door rolls shut behind us, swallowing us whole.

Silence. For a breath. For two. I strip off the helmet and drag a hand through my damp hair, panting.

We made it.

But my gut twists with that old, familiar instinct. The one that never lies.

Someone out there knows where to look.

If it's Jag, we wouldn't have seen him. He wouldn't follow. He'd already be inside.

If it's not Jag, who the hell is watching me now?

How much time do we have before they stop watching and start hunting?

Wolf removes his phone and shoots off a text. Minutes later, Carl and Jasper show up to escort us home.

The island is dark when we arrive, quiet but for the soft lap of waves against the dock.

We don't speak. Not when we enter the guest house. Not when we climb the stairs. Not when my boots hit the landing outside my room.

love

I pause at the door, hand on the knob, heart thudding.

Wolf presses in behind me. Close.

Heat rolls off him. I can practically taste the tension crackling between us. His breath brushes my nape, and I shiver.

Slowly, his mouth finds the curve of my neck, soft at first, then open and hot, teeth grazing skin.

I let out a gasp, surprised. Eager.

His hands migrate to my hips, then under the hem of my shirt, rough palms skimming over bare skin.

I lean back into him, eyes fluttering shut, lips parting.

I want this.

I want him.

The hardness of his arousal presses against me, undeniable, desperate. My fingers curl around the doorknob, trying to ground myself as heat blooms low in my belly.

His hands roam higher, over my ribs, my sides, his mouth trailing fire up to the shell of my ear.

"Let me in," he murmurs.

He means more than the room, and I want that. God, I want him. I want and want and will take anything this beautiful man will give me. But—

Jag.

The tattoo. The manipulation. The seduction.

The way Wolf said, *He already tried.*

"Wolf." My body goes stiff in his arms.

He doesn't stop kissing me. Doesn't sense the change yet.

"Wolf," I repeat, firmer this time.

His lips pause against my jaw.

I draw in a breath I don't want to take. "When Jag tried to seduce you, did you feel anything?"

He doesn't move.

"Did you get hard for him the way you are for me right now?"

The silence is too loud. His body, so eager a second ago, is frozen behind me.

"Don't lie to me." I turn slowly, stepping out of his grasp until we're face to face, inches apart. "Don't insult me like that."

"I won't." He swallows hard, jaw ticking, eyes flicking away, then back to me. Torn. "I didn't want... He got in my head. Knew exactly how to... Push. What to say. What to do. I didn't mean to react. It was instinct. Confusion. Not desire. I don't want him."

I stare at him, heart aching. Not because I didn't expect it.

But because I did.

Because Jag always finds the cracks.

And because Wolf is Wolf. Sexually inexperienced. Possibly raped by a psychopath. He thinks he's straight, but if he hasn't unpacked his trauma, how does he know for sure?

Maybe I'm wrong. After Gavin, I can't trust my gaydar. But Wolf's sexuality feels deeper, wider, more vivid and complicated than boring old straight.

Where does that leave him and me and Jag?

Jag has single-handedly manipulated and stolen every man who's shown interest in me. One by one, he slides in and fucks them. Sometimes, he ends them.

Now there's Wolf. A man I like. One I like far too much.

I know this pattern. I can trace it blindfolded. I'll be shoved to the side, discarded like trash, and forgotten by tomorrow.

It doesn't matter how different this feels with Wolf. Jag always wins.

How many times do I have to be replaced before I stop being such a goddamn pushover? When will I learn?

Now.

Not tomorrow.

Not after I've picked myself off the floor again.

I want everything Jag Rath touches to stop bleeding. I want the stains he left on me to finally stop spreading. I'm done standing on the sidelines of my own damn life, swallowing it down when I should be screaming.

I want this pattern to end. Now. With Wolf.

So I pull on my big girl pants and draw my line.

"You can't have it both ways." My entire body clenches against the hurt. "You can't chase me and entertain him."

He stares at me for an aching moment, each breath dragging his chest higher, stretching the fabric tight over the sharp, sculpted map of his body as if every muscle was hewn to test my restraint.

Finally, he opens his mouth, but nothing comes out.

"Goodnight." I turn, open the door, and step inside.

When it closes behind me, I slump against the wood, fists balled at my sides, eyes stinging.

I've been here before.

love

    On the edge of something that could've been beautiful, but never had a chance.
    I don't know what scares me more.
    Knowing he'll eventually let Jag in.
    Or that the weakest parts of me still want to let Jag in, too.

wolfson
NINETEEN

The next morning, I drop Dove at the mechanic shop just after dawn. Carl and Jasper nod at me like we're all pretending this setup is normal. Like I didn't spend half the night thinking about her on skates, Jag's tattoo, the mysterious car, and her painful—albeit well-deserved—rejection.

The streets are empty. Sitka's always quiet at this hour. The tattoo parlor looms, the door already propped open with a cinder block.

Inside, the lights are on.

And so is Declan.

"Okay, so this wasn't here on Sunday, right? Like, definitely not here. I was off yesterday, came back this morning, and boom—bam—bam! A new room. Just… There. Like it grew overnight. Like a mushroom. Or an alien pod. I don't know, man. This reeks of the Anunnaki. No tire tracks. No receipts. No weird guys in reflective vests. And the construction? Pristine. Like too clean. No dust, no noise complaints, not even a rogue drywall screw on the floor. I think it's an invasion. Did it happen last night? Or 4000 years ago? Are we missing time? What day is it?"

"Morning, Declan." I brush past him.

He vibrates, tweaking hard off his fifth or tenth cup of coffee.

The aroma of burned beans trails him as he follows me, spewing conspiracy theories I no longer hear.

Because standing where my workstation used to be is a room. Framed out. Walled up. Closed off. A godsdamn room.

New sheetrock hangs on new studs, the tang of sawdust and fresh wood cutting through the musty air.

Perplexed, I run my fingers along the edge of the doorframe, the unpainted drywall, the cleanly mudded seams. A room made of high-grade shit that doesn't match the rest of the shop.

I open the heavy door and step inside, finding everything exactly how I left it last night.

My chair. Worn stool. Workbench of sterilized tools. Inks arranged in gradients only I understand. Light still spills through the window at the perfect angle for morning sessions. Nothing out of place. No tampering.

But the privacy? That's new.

I walk the perimeter, inspecting. I don't hate it. Not even a little. I've spent my life being watched and observed. By a psychopath. By my brothers.

And now Jag.

He did this. Probably planned it out while my hands were on his thigh. Maybe built it himself after I left last night.

The pleasure of it creeps in too fast, warm and unwelcome.

Anger follows.

Because privacy is currency. A bribe. A manipulation.

I back out of the room, heart thudding.

Declan prattles on about quality craftsmanship and aliens. I breeze past him, slam open the door to the break room, and pull up short.

I didn't expect to find Jag in here. But there he is. Asleep on a shitty metal cot, shoved into the corner of the room like someone dumped him there after a hard night of partying.

He looks like a fallen statue of some war god left behind in the rubble. Completely nude except for a thin blanket slung low over his hips, barely covering anything worth hiding.

His massive frame twists awkwardly to fit the too-small mattress, legs dangling off the end, one arm draped over his washboard stomach, the other hanging limp to the floor. His chest rises slowly, all corded muscle and brutal lines. A body chiseled out of violence and left to cool.

Every inch of him is honed. No softness except his face, and even that's a lie. Square jaw dusted with faint whiskers. Mouth slack in sleep. Shadows trace every ridge and groove, highlighting how perfectly designed he is to break people.

"Isn't he magnificent?" Declan whispers, peering around my shoulder, gawking.

"No." I push him backward and shut the door in his face.

Then, with a pulse full of piss and adrenaline, I cross the room and stop at the edge of the cot.

"Hey," I snap, low and sharp.

Nothing.

"Wake the fuck up."

Still nothing.

I kick the cot hard, and it screeches against the floor.

Jag jolts as if ripped from a nightmare, sitting up fast. Eyes wild, chest heaving, he stares at me, shocked.

I stare right back.

He blinks rapidly, and a bead of sweat rolls down his temple. Then he lifts the wrong hand.

The broken one.

His whole body seizes, and his jaw snaps shut so brutally I hear his teeth connect. No other sound leaves his mouth as pain crashes through his expression, flaring his nostrils and strangling a roar in his throat.

He swallows it down like it's acid. But he can't hide it. Not the tremble in his arm.

The hand is bloated and purple around the wrist, the bandages crusted with dried blood and construction dust. The unraveling gauze appears too tight in some places, loose in others.

He tries to flex his fingers, but they don't move.

"What the hell did you do to it?" I growl.

"What time is it?"

"Time to go to the hospital."

Falling back against the cot, he winces. "No hospitals."

Of course not. He's a walking felony. The ER would probably fingerprint him and set off a dozen alerts.

"Did you wash the tattoo?" I pull out my phone and fire off a quick text to the family group chat.

"Been busy."

"Busy building a room I don't need?"

"You need it."

"No, *you* need it."

"You were out in the open." He drags the blanket higher over his hips as if modesty suddenly matters. "No door or control over who walks in. Anyone could watch you work."

How very possessive of him. He wants to be the only one allowed to look. The only one who gets access.

And I hate how that twists something inside me.

Part of me wants to shove him. Hard. Tell him I'm not his. That I don't belong to anyone.

But another part, the quieter, hungrier part, wants to know what it feels like to be wanted like that. To be claimed without apology.

You can't have it both ways.

"Don't pretend this was a gallant sacrifice." I shoot him a distrustful look. "You did it to seduce me with privacy. To have a claim on me. A room with your fingerprints on every wall."

He exhales hard, sweat slicking his forehead.

Fever.

"Was it worth it?" I lick my lips. "Fucking up your hand to cage me?"

"*You* fucked up my hand, Strakh." His mouth curls like he might say something cruel, but instead, he throws his good arm over his eyes. "There was a car last night. Tail lights on the ridge. Trailed you when you left town and again when you returned."

"You watched us." My spine stiffens.

"I always watch you."

He's not denying it. Not apologizing. Just tossing out the confession with no shame.

"Let me get this right." My voice drops. "Last night, you stalked us, built a room with a fractured wrist, and passed out in the break room instead of going home?"

His eyes meet mine, clear now. Awake. "I don't have a home."

I breathe through my nose, trying not to react. Trying not to feel.

"Then this—" I gesture toward the new construction "—was a waste of money."

"It's not about money."

I stare at him for a long beat, heart hammering. Because he's right. This is about Dove.

And now me.

I let out a sharp breath through my nose. "Get up. Shower. You're burning up, and you didn't clean the damn tattoo."

His eyes flutter halfway open, and *surprise, surprise*, he drags the blanket off and swings his legs over the side without a fight.

But when he stands, his knees buckle.

"Shit." I lunge forward and catch under his arm, his weight slamming into me like a fucking oak tree falling sideways.

He's naked, skin as hot as a fevered furnace and damp with sweat. I grit my teeth, trying to ignore the fact that I'm half-dragging, half-hauling a muscle-sculpted serial killer across the room.

The attached bathroom is a cramped, spartan space tucked off the break room. Cement floor, drain in the middle. Rust-streaked toilet, a wall sink with a cracked mirror, and a single showerhead jutting from the wall like an afterthought. No curtain. No divider. Just cold, ugly function.

I prop the oversized ogre against the sink, one hand pressed to his chest to keep him upright as I twist the knobs. The pipes groan and spit until lukewarm water coughs out.

"I got this," he mutters, voice rough.

"Sure you do." I crouch to yank off my boots and peel my socks free.

When I stand and shove up my sleeves, he's already half-gone again, eyes unfocused.

"Fuck." I grab his shoulders and maneuver him under the spray.

The water hits his skin, and he shudders.

"If you fall, I'm leaving you on the floor." I wedge myself between him and the wall to keep him vertical.

I work fast, running my hands over his chest, arms, down his ribs, and the fresh tattoo along his thigh. My fingers trace the lines, rinsing the grime away, careful not to rip healing skin.

This is just about cleaning him. Keeping the ink from going septic. That's all.

Besides, I have the upper hand here.

Except the muscle beneath my palms feels devastatingly sinful and impossibly hard. His skin is too slick, sweat and water mixing, breath hitching in his throat as I move lower.

And my traitorous body reacts.

Because I'm a lowly mortal.

But I'm not gay.

So what if my dirty fantasies include men sometimes? That's only because it's all I know. When I close my eyes and think about sex, I see dicks. I know dicks.

Once I get my hands and mouth on Dove's pretty pussy, I'll have her image to preside over my filthiest imaginings.

Except last night, I fucked my fist to fantasies of them both. The three of us together. In every position.

You can't chase me and entertain him.

She's right.

Jag's the enemy. Her tormentor.

Her stepbrother.

I leave the soggy bandages on his hand and reach between his legs to rinse him. Then I make another pass, chasing away lingering suds.

His chin drops to his chest, eyes cracked open. "If you clean it more than once, you're playing with it."

My first instinct is to punch his pretty face.

Or maybe I should let go and watch him faceplant.

But his knees buckle, and his body sags heavily against mine.

"Shut the fuck up." I haul him upright, my face hot and hands clumsy.

I swear under my breath as I finish quickly, my clothes soaked through to my skin. But I can't remove my shirt, not in front of anyone, especially him.

Once he's rinsed, I drag him out, water dripping everywhere, and half-carry him back to the cot.

He's unconscious before he hits the mattress.

A black duffel sits on the floor. I rummage through it, yanking out a pair of sweatpants, and manhandle his limp weight into them. My hands shake for no good reason, but I get the job done.

Just as I'm hauling the blanket over him, the door opens.

"Wolf?" Kody's growly voice loosens the tension in my shoulders.

Frankie barrels in right behind, her sharp green eyes wide with worry.

When I fired off that text to the family, I wasn't sure they'd actually come. As quickly as they arrived, they must've been nearby. Probably on the way to the hospital, given Frankie's scrubs.

I don't know why I bothered, but as I look down at Jag, his wet hair curling over his fever-flushed forehead, I guess I didn't want him to die.

Not until I've played with him a bit more.

jag
TWENTY

Drenched in sweat, I wake on the cot. My mouth tastes like rust and ash, and every muscle aches as if I've been pried apart with a crowbar.

Hell.

That's where I am.

A dry groan scrapes out of me as I blink against the gummy seal of my eyelids. The world swims. Walls, ceiling... Movement.

I'm not alone.

A man sits nearby, long legs sprawled, arms folded, back propped against the wall like he has all the time in the world to stare at me.

Shaggy black hair falls over his forehead, and his eyes... Good God, his eyes are so black and bottomless, like two endless pits, pinning me in place. He's a burly, broad-shouldered, living mountain in a fitted shirt.

Kodiak Strakh.

Beautiful and brutal all at once. Probably wrestled grizzlies in the Arctic. And if the glare he's throwing me says anything, he'd wrestle me just for fun.

Why is he here?

The bathroom door creaks, and a smaller figure slips into

view. Red hair drapes around porcelain shoulders. Eyes big and green as emeralds. Childlike, but not fragile. No. There's steel under those nursing scrubs.

Frankie Strakh.

Monty's wife. Kodiak's and Leonid's, too, if the rumors are to be believed. Sitka's favorite scandal.

Gracefully, she moves toward me, and Kodiak instantly tenses. He growls low in his throat, a territorial touch-her-and-die growl.

She hushes him with a small sound and leans over me, pressing the back of her hand to my forehead.

"Your fever's still high." She withdraws her touch and backs away. "I gave you antibiotics. Keep resting. Drink water. And stop using your hand like your wrist isn't broken."

My gaze drops to the aching thing, now splinted with a brace and neatly wrapped in fresh bandages. I flex my fingers, wincing. At least, they're moving.

She clucks her tongue. "Nurse's orders."

Kodiak reaches for her arm, fingers closing gently but firmly, pulling her farther back.

She shoots him a glare so sharp I half-expect him to flinch. He doesn't. He just holds her, his jaw tight enough to grind rocks.

"Thanks for coming, Dorothy." Wolf pushes off the door and kisses the top of her head. "And your little dog, too." He winks at Kodiak.

The big man grunts, but my attention is rapt on Wolf.

He turns to me like a fucking fever dream, dripping in drama. Black pinstriped pants hug his thighs, laced up the sides just enough to show skin. His Renaissance retro boots with pointed toes weren't made for walking. They were made to step on a man's neck and look good doing it.

Up top is some designer monstrosity, deep burgundy silk with high, exaggerated shoulders and embroidered gold thread twisting across his chest in baroque patterns. No buttons undone. No glimpse of a defined torso. Not even a sliver of collarbone. Just a smug, sculpted mouth and hint of untamed madness prowling beneath the fabric.

It's infuriating. Don't get me wrong. I love his eccentric aesthetic, but I want him shirtless. I want the tease stripped down and pissed off.

"This is a problem." Kodiak glares at me and clamps a paw

jag

on Wolf's shoulder. "Get it out of our town."

"Heard you the first ten times." Wolf shakes him off.

"I mean it."

Wolf looks at Frankie and directs his chin at Kodiak. "Remember how he used to be a virgin?"

"Behave." She gives him a teasing smile.

"Only if you watch." His eyes sparkle.

Kodiak growls, and I'm tempted to growl with him.

"Alrighty." Wolf claps his hands and shoos them toward the door. "You kids run along now. I got this."

"I need to talk to you." Kodiak plants his boots and shoots me a look that says I'm a diseased devil they should've left to rot. "In private."

"Is this another one of those talks about how I shouldn't be alone?" Wolf pulls on his pearl earring. "How I don't spend enough time with you and the Strakh emotional-support brigade?"

"You're *not* alone." Kodiak spreads his arms. "You have us if you'll let us in."

"Sounds like *you* need some family time. Tell you what. I'll pencil in a group hug after I deal with Satan over there." Wolf jerks a thumb in my direction. "We have some marshmallows to roast over the barrel fire of his poor life choices."

What the fuck? I'm lying here half-dead, and this is the guy who claims *he* is protecting Dove from *me*?

They go back and forth like this. Kodiak with his hell-dark eyes and quiet concern, and Wolf flinging sarcasm like it's his sharpest weapon. It's messy, uncomfortable, and genuinely charming.

I hate that their bickering makes me green with envy. I don't have this. Brothers. Friends. People who care enough to smother me.

Kodiak shoves his face into Wolf's, baring his teeth. "You spend too much time by yourself."

"You think?" Wolf mutters, looking away. "I don't need a babysitter. I need you to trust me."

Kodiak blinks once, twice, then hauls Wolf into his arms and smashes an aggressive kiss against his cheek. "You're still my little brother. Stop acting like you're not."

"And nothing says brotherly love like oral affection." He

turns his head and slowly licks a line up Kodiak's neck.

As intended, Kodiak jerks back, stumbling to put space between them.

"There we go." Wolf mimes spraying perfume in the air. "Boundaries restored."

"Remember what I said." Kodiak clasps Frankie's hand and pulls her toward the door.

She glances back once, worry wrinkling her brow. He doesn't let her stop.

When they're gone, the silence they leave behind is anything but empty.

"Show me how you're monitoring Dove." Wolf casts a glance around the sparse break room. "Where's all your equipment?"

"You've seen my equipment." I wink. "But I'll gladly show you again."

"Spare me the punchlines, Pornhub." He crouches beside me, arms resting on his knees, a glint of the Arctic in those too-blue eyes. Persistent. Unamused. He's not going to let this drop.

With a sigh, I fumble with my phone, swiping through some of my security programs. His eyes flicker over the screen, narrowing when I pull up the mechanic shop camera.

There she is, skating lazy circles around the grease-stained bays, headphones on, lost in her own world. Her hair is loose today, blue waves streaking down her back, catching the fluorescent lights.

Stunning.

Wolf's gaze softens, almost imperceptibly. "She's safe."

For now.

But I'm not watching her. I'm watching him.

The sharp planes of his face. The full mouth that never stops twisting into sardonic shapes. The tension riding his shoulders like a mantle he never sets down.

He called his family to mend my hand. No one's done anything like that for me. Ever.

"Who's following her?" He pins me with a murderous stare. "If it's not you, then who knows she's here and what do they want?"

I know who's following her. I've known since the moment the feed glitched for three seconds at 2:14 this morning, just long enough for a fingerprint to brush across a relay node I built myself.

jag

They found us.

If I tell Wolf the bad news, it's over. He'll react. Explode. Bring the whole fucking circus down on us. He's too impulsive, hot-blooded, and emotional.

Just like she is.

She can rebuild engines in her sleep and hotwire a city block with a screwdriver and a paperclip. But when it comes to survival, real survival, she's still that little girl in the system, trusting the wrong foster brother, seeking affection from the wrong family.

She trusts too easily. Loves too hard. And she'll get herself killed if she knows who's hunting us. So I keep my secrets and stick to the plan. Like always. It's muscle memory wired into my fucking DNA.

"Tell me what you know." He points at the screen. "You're hacking private cameras. How? Where is all your computer shit?"

"Blue princess."

"What the fuck does that mean?"

"Whatever you want."

"I want answers!" He punches the mattress.

"So protective," I murmur, voice roughened by fever and something hungrier. "If I ask nicely, will you climb on my lap and make me forget how you broke my wrist?"

"In your dreams, kitty cat." His eyes remain on the screen. On Dove.

"Oh, I dream." I grin slowly, feverishly, delighted. "You, me, and the make-out booth I built for you. Bet you're curious how soft I can purr when you're on top."

He snaps his gaze to me, eyes wide, before he narrows them. "Didn't peg you for a bottom."

"Depends who's doing the pegging."

"Sorry to disappoint. I don't fuck homicidal stalkers. Or stepbrothers. Or men, in general."

"I'll change your mind." I stretch out on my back, watching his eyes trace my bare stomach as it flexes.

Nothing shy about the way he regards me. The man is confronting, openly hungry, and beneath the uncultured mannerisms, deeply curious. Almost innocent.

I'm certain he's never been with a man. But is it possible he's never fucked a woman?

Could he be a virgin?

He's had six months to take care of that problem. Six months to shed his animal skin, tame his feral impulses, and acclimate to civilization.

Okay, that's not long. Especially if he's dragging around some heavy-ass trauma baggage. Torture, rape, whatever flavor of fucked-up his snow cabin captor fed him in the Arctic.

Holy fuck.

I bet this beautiful, damaged man has never had consensual sex.

Lust trips in my belly and stiffens my cock. He marks it immediately, his gaze locking on the growing, twitching bulge tenting my thin sweatpants.

"You can't stand me, and you can't look away." I wet my lips. "Fun little problem, isn't it?"

He rises from his crouch and sits against my hip on the cot, bracing his hands on either side of me.

"You're playing a game you'll lose, Step-psycho."

"Oh, pup. I only play games I don't mind losing."

Our eyes meet and hold as a quiet storm drops between us. Fuck if I don't grow harder, the throbbing in my erection rivaling the pounding in my head.

"It's yours." I lift my hips, my whisper sticky with want and wickedness. "Satisfy your curiosity."

The camera feed with Dove continues to stream, but his eyes don't shift. They're on me. Stark and wild and sparking with furious need.

"When I look at your dick..." He looks. And keeps looking. "I feel nothing."

It's a lie. A soft, breathy, ridiculous lie.

"Prove it." I bite the corner of my lip. "Touch me. If you feel nothing, if you show no reaction, I'll accept your boring heterosexuality and never proposition you again."

His jaw tenses, mouth parting like he's about to issue a warning. But nothing comes. Only silence. Breathing. That pulse in his neck.

"Look, I have one good hand, and it's not going anywhere." I ease my waistband down with that hand, enough to bare myself to him. My cock stands against the flat of my stomach. "I won't touch you. Not unless you beg me."

He stares, unblinking.

jag

"Come on, Wolf." I fold my good arm behind my head and give him the full show of my body. "Let me be the first. Make a memory out of me."

Still, he says nothing. But he doesn't look away, not even when he shifts closer.

His curious fingertips brush my chest, one nail dragging down my sternum, slow and deliberate. A tease of sensation that leaves me gasping. I arch beneath him, dizzy from fever and lust.

He follows the centerline of my torso, down, down, until he reaches the coarse hair above the base of my cock.

Pausing, he meets my eyes. "You will *not* touch me."

"I swear it."

He closes his hand around my shaft, his touch rough, firm, and really fucking unkind.

I moan. Loud.

His smirk is feral as he begins to stroke.

Expert fingers. Vicious grip. Unruly pace. He pulls and strangles and beats my dick like a savage, and I fucking love it. His other hand grips my balls, ruthlessly squeezing.

My back bows. My heels dig into the mattress. My lungs burn, and my fever gives way to an inferno of sweat and desire.

"Fuuuck!" I angle my pelvis, chasing the hellish pleasure of his mastery over my body.

"You're louder than I expected."

"You're better than I expected." I groan. "So damn mean."

"You like mean."

"Fuck you. Jerk it like you hate me."

"I do." He twists his wrist, the metal of his stacked rings digging into my sensitive flesh. "I fucking despise you."

"Then use me harder. Show me your fangs."

He crawls over me, straddling me, his breath hot on my cheek, his mouth almost at mine as he works my cock like a goddamn animal.

"Admit it," I pant. "Admit you want me."

I feel him against my hip, thick and stiff. Hung like a horse. He would hurt me with that thing. *If I let him.* But I don't do that. I don't bottom.

Except I might with him. Right now, I'd let him do anything he wanted.

jag

His proximity overwhelms me, his tantalizing scent of smoke, leather, and untamed carnality clouding my senses. My pulse races as a charged question hangs unvoiced between us.

How far will we go?

"Tell me what you want." My voice wavers, betraying a truth.

I want him.

Not the game. Not to break him or steal him from Dove. I just want him for the pleasure of... This. Him. Us.

His eyes bore into mine, searching, dissecting every hidden desire, every buried secret. His fist doesn't slow on my dick as his free hand grips my face, fingers bruising.

"If you touch me," he snarls against my lips. "This stops."

Jesus. Did his cabin daddy fuck him up that badly? Pretty thing like him, acting like touch will break him. But somehow, he's the one breaking me.

Fuck perfect. I want the pieces. The shame. The wreckage. "Don't stop."

He releases a panting, guttural groan and crashes his mouth against mine, harsh and demanding, a collision of power and need. Our teeth clash and tongues tangle. Not soft. Not tender. It's warfare.

And I surrender.

He kisses like he fights, violent, skillful, and punishing. I match him stroke for stroke, sinking deeper, deeper, further into this madness as our tongues battle fiercely.

Urgency detonates between us, raw and intoxicating. My hand flexes above my head, gripping the mattress as I fight the frantic impulse to grab him and restrain him against me.

Above me, he growls against my lips, the sound primal, vibrating electricity through my veins.

"You smell like hunger." My cock kicks, jabbing into his fist as I climb the high.

"It's Old Spice body wash."

"Ah. Vintage daddy issues."

"At least mine washes off. Yours is permanent."

"Mine is dead."

"And you're next." Every tendon in his neck pulls tight. Shadows carve down his arms, flexing through the fabric of his shirt, biceps thick and knotted as if he's trying to hold himself back.

Fuck, he's beautiful like this. Sex-crazed and cracking. Nothing exists beyond his heat, his hand on my shaft, and the taste of his hunger.

He sucks at my mouth, biting hard enough to break skin. It's as rough and greedy as his stroking fist. He's trying to split me open and wring me dry, and it's pissing him off that I'm not spilling all over him yet.

Good. Let him work for it.

"You're fucking toxic." He deepens the kiss, suffocating me with it, pressing in with teeth and tongue.

"Then let me kill you slowly," I rasp against his mouth, drawing him back in, surrendering fully to this irresistible, destructive force between us.

Our gazes lock as we kiss, sparks igniting, a silent war of wills and desires. The air between us grows hotter, charged with secrets, threats, and unstoppable attraction. I'm everything he despises, and he's everything I crave.

Blood pounds in my ears as he releases me to shove a hand down his pants. Popping the button, he frees himself. And just like that, his hot, swollen, massive erection is out of the closet and leaking all over me.

He's frantic with it, his gasps spilling into my mouth, and his fingers fumbling like his body is moving faster than his brain.

A few clumsy adjustments, and he has both our waistbands shoved past our knees, our lower legs tangled, and our cocks bumping, dripping, and rubbing together.

His long fingers circle our dicks, joining us in the hot stroke of his fist. The feel of his burning hard length against mine sets my skin on fire as he works us into a consuming rhythm.

He's as thick as me. And longer. With each brutal pump, his grip struggles to keep us fused. I want to help him. I want to take control. But I made a promise.

No touching.

Opening his lips, he feasts on my mouth and swallows all my air. My fever rises to scalding degrees. His thigh painfully rubs my tattoo, and I don't fucking care.

Bent over me, he gives me the pace I crave, working me with his hand, his tongue plunging and taking.

I'm gone, drowning beneath the coiled power of his body, the wild force of it. He doesn't even know what he's doing to me, and that's the worst part. He's a loaded weapon, and I'm the target.

We grind together, flexing, panting, and working ourselves up, harder, closer, faster...

"Oh, fuck, yeah." I feel the sudden, explosive spill of release. His. Mine. We come at the same time, groaning into a sloppy, frenzied kiss.

My eyes roll back in my head, and for a second, I pass out. Until a hand smacks my face, wrenching me back to consciousness.

"Don't die yet." He climbs off me and straightens his clothes. "I need answers first."

Boneless, I can only lie there, arms trembling and vision sparking with aftershocks.

I feel high. Quiet in my head for the first time in forever. No noise. No rage. No guilt gnawing at my ribs. Just floaty and fucked-out, every inch of me humming with the electric shimmers of a really intense orgasm.

He stands over me, trying like hell to pull his pretty mask into place, but it's useless. His body gives him away. The shifting muscles, twitching jaw, flushed skin... It's all there. His desire to repeat what we did. The urge to deny his attraction to men. The trauma he doesn't talk about. And the ever-present impulse for violence.

He's a ruthless, sexual creature, and he hasn't scratched the surface of what he wants. Or who he wants. Men. Women. Pain. Pleasure. He's tasting it all for the first time and doesn't know he's starving.

Breathtaking. Addicting. He's my new obsession.

Any second now, he'll erect a wall between us and pretend he didn't shoot his load all over my stomach.

Except he doesn't, because nothing about Wolfson Strakh is normal.

Leaning down, he drags his tongue through the mess on my abdomen.

What the—?

My brain blanks. My entire body reignites, and I stare at him, stunned. Fucking stunned.

This isn't how it goes. This isn't what people do. Not after they dodge my hands and claim to be straight.

He pauses to lick along the grooves of my abs, and Jesus fucking Christ, I almost come from the shock alone. Then he nibbles upward toward my chest, my neck, the hinge of my jawline. By the time he reaches my mouth, I'm panting and hard again.

He doesn't kiss me. He touches. Slow, careful palms skim up my sides, and fuck, it feels so fucking good. My skin ripples under his hands. I don't know this feeling. I don't know how to handle tenderness.

He works over my ribs, my hips, then settles into my chest like he's trying to knead the damage out of me. It's not sex. It's not aftercare. It's a goddamn massage.

And it's wrecking me.

I haven't felt this loose in years. Maybe not ever. I forgot how to relax until he showed up with these quiet hands and that deep, rumbling sigh.

My whole world shrinks to the caress of his palms and the weight of him hovering over me, not to dominate, not to destroy, but to give me this strange, foreign thing.

Gentleness.

"Goddammit." I groan, limp and aching. "What the hell are you doing to me?"

"I don't know." His brows pinch, and he pulls back, seemingly confused.

"Time to wave that freak flag, Wolf."

"Um, hello?" He gestures at the smudged guyliner around his eyes and the pearl earrings dangling from his ears. "I've been waving that flag my whole life."

"Love that about you." I swallow.

"I'm not gay." He stands, complexion paling.

"Neither am I."

"I'm not like you." He flicks his fingers at me. "Bi-, pan-, poly—"

"Don't put me in a box. My sexual fluidity exists on a spectrum and shifts from one person to the next."

"Whatever. I'm not into men."

"Maybe what you're attracted to has nothing to do with gender or identity."

"Okay, enlighten me, Freud. What am I into, exactly?"

"Danger." I flash a smile, all teeth. "But don't worry. I'll make sure you enjoy the damage."

jag

"Cool story, bro." His lips press into a thin line, the heat and confusion from a moment ago gone as he heads to the door. "I gotta bounce."

"I'll be out in a minute to start on the lower part of the leg sleeve."

Truth is, I feel like I'm going to die. Fever continues to ride me hard, and cold sweat clings to my spine. But I'll push through it.

"Yeah, you do that, and I'll get your body bag ready." The door shuts behind him, leaving silence in his wake.

Shit.

I drop back against the cot, breath shaky, chest rising and falling as if I ran a mile instead of lying here letting him touch me like I'm worth the effort.

I'm not, and he knows it.

It was nothing. It meant nothing. Just a little fever heat between rivals. Happens. It's fine. He's not mine. Not part of my plan. Not the one I want.

Dove.

She's the priority. The line I can't afford to blur. The only one who counts.

I drag a hand down my face, my lips still tingling from Wolf's seductive mouth.

Christ, I need saving, but I don't want that. I want Wolf again, and I intend to fuck his hot feral ass until he's out of my system.

wolfson
TWENTY-ONE

It's official. I've finally snapped and lost the last marble rattling around in my skull.

The second I escape the break room and the man inside it, my composure shatters.

The walls close in, and the air ripens with the stench of my fucking shame. I can't breathe.

Congrats to me. Certified lunatic. Straitjacket queen. Not that anyone's lining up to take the crown, but hey, I wear it well.

Like seriously.

What.

The.

Fuck.

I should've spent the morning interrogating Jag Rath about his intentions with Dove. Should've been protecting her by pressing him, punching through his lies, and ripping the truth out of him with my bare hands.

But no. What did I do instead? I played with his dick.

Now I can't stop replaying it, every filthy inch of him sliding in my grip, every aggressive lick of his tongue rubbing in my mouth.

And the part I'm choking on the most? The absolute rock-bottom truth?

It was hot as fuck.

Dove deserves better.

I know she and I aren't *together* together, but I'm working on that. I want her to be my girl.

Fucking around with her stepbrother after she told me he hurt her... Yeah, I'm the literal scum of the earth. No better than her cock-gobbling ex-fiancé.

I fucked up. Frigid gods above, grant me strength and bigger balls. She won't forgive me for this.

Who can blame her?

The reel won't stop spinning in my head. Jag's mouth. Jag's body. My hand on him like it belonged there. And now it's all tangled with Denver's mouth, Denver's body, the old sickness howling in surround sound.

Heat and cold sweep through me. Sweat slicks my temples, and I grip the counter's edge for balance.

"Hey, man." Declan approaches. "You okay?"

My heart jackhammers, and blackness creeps in at the edges of my vision. Can't gather my thoughts. Can't pull in air.

Fuck this.

Declan's relentless voice pellets my back as I shove open the front door and stumble outside.

Rain slams into me, soaking through my shirt in seconds. Good. Maybe it'll wash the filth off me. Maybe it'll strip away the dirt ground into my bones.

I hit the sidewalk at a run, eyes locked on the distant harbor lights. I need the yacht. The safety of the island. I need to get the hell out of here before I turn the town square into a psych ward circus.

Grinding my teeth, I force myself faster, faster as rain plasters my hair to my face. My lungs burn. My hands tremble, and the voice in my head spits one word.

Stupid.

Stupid to let Jag manipulate me. Stupid to desire him like a twisted fucking sicko. Stupid to let another man use my body like a dumping ground for their toxic fluids and waste.

Such a sweet little boy.

My legs lock up, and I stagger, one step short of the docks, chest heaving, vision tunneling.

So small and tight.

My knees give out. The ground rushes up, and I'm back in the hills. The same loop. Same panic.

You take your daddy's dick so good.

I'm eight years old again, curled up on my bed, shivering under thin blankets, skin too small for my body, and breath raging with fear as Denver's shadow fills the doorway.

I see you, Son. I'll never stop wanting you.

His hand clamps over my mouth. His weight crushes me. And that sickening part of him, it jabs and tears and invades, and *oh, hateful God,* it hurts. I hear his husky *Good boy* on repeat and feel his calloused fingers in places they should never touch.

The shame burns hot, and I curl in tighter, trying to disappear, trying to dissolve. The world fractures. My chest cracks open. Nothing exists but him and his hurt and his hurt and his hurt and his hurt and…

I'm back.

Back in Sitka, crouched under the pier, hunched against the concrete embankment where it meets the water. My arms wrap around my knees, my forehead pressed to my soaked trousers. Rain drips through the cracks above me. My body shakes, from the cold, from the memory, from the haunting pain.

How long have I been here? Minutes? Hours? No one noticed me. No one stopped.

I drag in a breath, shallow and searing, but it's air. I'm here. Not in the hills. My fingers flex against my pants, proving I exist. I didn't die. I'm not a child. The pain is old pain. I escaped.

Swiping rain and tears from my face, I swallow down the acid in my throat and push to my feet.

I fucking hate this. Hiding under the dock like a sewer rat. Falling apart where anyone can watch me sob. Pathetic. Broken. I need the island, just until I can patch myself back together and be normal.

As if I know how to be normal.

The pier thrums with bodies, umbrellas stabbing the air, and boots slapping against wet wood. I cut through them too fast, head down, tunnel vision on the yacht. Just a few more steps. Just a few—

A shoulder collides with mine, and a man's hand clamps on my arm to steady me.

I detonate.

White-hot panic knifes through my stomach, flays away skin and muscle, and exposes the child trapped inside my rib cage. Denver's hand cinches around my arm. My throat rips open, and a raw, ear-splitting wail spills out before I register that I'm screaming.

I careen sideways, knees cracking against the boards, palms scraping slick planks. People crowd in, hands reaching, voices clanging, too close, too many.

Don't touch me. Don't fucking touch me.

Another hand grazes my shoulder, and I lose it, thrashing and kicking and biting at the air.

"Get off me! Get the fuck away!" Spit flies, and rain streaks my face, salt from my tears. My body folds in on itself, wild and shaking, trapped in a nightmare with no exit.

The crowd recoils, their revulsion giving me space to crawl, to shove, to claw my way through legs and umbrellas.

Dragging myself upright, I wheeze, shove out of the shadows, and break into a run. Across the gangway and aboard the yacht, I don't stop, desperate for the lock of the door and the distance that will put the mainland behind me.

Fading in and out of a mouth-breathing meltdown, I steer into the Sound. My hands shake on the wheel, but I don't let go. I can't. If I stop moving, I'll implode.

Somehow, I manage to hammer out a message to Dove's security team, instructing them to bring her home when she's finished. Straight to the island. Tell her I need her now.

My thumb hovers over that last demand. That's not fair. She doesn't need my shit. Delete. Send. Done.

As I reach the island, I remember my family is still in Sitka. No witnesses. It's for the best.

I don't remember docking or walking to the guest house.

All I remember is Jag.

His name hits like a fist. Jag, the asshole. Jag, the fever-burned sex god, stretched out beneath me. I can't stop replaying it. Trying to line it up in my head. Line it up with Denver's hands on me, the way he pinned me and hurt me. And today, *Jesus Christ*, me on top of Jag, my body betraying me, straddling him like I was the predator. Like I was Denver.

Bile scorches my throat.

Jag didn't touch me. Didn't force me. He kept his word. He

fucking let me. And that's worse. That's what's killing me. Because it wasn't him. It was me. My body, my hunger, my sickness clawing to the surface like it never left.

Who's the villain now?

My chest constricts, breath cutting short, eyes going blurry. I stumble into my bedroom and drop face down on the mattress. My brain slams against the same wall over and over, sparks flying in the cracks.

I gave him a hand job. I made him come. Made us both come. Then I licked up our seed like a depraved, unhinged animal.

And I want to do it again.

"No." I gnash my teeth. "No, fuck you. That's not me."

But it is. I'm fucking hard just thinking about it. Hard and grinding my aching dick against the mattress.

Frantically, I hump the bed, overcome by the warzone in my head as graphic images explode in every direction. Jag's body beneath me, Denver's groan in my ear, Jag's cock in my hand, Denver's rotpiece in my ass, and my eight-year-old sobs threaded through it all.

I can't want a man that way. I didn't want it with Denver. But what if I did? What if all I'm meant to be is another man's fuck boy? What if I let myself believe it?

I'll break. I'll break so hard there won't be anything left to patch.

Doesn't stop me from pushing my skull into the mattress and muffling my roar as I free my erection and squeeze it. Fighting the breakdown. Fighting the urge to jerk. Fighting the impossible need to fuck my fist like a beast with teeth.

I kept it leashed for so long. Kept it hidden where it belonged. And just like that, one orgasm with a man on a creaky cot, and I can't stop the sudden, rapid, uncontrolled release of impounded sexual hunger.

The dam has broken, and there's no going back.

I can't kill this gnawing, bottomless need for sex. For intimacy. For deranged rutting in every body hole. I crave it. I fucking need it. In the name of Freddie Mercury, I. Want. To. Fuck.

But not with these feelings. Not these sucking, unrelenting, painful godsdamn memories.

I want to fuck like a regular guy.

I want to fuck Jag and Dove.

You're a horny bitch. That's all this is. Nothing new there.

Yeah. Just horny.

With great effort, I release the chokehold on my dick, push off the bed, and tuck myself away.

This need is maddening, more than I can bear. I'll starve it out. Let it dry up and shrivel.

So I throw myself into work, scrubbing the guest house until my knuckles split. Then I drown in the Internet, mindless scrolling through black holes of nothing. Then I fill page after page of my sketchbooks until the pencils bleed down to nubs.

But no matter how many distractions I choke on, the truth keeps stabbing through.

I want him.

Man or not. Enemy or not. Even with the manipulation, the murdering, and all the pain he caused Dove. I want him.

And I want Dove, too. My prickly, runaway princess bride.

She hasn't said it, but I know she's been denying Jag for years, pushing him into the enemyzone. But he's still here. A Peeping Tom in the window. A voyeur behind the cameras. A shadow curling in the edges of her thoughts, now coiled in mine.

Jag and Dove are a package deal, tied together, shackled in trauma and history. As long as he breathes, he'll be the weight that presses behind every kiss I steal from her, every laugh and sigh and breathy moan I claim. He's the name that burns both our tongues, whether we speak it or not.

And doesn't that fucking suck? I hate that he's under my skin. Hate that I can't cut him out without cutting her, too. Hate that the only way forward might be through the come-soaked sheets in his bed.

I wipe a hand down my face and catch sight of the closet door. The cracked opening shows me what I don't want to see, the saxophone case wedged up on the shelf, black leather dulled with age.

My chest caves, and my body moves without asking, dragging me into the closet, reaching up like a starving man. The case comes down hard into my arms, and I open the latches.

Brass glints in the dim light. My throat closes.

Still, I put it to my mouth. Because I'm a masochist. Because the sound makes me feel human.

The first note pours out, low and rusty. My fingers remember, moving with precision, muscle memory etched so deep no amount of trauma can erase it.

The sound swells, vibrating through the empty house, through my ribs, through the scared boy inside me.

For a dissonant riff of beats, I feel alive. But memory doesn't stay dead for long.

Denver's voice cuts through the melody.

Play it again, boy.

Slower this time.

Remove your underwear.

Let me hear you.

His shadow stretches over me, the slimy heat of his stare dripping down my body, every quiver of my embouchure feeding his sickness. I see him, clear as the brass in my hands, legs spread in that chair, one hand buried down his pants, the other stroking his drink as he watches me blow out every note. His panting. His arousal. My shame.

The melody fractures. My breath stutters, and my fingers wobble on the keys. The sax slips from my grip, and my chest crumples, every breath airless, strangled, a scream with no sound.

My vision whites out, spinning, and I slam to my knees, gasping, the past and present indistinguishable.

The next thing I know, a hiss of water slaps my face. Then a cascade. I blink.

I'm in the shower. Naked. I don't remember undressing. Don't remember turning the knobs.

Through the steam and spray of water, I can see what I'm doing. From outside my body, I watch my hand move, throttling my erection, beating it in a ferocious, mindless frenzy that I can't stop.

It's not pleasure. *Yes, it is.*

It's not punishment. *Yes, it is.*

On my knees, I press my forehead to the cold tile, my throat raw from sobbing. Every choking, ruthless stroke of my hand feels like self-harm. Self-destruction.

It doesn't matter how much I tell myself I'm not built for it, that I don't want a man ramming into my ass, that I don't want to fuck his stepsister while she swallows his cock, my body's a liar. My head's full of sick, dark cravings. Every second I'm awake, it hums under my skin, a low-level current, always circling, never shutting off.

"Disgusting," I rasp, the word drowning in a broken cry. "You're just like him. Spawn of the devil."

My lungs thrash, gulping at nothing but the sour reek of my own panic. Every drag of air scrapes my throat bloody.

I yank harder on my miserable cock, nails biting into skin, trying to rip the thing off me. Doesn't work. Never works. My body folds, buckling forward, forehead kissing the shower floor as more memories slide in.

Denver's hunger-soaked grunts fall across my face as he traps me against the mattress, hips slamming into mine, watching me wheeze through the pain he gouges into me. The more I fight for air, the more he groans.

He used to say I looked like a bird when I gasped for breath.

Poor little broken fledgling, heart fluttering, wings clipped, dying in the corner.

My ribs shrink, crushing the oxygen out of me. It's not me on the shower floor. It's that weak, pathetic boy, hugging himself, shaking so hard he can't stop, while Denver breaks him again and again.

I slam my fist faster, clenching and twisting, hoping to release the ghost in ropey streams and shoot it straight down the drain.

My vision spots white, black, then white again. My howls sound like screaming animals in a mating frenzy, fucking themselves bloody, and I can't jerk my dick hard enough, can't reach that climax to quiet them.

The worst part? Deep in the pit of my soul-cage, beneath the panic, I hear him. Not Denver.

Jag.

His hand wraps around my throbbing flesh, and his masculine presence curls over my back, panting with me, mocking me every time I moan.

I'm not gasping for air anymore. I'm gasping for release.

Tears burn hot. My whole body convulses, shame and arousal knotted together until I don't know what's what. My mind screams to stop, but my body won't. I come with a sobbing, unsatisfying agony that leaves me hungrier than before.

I hate this flesh. I hate every nerve that remembers Denver's touch, every cell he rewired, every scar that confuses pain for desire.

My fist tightens and pumps, moving like a piston along raw skin. I'm still hard. Ready to chase the next release.

So I do, shaking, sobbing, rocking under the spray. And a thought whispers, seductive and venomous.

It'd be easier if I just ended it.

No cliff this time.

A knife.

Let the blood swirl down the drain. Quick and clean. Sounds nice.

But what would happen to Dove? Maybe she doesn't need me, but she already lost her parents. She has no one left in her life.

Except Jag.

I won't leave her alone with him. I will *never* do that to her. She has me for as long as she wants me. And for as long as I need her, which happens to be forever.

Lucky her.

The water hisses louder, masking the sound of my broken gasps and stroking fist as I'm sucked back into the hills of shivers and shadows.

love
TWENTY-TWO

Break time.

If I can call standing in the back room picking grease from my nails a break.

The scent of scorched rubber and motor oil sticks to me. I sniff my armpit and sigh. No wonder Wolf prefers Jag over me. Stray animals smell better than I do.

I wipe my hands on a rag that'll never come clean, pull my phone out of my back pocket, and thumb the screen awake.

Still no texts from Wolf.

His radio silence chews a hole through my ribs. Because I know where he is and who he's with.

The thought makes me itch. Not just because Jag is a narcissistic, homicidal manwhore. Not just because he can and will hurt Wolf.

It's more selfish than that.

Jag has taken everything from me, and I can't stand the idea of him stealing Wolf, wrenching Wolf's savage protection away, and hoarding all that wild devotion for himself.

I shut my eyes. Squeeze the phone until it creaks. Open them again. Swipe down, and check my notifications.

One new message.

Carol.

Of all people. Carol-fucking-Samuels. My ex's mother. The woman who never looked at me without pursing her lips like I was a sour sip of boxed wine. Too cheap. Too dirty. Too rough around the edges. Too much of everything unworthy for her perfect little Gavin.

I hesitate. What could she possibly want? I haven't talked to her since I fled my wedding and left her with the bill. Maybe she wants reimbursement.

That'll be a cold day in hell.

I tap the screen, and a link pops up.

An obituary.

Gavin Michael Samuels, 34.
Beloved son. Cherished friend. Taken too soon.

My breath strangles. My knees turn to wet paper, and the greasy rag slips from my fingers.

Dead.

He's dead.

The shop carries on with the din of ratchet guns, clanking wrenches, and the guys shouting across the bay. But it all fades beneath the resounding toll of *Dead, Dead, Dead.*

How?

I scroll down, scanning over the funeral home address, candle emojis, and phrases like *In lieu of flowers...*

A quick Internet search doesn't confirm how he died, but I know. The last year of my life is buried, six feet down, because that's what Jag does.

There was the foster brother who fingered me behind the garage when I was fourteen. Two days later, a car accident. Hit and run, they said. Jag was stealing cars by then.

And the soldier who took me out for beers when I was fifteen. Deployment cut short by a bar fight gone too far. Stabbed.

And the mechanic who taught me how to rebuild a carburetor when I was sixteen. He was twenty years older than me, and I shouldn't have had sex with him, but he gave me hope I could be more than an unloved orphan girl. Then he hung himself. Rope burns on his neck. But I know that knot had Jag's fingerprints all over it.

love

And there were more. Every man who's ever looked at me, touched me, or tried to love me is gone.

Jag circles my life like a man-eating beast, tearing out throats in the dark and ensuring no one stays long enough to matter.

He doesn't kill me. He kills them. One by one.

So yeah, I don't need the obituary to spell it out. Jag dealt with Gavin, and I don't know whether to cry or laugh or smash this goddamn phone into the pavement.

I loved Gavin. Or I thought I did. My feelings are muddy, but I certainly didn't wish him dead.

Why did Carol send me this text? She'll get nothing from me. If she'd known the truth about her son, that he preferred men, she would've cut him out of her life long ago.

Fuck her.

Jag, on the other hand, probably thought he could keep this from me.

I open our text chat and send the obituary link to him.

Three dots instantly appear. Disappear. Appear again. Pause. Gone.

Nothing.

After a long minute of waiting, I know that's the only response he'll give.

I shove the phone into my pocket and grab the nearest work order. Brake pads on an old Toyota Tacoma. Easy and quick. I throw myself into it. Lug nuts, calipers, pads swapped out. When I'm done, sweat slicks my neck and grease lines my wrists.

"I'm out." I toss the keys onto the counter and meet Chester's eyes. "Not feeling well."

He studies me, probably wondering if I'm hungover or just being a bitch. Then he nods.

I wipe my hands, grab my jacket, and step out into the rain.

Carl and Jasper break off from the exterior wall and stride toward me.

"Evening, Miss Rath." Carl motions for me to walk ahead of him. "We're taking you directly to the island. Wolfson's orders."

"Where is he?" My pulse ramps.

"Waiting for you there."

Relief and dread swirl in my gut. Wolf hasn't texted. Hasn't called. But he's waiting for me.

Why didn't he just come here?

Something's wrong.

And that something is watching me.

I feel him before I glance at the alleyway behind the guards.

Jag leans against the brick wall, rain sluicing down his hair, dripping over his face, and drenching his denim jacket until it clings to muscle.

His dark, unblinking eyes cut through the haze. Lightning cracks overhead, and he doesn't flinch. Thunder shudders the ground, and he doesn't twitch.

He just stares. Possessive. Accusing. Like I belong to him.

Part of me always will.

Even now, after Gavin, after all the bodies in Jag's wake, I feel the tug, the familiar pull toward the man who raised me, hurt me, saved me, and stalked me my entire life. He's inked into my existence, permanently etched into every fear, every memory.

I hate him.

I love him.

I'll never be free of him.

My breath shortens as his gaze bores into mine. There's no cruelty there. No sneer. Just raw, lethal protectiveness, heavy as a hand around my throat. It's the same look he wore when we hid in the pantry the night our parents died. The same look he wore when he beat my first foster brother to death.

I want to talk to him, demand answers, scream accusations, and pound my fists on his chest until he coughs up the truth. Who are his enemies? What does he want with me? Will he kill Wolf like all the others?

Carl and Jasper close ranks, more assertive than usual, funneling me toward the harbor. I let them move me along, but my eyes stray over my shoulder, remaining fixed on Jag.

He removes the phone from his pocket and taps the screen.

A vibration buzzes against my palm, and I look down.

Jag: How's your boy?
Me: Don't touch him.
Jag: I didn't.

The dots bounce. Pause. Bounce again.

Jag: Can't say he didn't touch me.

love

My breath punches out, and I slam to a stop.

"Miss Rath." Jasper nudges me forward. "We need to—"

"I need to answer this text. Give me a minute." Subtly, I peer toward the alley and glare at the shadow still lingering there.

Me: *What did you do?*
Jag: *You know and you'll think about it tonight when you're alone.*

The words blur. My throat burns. I almost drop the phone.

Why am I surprised? This is what he does. As long as he lives, he'll steal every person I care about. He steals them. Then he kills them.

Me: *Why can't you leave me alone? Please. Just walk away. Let me go.*
Jag: *Little Bird, walking away from you is the one sin I'll never commit.*

Little Bird.

Shimmery, traitorous warmth flushes my cheeks and sweeps through my bloodstream before doubt crashes in.

He speaks in venomous lullabies, always half-truth and half-hook. He knows how to string me between craving and loathing until I forget how deadly he is.

This has to stop.

As Carl and Jasper shift impatiently, scanning the perimeter, Jag sinks deeper into the shadows. I know he's still there, watching me from the darkness. I feel him more than I see him, that glaring, overprotective aura embracing me too tightly. Suffocating.

I tear my eyes away and let the guards guide me down the street.

Their presence forms an iron wall around me, but I still feel my stepbrother, pursuing his prey, his jaguar eyes slicing into my back, and branding me with a vow I feel in my bones.

Soon.

I can only assume that means one thing. The sooner he has me, the sooner he can throw me away.

At the pier, tourists crowd in clusters. Locals haul crates, and fishermen shout over gulls. All the usual chaos. But amid the bustle of bodies, someone stands out.

Not a fisherman. Not a tourist or commuter. Not anyone with a purpose. Just an average man wearing average street clothes. Dressed to vanish into a crowd.

He doesn't move. Doesn't fumble for a phone or glance at the sky. He just stands there, still as a statue, his eyes fixed on me like I'm the only thing that exists.

It's not his face or his stance that lifts the hairs on my nape. It's his watchfulness. He tracks me like it's his job. Like a thug. Only he doesn't look like a thug. Doesn't need to. I feel it in my tingling scalp and dampening palms.

My steps falter as I peer over my shoulder. My gaze arrows through the sea of people and immediately lands on Jag. But his focus isn't on me. It's locked on the man.

Carl and Jasper notice the threat, too. They tighten around me instantly, their postures humming with alertness.

"Keep walking." Jasper's assertive grip belies his casual tone. "Don't slow down."

"Faster, Miss Rath." Carl presses close behind.

I match their pace, my nerves unraveling. But I'm not afraid. Not with Jag in sight. I may never be safe from him, but no one else will hurt me while he's near.

"Kai! Let's move." Carl shoves me onto the gangway and raises his voice at the captain. "Get us off the pier now!"

The engines hum alive, Kai already at the helm, as we climb aboard. The deck tilts as he guns it, propellers churning froth, speeding us away.

I grip the rail, knuckles white, eyes on the crowd shrinking behind us.

Jag floats through the swirl of bodies, effortlessly gliding toward the man with a predatory calm in every step.

But the man... He's gone. Vanished.

Only the echo of his stare lingers, crawling over my skin, a cold reminder that Jag might not be the only one stalking me.

The ride feels too long. My pulse spins harder than the engines. Through the rain-smeared glass, the island rises out of the water, black trees crowding the shore, the stone mansion crouched and waiting.

We dock, and Carl and Jasper flank me to the house with no

space to breathe. No chance to slip away. Their boots keep pace with mine as we hurry up the path.

Monty steps out before I veer toward the guest house, his silhouette sharp against the porch light. His expression hardens the second he sees the guards glued to me.

"Where's Wolf?" His eyes flick to me, quick and assessing, then back to them.

"He returned home on his yacht several hours ago." Jasper shares a look with Carl.

Monty pivots toward the guest house.

"Sir." Carl plants a hand in his path. "We have a situation."

The words stop Monty dead. "The last time you said that…" His tone drops. "Denver's heart was in our kitchen."

A chill spiders down my back. Denver's heart? Given what I've pieced together about their dark past, I know it's not a metaphor. These men don't speak in metaphors.

I glance between them, catching the subtle exchange—Carl wanting to pull Monty aside, Monty already bracing for bad news. And I know. It's about Jag and the man on the pier.

I want to hear this, but I doubt I'm invited to the conversation.

"I'm going to check on Wolf." Without waiting for permission, I break from the tight formation and hurry across the path.

Inside the guest house, the air smells faintly of detergent and damp wood. And the silence? It's heavier than it should be.

"Wolf?" The stairs creak under my steps. "Where are you?" I find his bedroom door cracked, letting a slice of light into the hall. "Wolf?"

I lift my knuckles to tap and freeze.

Water. The steady rush of a shower.

Relief loosens my shoulders, and I retreat into my room. My skin itches from the shop, stinking of oil and dirt. A shower sounds perfect, a little scalding steam to burn off the day.

In my bathroom, I start the water and peel off my outerwear, shirt, and wet boots. The jeans take a minute, clinging damply to my thighs. My reflection in the mirror looks haunted and restless. Normal.

I turn away and test the water. Still ice cold.

Gritting my teeth, I kick free of the rest of my clothes and try again.

The spray pelts my palm, arctic sharp. No heat. Not at all. Weird.

I pause, listening. The pipes groan, carrying the sound of rushing water through the wall. Wolf's shower. Still running. Did he use all the hot water? Burn the tank down to nothing? Except he's still in there. Taking a cold shower?

My stomach drops, that earlier instinct slithering back to the surface. He didn't stop to get me after work. He came straight here. Alone.

Something's wrong.

I shut off the water and bolt through my room, yanking on a clean shirt and shorts. Then I grab my phone and race into Wolf's room.

"Wolf!" I hammer my fists on his bathroom door. "Open the damn door!"

No answer over the continuous hum of water.

I barge inside, and *Oh, my God.* I can't process what I'm seeing.

Oh, no, Wolf. No, no, no.

He's curled on the shower floor, knees tucked, head down, the icy shower beating into his naked body. His lips are blue, and his frame shakes so violently his bones look ready to snap.

Goosebumps cover his skin.

And scars.

I stop breathing, and my hand flies to my mouth.

His torso is a battlefield of macabre cuts. Some still angry and red. Others pink and shiny. Knife marks everywhere. Crosshatching. Overlapping. Hewed, quartered, and carved in layers.

Too many to count.

And *Jesus Christ*, another one, deep in the ball of his bicep, left a hole that never healed right. As if whatever went into his arm had been ruthlessly torn out.

"Wolf..." My voice breaks as I lunge forward and twist off the faucet.

Silence crashes as the spray sputters and dies. I snatch a towel from the rack and wrap it around him, my hands trembling and pulse crashing.

"It's okay. You're okay. I've got you. I—"

"Don't touch me!" He erupts with a roar ripped from hell.

love

"Wolf." I flinch. "It's me. It's Dove."

"Get away from me!" He jerks back, shoulders slamming the tile. "Don't fucking touch me!"

His arms snap up to shield his face. Hands over his head, elbows tucked in, he folds tighter into himself, making himself smaller, bracing for a blow.

I stagger back, my heart crying.

He isn't yelling at me. He's yelling at ghosts, at whoever put those scars there, and I don't know how to pull him out. My hands hang uselessly in the air as I choke on panic. I don't know how to help him.

Monty.

He'll know what to do. If I run, I can reach him in two minutes. Maybe three.

But I can't leave Wolf alone like this.

I scan the bathroom and spot his pants crumpled in the corner. Scrambling for them, I dig through the pockets until my fingers close on his phone.

My breath rattles as I hold the screen to his face. Mercifully, the phone unlocks, and I'm in.

His contacts... *Oh, God,* what is this? My heart rate redoubles as I scroll through a very short, very strange list.

Bluebird
Captain Kai
Dr Freud
GI Joe Carl
GI Joe Jasper
Nurse Dorothy
Rich Daddy
Scarecrow
The Bear
The Lion

I go back to *Rich Daddy.* That has to be Monty.

Stabbing my thumb against the nickname, I press *Call.*

"Please, answer." I stare at Wolf shivering on the tile, my throat closing around the helplessness.

"Wolf?" Monty's stern voice pierces my ear. "Everything okay?"

"It's Dove. He's…" I swallow. "He needs you."

TWENTY-THREE

With my back to the wall, I slide to the floor beside Wolf and grip my knees to stop myself from reaching for him again.

"You're okay. I'm here." My voice shreds. "I'm not touching you. See? Just breathing with you. Just breathing."

But I'm not breathing. Panic scrapes my throat raw, every heartbeat a hammer against bone. He's shaking so hard the tile rattles, eyes squeezed shut, arms locked over his head like he's trying to disappear.

My chest aches with the need to hug him. But I can't touch him. I can't help him. I can't—

Footsteps pound the stairs. Then Monty bursts into the room. Not frantic or disheveled. Never that. He's out of breath, yes, but his suit is still crisp, his shirt perfectly white.

His eyes land on Wolf, and his features go dangerously sharp. "What happened?"

Jag. Me. The stain of the Rath siblings. That's what happened.

Instead, I say, "I found him like this."

He crouches next to Wolf, his gaze lowering, catching the scars. Dozens. Hundreds. His jaw saws, the muscle jumping like it might crack, like this is the first time seeing his son's mutilated body.

"Goddammit, Wolf." His composure falters, voice fracturing. "What did they do to you?"

They? More than one person hurt Wolf?

Monty's eyes skim over the mess of scars, so many ragged wounds that didn't heal right. His face hardens, tendons straining like they're the only thing holding him together, and he crumples in the same breath.

"I should've been there." His hand hovers above Wolf's shoulder, fingers twitching like he wants to touch but doesn't dare. Then the words pour, coarse and thick, meant for a son too far under to hear. "I should've taken the knives for you. I would've bled for you. Every cut should've been mine."

Just like that, Alaska's richest man is unrecognizable. Stripped of his arrogance and billionaire swagger, he embodies a father's wreckage.

"I need to move you, Wolf. I'm so sorry." He slides his arms under Wolf's trembling frame. "You're safe now. I swear it."

Wolf thrashes and weakly swings punches like a cornered, injured animal. Monty doesn't waver, lifting him as I hold the towel in place, covering Wolf's nudity.

We shuffle out of the bathroom, and I wonder if we'll make it to the bed. Wolf is all muscle and mindless panic, bucking and snarling. But the shivering wrings him out fast, draining what little fight he has left.

His head lolls on Monty's shoulder, and he releases a terrible, breaking sound, choking on air, until his anguish tumbles into sobs. Crushing, soul-deep sobs.

A ball of fire swells in my throat, and guilt buckles my stomach. I want to puke. Jag did this. Or lit the match that set it off. And I'm the one who brought Jag into Wolf's life.

What did Jag do to trigger Wolf's breakdown?

You know, and you'll think about it tonight when you're alone.

I do know. And it makes me sick with self-loathing.

Monty carries Wolf into the bedroom and eases him onto the bed, layering blankets over him, his movements clinical but so heart-wrenchingly tender.

I want to be the one to care for Wolf like that. And isn't that a selfish thought? He deserves so much better than me.

"You're safe." Monty tucks the corners snug and sits on the

bed beside him. "Nothing can reach you."

Unresponsive, Wolf doesn't appear to hear him.

"Breathe with me, Son. In. Out. Slower. Slower. That's it." He rests a hand on the blanket where Wolf's chest rises and falls. "Rest now. I've got you."

I stand uselessly at the foot of the bed, arms crossed over my middle, my sinuses burning with barely contained tears.

Monty looks at me and gestures toward the empty spot on Wolf's other side.

"It's me." I clutch at my throat, wanting to help, knowing I'm part of the problem. "I brought this into his life. I'm hurting him."

I should go.

"I don't know what's going on between you and my son, but it isn't nothing." Steel edges his calm voice. "You feel something. He feels something. It's new and fragile, and if you leave him now..." His gaze drops to Wolf, cocooned in blankets, breath hitching shallow. "That will hurt him far worse."

"You don't understand." I remove my phone, open the browser, and angle it toward him.

Gavin's obituary glows on the screen.

"My ex-fiancé is dead." My chin trembles. "Wolf will be next."

Monty stares at the screen, and the air in the room shifts, chilling my skin. His blue eyes turn back to me, frosty cold but not surprised. He already knew about Gavin?

His expression goes stone-hard, calculating, like he's already assembling a plan in the back of his mind.

"Not while I'm breathing." His snarling tone triggers my fight-or-flight instinct, but beneath the growl lies a comforting protectiveness. "No one will take him. Not the ghosts in his past. Not the monsters in yours. Whatever is hunting you, hunting him, will go through me and his brothers first."

My mouth opens to respond, but nothing comes. Then, to my horror, a ragged sob breaks loose from my throat. My hand flies up to meet it, too late. Hot tears spill faster than I can wipe them away.

I choke, trying to breathe, but the air won't come. It gathers in my chest and collapses into more sobs. Holy fuck, I'm crying. Ugly, heaving tears I haven't let myself shed since I was a little girl.

Monty doesn't move to comfort me. He regards me without comment, one hand steady on Wolf's blanket, the other free as if he'd offer it if I dared to take it.

I desperately need the warmth of human contact, but Monty's hand isn't the one I want to hold.

Before I can doubt myself, before shame can bite my heels, I move. Clumsy, graceless, but unstoppable, I climb onto the bed, slip beneath the blankets, and curl my body beside Wolf's.

He's ice-cold, his skin clammy and too pale. His chest rises shallowly, each breath strained, the muscles in his face tense even in sleep.

My hand hovers an inch from his cheek, trembling with the need to touch. Instead, I settle against the curve of his shoulder, my forehead close to his. Not touching. Just there.

"Breathe, Wolf," I whisper. "You're not alone."

The sound of hurried footsteps cuts through the quiet, pounding downstairs, then up, closer, closer. The door bursts open.

Leo storms in, brash and golden, like a Norse sun god punching through frozen trees. Kody follows, cold and brooding, as if he were born in a blizzard and never thawed. And Frankie, still in her scrubs, hair pulled back, eyes wide with worry, trails close behind.

Monty greets them with his glacial stare and avalanche jawline vibrating with worry and relief.

They gather around Wolf, the dark heart of the north, taking in his pallid appearance. Taking up space. These people don't just enter a room. They swallow it whole and all the air in it.

"We came as soon as we could," Leo whispers, running a hand over Monty's shoulders, absently massaging the stiffness there.

Monty immediately relaxes beneath the touch. "He had another episode. Severe. I don't know what triggered it."

Another episode. How often does this happen?

"Is he responsive at all?" Frankie wriggles in around them, her medical training taking over. "Pulse steady? His breathing is too shallow and—"

"He's stable, darling." Monty catches her wrist, his thumb making slow circles against her pulse point.

Kody's gaze drags over me, then drops to Wolf's arm. His

worst scar. The chewed-up hole in his bicep looks like rot once lived there, eating him from the inside out. The skin is so mangled, puckered, and ruined, I wonder how close to death it brought him.

"I gave him that scar." Kody glares at it. Then his stark eyes lift to mine. "Shot him with my crossbow—"

"Kody. That's not..." Frankie shakes her head and looks at me. "Kody was protecting me."

"Protecting you from Wolf?"

"It was..." She rubs her brow, letting her exhaustion show in that subtle gesture. "A dark, complicated time. We were stranded and starving."

"And freezing to death." Leo brushes a lock of hair behind her ear.

"Yeah." She feathers her thumb over the arrow wound on Wolf's arm. "We all did impossible, terrible things to survive."

Kody flinches as if her words hit a nerve. His fingers flex at his side, drawing my attention to the stigmata-like scar on the back of his hand. It's perfectly centered, round, the skin shiny and tight. Healed, but not old. Maybe a year? The edges are still pink and tender-looking, like something sharp punched clean through his hand.

I wonder how it happened and if there's a matching hole on his palm.

"You were here, Dove? When Wolf had the panic attack?" Kody opens his palm, revealing a smooth exit wound, confirming my suspicion. "You were with him?"

"I—" My voice cracks. "I found him curled up in the shower."

"We left him alone with Jag this morning." Frankie angles her ear near Wolf's chest, listening to him breathe. Then her eyes shift to mine. "Your stepbrother had a high fever, could barely lift his head. But could he have done something—?"

"Of course, he did," I snap, harsher than I mean to. My throat burns as I push to a sitting position and lower my voice to a whisper. "Jag sent me a text. Said he didn't touch Wolf, but Wolf touched him. *Something* happened."

"Oh." Her features soften then dawn with realization. "*Ohhh.*" She lowers her gaze to Wolf. "He hasn't been out in the world long. He's still learning what he wants, what excites him..."

She looks at Kody and Leo. "And what triggers him."

I nod stiffly, but discomfort coils in my gut. This room feels too full, crowded with family, blood as thick as tar between them. I'm the outsider, sitting under Wolf's blankets like a fraud, an intruder.

"Dove was here for him," Monty says, shutting down whatever questions are brewing in their eyes.

Leo exhales slow, lips pressed thin. Kody scoops a saxophone off the floor and stows it in a case on the dresser.

I had no idea Wolf played an instrument. But why would I? I barely know Wolf at all.

One by one, Frankie carefully shimmies the stacked rings off his limp fingers. "We'll get him through this."

We.

I don't belong in this family circle, yet here I am, folded into their moment by accident, by necessity.

They aren't pushing me out, but I can't stay.

"I need to shower." I slide off the bed, stinking of cowardice, guilt, and motor oil.

No one stops me as I slip out the door. No one follows. The absence of footsteps is louder than a scream.

love

love
TWENTY-FOUR

The shower fills with steam, but I can't get warm. The water beats down, scalding, burning my skin red, but inside I'm frozen.

Palms flat on the tile, forehead pressed against the wall, I let the hiss of the shower drown everything else.

But it doesn't drown the image of Wolf on the floor, curled up, arms around his head, scars crisscrossing every inch of his torso.

I squeeze my eyes shut and still see his face, so pale and strained with fear. His body trembling under the spray. And his sobs. Christ, those sobs. They splintered me into so many pieces.

My chest cracks open, bleeding and bare.

The Strakhs didn't push me away. Without even meaning to, Monty claimed me in that room. Frankie included me in her *we*. Even Leo and Kody, suspicious as they are, let me stay.

Their kindness tips me over, and I cry harder. I'm not used to it. I don't know what to do with it.

I care about Wolf. More than I should. More than I can admit. And I know what I need to do.

If I leave town, Jag will follow me. That's what he does. He'll keep his cameras on me and forget all about Wolf. He won't hurt Wolf if I'm gone. He only kills men who stand between us.

love

The thought feels noble for half a second. Then it splits me down the middle.

Leaving Wolf... It'll ruin me beyond repair.

I choke on a breath, but it caves into a sob. Then another. Soon I'm bent in half, fists pressed against the tile, water mingling with hot tears. Crying in a way that hollows out my insides. Ugly, violent, body-wracking sobs.

The water pours over me, steam swarming down my throat, and I'm hit with *déjà vu*. I'm shaking like him, like Wolf, fighting shadows I can't escape.

I slide down the wall to the wet floor, knees to my chest, forehead to my arms, the roar of the shower covering the sound of me falling apart.

If I leave, I'll save him.

If I leave, I'll never encounter another soul like Wolfson Strakh.

The water finally runs lukewarm, then cold, but I don't move. I sit there until my skin wrinkles, until my sobs run dry, until all that's left is an empty throb behind my eyes.

Then I drag myself up.

I scrub at my face and scour my body, trying to wash off the shame, the grease, and the grief.

When I step out, I towel myself down hard, punishing. I yank on a shirt and sleep shorts and twist my drippy blue hair into a tight braid over my shoulder.

In the mirror, my eyes are red, my cheeks blotched. I don't look like someone who belongs in this house, in their circle. I look like someone who stumbled into a family she has no right to know.

But I'll face them anyway.

I'll stay until Wolf is well enough, steady enough, to have a conversation about this. About me leaving. About why I have to go.

I won't disappear on him. I couldn't do that. Not after today.

Smoothing my face with the heels of my palms, I square my shoulders and bite down the leftover tears until all that remains is a dull ache.

Steam swirls around me as I emerge from the bathroom. And I stop cold in the doorway.

"Wolf?"

He perches on the edge of my bed, wearing a purple housecoat that hides every scar. But nothing covers the damage on his face.

He looks haggard, ashen, lips drained of color, and shadows dug deep under his eyes. His hair hangs in damp, messy ropes. He's been wrung out for hours, every drop of fight and fury squeezed from him.

His eyes lift to mine, all those vivid shades of blue reflecting in the light.

"You're spooked." A frown ghosts across his mouth. "Monty told me about the man on the pier. Your security team saw Jag there, too."

"You have more important things—"

"Nothing's more important than *you*." He pauses, staring at his hands, anxiously twiddling his thumbs. "But Jag and the stalker on the pier didn't spook you. *I* did. My breakdown. I owe you an explanation."

"You don't owe me anything."

"You deserve a conversation, and I'll give that to you. I'll tell you what happened today. And what happened last year. And the twenty-three years before that." His thumbs stop moving, and he slowly drags his eyes to mine. "But not tonight."

My throat tightens.

"Tonight...." He swallows, and his voice dips with vulnerability. "I just want to sleep beside you if you'll allow that."

How could I ever refuse him? I nod rapidly, rushing forward until my feet land between his. "Can I hug you?"

For a second, he regards me, a twitch feathering at the corner of his eye. Then he rises from the bed, the movement forcing me to shuffle back. He opens his arms. Not wide or theatrical. Just enough. Just for me.

I go to him, falling into him, my cheek smashing against his chest, and my arms forming a vise around his broad frame. The scents of soap, rain, and his signature, feral notes of the wild flood me with relief.

The physical contact does swirly, glowy things to my heart. He's solid. So damn strong and solid. Heat radiates through the thin layers of fabric between us, and I want to sink into it, lose myself there.

His arms cinch around me, rock-hard but trembling, like he's terrified I'll vanish if he loosens his grip.

love

We both need this. Affection, anchoring, and proof of life.

But there's something else. Something hard and urgent, jabbing between us.

I flinch, not away, but in shock. The timing isn't great after his catatonic breakdown on the shower floor. I didn't expect him to be thinking about sex. But if he wants to take me right here, right now, I'll give myself to him without hesitation. Happily. Willingly. Desperately.

I move my hand lower, tracing the rigid shape of him.

"Dove." He groans darkly and seizes my wrist, shaking his head. "No."

"I'm so sorry." I jerk my hand away.

"Trust me. I'm the one who's sorry. My head's in a fucked-up place." He rests his forehead against mine and recaptures my wrist. "My body doesn't care. It'll always react when you touch me. But tonight..." His grip softens, thumb brushing my skin. "I can't. Not until we talk, okay? Tonight, I just want to be near you. With you. Just us in the present moment."

What he wants, it's more intimate than anything physical he could've asked of me. It's... Gentle. Strange, but gentle. No weight of expectation pressing down. No hands reaching for more. Just him, here, choosing me without an angle.

He came to my room to be with me, not to take from me. That's new. That's different. With men, I've never had *this*.

So I nod, letting my shoulders relax, and wait for his lead.

He slides back onto the bed, watching me intensely as he lowers himself onto his side. I follow, curling onto mine, facing him.

Our hands find each other in the middle, fingers tangling, palms hot with shared pulse.

We don't speak. His eyes stay on me, hooded but soft, carrying too many memories, too much pain. I hold his gaze, searching the flickers there, mesmerized by how exhaustion stripped away the years, exposing so much of his innocence.

The silence grows heavy, but not oppressive. It's comfortable, despite all the things neither of us can say.

Are you okay? He's not okay.

Do you want to talk? He doesn't want to talk about it.

Did you have sex with Jag? I don't want to think about it.

I squeeze his hand, and he squeezes back.

This intimacy... I've never experienced anything like it with anyone else. Intimacy without sex. Without chatter. Just a deep, cozy closeness between two people content to watch each other, breath syncing in the quiet.

His eyes drift over my face, mine over his, both of us caught in some wordless spell. The world falls away, leaving only the rhythm of our lungs, the warmth of our hands, and the quiet hum of noisy thoughts.

Then, after a long beat, his mouth bounces at the corner. "Have you heard the fairy tale about the drag queen, the heart doctor, and the princess bride?"

"No, but I'd love to hear it."

"It's dark."

"Have you met me?"

"Fair enough. I'll skip the buildup and start at the good part." He stretches out his legs, linking them around mine. "The drag queen jumps. Right off the cliff. Sequins, eyeliner, fuck-me boots, the whole shebang. Splat. Right into the icy river, she goes. Drowns, dies, done. Curtain closed."

"But she didn't die."

"Lord knows she almost met him." He hauls in a long, shaky breath. "But as usual, the Mighty God is a no-show. Instead, she meets the doctor. The white-coat kind that hands out medicine and miracles. He drags the queen out of the water, sews her back together, and saves her life. Sounds like a stand-up guy, right?"

"I feel a twist coming."

"All the best fairy tales have one. But this one comes with trigger warnings. Can you handle that?"

"I don't have triggers."

"We'll see. As it turns out, the fancy little heart doctor has a few screws loose. But screwdrivers aren't his specialty. Scalpels are. He loves the way they shine under the fluorescent lights, and for the next ten months, he demonstrates his mad skills. Slice, hack, cut, stab. Anatomy turned into art."

My hands twitch in the warm clutch of his. He's telling me how he got the scars, and it wasn't by the psychopath who raised him. Who the fuck is this doctor?

"The queen learns fast. Learns too much." He shifts, his eyes losing focus. "One night, the doctor hosts a dinner party and invites all the people he killed and all the people he wants to kill. The lion, the bear, Dorothy, and Rich Daddy... All the queen's friends are there."

Wolf's family. I can gather that much. But the rest? I don't know. He's using cryptic symbolism to express his trauma. Maybe it's the only way he can talk about it.

I won't question him. I'm just glad he's talking.

"The doctor raped Dorothy right there on the table." His voice darkens, making my blood run cold.

Frankie. That kind, gentle woman. The unspeakable hell this family has endured. They've suffered too much.

"Too dark?" Wolf searches my eyes.

"Keep going."

"While the doctor's busy admiring his reflection in the blade, the queen steals the scalpel. Plucks it right out of the ruby slippers. The doctor laughs, saying, 'You wouldn't dare.' Oh, she dares. She chops him into kibble-sized bits and feeds them to the wolves waiting in the dark."

"He's dead." I release a shuddering breath.

"Deader than dead. And now the queen is free. She goes out into the world, looking for her Magic Kingdom, wandering, wandering, sequins dulled, eyeliner running. And she's..." His voice goes achingly soft. "She's lost. Because what's a kingdom without a princess? Who wants a throne when there's no one to share it with?"

Oh, Wolf.

A kingdom, a worthy princess, and a happily ever after. He deserves nothing less. Goddammit, I want to be the one beside him, holding his hand as he climbs his throne.

But I'm no princess. I'm an orphan mechanic with grease under my fingernails and too many facial piercings. Jag and I are a curse. Whoever we touch, ruin follows.

"I'll tell you the next part, but you already know it." He hooks an arm around my waist and tugs my body flush against his. "A princess bride materializes out of the fog. She isn't in a tower. She isn't locked in chains. She's running down the street, running from something, always running. She doesn't know that she doesn't need to run anymore. The queen will save her, and she'll save the queen right back." He narrows his eyes. "To be continued..."

He waits for me to say something, but I can only lie there and chew on the words.

That queen is him. Sequins, eyeliner, fuck-me boots, he dresses in pieces of feminine flair, like camouflage, like maybe he's trying to outrun himself. Like if he layers enough glitter and lace over the scars, no one will see the boy still bleeding underneath.

"Aren't you going to ask me the point of the story?" He gives me a crooked grin, the one that dares me to misunderstand him.

"Nope. I get it."

The point of the story is *him*. I think about the eyeliner, rain boots, and feather boas. He isn't mocking women. He isn't mocking himself. He's testing something. Or maybe confessing something without using plain words.

Does he want to be a drag queen in real life? Is his identity unraveling and rethreading? Or is it just Wolf being Wolf, eccentric, theatrical, and hiding the crisis in his chest behind eyeliner and satire?

I don't know.

But I know this. The way he told that story, he wasn't laughing at the drag queen. He was mourning her. My chest aches with the weight of it, because maybe Wolf doesn't know who the hell he is, but for tonight, in his fairy tale, he wants to be the one worth saving.

"You would make a beautiful drag queen, Wolf."

"That's not the point."

"You'll build your own magic kingdom, and princesses will line up to share it with you."

"Also, not the point, Buttercup. Were you even listening?"

"I heard every word."

"Then you know there's only one princess bride. *The one.* And I already found her."

"What if she hurts you?"

"What if she doesn't?"

I'm no princess, and if I stay, there will be only tragedy and death in his ever after.

"Thank you for sharing your story with me." I tentatively trace a finger along the sculpted line of his jaw. "You didn't have to, and I promise to keep it safe."

"It's just a story."

I wish that were true. But I don't say that. "Will you tell me more fairy tales about the drag queen?"

"I'll tell you my favorite." He burrows in closer, the

love

effervescent wildness returning to his eyes. "The drag queen wants to go to Disney World, but she can't travel to the Magic Kingdom without her pets—the lion and the bear. When she tells them to take her, the lion is all doom and gloom, crying, 'We're going to die.' And the bear's like, 'Is there vodka? I love vodka. Grunt. Grunt.' To which the queen says, 'Yes, you small-minded beast. Of course, there's vodka...'"

I listen, breathless, captivated, and devastated as he shares glimpses into his imprisoned childhood with Leo and Kody. The harrowing helplessness they must have felt, trapped and motherless, with only their captor to raise them.

But they escaped. They learned how to fly, left the horrors behind, and built a happy life on this paradise island.

They're finally safe, and they need to stay that way.

jag
TWENTY-FIVE

Four walls, no windows, and a single door bolted from the inside. This is my confession booth. A concrete tool shed behind an abandoned house on a dead-end road that no one visits.

Just a couple of blocks from the tattoo shop, dead freight piles up outside. Busted pallets lean against the weathered blue exterior.

Blue princess.

Nobody looks twice.

Inside, though? Inside is mine. Stacks of towers. Rows of monitors. Thirty eyes, all open and unblinking.

Here lies the equipment Wolf asked to see.

My hunting ground.

I lean back in the chair, fingers spidering over the keyboard, pulling up feeds.

Thanks to Frankie Strakh, I can type with both hands again, only slightly limited by the splint on my wrist.

The screen on my left streams in real time, showing footage from the street outside this room. The one above it loops through the morning hours, time stamp after time stamp.

All the rest, dozens of displays, monitor Dove's walking paths to the mechanic shop, inside the garage bays, the deli

jag

where she grabs lunch, the private slips where she comes and goes by yacht. Every angle of her little Alaskan life recorded in grainy black-and-white.

Except the island. The Strakh fortress is impenetrable.

For everyone but me.

I take grim satisfaction in knowing which island is theirs and how to breach the security.

But I'm backed into a corner. If I drag her out now, I'll lose the bodyguards who are protecting her. If I leave her there, I'll lose her to Wolf.

Either way, one of us gets hurt.

Better me than her.

She's safe with the Strakhs. Safer than she ever was with Gavin.

Safer than she is with me.

I hate that.

Since the night I butchered our parents' murderer, I've been on the run, using fake names everywhere, from Colombia to Bangkok, across borders and burner phones. But Sitka Tattoo carries my real name. A signal flare in the night. Not because I want to be found, but because I want to see who's brave enough to come looking.

Last year, the feds found me in California. But the tail on Dove yesterday and today? That wasn't government-issued.

A far deadlier threat has arrived in Sitka, and I'm not ready. I don't have the money or manpower to win this war.

It's time to call in a favor.

I reach for a burner phone and hesitate, the splint on my wrist transporting me back to this morning.

The shape of Wolf's mouth against mine, the taste of his defiance, the punishing hand job, the way he didn't pull away, and the moment I realized he isn't just another mark.

There's no denying it. He was into it, into me, and goddammit, I didn't want him to leave.

My fever took hours to break, but I wanted another round with that complicated dark angel and his vicious hands. More conversation, more heat, more of that razor-wire tension that makes me feel alive. But he bolted. Like I knew he would.

Did he run straight to Dove? Put his cruel mouth all over her? Shove his virgin cock up between her legs? Slack all that wild hunger I stirred in him?

Grinding my teeth hard enough to crack enamel, I shove closer to the keyboard and click back to earlier footage, the minutes after he fled the shop.

Where are you, Wolf? Where did you go?

There.

I scrub forward, camera by camera, and watch him stagger down the street. Shoulders tight, gait unsteady, he walks like his legs don't trust him, like he's drowning in air.

What the hell is wrong with him?

When he heads to the harbor, I split the feed between two angles. At the entrance, he stumbles, falling down the embankment and tucking under the pier, knees pulled to his chest, and arms wrapped around his skull.

Small as I've ever seen him. Like a child hiding from the belt. Shaking, clutching his hair, mouth open on a sound the recording doesn't capture.

But I feel it. Real, unguarded, paralyzing panic. He's having a full-blown attack.

A vein throbs in my temple.

I should enjoy this. I should take notes and catalog the weakness. Watch, record, exploit. Every tic, every flinch, every strangled gasp is ammunition. That's what I do, what I've always done to protect my little bird.

But I'm not cataloging. I'm staring with a hundred-pound lump in my throat.

He tries to get up. Tries to board the yacht. The crowd presses too close. Someone bumps into him, and he snaps like a wild dog, snarling and baring his teeth.

People scatter. He bites at the air, chest heaving, face half-mad.

It's brutal. But it's not weakness. It's a wound that never closed.

I drag my hand down my mouth, my stomach swarming with bile. I did this. I triggered something terrible and ripped open that wound.

The violent churn in my chest shouldn't be there.

He's not my problem. Not my problem.

I slam the keyboard and switch screens. Recordings flicker and bruise the dark as Wolf's image peels away, replaced by this morning's footage of Dove's small, stubborn frame on another

jag

feed.

She's the priority.

Whatever this is with Wolf—primal hunger, animal attraction, ferocious domination, whatever I call it to keep from sounding soft—it changes nothing.

I reach for the burner and set the hardware token into the cradle. When it chirps, the LED turns green, then amber. The VPN light on the chassis breathes a single blue pulse, and I breathe with it, tapping the sequence until the token spits a new code.

The line will hop through a dozen melt-points, a sat relay in the Aleutians, an encrypted node in Cartagena, a tunnel of offshore uplinks, and eventually, into the private mesh of The Shadow Collection.

It's messy and dirty and will leave footprints for anyone with a microscope. But it will look like nothing if the right hands take it on the other end.

My fingers tremble. Stupid things. A whisper of sweat at the wrist. A tiny hitch in my thumb when I press.

I'm a careful man. Careful hands don't shake. But this is different.

If I breathe wrong, these people will cleave my head from my body and mount it on a stake in the Bolívar Square. The scariest part? I won't see them coming.

That's why I've never dialed this number. Never been desperate enough to reach for this favor.

The burner coughs, negotiates, and settles into a slow, hungry ring. The light on the cradle beats as fast as my pulse.

I taste bile.

Servers hum. Cooling fans spin harder. I rub the hell out of my nape, bleeding tension from every joint. Until I hear it.

A click.

Then a voice, thick with accent and smoke. "*¿Quién habla?*"

I let the silence lean for a heartbeat, a practiced pause to disguise my nerves. Then I supply the name they know me by.

"*El Vigilante.*"

"Ah. *Sí, por supuesto. Hace rato te tengo en la mira, Vigilante.*"

My Spanish is shit, but I don't need it. I have a program at my fingertips, translating his words into English.

The voice belongs to a top dog in the Colombian cartel. I don't know which dog, but he knows who I am. The cartel gave me this number after all.

"What do I call you?" I ask.

"*Jefe.*" Two purring syllables meant to disarm.

It's rumored the cartel uses a decoy in every meeting and phone conversation. If the voice on the line claims to be the boss, there's a good chance it's not.

Matias Restrepo, the real *jefe*, remains elusive to anyone not paying attention.

But I've always paid attention.

I was eighteen when I started selling pieces of myself to criminal organizations. Too young to be sentimental, too desperate to care, and too clever to be honest about it.

I didn't stumble into human sex trafficking so much as trade my hacker skills in small, soulless auctions.

Who would've thought the hours I wasted as a skinny gamer kid, balls-deep in code and cheat mods, would turn out to be such valuable currency in the dark net?

"*Habla,*" he purrs, seductive and threatening all at once. "*¿Qué quieres?*"

I hear the danger behind the syllables, years of other men's terror soaked into the simple question.

What do you want?

"I'm calling in that favor." My mouth goes dry, but I keep my voice even.

The pause lasts long enough to count teeth. Then the man laughs, deep as a dug well, velveted with smoke, the edges worn by time and appetite.

"This favor is not a small thing," he says in accented English. "You want to waste it on your pretty bird and her wolf?"

There it is. He knows as much about me as I know about them.

The Restrepo cartel and The Shadow Collection are the same machine. Most people don't know it, but the *jefe* runs both.

Cocaine keeps the books fat, but flesh is easier to move across borders, harder to trace. Nobody reports a missing girl from a nowhere village. The cartel moves the product. The collection launders the bodies through ports and pipelines, and it all circles back to the same table where one man counts the profit.

jag

At least, that's the story they're selling.

It goes so much deeper. But I don't care about their ethics. I'm only interested in strengthening our partnership and using it to my advantage.

They control the global slave trade, and I sell them dirt and doors. They infiltrate enemy territories, and I give their runners access to move quietly. When a job goes south, I open holes to slip through, patching nodes, scrubbing traces, and tidying feeds.

I've met three names in person. The rest are voices, packets, and time stamps.

Twenty-two years of dirty work bought me more than a feared name in the black market. It bought a favor from one of the deadliest criminal groups in the world.

I attach myself to them because they're the enemy of my enemy. I've always known that one day, I would need their reign of terror on my side.

That day is today.

"Yes." My stomach hardens. "I need your help."

"*Sí, lo necesitas. Reconozco que te lo has ganado, Vigilante. ¿Qué tanto te quemó para venir a mí?*"

My fingers freeze, missing the translation. I'm too focused on that cadence, the tiny swallowed consonants, and the way his vowels curl at the end.

Oh, fuck.

There's a distinct shape to the sound of that rumbling voice, not just a timbre but a posture.

I blink. The room tilts, and the air leaves me like a fist.

Fuck, fuck, fuck.

I've watched the cartel for years and listened to hours upon hours of surveillance. I memorized the smoky laugh threaded through static in Buenos Aires, the clipped consonants in the Austin recordings, and the deep intake before each execution is ordered.

It's not data in a file for me. It's an obsession with details. That's what terrifies me now. Hearing the cadence, the unmistakable pattern, the pronounced pauses... I'm not speaking with a decoy.

Matias Restrepo, the most feared cartel *capo* in Colombia, is the voice on the other end of the line.

Every bargain I made with blood and code folds like a

trapdoor. Every drop of humanity I've traded away has come due.

My throat chews. My pulse drums in my teeth.

"Respirá, Vigilante. Que los nervios no te delaten." The mob boss exhales. "You saved *mi vida*. A debt is owed, and I deliver."

Mi vida. The endearment he uses for his wife, Camila Dias.

Years ago, I pulled Camila out of a job gone sideways. With some spoofed IDs, forged metadata, and fake time stamps, I made her vanish from all surveillance cameras until she escaped the assassin on her tail.

Camila is no damsel in distress. She runs The Shadow Collection alongside her husband. But I saved her life that night, and the *jefe* hasn't forgotten.

"We will talk terms," he says, his accent silky dark and twice as lethal. "But not on the phone. You come to me."

"That's not... I'm..."

"Broke? Homeless? No plane? Out of time? Completely fucked?"

Yeah. All of those. Colombia is a long goddamn way from Alaska. How the hell does he expect me to come to him?

I grit my teeth, sort my voice out of a cluster of wrong ones, and keep it respectful. "Yes."

"I'll send for you." He hangs up before I can reply.

Fuck me.

The cradle clicks down like a cocked gun, and my hands stop being hands. Frozen and shaking, I feel the splint against my wrist, the sweat beneath my forearm, and the struggle for breath that doesn't come.

Dove's footage loops before me, replaying her morning walk to work. I watch her breathe on the screen, and the cold, gnawing thing that is fear hardens into something useful.

Purpose.

wolfson
TWENTY-SIX

I wake to the sound of Dove breathing.

Not snoring. Not the labored chuffing of bad dreams. I'm greeted with the delicate, steady tide of air filling her pretty chest and emptying again.

And I'm hard. Harder than any morning wood has the right to be.

For the love of poor decisions, I hope my dream self didn't grope her through the night. My awake self is hanging by a thread, and the last thing she needs is me crossing another line.

After we passed out, I don't remember anything. None of my usual restless, twitchy half-sleep. That can only mean one thing. I just had the deepest, heaviest, best-ever sleep of my life.

We both did, judging by the positions of our bodies. Neither of us moved.

Through the blinds, the blue-gray light of early morning filters in stripes across her pillow and cheek, catching on the silver glint of her septum ring, the metal stud above her lip, and the tiny rod threaded through her eyebrow.

I lie on my side and stare like she's the first real girlfriend I've shared a bed with in twenty-four years.

Because she is.

Nothing in my wreck of a life prepared me for how good this feels.

A clean, mineral scent lives in her hair. Skin, salt, rain, and underneath it all, my favorite fragrance. Sun-warm, feather-soft Dove.

I've never wanted anything as badly as I want to roll forward, drape an arm over her waist, tuck myself into the curve of her, press my nose to her neck, and pretend I'm a normal man sleeping beside a woman who wants to stay. Pretend I didn't have a mental breakdown after giving her stepbrother a handy. Pretend I'm not a living nightmare with more scars than a used mattress.

Her lashes twitch. She murmurs something that might be a word and burrows deeper into the pillow. The blanket slips down her shoulder, exposing a pale slope of skin.

The urge to kiss that spot is a bright, roaring pain. My mouth waters, and I taste the metal of it. The *want.*

But I can't. Not until I tell her what happened with Jag. And after that, she'll no longer have a reason to stay.

Carefully, I slide out of bed. The room tilts, then steadies. I'm lightheaded, and my stomach cramps like I didn't eat yesterday.

Oh, right. I didn't.

I wrap the edges of the housecoat around me, covering my boxers and scars and tying the sash. The sleeves fall too short on my arms, and the purple fabric is worn to a thin nap. After all these years, I don't know why I still wear it. Dr. Freud would analyze the shit out of that.

Dove sighs, and I go still, but she doesn't wake. A shiny curl of blue hair hangs across her face. I don't touch it. I memorize it.

Then I leave without looking back because if I do, I'll climb into bed and make the wrong kind of promises to myself.

The walk to the main house is too warm for my Arctic-bred bones, the daylight too honest, and when I reach the back door, my reflection in the glass looks like a trespasser in a dead woman's robe.

In the kitchen, I find Frankie at the island, barefoot, red hair twisted up in a knot, and shoulders slumped in a way that says she didn't sleep as well as I did.

She glances over at me, and her eyebrows rise a millimeter. I know the robe caught her eye. It always does. But she doesn't comment. One of the thousand gifts she gives me.

"I was just going to make eggs." Her voice sands down to a gentle roughness that loosens tight places inside me. "You want—"

"Yes. Feed me before I start gnawing on the furniture." I cross to the back counter and pour a mug of coffee. I'd offer her a cup, but caffeine isn't good for the baby. "Where are your daddies?"

"Still asleep."

"Let me guess. They stayed up all night braiding each other's pubes."

She smiles without showing teeth, and the softness of it makes my throat ache. She doesn't need to correct me. I know they were up all night discussing my mental health.

I don't have to pretend with her. We've seen each other at our worst. She held my eyes when Denver raped me. I held her hand when the doctor raped her. She has PTSD like me, though her panic attacks are growing fewer and farther between.

She moves around the kitchen. Pan on the burner. Flame. Butter hissing. The sound is indecent. My stomach groans and folds into cramps.

I sit at the island, slurping coffee and slicing bread to make toast.

"Did you sleep?" She approaches my stool, careful not to spook me, but close enough that her warmth presses into my space.

"Yes times a thousand. I slept beside Dove for the first time."

"And?"

"It was... *Clean.*"

Anyone else would assume that meant no sex and move on. But not Frankie.

"Emotionally clean." Her gaze pries me open. "I'm glad Dove could give you that."

She hovers so close I feel her need to touch me like a hand held near a fire. I look down. She looks up. There's a question in her eyes and a hundred unsaid words circling like wolves.

I give her a tight nod.

With a relieved breath, she throws herself against me. Not in front like a hug would be, but onto my back. She hangs there, arms looped around my collarbones, cheek at the hinge of my jaw, her weight comforting, familiar, her warmth sinking into my spine, into places where last night hollowed me out.

When she exhales, the sound comes out of me, too. I let my head tip back until it hits her shoulder and rests there, waiting for her questions.

"How much did you tell her?" She nuzzles my hair.

"Bits."

"Graphic bits?"

"More like big-picture bits. In fairy-tale format."

"Did these fairy tales feature a drag queen?"

I nod.

She pulls a heavy breath through her nose, doing her best to remain neutral.

The silence that follows is a barbed wire fence. I could grab it and bleed. Or I could sit here with her arms around me until I say something offensive that sends her running away.

Except Frankie doesn't run from a challenge. She faces it head-on.

"We knew, Wolf." She kisses my temple and shifts around to face me. "We all knew about your scars."

"Leo told you."

"He loves you. We all do, and we're trying to give you space, knowing you're talking to Dr. Thurber—"

"Dr. Freud."

"Right." A smile moves through her voice, a tremor rather than a sound. "I know it's hard."

Hard implies there's a correct angle of attack, and if I apply enough force, it yields. This isn't that kind of hard. This is a cliff in the way of a river, and the river in the way of a cliff.

I'm stuck between two unmovable realities. Captivity and survival. One blocks. The other erodes. Both are in the way. Both require a lot of work.

The butter in the pan goes from a hiss to a sizzle. Frankie peels away, grabs a spatula, and starts cracking eggs.

Saliva floods my mouth as the smell hits. Fat, pepper, a hint of singe. It grabs my spine and shakes.

I start the toast and stare off into space. When the toaster pops, I flinch.

Frankie pretends not to notice.

After she plates the food, we sit side by side and dig in.

The first bite is ridiculous, the crisp edges of fried egg giving under my teeth. My jaw works, chewing too loud and fast. I eat like I'm on the clock.

My body doesn't trust abundance, so when it's placed in front of me, the old instinct flicks on.

Eat it before the hills eat you.

When I come up for air, Frankie's watching as if she knew I would inhale every bite and made peace with that outcome before she cracked the first egg.

"You want more?" she asks.

I nod, starting to stand. But she's already up and plopping more eggs into the pan.

When she brings the plate back, I force myself to go slower, trying to taste things individually. The black pepper, the toast's char, and the butter's sweetness.

As I finish, heat pools behind my sternum. Not panic heat. Coal fire. Steady. I lick my thumb where yolk slicks it.

Frankie clears her throat. "How's it going with Dove?"

I set down the fork and choose the smallest word, the safest one. "Fine."

"Wolf." She leans her elbows on the table, eyes gentle but not easily fooled. "You don't have to be alone in your head about it."

"I'm not."

"You are." It's not a scold. It's an acknowledgment, like pointing to a scar and naming it *Scar*. She sits back. "Do you trust her?"

"More than I trust myself, which is fucked up, but there it is."

"Will you tell her your story?"

"She already got the full experience with my scars, my breakdown, and my fairy tales. That's more than I've shared with anyone else."

"That's not the same as talking about it."

"Words don't fit this. They slide off the bone and make an ungodly mess."

"You talk to Dr. Thurber."

"I toss him juicy bits here and there. You know what they say. Vague book—"

"Isn't the best book." Her mouth turns down. "Will you wait a second?"

At my nod, she pads down the hall. I hear the soft thud of a closet door, the sigh of a drawer. My pulse climbs, and I occupy myself by stacking plates and aligning the butter knife with the bread crumbs.

Footsteps return. When I look up, she's holding two books.

I recognize the one on top. The cracked spine. The stains on the cover. The dents and scratches from outlasting arctic blizzards, famine, and a plane crash.

Survivor's marks.

My stomach drops hard, and the room blurs.

If I open that book, it will open a past I'm not ready to face.

wolfson
TWENTY-SEVEN

I've never read Frankie's journal, but I know it was written with my sharpies, the ink pressed too hard in some places, bleeding in others.

It started in the hills as one of my scrapbooks and mutated into a forensic case file. She even added hair samples from all the Strakh men. Short and curlies from me, thank you very much.

She wanted everything documented like a true crime investigation. Details about our gruesome childhood. Notes about the women Denver abducted and killed.

Her own kidnapping and torment was part of the unsolved mystery. Each day tallied like a prison sentence. Some entries precise. Others scrawled like she didn't know if she'd have another chance to finish them.

But she did. She finished it before she escaped.

She sits beside me, cautious and patient. "Do you know what triggered you yesterday?"

A shiver skids through me as my mind tumbles back to Jag's mouth against mine and his dick pulsing in my fist. The heat of him. The hardness of him. And worse... Wanting him.

I can still taste his come. The wrongness of it. The craving for more.

Desiring a man isn't conceivable. Not with the memory of Denver's depraved *love*, the stink of sweat and cruelty, and the pain... Christ, I'll never forget that sickening, unbearable pain.

I don't know where the line is between what I want and what was done to me. Every time I think about Jag, I relive Denver's abuse.

So yeah. Kissing Jag, touching him, longing for him... All triggers.

Frankie isn't asking for the gory details. Just an acknowledgment. So I give her a nod.

She nods back and sets the journal between us.

I don't touch it.

"I wrote this to remember." She strokes the cover. "And to forget. I wrote it because there were days when I needed to prove to myself that I existed in sequence. This happened, then this, then this. I wrote it because there were things I couldn't say to anyone, but they needed to be said." She swallows. "I wrote it because I was afraid if I didn't, he'd win."

The *he* in our life doesn't require a name. Even dead, he has one foot in the room.

I suppress a shiver. "Did you write about that day?"

There are so many I could be referencing but none more pivotal, haunting, or fatal than the day she killed Denver and I jumped off the cliff.

"Yeah, Wolf. I did."

"You confessed to murder?" I whisper, horrified. "In writing?"

She gives a single nod.

"Bad idea, Frankieberry. If this fell in the wrong hands..."

She pushes it toward me, her eyes shimmering with trust.

Dammit.

I stare at the faded cover until it blurs, and I'm suddenly on the shower floor, the tile dark with icy water, my heart punching, punching, punching, trying to jailbreak my ribs. Then I see Dove's silhouette crouched beside me, and I hear her whispered words.

You're okay. I'm here. Breathing with you. Just breathing.

I feel the cancerous, unwieldy parts of me I need to amputate. Fear, rage, shame, and the one that's growing harder to carry. My virginity.

That one belongs to Dove. But she deserves the whole story,

not just the bits I'm willing to part with.

I return my attention to the book. The autobiography of a woman who murdered her captor and lived to write the ending.

Pinching the edge of the cover, I open it an inch, then another, and another, until the past rises out of the paper like breath on a cold day.

The first sentence I half-read speeds up my pulse. I close the book because if I don't, I'll fall into it and not sleep for a week.

"You don't have to read it." She touches my hand. "It's *my* story. The stupid brave parts and the brutal parts. There are pages where I'm proud, when I was strong and fought hard and loved harder. There are pages where I'm rotten, when I was mean and reckless and made bargains with the devil. There's grief, too. Constant, fathomless grief after we lost you on that cliff."

My face numbs, and my fingers go cold. I want to apologize, but it's far too late for that.

Maybe reading about the pain I caused them is a start. Perhaps experiencing my suicide through her eyes is the only mercy I can offer.

I press my thumb to the cover until it hurts. "I'll read it."

I'll read every page like penance. Not to pull pity from my death, but to stop acting like the worst thing I did was survive.

"There are parts you shouldn't read." She places her hand over mine on the book. "The messy, sexually graphic parts."

"No shit?" I slide the book out of her reach because now, of course, I have to read it.

"I'm serious." She tries to grab it back. "I describe your brothers' anatomy in shameless, vivid detail."

"Did you exaggerate size and stamina? Or did you keep it realistic?"

She groans. "Please, don't read those parts."

"Do you even know me?"

"Why did I say anything?" She drops her face in her hands.

"Hey." I duck my head, trying to meet her eyes. "What's a little brotherly porn shared between friends?"

Her face is still in her palms, but when I pry her chin up and angle it toward me, we're locked, her eyes on mine, mine on hers.

We try. Frozen bones and fuckberries, we try to remain serious for the sake of this conversation. Her mouth tightens. My molars clamp together, but the longer we stare, the faster we crumble.

Her expression cracks first. A flutter at the corner of her lips. That's all it takes to wrest a grin out of me. It splits across my face, lopsided and unguarded. Then we're both grinning like assholes, shaking our heads, laughing without sound, and just being... Us.

"Wolf." She says my name like a thought she's been holding in her mouth to keep it warm.

"Hm?"

"I'm giving you my story because maybe it will help you tell yours." She grabs the second book and stacks it on her journal. "This one is yours."

I thumb it open and flip through the pages. They're blank. Every damn one.

"Write your story."

I bark a laugh and hate how it sounds. "I did, remember? It's a dark comedy titled *Already Dead*."

"And I said to rewrite it. Change the narrative. Remember?"

Yeah. That night, I told her I would live, that I would survive for her. I said it, knowing it was a lie. I'd already planned my dramatic exit.

But fate had other plans, and here we are.

I stare at her, processing her advice with better clarity than I had that night. Maybe I've matured, learned a thing or two since that jump off the cliff.

She wants me to write my story, put the past on paper. Words on a page won't stare back at me with judgment. I can shape them, scrub them, cut the parts that don't fit. Easier than saying it out loud and watching Dove's face rearrange into pity or disgust in real time.

"Let's say I follow your advice and let Dove read it. Then what?"

"Then you write the next chapter. In your head. Or on the page. Write the best damn story you can imagine for yourself. Then go out and live it."

"What if my brain is an unreliable narrator? What if it edits out the parts where I deserve good things?"

"Then you remind it. Every day. With little stuff. Food. Warm showers. Letting people hug you. Reading a page. Writing a sentence. Making love to a pretty mechanic. Remind it that you aren't where you were anymore."

My mouth tastes like pepper and coffee and something like grief. I look down at the book, the cover darkening where my fingers sit, sweat seeping into the fabric.

The robe's cuff brushes the edge of the cover, and for a second, I see my mother's hand where mine is, the way she used to press herbs with her palm and tuck them into a tin.

I swallow hard enough it hurts. "I'm going to mess it up."

"Probably." She smiles. "But you'll mess it up honestly. That's a better story already."

"Dove's going to ask me things."

"She might. Or she might not. She might just be there and hand you a wrench when you choke like an engine."

"She won't hand me the wrench. She'll throw it at my head."

"Sounds like a woman who belongs in our home."

Our home.

The thought sends an avalanche down the inside of my ribs, and I breathe easier under it.

We sit with that a minute, the books between us.

Then I stand and pour more coffee, black and mean. The first sip is bitter enough to strip paint, fizzing on my tongue. I swallow and feel it hit my stomach like a small grenade, the good kind, the one that clears fog.

"What will you do now?" she asks, not as a command or a test. She trusts I have an answer.

Tattooing is a no-go today. I don't want to see Jag until I come clean with his sister.

"I'll bring food to Dove." I shrug. "And take a shower."

"And after?"

"I'll... Read a page." I glance at her journal. "Maybe two if the first one doesn't eat my lungs."

"Perfect." She releases a slow breath as if I just saved a life. "And later, if you want, we can talk to Dr. Thurber about grounding exercises that don't end with you emptying the hot water tank."

"You mean, Dr. Freud. Because let's be honest. He's all but asked me to fingerpaint my mommy issues."

She grins at the joke.

A grin that proves time passed, and we both survived.

wolfson
TWENTY-EIGHT

The house makes its old-man noises, wood settling and pipes sighing. Right on cue, one of Frankie's old men flushes a toilet upstairs.

Beyond the kitchen window, a strip of water flashes silver. The dock slaps and mutters. Somewhere, a gull yells profanity. The air through the cracked window feels heavy and wet like a tongue on my skin. Summer's here, creeping up the back steps.

I build a plate for Dove, going overboard with sliced apples, eggs, toast, and thick smears of jam. I pour her coffee and add cream until it turns the color of wet sand.

The bloom of milk in the mug is a small, lovely thing. I want to give her more small, lovely things until the pile of them is big enough to stand on and see our future. Together.

Frankie watches me and says nothing, which is another gift. I set the cup on the tray and look up.

Her eyes shine bright. "I love you."

"Love you more, *ma cerise chérie*."

I tuck the journals under my arm, grab the tray, and kiss the top of her head on my way out.

The walk back is shorter than it was an hour ago. Inside the guest house, the air smells like wet cedar and the faint, old sweetness of wooden bones.

Upstairs, I set the tray on the dresser and stand still, listening.

Dove makes a small sound in her sleep and shifts, the sheet whispering against her shoulder. I carry the coffee to the nightstand and set it down where she can reach it. The movement wakes her.

Her eyes open, honey warm, then sharpen. Sleep to fight in an instant.

When she sees it's me, she softens around the mouth, and the sight kicks me behind the knees. Her eyes sweep over me, taking in the purple robe like it's a statement I didn't intend to make.

"You smell like breakfast," she rasps.

"Eat."

"You okay?" She sits up and reaches for the toast first, like a civilized person.

"Better."

"Cool," she says around a mouthful of bread. "Because last night, you looked like a drowned prince, and I was seconds away from dragging you out of the shower by your hair and mouth-to-mouthing you without your consent."

"Would've been awkward."

"Which part?"

"The hair pulling."

"I'd have managed." She sips coffee, considers the color, and nods. "You remember how I take it. That's either sweet or creepy."

"Both."

Her grin is a small, tilting sun.

"What's that?" She directs her gaze to the books under my arm.

I hold up Frankie's journal. "This one is a map."

"Of what?"

"Hell. And how four people walked out."

She squints at the book, then at me. "You gonna read it?"

"I'll try." The admission costs me, and it buys something, too. I show her the blank journal. "I might write a story."

Her brows rise with interest. "About?"

"The fall of a drag queen." With Frankie's voice still warm in my head, I add, "And her resurrection as a wolf."

Dove chews that answer like she chews toast. Thoughtfully.

"Love that," she finally says. "I've never been interested in Prince Charming. Too boring." She yawns. "So overdone. But an artistic, chain-smoking wolf in fuck-me boots and eyeliner? Now we're talking."

"That's convenient. I've been hoarding cigarettes and sharpies for years."

"Prove it." She tips her chin at the blank journal. "With words."

"Bossy."

Lifting a shoulder, she takes another bite, and crumbs stick to her lower lip.

I stand there like an idiot, wanting to kiss them off. "I need a shower."

"Go." She lowers her voice. "Before I beg you to return to bed and this turns into a problem."

"It's already a problem."

She slides back the covers beside her, inviting me to crawl into that empty spot.

I want to. By God and his frostbitten nuts, I want to. The smell of her skin. The shape of her beneath the sheets. Every part of me is wired to dive back under, crawl into her heat, and forget.

I shouldn't. Because I'm carrying the taste of her brother's come in my mouth.

But I need her. My bones ache with it.

I can't. If I take what she's offering, it won't be clean. It'll be a theft.

My feet move before I decide. The exit is closer than the bed, and I take it, gripping the doorframe until my knuckles blanch.

Behind me, the covers rustle.

I look back.

Her room is ordinary. A bed for two people, a chair that's never used, clothes on the floor. The ordinariness is a benediction.

Ordinary means no one is starving or freezing or bleeding beneath a rutting devil. Ordinary means there's a lock on the bedroom door for privacy not protection, and the world didn't end in a cabin.

"I'll tell you what happened with Jag yesterday, and about the monster who raised me and the doctor who cut me. I'll introduce you to every boogeyman in my closet." The promise scrapes out like gravel, and I can't look at her, not directly. "But first, I need today to get my head straight. Can you give me that?"

"If you need space, I can go to work for a while. Keep my hands busy and earn my keep."

She's offering me distance like it's mercy, like the only help she knows how to give is her absence.

My gut twists, because she doesn't get it. Sending her away from the island is the last thing I want. But it might be the only way I can have a come-to-Jesus with my demons.

"Only if you take the bodyguards." I meet her eyes. "And only if you promise you'll come back to me after." Begging totally kills my vibe, but I'm doing it anyway. "I know you're not sure about us. I get it. Just… Give me the day. Listen to my horror story tonight. Then decide."

Every nerve in me waits for her to flinch. To tell me to keep my monsters to myself.

"Wolf…" Her shoulders drop on a sigh. "I don't want to go. I just… I worry being here makes it worse for you."

Her honesty hits harder than if she'd pulled away. She doesn't make it worse. She's the only thing that makes it bearable.

"But if what you need is time, I'll give it." She straightens. "I'll be back tonight. And I'll listen."

Relief and dread collide in me, a lightning crash behind the ribs.

How will she look at me after I tell her what I did with Jag and what Denver did to me? It won't make her jump my bones, that's for damn sure.

"Tonight." I push off the doorframe and don't wait for her answer.

Down the hall and in my room, I dump the journals on my bed and tackle easy tasks. Shower, clean teeth, heavy eyeliner, and clothes.

The last one requires some thought.

If I'm about to drown in Frankie's journal, I need pieces that will hold up when my ribs come undone and my insides spill out.

I pull on black jeans, stiff with wear, and a gray T-shirt so tattered and ugly it matches my scars. Over that, a flannel with sleeves rolled to the elbows. No color. No flair. The whole outfit screams, *I'm still here but not pretty about it.*

With the journals under my arm, I head downstairs and find Dove by the door, shrugging into her bomber jacket.

She showered, too, her damp hair half-up, half-loose. A messy knot high on her head lets waves of electric blue tumble around her shoulders. More strands fall in her eyes, and she doesn't bother pushing them away.

I catch a flash of a tank top, cropped at her midriff, baring a heavenly slice of skin. Pants black as asphalt, pockets stitched over pockets, and boots with green neon laces.

My chest tightens with the sudden, stupid thought. When she walks out that door, I won't be the one who gets to follow her.

I need to let her leave, but my eyes won't let go.

She's zipping up her jacket when I cut across the room and block the door.

"If clothes can confess a mood..." I tilt my head. "Yours say, *Princess of the scrapyard. Kiss me dirty or don't bother.*"

"Not wrong." Her lips curve.

"What do mine say?"

She examines my outfit and returns to my face. "*Falling apart, but the seams are stubborn.*"

Christ. My chest stutters. That's it. That's me. How does she do that?

Before I think better of it, I fist the back of her neck, clamp a hand on her hip, and haul her against me.

My mouth crashes down on hers, hard and hungry. She gasps, lips parting, and I dive in. Sweet heat and cool metal from her piercing roll against my tongue.

The kiss is teeth and desperation, the clash of breath caught and stolen. Her hands are everywhere, clutching my flannel, sliding under it, nails scraping skin and setting me ablaze.

My ribs ache from the pressure of her chest against mine, the way we weld together. Still, I grip her tighter, anchoring myself against the inevitability of letting her go.

The pleasure of her kiss in my mouth is seductive and surreal, flooding me with fire and sparks that make every muscle twitch. My hips drag toward hers, reaching, chasing, controlled by a magnetic pull.

Not a drop of blood remains in my head. Every ounce drains south, pounding thick in my cock. Her heat seeps into my skin, burning through muscle, spreading fast, and untangling nerves wound too tight for too long.

I didn't realize how shattered and empty I was until she started fitting into the cracks, until this fragile, feverish happiness started chasing away a lifetime of coldness.

"God, I love the way you kiss." She slides her nose along mine, nibbling at my lips. "I don't want to go."

Breaking apart feels like ripping open stitches, but there's comfort in her reluctance, in knowing she hates the separation, too.

"Good luck today, Wolf." She drops a kiss on my bottom lip. "Text me if you need me. I'll drop my tools and head back the second you do. Got it?"

I nod and force myself to let her step back, force my fingers to unclench from her jacket. She opens the door, and the morning light outlines her in a holy, angelic glow.

The second she's gone, I snatch my phone and fire off a text to her guards.

Me: Escort Dove from the island to work. Don't let her out of your sight. If she doesn't come back to me tonight, don't bother coming back yourselves.
GI Joe Carl: Understood, sir. We'll maintain constant visual contact, comms on, and keep you updated with ETA and any deviation.

My pulse still shakes from her mouth as I drop on the couch and pull Frankie's journal onto my lap.

"All right, Dorothy. Remind me why there's no place like home."

I don't go in gentle. I open page one and jump, throwing myself into the graphic account of her first day in captivity.

Several dozen pages later, I take my first breath.

Christ, I forgot how horrible we were to her. She miscarried Monty's baby, my would've-been sister or brother, and we acted like it was nothing. She was scared out of her mind and so fucking alone, and we piled on, and on, and on.

We were monsters.

The memory hooks me under the ribs and yanks hard. I breathe. In for four. Hold for four. Out for six. Dr. Thurber's box breathing technique. Dr. Freud. Whatever.

I power through the first half of the journal without pausing. The imagery is vicious, the details merciless. My brain wants to sprint ahead to where it hurts less, but I make it stay and absorb every painful word.

Monty comes in once, carrying a tray of sandwiches, pasta salad, and ice water.

He gives me a discreet perusal, and I see him doing the thing, chewing on the inside of his cheek when he's uncomfortable and trying to figure out how to fix something.

But instead of interrupting, he makes a quiet exit.

I stop him at the door. "Did you read this?"

"Yes." He glances at the book and looks away, sliding his hands into his pockets. "Can I get you anything?"

"Not yet."

"I'm here if you need me." With that, he steps out.

I return to her journal, consumed by the memories and her surgical details. My eyes burn, and my neck aches from holding the same position for hours.

The pages keep turning.

At some point, the sentences shift, and her map begins to point at me. My detachment. My depression. She pins it down with the same brutal precision she uses on the worst of the Arctic.

The sky is turning the wrong shade.
The cold is so vicious it hates human skin.
Wolf grows withdrawn and distant.

When I reach the part I dreaded, her account of that day doesn't deviate from my memories.

Frankie asleep by the fire, my brothers dealing with Denver's body, the snowdrifts pushing against the walls of the cabin... I threatened to kill her on the cliff, and she knew I wouldn't. But I still hurt her irreparably.

I left them to mourn and ration and freeze because my head told me the only clean escape was death. I told myself that leaving this world would save them from having to watch me fall apart.

What I did, as her journal shows without pity, was leave them to carry too much heartache and suffering alone.

I reread one sentence in particular, one she scribbled in a cramped, furious hand.

Every day, we count our breaths and keep one for Wolf.
Fuck, that hurts.

They never gave up on me. They looked for me. They waited for me. They *hoped.*

If survival is a story, Frankie's just handed me the part where the martyr finds out he was a selfish cunt.

My face goes numb, and the tears come without ceremony. One, then another, followed by a steady drizzle that smears the pages. I let it. I let myself feel the thing I keep tucked away, the knowledge that I left my family to a frozen fate I knew they couldn't survive.

I fucking left them.

If I could rewind, I wouldn't jump. I'd stay. I'd be the brother shivering beside them in the dark, bitching about the last can of beans, and cracking sick jokes to distract their stomachs from twisting inside out. I would man up and choose to be there because love is harder than death.

I read the rest with an achy throat, and despite what I told her, I skip the sex stuff. That belongs to them, not me. I stick to the parts that hurt. The bear attack, the icy lake that swallows her, the SOS signal, every harrowing effort they make to survive. I inhale it all, knowing where I was during those ten months.

Was being tortured by Dr. Rhett Howell worse than the hell they suffered? I don't know.

Physical pain aside, they weren't alone. Through it all, they had one another.

And they had one more thing.

Hope.

Turns out that was the map out of hell. Who would've thought?

My tears dry, leaving tracks on my face, as the book finishes beneath my thumb. I close the cover, hollow and heavy in the space where regret sleeps.

Setting the journal on the coffee table, I stare at the other book.

My book.

Write your story.

"Okay, Frankie. You mouthy little gangster. Here's mine."

Dropping my head back on the couch, I close my eyes.

I'm in a guest house on an island in Sitka. I don't know if I'm straight or gay or maybe I'm stepsexual. Is that a thing? Because apparently I can't have one stepsibling without the other.

The woman I want is a badass mechanic. Hard, honest work. The woman who gave birth to me was a rapist, and I killed her.

The man I want is a criminal stalker. Dangerous, dishonest work. The man who raised me is a pedophile, and Frankie killed him.

My real father? He's one of the good guys. He loves like a man who refuses smallness. Too much love for a broken son like me. Too much grace. But I'm so fucking grateful for him.

I'm not where I was. I'm safe. My family is safe. I'm free to shop for clothes and feed my girl and lose my virginity.

I have a job that sparks joy and have more money than any man needs. I'm in a story where the narrator is unreliable, unhinged, and broken beyond repair. But I'm finally brave enough to put the nightmare into words.

Should I start at the beginning? That's normal. Expected. But I'm not normal. I'm not expected. I'm not a book that follows rules or order.

If I'm going to open a vein, let it be honest. Let it be the aftermath, the scars, the hand job, and yesterday's breakdown. I need to start with the now, today, and work my way backward, tracing the steps that made my damage unavoidable.

Might be braver. Might be lazier. Or crazier. Either way, it's honest.

I flip to the last page.

"Let's ruin the sheets."

I light a cigarette.

I pick up a sharpie.

In the rise of ink and smoke, something inside me unclenches.

One sentence. No flourish. No fairy tales.

I write...

I woke up and wanted the day.

wolfson

dove
TWENTY-NINE

"Good night, Dove." Taaq waves over his shoulder and follows Chester out of the garage.

I look up from a transmission rebuild and drag a sweaty forearm across my brow.

The shop goes quiet in the way it always does when the day folds up and tucks itself under half-dead engines.

Grime cakes my nails. Exhaust fumes soak my hair, and my back aches from bending under hoods all day. I check my phone for the hundredth time and return it to my pocket.

Still no message from Wolf.

I could stay, lose myself in this stubborn rebuild, and avoid whatever's waiting across the water.

Will it be a confession from Wolf? Will he tell me he's fallen for my stepbrother? That he prefers Jag over me? They always do.

Listen to my horror story tonight. Then decide.

I made a promise.

So I kill the lights, lock the bay door, and scan the street as I step out to greet Carl and Jasper.

The entire walk to the pier, Jag's shadow lingers, breathing against my neck and daring me to turn. Each time I do, no one is

love

there.

By the time the bodyguards ferry me across Sitka Sound, the violet haze of dusk darkens the island.

Pushing open the door to the guest house, I brace myself for finding Wolf curled up somewhere I can't reach him.

Instead, I'm hit with warmth. Real warmth. The smell of food.

The kitchen looks like it was claimed by a professional chef. Pots steaming. Plates waiting. A skillet abandoned on the stove, crackling with the last hiss of oil.

Wolf stands at the sink with his back to me, sleeves shoved up, sculpted forearms on display, scrubbing a pan.

I take the opportunity to appreciate the rear view, the broad shoulders tapering down, denim clinging to a hard ass, and legs strong enough to slam a woman against a wall and fuck the fight out of her.

His hair is messier than usual, but his shoulders are loose, so much lighter than this morning. He's painfully beautiful, and the sight of him in his tattered shirt with the seams holding strong adds to my breathlessness.

"Hi." I hang my jacket on the hook and pad into the kitchen. "You cooked."

"I'm feeding you, Birdie." He wipes his hands on a towel and slaps it over his shoulder. "Pretty sure it's edible."

"Thank you." I lean my brow against his shoulder and steal a whiff of his dark, masculine scent. "Do I have time to shower?"

"Ten minutes. Don't make me hunt you down. Or do. Your choice."

I smirk, snag my bag, and bolt upstairs.

Speeding through the shower, I scrub off the grease and the stink of gasoline until I no longer feel like a grungy oil pan. I pull on a soft shirt and clean jeans and towel-dry my hair, rushing because the smell downstairs is already dragging me back.

When I pad into the kitchen again, the table overflows with roast halibut, buttered potatoes with fresh dill, charred asparagus slick with oil, and a basket of bread that steams with warm yeast.

He even poured wine.

Everything looks delicious. Especially him.

"Looks like a damn feast." I sway closer, the hunger hitting me hard with so much food under my nose.

He shrugs, but there's pride in it. "Feeding you makes me happy."

"You make me happy." It comes out more honest than I intend, and I hug my waist, feeling awkward. "You shouldn't have done this. You needed to focus on yourself today and—"

"Stop."

"I don't want to be a burden."

"Shut up." His tone darkens, all iron and no give. "Come here."

His arms open, and I step into the muscled circle of them. He smells like soap, sautéed herbs, and a wildness that doesn't belong in a modern kitchen.

For a moment, I let myself lean into his strength, savoring his closeness. My head brushes his collarbone, and his heart thumps against my cheek, grounding.

Then he eases back, one arm sliding away to tug a chair from the table, and waits for me to sit.

I obey his wordless command, feeling stupid for how much I'm rattled by his care and attention.

He pushes me in with a gentleness that doesn't match his uncivilized edges, and when I glance up, his eyes catch mine, hard and unflinching, as if to say, *Eat. Stay.*

We sit across from each other, passing platters and sampling the decadent flavors. I don't ask where he learned how to cook like a gourmet chef. He grew up in a self-sufficient homestead in the Arctic Circle. I imagine he's mastered a great many things that most men have never even attempted.

He watches me eat, chewing his bites slower than usual, methodical, as if he's buying time. His hand shakes when he lifts his glass, but he steadies it quickly.

"You seem... Different." I eye him over a heap of potatoes.

"Better or worse?"

"Better. Clearer." I set my fork down. "What happened today?"

He leans back, long legs sprawled, eyes darting away. "I fought some demons. Didn't win. Didn't lose. Just stopped letting them own the place." He taps his temple.

Silence settles, magnifying the clink of cutlery. It's not uncomfortable. Just heavy.

When the plates are mostly empty, he slips into the living

love

room and returns with the books from this morning.

"You wrote your story?" I wipe my hands on a napkin.

"A lot of it. And I left a lot out." He sets the books on the table. "But I need you to hear it all. Maybe not tonight. Probably not in order. I figure we can read it together, Frankie's story and mine, and I'll fill in the blanks as we go."

"Okay." I stroke his hand, humbled by his bravery.

"But if you're too tired—"

"I'm not."

He studies me, making sure. Then his lips tip in a crooked smile.

We clean the dishes side by side, fingers brushing as we pass plates.

"You always this domestic?" I ask.

"Only when I'm trying to trick someone into liking me."

"It's working." I rinse a glass and set it in the dishwasher. "Barely."

He flicks water at me. I shove his elbow with my shoulder. It's silly and so normal my chest hurts with it.

When the counters are clean and the stove is wiped, he turns off the overhead and leads me to the couch.

As we settle in, he sets the books between us. I tuck my legs under me, heart heavy, readying myself for the pieces of hell he's willing to hand me.

He rests his splayed fingers on the cover of his book, one last pause. His arctic blue eyes lift to mine, brighter than I've ever seen them.

Then he opens the past, and we step off the ledge together.

wolfson
THIRTY

Sixteen months ago

The Fall

The hills of shivers and shadows recede until nothing remains but the edge and the ache.

And Frankie's shout.

"Wolf!" She races toward me like a flare in the dark. Too loud. Too bright.

"Stop screaming." My voice is flat. Final. It doesn't belong to me. "The entire Arctic can hear you."

"What are you doing?"

"Already told you."

"No." She scans the polar night, searching for me in the shadows. "You didn't tell me you were leaving."

"We have all these talks, but you haven't heard a thing."

But she does hear me. The problem is she can't hear the dead parts inside me.

"You're standing on the edge of the cliff for the same reason I stood there two months ago." She moves closer. "Leo talked me down that day, and I'm so fucking grateful."

Sure, she is. She's also terrified, freezing, starving, and facing a looming, excruciating death.

"The idiot should've let you jump." The lie is easier to swallow than the thing breaking the bones in my chest.

"You don't mean that."

"We're murderers."

Oh, she hates *that* truth and comes at me with her flapping, frantic kindness, throwing words like lifelines, trying to talk me off the ledge. Begging, bargaining, and making promises about bright futures.

She says all the right things and nails every line that used to latch onto me, but the hooks don't catch anymore. I'm done talking. Done hurting. Done feeling. I'm just done.

"I want to die." Like a coward, I aim the pistol at the space between her ribs. "In my heart, I'm already dead. I need you with me. We can finally be together."

Her eyes dart to my finger on the trigger. "Wait! Please, I don't want to die. Not like this."

I would never hurt her. She knows that.

"I love you." It's small, true, and entirely useless. It's the last honest thing I have to give.

Training the gun away from her, I pull the trigger. The shot cracks, and white-hot pain detonates up my arm. Kody's voice cuts through the shocking, blinding agony, and I look down at the arrow sticking out of my bicep.

He shot me. He actually fucking shot me.

Leo emerges from the dark with a rifle as Kody reloads another bolt.

It all arranges into neat geometry—Frankie in front, them at angles of protection, me the loose thing in the middle.

"You're choosing her over your own brother?" I spit at them, dizzy with blood loss and shame.

"No, they're not," Frankie cries as Kody shouts, "Yes," and that one word, that final truth, makes me instantly, violently sick.

Sick with envy. Sick with wrath. Sick with all the deadly sins.

I drop the gun, spread my arms like Christ on the cross, and step back. I'm hellborn and hell-raised, and so I let hell pull me back in.

The fall is a slow burn of moments I want to forget. A collapse of memory and regrets. The wind strips breath from my mouth. My stomach climbs into my throat. My whole life becomes a long, mournful note on the saxophone.

Will they miss me? The thought is lame and painfully human. But the answer is omnipotent.

Yes.

Yes, they'll fucking miss me, and they'll suffer for this.

In a tunnel of wind that's mine to die in, something inside me startles awake. Not heroism. Not courage. It's a single godawful thought.

I can't let them drag my body from the river. I can't throw them a corpse and call it escape. Picturing Frankie and my brothers sifting through pieces of scattered bone and organs... That's the too-late image that changes my mind.

Mid-fall, I do the only thing I can. I flinch, twist, and fling my one good arm, grabbing for anything that isn't final.

My fingers connect with snow and brittle birch. The knot of shrubby branches juts from the cliff like a splintered handshake. I grip it, and the wood bites back, shredding my palm and splitting my nails.

It takes half my weight in one impossible, creaking complaint. Then it takes the rest. I hang by an arm between vertigo and salvation, my breath a ratchet of pain.

Beneath my dangling feet, the glacial river awaits, spitting and churning. A massive tooth of stone juts out of the rapids. That's where my head would have been if I'd kept going.

It's only a matter of time before my fingers slip. But I'm ready for it.

I shove off with a strength that's more will than muscle and swing like a pendulum, using the branch as a fulcrum to alter trajectory.

Wind slaps my face. Snow punches my cheeks. I twist my hips mid-air and aim my body in a desperate prayer.

Roll. Absorb. Don't splatter on impact.

I shoulder the angle and hit the icy current. My wounded arm slams into rocks. My ribs eat the vibration, and for a second so precise I can measure it, I think, *Holy shit, I stuck that fucking landing.*

Then the river peels open its snarling, fanged jaw and sucks me down its throat.

The undercurrent grabs my legs, dragging me beneath the surface as the world shifts sideways, spinning and pulling me at breakneck speeds far away from Hoss.

Ice chunks bash my face as I claw for a rock, a root, anything to stop the ruthless rolling. The arrow in my arm wrenches and catches on debris like a barbaric anchor.

The choice is ugly and instant. I curl my fingers around the bolt's shaft and yank. My bicep screams, and blood sprays across the water. Vicious, fiery pain stabs up my arm, obliterating tendon and muscle.

No time for shock. My lungs demand air. For endless miles, I paddle my limbs with a panic born of instinct. Agony flares with each stroke as I choke on the brutal, shredding pain of slowly drowning.

The whitewater rapids sweep me farther and farther from the hills with violent urgency, smacking me around with the force of a god-shaped hand, and siphoning the last drop of heat from my pores.

It's a cold so vast it isn't cold. It's a breath, the final one, before the body quits fighting.

My vision edges with colorless static. Every movement becomes heavier than the one before. My lungs burn for breath I can't coax.

When the river falls silent, death answers.

The Resurrection

I wake in the dark with a gasp.

Pain. It's everywhere. In my lungs. In my teeth. In the roots of my filthy hair. But it's a language I understand. It tells me I'm alive.

Unless pain exists in the afterlife. In that case, I'm fucked.

The river crashes nearby, close enough to lap at my legs. But the ground beneath me is solid.

Lying on my back, I try to shift my body, but it's too heavy. My limbs stick to the riverbank like slabs of cement. Nothing moves. Not a shiver.

Not good.

When the shivering stops, that's the real silence. I must be dead.

I can't feel my balls.

Oh, fuck. What if I have frostbite on my dick? Will I lose it for eternity?

I've died and gone to cold hell in a handbasket.

Except there's no handbasket, and I've lost my dick.

I stare into the void. Is this it? This is what the end feels like? I traded twenty-three years of emptiness for a dickless eternity of more emptiness?

That's on brand.

A shape moves above me, cutting the blackness of afterlife into a silhouette. At first, it's nothing but a lighter dark. Then my eyes adjust, taking in the outline of a man.

White hair. No, blond. Feathered tufts of it fall from beneath a white, fur-lined hood. He wears white all over, from the long, goose-down parka and immaculate gloves to the tailored snow pants. Not a smudge of dirt on his hiking boots. And that knitted white scarf? It won't survive a day in this climate.

Did he slide down from heaven on a rainbow? Or just materialize out of the ether?

His face is the kind that glows in the stain-glass windows of an old church, perfect bone structure, backlit by a halo of light. His coat billows around him like a ceremonial robe as he holds out his hands in a peace offering.

"Are you God?" I rasp past cracked lips.

"Yes."

"Is this a social visit? Or are you on the clock?"

"I'm always working."

"Answering prayers?"

"Sometimes I save lives. Sometimes I end them." He sweeps his gaze to the river and returns to me. "Today, I'm your savior."

"I thought you'd be bigger."

"I thought you'd be more grateful."

"No, really. I pictured less clothes. Maybe a tunic. Definitely sandals. But the snow pants are a solid choice. Nobody wants frostbitten nuts. Do you even feel the cold?"

"Do you?" He rips open my coat, exposing my river-soaked chest to the bitter wind. "You're lucky to be here."

Lucky? I don't think so. I fought tooth and nail to get here, and now I want to go back. It's becoming harder to form words and straighten my thoughts. None of this makes sense.

"You're hypothermic." A clinical melody sings through his voice as he rezips my coat. "We need to raise your core temperature. You're losing heat."

He talks like a doctor, like a minister, like a man with a plan.

Then he reaches for something, and for a second, I think he's taking my picture.

A bright flash follows, and I close my eyes against it. More clicks. More flashes. Definitely a camera.

Is he cataloging a miracle? Or documenting a death?

He pulls a thermal blanket from somewhere behind him and kneels like a man in church, tucking the material under my shoulders and ribs.

I can't lift my head. Or my arms. Opening my eyes is a struggle. "Am I dead?"

"You were." He carefully removes his gloves, finger by finger, and touches my throat, checking my pulse. "You rose from the dead because of me. I raised you up by my mercy. My miracle. Remember that."

Warmth blooms as his hands move over me with certainty, quick rubs across my shoulders, tucking the blanket tight, coaxing my limbs into stabbing pins and needles.

If I'm not dead, then... "Where are we?"

"The Brooks Range."

"Where's that?"

"In the heart of Alaska's Arctic region." He eyes my bloodstained sleeve and turns away to dig through a bag.

Alaska. I always wondered where we live. Now I know.

How far did the river take me from Hoss? Miles, if I had to guess, which equates to weeks this time of year. Too far to hike back.

Too far to be found by my brothers anytime soon. But they *will* come for me as long as I stay here, find shelter, and stay hydrated.

Should I tell the Almighty One about my stranded family? If he's truly the Lord of All, wouldn't he already know?

The breathing, pulsing, still very much alive instinct behind my ribs clenches. Not with hope. More like alarm.

He tapes and packs around the hole in my arm with sterile hands, iodine wipes, and folded gauze. Amid the pain, I focus on the wrongness in his practiced patience, on the carefulness that aims to own the moment. He's too clean by miles.

If he's God, couldn't he just heal my wound with the touch of a shimmering, magical finger?

If he's not God, what is he? A bush pilot? Off-grid trapper? Seasonal operator?

Except men who belong out here don't have soft, manicured hands. They don't wear knitted scarves and take pictures. And they sure as fuck don't fold their gloves like clergy.

"Who are you?"

"Dr. Rhett Howell. And you, Wolfson Strakh, are *mine*. This will help with shock." He moves a small vial into view.

I know the look on a man's face when he wants to control a thing that refuses to be controlled. I see that look now as he plunges a syringe into the vial.

"Don't." I try to push him away, but the river stole my thunder.

"This is for you." He leans close, breath warm and terribly calm. "To make you comfortable. To revive you fully."

A wild, hungry thing snarls in my gut, and it's far meaner than a doctor with a syringe. But before I can unsheathe its teeth and rip off his face, the needle enters my skin.

"Sleep now," he purrs.

The cold curls into my chest and closes like a fist. I try to scream, but my voice is a bubble that pops.

My eyes slide closed on the quiet, awful certainty that I escaped one nightmare only to wake in a new one.

love
THIRTY-ONE

The night exhales a mournful hush that feels borrowed from a church. Pine leans into the wind as the little guest house breathes around us, a soft rib cage of wood and light.

The kitchen still smells like heat, lemon butter clinging to steam and the scent of dill floating in the air. The dinner Wolf made sits warm in my stomach, sending pulses of comfort through a body that clenches and shivers with arctic horrors.

He fed me before we started. Because he knew. That's so him. Haunted, damaged, but so stubbornly protective that he would never let me follow him into hell on an empty stomach.

What he suffered is more unfathomable than anything I imagined. And this is only a glimpse.

He started his story on the edge of a cliff. He spread his arms, let go, and hit the river, taking me with him. Death should've been the end, but instead it delivered him into worse hands.

For ten months.

Ten months alone, in a cage, without the mercy of light. He wrote about his conversations with Regret, the visits from the doctor with a heart of frost, the scalpel, the blood, and the depth of pain that didn't stop when the blade lifted.

My throat burns. I can't scrub the images from my head.

Wolf shackled, stripped, bleeding, but still spitting sarcasm through grinding teeth. A boy raised in hell, dragged back into hell, and still too stubborn to die.

I want to scream. I want to put my hands on the walls and rip the world apart for letting that happen to him. I want to do things that would shame the devil who hurt him.

Violence. That's what his story inspires in me. I'm so angry for him. So fucking angry.

Instead, I look at him. Really look. The makeup-stained eyes, the pout, the theatrics, the necessary mask that prevents others from seeing what he carries under his skin.

But I see it now. There's so much more. The steel braided into his bones. The fight that kept him alive when lesser men would've curled up and died.

He thinks he's broken. He thinks he's a lonely, lost boy. But all I see is ferocity. He isn't fragile. He isn't some tragic fallen angel stumbling through an expression of self-destruction.

He's a survivor.

Not just a survivor of captivity but of a lifetime of it. Of whatever Denver did to him. Of unspeakable hardships in the hills. Of every scar branded on his body long before the doctor touched him.

He feels me looking and lifts his head. "Welcome to my freak show."

"Wolf."

"If I don't make jokes about it, who even am I?"

"You don't have to do that with me. No pretense. No judgment. No masks between us." My chest feels so tight it's hard to breathe. "Why did you jump?"

"For that, you need to meet Denver. Frankie introduces him best." He plucks the book from my lap and replaces it with hers. "Need a break? Bathroom? Booze…?"

I'm already shaking my head, eyes glued to Frankie's journal. No way in hell am I stopping now. I'm strung between dread and fascination, terrified of what I'll find and starving for it anyway.

His fingers hook beneath my chin, gentle but unyielding, coaxing my face up until I stare into his stormy blue eyes.

"You've been reading for hours." He examines my pupils, the tremor in my hands, the stiffness in my shoulders, every small tell he's learned to read. "You don't have to keep going tonight.

love

You can sleep. Eat something. Breathe."

I can't. Not yet.

Swallowing hard, I refuse to look away, refuse to let him see how much his past has shaken me. After a too-long moment, he sighs, and a soft, sad look passes over his face.

"Okay." He lets go, fingertips trailing from my chin as if reluctant to lose contact. "We'll read together, and when you want to stop, say stop. If you want to know more, ask. If you want to skip, we'll skip. If you want to throw the book at my head, aim for the soft parts. Deal?"

"Where are the soft parts?"

He presses his soft, warm lips against my mouth, slowly flicks his tongue, and leans back.

"Oh." I pull in a breath and nod.

The spine creaks as he opens Frankie's book. Her handwriting fills the first page, a looping scrawl that looks nothing like his.

He runs his thumb down the margin and begins to read. "They say obedience is survival. Staying silent is proof you don't want more than your share of air. Obedience is the only language Denver respects. The moment you make a sound, you give him something to take. I learned that lesson on the first day when he took my unborn baby."

The hairs along my arms lift. Wolf's growly tone is a tool he doesn't wield often. Every word rasps like it's been rusting in his throat for years, scraped clean to reach me. The gravelly ache in it makes the story hurt worse, makes it more real.

He glances at me like an apology.

I expel a breath and gesture at the book. "May I?"

At his stiff nod, I read aloud.

I read through the first forty-two days of Frankie's chilling captivity. I read until she finds bones.

Human bones.

And what does she do?

She collects them in a bag of blueberries and dumps the morbid pile onto Denver's dinner. She feeds him his own damn ghosts.

You go, girl.

But as she warned in her opening sentence, defiance has a cost. In this case, kin punishment.

Denver pinned Kody's hand to the table. *With a fillet knife.* That explains his stigmata-like scar.

Frankie details how the handle trembled from Kody's pulse, how the sound he made wasn't human, and how she would've traded her soul to take his pain instead.

I look up at Wolf, and he's watching me, silent, expression chiseled from stone, but I can see the flicker of old anguish.

"Is it true?" My voice cracks. "The bones? The knife? All of it?"

"Yeah. She was trying to survive. Trying to fight him the only way she could."

"A fillet knife?" I blink hard, a tear breaking loose and sliding down my cheek. "That's why Kody's hand is scarred? It was a punishment for something he didn't do?"

"That was Denver's way."

"Holy shit." My fingers quiver. "And the women, the ones before her, he killed them?"

"You'll get to that part." His voice lands roughly, carrying too many scars. "Let's call it a night."

"No." I grip the book tighter. "I can't stop now."

"You should." He leans back, watching me as if measuring how close I am to breaking. "You've read enough for one night."

"I haven't. You lived it. The least I can do is finish it."

"You don't need those pictures in your head, Lovey-dovey." He frees a heavy sigh. "Trust me."

"Too late. They're already there."

His eyes search mine. Whatever he sees makes his shoulders drop.

"You don't get used to it." He reaches out and brushes the tear from my cheek with his thumb. "No matter how much time passes. You just learn where to hide the parts it ruined."

I study his face, the tension behind his eyes, the faint tremor in his jaw. He doesn't want to live through it again tonight. He already did it once today, reading it for the first time.

"You don't have to stay up with me." I close the book partway, thumb marking the page.

"You're not stopping?"

"I won't sleep until I finish it. But you should. Sleep."

Relief flickers across his expression. Maybe gratitude. Maybe both. "You sure?"

"Lie down, right here, if the light doesn't bother you. I'll read quietly."

He hesitates for a heartbeat, then exhales, tension draining from his shoulders. He lowers himself onto his side on the couch, carefully, as if testing the idea of comfort. His head finds my lap, and before I can second-guess it, my fingers weave through his hair.

It's so soft and shaggy, damp with the remnants of salt air, curling against my palm. He hums low in his throat, eyes slipping closed.

"My favorite pillow," he murmurs against my thigh, voice already fading.

"Sleep, Wolf."

He does. Slowly, his breathing deepens, and his weight settles into me. I absently comb through the dark mess of his hair, the movement hypnotic and grounding. His fingers twitch once against my leg but never lift.

I open the journal again. The pages whisper.

The secrets. The mystery. The unexpected love blooming in Frankie. Love for three feral men who bullied her, kept her in the dark, and protected her from Denver and one another.

Why? Frankie's word bleeds into the next lines. *Why did Denver abduct me? Why didn't Monty come home? Why won't they tell me what they're hiding?*

My pulse hammers in time with her questions. They're my questions, too. The why of everything. The madness. The lies. The secrecy that binds them all.

As I read the shift in her words, I feel a sharp coldness open in my chest. Her handwriting grows unsteady and desperate as she writes about the night I knew in my gut was coming.

The night Denver tied her to the bed.

The Glasgow smile painted on Wolf's face.

The devil's bargain.

Vital pieces inside me break cleanly, audibly. I hear them snapping, falling away permanently.

The man who raised Wolf hurt him in the most unthinkable way. The betrayal. The damage. It's a wonder Wolf can function at all.

Tears smudge everything, and I press a hand to my mouth, trying to keep quiet, but the sob crawls out anyway.

God, Wolf.

My throat closes. The room shrinks, and the air becomes unbreathable. I can't look away from the page, even when the tears splash onto the ink.

Someone else cried on these pages, the dried splotches making some parts hard to decipher. Am I reading through Monty's tears? Wolf's?

Fucking hell, this hurts.

I keep going, the letters blurring, the ache in my chest insufferable. Wolf stirs but doesn't wake, his breath warm against my thigh. I drag my fingers through his hair again, careful not to wake him.

He survived this. They all did. But now I understand what it cost.

Wolf made a deal with the devil to protect Frankie. Then she sacrificed herself to protect him and his brothers. She promised to give Denver anything, everything, if he never hurt his sons again.

My eyes burn, the pages swimming.

Jag triggered Wolf's breakdown in the shower. Whatever happened between them was sexual. If Wolf has only ever known abuse, his reaction to Jag makes sense.

It breaks my fucking heart.

As I sit there, tears streaking down my cheeks, with Wolf's head resting on my lap and his scars hidden beneath my fingertips, I realize the truth that Frankie didn't write.

Sometimes survival isn't proof of strength.

It's proof of love.

If only I could apply that truth to my own past.

jag
THIRTY-TWO

The private jet takes off, vibrating with the ominous, too-late sensation of a terrible decision.

I flex my good hand, keep my expression blank, and stare at the man sitting opposite me.

The courier of cartel favors.

Cole Hartman.

I recognize him instantly.

He doesn't speak for the first thirty minutes. Instead, he studies me with hard brown eyes that undress, dismantle, and decide a man's fate in a single heartbeat.

The good news? I'm still alive.

Unlike most cartel lieutenants, he doesn't wear a suit. His mobster gear consists of a black leather jacket, boots that have seen desert sand, and a T-shirt that fails to hide the gun tucked along his ribs.

His posture says trained soldier. His glare says homicidal deserter. His smile says he's not sure which one he'll be today.

Over the years, I've dug up everything there is to find on Cole Hartman.

In another life, he was a high-speed ghost for the U.S. government, an undercover operative in a clandestine operation called The Activity. No badge. No trail. No laws applied to him. When the government wanted deniability, Cole was their man. He infiltrated wars and made important people vanish. Terror cells, traitors, anyone too close to the truth.

Somewhere between Baghdad and Bogotá, his cover was blown. He faked his death and walked straight into the underworld.

Now he's a trusted adviser in the Restrepo cartel's inner circle.

I can recite his resume down to how he takes his coffee, the VIN on his motorcycle, and every tattoo on his body. And his wife's body, too. But nothing I found on the dark web captures the disturbing, live-wire electricity that sizzles the air in his presence.

"So you're the notorious *Vigilante.*" He clicks his tongue. "The hacker who made the NSA shit itself."

"They should thank me for the warning shot."

"You got balls walking into Restrepo territory. Most people don't come back in one piece."

"I'm not most people."

"Yeah, I've seen your work. Dubai, Kiev, Râmnicu Vâlcea... I watched you erase an arms dealer's offshore empire in under an hour." He regards me for an eternity, tilting his head. "All this time, you kept your identity hidden. Why crawl out of your hole now?"

"Everyone crawls out for something." My heart kicks as I lean back, stretch my legs, and feign nonchalance.

"What's your something?"

"Not your concern."

"Fair enough." He smiles, and the dimples ruin it. Way too cute for a killer's face. "You don't cash a Restrepo favor unless you're willing to bleed for it. Are you willing to bleed for your *something*?"

"The way I see it, you owe me a favor. I'm calling it in. When it's done, we're even."

"You won't owe us after this." He taps his fingers on the armrest, slowly and rhythmically, calculating. "You'll belong to us."

They'll have to pull the bullets out of me first. I want out, not deeper in.

I want a world where Dove isn't in danger every second of

jag

every day.

"You look tense." Cole eyes me sidelong.

"I don't fly well."

"Liar."

He's right, of course. It's not the altitude that twists my gut. It's the fact that I'm about to walk into a nest of ruthless demons armed to the teeth. I've dealt with my share of violent criminal organizations, but I've never asked one for help.

"It's curious," he says. "You hate the world enough to fight it, but not enough to join it. That's a lonely place to stand."

"I'm used to lonely."

"Still, it's easier when you have a cause. You, me, the anarchists, and the patriots, we all tell ourselves we're burning down the world for this or that reason. But the best of us learned to smile while doing it."

"I'm the best. And I don't smile."

"Yeah." Popping those dimples with a grin, he stands and ambles toward the cockpit. "I noticed."

The plane eats miles and swallows whole countries. Time becomes a smear of coffee cups, crumpled napkins, and half-eaten meals. My phone stays off. Files flash through my head the way code slides down a monitor. Dove's face is the only image that refuses to pixelate.

My fingers itch for a keyboard I don't have, for a terminal I can't touch. Not knowing where Dove is or what she's doing is a special kind of torture. I tell myself Wolf's protecting her, not filling her with come. It's the only way I stay sane.

Hours fold into one another. I close my eyes and open them to a different sky. Stars stream past the window in slow motion. Cole reads a small tablet, thumbs drumming. Each glance he sends my way is a reminder that whatever we're about to do has been measured, weighed, and approved by people who don't blink.

We stop somewhere in Panama to refuel. After that, sleep comes in snatches, a nod against the seat, a dream that's filled with a teenage Dove who gazes upon me with love in her eyes. I wake to the phantom feel of her small pinky finger wrapped around mine and the stronger reality that her life now sits in the cartel's unmerciful hands.

jag

I spend the waking hours cleaning my mind the way I clean hard drives. Overwrite, overwrite, overwrite until the old traces are no longer relevant. I run scenarios, door codes, safe houses, and the names of men who might try to kill me.

Around midnight local time, the pilot announces our descent into Bogotá.

My palms slick with sweat, not from fear, but from focus. Whatever this place demands, I'll bear it. For her.

As the wheels slam onto the runway, Cole shifts toward me. "Welcome to enemy territory. Smile for the cameras. Everyone's watching."

The plane slows, and the engines wind down to a chilling hush. The door opens, letting in the humid night reeking of diesel and tropical rot.

I stand, roll my shoulders, and follow Cole down the stairs and onto a tarmac lined with armored SUVs and armed silhouettes.

No passports. No customs. No uniforms with crooked badges. This isn't an airport. It's a checkpoint for the damned, owned and operated by the Restrepo cartel.

Cole's hand lands on my shoulder, heavy and brief. "Frizz will take you from here."

Then he's gone, swallowed by the hum of turbines.

I turn, and a man unfolds himself from the back seat of the lead SUV. A young, slender man built of bones and shadows, his pressed black suit clinging to edges and hollows. And his mouth...

Holy fuck.

Thick black thread crisscrosses his lips, puckering the corners into a mockery of a smile. The stitches aren't neat, too human for a doctor, too practiced for an amateur.

His blue eyes bore into me, unblinking and shockingly bright. Eyes that have seen more than a lifetime's worth of nightmares and decided to collect them instead of forget.

He opens the door and motions me into the car, his movements deliberate, graceful even, but his presence frosts the air.

I climb into the back seat, and he joins me, shutting the door. The lock clicks, and the driver hits the accelerator.

What fresh hell am I racing into?

The city unfurls outside the tinted glass, and Frizz sits perfectly still beside me, hands clasped on his lap. Black gauze wraps his wrists with thin white thread biting into the fabric.

When he turns his head, the stitches on his lips gleam wet. New.

My insides shrivel. "Did the cartel do that to you?"

His mouth flattens into a hard line of anger, bunching the threads.

"Self-inflicted?" I lift a brow.

His lips relax as he hums softly, almost a whistle, emitting a twisted little tune that sounds cheerful until it isn't.

Christ. Please tell me he isn't singing "Dead Babies" by Alice Cooper.

Yeah. He definitely is.

The melody continues on a loop, crawling under my skin and getting comfortable there.

My mind scrolls through every file, every dossier I've scraped from cartel archives, and comes up empty. Nothing. No Frizz. No mention of a torturer with a knitted mouth and Edward Scissorhands vibes.

That's not oversight. It's intentional. Someone buried this man so deep that even the infamous *Vigilante* couldn't find him.

I keep my eyes forward. "I assume a conversation is out of the question."

A sound escapes him, a muffled exhale through the stitches. Not quite laughter. Not quite breathing. He looks away, watching the streets blur into the jungle-dark outskirts.

This thin, zipper-lipped creature isn't just some freak the cartel keeps on payroll. He's a weapon they take out when they want a clean, wordless transaction.

They could've taped my mouth shut and put a hood over my head. But that would've sent me into a fist-swinging struggle, ready to turn and burn and run.

Instead, they put me in a car with *this* guy.

His appearance alone disarms and intimidates. By design. Every time his haunting eyes flick toward me, I feel the weight of him measuring what I am, how I bleed, and how loud I'd scream. He hums as if already composing it.

Consider me officially unsettled. But I'm not running. Wherever we're headed, I'm ready to be there.

The convoy speeds through checkpoints that open without

jag

question. Eventually, the driver speaks a code word into the radio. We veer off the main road and onto a narrow strip of cracked asphalt that snakes between shanties and the black sprawl of jungle.

Up ahead, the neon glow of a club sign pulses pink against the night. Music leaks from every direction, low bass crawling through the ground.

We pull around to the back, where dumpsters steam and rats scatter. Two guards in tactical black wave us through an iron gate.

Frizz exits first and gestures for me to follow. He leads the way through a narrow corridor and down a stairwell, the concrete walls wet to the touch. As we pass under the bulbs, his stitched grin glints. Creepy as fuck.

I stay close, scanning corners, counting exits, doing the math of survival.

He stops before a door at the end of the hall. A heavy steel thing, painted black. Raising a pale hand, he taps twice.

The door opens with a mechanical buzz.

My heart hits overdrive, no permission given.

Turning toward me, Frizz hums a few cheerful notes, ushers me into a private lounge room, and locks me inside.

I'd be lying if I said I'll miss his face.

In the room, lamps glow amber behind red-tinted glass, turning the smoke-dense air into shades of blood. It smells like sex, booze, and money. The cartel's holy trinity.

A man sits on the couch. An empty chair waits across from him, a coffee table between, littered with ashtrays, a half-empty bottle of tequila, and a pistol. He rolls a toothpick between his lips, eyes steady on me.

Yeah. I know that face. The scar bisecting his cheek makes him look homemade, not born. Steel-cut jawline. Gunmetal eyes. Brutally handsome.

The toothpick rolls lazily between his lips. Calm. Too calm. The kind of calm that comes from killing enough people to find peace in it.

Van Quiso.

He doesn't introduce himself. No need. His reputation fills the room.

"Sit," he says, voice a slow rasp that could pass for civility if not for the dominating demand behind it.

I drop into the chair opposite him, every nerve stretched tight.

A fitted Henley clings to his muscular chest, the sleeves pushed to the elbows. His black jeans show no dirt or wear. Can't say the same for his heavy combat boots or the knife sheathed at his thigh.

He studies me. The toothpick spins. "Welcome to Colombia, *Vigilante*."

The alias sounds wrong coming from him, like he's trying it on to see if it fits.

I say nothing. Pretend I don't know who he is. Pretend I haven't read every classified whisper about the man who kidnapped, tortured, and trafficked humans in Texas.

"Relax." He smirks. "I don't bite. Not unless you're naked and bound to a rack."

I shiver.

In another life, I might've pursued that bite, even knowing what he is.

"Tell me something, *Vigilante*." His polite, too-soft voice carries an undercurrent of terror, a predator making small talk before the kill. "What does Jag stand for?"

My brain blanks.

No one here should know my real name. No one knows that name unless I choose to reveal it.

The thrashing of my pulse drowns out all other sound.

I recover fast. Shrug. Let my mouth twist into carefree indifference. "J-A-G. Just Another Guy. What does Van stand for?"

He grins, showing no surprise that I know his real name. "Vanquish."

Yeah. Figures.

"So, Jag." Legs spread, he props a boot on the opposite knee. "What has you desperate enough to come knocking on our door?"

jag
THIRTY-THREE

"You know why I'm here." I rub my chest, forcing my heartbeat to behave.

"The favor." Van flicks his fingers, impatient. "Let's hear it."

"I want a threat removed." Leaning forward, I let my hands dangle between my knees. "There's a criminal network hunting me."

"Adrian Crowe."

The name shoots ice down my spine.

Van Quiso saying it out loud tells me he already knows the threat and the terms of my favor.

Adrian Crowe founded House of Crowe, a network of shell companies that cater to talent agencies, retreat management, luxury villas, private aviation, and discreet shipping routes.

In other words, he runs a high-end sex-trafficking syndicate and cult-front organization for elite perverts and pedos, laundering influence and moving victims under the guise of luxury retreats, talent development, and global export logistics.

Of course, the cartel is aware of House of Crowe. Same trade, different criminals. They've been circling each other for years, feeding off the same industry and spilling blood every time their routes cross.

But how does the cartel know that Adrian Crowe is hunting me?

Van's gaze narrows on the bandaged splint on my broken wrist. No one has asked me about the injury. Because they already know.

"You're watching me." My scalp tingles.

"Not as expertly as you watch us."

No argument there. But that doesn't make the invasion of my privacy any less horrifying. How much do they know?

"House of Crowe found me in Sitka." I roll my neck. "I want them gone."

"Why are they hunting you?"

Is he testing me? Or does he truly not know about my unfinished history with Adrian Crowe? History I can't let go. Call it revenge. Or obsession. Or a goddamn suicide mission. Whatever. I've been hellbent on gutting that fucker for twenty years, but he's so deeply entrenched, networked, and insulated by decades of powerful alliances, he's impossible to dislodge.

Un-fucking-touchable.

Not that I'll admit any of that to Van. "I'm a threat."

He knows I'm hiding shit, but his expression doesn't change. He stares me down in that terrifyingly still way men like him do, parsing my words for weakness, not meaning.

"The FBI is hunting you, too." He raises a brow.

"I can handle the alphabet agencies. I want you to take down House of Crowe."

"Don't you think if we could take down that West Coast circus, we would've done it by now?"

I shrug.

"We can help you. But you have to help us." His sharp gaze digs into mine. "We want something in return."

I don't move.

"You're secretive, intelligent, tenacious. Gutsy as fuck." He cracks a grin, the toothpick jogging. "We need a man like that."

"You have plenty of men."

"A man who can erase a name off the map before breakfast."

I sigh, annoyed. "You owe me a favor."

"And you have a rare talent we want." He aims a finger at me. "We want to hire you."

"You want to own me."

"There are many shades of ownership."

jag

"Says the man who owned sex slaves and sold them to the highest bidder."

The sick fucking monster smiles.

"No one owns me." I straighten, hardening my tone. "I don't work for anyone. The answer is no."

"You'll change your mind."

"You'll have to kill me first. I won't give the remaining years of my miserable life to a cartel. I know how that story ends. There's only one way out."

He examines me for a long, unbearable moment. Then his mouth crooks. "You're not wrong."

Death.

That's the only way out.

But if I don't accept their offer, I'm dead anyway. They'll make sure of it.

Fuck.

Fuck.

Fuuuuuck!

I shouldn't have come here. I've fucked up fantastically, and every instinct screams for an exit.

The shadows stir behind him. A door creaks open, and two shapes emerge from the darkness.

As the figures float closer, they blur into living glitches, forming the wrong copies of something familiar.

At first, I think the smoke's playing tricks on me. Then I see the details. The same build. Same coloring. Similar facial features. One looks like Dove, the other like Wolf. A pair of distorted reflections. Almost indistinguishable.

Almost.

My gut squirms, telling me something's off. Little things like the missing beauty mole on the woman's collarbone and the slightly duller eye color on the man. Not noticeable to anyone.

I notice.

They stop in front of me, and I stop breathing. The resemblance is eerie enough to turn my stomach.

It's not them. It's not them.

The woman wears lace panties and nothing else. Long blue hair frames her honey-colored eyes. Her bone structure matches Dove's. Same facial hardware. Same pretty pierced nipples. They harden beneath my stunned perusal.

Fuck me to hell and back.

The guy towers over her, lean and pale. Black hair hanging wild, corset pinched tight, thigh-high fishnets decorating his long legs, rings stacking his fingers, and eyes painted in smoky black. A perfect echo of Wolf's chaos. Most of the meat on his body appears to be stuffed into his spandex thong, the massive bulge stretching at the seams.

"What is this?" My insides contract as I fight an unwanted surge of heat.

Van doesn't answer. He just watches, that half-smile curling under his scar.

The woman runs a hand along my shoulder, tracing the line of my collar, testing for a reaction. The man mirrors her, every movement synchronized.

"Proof." Van leans back on the couch. "That we can give you whatever you want. Faces, bodies, obedience. A world tailored to your needs."

"Sex slaves."

"They're here willingly. They want this."

"I don't." I knock their hands away. "I'm not here for this."

"Everyone's here for sex." He lifts a brow. "We exist to fuck, do we not?"

My sexual tastes run dark and freaky. Freaky enough to admit he's not wrong.

A month ago, I would've bent the Wolf-lookalike over the coffee table and fucked him bareback while holding Van's gaze.

But now?

I'm not tempted. Not even a little.

I've felt Wolf's touch and experienced his passion. And Dove? No one can replace her. Not now. Not ever. Hell knows I've tried.

"I'm here to call in a favor." I dodge the breasts bouncing in my face. "Remove House of Crowe from Alaska. That's it. Get them off my back, and we're done."

"If we do that, what then? You crawl back to your cot in the tattoo shop and pretend Adrian won't send more crows to Alaska?"

How the fuck does he know I sleep on a cot? Dread ices my stomach.

"You could have power here." He spreads his arms, indicating his violent world. "Money, control, and all the little

jag

birds and wolves your cock desires."

In exchange, he wants the same thing Adrian Crowe wants. A hacker who can outthink, outcode, and outghost the competition.

Except Crowe doesn't just want me. He wants the one thing I'll never surrender.

Dove.

"We'll fix your problem." Van twitches a shoulder in a lazy shrug, as if my decision doesn't matter. "Your dove and her wolf can go on living their safe fairy tale, while you build something real with us. Win-win."

The hot, unmistakable touch of Fake-Wolf's leather bulge rubs against my arm.

I jerk away. "Is this a game?"

"It's a down payment. They're yours to do with whatever you want."

"Everything I want is in Sitka."

For a heartbeat, Van studies me, his gray eyes cold as winter. The toothpick turns once, a slow rotation. "You have attachment problems, Jag. In this business, emotion will kill you faster than a bullet."

He wants to go there? Fine. We'll go there.

I reach up and fist my good hand in Not-Wolf's hair. The man's startled gaze flies to mine.

"Take off your clothes." I release him, roughly.

He jumps into action, loosening the ties on his corset and peeling off his fishnet stockings. With a seductive curl of his body, he positions himself in the space between my knees, standing before me in just the thong.

"Did I tell you to stop?" I direct my gaze at the remaining fabric.

Biting down on a grin, he shimmies off the thong and angles his impressive erection toward my face.

I recline into a sprawl and rest my chin on my loosely curled fist. "Are you a good kisser, handsome?"

"Yes." He runs a hand along his twitching dick. "Very good."

"Show me."

He bends, bringing his mouth toward mine.

I stop him with a finger against his lips.

"Not me." I nod to the silver-eyed monster on the couch.

"Him."

Naked Wolf freezes, and genuine fear crosses his pretty features.

"Go on. Both of you." I pat his hip and wave the decoys toward Van.

"What are you doing?" Van straightens. "They're yours."

"To do with whatever I want." My eyes lock onto his. "This is what I want. I want you to fuck them while I watch."

I give the lookalikes a nod, wordlessly ordering them to do my bidding.

Slowly, stiffly, they walk to the couch and kneel on the cushions, bracketing Van. The woman doesn't appear to be breathing as she reaches for his shirt.

"Stop." He catches her wrist and pushes her away.

That was fast.

"Attachment is a problem. Emotion will get you killed." I lean forward, shooting Van a knowing look. "That advice from the man who keeps his wife locked in a cartel fortress she's too afraid to leave."

The toothpick stops moving.

I keep going. "Amber, right? The pageant queen. Agoraphobic. Is she still counting the tiles on her bathroom floor to keep the panic away?"

Van's jaw works, a muscle feathering near the scar.

"How far will you go to protect her from this life?" I ask quietly. "Same as me, I bet. Far enough to *vanquish* anything that threatens her."

The toothpick hangs limply on his lip, forgotten. For the first time since I walked in, he looks human. Not weaker. Just real.

The room holds its breath, the tension suffocating.

Then it shatters when *she* walks in.

No jewelry or designer gown. No entourage of bodyguards. Nothing to signal she's the queen of the cartel. Just her fuck-all presence and warrior prowess. That's all she needs.

Camila Dias is a legend, on and off the battlefield. She strides toward me with precise shoulders and a cat-stepped gait, the kind of posture that makes people sit straighter without realizing why.

Her matte-black combat suit fits like it was made for motion, not show, the buckles and straps stashed with countless weapons.

jag

No unnecessary accessories. No flourishes. Not for a badass Latina who shares a bed with the bloodthirsty kingpin of the Colombian cartel.

At her nod, the lookalikes fade into the shadows and exit the room, suddenly irrelevant.

Camila lowers onto the couch beside Van as if the seat is hers by right.

"You have a little something…" She plucks the fallen toothpick off Van's chest and drops it in an ashtray.

Scowling, he pulls a fresh one from his pocket.

She turns her attention to me, stares for two beats, then tilts her head like she's taken a taste.

"*El Vigilante* in the flesh." The soft vowels of Mexican-Spanish curl around her accent. "I'm—"

"Camila Dias. Wife of Matias Restrepo. Queen of the cartel and founder of The Shadow Collection."

Her eyes glitter. No need for theatrics. She's not here to prove anything. She's here to collect.

"I told you he was good," she says to Van.

"Too good." His scowl deepens.

Great. He's still pissed I said all those things about his wife. All true, but that won't stop him from separating my head from my body.

"He knows our secrets." Camila stares at me full-on.

I know everything about every man and woman in their inner circle. I know their lovers, their spouses, their children, all the weaknesses they keep safely hidden.

The light catches the braid at her nape, drawing my gaze to the teeth marks on her throat. A fresh bite.

I bet her capo husband is here, probably standing on the other side of that door, ready to rip out my throat if I look at her wrong.

The chances of me walking out of here alive? Slim to none.

"Thank you." She crosses her legs, adjusting the blades on her thighs. "For showing up. And for saving my life."

Her gratitude strikes off my bones. I saved her life once, and she may be the reason I lose mine. What a turn.

"I've been watching you," she says. "Studying what jobs you choose, what you won't sell, and who you protect. I like what I see. Loyalty is rarer than talent. Most men sell it fast."

"I'm loyal to no one."

"That's not true." Her gaze hardens, but there's a soft edge beneath it. "You're loyal to her."

I hate that they know my weakness.

It must show on my face, because she says, "That's not a weakness, Jag Rath. It's leverage. It's motive. It makes you dependable, and it makes you useful."

Useful. Like I'm a thing that can be handed over, wrapped and delivered.

Van watches me closely, toothpick between his teeth like a metronome.

"Here's the plain part." Camila wets her lips. "Adrian Crowe loves nothing and no one. Except himself. He hides in charities, elite circles, and polite smiles. He built an industry around innocence and traffics girls the way his politician friends collect rare wines. We want him gone. Annihilated. Out of our way."

I want to hear the how. I don't ask it yet. She can tell I'm not a man who signs blank checks.

"We can do it," she says. "But not without you. We need the kind of hit that leaves no trace. Someone who can make the world forget a household name. Someone who makes people vanish from every ledger and server. You're that man."

She goes on about the operation, her words coldly tactical as she details the routes to choke, shell companies to collapse, and private manifests to expose. She paints a map that I already know by heart.

"And the price?" I already know that, too.

"Sacrifice." She lets out a breath that could be a smile. "Everything worth saving costs us. Matias gave up his childhood sweetheart to become a fearsome *jefe* so others could survive. Cole lost his fiancée and burned every bridge back to his law-abiding world. Van gave up..." She winces. "Things I won't put into words. We've all bled for this life."

Sacrifice. I've spent half my life bleeding for Dove. Every line of code, every murder, every sleepless night spent tracing Crowe's shadow. If sacrifice is the price of love, I've been paying in installments for twenty years.

But this? This feels different. Bigger. Permanent.

I stare at the floor between my boots, trying to keep my pulse from showing in my neck. The idea of joining them curdles in my gut. I've lived too long in my own orbit, too used to being the ghost in the system, not part of one. I don't trust causes. They start righteous and end in death.

Still, she's not wrong.

Crowe's reach is longer than mine. If I keep going at this alone, Dove dies. Maybe Wolf, too. Maybe me.

"I want your loyalty." Camila's brown eyes swirl with empathy, the kind that's been weaponized, earned through pain, and honed for persuasion. "I want you not as a slave. Not as a bought man. I want you beside us, for the season we need you. Help us take down Crowe cleanly, permanently, and you'll get what you want. Your stepsister gets to keep living. You get to keep the things that matter."

She reaches into the language people like her use. Honor, sacrifice, liberation. It's the kind of pitch men in uniforms make when they want soldiers to trade blood for a cause. It lands differently coming from her. I feel the truth under the rhetoric. She believes it. She's lived it. Or she's the best liar I've ever met.

I drag my good hand over my face, feeling the grit of sweat and resistance.

Keep the things that matter.

Yeah. That's the problem. People like me don't get to keep things that matter. We destroy them trying to protect them.

"You want me to join you," I say flatly. "Not work for you. *Join.*"

"Yes." She sways closer, teasing my senses with hints of orange blossom on her skin, an old scent, a memory of her grove, sweetly human in a room full of predators. "Stand with us. Use your skill. You won't answer to Matias the capo or Van the enforcer. You'll answer to the mission, the operation." Her expression hardens. "If you can't bear that, we can't help you. The only way I'll guarantee Dove's safety is if I know you're not going to turn on us when things get ugly."

I want to refuse. I want to spit my objections and leave with my chest empty of bargains. I remember the way Van spoke of ownership. The cartel eats men like me with bullets and lifetime contracts and favors that turn into collars.

But I see Dove's face when I close my eyes. I feel Wolf's hand on my chest, massaging me. I see the cot, the duffel bag of meager belongings, the thin life I taped together in Sitka. I see a thousand little reasons to hand over my life to these violent avengers.

"What's the catch?" My pulse buzzes in my ears.

"We don't promise you immortality. We promise results. We promise that when it's done, House of Crowe will be dead and dismantled, along with its founder. We promise protection for Dove and Wolf. Real protection, not the bandage you came here for. We ask for your blood on the plan. You will be exposed. You will be used. You will be expected to choose us over yourself at the moment it counts."

Silence opens in the room like a held breath. Van's toothpick turns slowly, his razor eyes unblinking.

I touch the base of my throat, the place where promises settle and decisions weigh. The answer sits there, raw and half-made.

"You want loyalty." I swallow. "You want a man who won't flinch."

"Yes." Her eyes are blades, homing in on the right place to cut.

"I'm flinching. You know why? Because I don't want to belong to anyone."

"You already belong to someone. We're offering you the best chance to keep her. But it costs. Everything worth saving costs. Join us."

"Join us." Van winks. "If you're not a fucking pussy."

If they thought I was a pussy, I wouldn't be here.

The offer is simple and terrible. The room waits for me to sign, to refuse, to decide whether I'll become their weapon or die trying to stay outside their ranks.

My pulse slams as I unclench my jaw and meet her eyes. "Tell me the plan."

Not yes. Not no. Not surrender. Just a foothold I can use to leave this room alive.

dove
THIRTY-FOUR

Daylight fades without either of us noticing. Wolf's bed smells like hearth smoke, the sheets rumpled, the air steeped in that faint wildness that's all him.

Three days have passed since I started reading the journals. I've slept an hour here and there, my body running on caffeine, emotion, and the unbearable ache of everything I've seen through those pages.

Wolf made sure I ate, bringing me soup, coffee, and whatever he threw together in the kitchen. But mostly he's been giving me space, hovering nearby, sketching, or scrolling on his phone.

We haven't left the island. Hell, we've barely left the guest house. Taaq told me to take as much time as I needed. My job will be there when I return.

Jag has been uncharacteristically quiet. He sent a text yesterday telling me not to leave the island, all his usual threats on the surface, but unsettling underneath.

Stay on the island? Why? I expected him to demand the opposite and don't know what to make of it. Honestly, I don't have the emotional capacity to dig into whatever mind game he's playing right now.

love

The journals lie closed beside me, heavy as coffins, the pages discolored with fingerprints and tear stains.

My eyes sting from reading and crying and not sleeping, but for the first time, I don't feel like I'm trespassing in Wolf's pain. I'm part of it now.

I sit cross-legged on his bed, hands slack on my lap. He sprawls beside me, one arm folded under his head, the other resting over his chest. His eyes are open, shadowed, watching the ceiling.

He looks calm in that deceptive way of his, mouth lazy, lids hooded, but the small tics give him away. The flex of his throat, the twitch of his fingers against his ribs, the way he swallows as if it burns going down.

He's waiting for me to say something.

I don't know where to start. My head is a burning field of nightmares.

Twenty-three years in the Arctic Circle. Twenty-three years of captivity, abuse, and isolation. Raised like an animal under Denver's sick perversions. Taught to kill, survive, and shun all hope.

Then the river. The cage without windows. Rhett Howell's scalpel and the dark.

And finally, Sitka. Six months of learning how to exist among people.

He wrote about his first visit to a grocery store. How he stood in the aisle for thirty minutes, too overwhelmed by choice to buy anything. How Monty had to teach him to cross streets without freezing at the sound of an engine. How technology had both fascinated and terrified him.

He wrote about people as if they were another species. The way strangers stared at him when he forgot to blink. The way laughter in a restaurant felt like gunfire.

He wrote about the day Declan gave him a tattoo machine and told him to try. The trembling in his hands. The vibration reminding him of something awful before it became something healing. Drawing on skin instead of splitting it with a scalpel. Control instead of helplessness.

He found purpose in ink.

Maybe that's what keeps him tethered. Not sane, but whole enough to be kind. To be human.

For all his darkness, he's the most colorful person I've ever met. His moods swing like the weather, storm one minute, sunlight the next. He talks with his hands, hums while he cooks, and makes faces when he thinks.

He hasn't told me he cares, but he shows it a hundred sideways ways, by feeding me, teasing me, and guarding my quiet.

For someone who lived his entire life in the dark, he's the only person I know who tries to make other people feel happy and bright.

But after reading every word in his journal, there's one thing missing. The trigger that sent him spiraling in the shower.

What happened between him and Jag that day?

I shift on the bed, pulling my knees to my chest. The light from the small lamp drapes a quiet warmth over Wolf's face, his lashes absurdly black.

"I understand now." My voice scratches.

"What's that?" His eyes remain on the ceiling.

"The reason you jumped. I don't know how you managed to endure as long as you did. You're a lot braver than I am."

"Brave is not what that was."

"You survived hell. Literal, actual hell on Earth." I stare at my hands. "I don't even know how to talk about it. I feel like I lived twenty-four years in three days."

"I hope it doesn't stick to you, Bluebird. The evil. The soullessness. I don't want you seeing what I see when I close my eyes."

"What do you see?"

"The doctor's ghost. He knows I fear him the most, so he stays." He taps a finger against his temple.

"Yet you killed him. I think he's the one afraid of you."

"You don't need to fix me." He looks away, eyes shuttering halfway.

"I'm not trying to fix you. I'm trying to understand you."

"That's worse."

I breathe out a whispered, broken laugh.

"All I'm saying is..." He sighs. "I don't want you haunted by my little life of horrors. One of us losing sleep over it is enough."

"And all I'm saying is..." I trace the cover of his journal. "I opened Pandora's box, and the monsters didn't fly out. They just lay there, defeated and chopped up. Hardly the apocalypse you promised."

He snorts a deep laugh, his eyes glimmering. I see love in that stare, but we're too new for that, the idea of us too uncertain and ill-fated.

If I stay, he dies. That's my track record with men. The only certainty I have. I can't lose sight of that.

"I know how hard this was for you." I gesture at his journal. "You wrote about everything. Your mother, Denver, the doctor, adjusting to civilization, and even things about me." I pause. "But not Jag."

His whole body stiffens, rippling tension through the mattress.

"What happened with him?" I ask.

His throat works around something he can't swallow. The smirk is gone. The black makeup, sequins, and lace all gone, leaving the scarred remains of a man staring into a dark that still answers back.

He rolls onto his side to face me, and his purple robe falls open. A robe I now know belonged to the woman who gave birth to him. The woman he killed when he was only eight because she viciously preyed on his brother.

The fabric parts enough for the lamplight to find him, illuminating his chest. His scars. I see them differently now. More than the healed-over crosshatching of trauma. They're stories written in a knotted weave of threads, some thin and silvery, others bubbled and raised. A road map of pain that travels from his collarbone, down his ribs, and fades into the shadows beneath the robe.

My throat aches, not from horror but from heartbreak. He doesn't flinch under my stare, but his eyes flick away, like he's bracing for disgust or pity.

He won't find either.

All I want to do is reach out and soothe the hurt with my fingertips. Let him know his past doesn't scare me. That it doesn't make him less. That, if anything, it makes him more. Proof of how much life he's fought to keep.

My hand rises halfway before I stop myself. The fragile space between us shivers. I don't want to break the spell by asking permission, but I also don't want to steal something he isn't ready to give.

When his gaze finally comes back to mine, there's a flicker there. A question. Maybe an invitation.

"You ever touch a bruise and feel it ache even when it's healed?" He captures my hovering hand, holding it immobile.

"Yes."

"That's what happened with Jag."

I wait, saying nothing.

"Jag and I..." He regards me like I'm another cliff, another leap. "Your stepbrother pushed me past a line. I didn't even know where it was until I crossed it."

My heart beats unevenly. "A line?"

"Between pain and pleasure. Between control and collapse." He pulls on my hand, flattening my palm against his exposed scars. "Between me being a survivor and the fucked-up freak my abusers created."

I hold impossibly still.

"Jag made me remember things I didn't want to remember." He slowly runs his tongue over his bottom lip, thoughtful. "He made me feel things I didn't know I could."

"What did you feel?"

"Desire. Panic. Rapture. All at extreme levels all at once." He presses my hand harder against his chest. "I thought I was done being anyone's victim. But he's not like the men who hurt me. He's something different. Dangerous in another way."

"Did he hurt you?"

"No. But he could have, and I would've let him."

My chest squeezes, aching for him. And for the part of me that knows I'll lose him before I even have him.

He strokes his thumb along the back of my hand. "I had that classy moment in the shower because I didn't understand my reaction to Jag. Didn't know if it made me broken or human. I mean, how can I want a man to touch me after I spent my life hating a man's touch?"

So much to unpack there. I can barely breathe. "Wolf..."

"Don't say anything yet." He releases my hand, breaking the contact as he pushes to sit before me. "I need you to know that it's not simple. Nothing about him or me or what happened is simple."

I nod. The lump in my throat is too big for words anyway.

"He built a room for me in the tattoo shop." He goes on to explain how he found Jag with a fever, called in Frankie, and

love

washed him, all of which led to an unexpectedly intimate moment. "I touched him. Then I kissed him. Then I gave us both a crazy, intense release. Through it all, I refused to let him touch me. How fucked up is that?"

The confession hangs there, human and hurting.

My first reaction isn't compassion. It's jealousy. Dark, toxic, and irrational, it burns behind my ribs. I picture Wolf's beautiful nude body entangled with Jag's, the man who's tormented me for years, and it guts me.

But underneath that twisting misery is a quieter, more profound emotion.

Understanding.

If I strip away the jealousy, what's left is pain. Wolf's pain, not mine. A boy who never learned the difference between a cruel touch and an affectionate one. A man who's trying to figure out if desire can ever mean safety.

He watches me as if waiting for judgment, for recoil, and that's what undoes me completely.

I edge closer, slow enough that he can stop me if he wants.

His breathing stumbles, and his eyes flick down, wary. He expects me to weaponize tenderness.

"You don't owe me shame for what happened." I reach out, fingers trembling, and let my hand rest against his chest. "You don't owe me excuses or explanations. Just the truth. That's enough."

His muscles twitch under my palm, but he doesn't pull away.

The jealousy still simmers, but it's diluted now, melted into a feral protectiveness that demands I keep him safe from everything that tries to twist love into pain.

I don't know what we are, but I know what I want.

I want to be the first touch that doesn't hurt.

love

THIRTY-FIVE

Wanting Wolf isn't enough. Not after everything he's lived through.

If I put my hands on him without understanding every land mine planted beneath his skin, I could hurt him in irreparable ways. I'm not afraid of his scars or the ghosts in his head. I'm afraid of becoming one of them.

And there's something else, something he doesn't see yet.

He needs space to understand himself. Not what Denver beat into him. Not what fear taught him. Not what Jag sparked and confused.

Him.

He needs a healthy perspective about what he wants, who he wants, and why. His orientation isn't a trauma scar, and it isn't a debt he owes to anyone.

He needs to know his desire is his own.

He deserves that.

And so do I.

"There's nothing wrong with your sexuality." I meet his eyes. "If you're attracted to men, explore those desires. If you like women, pursue both. Figure out what fits. But if Jag is what you crave..."

love

"Is it true what they say? Once you stray to gay, you can't stay away?"

"No. First off, I don't think you've ever been straight. And second, that's an offensive generalization."

"I don't know what I am. I don't want men or women or anything as boring as that. I want a dove."

My chest flutters. "You want Jag."

He opens his mouth, and I see the denial forming.

"You already admitted as much." I sigh. "Just... Please don't pursue this thing with him. Not because he's a man, but because he's Jag. He's dangerous."

"I want *you*." He doesn't say it defensively. He delivers it like a vow that can't be undone. Resolved. Unshaken. Fearlessly honest.

My pulse swoons, tripping over itself.

I want him, too. So damn much. But the thought terrifies me. I don't want to be the easy choice, the soft landing after pain. I don't want to be the one he experiments on just to see if it feels different.

"Wolf..." My voice trembles. "You've been through too much. I don't want to be a trigger. Or worse, a regret."

"You won't be either." He drifts closer, his nearness pulling at me, the heat in his eyes smoldering.

"I need to know what you and Jag did. I don't want to hurt you."

"You won't."

"How do you know that?"

"You don't have the anatomy." His gaze sweeps over my body. "No parts that trigger me."

"That doesn't tell me enough."

"Yeah, didn't figure it would." His unflinching stare hooks mine for a silent beat. Then he speaks, voice quiet and stripped down. "At the shop, Jag dared me to prove my heterosexuality. He was weak with fever, too weak to be threatening, sprawled out on his cot, half-dead and stupidly vulnerable, looking at me like... I don't know. The way he looked at me made me feel wanted. Desired. Not the way Denver made me feel. Not in a manipulative, despicable way. For a hot minute there, it didn't feel wrong. Maybe that's Jag's game. He says all the right things and gets in your head." He shrugs. "It worked."

I've been on the receiving end of Jag's looks and understand exactly what Wolf's describing. But I keep that to myself, not interrupting. Barely breathing.

"He promised to keep his hands to himself. His broken wrist over there, his other arm behind his head." His eyes drift somewhere behind me. "I couldn't resist the offer. I needed to know. So I touched him. Jerked him. Not gently either." A muscle jumps in his jaw. "I was mean, every stroke of my fist fueled by anger and confusion and shame. He didn't stop me, and that only made me want him more."

A jealous spasm erupts in my stomach, but I tamp it down because this isn't about me. It's about him learning what it means to want without fear.

"I leaned into it." His fingers pick at the edge of his robe, the movement restless. "I had to know if it felt different with a man who wasn't forcing himself on me. Someone who wasn't my self-proclaimed father."

My throat closes around a hot ember.

"It did. It felt different. Jag kept his promise and didn't touch me. Maybe it was his fever, but I think he would've let me do just about anything I wanted to him. So I did. I pulled myself out and jerked us both off in one hand. But you know what really messed me up? I hurt him the way Denver hurt me, and Jag got off on it. He fucking enjoyed it. And so did I. It was the first orgasm I ever had with another person."

My nails dig into my palms, but I keep my face steady.

"I never enjoyed what Denver did to me," he whispers. "Sometimes, my body responded to his abuse against my will, and I hated that. But I never climaxed. Not even close." He forces a shaky, bitter laugh. "Denver did, though. He took pleasure in hurting me. And when I was with Jag, I got off on hurting him. What does that make me?"

He stares at his lap, his entire posture caving inward, as if waiting for me to reject him.

"It makes you normal, Wolf. Look at me." I wait for his gaze and soften my expression. "You were two consenting adults, sharing a heated moment. If Jag didn't want your touch, fever or not, he would've shut it down. I know you know that."

"Maybe. Didn't stop me from falling face-first into crazy town afterward. Not because of what we did together, but because of what I felt."

love

"You're not crazy." I reach up and touch his jaw, my thumb brushing the faint stubble there.

"Debatable." He leans in, his timbre rumbling in that low, rough register that always finds its way under my skin. "Now you know all my unsexy secrets and regrets."

"Do you regret what you did with Jag?"

"No." He searches my eyes. "Is that the part that sends you running?"

"I don't want to leave you."

His face softens, just enough to hurt.

"But," I whisper, "I can't stay."

The softness shatters. "Why the hell not?"

"It's not you." I hate how cliché that sounds. Even more, I hate how true it is. "It's the risk."

"What risk?" His jaw clicks, nostrils flaring. "You think you'll hurt me? That's as insulting as—"

"Jag."

"Jag?" His expression shifts. Not fear. Not surprise. More like annoyance that I picked the wrong subject to argue.

"What about him?"

"You know what he does." My chest tightens. "People die around him. Men who show interest in me. He's possessive and violent—"

"He wouldn't kill me." He says it like it's obvious, matter-of-fact, like a man defending his lover.

The jealousy hits again, a stupid flash low in my stomach. "Wolf..."

"I'm not one of your abusive foster brothers or pervy stalkers, begging for Jag's wrath. He and I have an understanding."

"Oh, because you shared an orgasm together, you're no longer his enemy?"

"Well... Yeah."

"Gavin is dead, Wolf." I hug my waist.

"What?" He stiffens. "Your ex? When?"

I pull up the obituary on my phone and hand it to him.

He reads it and loosens a disbelieving breath. Then he presses the back button and sees the text from Gavin's mother.

"You learned about this four days ago." He pins me with an accusing glare. "Why didn't you tell me?"

"I learned about it right before I found you in the shower and…" I wave my hand around. "There hasn't been a good time to bring it up."

"That's no excuse. *Christ.*" He rakes his fingers through his hair, his features gentling. "You shouldn't have carried that alone. You could've told me. I would've held some of it for you."

"You were dealing with enough."

"Give me some credit, darling. I'm built to handle the heavy stuff."

"You're right. I'm sorry."

"Do you want to talk about it? About Gavin's death?"

I flinch. "No."

"How did he die?"

"Jag." My chest constricts. "Jag killed him."

"How do you know?" His face goes pale and feral all at once.

"It's always him, Wolf. It's what he does."

"So that's it? You're leaving me because you think he's coming for me next?"

"I'm trying to protect you." My voice cracks. "Not ruin your life. Not drag you into mine."

"Protect me?" He stands abruptly, anger blasting off him. "I've survived things that would snap most people in half. Stop trying to guard me like I'm fragile."

"Not fragile." I lift my chin. "But you're not invincible. And Jag—"

"He would never kill me!"

"He killed Gavin!" I stand, too, breath shaking. "Gavin was his lover. He knew Gavin had fallen for him, and he killed him anyway. What do you think he'll do to you once he realizes you—" I bite down on my trembling lip.

"Once he realizes what?" He presses into my space, the air between us boiling.

I look down at the phone in his hand then back at him. "Once he realizes you want him *and* me."

"That's not—" His eyes flash with hurt, anger, and possession all tangled together. "That's *my* problem, not yours."

"Dammit, Wolf."

"You want to leave me? Then give me a reason that isn't Jag."

I open my mouth.

Nothing comes out.

Because I don't have another reason. Not one that holds up.

love

He sees it, feels it, and makes a wicked growling sound that vibrates my bones, terrifying in its certainty. "Then you're not leaving."

"You can't keep me here." I cross my arms.

"No." He puts his face in mine, his breath hot on my lips. "But I can be very persuasive."

"Why?" I retreat, dropping my head in my hands before meeting his feral blue eyes. "Why are you fighting so hard for me? You can have anyone you want. Men, women, whoever. I'm not your fairy tale princess. I'm a disaster. I can barely keep my life from setting itself on fire."

He stares at me like I'm speaking a foreign language.

"I'm a fucked-up mess." My hands fly to my hair, tugging at the roots. "A messy, unwanted orphan who aged out of the system. No parents. No friends. I'm in no place to be good for anyone. I need to get my shit together before I even think about being with someone."

"How?" His expression twists. "I don't see it. How are you fucked-up?"

I freeze, my lungs buckling. "I was eight when my mother was killed."

He blinks. "I was eight when I killed mine."

Regret punches me so hard my stomach pitches. I shouldn't have said it like that. Shouldn't have thrown my pain down between us like a challenge. My mother was stolen from me. His was a monster he had to stop.

I search for the right words to take it back, to fix it, but the compassion in his gaze tells me he understands what I meant.

He looks down at the purple robe draped around him. Her robe. A shadow crosses his eyes, and something decisive and final settles there.

Before I can ask, he reaches for my hand, his grip determined. He doesn't give me a chance to resist as he leads me downstairs, each step creaking under our weight, the guest house quiet around us.

In the living room, he kneels before the fireplace, flicks on the gas starter, and watches the flames catch.

"Your mother loved you," he says quietly. "You had that, even if only for eight years. That makes you whole, Dovey. Not damaged. Lucky, even." He stands and sheds the robe. "I never had a mother."

My eyes sting as he begins to shred the robe, ripping it into strips and feeding the pieces into the fire. The flames accept it hungrily, devouring the fabric and its history.

"Let her be gone." He stares into the blaze, watching the purple scraps curl inward as they burn, crumbling into blackened edges and ash. "Let the past be done. Let this be the start of something else."

I swat at the wetness on my cheeks, fighting the sob trapped in my throat.

He turns toward me, arms outstretched, standing in nothing but his scars and tight black briefs, nothing to hide behind now, nothing to shield him from being seen.

"This is me. Bared. Exposed." He raises that strong, square-cut jaw. "Take a good, hard look."

"Wolf." The sob wins, choking my breath.

"Do it! Look at me!"

God help me, I do.

The firelight paints him in molten shadows, every angle sharpened, every scar highlighted. He towers over me by a foot, all lean muscle and long lines. The defined shoulders, arms mapped with veins, sculpted chest and abs, and solid power in his legs.

He looks both dangerous and vulnerable, half-wild and wholly human, staring at me with a challenge and a question in his gleaming eyes.

An achy pressure climbs my throat, swelling through me until my skin feels too tight to hold it.

"No one's ever gotten this close." He floats closer. "Tell me what you see. The truth, Heart-thief. You know me better than anyone."

My mouth goes dry, but the truth is right there, clawing its way out.

"I see an artist," I whisper. "Someone who feels everything too deeply and turns it into magic and meaning."

He keeps his face unreadable.

"I see strength. Soul. Wild beauty." My voice breaks. "Compassion. More than you think you have."

His gaze drags down my face, hungrily searching, as if trying to absorb every syllable.

My eyes flicker lower, unbidden and involuntary, and land

on the unmistakable shape forming beneath the black fabric of his briefs.

"And..." I swallow hard. "I see desire."

"I'm so turned on right now."

A burst of sparks arouses every nerve ending in my body. "I know the feeling."

The shift in him is immediate. His eyes darken. His lips part, and his muscles tense, readying.

"You want me." He steps behind me, so close his breath stirs my hair. "Deny it."

"Can't do that."

He circles slowly, a predator's prowl, deliberate and controlled. His fingertips graze my hip, a featherlight caress that makes my heartbeat ricochet.

"I want you, too." He flicks his tongue against my earlobe. "What are we going to do about all this *wanting*?"

My knees weaken.

He comes around to my front, his chest rising and falling, every inch of him confident in an unrehearsed way. This is instinctual. The real him. The alpha wolf.

He lifts a hand and touches my jaw with the brush of his knuckles, lighting fireworks in my veins.

"You're going to stay." He lowers his head and nips at the sensitive spot beneath my ear. "You'll give us a week. Just you and me. No work. No leaving the island. We're going to hole up here and get to know each other *really* fucking well."

My lungs can't keep up, and my heart races so fast I fear I'll pass out.

"We'll spend time talking." He traces a slow line down my arm with one finger. "Touching." His lips ghost near my cheekbone without landing. "Exploring." His hand settles at the base of my spine, warm and assertive.

Every word curls around my ribs, every touch coiling a fierce need inside me. I can't feel my face. My skin tingles everywhere, and the hollow ache in my chest transforms into a bright, urgent pounding, pounding, pounding.

"I'm going to learn everything about you." He tucks a strand of hair behind my ear, his fingers lingering at the hinge of my jaw. "All of you. Your mind. Your body. Every secret. Every warm, dark place. Inside and out."

All the arguments I rehearsed melt beneath the heat of him, and my body betrays me. A breath caught too long, a pulse that skips, and he notices.

"Before the week ends..." Pressing closer, close enough to let me know how goddamn hard and hungry he is, he takes my face in his hands, tips my head back, and forces my eyes to his. "You'll fall in love with me."

He's frighteningly right. I'm already falling.

The electricity between us is unbearable, want threaded through fear, tenderness tangled with risk. His hand cups the back of my neck, holding me there, asking without words.

Despite my exhaustion, despite the grief and fear and everything breaking apart in my life, a warm glow cracks open inside me. A yes I'm not ready to say aloud. A want I can't swallow down. A need that erases all rational thought.

This time, I don't pull away.

I open my mouth, and he captures it, not gently, not cautiously, but with a certainty that steals every scrap of air from my lungs.

The kiss hits me sideways, knocking me off balance in the shockwave. His hand fists my hair. His other collars my throat. A desperate claiming wrapped in tenderness, complete control, and domination.

I liquefy.

He tilts his head and deepens the kiss, bolder, wetter, coaxing, and demanding. His lips move over mine with a reverence I've never felt, memorizing, learning, and infusing me with deep hunger.

My fingers clutch his shoulders, tight, greedy, aching for more, and he answers with a rough, guttural growl against my mouth, unraveling me.

The world narrows to taste and breath and the impossible pressure of his mouth on mine.

The hand in my hair wanders to my waist, pulling me flush against his chiseled body, aligning our hips. Then he grinds.

Oh, God.

I gasp into him, and he smiles against my lips, a dark, knowing curve. He kisses me again, harder this time, swallowing the sound I make as if it belongs to him.

Everything inside me tightens, sparks, shivers, and gushes. It's dizzying, devastating. A one-of-a-kind kiss that resets the

love

tectonic plates in a woman's heart.

"Tell me you felt that." He pulls back, his forehead against mine, breath shaky, eyes dark and heavy-lidded.

My entire body trembles, my mouth swollen, my pulse thundering like I've been kissed down to the bone.

"I felt it."

"Good." His seductive bedroom eyes make my knees give out all over again. "Remove your clothes."

wolfson
THIRTY-SIX

I've imagined this moment in a hundred filthy, half-formed ways over the years, never believing it would actually happen. Never believing I would be standing in front of a woman, let alone the hottest Disney princess that ever existed, waiting for her to strip for me.

God's balls on a gold chain, I'm fucking feral for Dove Rath. Like I'm shaking, panting, so fucking turned on I'm making a dick-dribbling mess in my underwear.

I hope she's leaking, too. I want her honey all over my face.

My heart slams, and every nerve in my body fires at once. I've only ever seen one woman naked, and those moments in the cabin with Frankie are bound in pain. Nothing my mind can twist into pleasure. Nothing that taught me a single damn thing about how this is supposed to feel.

Everything I know about sex, the mechanics, the rhythm, the way bodies fit and react, I learned from porn. *All* the porn. Every category, kink, and gender combination. Not because I needed it. Hell, I can get off with my imagination alone. But I wanted to understand the rules. The steps. How to make someone feel good. How to take someone apart slowly. How to read a body in all its aroused glory.

Not gonna lie. My extensive research has made me cocky as hell.

I'm a fast learner. Especially when the thing I want to learn is standing right here.

Her eyes lift to mine, pupils blown, and lips swollen. Her breathing comes quick and fractured, like she's trying not to melt into the floor. She's not stepping back.

She wants this.

She wants me.

I've held her hand, kissed her lips, brushed my mouth along her throat, and seen her pierced tits.

But not this.

This is a locked door in my scarred chest swinging wide open.

This is the monumental, long-overdue surrender of my virginity.

My body throbs so hard I can barely catch a breath. I'm harder than I've ever been, my need so rabid it blurs the edges of my vision.

She floats closer, her throat bobbing and her hands hovering near my stomach. Her lashes lower and lift, and her breathing tumbles into a soft shiver as her gaze rests on my mouth.

That look alone nearly makes me come.

Then she speaks. "We need to talk about the things that trigger you. The types of touches. Pressure of fingers. Memories tied to certain positions. Your off-limit zones and—"

"Remember when we met, and you refused to talk? I think you said five words in one week." I widen my eyes. "Look at you now. Giving TED Talks instead of getting naked."

"Shut up."

"You shut up."

"I'm being serious." She folds her arms. "I need to know what shuts you down, speeds up your breathing, makes you freeze and feel cornered, makes you feel safe…"

"Are you done?"

"I won't touch you until I know how to touch you right."

"Listen up, Little Menace. You *will* touch me." I grip her jaw, thumb dragging across her lower lip, forcing her mouth open, wide enough for her to know what I intend to put in it. "But first, I'm touching you. Take. Off. Your. Clothes."

I step back and make an impatient gesture.

A tiny sound escapes her, something between a sigh and a plea. Then her hands go to the hem of her shirt.

The first inch of bare skin appears, and my vision tunnels.

The shirt lifts higher, revealing a flat stomach, the faint rise of ribs, and the slope of full breasts below the bunched fabric. My breath stops.

She hesitates for half a second, staring up at me. Then she pulls the shirt over her head and tosses it away.

No bra.

My heart rips open.

She's inconceivably, irrationally breathtaking in a way the world isn't prepared for.

Blue hair falls in glossy, rebellious waves around her shoulders. A silver hoop in her septum, a small diamond above the center of her lip, a spike glinting from her brow. Her whole face is a contradiction, sharp and soft, fierce and heartbreakingly vulnerable. Beautiful on an eccentric level that isn't delicate. It's bold and unexpected like a sucker punch.

And her body…

Holy unholy hell.

She swapped the little hoops for silver barbells, the metal decorating her plump nipples so perfectly. I want to buy her all the jewelry. Not that she needs adornments. Her skin is fair, warm-toned, and kissed with a beauty mole on her collarbone.

My pretty little sinner.

A vicious rush of arousal sends my hand to my cock, my fingers choking the damn thing through my briefs, trying to hold off the threatening orgasm.

Her gaze follows the movement. "Do you need to—?"

"Not gonna come in my pants, Tiny Terror. But you need to hurry with yours."

Hooking her thumbs in the waistband, she shoves the final piece of clothing down her legs and kicks it away.

Then she's completely bare.

Small hands. Small feet. Toned legs. Honey, lust-soaked eyes. A witchy little waist that nips dramatically before curving into hips I've been obsessed with since the moment she crashed into my life in that ruined wedding dress.

And holy fuck, her pussy is right there. Her sweet, luscious, fully exposed pussy.

My blood pressure spikes so fast I swear I black out for a second. I can't move. Can't blink. I can only stare, knocked absolutely stupid by how stunning she is.

Gods forgive me. The things I'm going to do to her... I don't even want forgiveness.

"Dove." My whole world tilts toward her. "I'm going to touch you now."

"Fuck yes." Her skin flushes beneath my hungry stare, pink blooming everywhere. "Touch whatever you want, however you want."

I lunge, sink my hands into her hair, angle her head, and kiss her with everything that's been starving inside me for twenty-four years.

She moans against my mouth, my new favorite sound, and her warm, satiny skin meets mine. All of her glides against all of me, all at once, until I'm nothing but burning flesh and painful, fisting pressure between my legs.

This is it. The moment my life starts.

This is happiness.

This is the reason I crawled out of that river alive.

I back her against the kitchen table and brace a hand on the edge while the other roves down her spine. She arches into me, pressing her chest to mine, her hips catching my bare thigh.

Her scent rises to meet me, clean skin and soft female arousal, driving my pulse into a frenzy.

"I'll come back to this." I lick into her mouth one last time and move to her jaw, her throat, and the slender line of her collarbone.

She gasps when my lips find the spot beneath her ear.

I take my time, dragging my tongue along the tendon in her neck, tasting salt and sugar. I bite gently at the place where her pulse flutters, memorizing the subtle jerk of her body and the way her breath breaks in a sigh.

"Wolf..." My name crumbles off her lips.

I smile against her skin and move lower, tracing the edge of her collarbone with my mouth, chasing it from one shoulder to the other. I kiss every inch, sucking faint marks into her flesh with obscene devotion.

The hollow between her collarbones. Definitely one of my favorite places.

From there, I lick a path down the center of her chest, stopping to press my mouth between her breasts. Her heart drums wildly beneath my tongue, matching my own chaotic rhythm.

"You're killing me." Her fingers tangle in my hair, nails scraping across my scalp.

"You're reviving me." I nose along the swell of one breast, then the other, deliberately avoiding the beauty mole for now.

Tease first. Worship later.

Little goosebumps rise under my breath, and her nipples tighten in the cool air. I bring one into my mouth, closing my lips around dewy skin and cold metal, sucking with gentle friction, testing what she likes.

"Fuck." Her whole body shudders, back bowing and hands clamping tighter in my hair.

That's going on the list. Her breasts. The piercings. The way she loses control when I suck them.

I give each one reverent attention, switching sides, changing suction, and learning every reaction. Low whimpers. Shaky breaths. The way her thighs press together and shift restlessly with each pull of my mouth.

When I lift my head, her cheeks glow with color, lips parted, eyes dazed. The sight nearly drops me.

"Angel Face," I murmur. "You look wrecked already."

"Proud of yourself?"

"Very."

I straighten and, in one rough sweep, drag my forearm across the table behind her. Sketchbooks, pencils, and coffee mugs crash to the floor. I don't care. I need her on that surface.

She lets out a startled laugh that turns into a yelp as I grip her thighs and lift. She's light in my arms, all tight muscle and lush curves.

I spread her out on her back, hair falling around her like spilled ink.

When her eyes lock onto mine, it hits me.

After twenty-four years of emptiness and ache, I've been given the priceless, unworthy privilege of making Dove Rath come.

"I'm going to ruin you." I bite her hipbone.

"Too late." A shaky smile tugs at her lips.

"Oh, my dirty bird. I'm only getting started." I circle the table slowly, skimming my fingers along the sinuous shape of her.

With each step, I pull a chair out of my way, my attention never leaving her gorgeous body. When I reach her face, I drag my knuckles along her jaw. Her lashes flutter and lips separate on a hiss.

I bend to kiss her pierced Medusa, the tiny diamond seductively centered in the indentation above her full upper lip. Then I follow the arch of her pierced brow with the tip of my tongue.

She shivers, eyes closing.

"This one." I return to the Medusa, teasing it with my thumb. "Drives me crazy."

"Most people hate my hardware."

"They don't hate it. They're intimidated by it." I lower my mouth to the hollow of her throat and spend more time there.

Her shoulders are another favorite. Compact strength, beautiful lines, and faint scars that tell stories she still hasn't shared. I kiss those. All of them. A silent promise.

I move to her arm, lifting it and pressing my mouth to the inside of her wrist. More kisses to the tender bend of her elbow. When I find a sensitive spot, her fingers curl into my hair.

Grinning, I drag my teeth along the inside of her forearm.

"Jesus, Wolf." She turns her head to watch me, lashes half-lowered. "You're merciless."

"Then call me by my first name."

"What's that?"

"Yours."

Her eyes flutter shut on a shivery inhale.

My hands roam while my lips work, learning where she's ticklish and where she arches. I follow the slope of her ribs with open-mouthed kisses, counting each rung with my lips and continuing downward.

Her stomach jumps beneath my tongue, and a small, involuntary giggle breaks free.

"Lie still." I swat her thigh.

"Yes, sir."

She bites down on a smile, compelling me to bite down on the soft dip above her navel. She shrieks with laughter and quickly reins herself in.

Her stomach goes on the favorites list.

I continue my circuit around the table, pulling out more chairs with my free hand while never losing contact with her skin.

My fingertips trace lazy paths over her hips, following the dramatic flare from her narrow waist.

"These." I squeeze, digging my thumbs into the curves. "Obsession territory."

"You're obsessed with my hips?"

"And your thighs. Don't get cocky. I'm not done."

I kiss along the length of one leg, then the other, my mouth skimming around the blond patch of hair between her thighs.

Her heels slide on the table's surface, her legs tensing and relaxing, as if she doesn't know whether to close them or spread them.

"Open your legs." I press my lips to the inside of her knee.

Another on the favorites list. Inner knees.

She whimpers as I pepper kisses along her thighs, deliberately stopping just shy of where I know she's pulsing hot and frantic.

"You're..." She swallows a quick sip of air. "You're doing that on purpose."

"Obviously."

"You're not so cute when you're cruel."

"Should I stop? Because I intend to be very, very cruel."

With a gulp, she quickly shakes her head.

By the time I complete the circle, I've committed a full catalog of reactions to memory. The breathless gasp when I kiss the hollow under her jaw. The choked curse when my teeth scrape her collarbone. The low, helpless groan when I suck her pierced nipples. The trembling in her thighs when I pay attention to the insides of her knees.

"Are you hard?" She cranes her neck, trying to steal a glimpse.

I give her a look. *Seriously?*

"How hard?"

"Put it this way. It's a miracle I haven't torn a hole in my shorts. I've leaked a gallon of precome, and at this point, if anything bumps into that general area..." I gesture at the source of my discomfort. "I'll go off like a one-hundred-year geyser."

"Can I see?"

I groan. "Exposing myself involves touching it, and touching results in—"

"Old Faithful?" She traps a squirming smile between her teeth.

"Old Faithful erupts every ninety minutes." I return to her face, bracing one hand beside her head, the other spreading wide over her ribs. "Since meeting you, I'm significantly more active than that."

"Yeah?" She breathes in short gasps, looking as worked-up as I am with her damp skin and hard nipples. "What's your eruption frequency?"

"Dangerously high." I drag my nose along hers. "By the way, I found at least ten favorite parts."

"Only ten?"

I crush my mouth to hers, and she opens against the pressure of my tongue, welcoming my consuming kiss with breathy whimpers, her hands finding my chest, and tracing the bubbled welts.

Her tongue rolls against mine, hot and soft, clashing between our lips. Mouths open and fused, we lick and groan, growing wilder, messier, and more frantic by the second.

As I devour her, my thumb drags across her nipple, tracing the barbell. She arches, a helpless noise ripping from her throat.

Yeah. That one never gets old.

I keep her right on the cusp with only a kiss, edging her toward release, pulling back when I know she's close, and circling the table again. I touch her everywhere except the one place she wants me. I kiss her until her body goes heavy and restless. Then I torment her again.

"Wolf, please." Her legs shift, and her hands grab at me like she doesn't know where to hold on.

"Time for another angle."

She blinks up at me, confused, until I grab a chair and drag it directly to the end of the table.

I sit, muscles thrumming and blood roaring in my ears. Then I grip her ankles and tug.

wolfson
THIRTY-SEVEN

My hands tremble around her ankles as I pull her body across the table toward me. Her ass meets the edge, and her legs fall open, knees bending.

Jesus on a snow machine. Her position, all sprawled and trusting, is enough to make me want to skip this part and go straight to the fucking.

But no. I don't want to miss a single step.

Her hands clutch the edge of the table above her head, and her chest heaves in fast, shallow pulls. She stares down at me, eyes glazed and blue hair spilling everywhere.

"You okay?" I draw slow circles on her inner thighs. "Too much?"

"No." She gulps, her throat working. "Not too much. I love the way you look at me."

"Good, because I can't stop."

And I don't.

I take her in from this new vantage point. The slope of her stomach, the *V* of her hipbones, the damp sheen at her temples, and the faint quiver in her thighs every time my thumb brushes close to her cunt.

Every part of her is a discovery.

Every twitch, gasp, and needy tug of her hands on the table goes straight to memory, burned there. I'm not just turned on. I'm fascinated. Consumed. Utterly addicted.

"You have the prettiest cunt." I skim a knuckle along her slick seam. "I'm about to get really fucking familiar with it."

"About time."

"Open wider."

Her legs fall open for me, and my fingers are there, gently splitting her soft, slippery lips to get a good look at her. I take my time, savoring the view, my cock aching, needing to be sheathed inside that warm, tight hole.

But not yet.

Leaning in, I press my nose to her flesh, pull the scent of her into my lungs, and let it leave through my nostrils in a controlled stream.

"Fuuuuck." A groan vibrates through me as more blood rushes to my dick.

I can no longer ignore the wet spot between my legs, the soaked fabric unbearable against my pounding erection. With a quick lift of my hips, I shove the offending garment down my legs and off.

Perching my bare ass on the chair, I hook her legs over my shoulders and gently wrap my lips around her clit.

Her entire body lurches toward me as if trying to pull me inside her.

"We'll get there, Bluebird." I flatten a hand on her belly, urging her to relax on the table.

As her limbs loosen, I add my fingers, sinking one, then two, all the way to the knuckles.

Her spine arches. Her head falls back with a moan, and her thighs shake around my ears.

I curl my fingers inside her, thrusting slowly, kissing her inner thighs, and breathing in deeply. She smells like a woman. Clean and wild. Like the Arctic before a storm breaks, the rush of air over fresh snow, carrying the faint sweetness of berries thawing in the sun.

And the feel of her pussy... She's warm inside and out. Silky, delicate, and unexpectedly strong. A molten, wet pocket of velvety muscle, gripping at me like she won't let me go. Against my hands, around my fingers, getting sloppier by the second.

Time to eat.

She makes a sound of protest when I slide out my fingers. But in the next breath, I bury my face.

Holy Mother of all things forbidden. I've finally died and gone to heaven. Turns out it's between the thighs of my favorite Disney princess. What fantasy is this?

Mine.

All mine.

With her legs locked around my head and the juice she's juicing all over my mouth, this is my destiny. Her. My princess bride.

I run my tongue from her ass to her clit, and Ohhhhh. My. Fuck! I do it again. And again. With each pass, I lick deeper, and with each return to her clit, I suck harder.

Her hands tangle in my hair, fingertips pressing at my skull. She becomes rabid on my tongue, riding my face, grinding her hips, and shivering with mindless want. Her hands can't keep still, clawing at my neck and scratching at the hard knots of my biceps.

I fuck her with my tongue with the single-minded intensity. Despite this being my first time, I quickly learn the pace, pressure, and movements that make her scream.

My girl can scream.

With another thrust of my fingers, I seal my lips around her clit, swirl my tongue, and suck hard.

She lets out a long, throaty howl, her back arched and thighs clenched. When she falls silent and melts against the table, I know she's lost in the shimmering aftershocks of her orgasm.

"How many can you have?" I drag my tongue along her soaked flesh.

"Oh, God. You can't—"

"I'm your god, and I can." I wrap my arms around her thighs, pull her tighter against my face, and feast again.

And again.

And again.

With my tongue, fingers, and the slow grind of my mouth, I become her devoted creature, her acolyte of pleasure, fusing myself to her desires like I was made for this. Made for her.

I worship her hungrily, obsessively, consuming every shiver and scream she gifts me. There's no space between us. No secret cravings or hidden kinks. I know her body like my own, and there's no question now. She wants me with a desperation that hardens my dick past the point of agony.

So as I feel her tightening, trembling, and chasing the stroke of my tongue for the fourth release, I know I won't be able to stop myself from joining her.

I try. Fucking hell, I try to tamp down the rising surge that sets fire to my cock. I haven't touched myself once since we started. But the fuse is struck.

The moment she clenches around my fingers and kicks her pussy against my lips, I'm a goner. All the seed I held back since we started explodes out and onto the floor as she comes all over my face.

I fall against her, my nose pressed to her quivering stomach, and the groan that leaves me carries a full-body vibration that drags from the depths of my soul.

Cracking open my eyes, I find hers glimmering with laughter.

"You came." She lifts on her elbows, tits jiggling as she tries to stifle her amusement. "Fucking finally."

"It's not funny." I reach up and tweak a pierced nipple. "I was saving myself for the big finale."

"Oh, Wolf." She slips off the table and onto my lap, straddling me. "I'll give you another one."

My spent dick jumps and thickens in agreement.

"I bet I can give you lots and lots of other ones." She rocks against my erection. "With my hands." She runs wicked fingers along my hardness. "With my mouth." She glides her lips across mine. "With my body." She adjusts my length along her slit, sliding the head through our wetness.

I've never had a mouth on my cock. Denver molested me with his hands and forced himself down my throat, but he never sucked me.

As my mind starts to spiral to that dark place, she grabs my face and pulls me back to her.

"Where are you, my darling wolf?" She stares into my eyes.

"I'm with you." I smooth my palms along her thighs, anchoring myself between her legs.

"Stay with me."

"Never leaving you." I clutch her waist, marveling at how my hands completely encircle the circumference of her body. "How can someone so small be so fucking strong?"

"How can someone so inexperienced be so fucking good with his mouth?"

"I'm no stranger to porn."

"Of course, you're not." She rolls her eyes, laughing.

"I need inside you."

"I need to taste you."

She circles her hips, slowly, sensually, moving her body in a dance on my lap. Each lift and roll glides my dick along her cunt and short-circuits my brain.

Then she puts her mouth to my ear and purrs, "Can I be the first mouth on your cock?"

My body vibrates so violently that the chair beneath us rattles against the floor.

"Always yes with you." I grip her hair and thrust against her. "But not now. If I don't fuck you in the next thirty seconds, I'm going to do some serious damage."

"Considering your size, damage is unavoidable." She wraps her small fingers around my shaft and twists her wrist through a diabolical stroke.

"What do you mean?" I clamp my hand over hers, stalling her delicious torture.

"You're a big boy." She gives my cock a punctuating squeeze. "Bigger than anyone I've—"

I shut her up with a kiss, pouring all my jealousy into it and growling against her lips. "I'm going to kill every man who's ever touched you."

"Jag beat you to that, I'm afraid."

"Fuck." I pull back. "I'm sorry. I mean, I'm not sorry. I still want to gut them."

"What were you saying about thirty seconds?"

I grab her ass, leap from the chair, and slam her up against the nearest wall. The position aligns us perfectly, my hands pinning her hips, and my dick jabbing at her opening.

Insatiable lust takes over, flooding me with more hunger than I know what to do with.

Slow down, idiot. Fucking slow down and do her right.

With great effort, I take her bottom lip between mine and give it a gentle pull. Then I press a kiss to the corner of her mouth, an attempt to reel myself back before I ruin this.

In my urgency to mount her like a barbarian, I know I'm

forgetting something.

What the fuck am I forgetting?

Oh.

"Condom. I don't have any." Everything inside me grinds to a halt as I frantically scan the kitchen for a magic condom dispenser. "What am I saying? I've never even held one."

"Hey." She shoves her fingers in my hair, drawing my eyes back to her. "I have an implant in my arm, and I go to the clinic regularly for tests. We're safe."

Safe. No more obstacles. Nothing between us.

I can't stop shaking. Every muscle vibrates and throbs so brutally that my body doesn't feel like my own. My skin is too tight, my breathing too sharp. My seams are unraveling, losing their hold on the havoc inside me.

All of it, my whole fucked-up life, lines up behind this single moment. Every hurt, every loss, every far-off fantasy I buried to survive, it all collapses here, at her feet, and I'm so spectacularly overwhelmed and excited I can't breathe.

"I know." She slides her hands to my jaw, bringing our foreheads together. "God, Wolf, I know how deeply significant this is. It's not just a first time. This is you breaking the last chain of your past. It's a victory, an awakening, and the kickoff of every wild, vibrant dream you've ever deserved. Thank you for letting me share it with you. It means more than you can know."

"Dove..." My chest expands so fast I swear it cracks open. "Godsdammit. I love—"

"Not yet." She presses her fingers against my mouth. Then replaces her hand with her lips. "Put it in me, Wolf."

I'm already grinding my hips and stabbing her with my dick, searching for her entrance. When my crown finds the notch of her opening, I hesitate.

"What's wrong?" She reaches down, trying to guide me inside.

"Do I just shove it in? Or go slow and easy?"

"You won't hurt me. Do whatever feels good."

My breath cuts off as I slowly push in, just the tip, completely overcome by the tight clench and suction that greets me.

"Oh, gods. Oh, fuck. You feel..." I choke against her mouth. "Un-fucking-real."

"Wait until you're all the way in, Loverboy." She pushes her pelvis closer, pulling me in another inch.

I groan, blown away by the swarming sensation and shaking with the restraint to not go full animal on her.

"Fuck me, Wolf." She bands her arms and legs around my torso and holds on tight. "Give me the fighter, the ferocious survivor, the beast who clawed his way out of hell."

That's it. I drive into her in a hard, unpracticed thrust, and everything changes.

No pain. No shame. No fear. I'm unbound and far removed from Hoss as I crush her between the wall and my chest and let my instincts take control, plunging and pounding and claiming her on *my* terms.

There's nothing civilized in the way I fuck. No technique or skill. Just raw, primal movement. And she takes it. She moans and gasps and lets me in and in and in, deeper, rougher, opening for my feral tongue and savage hammering.

I've felt pain, cold, terror, but nothing like this. Nothing even close to this intensity. It stimulates every nerve and invades every inch of skin, this beautiful, wild joining.

With our lips wed, our tongues entwined, and her pussy gripping me tighter than a fist, this is the most connected I've ever felt to anything or anyone. We're one body, one heartbeat, sharing a violent, otherworldly closeness that knits all the frayed, misshapen scraps of my soul to hers, making me whole.

All along, this is what I needed. She's the missing piece.

She threads her fingers through my hair and guides my face to her chest, holding me there, loving me with her body, and easing the heavy pain I carry. Because that's what I need. Even when I thought the heaviest ache I carried was my virginity, she knew. I just needed her.

Needing closer, deeper inside her, I peel her off the wall and lower her to the kitchen floor.

The new position gives me the leverage and gravity to melt into her, stretching and penetrating every secret part of her body. But the moment I have her on her back, it's a fast, urgent climb.

I really hoped I could brag later about how I made love to her with languid thoroughness long into the night. But she feels too fucking good, and I'm not as amazing as I thought.

"Fuck, I can't... I can't. I'm—" My lungs lock up. My muscles strain. My molars crash together, and the pressure snaps as I roar, jerking, breaking open, and exploding in a fierce, uncontrollable, forceful spray inside her.

Like a geyser.

Yeah, it's messy. The orgasm has me in a chokehold as I unload twenty-four years of come. I wonder if she feels the scalding blast. Imagining rivers of my seed shooting up and everywhere inside her fills me with the deepest pleasure.

I intend to keep her nice and full forever.

Caveman thoughts. Great.

Didn't think I could sink to Kody's grunting, knuckle-dragging level. But after what just happened with my woman, my mate, it's like something primitive got its claws in me and shook every smart thought out of my skull.

And something else.

I touch my cheek and find wetness there.

Mortifying.

Still seated inside her, I stare down at my wayward princess and fight a vicious rush of emotion shaking through my bones and skin.

"I know." She's crying, too, pressing the heels of her hands against her eyes. "I know."

The tears hit harder, hers rising fast, mine right behind them, flaring in my chest and burning behind my nose.

This is the break that follows the fall.

My sweet, orphaned, lonely dove has been stowing away pain since her mother died, packing it tight inside herself. And now she's releasing it with me, her dark, wild, lonely wolf who knows pain like a second skin.

I thumb small swirls through the damp tracks on her cheeks, and she mimics the movement on mine. I feel it in the mingling of our breaths, the intimacy of our eye contact, the swell of my cock inside her, and the answering squeeze of her inner muscles.

I feel the promise we make to each other. The unspoken words of love. The fight that we'll fight to stay together.

That's when the front door opens.

wolfson
THIRTY-EIGHT

I whip my head around to find Leo strolling in with his phone in hand.

No.

No, no, no!

The thought of his gaze sliding up Dove's bare legs, catching on her hips, and lingering on her breasts... I see red, not as a metaphor, but as an actual flare in my vision.

Tilting my head, I track him over my shoulder like prey. My stance shifts, knees widening, weight dropping over her, ready to launch myself at the threat.

It's not jealousy. This is older. Darker. Forged into the marrow.

Mine.

That's the word that slams through me like a hammer to the sternum.

"Did you just—?" Leo's eyes bulge. "Did I just walk in on your first time, bro?"

By the eight frozen nuts of Hoss...

"Get out!" My cock softens, slipping out of her, as I tuck her beneath the cover of my body.

If he so much as glances at her curves, her piercings, the soft skin I've memorized with my mouth, I'll become the worst version of myself. The version that survived hell by becoming a creature capable of returning it.

"Goddamn, you have a pasty ass." His thumbs fly over the screen of his phone. "This is too good."

"Don't you dare text—"

"Too late." He holds up the screen. "They're on their way."

"She's naked, you fuck." My posture goes predatory, chin lowered, eyes up, tracking his every movement.

I bare my teeth. Not smiling. Not friendly.

Claiming.

Promising violence.

Daring him to look at her.

"If I recall," he says, eyes on his phone, "the night you introduced her, my bedmates and I were naked, in the privacy of our bedroom. Isn't that right, Dove?"

She makes a noise that sounds like a swallowed laugh and buries her face in my neck.

"Get the fuck out!" My jaw locks so tightly a crack echoes through my ears.

"Wolf..." She sighs.

A growl builds in the back of my throat. My shoulders square, chest rising with an inhale of fire. Every muscle coils, ready to strike first and ask questions never.

"After all the times you've walked in on us— Wait. Is that...?" Leo examines my face. "Were you crying?"

"Swear to the holy of holies..." I keep my back to him, blocking his view of her. "I'm going to wrap your braids around your stupid neck until your eyes pop like rotten testicles."

"Tell me you gave her more than two pumps before your tear-jerking release."

Clutching her to my chest, I rise to my knees and grab the closest thing I can reach.

My discarded underwear.

She digs her fingers into my shoulders as I twist and fling the dirty shorts at his face.

He catches them midair and instantly drops them with a shriek. "Fuck! Why are they wet?"

"Those are your nieces and nephews. In liquid form."

"Vile." He makes a gagging sound and rubs his hand on his leg. "Don't talk to me. Don't breathe near me. I'm never recovering from this."

"You won't have to recover." I glare at him over my shoulder. "Because I'm going to kill you."

Dove lifts her head. "Both of you shut up."

We both freeze.

"Leo." She rubs my spine in a placating gesture. "Give us a minute?"

"Yeah, sweetheart. I'll go." Hands raised, he backs up slowly and winks. "But this is going in the family group chat."

His laughter follows him out and lingers long after he shuts the door. Because he's still there, still laughing on the other side.

Rage crawls up my throat, and my hands curl into fists, knuckles whitening and forearms trembling to rip his head from his body.

"He's dead." I untangle myself from her and help her stand. "Go upstairs and get dressed. And don't come down. I'm about to commit murder. Lots of blood. Foul yeti organs everywhere."

I charge to the knife block on the counter and grab a three-inch paring blade.

Nah. Too dull. Definitely too small.

I swap it for the five-inch meat cutter. That's the one.

"You're not stabbing your brother." She plucks the weapon from my hand and drapes a blanket over my shoulders.

"Just his eyes." I reach for the blade again. "And his tongue."

In a flash, she sweeps the entire block of knives under her arm and bolts toward the stairs. Gloriously naked.

For a derailed moment, every molecule in my body shorts out.

Her hips sway as she runs, muscles flexing under smooth skin, the curve of her ass tightening as she climbs. Her blue hair flies behind her like a flag I'd follow into any battle. Every bounce and shift of her body owns my attention.

My mouth falls open. Until she vanishes beyond the top step.

I blink. Once. Twice. Reality snaps back.

"Those aren't the only knives in the house!" I shout.

"Wash your dick and clean the mess on the floor! We're expecting company!"

Right.

My family's on their way.

To congratulate me on losing my virginity.

Of all the torture in Alaska, this is next-level.

I'd rather run upstairs and spend the rest of the night making love to my woman.

But murder first.

I wash up in the guest bathroom and run a towel over the sticky floor. Then, with the blanket tight around my shoulders, I storm to the front door and kick it open.

Leo's smart enough to stay clear of my raging path as I charge out, nostrils flaring.

Standing a safe distance away, he eyes my blanket cape. "Are you armed under that?"

"With my fists."

"If you mess up my pretty face, Frankie won't forgive you."

"She won't see the bruises beneath your beard jungle."

"Listen, Wolf. You're the smartest guy I know."

"You only know three guys."

"If you don't want a compliment..."

"Continue."

"You're genius smart, but all that intellect evaporated the second you got your dick wet."

"*That's* your compliment? Why don't you come a little closer and say it again?"

"No, thanks." He chuckles. "I shouldn't have riled you, but *fuck*. I've been waiting a long time for this moment. I mean, the timing..." He flashes his teeth. "I couldn't resist. You deserve some payback for all the hell you've given me."

I hate it, but he's not wrong. How many times have I seen Frankie naked? I'm lucky they haven't clawed out my eyes. Strakh men are viciously territorial, but I didn't really understand what that meant until now.

I won't be as gracious with them as they've been with me.

My mind spins through impending scenarios, imagining Dove bending over an engine at the garage or sipping a drink at Kody's bar. If I even think about another man's eyes on her, my whole body changes. It's not subtle. Not civilized. Not anything remotely human.

It's instinct. Animal-deep.

My vision narrows until all I see is her body and the imaginary bastard looking at it. Veins stand out along my arms. Tendons strain in my neck, and my pulse spikes so fast it feels like my heart is breaking my ribs.

"I remember those feelings the first time I had sex with Frankie." Leo lets out a low whistle, his mismatched eyes studying me. "Immediately afterward, I felt different. Irrationally territorial and uncontrollably dangerous." He ambles toward me, stepping onto the porch. "I didn't want you or Kody near her. Didn't matter that you're my brothers. I was a hair trigger away from feeding you to the wolves if you so much as looked in Frankie's direction."

"Look at you now. Seventy percent less murder-happy, thirty percent titty baby, only mildly unstable, and still not housebroken. When was the last time you spent the night in the Sitka jail?"

"It's been a minute." He smirks, leaning against the door beside me. "Doesn't mean the urge to kill everyone who looks at Frankie is gone. Just means I learned how to control the murderous impulses."

"I don't know how you do it."

"What?"

"Share her. The thought of sharing Dove makes me feel unhinged."

"Because it's Monty and Kody. I trust them with my life and with hers." He lifts a shoulder. "It doesn't feel like sharing. It feels like the most natural thing in the world. Like breathing. It's that easy."

"Not at first."

"No." He laughs, shaking his head. "I had to sort out my ego. That took some time."

All this happened while I was locked in Dr. Pain's cage in Whittier, with everyone thinking I was dead. But I remember what Leo was like when Frankie arrived in Hoss. He postured like he was two breaths from snapping his own neck.

"Speaking of cavemen..." His eyes sparkle as he turns his attention toward the main house.

Kody's silhouette emerges on the path. Broad shoulders, slow stride, arms full of stacked boxes like he robbed a post office. Monty strolls behind him, balancing bags in each hand with that rich-man grace that makes everything look like a business deal. Frankie saunters beside them with a smaller load, red hair bright in the warm light.

Behind the trio, Carl and Jasper lumber along under the weight of even more boxes.

"Christmas in July." I clap my hands and usher everyone in. "My very first Christmas!"

Dove waits in the living room, looking freshly fucked in her jean shorts and tee, her feet bare and arms overflowing with things for me.

One look at her and I'm undone. Every scar and quiet place inside me rouse like my body knows she's the one it's been waiting for.

"What's all that?" She nods at the chaos of boxes pouring in.

"I did a little online shopping while you were reading the journals."

"A little?"

"It's all for you, my love." I kiss her mouth. "My dove." Another kiss. "My beautiful one."

Her lashes flutter on a breathy exhale.

Watching Dove Rath melt for me? Another favorite.

Carl and Jasper stack the last of the boxes by the couch, nod their goodbyes, and head out.

My family drifts into the living room, making themselves comfortable. Frankie curls up on the couch between Monty and Leo. Kody takes one of the armchairs.

I follow Dove into the kitchen, keeping my back to them as I drag on the jeans she brought for me.

"I thought you might want these, too." She holds out the journals, her eyes gentle and perceptive in a way I've needed my entire life.

"Thank you." I rest my brow against hers, breathing her in.

"I didn't get a chance to tell you earlier," she whispers.

"What's that?" I lower my voice, matching hers.

"You were legendary." She gestures at the table, the wall, then the floor where we finished, keeping her words low enough for my ears only. "Makes me question your honesty about this inexperience you claimed to have. I mean, up until an hour ago, I thought great sex was a myth. Now I know the real myth is *you*."

"Careful." My lips twitch. "You might want the myth forever."

"I do." Her eyes widen with a flash of worry before she blinks it away and smiles. "Go. Talk to your family."

With the blanket still draped over my shoulders, I hold the

edges together against my chest and walk into the living room where all the people I love most in this world are waiting.

Everyone watches me approach in that Strakh way, attentive and over-protective, waiting for the next emotional grenade to go off.

I pause in front of Frankie and hold out the journals. "Thank you for writing all of that and letting me read it."

"Sorry I was so pushy about it." She accepts the books.

"Don't be. You gave me the guts to write my story." I gesture at the journal on top. "And to share it with you. All of you."

Her eyes shine instantly.

"No tears." I shake a finger at her. "I'm shirtless, and if you cry on me, you'll be tempted to cop a feel, and your husbands will make it weird."

Leo throws a pillow at my head.

I dodge it.

Frankie ignores him, her hands trembling around the books. "You're sure you want us to read it?"

I never told anyone the details of my ten months in Rhett Howell's cage. Not until Dove.

"Yeah." I nod at the journal. "It's all there. The dark stuff, the deranged conversations with myself, and all the brilliant verbal smackdowns I gave the doctor. Whatever you think happened, it's worse. And it's better. And it's over. Read it." I yawn. "Or use it as a coaster. Prop up a wobbly table. Pee on it. Just don't let Leo pee on it."

Before I lose my nerve, I let out a slow breath and shrug off the blanket.

It falls to the floor without a sound.

The room goes dead still as all eyes fixate on my bare torso.

I'm sure they stole glimpses when I had my meltdown in the shower. But this is the first real show-and-tell.

The scars across my chest and arms announce every nightmare I survived. The arrow wound, the river impact, the surgical slices, and the mismatched, patchwork of crooked seams where skin was forced shut without mercy. None of it blends, some spots still pink, some thick, some translucently thin, all of it monstrous like Frankenstein's creature.

What can I say? I was taken apart and put back together wrong.

I force myself to stand there, to let them look, because hiding the damage hasn't made anything easier.

Frankie swallows. Kody's face turns to stone. Leo's eyes darken with grief so sharp it cuts. And Monty...

The air thickens, squeezing around my ribs as he rises to his feet. Then his arms are there, banded around me, quivering with all the un-Monty-like emotion he keeps tucked away.

My throat clicks. My hands shake, too. My body wants to flinch, but it doesn't because this is my dad. My biggest supporter.

He carries so much guilt for rejecting Gretchen when she got pregnant with me. He blames himself for my childhood trauma, my captivity, and every terrible thing I endured. But I don't. I don't blame him for a damn thing. He didn't abuse me or hold me captive in the Arctic. He showed up in my life when I needed him the most, and he stayed. Every day, every hour, he's been here.

Voicing this stuff isn't really my style. But I wrote it. Every bit of my gratitude and love for him is in the journal.

"I want you to read it, Dad." I step back and grip his shoulders. "Will you?"

His lips press together, trapping the emotion he can't hide in his stormy eyes. Then he nods.

"Cool." I turn to the others, my gaze latching onto Frankie's wet cheeks.

"What?" I lift both brows. "Were you expecting a dramatic monologue? A speech? A group hug? Not happening."

"That's not..." She dashes away her tears, her anger rising to the surface as she examines my scars. "He used a scalpel on you but didn't bother to heal the wounds. I mean, he was a fucking surgeon!"

"Yeah, well..." I rub the back of my neck. "He was stingy with the stitches. I never got an infection, so he must've put antibiotics in my food."

Monty exhales like a man preparing for war.

I swallow and try to come up with a joke, but nothing lands.

Dove steps to my side, and her hand skims around my waist, her fingers slipping into the dip above my hip, holding me together. Who needs stitches when I have her? She's my seams.

That's when it hits me. With my scars out, my story written, and Dove standing at my side, I don't feel the urge to curl up on the floor. I'm not blacking out or tripping into the scary-movie reruns of my life. My vision is clear, my mind lucid and present.

"No more hiding." I meet their eyes, one by one. "I'll talk about it instead of running from it. But right now…" I spot a bottle of vodka on the coffee table. "I say we drink." My eyes lift to Kody. "Is that a new flavor?"

"I made it a while back. Been saving it for this moment." Kody frees a rare smirk. "It's cherry-free vodka."

"What the fuck is cherry-free vodka?"

"Vodka that lost its cherry." He looks me straight in the eyes. "Like you."

I stare at him, waiting for my chest to burn with the defensive coil connected to my virginity.

But it doesn't come.

Instead, something lighter pushes up under my ribs and tumbles out in a carefree laugh. "I'll take that. I earned the hell out of it."

Kody's smirk grows into an expression that could damn-well be considered a smile.

"I'll get some glasses." Dove steps toward the kitchen.

"No." Kody waves her back. "We'll do it family style."

Monty reclaims his spot on the couch as I grab the free armchair and pull Dove onto my lap. She settles across my thighs, her palm finding the center of my scarred chest.

Her touch sinks like a grounding bolt, pinning me to the moment, keeping me from retreating into the parts of my brain that still feel the scalpel opening my flesh.

Kody twists off the cap and takes the first pull, jaw feathering as the vodka hits. Then he passes it to Monty, who drinks like he's signing legal documents with his throat. Leo takes a swig and releases a loud, aggressive shout, widening his eyes and fully extending his tongue like the animal he is.

Frankie laughs, snatching the bottle and giving the rim a mournful sniff. No alcohol for our baby mama.

Then the bottle comes to me.

I hold it to Dove's lush lips and tip it back. She swallows like a champ, then I slug my share, the vodka burning warm all the way down. Clean and wild. Kody's specialty.

"So…" Monty crosses an ankle over his knee. "What's the plan for you two?"

"We're getting married."

Dove makes a sound of surprise. Everyone else looks at me like *Duh, tell us something we don't know.*

"Oh, you meant what are our plans right now?" I wipe my mouth with the back of my hand. "We're going to chill on the island for a week. Let everything settle after... Everything. We need time to get to know each other better."

Leo snorts. "By that, you mean biblically, repeatedly, and with enthusiasm." He shakes his head. "Poor Dove."

"All right, let's get this over with. I know why you're all here and what you're thinking. I have no experience, so I probably fumbled it." I take a long pull from the bottle and hand it to Kody. "Feral men and lady of the jury, allow me to present the evidence. Dove said, and I quote, *I was legendary.*"

"I meant it." She touches her smile to my cheek.

"Now you know." I glance around the room, enjoying the hell out of their squirmy discomfort. "In other news, I called Dr. Thurber yesterday."

Frankie's head snaps up, eyes going bright.

"He's coming to the island tomorrow. We're doing a session here. Oh, and you won't see Gretchen's robe again." I motion at the flames in the fireplace. "I sent it back to hell."

"Wolf..." Frankie practically vibrates. "I love that for you."

Leo stares at the floor, smiling to himself. Kody gives an approving nod and takes a hit of the vodka before passing it. Monty sits back, studying me like I just lifted the weight of the world off his shoulders.

"I'm so proud of you." Frankie casts a look at her husbands. "It took an act of Congress to get these three into a therapist's office."

"Here we go." Leo takes a swig and returns the bottle to Dove.

"I support mental health." Frankie flattens her hands on the journals.

"You support mental torture."

"Shut up, Leo," we all say in unison.

Dove laughs, takes a sip from the bottle, and offers it to me. As she curls up against my chest, her warmth sinking into my bones, the whole room shifts around that simple connection.

My past sits on Frankie's lap.

My future sits on my lap.

wolfson

My family sits around me, loud, supportive, and *mine*.

For the first time in my life, I'm surrounded by people and don't feel alone.

wolfson
THIRTY-NINE

I don't remember the first day I felt cold. But I remember the first day I felt warm.

It wasn't sunlight. It wasn't Monty's high-end heating system. It wasn't even my family rescuing me from arctic hell.

It was a runaway bride in white satin, sprinting down the street, skirt bunched in her fists, rage and hurt and defiance in her eyes.

The moment I saw Dove, her hair flying around her as if she were born from lightning, burned through me so fast I didn't even know what it was. I only knew it melted the cold that had lived under my ribs since forever.

That warmth simmers through my veins now as I float on my back in the pool, listening to her cut through the water beside me.

Summer wraps the island in lazy softness, the dark sky streaked with starlight. The air smells like ocean salt, wet stone, and the faint sweetness of the lotion I rubbed into Dove's skin after our shower this morning.

She surfaces with a slow push of her hands through her hair, looking like a retro pin-up rising out of the water.

The black-and-white halter bikini hugs her figure as if

grateful for the job. Just one of the many rockabilly pieces I ordered during my online shopping bender.

Zero regrets.

"You're staring." She wades toward me, her hips swishing beneath the water. "Is this swimsuit your favorite?"

"*You* are my favorite."

She rolls her eyes. "I've never owned this many clothes in my life."

"That's why I fixed it."

"No one needs twenty bikinis."

"Correction." I sink beneath the water, letting my lips skim the surface as I drift toward her. "You needed exactly that. You also needed that vintage skirt that swirls when you walk. You needed those boots for the next saloon door you kick open. You needed those tiny shorts that make it so damn easy for me to access heaven. And don't get me started on the body jewelry."

"I admit your taste in fashion is exquisite. But the sheer amount of clothing you bought..." She splashes my face. "It's excessive, you weirdo."

"Your beauty is excessive." And I'm fucking drunk on it.

After I bought half the Internet, I made her try on every single item in a private fashion show.

Spoiling her satisfies the newly awakened, possessive beast inside me that requires constant proof that she's here, safe, and *mine*.

She's clothed because I put clothes on her, fed because I put food in her mouth, and protected because I dragged her into my cave and locked the door behind her.

I glide closer and fit myself between her knees. Her thighs instinctively wrap around my waist. Warm. She's so fucking warm.

"You know..." I brush a wet strand from her cheek. "I like taking care of you. Even if you don't need it."

"I like letting you. Even if I pretend I don't need it."

I kiss the corner of her mouth because if I kiss her fully, we're not talking anymore. And we need to talk.

It's been two days since we had sex the first time. Two days mostly spent naked, in bed or out of it, her breath tangled with mine, her nails in my shoulders, and my name in her throat.

My cock aches at the memory, ready to go again.

But tonight holds a quiet that invites a deeper connection. Rather than flinching from it, I feel strong enough to face it.

Maybe because of yesterday's session with Dr. Thurber.

He's a good listener. He doesn't try to fix me in the first five minutes or talk to me like I'm a feral animal. He just waits and lets me speak when I'm ready.

And this time, I surprised myself. I shared things. Not everything, not the worst pieces, but enough to break away some of the stubborn plaque in my chest.

He told me my nightmares make sense. My panic spikes make sense. My breakdown after touching Jag... That makes sense, too. No shame or judgment. Just a man saying, *You survived hell, Wolfson. Your brain reacts because it remembers.*

Not gonna lie. I hate how exposed these sessions make me feel, how he sees the things I don't say, and how he names feelings I'd rather pretend I don't have. There's a mountain of shit I need to work on. The anger, the guilt, and the stupid fixation on Jag Rath that I can't shake.

I want to be better for Dove. The best version of myself. And whatever the hell this magnetic pull toward her stepbrother is... It's not helping.

"You're thinking too loud." She taps my forehead with a wet finger.

"I want to ask you something. A few things."

"Ask." Her legs tense around me, her voice calm, but not casual. Never casual.

"I want to understand you." I ease my head back to look at her.

"Which part?" Her chin lifts, guarded.

"All of it. Everything. But first and foremost, how are you? Be sincere. Really. How are you?"

"I'm fine." At my arched brow, she sighs. "Okay, I'm... Tired. Jumpy. Half-hopeful, which I hate. Half-terrified, which is normal."

"Why are you scared?"

"Because I feel safe. *That* scares the hell out of me. Safety has never lasted in my life. It usually comes right before something terrible." She chews on her cheek. "I feel like I'm learning how to breathe again. It hurts. Everything hurts. But you make it hurt less."

"What else?"

"You make me hungry in ways I don't understand. I'm confused. And overwhelmed. My past sits in my bones like pockmarks. But I'm here. With you. Which means something I can't name yet." She releases a thready breath. "That's the truth."

Her honesty knocks the wind out of me. I want to wrap her up, hide her from the world, and swear on my life she'll never have to brace for pain again. But I know better. She doesn't need a cage. She needs a place to land.

"Thank you for telling me." I graze my lips along her cheek. "I don't want the easy Dove. I want the real one. The messy, uncertain one. The one who's still figuring things out." I rest my mouth on her temple. "For the record, I'm not going anywhere. So feel whatever you need to feel. I'm right here."

"I know, and I can't express how grateful I am for you." She cups my cheek, her exhale teasing my lips. "My turn to ask something."

"Fire away."

"What's the quality you admire the most in the person you like the least?"

"The people I like the least are dead."

"Someone alive."

Well, that narrows it down. The contact list on my phone is a short one, and most of them are Strakh employees. But there's one name missing, and he pisses me off in a way that feels... Annoyingly, dangerously satisfying.

Fucking Jag.

I know what I admire the most about him, but the moment I say it, she'll see right through me.

Except this is what I wanted. Talking. Honesty. No secrets between us. She gave me her truth, and now I owe her mine.

"Okay. Here's what I admire... His loyalty and sense of duty, even knowing how deeply he's twisted those qualities into obsession. He won't stop. Never. He'll burn the world for his obsession and destroy himself in the process."

She looks away, knowing exactly who I'm talking about. "His sense of duty kept me alive all these years, but it's also the very thing that ruined me."

"You're not ruined."

"My scars..." She coasts a hand down my damaged chest. "They live beneath the surface, unseen."

"We need to talk about him, darling. Tell me how he hurt you."

"I knew this was coming."

"He's in your head, in your choices, and the reason you jump when you hear footsteps behind you."

"He's my past."

"And your future. Whether you like it or not, he's not going away. The question is... Do I fit there with him? Or am I just a place to hide for a while?"

"Wolf..." She licks her lips, eyes dropping to my throat before lifting again. "I've been surviving for so long that even thinking about the future feels like picking a lock in the dark."

"That's fine. I'll sit in the dark with you. But I need to know what you feel for him. I need the honest answer, the one you don't want to give me."

"Okay. Jag was..." She holds out her hand, ticking the list off on her fingers. "My guardian. My superhero. My protector. My only family. My prison." She lowers her arm. "But he's not mine. Not anymore."

"What do you feel for me?"

"I feel..." Her breath leaves her in a quiet rush. "Like I'm choosing something for myself for the first time."

"You choose me?" I grip her hips.

She doesn't pull away. Instead, she tightens her legs around my waist. "I choose you."

"I'm never letting you go." The warmth hits so hard it's painful. "Not a chance."

"You say that like I'm planning an escape."

"Are you?"

"Depends." She drags her nails down my neck. "Are you a religious man, Wolfson Strakh?"

"I tried."

"You tried to be religious?"

"There was a time when all I wanted was to have a friend in Jesus. But when I needed him most, when I needed to feel seen, to feel love, the Only Begotten Son had forgotten this son. And that book his devoted followers love to quote? It cheers on incest, shames anything queer, treats women like property, and sucks the balls of the patriarchy. Also, God isn't real." I shrug. "So yeah. I'm your friendly, neighborhood heathen. Still want me?"

"Yes and amen." She kisses my lips. "We'll be heathens

together."

"Sweet unholy yes. Let's start a cult. Church of Now-a-day Heathens. I've always wanted to be a priest. You can be my priestess. We'll do his and her robes, matching tattoos, forbidden sex rituals, the whole damn thing."

"Say no more. I'm never leaving you."

"Cool." Holding her against my chest, I paddle lazily around the pool. "So you and me. What do you want it to look like? Tomorrow? Next week? After that?"

She stares at me for a long time, the water rippling around us, her thighs clutched to my hips, and her swimsuit clinging so sinfully it makes my pulse throb.

Finally, she says, "I want to stop running."

"From him?"

"From everything. I want to figure out who I am when I'm not fighting to stay alive."

"Then let's find out." I run my hands along her thighs where silky skin meets the seam of her bikini bottoms. "What do you love? What are your favorite things?"

"I love engines. The rumble, the electricity, all that sexy power. I love thunderstorms for the same reason." Her eyes hold mine, open and trusting. "And I love the way you look at me."

"For the same reason?"

"Definitely."

Her breathy answer doesn't help the chub I've been fighting since she put on this damn bikini. I glance at the main house, knowing my family won't be home from the distillery until late.

"What do you need right now?" I nuzzle her neck.

"You. Closer."

"Then there's only one question left." I pull the string that holds her top and watch the scrap of material float away from her breasts. "Have you ever had sex in a pool?"

"No." She reaches into my swim shorts and curls her fingers around me, claiming me.

I drag her out of her bikini and claim her right back with a need that feels like fate is finally sharpening its teeth.

love
FORTY

Monty bangs on the guest house door at eight in the morning.

"Get up." More banging. "We're taking the yacht out."

I sit up too fast and nearly fall off the bed. Wolf groans into his pillow, his hair a tangled black mess.

We left the door to the balcony open all night, the only reason we hear the wake-up call.

"Don't care!" Wolf shouts toward the open door.

"It's summer!" Monty shouts back. "Be at the dock in an hour."

Summer.

In California, that means burnt asphalt, burnt skin, and traffic jams that smell like burnt rubber.

Here, though, summer feels warm but not punishing. Bright but not glaring. The Alaskan sun doesn't cook my skin through my clothes. It kisses it like a playful wolf. Like *my* playful wolf.

We haven't left the island in five days. The fresh air would be good for us.

I climb onto Wolf's back, my bare chest pressed to the defined line of his spine.

He groans again, but now it sounds less sleepy and more hungry.

love

I nip the back of his neck. Then his shoulder. Then the place where his ribs curve. I cover every bit of skin I can reach with fast, noisy kisses.

"Sweet goddess of torment." He squirms beneath me, grinding his hips into the mattress. "Come here."

He reaches back to grab me, but I'm faster. I roll off him and yank the blanket away in one swift rip, leaving him completely uncovered.

Then I stare like I've never seen a man before.

Broad shoulders, strong backbone, narrow waist, long legs, all smooth muscle over pure tension, power wrapped in pale skin, shaped for speed, stamina, and insatiable fucking.

Naked Wolf is my favorite Wolf.

Unable to help myself, I pounce and sink my teeth into the chiseled muscle of his ass.

He jerks and lets out a rough sound that definitely isn't a complaint.

"My darling dove." His smile ruins his growly tone. "You have two seconds to hop on my dick."

With a grin, I hop off the bed, just as naked as he is, and saunter backward toward the bathroom.

His hooded eyes rake over me in a slow sweep that weakens my knees.

"Come with me in the shower." I hook a finger at him. "Or I'll come without you."

He's off the bed so fast I don't have time to blink.

We shower together, climax together, and an hour later, we're on Monty's yacht, slicing through Sitka Sound.

Not for the first time, it strikes me how bizarrely gentle summer is here. It's cool at the edges. Soft around the lungs. Feels like a reset.

Wolf and I lie on the outdoor couch tucked against the cabin wall, our bodies entwined on sun-warmed cushions. His leg drapes heavily over my thigh, his cheek resting on a bent arm, his eyes regarding me from inches away. Every time the boat rocks, his breath kisses my cheek.

Across from us, Leo and Frankie are passed out on a shared sun lounger near the railing. Leo sprawls like he lost a fight with gravity, one leg hanging off the edge and a tangle of braids covering his cheek. His arms cradle a curled-up Frankie, her face tucked against his chest.

He looks different in sleep. Younger. Less threatening. Whatever storm lives in that man, it goes quiet when his wife is protected in his embrace. Even unconscious, his hand splays over her baby bump, guarding the fragile life within.

"Look at them." I nudge Wolf with my knee.

He follows my gaze. "Leo just finished an insane accelerated program for his ATP license."

"He needs that license to run private aviation tours in Alaska?"

"Nope. This is Leo being Leo. He doesn't do anything halfway."

None of them do, including their pregnant wife. Monty mentioned that Frankie worked a brutal shift at the hospital before he dragged us all out here. Sounds like she and Leo needed this break the most.

Inside the open cabin, Monty sits at the polished bar while Kody teaches him how to make cocktails I've never heard of.

"Don't bruise the basil." Kody slices herbs with assassin precision.

"I don't care about the basil," Monty mutters.

"You should. It's the whole point of the drink."

"Vodka is the whole point."

"It's gin, you overpaid lightweight. Try to keep up."

They continue to bicker like lifelong friends. Like husbands. Definitely like brothers.

The resemblance between them is ridiculous. Same dark hair, same athletic build, same controlled intensity beneath their broody moods. Monty is the older, smoother version, Kody the rougher, colder one. They carry themselves with the same squared shoulders and stony expressions, ready to protect and defend that which they hold most dear.

Family.

The word lands in my chest like a pebble in deep water.

"What is it?" Wolf tucks his voice beneath the wind, ensuring no one else can hear.

"It's… I don't know." I stare past him, watching Monty steal a taste of the drink, and Kody smacking his hand away. "They're so comfortable with each other. Like they've been doing this their whole lives."

"They didn't start that easy. But now? Yeah, the four of them

Love

are annoyingly made for one another." He sounds entirely too happy about it to be annoyed. "Next question is mine."

"Okay."

We've been trading questions for days. Questions that started as nothing but turned into... Whatever this is. Honest. Disarming. Sometimes absurd. Sometimes bold enough to stop my heart.

"Your mother Celeste..." His fingers graze my wrist. "Tell me about her."

"I don't remember much. Just flashes here and there. She was very pretty. And young. But always tired. Always scared."

"Scared of what?"

"No idea."

"Was her murder premeditated?"

"They said it was a random burglary gone sideways."

"What do *you* think?"

"I was only eight, so everything is jumbled. I remember David and Celeste fighting off the intruder, probably guarding what little we owned."

He nods, listening the way only Wolf can, ears perked, eyes locked, endless patience.

"And Jag?" He keeps his voice low, safely inside our private pocket of sound. "What does he think?"

"Who knows? He never talked about it, no matter how much I pressed."

"Where's his bio mom?"

"She died when he was a baby. David married my mom when Jag was nine. Celeste is the only mother he ever knew."

Wolf presses closer, brushing his cheek against my temple, encouraging me to continue.

"Jag was close to his dad and my mom. Really close. I remember that much." My chest constricts. "But he never talks about them, not about their lives or their deaths."

"Why not?"

"Losing them messed him up. When he pulled me out of the pantry after he stabbed that man..." My voice thins. "The way he looked at me, it was like the world was dead, and I was the last thing he had to drag through it."

"He shouldn't have put that on you."

"It wasn't his choice. But it became his curse. He was wanted for murder, so everything we did was about survival. Running. Hiding. More murder. He turned himself into a death-dealing fortress, and I was the stray locked inside."

"What about your bio dad?" His thumb traces the bones in my hand. "Did you try to find him?"

"No. My mom never told me his name or why she left him. Only that he didn't deserve our love and wasn't worth the space in our heads." I loosen a breath. "The concept of family died with David and Celeste. I don't remember what being part of a family feels like."

"You do now."

My throat stings.

"That's not just my family." He nods toward Monty and Kody. "It's yours now, too. If you want."

I look at the two men inside the cabin, one lecturing about muddling mint, the other pretending not to care. Then at Leo and Frankie asleep on the lounger, curled around each other in perfect tranquility.

It feels unreal, like stepping into someone else's dreamy life.

Except their lives have been anything but dreamy.

I read the journals and can't help but think about the hell they lived through. So many harrowing moments plague my mind. Like the wolf attack that shredded Kody's body, and Frankie's quick reflexes with the blood transfusion that saved his life. The scar across Leo's abdomen, and eight-year-old Wolf's revenge against his mother. Monty's year-long hunt for his missing wife, and the discovery that his depraved brother had taken her.

And Wolf... Abused by not one, but two monsters. The things they did to him, no one should survive that. But he did. And now he's lying beside me, warm and alive and looking at me like I'm the celestial light at the end of a long, dark tunnel.

I swallow hard and push my fingers into the cushion to steady myself.

"And me." He tugs at my hand, bringing my eyes back to his. "You get me."

"And you get me."

"I plan to take full advantage of that." His smile is devastating.

Heat flares through me, along with an intense pull to burrow closer and prove to myself that I'm worthy of Wolf's devotion and what I feel for him isn't going anywhere.

"This is my first real summer." He tucks my hair behind my ear. "I didn't know it could feel like this."

"Like what?"

"Like something worth staying awake for. Like a daydream that doesn't turn to ice or threaten to leave."

The way he says it, with his gaze drilling into mine, tells me he's not just talking about summer.

"Five days ago, I told you I couldn't stay." I touch his jaw, smoothing the sudden tension there. "Because I don't want to endanger you."

"What did I tell you?"

"You said Jag is your problem, not mine. But if I stay—"

"If? Is that still a question?"

Old fear rises fast, shrinking my ribs and kicking my heart. My brain tries to drag me backward, back into running, back into hiding, back into every instinct that kept me alive.

But I look at him. At the quiet waiting in his eyes. At the trust he's learning how to give. At the way his throat jogs, not because he doubts me, but because he's terrified I'll pull away.

"No." I inhale through the fear, push the old reflex down, and wrap my hand around the back of his strong neck. "I'm not leaving."

He searches my eyes, waiting for a catch.

"I told you I couldn't stay, but the truth is..." My voice drops. "I can't walk away from you."

His earlier claim flickers through my mind.

Before the week ends, you'll fall in love with me.

I don't tell him he was right. I'm not brave enough for that yet. Instead, I make a different promise.

"I'll stay. But Jag isn't your problem. He's *ours*." I swallow as the wind covers us in a warm cocoon of sound. "If you get hurt, Wolf..."

"You leaving me is the only way to hurt me."

"Then it's settled. I'm never leaving."

"Obviously."

"I hope you're ready." Frankie rises from her lounger, smiling at me over her shoulder.

"For what?" I ask.

"Your feral Alaskan family." She winks, and sensing Leo's

movement, she bends to brush his braids from his face. "Go back to sleep, you brute."

She steps away, and he reaches for her.

"Just using the bathroom." With a laugh, she straightens the sun dress over her bikini and saunters into the cabin.

"Your turn." Wolf drops a kiss on my lip piercing.

"Hm." I prop my feet on the cushion, curling toward him. "What's your favorite ice cream flavor?"

"Shimmering honey."

Honey? Is that a flavor?

"Okay, but why is it shimmering?"

"Ask the color of your eyes."

My stomach flips. "Have you ever had ice cream?"

"Once. Frankie made me try it during my first week in Sitka."

"Which flavor?"

"Vanilla."

"And?"

"It was..." His thumb teases my nipple through the bikini top, his confidence quiet and coaxing. "Too vanilla for my tastes."

I expect nothing less from my dark, dirty wolf.

Tucking my knee under his, I keep my voice soft so it stays just ours. "Tell me about your first day in Sitka."

He exhales slowly, almost smiling, his eyes softening with gratitude or nostalgia or disbelief that someone wants to know this from him.

"All right." He leans his head back against the cushion and stares out at the water, remembering. "When the yacht docked, I didn't understand anything I saw. I had no sense of how big a city was supposed to be. No scale for any of it. I mean, the harbor looked massive. Like a whole new continent." He laughs under his breath. "All those retail shops by the water... I didn't know if I walked into a booming urban jungle or the saddest patch of nowhere on Earth."

"Truly?"

"It felt huge." He looks at me, eyes bright with memory. "And alive. People everywhere. Cars. Traffic lights. Music spilling out of doorways. The smell of coffee and gasoline. My senses were overloaded, like someone had taken the world off mute."

"When did you realize how small Sitka actually is?"

love

"Brace yourself, Trouble. I'm about to blow your mind."

"We'll see."

"Sitka is the largest city in the United States."

"What? No way. That's not—"

"It's the largest by land area, covering 2,800 square miles."

"Whoa." I shake my head, officially mind-blown. "But population-wise..."

"It's small. So small it only has fourteen miles of road. But that first day? It felt fucking magical. Like standing inside a dream and finally seeing a place I'd only heard stories about."

"Like Disney World."

"Alaska's low-budget, soggy, fish-scented Disney World." He huffs a laugh.

I laugh with him, but it breaks at the end. Because I can envision it, the wild man he was, shaking, overwhelmed, stepping into sunlight after a lifetime of darkness and meeting a new world that didn't know his name or what he'd survived.

Lost in our thoughts, we lapse into a weird little hush that feels like a hallway between rooms.

Inside the cabin, Kody and Monty argue about how much lime juice constitutes *too much.*

Frankie returns to the railing with a drink in hand, one of Kody's mint mocktails that he makes just for her.

"Your turn." Wolf pulls me onto his lap, his mouth at my ear. "Give me something real. Doesn't have to be big. Doesn't have to be about pain. Just something you're willing to share about your history with Jag."

Funny how I haven't heard from Jag in days, yet he manages to worm his way into most of our conversations.

I think of the lies I could tell Wolf, easy ones, but they taste rotten before they form. So I pick a small truth. An important one.

"Every time Jag uproots his life, he leaves me a message at our parents' graves. He plants a flower or tree near their headstones, and under it, a rock with a code on it, usually the name of a city, a new phone number, or whatever. That's how I knew he was here. A black willow, a sharpie rock, Sitka Tattoo." I meet his eyes. "He assumed I'd never follow."

"Yet you did."

"I had no choice after I found out about his affair with Gavin.

Following him was the only way to hate him properly."

"Nothing drives that point home like a runaway bride with a rifle."

"Exactly."

"I'm fucking grateful your hate-trip led you to me."

"Me, too."

"Tomorrow..." He shifts beneath me, banding his arms around my waist. "I need to call Wilson and get an update on the investigation."

His private investigator isn't going to dig up a damn thing on Jag or the criminals he's tied to. Jag erases trails better than the FBI, including whoever is now following me in Sitka. But I keep that to myself. Maybe the Strakh family has reach I don't fully understand.

"Sounds like an exciting day," I deadpan.

"I'll feed you first. French toast, maybe. Or those stupid tiny pancakes you like."

"I never said I like tiny pancakes."

"You inhaled eight yesterday."

"Coincidence."

"Uh-huh."

"Next question." I relax against his chest. "Did you quit smoking?"

"Not that I remember." He scratches his jaw. "I smoke when I have shit on my mind."

"You haven't had anything on your mind in five days?"

"Only good things." He dips his head, brushing a smoky whisper against my throat. "Mostly filthy things."

My face tingles with heat.

"Your cheeks just went pink," he murmurs, delighted.

"Shut up."

"My turn." He bites my neck and moves to my ear. "What do you collect without meaning to?"

"People who irritate me." I squeak when he nips a ticklish spot. "So far, that list is just you."

"For that, I get to ask another." He rests his chin on my shoulder. "What's one thing you want?"

"Everything you've already given me."

His breath releases with a purring rumble. "Something else."

Soft music starts thrumming through the hidden speakers, and Frankie straightens at the railing. Her head snaps toward the

love

cabin, green eyes sparkling.

Monty stands in the doorway, framed by sunlight, holding a drink to his lips, hiding a smirk. Frankie's whole face softens. No, it glimmers. Cocking a hip, she crooks a finger at him in a silent summons.

Then she moves. *God*, she moves. A slow, swaying walk across the deck, hips rocking gently to the music like she's answering an invitation only she can hear. Her fiery hair catches the breeze, her smile lazy and luminous, and for a heartbeat, she looks like a woman with no ghosts at her heels.

Monty meets her halfway, setting both drinks on the sideboard without breaking eye contact. He sweeps an arm around her waist, pulls her in, and spins her across the deck with a fluidity that doesn't match his crisp, collared shirt.

Frankie's head tips back, sunlight catching her freckles as she laughs. The sound floats over the water, mixes with the music, and settles in my chest with a swirly warmth I didn't know I needed.

"Her," I say, answering Wolf's question.

"You want Frankie?" His head jerks back.

"For friendship, you gremlin." I poke his ribs. "I've never had a loyal female friend. Definitely not one like her. She gives strong woman sass but also vulnerability. Protective, but at the same time, accepting and kind. I don't have much experience with kindness. Most women judge me. Or use me. They all fuck my brother. I'm not normal."

"Neither is Frankie. She doesn't have experience with female companionship, either. Before she met my family, her closest friend was her boss."

"The doctor." My stomach sinks.

"Yeah, and you know how that turned out."

Dr. Rhett Howell lied about being her gay best friend. Turns out, he was her stalker, her kidnapper, and her rapist. Until the Strakhs hunted him down and hacked him into three hundred pieces.

"She needs a good friend, Bluebell." Wolf entwines our fingers. "And so do you."

Leo stirs on the lounger and lifts on an elbow, his dual-colored eyes searching, searching... When he spots Frankie twirling in Monty's arms, his face brightens. Softens. Fucking melts.

He pushes to his feet, strong and balanced, like a Viking born for the sea. Monty notices him and, without breaking rhythm, passes Frankie smoothly into Leo's waiting arms.

Leo catches her, his big hands settling on her hips. She beams up at him, rising on tiptoes to loop her arms around his neck. He sways with her, awkward and adorable, his feet doing something that can't be called dancing, but she laughs like it's the best performance she's ever seen.

Kody leans against the railing, an unguarded smile glittering in his black eyes. He doesn't move toward them. Just watches in his brooding way. Content.

Leo tries to spin Frankie and nearly flings himself sideways, but Frankie saves it, wrapping her arms around his neck and pulling him close. They sway again, slower this time, her cheek resting on his chest.

Then Monty slips in behind her, one hand at her waist, the other on Leo's bicep. She sighs as they sandwich her between them, the three of them stepping to the music and bumping into Kody, their movements imperfect and unsynchronized, yet in total harmony.

Wolf regards them with a soft hum in his throat, his chin nudging my temple.

"That," he murmurs, "is how they survived."

Frankie presses her freckled nose to Leo's chest, her hand reaching back to squeeze Monty's ass, her other reaching for Kody.

Kody takes it and joins their circle.

She looks held from all sides.

She looks safe.

She looks loved.

I understand what Wolf means when he says this family doesn't operate by normal rules. They don't patch wounds with distance. They patch them with closeness. With touch. With presence. With whatever strange balancing act keeps them from tipping over again.

Frankie laughs louder as Leo spins her. Badly. Monty stumbles. Kody steadies him, and the foursome dissolves into a golden knot of motion and light.

"Come on." Wolf slides his hands beneath my thighs and lifts me.

love

My arms wind around his neck as he carries me out onto the deck. Sunlight washes over his dark hair, the breeze tugging at it like even the wind wants a piece of him.

He sets me on my feet, his palms wrapping around my waist, guiding me close, his body pressing along mine. He starts to move with the music, far more skilled than I expect from a man who grew up in the frozen wilderness.

He's tall and heat-warm, firm everywhere, his chest a solid wall my hands can't stop groping.

His virile scent wraps around me, and his arms curve around my back, pulling me in until there's no space left, his breath caressing my cheek, his confidence enveloping me in a protective embrace.

I melt. Full-on, shameless melt. My knees go soft. My pulse sings, and I let him move us across the deck in fluid, deliberate steps that feel indecently sexy.

"Your turn," I whisper. "Ask me if I've ever danced with a man before."

He bends his neck, mouth hovering near my ear. "Have you ever danced with a man?"

"No."

Pleasure shimmers across his gorgeous face. His fingers tighten at my waist, drawing me even closer. He stands taller, prouder, and it hits me how much he loves this. How much I love giving him this. How he looks at me like I've handed him the world.

And I'm happy, too. Not the fleeting kind. The deep, forever kind that reshapes my heart.

He spins me, catches me against his chest, and I laugh, unfiltered and honest.

Surrounded by glittering water and the laughter of family, we dance in the warm sunlight. I lean into him fully, letting the day be exactly what it is.

Beautiful. Simple. Safe enough that neither of us pulls away.

Maybe that's the biggest question answered today.

dove
FORTY-ONE

At the end of our one-week hiatus on the island, I finish towel-drying my hair in the bathroom and stare at the fogged mirror.

My reflection looks... Different. Unsettled but not in a bad way. More like I've been unplugged and rebooted, and all my internal parts have recalibrated around... Him.

My darling wolf.

This week gave us quiet mornings, slow nights, honest answers, stolen hours where nothing hurt, and the best sex of my life.

He taught me how to fish off the dock, and I learned that I don't have the patience for it. We played cards with his family, and I learned that Leo is a sore loser and that Kody is a sneaky cheat.

We ate dinner with his family on the outdoor patio, worked out in the home gym, and took full advantage of the pool.

And now it's ending.

My heart rate is all over the place because I don't know what life looks like once we leave this house, this strange, precious bubble we hid ourselves in.

I'm terrified I'm about to lose it.

I'm equally terrified I'm not.

Under all the clashing noise, something louder pushes against my breastbone. A pressure. A truth. Three words I've been carrying like held breath. They've been sitting in my lungs all week, swelling with every glance, touch, and easy grin Wolf tosses my way.

I've told other men *something* before. Variations. Performances. Nothing that came with this intensity, this clarity, this life-altering certainty.

This is absolute.

Wolfson Strakh isn't a gentle drift or a stumbling detour. He's a roar in my chest. A pounding beneath my skin. Losing him would be losing an organ. He's vital. Integral. An essential part that doesn't grow back.

I can't lose him.

With a steadying breath, I return to the bedroom in a long T-shirt and undies, my hair damp around my shoulders.

He's sprawled across the bed, head tipped back, eyes closed. His arms lay out to the sides like he's offering himself up to a god who never deserved him.

It looks like prayer.

A heathen's prayer.

"You falling asleep on me?" I ask.

"Never," he says without lifting his lids.

Then he opens them, and that arctic blue gaze knocks the air out of me.

He looks lighter. Not healed. Not even close. But more distributed. Like the heaviness he carries found a way to spread out instead of crushing him all in one spot.

I climb onto the bed beside him, and he rolls, facing me, his hands tugging my hips until we're pressed together.

"What's going on?" He narrows his eyes as if trying to see straight into the center of me.

My throat thickens.

This is it.

No running. No hedging. No half-truths.

"I love you." The words leave me in a rush, almost violent in their urgency.

His breath stops. His lashes flutter. Shock freezes his entire body for one second, two seconds, three... Then his face cracks with pure, blinding happiness.

He tries to hide it. Of course, he tries. He pushes his tongue

love

into his cheek, nostrils pulsing, fighting a grin, fighting the wide-eyed innocence threatening to spill out.

But he can't mask it. Not from me.

His fingers sweep up my arm and tremble against my cheek as he brings his mouth to mine, eyes blazing with reciprocated love.

"Of course, you do," he says hotly, hoarsely. "You never stood a chance."

He leans his forehead against mine, the grin winning, boyish and smug. Somehow, that arrogance makes my heart bang harder.

He's still smiling when he rolls onto his back and releases a satisfied breath. I follow the movement, propping myself on an elbow beside him.

"We leave the island tomorrow." I run a finger down his chest, tracing the longest scar beneath his ribs. "Back to everything."

His nose wrinkles. "We could stay. Build a treehouse. Start our cult. Only rule is nudity after breakfast. And before."

"Be serious."

"I am serious." He turns his head toward me. "I don't want to go back to separate schedules and walking around Sitka pretending we don't have an entourage of bodyguards."

"We can't stay here forever."

"Why not?"

I laugh under my breath, because, of course, Wolfson Strakh asks *why not* to reality like it's negotiable.

Reality won't wait for us. Not while Jag is hacking systems, controlling cameras, and making enemies with every criminal organization under the sun. As expected, Monty's private investigator has uncovered fuck all on my stepbrother and his associates.

"Did you tell Taaq you're returning tomorrow?" Wolf shifts closer, sliding a hand under my T-shirt, warm palm settling against my stomach.

"Yeah. I have a full roster waiting for me. Brake jobs, filter changes, oil leaks... Back to minimum wage and greasy hands."

He studies me for a long beat. Too long. "You know you don't have to do that, right?"

"I like working on cars."

"I know." He nods slowly. "You used to have your own garage. Specialized in vintage engines. You like working on those. The ones *you* choose. But that shop in Sitka? It's not the same thing."

I look away, because he's right. I love vintage engines, the old-timey mechanics, the well-built parts, the delicious history. But being elbow-deep in strangers' junkers while a shop owner hovers over my shoulder with a clipboard? That isn't passion. It's survival.

"Stubborn little dove." His fingers skim over my pierced nipple. "You don't have to survive now."

"That's easy for you to say."

"You bet your pretty ass it is. Because I can fix this part." He sits up a little, resting his cheek against his shoulder as he looks at me. "What are you trying to prove by staying in that job?"

"I'm not trying to prove anything."

"Then why does it feel like you're punishing yourself?"

That knocks something loose in my chest. I swallow hard.

"Look, my brothers and I inherited everything Denver hoarded. And Rurik Strakh's empire. And my dad's old accounts. Offshore stuff I didn't even know existed until Monty dumped the folders on the table." He widens his eyes dramatically. "I have more money than I can ethically talk about out loud."

"I don't need your money."

"I know. That's why I want you to take it."

"That makes no sense."

"Sure it does." He cups my breast, thumbing the nipple. "You're not with me for my money. You're with me for—"

"Your tiny pancakes."

"I was going to say the best sex of your life."

"Definitely the pancakes."

He squeezes my breast with a wolfish smile. "You're not trapped anymore."

"Feels like I'm trapped." I wriggle in his grip, matching his smile.

"You don't have to cling to scraps to feel safe."

"I'm not clinging."

"You are." He releases me and moves to my other breast, teasing me there. "It's okay. I get it. But you don't need to anymore. Your independence isn't tied to a clock-in screen at some garage." His voice sinks into a dark, velvety rumble. "You're

love

with me. That doesn't make you less. It gives you room to breathe."

The fight goes out of me all at once. It's like my shoulders release for the first time in years.

"So what?" I whisper. "I just... *Quit?*"

"If it makes you miserable? Yeah. Let me take care of you. Not because you're weak. Because you don't have to do everything alone."

"What about you? Will you quit, too?"

"Absolutely. Whatever you want, my queen. Besides, Jag already fired me, remember? And it's not like I need the money."

"But you love going in."

"Because it's fun. I show up whenever I want, tattoo whatever I want, turn away the idiots, and listen to Declan fill the silence with his unhinged conspiracies. I mean, he doesn't shut up, but I kind of miss the guy. He's awkward and odd as hell, and... Nice. Really nice. Being around him is better than being alone. But now I have you, so lonely isn't a thing anymore."

"You're right. You're not alone anymore. But you can't quit."

"Well, I'm not going to keep my job if I convince you to ditch yours. That's villain behavior. Grade-A dick move."

"Except what you have isn't a job. It's a passion. You're pursuing what you love at your shop. That's not what I'm doing at my shop."

"What are you saying?"

My mouth dries, but not in a scared way. In a maturing way. In a way that growth brings discomfort and surrender releases its grip on the things that hold me back.

"Okay," I breathe.

"Okay?" His eyes shine, luminous and hungry. "You'll quit?"

"Yeah."

He grabs me by the hips and yanks me flush against him, his smile feral and sweet as he presses it against my mouth.

Then he goes still.

"Wait a damn minute." He leans back, brows puckered. "Did I just run accidental reverse psychology on you?"

"No."

"Yeah, I totally did. I told you to quit, then somehow made it about me quitting, and you argued I should keep my job, which magically proved you should quit yours. This is sorcery." He beams at me, his grin way too wide, all feigned surprise, the exact expression of a man who knows what he's doing and can't wait to do it again.

"You're so obnoxious when you get your way."

"I regret nothing."

"You might've won this round, but don't get comfortable." Setting my palm to his sternum, I give a firm push. "I have a condition."

He goes down easily, flat on his back and hair fanning against the pillow.

"Give it to me, Wildbird." His troublemaking, kiss-stealing, too-pretty mouth slants in a lopsided grin.

I climb over him, sliding onto his chest and settling into my rightful place. My legs tuck along his ribs, my hands braced on either side of his shoulders, our noses a twitch apart.

His breath hitches. Mine licks over his mouth.

"My condition for quitting is…" I slide a hand between his legs and feel him thicken in my grip. "You have to put your cock in my mouth."

"Hmm… Let me think." He sucks at the corner of his bottom lip, feigning deep concentration. Then his gravel-rough voice rasps across my skin. "You have no idea how much *yes*."

"Really? Because every time I try to go down on you, you stop me."

"Mother Mary's dangling cherry." He closes his eyes, breathes deeply, then meets me stare for stare. "I'm new at this, okay? My control levels are questionable, and I'm still figuring out the whole *lasting forever* magic show."

"You don't need to last forever."

"Cute theory, but I'm an overexcited rookie. The mere thought of your lips on my dick already kicked off the pre-party. Like the tap's open and the opening credits are rolling. Don't believe me?" He shoves down his boxers, freeing his enormously hard, very *wet* erection.

"You're overthinking it."

"Tell that to the low-pressure leak." His abs flex restlessly. "This is a bust-a-nut the instant you tongue-a-nut situation."

"Let me worry about that." I scoot backward, lowering myself down his legs and taking his boxers with me.

"Wait." He fists my hair, stopping my descent. "What happens when I need to come?"

love

"Then you come." I glide a loose fist along his length. "Shoot it straight down my throat, and I'll swallow all of you."

"Sweet sin on a Sunday." He drops his head back, his hand falling to the mattress. "You'll be the death of me."

"Relax. I'll revive you."

He said Denver never crossed this line, so it shouldn't be a trigger. Even so, I'm cautious, paying attention to his breath, his muscles, the smallest changes as I stretch out between his legs and lower my head.

Beautiful. I've never thought of a dick in that way, but the long, thick, leaking hardness between Wolf's legs is unreasonably, irresistibly beautiful. He's immaculately formed, uncut, no blemishes, no curves, nothing outside the golden rule of proportions.

Except his size.

His length and girth are significantly more impressive than every man I've been with.

My brain fires in eighty filthy directions as I stare into his eyes and slowly lick a wet circle around the bulging, plump head.

His jaw falls open, and his muscles lock. Not a single part of him moves as I take him into my mouth.

Oh, damn.

The sound he makes is guttural, wild, dragged from a place of pure ecstasy. So. Fucking. Sexy.

His head snaps back against the pillow. His throat arches, long and cut with muscle, every line of it tightening as another obscene sound punches out of him.

He's hot and slippery against my tongue, pulsing hard, the skin smooth and tight. I trace the swollen veins with my lips and palm his heavy balls, learning the shape and texture of him.

"Dove..." A mangled whisper.

His hand fists in the sheets beside him, and his stomach tenses, the hard ridges flexing with the swirl of my tongue. His hips jerk, uncontrolled and instinctive, before he forces them down with a bitten-off groan.

All his usual swagger is gone, his flirty smiles and patented one-liners nowhere to be seen.

He's actually shaking. His eyes squeeze shut. His back arches, and his thighs go rigid around me.

He's losing the battle, and we both know it.

love

FORTY-TWO

Need. Yeah, I fucking need him. For the past week, he's given me the greatest head of my life, leaving me wrecked and boneless more times than I can count.

I intend to ruin Wolfson Strakh the way he's ruined me.

As I hum and suck and draw him into the back of my throat, I keep my fingers moving on his scrotum, teasing and exploring.

Without taking my eyes off him, I read every twitch, held breath, and flicker of emotion as I shift my hand lower to caress the skin behind his ball sack.

His breath quickens, and his thighs quiver violently.

I lift my head. "Should I stop?"

"Don't you dare." He rocks his hips, restless and panting.

"You'll tell me if it's too much."

"Wicked Dove." He groans. Not a warning. Definitely a plea.

I suck him back into my mouth and slide my finger farther back, testing with soft pressure and gentle touches. His entire body shudders.

"More." His head falls back, mouth parted, his voice breaking on a growl that sends heat racing through me. "Don't stop."

The desperation in his expression is all the permission I

Love

need, but I still watch him, his eyes, his breath, the flux of tension rolling through his limbs. No fear. No recoil. Just hunger. Feral, unfiltered animal lust.

I follow his voice, his body, and the way he opens under my touch. I move with purpose now, letting my mouth and the hum in my throat build frenetic ripples through his body as my wet fingers stimulate the sensitive spot behind his sack.

When I reach the place where he was abused, I lightly circle the tight knot of muscle, a delicate touch. An offer. A question.

He clenches beneath me, shaking, breathless, undone in a way I've never seen him.

"Do it." His hands claw at the sheets, then the air, then my shoulders, like he needs to anchor himself to something real before he comes apart completely. "Please. Fuck. I need it."

I thought he might. I think he needs a lot more than my finger inside him. More than my anatomy can provide.

One step at a time.

I continue to hum around his hardness, working his shaft with my lips and a lot of saliva. Gathering that wetness, I swirl it around his anus and slowly, slowly, so fucking slowly press my smallest digit inside.

He's only ever experienced dry, violent, excruciating penetration against his will.

This is his decision, not a taking, but a giving, his body stretching and inviting me in.

The vein in his neck stands out, pulsing under flushed skin. His chest rises fast as if he can't haul air in or out. His legs tense, long muscles straining, every inch of him wound up and fighting to stay still. Fighting not to finish early.

I continue to work him, studying every adjustment and spasm, hyperaware of the heat, the lubrication, the way his cock fills my mouth and his ass grips my pinky finger.

His hips jerk involuntarily, his breath catching in short bursts, but he doesn't pull away. He presses into my touch, driving deeper into my mouth, chasing more, more, more.

I hold him there, right at that trembling edge, giving him exactly what he asked for.

More.

Using the pad of my finger to locate his prostate, I stroke upward in a come-hither motion. Then I apply a steady pressure that bows his back off the bed.

"Fuck, Dove. I'm coming. Coming so hard." He fists my hair and fucks my mouth, spilling heavy heat into my throat.

I savor the salty, clean taste of him, swallowing him down and stroking him through the release until he settles.

As I start to sit back, he grabs my hips and pulls me onto his chest, taking us both to the mattress.

"Where did you learn to do that?" His hands find my ass, his fingers absently kneading.

I've been with men who loved ass play. Over the years, a few taught me how to do it properly. One man, as it turns out, also liked my stepbrother's dick in his ass.

Come to think of it, how many of my past lovers were secretly gay? How many was Jag fucking behind my back?

I wait for the anger to rise, but it doesn't. Gavin lied to me about many things, the biggest one being his sexual orientation. But he didn't deserve to die.

Regret is the emotion that squeezes my chest. I should've been more selective about my partners. Should've used better judgment rather than seeking a warm body out of loneliness and a desperate, misplaced need for love.

How pathetic.

"Whatever you're thinking, knock it off." Wolf grips my chin, forcing my eyes to his. "I will never shame you for the lovers you've had. But I will shame *them*."

"Why them?"

"Because they lost you. Tragic." He runs his thumb over my Medusa piercing. "Their loss is my reward."

My heart flutters. "How do you do that?"

"What?"

"Read me so clearly and say the right things. You're too good to be true."

"I'm just me." He shrugs. "And I'm yours."

This feeling he stirs… It's not soft or floaty. It's a pressure in my ribs. A rush of adrenaline. A pulse that won't settle, no matter how still I sit. It's my guard rising, then dropping, then rising again, fighting a battle I already lost.

"And I'm yours." I kiss him slowly, languidly, and pull back, moving toward the bathroom. "I'm going to get ready for bed."

As I wash my hands and brush my teeth, I replay Wolf's orgasm in my mind.

love

There may come a time when my finger isn't enough, when toys aren't enough, when my soft, womanly body isn't enough.

What if he needs something different, someone different, to figure himself out?

A man.

A new dynamic.

A direction I can't compete with.

The idea of sharing him makes me murderous. Not petty jealousy. Ugly, selfish possessiveness. I don't want to be the kind of woman who digs her claws into him, cages him, and keeps him from exploring whatever he needs to understand about himself.

But the thought of stepping aside?

No.

Hell fucking no.

I'll fight for him with every drop of blood in my body. And we'll figure it out. I'll find a way.

As I slip out of the bathroom and pause in the doorway, my frightening spiral of thoughts unclenches.

Wolf sprawls on his back, an arm tossed above his head, the other resting against his stomach. Passed out cold.

Dark waves of hair stick to his forehead and fall across his cheek, completely untamed. And his face...

God.

Every ounce of tension he carries, the pain, the shadows, all of it has drained out of him. What's left is unarmored, gentle, boyish innocence.

His lashes lie thick and dark against his cheeks, his full lips parted and swollen from our kisses. No nightmares. No tight breaths. No haunted flickers under his lids.

I turn off the lights, letting the moon take over, the glow spilling through the open balcony door. The curtains drift lazily, turning the room into a slow-moving hush of shadows and warm breeze.

I climb onto the bed and curl into his side. He shifts instinctively, even in sleep, an arm sweeping around me and pulling me against his chest. His breath fans across my forehead, and just like that, I join him in the land of dreams.

Sometime later, movement wakes me.

Wolf eases me onto my back, his naked body settling over mine, solid and warm. His palms glide down my hips, coaxing my legs open.

"Bluebird." He hooks a finger in the crotch of my undies and pushes it to the side. "I need you."

It's dark, and he's on top of me, hard as a rock and wanting me like it's the easiest truth in the world.

Everything inside me goes molten. I reach for him instinctively, palms sliding over the solid muscles of his ass, pulling him closer.

He sinks into me, entering slowly, deeper with each breath, until there's no space left between us. Just heat and fullness and the weight of his body fitting perfectly against mine.

"I dreamed this." He steals my mouth, kissing me with a consuming desperation that leaves me dizzy and clutching at him. "But it's not a dream."

"It's real."

"It's fucking real." He draws back and surges in again, setting a slow, powerful rhythm. "I didn't dream you. You're real."

"I'm real." I open my legs wider and pull him in deeper.

He fucks into me, groaning into our kiss, and finishing as quickly as he started. I'm not awake enough to come with him, but as we separate, he repositions us, pulls my back to his chest, and pushes into me from behind.

This time, he doesn't thrust. With my backside flush against his pelvis and his arm curled around my waist, he falls asleep inside me.

Another first.

I've never done the post-coital cuddling thing, let alone fallen asleep with a man inside me. I never knew it could be like this.

Safe. Held. Claimed. This is what love feels like.

My eyes drift shut, and I'm out within seconds.

When I wake again, the room is dark and quiet except for the soft rush of the ocean outside. The balcony curtains billow, letting a stray draft brush my bare legs.

Wolf's no longer pressed against my back.

Beside me, he sprawls face down, cheek smashed into the pillow, the sheets tangled low around his hips, exposing the long lines of his back and cords of muscle down his sides.

My eyes adjust slowly, shapes sharpening in the blue-gray glow, as my senses come online.

That's when I feel it, something hard and round tucked into

the center of my curled hand.

I blink, confused, and open my palm.

A rock. Small and smooth like so many of the stones scattering the shoreline.

I squint, rolling it with my thumb, turning it over.

There's writing on it. Black sharpie. A single word.

My heart pounds as I tilt it toward the weak light. It takes a second, but the letters resolve.

Come

My eyes snap fully open, and adrenaline pours through me so fast I sit up on instinct, twisting toward the balcony door.

It stands open, just like I left it, the curtains swaying lazily in the warm breeze.

Nothing looks disturbed.

Heart racing, I scan the room, the corners, the shadows, the closet door cracked an inch.

Nothing.

No Jag.

No movement except the slow rise and fall of Wolf's back as he breathes, dead asleep.

If Jag is here... If Jag came into this room while we slept...

A cold, violent protectiveness locks around my ribs, and I roll toward Wolf, setting two fingers on his neck, feeling the deep, steady rhythm of his pulse.

Alive. Safe. Unaware.

If Jag came with the intent to kill, Wolf would already be dead.

I slide out of the bed, feet hitting the floor as quietly as I can manage, the rock still clutched in my hand. Then something catches my eye. A small shape on the floor, a few feet from the bed.

Another rock.

Creeping toward it, I snatch it up and spot a third one in the doorway leading to the hall.

My skin goes cold.

Jag doesn't leave trails.

How did he sneak onto the island undetected?

If he went through all this trouble to see me in the middle of the night...

Something's wrong.

I look back at Wolf. Still asleep.

The thought of Jag getting anywhere near him ignites a bloodthirsty dread inside me. If I wake him, it could lead to a fight. Last time they fought, weapons were drawn, and bones were crushed.

Last time they were together, Wolf had a breakdown.

No, I won't wake him. Not yet.

After a quick sweep of the closet and bathroom, I slip into the hall, locking the bedroom door behind me without a sound.

The rocks bite into my palm as I follow the next dark shape on the floor, then the next, collecting them, one by one, down the stairs.

On the ground floor, I pause.

Silence. Nothing stirs in the shadows. No creak of floorboards. No phantom shift of air.

Where is he?

The faint trail of rocks snakes through the living room, catching the moonlight in small, cold glints. I follow it, palms clammy, and set the pile on the armchair.

The last rock sits at the front door.

My stomach drops. No way in hell am I stepping outside without Wolf.

As I turn back, a hand slams over my mouth.

I throw an elbow, a hip, and my nails come out, clawing and fighting with all my strength, but the grip is iron. My breath strangles beneath the hand as a muscled arm locks around my waist and wrenches me around.

My back hits the door, and a rigid body pins me in place. A body I recognize before I see the eyes.

Jaguar-gold and hellfire-red melt into a metallic amber gaze that watches me carefully, warning and burning with every reason I should scream.

And every reason I don't.

Jag lowers his uninjured hand from my lips and ducks his head, leaning in, bending close. His cold nose grazes my neck, inhaling deeply before moving my hair.

Then he straightens and gives me an unfathomable look.

A chill runs through me. Fear, yes. But something else.

"What?"

Love

"You smell different when you're awake."

"You've been watching me sleep?"

"Since you were a child."

"That's—"

"Sick? Yeah. I'm fucking sick, Little Bird."

"I didn't say that."

Alarm bells ring in my head.

His brown hair sticks up in wild, frantic angles that only comes from raking a hand through it over and over. His rumpled jeans show stains on one leg and rips on the other, and he probably grabbed that wrinkled shirt off a floor. Or slept in it. If he's sleeping at all.

Shadows darken his eyes. His face is drawn tight. His jaw locks so violently it ticks, and his chest rises hard and shallow. Did he run here?

His wrist is swollen along the ridge of bone, the skin mottled in sick yellows. No brace or bandages. Nothing to help it heal.

He's not taking care of himself.

This isn't the cocky, shameless, sex-drunk Jag who thrives on getting a rise out of me. Nor is this the version who manipulates, taunts, and stalks his prey with practiced bedroom eyes.

This one is... Wrong.

He looks hollow, unsteady, frayed at every edge.

Something is very wrong.

"What happened to you?" I whisper. "Why are you here? How did you even get on the island?"

He closes his eyes like the questions hurt.

"Jag." I gnash my teeth. "What do you want?"

"I had to see you." He looks at me now, his eyes darker, sunken, haunted. "Before I go."

"Go where?"

"I'm leaving Sitka."

"You're running again? Who's hunting you?"

His jaw flexes, a single angry clench.

"Why didn't you leave a rock at the goddamn grave like you always do?"

Drawing a slow breath through his nose, he removes something from his pocket and presses it into my palm.

Another rock.

I look at it, at the black letters written across the surface.

Ends Here

My heart scrapes against my ribs.

"This is the last time you'll see me, Dove." He grips my fingers, his hand shaking against mine.

Jag never shakes.

"What the hell does that mean?" Icy dread crawls over my scalp. "You can't just... Jag, you don't get to show up in the middle of the night with your non-answers, and— And this." I shove the rock against his chest. "Explain it."

"I'm not answering your questions." His expression hardens as the rock falls to the floor. "I can't."

Blood thrashes in my ears. I want to scream, but Wolf is upstairs, and I need to sort this out before he wakes.

"Why now? Why tonight?" I force my anger into a whisper. A harsh, seething growl. "After stalking me for years and killing everyone I know? Why are you doing this?"

"I should've done this a long time ago." His features twist with a deep, private agony.

"Done what?"

"Let you go. I tried with Gavin, thinking he could keep you safe and give you what I couldn't. But I was wrong about him, and I'm so fucking sorry."

"I don't understand." My chest hurts.

"You're safe now. Safer than you've ever been. You have Wolf and his resources—"

"Safe from what? Tell me, goddammit." I grip his forearm, digging my fingers into muscle. "What do I need protection from?"

"Me."

"Why?"

"You needed a mother, and all you had was me. An angry kid. A horny teenage boy who didn't know how to raise you. Didn't know how to love you without... Damaging you."

"I needed *you*. Just you, Jag." Tears burn the backs of my eyes.

Why am I crying? Why do I even care? I need to step aside and shove him out the door. But I can't. For the same reason I couldn't shoot him after I fled my wedding.

love

Before he was cruel, he was my protector. Before he broke my heart, he was my everything. The terrible things he did to keep me fed, the sacrifices he made to keep me safe, the darkness he became to keep me alive, it killed the beautiful boy he was and turned him into something I no longer recognize.

But as I stare into his hooded eyes, all I see is that strong, determined, selfless boy who fought like hell to give me a better life.

He hates the tears. The instant they hit my cheeks, his expression crumples. He crowds in, taking my face in his hands and touching me like I'm sacred. Touching me like he used to touch me.

"Don't." His thumbs brush my cheeks, too gentle, too crushing. "Don't cry."

"You're leaving me. Leaving without telling me where you're going or why. No explanation. No answers."

Emotions surge between us, raw and old and impossible to untangle. His hands mold around my neck, supporting, consoling as he runs his nose along mine.

He's leaving.

Leaving me with a kindness I don't trust.

But once, a long time ago, I did. I trusted his touch more than anything in the world.

We gravitate toward that connection, our bodies shifting, pulling, closing the distance, reaching for the safety and comfort we once found in each other.

Our foreheads touch. His breath shakes. Mine breaks. Then our lips meet.

Not soft. Not tentative. Not something that should happen between two people with our history.

It's a kiss that detonates the years between us, the grief, the resentment, the secrets, and the longing neither of us ever admitted. A collision of everything we shoved down and never voiced.

His hands travel down my body and curl around my waist. My fingers twist into his shirt.

Hunger. Memory. Pain. All of it crashes at once.

The moment our mouths fuse, another life flashes in my mind, opening rooms I haven't stepped into since I was a child.

Jag's arms around me as our world fell apart. His voice

singing to me in our cardboard fort. His large body climbing through my window. His bloodstained fingers braiding my hair. His shadow curled around me when I started my period. His breath whispering against my neck, *I'll never leave you*. His pinky wrapped around mine. And the blood, the blood, the blood, always so much blood running off his hands and swirling down the sink.

The present dissolves. The years disintegrate. I'm small again, lost and clinging, and Jag is the only person in the world I have left.

The kiss hauls me back into every abandoned building, cardboard box, and dirty blanket I shared with him, and the memories swallow me whole.

love
FORTY-THREE

Twenty-four years ago

Jag says this place is Portland, but it doesn't look like a port or a land. The sky is always gray. The people are strange, and this corner store smells like old gum under the counter. But I don't ask questions. If Jag says Portland, we're in Portland.

All I know is it's far from home.

Home is where I left my toys, pretty shoes, and soft sweaters. All the things I grew out of without meaning to.

I try not to think about Mom. Not because it hurts. It hurts a lot. But my head doesn't know what to do with a hurt that big.

Jag says eight-year-olds aren't built for that kind of thinking. Besides, my brain is too busy with the pinch in my belly. I'm always hungry, and it makes my tummy squirm and buzz like a mosquito.

I stare at the bag of peanuts in my hand, my mouth watering for the salty crunch. I just know the tiny pieces would fill the tiny pockets inside me.

Standing on my tiptoes, I search for Jag. I always know where he is, even when I can't see him.

A few aisles over, I catch the top of his head. His messy

brown hair never sits down, no matter how many times he pats it.

He's taller than most sixteen-year-olds. I didn't know that until a cashier somewhere told me.

I look down at my jeans, at the stiff dirt around the knees. They don't touch my shoes anymore. Maybe I'm tall, too. My shirt has holes that weren't there last year, and the rips around my neck are getting bigger. They flap when I move. The wind gets in.

But I'm not scared. The stomach ache doesn't scare me. The holes don't scare me. Nothing scares me when Jag is near.

Because he's always near.

I hear his footsteps before I see him, a sound I know better than music. He appears in my aisle, wearing sneakers that have more holes than my shirt. His toe sticks out of one, like it got too big and broke free.

"Let's go." He snatches the peanuts from my hand and shoves them into the pocket of his denim coat.

A candy bar disappears into the other side, so quick it's magic.

His hand closes around mine, his fingers warm and strong and never shaking, as he walks fast toward the door.

We don't run. Running makes noise. Running makes people look.

We walk like we belong here. Like we're supposed to have food in our pockets and empty bellies and nobody waiting for us anywhere.

Outside, the cold air bites my cheeks and stings my eyes. I'm thinking about tearing open the peanuts, about how good they'll taste, when the cashier shouts from the doorway.

"Hey! You need to pay for that!"

My heart jumps.

Jag doesn't flinch. His hand clamps harder around mine, and I squeeze back.

Now is when we run.

He pulls me forward so quick I almost leave my shoes behind. His legs are longer and faster. The sidewalk blurs, and my breath comes out in little squeaks. I try to keep up. I really do. But my feet tangle. Oh, no, I'm stumbling.

Jag immediately stops.

The cashier bursts around the corner behind us, yelling

love

louder, waving his arms, and calling for help.

Jag doesn't even look at him.

He scoops me up, an arm under my knees and another around my back. My face presses into the warm denim of his coat. Then he runs.

Not normal running. He runs like an action hero, veering between cars, leaping over trash, and dodging people and their dogs. He flies around corners without slowing, his legs mighty and strong. My arms stay tight around his neck as the world jerks and swings and spins.

No one's chasing us anymore.

I peek over his shoulder. Nobody. The cashier gave up ages ago.

But Jag keeps going. And going. And going. His breath gets rougher, but he never stops.

Not until we arrive in the land of tents.

Rows and rows of multicolored domes fill the space between buildings, squeezed together so tight we can't walk between them.

Jags pushes through anyway, carrying me over sleeping men and noisy women with eyes that don't look right. Our spot is in the very back.

We don't have one of the fancy real tents. We have something better.

Our fort.

Jag built it himself out of cardboard and plastic sheets that people threw away. It looks like a secret hideout that superheroes use when they need to sleep. The walls fold together in magical ways, and he fixes them every night so the rain doesn't get in.

Inside, he sets me down on the old blankets and foam pieces he found behind a store.

Everything important—food, water, clothes, the flashlight, the little knife he keeps hidden—stays in the backpack he never takes off, not even when he sleeps. It's right there on his shoulders now.

I don't need the things in that bag.

I only need him.

He adjusts the flap of our cardboard door, sealing us away from the big, scary world.

Kneeling beside me, he starts unloading his pockets. The peanuts, candy bar, soap, toothpaste, medicine, matchsticks... Then a can of noodle soup from the backpack. He uses his knife to slice the top open and bends the metal back carefully so it won't cut me.

He always thinks of stuff like that.

"Here." He feeds me spoonful by spoonful.

The noodles are soggy, but they slide right into the empty places in my belly. I eat until I'm full, and he finishes the rest without taking a breath.

"Got something for you." He reaches inside his coat.

I perk up at the strange sound of his voice.

He pulls out a stuffed animal. A soft, fluffy silver cat with whiskers.

"For me?" I'm so excited I could burst.

He nods and hands it over.

The fur is warm from being against his chest, and I hug it so tight it squishes in the middle. It's perfect. It's the softest thing I've ever held.

"What's it for?"

His jaw does that bouncing thing, making his face look extra hard.

"It's your birthday." He brushes the hair from my eyes. "You're nine today."

"Nine?" My heart does a weird jump. "I'm nine?"

"Yeah, Little Bird. Growing up fast."

I lift the cat to look at it better. Its black shirt is a little crooked, and the red feet look like they walked through paint.

"It's a jaguar." I wriggle its legs. "A really fast one like you."

"It's called a Trail Cat. The mascot for the basketball team."

"No." I squeeze it and pet its little head. "It's a jaguar. And his name is Little Jag."

He rolls his eyes, which means I win.

He digs into his pocket one more time and pulls out something wrapped in plastic. A small chocolate cake, the kind they sell at gas stations. It's squished a little, but who cares? It's cake.

He unwraps it and sets it in my hands. Then he sings, soft and deep, "Happy birthday to you..."

His voice fills our fort, and I smile so big my cheeks hurt. I have a cat and chocolate cake and my big brother sitting beside

love

me, trying his hardest to sing as good as my mom.

It's the best birthday I've ever had.

I break the cake in half and shove one piece at him, but he gives me his stern look, so I huff and eat the whole thing myself. It's the yummiest thing I've ever tasted, even if the frosting sticks to my fingers.

When we're done, we brush our teeth and go outside to use the portable potty place. Then we hurry back before anyone can talk to us or stare too long.

Inside, Jag pulls the scratchy blankets over us. He lies down with the backpack behind him, and I curl up against his chest. His arms come around me, strong and unmovable.

Outside, voices rise, shouting, crying, metal rattling, and someone moaning too loud. But Jag keeps me safe.

I'm drifting off when his sleepy voice rumbles against my ear.

"You need to go back to school, Dove."

"Noooooo." I groan into his shirt.

"You're smart. Smarter than most kids. You need school so you don't lose it."

"I won't."

"But for that to work, you might need to stay with a foster family. Just for a little while."

"No." I flip onto my back and glare at him through the shadows. "No way. I'm not going anywhere. You can't make me."

"Shhh." He taps my lips. "Keep your voice down."

"I'm not staying with strangers. I'm staying with you."

"Sweetheart…" He shifts so his eyes are close to mine. "I'm never leaving you."

"Promise?"

"I swear it." He holds up his pinky.

I hook my pinky around his, squeezing tight. Then I bring our hands to my mouth and kiss our twisted fingers. He smiles and kisses them next, sealing it.

Outside, the world yells and falls apart.

Inside, Jag and I hold on.

love
FORTY-FOUR

Two years later

I'm not supposed to be here.

Not in this house, not in this room, not in this stupid system that tosses me around like a mangy stray.

Fifth house in two years.

Fifth set of strangers pretending they want me.

On my ninth birthday, Jag and I argued about my return to school. We didn't know the decision would be made for us one week later.

He would never call himself my parent, but he sure fights like one every time they take me. He fights the cops, the social workers, and the paperwork, saying I'm not safe with anyone but him.

Every time the system pulls me out of his arms, he finds me. He always finds me.

When he doesn't like the home they put me in, when the fridge is empty, or the father stares too long, he cuts the window screen and steals me away. Then we run until our legs give out. New cities. New names. New lies.

Until child services catches me again.

Now I'm in Salt Lake City, in another house, with another last name.

And Dean.

God, I hate Dean.

He's eighteen, same age as Jag, but that's where the similarity ends.

Dean smells like cheap cologne and fried food. His white-blond hair and even whiter complexion make him easy to spot from the school bus.

Every day, he follows me from the bus stop to the house, walking slow like he's picking his moment. When he gets close enough to slime my cheek with his breath, he says things that make my stomach twist.

Today, he corners me on the side of the house and calls me a whore like I know what that means. Then he grabs my arm, squeezes hard enough to bruise, and tells me I better come to his room tonight or he'll *make it hurt more tomorrow.*

When the dog next door starts barking, I rip away from him, sprint inside, and lock my bedroom door.

For hours, I sit in the corner of my room, knees up to my chest, and arms squeezing my stuffed jaguar. It's ratty and missing a leg, but I still sleep with it pressed under my chin because it smells like Jag's jacket.

It's too bright outside. Jag won't come until it's dark. He'll wait until everyone's asleep before climbing through my window, quiet as a sparkling vampire, smelling like road dust and cold air. Most nights, he curls around me and doesn't move until I fall asleep.

But right now, the sun is still up, and Dean is somewhere in this house.

I stare at the doorknob, daring it to turn.

The room is small, the bedspread stiff with faded cartoon characters. One window. Beige walls. My backpack sits by the bed where I dropped it after running inside, my math homework sticking out the top. I don't care.

I just want Jag.

I need his voice telling me everything's fine, even though we both know it isn't.

I need his heartbeat against my back, strong and angry and alive.

Pulling my sleeves over my hands, I rock in place.

love

Until I hear movement.
Footsteps in the hallway.
I stop breathing.
They pause outside my door.
I pull my knees tighter.
The lock wriggles.
My heart slams so hard my body shakes.
Then a click.
A key.
The door swings open, and Dean fills the doorway.
    He grins when he sees me in the corner, and my skin crawls. He steps inside and shuts the door behind him. The need to puke makes my mouth fill with saliva.
    I hate how slow he walks toward me, how mean his face looks when he squats beside me like we're friends. Before I can make my voice work, he snatches Little Jag.
    "Give it back," I whisper.
    He holds it up by one arm, examining it like trash. I bury my face in my knees so he won't see my tears.
    Then the worst sounds spill into the room. A zipper lowering. Fabric pattering. Warm droplets splashing onto the floor.
    I freeze until the truth hits me, ugly and monstrous.
    He's peeing on it.
    "No!" I snap my head up. "Stop! Stop!"
    He pees harder, spraying Little Jag until the fur turns dark and soaked. Ruined.
    My chest caves in. I can't breathe through the breaking pain inside me.
    When he's done, he drops the dripping jaguar at my feet, and it lands with a wet slap.
    "Maybe I'll clean it." He grabs the floppy thing between his legs. "But first, you clean me."
    I scramble backward, but there's nowhere to go. I'm cornered, and he's bigger, so much stronger as his hand captures my hair and yanks me to my knees.
    Pain shoots across my scalp. Tears blur my eyes. I try to pull away, but he jerks harder, forcing my face forward, too close, right up against the disgusting part of him that's no longer floppy. It grows against my cheek, turning hard as he jabs it

against my pressed lips.

Panic rips through me, and my vision goes white at the edges.

"Open your mouth." His fist tightens. "Do it, or I'll make you."

My stomach heaves in terror.

Jag told me exactly what to do if someone tries to hurt me like this. I don't want to do it. I don't want to open my mouth. But I don't have a choice.

I unlock my jaw.

Then I bite.

Hard.

Dean screams, releasing my hair and staggering back.

I scramble on all fours, slipping on the floor as I lunge toward the bed. My fingers search under the pillow for what I know is there.

The knife. The little folding blade Jag shoved into my hand my first night here.

My fingers grip cool metal, and I whip around. My arm shakes so fiercely the blade trembles in the air.

"If you come near me again, I'll chop that thing off and feed it to the garbage disposal."

Jag said that's where it goes if they don't have a blender.

Dean stares at me, chest heaving, eyes wide with disbelief. Then fury.

"Deeeeean!" His mother screams from the stairs. "You haven't mowed the lawn, motherfucker! I'm not asking again!"

He glares at me as he zips his pants.

"This isn't over." He storms out, slamming the door.

I stand there with the knife shaking in my hand, staring at the ruined jaguar where it lies in a filthy puddle on the floor.

A sob stuffs itself into my throat, and all the bravery I faked falls out of me at once. My bones go soft. My legs can't hold me. I drop to my knees beside Little Jag and reach out with trembling fingers.

The smell hits me.

I gag. Then I heave, puking so suddenly I can't move fast enough to avoid the jaguar. I make a mess all over it, crying harder as I vomit.

When my insides are empty, I wipe my mouth and lock the door. Then I crawl onto the bed with the knife and curl into a ball.

I can't stop shaking.

The sun goes down slow.

The house quiets.

Finally, finally, the window opens, and the night air slips in. Jag climbs through, his backpack landing silently on the floor. When he sees me curled up on the bed, he freezes.

"What happened?" His voice vibrates in that deep way when he's angry.

My throat feels stuck as he follows my gaze to Little Jag and the sour mess around it.

His face changes into a slow, dark thundercloud that means he'll break things if he doesn't hold himself together.

He kneels by the ruined toy, fingers hovering above it, careful not to touch. He doesn't breathe. Doesn't move.

"Tell me." His eyes shift to mine. "Don't leave out a single detail."

I suck in a shaky breath and tell him everything. What Dean said, what he did to Little Jag, how he grabbed me, what he tried to force, how I bit him, how I threatened him with the knife, and how he promised it isn't over.

Jag listens without interrupting, his mouth hard and eyes harder.

When I finish, he stands and turns away from me. His shoulders rise and fall, rise and fall, like he can't breathe right. He grips his hair, pulling, yanking, and making a noise that sounds like he's hurting.

"Only ten years old," he whispers.

"I'll be eleven next month."

"Yeah." He roughly rubs his face with both hands, keeping his back to me. Then his loud breaths start to slow. He rolls his neck and faces me again. "You did good. The biting, the knife... You fought back just like I taught you."

My skin warms all over.

He grabs my black trash bag, the one I never bother to unpack, and starts stuffing the rest of my things into it. Clothes. Schoolbooks. Toothbrush.

"Time to run?" I pull on the shoes he hands me.

"Not yet." He ties the bag and leaves it on the floor beside his backpack. "Where is Dean's room?"

"Across the hall." I point. "First door on the left."

He wipes his thumb across my cheek, where dried tears left itchy lines. His touch is soft, but his skin is hot. I know that look in his eyes. It's the same one I saw the night he pulled me out of the pantry.

"I need you to sit right here and wait for me." He crouches where my legs dangle off the bed and fixes the ties on my shoes. Then he places the folded knife on my lap. "I'll be right back."

"Promise?"

"I swear it." He sticks out his pinky.

I wrap mine around his, squeezing so hard my hand shakes. After I kiss our tangled fingers, he leans in to kiss them, too, locking the promise in place.

"Okay, now I need you to put your fingers in your ears." He stands and walks to the door. "Do not move them until I come back."

I shove my fingers in as deep as they'll go and clamp my elbows to my ribs. The world goes muffled, then completely quiet. My breath is loud in my skull. My heart, too.

The knife sits on my lap like he left it.

I don't know how long he's gone. A minute. Ten. Forever. Time feels strange when he's not in the room, but I'm not scared anymore.

He's here. I'm safe now. He said so with his eyes before he stepped into the hall.

The door opens again.

I don't move my fingers until he taps my wrist. He holds a balled-up shirt and uses it to wipe his hands. It's bloody, soaked through, dark and sticky, smearing across his knuckles. There's so much blood my stomach turns, but I'm not scared of that, either.

I'm only scared the blood might be his.

His knuckles are split open like whenever he hits something too hard, too many times.

"Dean won't hurt me again, will he?"

"No." His eyes flash like fire, warming me on the inside. "Never again."

He slings on his backpack, and I throw myself against his chest, hugging his hard middle. His arms hug me, too, lifting me and the trash bag.

"What about Little Jag?" I point at my only toy.

love

He swings around, staring at it, his face pinching before smoothing out again.

"You don't need it." He kisses my nose. "You have me."

"Okay."

I give Little Jag a wave goodbye as the real Jag carries me out the window and takes me to where he sleeps.

It's not far, under the freeway bridge, deep enough that rain doesn't hit. He has a tent now. A real tent, with a zippered door and everything.

I miss the cardboard fort, but he says the tent is easier to move.

Inside, a tiny lantern sits beside a pile of blankets. There's plenty of room until he slips in. He takes up all the space.

His backpack goes in the corner, and my trash bag beside it. He gives me crackers, a squished granola bar, and half a soda. I eat even though my throat is sore from crying.

"You got taller." He puts his hand on my head, where it brushes the ceiling of the tent. "And your hair's longer. All the way down your back now."

"Yours, too."

"Yeah." He fingers the curly ends where they sit on his shoulders. "Guess so."

"And this." I drag my fingertips across the pale prickles on his cheek, laughing at the scratchiness. "You have a beard!"

"Just a little fuzz." He ducks his head, almost shy, which is strange because Jag isn't shy about anything.

"Do you have to shave it like Dad?"

"Not yet." He taps my hip. "Turn around."

I shift on the blankets, scooting to sit between his bent knees with my back to his chest. The tent is so small our legs fold in weird angles.

"Why don't you have a house?" I ask.

His huff caresses the top of my head. "I can't even get an apartment."

"Why not?"

"I don't have credit. Can't use my real name. I've killed a lot of bad people. I need to live close to your foster home and be able to pack up and move on the fly. Besides, I sleep with you most nights."

He lifts my hair off my shoulders and smooths out the

tangles, careful not to pull where my scalp still hurts. When the strands are separated, he begins to braid, threading the pieces better than I can.

I don't care about the blood trapped under his nails.

I don't care if we live in a box or a tent.

I only care about the big, strong hands in my hair.

"We'll have to leave by morning," he says.

I knew that already. "Where are we going next?"

"Texas, I think. It's warmer there."

The thought of traveling with him again, hitchhiking, hiding behind dumpsters, and sleeping in abandoned places should scare me. But it doesn't.

It's freedom.

It's us.

I wish we could go back to California and see the cemetery. I haven't been there. Ever. Jag says it's too dangerous.

"Tell me about Mom and Dad." I pat his knee, feeling the sudden stiffness there. "I can't picture them right anymore. I used to. But it's blurry."

"Dad had curly brown hair." His voice is choppy, like there are knives in his mouth. "He worked with his hands. An electrician. And he was good with computers. He smiled a lot."

I close my eyes, trying to remember.

"Celeste, our mom..." He clears his throat. "She was pretty, almost as pretty as you."

My cheeks burn.

"She had long, blond hair. Just like this." He finishes the braid down my spine, and his hands tremble just once near the end as he ties it off with a rubber band from his wrist. "She sang really well. All the time."

I wait for more, but that's all he says.

"Why did they die?" I lean back into him.

"They were in danger." He hugs me from behind, holding me tight. "Real danger. And they tried to shield us from it. None of it was your fault, and you don't need the details. Not tonight. Not ever."

"Are we in danger?"

"As long as I live, I will keep you safe. That's my job."

"Okay. I love you."

"Love you, too, Little Bird." He rests his mouth on the top of my head.

love

    The tent flaps rustle with the wind, and suddenly, I'm so tired I can't keep my eyes open.

    But I can sleep now, because he'll be here, guarding me in the dark.

love
FORTY-FIVE

Three years later

I stand in front of the electronics store and pretend the ground is interesting. Cracked concrete, gum spots, cigarette butts, anything to keep my good eye from drifting toward the glass door.

Because my other eye? It's a whole situation.

It throbs when I blink. I smeared on heavy black makeup this morning, and my hair hangs in my face. But I can feel the bruise pulsing through the strands.

Jag expects me to be here every day after school. If I don't show, he'll find me. Which would be fantastic if I didn't share a room with two other girls.

If Jag climbed through our window, the whole foster home would explode. Then we'd have to move again, and I'm tired. Tired of switching schools and learning new rules and changing my name, appearance, and identity.

I hike my backpack higher on my shoulder and go in, jingling the bell over the door.

"He's in the back." The store owner stands behind the counter, not bothering to look up.

love

I shuffle past old DVD players and towers of discount phone cases until I reach the storage aisle.

Jag crouches there with a box cutter, slicing tape off a shipment of speakers.

His hair curls around his ears, shaggy and wild. It looks different now. Grown-up different. He could be on a movie poster if he ever bothered to smile.

The amber color of his eyes is different, too. Harder. Older. Meaner. Because he learned too many things nobody his age should learn.

And his body… I pretend not to notice, but he grows in these strange, sudden ways. He's big. Everywhere. Not fat. Every part of him is hard and strong. His uniform shirt pulls across his chest, and his muscles stretch and stack like bricks.

His face is dreamy at every angle, and sometimes, when I look at him, my stomach feels weird.

I'm thirteen. I shouldn't notice things like this. Especially not about my brother.

But I do.

Everyone does.

I brush my hair over my eye and walk toward him. He glances up. Just a flick. Barely a second.

The box cutter freezes in his hand. His jaw turns to stone, and he stands in one smooth push of muscle and anger.

"Who?" He tosses the blade and strides straight to me.

It's not a question. It's bloodstains under his fingernails.

"It's nothing." My heartbeat kicks into a drum solo. "I'm fine."

"Let's go." He grabs my hand, firm but not rough, and pulls me toward the front.

"Stop. Wait. You're at work."

He doesn't stop.

"Where are you going?" The owner straightens behind the counter. "Hey! You can't leave, Simon!"

Simon. I'm not the only one with a dozen names.

"Then I quit." Jag flings his plastic badge across the counter and keeps walking, hauling me with him.

This job is better than all the awful things he's done for money over the years. He can't quit.

Outside, the Las Vegas heat shocks my system, but Jag

doesn't slow. We're half a block from the store before I manage to yank my hand out of his.

"You can't lose your job." My voice shakes with all the things I can't tell him. "Please, Jag."

He whirls on me. "This is more important than a fucking job."

My throat closes. Sometimes he forgets how big he is. How scary he looks when he's mad. But I know he's not mad at me. He's mad *for* me. Which is worse.

His hand swallows up mine and pulls. We walk fast, him dragging, me stumbling, past tourists and pawn shops and the guy who sits on crates and yells at the sky. We cut down the side alley that smells like rotten fruit. Then another that smells like death. And another. And another. Until we end up behind the abandoned apartment building where he lives.

We climb crumbling stairs. On the top floor, he pulls out the padlock key from around his neck and shoves it into the lock he drilled into the door.

Inside, the air is hot and stale, but familiar.

His setup crowds one half of the room. Towers of humming computers and mismatched monitors. Wires everywhere. Boxes stacked on boxes. He stole most of it. Probably from the store that he just quit.

Power cords snake from the lamp and computer equipment into a hole in the wall and out to wherever he siphons electricity. He steals the Wi-Fi from the smoke shop on the corner. If it goes down, he curses loud enough for the pigeons on the roof to fly away.

On the other side of the room is his bed.

It's not a real bed. The thin, tattered cushions came from broken lawn chairs he found in a dumpster. He taped the pads together and threw old blankets on top, forming a narrow spot barely wide enough for him. His legs hang off the edge, but he never complains.

The floor is busted tile and rough cement, and the walls are cracked and leaky.

It's ugly. It's perfect. I'm happier here than anywhere else.

He shuts the door and slides the interior bolt. Then he turns to me, eyes on fire. "Tell me what happened."

"I told you. It's nothing."

"Nothing doesn't leave a bruise that big."

love

"I got into a fight." I stare at my beat-up sneakers. I found them in a lost-and-found bin at school, and they don't fit right.

"Who?"

"I said it's nothing."

"You're not leaving until you tell me who hurt you."

That makes my heart sink because I know what he'll do.

The girl who blackened my eye? She didn't mean to do it. It was stupid. An argument. A thrown brush. I was in the way. The foster mom didn't care enough to separate us.

He inspects my face, not the bruise, but the way I press my lips together. We hit that wall where I won't say anything else, and he knows it.

Exhaling through his nose, he jerks his chin toward the attached bathroom.

He follows me into the small, doorless room. The sink doesn't work. The tub is rust-red at the bottom. Buckets of water line the wall, filled from a hose somewhere outside. The toilet only works when he pours water into the tank. His clothes hang on a rope he strung across the window, and they sway as he walks past them, brushing his shoulder.

"Sit." He flicks a finger at the closed toilet lid.

I obey as he grabs a cloth from a crate, dips it into the cleanest bucket, and crouches before me. He's too big to squat like that without his knees practically touching his chin.

He wipes the smeared eyeliner from my face, careful not to hurt me. I know when the black eye fully appears because he goes rigid.

Blond whiskers cover the sharp angles on his jaw and cheeks, making him look older than twenty-one. He looks like a man, not the boy who used to sleep on sidewalks with me curled under his arm. He has this vertical line that shows up between his brows when he's focused, and it's there now, deep and angry.

"Tell me what happened." He grips the edge of the sink.

"It's over."

"It's not over until I know who did it."

I shake my head.

"Then you're staying here tonight."

My heart lifts, stupid and fast. I love staying here, and it's not like I'll be missed at the foster house. No one keeps track of my whereabouts.

Except Jag.

"Put this on." He snatches a shirt off the line, tosses it to me, and leaves the bathroom.

I pull the huge garment over my head. The hem covers my shorts, so I take them off and stay in my underwear.

When I come out, he sits at his desk, bathed in the blue glow of his monitors. His fingers fly across the keyboard, coding or breaking into something or whatever illegal thing he does for money now.

I sink onto the cushions, pulling my knees to my chest.

He glances at me every few minutes, waiting.

I don't talk.

He doesn't force it.

We're good at this. Our silent fights. Our wordless peace. But I feel him waiting for my truth.

I watch him work for a while, the captivating way he focuses, the magnetic way he moves. Then I try to sleep, but when I close my eyes, I think about how his body would feel lying on top of mine, the hard press of his mouth against my lips, and the sounds he would make if he put his hand between my legs. I think about that every night until my skin feels too hot and my own hand rubs between my legs.

I used to tell him everything, but I could never tell him that.

My stomach grumbles, loud enough for him to hear it.

Without looking at me, he reaches under the desk and pulls out some packages from a box. Foil-wrapped crackers, a plastic cup of peanut butter, and a box of raisins land on the cushion beside me.

I tear the cracker packet open with my teeth and eat every crumb, dipping them into the peanut butter and scraping the cup clean with my finger.

After a long and unsuccessful attempt to sleep, I push myself up and pad over to him, the oversized shirt brushing my thighs. He doesn't remove his gaze from the screen, but he tilts his head when he senses me behind him.

I rest my hands on his shoulders. His muscles tense then loosen under my touch. I rub slow circles the way he likes, the way I've watched him do to himself when his neck locks up.

His body runs hotter than mine. He's my very own heater. I lean down and fold my arms around his neck. My cheek presses into the back of his head. His hair smells like sunshine and

love

whatever soap he used in a bucket.

Then I kiss him. Not on the mouth. On his cheek. Then the top of his head. The place where his hair parts.

This is how it's supposed to be. Him and me. Together. When we're apart, something inside me goes wrong. I don't know how to breathe right.

He sets one hand over mine, holding it in place for a second before letting go. His eyes flick to a different monitor, and that's when I notice it.

The street outside my foster home.

I lean closer.

He clicks a key, freezing the footage right as a girl steps off the bus.

Me.

My stomach cramps, not scared, just worried. Like finding out he can record the thoughts in my head.

"What is that?" I whisper.

"I'm learning how to control the public cameras." He doesn't look guilty. He looks smug.

"Why? What for?"

"If you won't tell me who hurt you, I'll figure it out myself." He taps a few keys, rewinding.

The screen shows the bus pulling up again, the whole street shifting backward like he can control time.

My pulse spins.

He switches to another tab, a black window filled with green letters streaming down like rain. I don't understand any of it. I only know he taught himself this stuff when we still had parents.

"What else can you do?" I inch closer to the screens.

"I can break into school records."

He shows me how he changes my grades when we move, so I don't have to repeat classes. He digs up addresses of foster families before I meet them, tracks bus schedules and routes so he never loses me, and disables door alarms so he can sneak into houses and get supplies.

All of it is for me. Every single thing.

He clicks another screen. A live feed from a camera near my school. Then another from the porch at my foster house. Then one I don't recognize at all.

"You can't do this," I whisper.

"I already am." That angry line between his brows deepens. "I'm not letting anyone touch you. Never again."

A part of me knows this isn't normal. Other kids don't have someone watching every sidewalk they step on. But the bigger part of me, the part that aches when he's not near, loves it.

If Jag is watching, I'm safe. And if I'm safe, he's calm.

He rewinds the footage, frame by frame, eyes narrowed as he scans every person on the sidewalk.

He'll find her.

"Jag…" I step between him and the screens, twisting the hem of my shirt in my fingers.

His eyes drop to the movement of my hands. Then lower.

He chokes. "You're bleeding."

"What?" I look down.

A thin red river trails down my thigh. It's dark and sticky and startling.

"Oh." I have no idea what else to say.

"Did you cut yourself?" His eyes dart around the room, trying to find what stabbed me. "Where did you—?" Slowly, his head lifts again. He studies my face, his mouth opening, closing, and opening again. "Did you get your period?"

"My… Period?"

"Your cycle." His voice drops even quieter. "Like… Your monthly. Blood."

"I don't know. I've never had that. What do I do?"

"Okay." He blows out a breath and rubs his jaw like he's trying not to panic. "Okay. Come with me."

He takes my wrist, and I follow him into the bathroom again.

"Stand in the tub." He clears his throat and looks away. "And take off your underwear."

I climb into the rusty bathtub and pull down my underwear. The red-stained fabric looks unreal, like someone else wore it.

"This is my only pair." I hold it out and away.

"I'll take care of it." He takes it from my hand and brings it to the sink.

With bucket water and a sliver of soap, he washes it the same way he cleans away other blood, fast and silent. I've watched him wash blood from his hands more times than I can remember. But never *my* blood.

Red drips along his fingers, mixing with the water and twisting into little spirals before disappearing down the drain.

love

It's weirdly beautiful. Mesmerizing.

When he's finished, the underwear is white again. He wrings it out and hangs it on the line next to his socks.

I'm still standing in the tub. Still bleeding. Still confused. So I take off the shirt, too. I don't want to get it dirty. It slides up over my head, and the air in the room hits my skin, making me shiver.

Jag turns around. His eyes go wide, then snap away so fast he stumbles and spins toward the wall.

"What—?" His fists flex against the tiles. "What are you doing? Cover yourself!"

"Why? You've seen me naked."

"That was different." He presses both hands behind his nape like he's trying to hold his skull together. His elbows stick out like wings, and every muscle in his back goes tense. "You... Dove... You can't just— God. Fuck!"

"Why are you acting weird?"

"I'm not... Fuck. Fuck." He bends at his waist and straightens again. "You don't look like a little girl anymore."

I stare at his back. His spine moves when he breathes, jagged and rippling.

"What do I look like?"

"Like a woman." He shakes his head sharply. "But you're not. You're still a kid. You can't take your clothes off in front of anyone. Not ever. Not even me."

"Well, that's not true. I know what people do together without clothes on."

"Kill me now," he whispers under his breath. Then louder, "The shirt. Tell me when it's on."

"Fine." I pull it on and cross my arms. "Done."

When he turns around, he doesn't look at me first. He looks at the doorway like he's about to sprint into the night to avoid this whole thing.

So I say one word that will grab his attention. "Sex."

He looks at me now. Really looks.

"What do you know about that?" His eyes narrow, then widen, then do this panicked flicker.

"I know you've been doing it for years."

His face drains of color.

I push on. "Sometimes when you sneaked out of our forts and tents in the middle of the night, I followed you."

He flinches like I hit him.

"I saw you." I stand taller. "With men. And women. In their cars. In alleys. In empty buildings. I saw you put money in your pocket after."

His whole body turns to stone. Then something else. Something cracks.

"Little Bird." The words break in his mouth. "You... God, no. You weren't supposed to—" He drags both hands down his face, scrubbing hard like he wants to erase himself. "You followed me?"

"Of course, I followed you." I shrug. "You're mine."

He staggers back a step, bumping into the cracked wall. He looks sick. Not angry. Sick. He grips his stomach. His jaw grinds back and forth, and his nostrils pulse wide.

"I did that to feed you." His voice strains. "When we were sleeping on the streets. When we had nothing. When you were freezing and hungry and small. I couldn't get a job. I didn't have anyone. I didn't have a choice."

"I know."

"That was never supposed to be something you watched. Never."

"I wasn't scared. I just wanted to know where you went."

He shuts his eyes like he can't stand looking at me. Or maybe he can't stand me looking at him.

"I'm not proud of any of that," he says. "I'm not proud of the way people touched me or the way I let them. I did it so you could eat. So *you* didn't have to do anything like that. Ever."

I don't know what to say. My throat hurts.

When he opens his eyes again, they're angry and sad. But he looks at me like I'm the whole reason he survived those awful years.

"You can't talk about sex." He steps forward, stops himself, steps back again. He's rattled. Really rattled. "Not with anyone older. Not with anyone who wants something from you. You don't let anyone see you naked. You don't let anyone touch you. You don't—"

"I already have."

"Have *what*?" He goes deadly still.

"I had sex."

He pins me with a look so terrifying my insides fold up.

"Who?" His shout hits like a fist.

love

"Why are you mad?"

"Who?" he roars.

I step back until my legs bump the tub's cold edge. "A boy at school."

"Which boy? What's his name?"

"He's…" My hands shake. "Just a boy in my English class. His brother."

"His brother?" His face contorts. Not confusion. Fury. Pure and simple and lethal. "Where is this brother? Is he in school?"

"No." My toes curl inside the tub. "He's too old for school."

He inhales sharply, his chest lifting with a dangerous, animal breath. "How old?"

"He has a car."

"That's not an age, Dove."

I press my legs together to stop the blood, my entire body heatless and tight. I can't answer. I can't say it. Because if I tell him more, he'll walk out and come back with more blood on his hands.

And it'll be my fault.

He watches me struggle, sees the fear, the hesitation. Then he realizes he's losing control.

"Clean yourself." He grabs a cloth and a bucket of water, holding it out without looking at me. "I can't… I can't help you with that. It's not proper."

His arm shakes.

I take the supplies.

He steps into the doorway with his back turned, arms crossed so hard his shoulders bunch like boulders.

I know every twitch in his neck, every shift in his legs, every tiny flinch that means he's barely keeping himself from breaking things.

Quickly, I wash myself with the cold water, wiping away the sticky blood that keeps appearing between my legs. It hurts. Not the washing. The looking. The understanding of it.

When I finish, he leads me back to the main room and pulls out a pencil and paper.

"Write down everything you know about him." He slams them onto the desk. "Write his name. His parents' names. His address. What he looks like. His tattoos. His car. Where he works. Where he hangs out. Everything."

Shame slithers up my throat. Shame for letting this happen. Shame because I know what Jag will do. Shame because I put that hurt look in his eyes.

I pick up the pencil with trembling fingers and write what he asks.

When I'm done, he scans the paper and shoves it into his pocket.

"I'll get what you need for your period." His tone is flat. Not calm. Not angry. Worse than both.

I don't want him to leave. Not like this. I don't want him to do this terrible thing for me, even though, deep down, I don't feel guilty about this particular death.

I don't want Jag to feel guilty about it, either.

Telling him was the right thing. The only thing.

When he grips the doorknob, the words tumble out of me.

"I told him no."

Jag goes still.

I nod toward the paper in his pocket. "I said no over and over, and he wouldn't stop."

The change in him is instant.

And horrifying

And familiar.

His face warps. The tendons in his neck stand out like ropes. His nostrils go wide. His eyes go bright. His shoulder veins rise. His fists open and close, and his entire body expands with rage. Monstrous, hellborn rage.

I brace myself.

But he shoves it down. All of it. He forces his lungs back under control, unclenches his hands, and drags that rage inward like he's swallowing fire.

"Did he do your eye?" he rasps.

"No. I fought with a girl. I told you. *That* was nothing."

"Do not leave unless the building is burning." He opens the door and glances up and down the crumbling hallway, then back at me. "Lock the bolt on the inside and let no one in. No one."

"Please, come back."

"I swear it." He lifts his hand, pinky out.

That tiny gesture hits harder than all his shouting, all his anger, all his everything.

I rush forward, hook my pinky with his, and bring our knotted fingers to my lips. He turns our hands, pulls the joined

love

pinkies to his mouth, and kisses them.

Then he walks into the hallway, carrying all my shame, all his fury, and the promise he'll keep.

I bolt the door behind him, and silence settles over the room. For three seconds. Then...

Bang.

Another.

Bang. Bang.

The sound vibrates through the cracked tiles under my feet.

I move without thinking, sliding back the bolt and cracking open the door.

Jag stands at the end of the hallway, destroying the wall.

He slams his fists into the sheetrock over and over, hammering, pummeling, and shredding. White dust explodes around him. Chunks fall to the floor.

"Jag!" I step out.

His head snaps toward me, his eyes too wild to be human as he roars, "Told you to stay in the room and keep that door locked!"

My stomach drops to my ankles. I've seen him angry, but not like this. Not this stripped open and out of control.

I caused this. All of it.

"S-Sorry." I close the door fast and shove the bolt in place with shaking hands.

The banging stops.

Hours pass.

When a light knock sounds, followed by my name, I unbolt the door.

He steps inside, hands stained in dried blood.

Exactly how I knew they'd be.

He avoids my eyes.

Without a word, I follow him into the bathroom and grab a water bucket. He leans over the sink, shoulders slumped, muscles twitching with all the leftover electricity trapped inside him.

I pull off his jacket and pour the clean water over his hands.

The blood runs in thin rivers along his forearms, swirling down the rusty drain. I wash him with a cloth, wiping the raw skin, tracing the ridges of his knuckles. I've washed his bloody hands before, always from bad people, never from walls.

When his skin is clean, he removes a crinkled plastic bag from his jacket. Sanitary napkins and a new pair of underwear.

He opens the box and reads the instructions like he's defusing a bomb. His brow furrows. Then he nods to himself.

"Here. This is how you use them." His ears turn red as he explains how the wings fold and where they stick.

When he's sure I understand, he leaves me to it.

Doesn't take me long to wash up and get the pad in place. Then I join him on the cushions.

He opens his arms, and I crawl into them the way I always do, chest to chest with his heartbeat rumbling under my cheek. Our legs pretzel together, and all my cold edges immediately warm.

"We'll have to leave by morning." He exhales into my hair.

"I know."

It's what we do after he washes blood from his hands. We run. We start over. We change names like other people change shoes. But it's harder now. He has all this equipment.

"Will you leave the computer stuff behind?"

"I'll get a car."

"By morning?" I pinch his ribs. "You already know which car you'll steal."

"Maybe." He pinches my ribs back, making me giggle. Then he falls still. "I'm sorry. For yelling. For scaring you."

"You didn't scare me."

"I'm sorry for what that monster did to you." He tightens his arms around me. "I'm sorry I wasn't there."

My throat aches again.

"I'm getting better. Every day. I'm learning all the things I can do with a computer. Hacking, tracking, watching. Next time..." His hand slowly travels up my back like he's counting my bones through the shirt. "Next time, I'll see the threat coming before it happens. I'll be able to stop it. No one will hurt you again. Not while I'm alive."

I nod into his chest. I love hearing it, but I'm afraid of it, too. The way he watches me and kills anyone who hurts me... It's wrong. I know that. But it's also the only thing that's ever made me feel like I matter.

His arms loosen enough for him to stare at my face, brushing hair from my cheeks, gentle again. He studies me like he's memorizing me. Like I'm his secret, his obsession, and his home.

I nestle closer and fall asleep with the thud of his heartbeat against my cheek, safe in the only place I've ever been safe.

love
FORTY-SIX

Two years later

The air smells like steaming shit in this part of Fresno. Feels like it, too.

By the time I finish sweeping out the bays at the mechanic shop, the heat eases enough that I don't feel like I'm inhaling buttholes.

I zip my backpack and start the long walk back to my foster house.

The neighborhood is too quiet at night. The held-breath kind of quiet. The don't-blink kind. My shoes scrape along the sidewalk as I keep to the streetlights. I'm not scared. I'm also not stupid.

Halfway down the block, my spine prickles.

It's not a noise or a shadow that unsettles me. It's that other thing, the instinct I picked up from living on the streets for seven years.

I keep walking. My heartbeat doesn't change. My breath stays even. That's another thing street life taught me. Don't show fear before my brain figures out what to do with it.

I turn casually, pretending to adjust a twisted backpack

love

strap, and peek behind me.

Empty sidewalk.

But the danger's here, pressed against my skin, whispering, *Pay attention.*

I scan the rooftops, parked cars, gaps between houses, and the busted streetlight on the corner that creates a pocket of dark.

Not Jag.

My throat closes. He's never been gone this long. Not even when he's angry. We fight about school and money and *boys,* and sometimes he storms off for a day or two to cool down.

But a month without him? He vanished out of thin air without a fight or a pinky promise.

Something's wrong.

I grip the switchblade in my pocket and continue along the sidewalk, awareness stretched wide, every sense open, my vision sweeping side to side.

Fifteen-year-olds with normal lives don't process danger the way I do. Then again, they weren't raised by Jag Rath.

Crossing the street, I veer left. Two blocks ahead sits a mini-mart with a busted security mirror. As I approach it, I angle myself to see the reflection behind me.

There. A shape. A man keeping pace with me. Too close to be innocent. Too far to be loud about it.

Okay. So I'm being tailed.

I don't speed up. I don't look back again. I do what Jag taught me long ago.

Don't freeze. Don't fold. Show them why they picked the wrong girl.

The mini-mart is too open, too many windows. If I go inside, he follows. If I stay outside, he corners me.

But three streets over, there's a yard with a broken gate and a huge pit bull. The dog knows me. I give him jerky sometimes.

I turn left at the next intersection, quick but not panicked. The man mirrors me. Another left. He mirrors that, too.

Now I know two things. He's not a random creep. He's good at this.

Reaching the yard, I squeeze through the loose panel in the fence. The pit bull lifts his head, wags once, and settles back down.

Good boy.

I crouch low and wait.

The man steps into view. He pauses and looks both ways, searching for where I went, but he doesn't check the ground for footprints. Amateur move.

He approaches the fence, and the pit bull surges to his feet. Kill switch activated. He gives a warning growl before erupting in loud, snarling barks that send the man stumbling back.

Such a good boy. I'm bringing him *two* pieces of jerky tomorrow.

The man shakes out his shoulders as if annoyed he got spooked. As he moves away, I slip out silently behind him and match my footsteps to the rhythm of his strides so our sounds overlap.

When his pace quickens, I fade into the shadows, angling around him and staying low. Then I dart forward.

My shoulder slams into his ribs as I hook my foot behind his ankle, taking him down. We hit the ground in a burst of dust, and before he can recover, I press the switchblade under his jaw, right against the soft place that bleeds fast.

"Whoa!" His hands shoot up in surrender. "Okay, okay, hang on!"

"Why the hell are you following me?"

"You don't know?" His eyes widen, darting across my face. "You're wanted by—"

A crunch splits the air, wet and heavy, as a hunting knife slams through his skull. His body goes slack beneath me.

My breath stops, and my gaze locks onto the hand holding the knife's hilt. Then the muscled arm. The bulging shoulder. I shove off the body, fall onto my back, and stare up at beautiful, hooded, amber eyes.

I don't know who lunges first, but we collide in a tangle of arms and legs, hugging and stumbling until Jag lifts me off the ground. Whirling, he carries me off the street, into a narrow alley, and presses a finger to my lips.

With a nod, I keep quiet as he hauls the body into one of the abandoned houses across the street.

Minutes later, he returns, wiping the blade on his jeans. But his movements look wrong, too tense, like he knows we're not out of trouble.

"We gotta go." He scans the perimeter. "Now."

"Who was he?"

love

"A problem with more to follow." He clasps my wrist and walks fast, not running, but at a pace that says we're being watched and he's not telling me how bad it is.

We cut through side streets and down several blocks until we reach a squat one-story house with peeling paint and Christmas lights still stapled to the roof from who-knows-when.

"Where are we?" My hand feels clammy in his. "What is this?"

Before we step onto the porch, the door cracks open.

A bald man in a terry-cloth robe, boxers, and cowboy boots peers out with a revolver leveled through the gap.

His eyes shift to me. "You can't bring a kid here."

"I got nowhere else to go with her." Jag straightens to his full, imposing height.

"Is she—?"

"My daughter."

The lie shocks me so hard I almost choke. Daughter? He's never called me anything but his little bird.

"As if I can say no to you." The man sighs, lowers the gun, and opens the door. "She stays in the bedroom."

Jag drags me inside.

The moment we cross the threshold, the reek of cigarette smoke, bleach, and mold invades my nose.

A single lamp with no shade throws a sickly glow over a sagging brown couch. Two women lounge there, one in a tank top and panties, the other wrapped in a leopard-print blanket with nothing underneath. Their eyes track us with that slow, unfocused drift that comes from whatever they snorted, smoked, or swallowed.

The coffee table is cluttered with bent spoons, glass pipes, foil squares, disposable lighters, a razor blade, a credit card dusted with powder, and a half-eaten pizza slice stuck to the cardboard. Empty beer cans rattle when someone shifts their leg.

"I'm running a business here." The man joins the women on the couch. "Not a daycare."

Jag keeps me glued to his hip as we move through the room.

We pass a kitchen with yellow walls and a table covered in Solo cups, pill bottles, and a digital scale that probably hasn't been cleaned since the last raid. Someone left a pot on the stove, and its contents emit a burnt smell that makes me gag.

"This way." He moves fast, eyes forward, steering me down the hall and into a bathroom.

He shuts the door behind us, turns on the faucet, and scrubs the blood off his hands. His reflection in the mirror looks too pale under the grime.

"We have to move again." I watch the blood swirl down the sink.

"Not yet."

"But—"

"No." He washes my hands next. Then he grips my elbow and leads me into a room at the end of the hall.

I stop short.

This... This is not where Jag lives.

My brother lives in cardboard forts, tents under bridges, and abandoned buildings with no running water.

But this room?

It's spotless. A real bed. Multiple desks with towers of hardware. High-end monitors. Servers stacked like black bricks. Cables braided in neat coils. All of it creates a low, humming heartbeat under the floor.

"What the—?" I drop my backpack and stare with a slackened jaw. "How?"

He slides the bolt on the door and sits at the desk, fingers moving fast.

The screens bloom to life with camera feeds, street views, and angles from places I recognize. The alley we were just in. The house with the pit bull. The mechanic shop where I work. Intersections. Streetlights.

"Holy shit." I lean against his chair, looping an arm around his neck.

"Watch your mouth."

"You can see all that? All the time?"

"I see everything, anytime I want." He types faster.

The feeds rewind, and he filters through different time stamps until two figures appear on the street. Me and the man walking behind me.

With a few commands, the images disappear. Frame by frame, they vanish. Erased.

"How?" I turn to him.

"I'm good at this." His eyes finally lift to mine. "When they find the body, there won't be a trace of us on any camera within a mile of it."

"You can do that?"

"Just did." He leans back, breathless from the rush of it. "I can control the investigation from here and keep our tracks clean."

"Who was he? Why did he say I was wanted?"

"I'll find out." He reaches into his pocket and pulls out a wallet.

"That's his." My stomach knots.

"Yeah." He tosses it onto a tray with other wallets that don't belong to him.

"There have been others? Were they all following me?"

He nods, eyes stony.

How many times has he taken out a bad guy on my tail while I was just walking along, completely oblivious? God, I'm so stupid.

"Why is this happening?" My panic rises. "What do they want?"

"Lower your voice." He pulls me to stand between his spread legs and studies me from head to toe, taking in the condition of my clothes, the scrapes on my arms, and the tattered ends of my hair where it hangs on my shoulders.

Then he rests his hands on my hips and stares at my stomach. "You're in danger, Little Bird."

"From who?"

"I have enemies."

"Because of the computer stuff?"

"When you can do things other people can't, dangerous people take notice."

"So you just... What? Hack bad guys?"

"I accept jobs that use my skills. Sometimes those jobs make enemies."

"Then stop. Just stop doing it."

"I can't." He says it fast, final, slamming a door on my concern. "Drop it."

"No." Anger climbs up my throat. "This is our lives. You disappear for a month, and I'm supposed to just wait around—"

"Dove."

"No! Where were you? What happened? Why did you leave me alone for that long?"

He stands abruptly, the chair scraping against the floor. He paces with his hands locked on top of his head, turning, pacing, and turning again. His shirt rides up with the movement, exposing a strip of his stomach—hard muscle, familiar grooves, and—

A barely-healed, scary-big wound under his rib cage.

My heart stumbles.

"What is that?" I grab his shirt before he can yank it down. "Jag! What is that?"

He reaches for my wrist, but not fast enough. I shove the shirt higher, revealing the full injury, pink and new, the width of a thumb. A wound that can only come from a blade sinking in deep.

"Someone stabbed you," I whisper.

"It's nothing."

"It's not nothing." My fingers hover near it, afraid to touch. "This is bad. This should've killed you."

He doesn't deny it. He doesn't say anything at all. He just lets me hold his shirt in my trembling hands.

The silence between us is too loud, the distance too far. He's hiding things from me.

The story about the man following me, the jobs he's doing, the danger we're in... That's not all of it. Not even part of it.

"A couple of months ago, a soldier took me out for beers." I watch his face carefully, the hard set of his jaw. "He was stabbed in a bar fight later that night."

"Don't know anything about that."

"Yeah, you do." I trail my fingers over the puckered skin. "Did he do this?"

"Fuck, no. He didn't even get a hit in."

"So you did kill him."

"You're fifteen-fucking-years old!" He bares his teeth, eyes wild. "And he was—"

"Twenty-two. A year younger than you." I return my attention to his wound, examining the raw skin.

It's only a few weeks old. Maybe a month. Too fresh to be related to the soldier.

A month...

This is why he vanished. Why he left me to fend for myself. Why the streets felt wrong and empty in a way they never have before.

love

"You were hurt." I grip his scruffy face, holding it in my hands. "That's where you've been. You weren't working some job or hiding from the cops or whatever story you were going to feed me. You were dying somewhere."

His eyes flick away. "Cracker patched me up."

"Cracker?"

"The paranoid drug dealer who aimed the six-shooter out the door. This is his house."

"You live in a drug dealer's house." I lower my hands.

"As if you didn't notice." He sighs. "I handle Cracker's security, and he buys me all this." He gestures at the room full of expensive tech.

"Are you using drugs?"

"No." His head snaps up, eyes burning. "I've never touched that shit. Not once. Not even when Cracker tried to shove pills down my throat after I got stabbed."

The image guts me. Jag bleeding out and some crackhead forcing opioids into his mouth. I should've been with him, taking care of him.

"You've been here all month? In this room? Recovering?"

"Yeah."

"And you didn't tell me? I would've helped you. Instead, you let me think you left."

"I didn't leave you, Dove. I watched you." He gestures toward the monitors. "Every day. Every night. Always with you."

Of course, he was. He doesn't crawl through my windows anymore. He crawls through every camera I pass.

I miss the windows.

"What happened?" I point to his wound.

"I lived." He sits on the edge of the bed, elbows on his knees, hands loosely hanging between them.

That's it. No details. No who. No why. No explanation for the blade that almost killed him or the enemies that want us both dead.

I wait for more, but he won't give it.

Not tonight.

Maybe not ever.

He exhales heavily, and the fight drains out of both of us at the same time.

The monitors dim to a blue glow, and the house outside this

room sinks into muffled TV noise, clinking pipes, and someone laughing.

"Get some sleep." Jag stands and pulls the blankets back.

"I'm not tired."

"Hungry?"

"I ate at work."

He pulls clean clothes from a crate in the corner, gives me something to wear, and gestures for me to turn around.

With our backs to each other, we change into our sleepwear. I pull on a shirt and flannel pants he grew out of, and I turn to find him wearing gray sweats and a white tank.

I climb into the bed, and the mattress dips as he joins me.

"Tell me about the shop." He drags the blanket over us.

"You literally watch it through like six angles."

"I want to hear it from you."

So I talk. I tell him about the busted transmission I rebuilt after school, the oil spill I slipped on, the new guy who thinks he's charming, but I would never date him because he likes country music.

Jag listens, really listens, even though he already saw and heard it all through his cameras.

"What about school?" he asks.

"Hate it."

"You need it."

"You needed it, too."

"Still do. But I'd probably scare the teachers."

That pulls a smile out of me. I roll onto my side, facing him. His hair sticks up in every direction. He looks exhausted.

"And your foster place?" he murmurs.

"Awful."

"It's a house full of women."

"Exactly."

"What'd they do?"

"Nothing. And everything. You know how it is."

"I know."

A hush settles over us. He lies back, opens an arm without asking, and I slide into the warm circle. My head finds the same spot on his chest it always has, just below his collarbone, near the rhythm of my favorite sound.

And just like that, we're in our cardboard fort again. Our bed made out of trash. Our alley corner behind the bakery. Every place we hid in together, every night he kept watch while I slept.

"You scared me," I whisper.

"You scare me every second of every day." He presses his chin to the top of my head.

"How?"

"By existing outside of these." He flexes the band of his arms around me.

"You're not funny."

"Didn't say I was."

I jab a finger in his ribs, nowhere near the wound, but he hisses like a kicked cat.

"Sorry." I bite my lip.

"No, you're not."

I'm not. But he's smiling now, the small, rare one that dimples the corner of his mouth.

The quiet stretches, warm and heavy, humming with the heartbeat under my cheek.

"I can't remember them." I trace a fingertip along the neckline of his tank. "Our parents."

His body stiffens.

"I try." I take a breath. "I really do. But it's just... Blurry shapes. Maybe a smell. Maybe not even that. Tell me about them. Just something."

"It's late, Dove."

"You never talk about them."

He goes quiet again, and for a second, I think he'll get up and escape into his computers.

Instead, he shifts onto his back, eyes on the ceiling. "Mom cooked, and Dad helped her sometimes. They liked to dance together in the kitchen. That's all."

"That's not all."

"It's enough."

"No, it's not." I lift my head. "I don't remember what they sounded like or what they looked like or if they laughed or how they—"

"Let it go."

"You remember more than I do."

"It doesn't matter what I remember." He rubs a hand over his face, frustrated.

"It matters to me."

"They're gone, and we survived. That's what matters."

"But I want to know them."

"You knew enough." He flicks a strand of my hair off my forehead. "You knew they existed. Some kids don't even get that."

It's not the answer I need. But I can tell by the roughness in his voice that talking about them hurts him.

He doesn't talk about the past.

He barely talks about the present.

"Come here." His hand settles on the back of my head, fingers threading through my hair as he guides my cheek back to his chest. "You're okay now."

"You're the one who got stabbed."

"And you're the one who tackled a grown man with a knife."

"So?"

"I'm proud of you." His arm tightens around me, and his heartbeat evens out beneath my ear.

"I missed you so much."

"Missed you more." His chest rises slow and falls slower. Then, barely above a whisper, "I love you."

"Promise?"

"I swear it." Eyes half-closed, lashes heavy with exhaustion, he lifts his hand, pinky extended.

It's automatic, this old little ritual fused in the joints of our finger bones. I hook my pinky around his and bring our twisted fingers to my lips. He's so tired, lids drifting shut, but he still does it. He leans forward the inch it takes and kisses our intertwined pinkies, cementing the promise.

Then he settles into the pillow, breathing slow and deep, and dozes off.

Even in sleep, he never fully relaxes. The arm around my waist, rigid as steel, keeps me locked against him. The leg he shoved between my thighs would take an act of God to move, not that I'd try.

I crane my neck and watch him in the glow of the computer screens.

His face.

His mouth.

The faint scruff on his jaw.

God, he's beautiful. Not pretty or delicate. Beautiful like a mythological warrior, built out of scars and near-death battles and muscles that aren't earned in gyms but in fights no one else survived.

The guys I've been with are all noise and hands and rushed moments in dark corners. None of them touch me the way Jag does just by existing. None of them makes me ache the way Jag does when he's asleep and defenseless beside me.

I shouldn't be thinking about this. But I always do.

His body presses against mine, hot, solid, and unmistakably male. His heat seeps into me, sliding under my skin. I can't help it. My fingers lift, hover, and settle on the hard flesh of his abdomen where his shirt rides up.

He's hard everywhere, made for running, climbing, fighting, and surviving. I trace lightly, brushing over the contour of muscle and the dips between them.

He makes a sound in his sleep, a rumble dragged from deep in his chest. His arm tightens around my waist, anchoring me to him, but he doesn't wake.

Encouraged, I let my fingers wander higher, sneaking under his shirt. Each tiny movement draws another unconscious reaction from him, subtle but responsive. A twitch. A groan. A stirring between his legs.

My mouth hovers near his throat, and he leans into it, shifting closer.

I shouldn't kiss him. But I do anyway. Just a soft brush of my lips where the veins and tendons strain in his neck. He tastes warm, almost sweet. Alive. My mouth lingers without meaning to, my breath fanning against his jaw.

He exhales a sound between a sigh and a moan and shifts again, climbing my body in his sleep, his hips lifting and searching. His hand slides up my back, fingers curling as if guided by his dreams.

He touches me without waking. Not grabbing. Not claiming. Just reaching. The gentle, instinctive, intimate way he does it sends a rush of melty, fizzy heat low in my tummy.

I let my hand drift up his chest, fingertips finding every familiar ridge, every honed inch of strength. My lips follow the line of his throat, soft kisses against fever-hot skin, each one bolder than the last because he keeps answering me with those unconscious sounds, those tiny shifts of his body pressing into mine.

I shouldn't want him this much. But wanting Jag feels like gravity, constant and impossible to fight.

Still asleep, he nuzzles closer, burying his face in my hair. His breathing speeds up and tumbles down my neck, lifting goosebumps across my skin.

I melt into him, into the body I've dreamed about for years, into the man who haunts every thought I shouldn't have.

Because here, in the dark, with his hardness jabbing against me, I can finally admit it.

There's no one else I've ever wanted.

His hand finds my hip, wrapping around the sharp bone. His warm, full lips touch mine, brushing, opening. Then he licks. I lick back. And he groans.

One second, he's half-draped over me. The next, he rolls fully on top, his weight pinning me in the way I always imagined. His mouth crashes onto mine, hot, desperate, and searching, and for a heartbeat, I forget how to breathe at all.

It's my first kiss.

My first real one.

Not the practice ones I give stupid boys in stairwells. Not the forced ones I walk away from with regret in my teeth. This is... Something else. Something older. It's heavy, deep, and grown-up.

My whole body goes electric as his lips move against mine with a hunger he never shows when he's awake. His hands roam desperately, up my sides, along my back, gripping, pulling, trying to join us in the way he joins with women for money.

I know how he moves his body, but I've never seen the male part of him he keeps hidden in his pants. My fingers tingle to touch it.

So I do. I slide a hand between us, into his sweatpants, and grip his impossible hardness.

"Jag..." His name falls out of me like a prayer, like a confession, like everything I've buried for years.

His breath cuts off.

His eyes pop open.

In one violent sweep, sleep clears away, and clarity slams in.

Recognition.

Horror.

He rips himself away so viciously the air leaves my lungs. He hits the floor with a hard thud, scrambling backward. His hands fly to his waistband, yanking his sweats into place even though he's not exposed.

His chest heaves, wild and panicked.

"Jag..." I crawl across the bed, reaching for him.

"No, no, no, no." He shakes his head in a frenzy, scuffing his heels across the floor and slamming into the wall, his eyes blown wide with disbelief. Disgust. Terror. "What the hell—? What did I—?"

He covers his mouth like he's going to be sick. Like he's choking. Like he'd cut off an arm to erase the last thirty seconds.

And the worst part?

I'm still kneeling on the bed, lips swollen from his kiss, panties wet with my wanting, and all I can think is... I want him back on top of me.

For him, it's a nightmare.

For me, it's the truest, purest joy I've ever known.

"What did I do?" He drags both hands through his hair, his eyes looking anywhere but at me. "Oh, God, what did I do?"

"It's a good thing, Jag." I shift forward on the mattress, reaching for him. "You and me. Together. That's how it's supposed to be."

"What? No!" With a horrified expression, he pushes to his knees and doubles over at the waist, a hand clamped to his mouth, trying to trap the sounds coming out of him. Dying animal sounds. "So fucking wrong. I wasn't thinking. I thought I was dreaming."

"Dreaming of me?" My heart skips.

"Fuck, no. Christ. Disgusting."

My eyes burn. My ribs cinch tight, and something inside me cracks and crumbles, hollowing me out.

"I can't..." He staggers to his feet, palms pressed to his eyelids. "Can't do this."

He doesn't look at me. Not once. Not from the moment he woke to the moment he turns and walks out.

The door clicks shut behind him.

I sit there, staring at nothing, my pulse thrashing in my ears. I don't cry. I can't. My body won't pick a feeling. It's all static, buzzing under my skin, numbing everything.

Ten minutes pass. Then twenty. He doesn't come back.

Finally, I stand on legs that don't feel like mine. I pull on jeans, a shirt, sneakers. If he's not coming back, I'll go find him.

I open the bedroom door.

The house is dim except for the blue TV glow in the living room. I follow the sounds of breathing, movement, and muffled moans. All wrong. All sour-tasting.

I step into the doorway, and there's Jag.

On the couch.

With the two women.

My mind connects the shapes and shadows fast enough to understand what's happening. The women are pressed against him, wrapped around him. One has her boobs in his face. The other straddles the back of his legs. Skin everywhere. Three naked bodies moving in wet, sloppy, panting rhythm.

This is worse than the dicks he sucked and the women he fucked for money. Worse than the men who took him from behind and left him crying alone in the dark after.

This is for *his* pleasure. He wants this. He chose these drugged-out women over me.

Because I'm disgusting.

He lifts his head, his gaze instantly finding mine. And his eyes...

They're empty.

Dead.

Blank.

"Go to bed," he says coldly, flatly. "Now."

He doesn't stop what he's doing.

He doesn't look disgusted.

He doesn't look away.

He thrusts harder and watches me break with a hollow stare.

My chest caves in, and something rips open so wide inside me I know I'll never be the same.

I turn away. My legs carry me toward the bedroom, but I can't feel them. The air won't go into my lungs. I choke on nothing and drown in everything.

The door shuts behind me, and I grab my backpack. I don't think. I don't look back. I just go.

The window screeches open. The dank air smacks my wet cheeks. I climb through and drop into the dirt below, my knees buckling.

I can't see. My tears blur the whole world into smeared lights and colorless shapes. But I shove myself forward, across the yard,

love

around a shed, and through a wire fence.

Sharp metal catches my shirt. Then my skin. Then deeper. It slices across my shoulders, deep and unforgiving. The barbs tear me open, dragging through flesh. I know it'll scar. Many, many scars. But I don't stop. I push through it, ripping myself free.

I'm crying too hard to feel anything.

Then I run. Through yards. Down alleys. Across streets where cars honk. My sobs wrench out of me, echoing loudly in the night, but I don't stop. My legs keep moving until they give out. I crumple, get up again, keep going, going, going, beyond the reach of cameras.

I run until the lights of Fresno disappear behind me. Run until my lungs burn and my throat tastes like metal. Run until my legs buckle a second time and won't stand back up.

Before the sun rises, I'm miles outside the city, stumbling along the highway with my backpack sliding off one shoulder and blood drying on my torn shirt.

A pickup slows beside me. I don't ask where it's going. I don't care.

The driver jerks a thumb toward the back, and I climb into the bed without a word. The truck pulls forward, heading south to nowhere, to anywhere, to someplace Jag isn't.

Rain starts to fall, cold and relentless. I curl into myself in the truck bed, drenched, shaking, and sobbing into my knees.

In the rain, in the back of a stranger's truck, heart split open and bleeding, I make a promise, one I never go back on.

I never spend another night with Jag Rath.

jag
FORTY-SEVEN

Present day

Every inch of distance I planned to keep is gone. The reason I sneaked onto the island, the stoic goodbye I practiced, it all goes up in smoke as Dove's mouth yields beneath mine.

Her fingers twist into the front of my shirt, dragging me closer. Close enough to feel that she's hurting and angry and still mine in ways she'll never admit out loud.

I grip her waist so urgently her breath breaks against my lips. Then she kisses me harder, pressing every bit of her tongue into my mouth.

She kisses me like that night seventeen years ago. The night she was dripping need and innocence and climbing inside my pants because she thought I was good enough for her.

It's the same desperation now. But stronger. Older. Damaged.

Her lips cling to mine, her tongue chasing, demanding, and furious. Furious she still needs me this much and frantic to swallow the years we lost.

Every exhale she gives me is hot and vicious, filled with memories I never let myself think about.

Seventeen years of wanting her rips through me in a single rush, and my body answers with zero hesitation.

I'm hard in an instant. Painfully. Stupidly. And she feels it.

Her whole body shudders against mine. A choked sound slips into my mouth. Then she wrenches me deeper into the kiss.

Fuck me.

My hand flies to her hip, her thigh, then the curve of her ass where I've imagined holding her a thousand times.

She arches into it, and I know she's thinking about our life together on the streets. Not everything. Not the worst parts. But the parts where she trusted me. The parts where she loved me.

Her breath trembles, brushing my cheek, my jaw, my throat as she tries to keep up with the pace we're both sprinting toward.

I recapture her mouth and kiss her like our lives depend on it. She opens for me, melting and clawing, fierce and hungry, her tongue sliding and dueling and rocketing heat through my groin.

My pulse jackhammers. I can't think, can't breathe, can't do anything but feel her pressing up against the seventeen-year void in my chest.

With her hands in my hair and her breath hot on my tongue, she brings every buried thing inside me back to life.

The longing.

The fury.

The stupid, stubborn hope I thought I burned out of myself years ago.

I've waited half my life to feel her like this again. To feel her shaking and clinging and kissing me like she remembers who we were before I destroyed everything.

But it doesn't last.

I know the moment her mind replays what I did that night. She tenses and rips her mouth away with a cry.

"No." She flattens her hands on my chest and shoves. "No! Don't touch me!"

I miss her lips so desperately I pull her back.

Until the cold, unmistakable edge of a blade presses against my throat.

Wolfson Strakh is the only person on the planet who can sneak up on me.

"Lower your hands, or I'll remove those first." He fists my hair and wrenches my head back, exposing the line of my neck. "Then I'll open your throat."

jag

I know he will. He'll do it without mercy.

If I'm dead, I can't keep them alive. So I drop my hands.

"Dovey." He walks me backward, separating me from her. "Did he hurt you?"

"No." She hugs her waist. "Wolf, I'm sorry. I—"

"Go to the kitchen and get yourself a knife. The biggest one you can find."

"She doesn't need it." I grit my teeth.

Wolf's free hand cups me between the legs, gripping the hardness there. "Feels like she does."

Christ in hell.

I hold my hands out to my sides, breath locked in my chest. I don't look at her. Not when my skin is bared under Wolf's knife. Not when his fingers are curled around my erection. If I see her face right now, I'll forget the blade and the consequences and everything I'm trying to keep alive.

But she doesn't go for a weapon. She stands at the edge of my periphery and shakes her head at Wolf like she can't process what he's asking.

He takes in her expression, *the tears*, and releases my shrinking dick.

"You made her cry." An ominous chill shivers through his voice. "What kind of monster are you?"

"The worst kind."

It's the truth. There's no excuse left to hide behind, and the sight of her tears—tears I put there *again*—cuts deeper than the blade digging into my throat.

"Look at me," she says quietly.

I don't want to. I can't. But the heartbreak in her tone drags my eyes up anyway.

"I loved you." She balls her fists at her sides. "You were my entire world. My safe place. My family. My heart—" She inhales sharply. "And you threw me away."

Wolf's blade presses deeper.

Her glare is a blade all its own. "You threw me away when I was fifteen. So I did the only thing I could do to protect myself. I ran. But you weren't finished with your torture. You chased me. Hunted me. Showed up in every town I tried to hide in. Every time I tried to start a normal life, you ruined it. You fucked my friends. My boyfriends. Anyone who got close to me."

My lungs burn.

"I let myself believe it was because you cared." Her voice cracks. "That maybe you were keeping me safe. That maybe you still loved me."

I can't breathe.

"I wanted you once." Her eyes shine with grief. "I wanted you so damn much. But you didn't want me back. You made that very clear. So why, Jag? Why didn't you just leave me the hell alone?"

"I couldn't." I swallow against the steel, because she's right about one thing. She loved me, and I pissed all over it. On purpose.

She wipes her face and looks away. Angry. Ashamed she cried. Ashamed she kissed me. Ashamed she let all those years hit her at once.

Wolf shifts around me, and for a split second, the absurdity of him is all I see.

What in tropical-hell is he wearing?

Floral rain boots, turquoise shorts with flamingos in sunglasses, and a vintage black tee with a snarling white wolf, its fangs dripping cartoon-red. The shirt hangs lopsided on him, exposing a scarred shoulder that hints at more scars underneath.

Without moving my head, I focus on his face, and... *Goddamn.* His eyes gleam with that special kind of madness, the razor edge between queer and violent that only trauma-bred boys can master.

"That's it?" He flutters his thick eyelashes. "You're not going to defend yourself?"

There's nothing to defend.

I removed every boyfriend Dove brought home. Every girlfriend she thought was a friend. They were bottom-shelf humans. Dead ends with faces. The boys cheated on her. The girls were toxic, most of them addicts, and they treated her like shit. So I fucked them to prove their disloyalty and killed the ones who dared to hurt her.

None of them was worth her time or attention. But she doesn't know that. She only knows the ruin I left behind.

For the longest time, I thought breaking her connections was protecting her. I thought if I kept the world from taking advantage of her, she could be happy.

Twisted logic from a twisted life.

jag

But now?

Now I know the only person who's ever been worthy of her is the same one holding a knife to my throat.

Wolf will fight for her, kill for her, and protect her from everything and everyone.

Including me.

Her chest rises and falls fast, her hands curling uselessly at her sides. Not afraid. Not timid. This is Dove broken open and trying to rebuild her armor.

"You won't touch her again." Wolf lifts my chin with the blade, bringing my eyes back to him. "Not without her permission. Not in confusion. Not in nostalgia. Not because you're lonely and she makes your dick hard."

"I'm leaving. For good." My chest constricts. "I came here to say goodbye."

"That right?" Wolf narrows his arctic eyes. "Where are you going?"

"Doesn't matter. She has you, and you're the only one good enough for her."

"Hm. Yeah. We're going to table *all of that* for a minute." He makes a face. "Dove darling... Safety check. Would your stepbrother physically harm you?"

"Never." She steps closer. "But he might hurt *you*."

"I don't think so." He lowers the knife and paces in the space between her and me. "Here's the thing, Murder Muffin. I feel very possessive of my woman."

He twirls the knife like a lethal baton. Not a flashy trick. Not for show. Just the effortless, predatory movement of a man thinking aloud with steel and fingers.

I've never seen anyone handle a blade like that.

"My feelings for Dove are bigger than me. We're talking princess level. In the realm of the Magic Kingdom. The real deal." He spins the knife along his knuckles, catches the hilt backward, flips it forward, and meets my eyes. "My feelings for you are..." He gives Dove a look. *"Confused?"* His gaze snaps back to me, the blade twirling again. "Maybe that's why you're still breathing. But the night isn't over. Help me understand it."

Confused. Yeah, that makes two of us.

I've spent years taking Dove's companions off the board. Not because I wanted them. Not because they meant anything. But because they didn't deserve her. I didn't just fuck them. I made sure she walked in at the right moment so she'd drop them quick.

But Wolf?

If I took Wolf to my bed, it wouldn't be for Dove's protection. It would be because I want him. And Christ help me, I do.

All my plans to test him, manipulate him, and break him down evaporated when I learned who he is at his core.

He's dangerous in ways I respect and loyal in ways I don't understand. He's attractive, uncivilized, honest, eccentric, and unashamed of who he is.

He and I? We can't happen. Because I know what that would do to Dove, and I refuse to hurt her again.

And Wolf wouldn't hurt her, either.

So yeah, my feelings for him are confused, inconvenient, and completely off-limits.

"Help you understand?" I stand perfectly still, hands loose at my sides, waiting for one of those blade rotations to stop dead in my chest. "Which part?"

"The part where you showed up on my island at three in the morning and kissed my woman." He steps toe to toe with me, the knife spinning fast enough to whistle. "Start with how you got here."

"I paid a fisherman for a ride across the sound."

Dove crosses her arms. Wolf gestures with the knife for me to continue.

"I slipped onto the shore before your security team saw me. The fisherman fed them a story about his dog falling overboard and swimming in this direction. So right about now, your men are fanning out along the shoreline and shouting *Buddy* into the dark."

Wolf's lips twitch. Dove actually looks offended on behalf of the nonexistent dog.

"Relax," I say. "Buddy is apparently very strong, very brave, and very good at the backstroke."

"What's your escape plan?" He ends the knife spin by snapping it into a perfect grip, the point angled at the floor.

"You tell me."

All his sharp, restless energy funnels inward, churning through the gears in his head as he regards me. He's smart. Smarter than most. It takes him two seconds to figure it out.

jag

"I'm your escape plan." His eyes flicker. "You counted on me catching you. Knew I would hear you out before I killed you. You assumed I would approve of your plan to disappear and leave Dove with me. If all went well, maybe I'd even take you back to Sitka myself. How am I doing?"

"Good so far."

"Wolf…" Dove steps to his side. "He's manipulating you."

"Copy that, boss." He drapes an arm around her and returns to me. "Since there's no dog, the GI Joe squad will be here any minute. Better start talking."

"There's nothing left to say." My head pounds.

"Sure there is. Why are you here?"

"To say goodbye." I catch Dove's stare and hold it.

"You chartered a ride across the sound, risked getting shot by our security guards, and climbed the guest house balcony like Romeo." He looks around. "That's how you got in here, right?"

"Yes." My jaw ticks.

"You did all that to say goodbye?"

"Yes."

"Wrong." He shifts, putting himself between Dove and me, his hard body pressing into my space, as he rests the blade under my chin. "Try again."

I counted on him being territorial. I counted on him seeing me as a threat, one he would tolerate long enough to do what's best for her. But I didn't count on his infuriating perceptiveness.

"I needed to see her." My voice scratches, thick in a way I hate. "One last time. Even if she didn't want to see me."

"You kissed her."

"We kissed each other."

She flinches.

Wolf notices. He notices everything. "I'll ask you again. Why are you here?"

Goddamn, he's frustrating.

"What do you want me to say, pup?" I release a heavy breath. "I'm desperate to do the right thing and finding it extremely difficult."

"Better." He steps back, lowering the knife. "Vague but honest."

"What's the right thing?" Dove seizes my gaze.

The truth hums under my skin, under my ribs, under

seventeen years of quiet ruin. It's a twisted knot of childhood, tragedy, and choices I can't undo.

I raised her, fed her, carried her, celebrated her birthdays, braided her hair, crawled through her windows, and slept in her doorways because that's who I *wanted* to be for her.

I sold my body, killed her monsters, and looked at her the way a father would look at his daughter because that's who I *had* to be for her.

Being her *anything* was a goddamn honor.

Then she offered herself to me that night, and everything changed. I saw her differently. I *felt* her differently. I imagined her in ways I never had before. And after? I couldn't erase those ideas from my head.

In the years that followed, I told myself she was too young. When she was in her twenties, I told myself she was my sister. When that no longer worked, I told myself that taking her the way I wanted would poison her life beyond repair.

Because if she were with me, she would never rise above what I am.

She deserves more than the man who raised her. More than the man who whored himself for money. More than the man who still wants her in ways he should never allow himself to imagine.

I shouldn't have kissed her tonight, but I knew I would never have another chance.

I don't want to let her go. Cutting ties will be the hardest thing I've ever done. Walking away and never seeing her again? It's unfathomable.

But *that* is the right thing.

Expression blank, I stare at her, silent, refusing to answer, because if I put the truth into words, it becomes real. Final. And I need more time. Just a few more minutes to look at her, memorize her face, and make sure she'll be okay without me.

She absently rubs the scars on her shoulder, the ones from that night that I couldn't mend, because she ran from me. She's never stopped running.

Until now.

The room shrinks, and the walls press in, suffocating.

Wolf watches us with narrowed eyes, analyzing our combative stares and unspoken emotions.

"Okay," he finally says. "Let's break this down." He looks at

jag

me. "You still have feelings for her. True or false?"

My pulse gives a hard thud, but I flatten my lips and keep my face empty.

"Got it." He turns to Dove. "You still have feelings for him?"

She glares at him, then at me.

"Is it a stepsibling thing?" He rakes a hand through his hair. "Is that what's happening here?"

When neither of us answers, his gaze swings back to me.

"Tell me something, kitty cat. Are you here because you love her?" He leans in, putting his face in mine. "Or because you finally learned how to let her go?"

"Both," I whisper.

Loud pounding rattles the front door. Fists, radios, boots on the porch. The security team.

Wolf blows out a breath. "Time's up."

jag
FORTY-EIGHT

The yacht rocks against the dock pilings, engines humming, ready to depart. The security team forms a loose ring around me, armed and vigilant. They know trouble when they smell it, and they're not about to let me slip past them again.

But the real trouble is on the dock.

Wolf stands in the middle of it, louder than the wind, shoving verbal knives into every Strakh within range. Kodiak. Leonid. Monty. Even Frankie showed up.

Dove stands under Wolf's arm, close against his side, holding him steady as the argument spirals out of control.

When the security team hauled me to the yacht, she pulled on warmer clothes and followed. Certainly not because she wanted to give me a proper goodbye.

She's here for Wolf.

"No!" he shouts again, voice cracking across the water. "You're not listening. I can't let him leave without telling us what the hell is going on!"

"He's not staying on the island." Monty jabs a finger in Frankie's direction. "I won't risk the life of my pregnant wife."

"Keep me out of this." Frankie huffs.

Security shifts. The night shifts. My pulse remains calm.

jag

Wolf wants answers I can't give.

He thinks if he twirls his blade, curves his sexy lips, and lays on the full force of his charm, I'll fold. He doesn't know that the part of me capable of folding already surrendered to the Restrepo cartel.

I didn't come here to offer explanations and build relationships.

I came to sever bonds and rest my eyes on Dove one last time.

And I did.

I saw her with Wolf. Curled against him in his bed, tucked tightly to his chest, his arm slung possessively around her. I saw them fitted together the way she used to fit with me.

I stood in their doorway long enough to memorize her quiet breathing and his protective grip. When I slipped the rock into her palm, he shifted and tensed, alerted by his feral sixth sense.

He didn't wake fully, but he reacted.

Because she's his.

I saw what I came to see. Saw enough to know she'll be worshiped and loved and safe. That's the only ending I ever wanted for her.

Now I must go.

My ending is already sealed, my fate signed in blood. The cartel gave me twenty-four hours to say goodbye.

I'm returning to Colombia tomorrow, whether Wolf wins this fight or not.

Dove breaks from the arguing cluster, steps to the edge of the dock, and glares at me.

"Fix this, Jag." She lifts her chin. "It's not a secret that you have enemies. Which one are you running from? How bad is it? If you don't want me in the cross-hairs, tell us what we're up against!"

Wolf turns, watching us, waiting for my response.

I hold Dove's stare from the yacht's railing. The moon glances off the water, illuminating the moat between us.

No matter how this night ends, she can't find out about House of Crowe or what waits for me in Colombia.

"I want the truth." She bares her teeth. "You owe me answers."

I owe her a happy life, so I give her the only thing I can.

Silence.

In that silence lies blissful ignorance. It may not be blissful for her now, but it will be. After I'm gone.

Wolf continues to study me, his expression morphing from concern to calculation.

His eyes track every inch of me, flick to Dove, then back again. His jaw flexes. His nostrils flare. Then his expression settles. A decision made.

He strides toward Dove, cups her shoulders, and turns her to face him. His head dips, his mouth close to her ear. She stiffens, spine ironed straight.

Whatever he's telling her, she hates it.

Her eyes dart to me, accusing and wounded, before she whispers something back to him, a rebuke too soft for me to catch. Her hands curl against his ribs, not pushing, but not accepting, either.

They argue quietly. Harsh breaths. Narrowed eyes. Controlled frustration. He doesn't raise his voice, and she doesn't snap back. It's mature and healthy, the way they challenge each other without spilling anything loud enough for the family to hear.

Then she exhales, shoulders sagging, and gives the smallest nod. I know her well enough to determine that she still disagrees but trusts him anyway.

Sliding a hand across his cheek, she runs her thumb along his jaw. He closes his eyes like she's grounding him, sealing whatever deal he just whittled out between them.

She murmurs something, a final warning or plea, one last piece of her I'll never be allowed to translate.

Then he squares his shoulders and pivots to face his family.

"I'm taking Jag back to Sitka, and Dove is staying here." When they protest, he talks over them. "I'll bring the guards and return before any of you start hyperventilating."

My stomach hardens.

Whatever he intends to do with me, I know it's going to push me to the brink of my control.

He murmurs something to Kodiak. Whatever it is, Kodiak turns away and lumbers toward the main house, his heavy steps swallowing the dock.

Wolf moves to the cleats and starts untying the mooring lines. That's when Dove breaks into motion, hurrying across the

jag

gangway and coming straight for me.

Security tightens instantly, a wall of muscle and weapons closing the path, but she waves them off and pushes through, stepping right up to me.

She grabs my shirt in both fists and yanks me down until her mouth is at my ear. "Don't you dare hurt him."

"I won't."

"Promise me." She leans back to see my face.

"I swear it." I lift my hand between us, extending my pinky.

Her chin trembles as she stares at it. Then she loops our fingers together and kisses them with a reverence that kills me.

I kiss them next. The easiest promise I've ever made.

Without warning, she throws her arms around me and hauls me against her chest.

I fold into it, starved for her affection. My arms crush her tight, imprinting the shape of her into my bones.

Her hair brushes my jaw. Her heartbeat thuds against mine, and for a moment, I let myself feel the weight of what I'm losing, what I never had, and what I never deserved.

"Whatever's going on with you..." She pulls away, letting her hands skim down my arms. "Don't let this be the end of us."

That's a promise I can't keep.

So I offer her the best smile I can manage—forced, thinly-shaped, and broken at the corners.

Behind her, Wolf steps onto the gangway.

With a sigh, she gives me a final, longing look and goes to him, walking right into his open arms.

He holds her, whispers private words, and leaves her with a claiming kiss. An oath, a line drawn, and a silent agreement, all shoved into that single collision of mouths.

A fist closes around my throat. Not jealousy. It's envy. Anguish. Resolution.

Kodiak returns from the house and lumbers onto the yacht behind Wolf, unreadable as ever.

Great. The dark one is joining the field trip. Exactly what I needed. A second apex predator staring at the back of my skull while my life unravels.

On the dock, Leonid guides Dove toward Monty and Frankie, keeping a protective hand at her back. She doesn't resist, but she doesn't stop watching me, either.

The yacht shudders, engines deepening, and we begin to drift.

I move to the aft railing.

She stands between Leonid and Monty, eyes locked on me.

The distance stretches.

She stays rooted.

I keep my face still.

This... This is what saying goodbye to the only person I've ever loved feels like.

A slow, surgical tearing.

A separation of bone from marrow.

I hold the railing with both hands as everything inside me strains toward her. Instinct. Memory. Ruin. But my body doesn't move. I won't let it. Outward composure is the last currency I have left, and I hold onto it like a dying man.

My throat burns, but I don't swallow. My chest constricts, but I don't breathe deeper. My gaze remains fixed, unblinking, absorbing the sight of her.

Inside, it's carnage. Regret thrashes. Desire bleeds. Grief ruptures.

I watch her watch me until the dock is just a shape, and she's just a blur, and the night swallows the sound of her heartbeat.

I don't look away. Not until she's gone.

Moments later, the spark of a lighter cracks behind me.

Wolf steps up to my side, shoulder brushing mine, a cigarette glowing between his fingers.

"Frankie and my dad..." Smoke rolls from his mouth. "They're a disaster. A beautiful, money-soaked disaster."

"Why do I care?"

"Oh, that's just the appetizer. Leo and Kody? Worse. Gorilla-brain energy. Territorial as hell. Ready to rearrange faces over absolutely nothing. One time, Leo punched a bartender because the guy blinked at Frankie with too much enthusiasm."

"He... *Blinked?*"

"Yeah. Leo said it was a flirty blink. It was probably dust. Didn't matter. Dude got launched."

I stare ahead at the dark water, refusing to engage.

"They're overbearing and needlessly foul," he goes on. "A grunting, mauling, animal kingdom soap opera. They've been banned from half the establishments in Sitka. The other half only tolerates them because Monty tips like he's trying to buy the building."

"Why are you telling me this?"

"Because you act the same way about Dove."

My jaw locks.

"But..." He flicks ash over the side. "There's one difference." He takes a slow drag, eyes cutting to me. "Frankie's men don't leave. They stick. Through the awful parts. The broken parts. The parts that reshape a man's existence. They stay."

He doesn't look away.

Neither do I.

"This is what you want." I harden my voice. "You want me gone so you can have her. Now you have her. You won."

"Yeah, okay. Sure." He makes a disgusted sound. "That's my grand master plan. Run you out of Sitka so I can collect Dove like a trading card."

I glare.

"What I want is for Dove to be happy." He taps the cigarette against the railing, embers falling like tiny stars. "She wants you. A real relationship with you. Not you stalking her and blowing up her life. She wants the emotional-support criminal she felt safe with when you lived on the streets. The caring, dependable version. The one who doesn't vanish in the middle of the night." He softens his tone. "Doesn't matter how brutal you love her, man. If you leave? She'll feel that worse than anything your enemies could do."

"She's my sister."

"Exactly. Have you met my family? Brothers, uncles, cousins... All blood-related. They're a genealogical pretzel sharing the same woman. It's scandalous. It's wrong. It's fine. Who cares? Everyone survived."

"It's not the same."

"You know what your problem is?"

"I'm sure you'll tell me."

"You're hiding behind lame excuses instead of telling me the real reason you're leaving."

The yacht hums, slicing through the black water as he stares at me with unnerving clarity, like he's staring past my defenses instead of at them.

"You think you have me all figured out." I clench my good hand on the railing.

"I figured out enough. I'm trying to figure out the ending."

He's making this harder than it already is.

I can't tell him I gave my life to a cartel, and we're about to start a war against House of Crowe. If I open my mouth, people die. People he loves. People I love.

So I give him nothing. No more excuses. No half-truths. I let my silence end the conversation.

"Let me see your hand." He tosses his cigarette.

I blink, thrown off balance by the sudden detour.

Classic Wolf.

Out of curiosity, I lift my arm, and he takes it carefully. Ironic since this is the same man who shattered it in the first place.

Turning it over in his palm, he studies the uneven coloring. With a gentle rotation, he tests the motion. A dull ache spikes, but the bone feels set.

"No more swelling," he mutters. "Bruises went yellow. You feel pain when you move it too fast?"

"Yeah."

"Believe it or not, I regret this. You and I crashed on day one, and I doubled down on the damage. Not cool."

His sincerity strikes harder than the original break, opening a mess of emotions in my chest. Surprise, relief, gratitude, longing, all the soft, warm shit I absolutely should not allow. Too many things. Too fast.

"What about after?" The question erupts before I can swallow it. "Do you regret the kissing and frotting and coming all over my chest?"

"No. Zero regrets there."

That stops me cold. I search his expression and find a sheen of vulnerability in his eyes.

The urge to grab his face and kiss him again thrums under my skin. He has some sort of spell on me, sucking me in.

I grasp for something to break it. "Does Dove know what we did?"

"She knows everything. I gave her every detail."

My pulse thumps in my throat as I replay his mouth on mine, the frantic grind of our bodies, the heat, the mess, and the shock of wanting him, wanting more with him, more than just sex.

He must read the surprise on my face because he adds, "I

jag

don't lie to her. Not about anything."

If he's telling the truth and she knows we fucked around, how are they still together? That's a hard limit for Dove. Non-negotiable. The moment I get involved with someone she likes, she drops them. No second chances.

But she didn't drop Wolf? Does that mean she's open to something blooming between him and me? Or between us three?

A spinning, falling sensation rips the air from my lungs. *Hope.* It burns bright and dies clean.

It's too late for hope. Too late for this conversation. Too fucking late for any of it.

I pull my hand from his, removing a fuse before it ignites something neither of us can control.

"I know what happened when you left that day," I say quietly. "I watched the video footage of your path from the shop to the pier and saw you break. The panic attack, PTSD, whatever the hell that was... I know I triggered it."

He nods once, eyes on the water.

"It won't happen again. I'll be gone by tomorrow." I glance at the dark sky, remembering how late it is. "Technically, today. When you drop me at the dock, it'll be the last time you see me."

"That's adorable. You think you're in charge of the itinerary." He turns his back to me and walks away, his shoulders loose and gait confident as he joins Kodiak's side.

For the remainder of the ride, he watches me across the yacht. He and Kodiak bow their heads together, discussing whatever plans they think they can force on me.

When we dock, they fall into formation behind me. Wolf, Kodiak, and eight security heavies follow me to the tattoo parlor. Whatever. Let them babysit.

I unlock the shop door, and the parade files in after me. Guards sweep the lobby, the stations, and the break room where I sleep. I don't fight it. I'm too tired and don't have anywhere else to go. This is where I planned to stay until the cartel transport arrives.

Security finishes its sweep, hauling knives and guns out of the break room. Every weapon I stashed in there is found and confiscated. Annoying, but temporary. There's nothing in that pile I can't replace.

Behind me, Kodiak grunts, and I turn in time to see him pass a book to Wolf.

"Thanks for grabbing that." Wolf tucks it under his arm.

"I hope you know what you're doing." Kodiak glares.

"Not even close." Wolf gives his stone-cut cheek a patronizing pat. "I'm the jump-first, regret-it-on-the-way-down type."

"I fucking know."

Security herds me into the break room. I let them, knowing Wolf's right behind me.

When he shuts the door, it's just him. And me.

No Kodiak. No guards. No witnesses.

Wolf sets the book on the table and takes a slow look around the room. There's not much to see. Cot, chair, metal table, bare walls. His gaze lingers on my duffel bag slumped in the corner, frayed straps, dirt ground into the seams.

"That it?" His brows pinch together. "Everything you own?"

I've lived out of a bag since I was sixteen. It never struck me as strange. But to him, son of the wealthiest man in Alaska, it probably looks sad and small. Proof I never stayed anywhere long enough to matter.

I say nothing, and he doesn't press. Instead, he edges closer, crowding my space and hiking my heart rate.

"Everyone who comes to Alaska is either hiding from someone or hiding from everyone." He rests a finger against my sternum. "If they leave, it's because the danger finally caught up."

I can't argue that, so I don't.

He lowers his hand, tracing the bottom of my rib cage through my shirt and pausing unerringly on my worst scar, the one I never talk about.

"When I saw this during the tattoo session..." He caresses the wound through the fabric. "I thought Dove stabbed you."

My breath shortens. Not enough to be obvious, but he notices.

"But after tonight?" He floats closer, grazing his thigh against mine. "After seeing you two together, I know she would never hurt you."

God knows she had dozens of opportunities and even more reasons to put me down, but she never laid a finger on me. Not even a courtesy nick.

"Tonight was eye-opening." His palm climbs up my chest,

jag

making a lazy, heart-pounding trip. "Watching you with her. The way you go on high alert when she's near. The way she responds to you. This thing between you two is protective, instinctive, and devoted."

The accuracy of his words lodges in my chest.

"That's how I know." He walks his fingers higher, over my collarbone, up my neck, drawing shocks of heat across nerves that haven't fired in years. "I know you're not leaving for yourself. You're doing it for her. Maybe even for me."

I should shut this down.

I will shut this down.

But just for a moment, for one stolen breath, I let myself feel it. His hand on my jaw, thumb tracing my cheekbone like I'm something worth memorizing. Something he doesn't want to forget.

Each caress tightens my body, surging an ache between my legs.

I've been so fucking lonely. So starved for human contact. And this man, this beautiful, unhinged disaster of a man, makes the hunger roar.

"You can't leave until I finish your tattoo." His thumb drags down, resting against my bottom lip. A sin. A dare. A temptation.

"I release you from the bargain." I exhale shakily. "You're not finishing it."

He watches me, eyes dark, trying to read what he isn't ready to understand.

I watch him right back.

Then slowly, deliberately, I draw his thumb into my mouth.

His breath catches.

My tongue presses along the pad of his finger as I suck, hard and obscene, holding his gaze the entire time.

His pupils blow wide. His free hand clutches my waist and joins our hips. A tremor shivers through his body. A flush climbs his throat, and he inhales like he's drowning.

"Jag..." He jerks his thumb free and steps back hard enough to hit the table. "I'm not—"

"I know."

"I won't do that to her." He drags a hand through his hair, shaking, fighting himself.

Because he's a good man, and good men break before they

betray the ones they love.

"I need to get back to her." He straightens, wiping his thumb on his jeans. "I'm leaving the security team here. They'll keep you in this room until I return."

"You're locking me up?"

"It's not a choice. It's what's happening." He gestures to the cot as if offering accommodations instead of confinement. "They'll bring you food. Water. Whatever you need."

"You can't keep me—"

"I need sleep. You need sleep. Neither of us is making decisions until that happens."

Fucking hell. This is completely, catastrophically inconvenient.

"Don't do this." I step toward him. "Let me go, pup."

"I'm not locking you up because I want to. Kody was going to throw your ass in Sitka jail overnight and charge you with trespassing. I convinced him this was better."

Fuck.

I stare at him, furious and unwilling to admit the spark of gratitude burning under my ribs.

Without looking away, he reaches for the book on the table.

"My story." He presses it into my hands.

I look down at it, confused, then back up at him.

"The journal explains things like this." He pulls down the neckline of his shirt, exposing the scars on his shoulder and chest.

"Why?" My fingers tighten around the book. "You can't possibly trust me with this."

He shrugs, casual on the surface, but there's tension beneath it, a risk he's taking whether he wants to or not.

"Trust isn't a transaction I want to hold hostage. I'm offering it to you." He gestures at the journal. "I'll see what you do with it. See if you'll build it with me or burn it."

That's a dangerous philosophy. A naïve one. Coming from him, though? It feels like he handed me a bomb.

"I won't regret giving you my ugly secrets." He takes a breath. "I *will* regret letting you leave without hearing yours."

My throat closes.

"I'm offering you a choice." He shoves his hands in his pockets. "Read my story or don't. When I come back this afternoon, if you tell me *your* story, who's hunting you, and why

jag

they want you, I'll use every Strakh resource available to help you."

Help me.

He says it so simply. So confidently. Because he doesn't understand the impossibility of it.

Before I can respond, he turns and opens the door.

"Wolf—"

He doesn't look back. Doesn't stop. Doesn't give me a single second more.

The door shuts, and the silence that follows crushes my ribs, leaving me hollow and breathless. Because I know, with a clarity that flattens me, that was the last conversation Wolf and I will ever have.

wolfson
FORTY-NINE

The yacht hasn't fully docked before I jump, my rain boots slamming down with more urgency than grace.

I've been gone too long. Dove didn't want me to escort Jag to Sitka in the first place, and now she's been sitting here for two hours with nothing but her imagination to keep her company.

Kody lands beside me with four guards at his back.

The other four guards stayed at the tattoo parlor, stationed outside Jag's room with orders not to let him sneeze without checking on him.

Jag definitely wants to kill me for this. I get it. The idea of anyone containing him makes my skin hum with something I don't want to look at too closely.

Inside the main house, the smell of coffee hangs thick. I follow it into the kitchen and find Dove sitting beside Frankie at the island.

Dove's honey-soft eyes instantly connect with mine, and my chest loosens.

"You're home." Frankie hurries toward Kody.

Dove blinks slowly, her shoulders caving inward in that quiet way she does when she's out of gasoline. It's nearly morning, and neither of us slept.

She doesn't protest when I scoop her up and carry her out, back across the walkway, into the guest house, and up the stairs to our bedroom.

I set her down gently, and she remains standing with her back to me, the tension in her neck warning me that a conversation is coming.

"You want to sit?" I ask.

"No. Just... Tell me."

So I do.

I tell her every word Jag and I exchanged. Every look he threw at me. Every moment we stood too close. Every second neither of us pulled away. The way he put my thumb in his mouth as if testing to see if I'd burn or break.

I tell her he has the journal and a choice to make before I return.

Her shoulders hitch with each detail, and her breathing tenses like she's trying not to shake.

"I didn't kiss him," I finish quietly.

"I did." She turns toward me, her expression vulnerable. "Do you hate me?"

"Never." I step into her space. "If anything, I love you more for it."

"Why?" She frowns.

"Because I saw you two tonight. I saw what you used to be together, what you still are, the way he looks at you, the way you respond without meaning to."

Her breath catches.

"It gave me a glimpse into your past." I touch her chin, lifting it. "I saw your pain in that kiss, what it cost you to allow it, and what it took from you when you pulled away. It showed me more about who you are, what you need, and what you've been missing."

Her lower lip trembles, not with fear or guilt. With relief.

And a tremor of something else neither of us is brave enough to name yet.

We peel off our clothes in tired silence. She shuts off the lights, and I lock the balcony door.

When we finally crawl under the blankets, she curls into me, legs tangled with mine, cheek tucked against my chest. My arms wrap around her on instinct.

But neither of us drifts off. Her breathing doesn't even. My pulse doesn't slow. The night doesn't soften around us.

After a long stretch of shared darkness, she whispers, "I know you're not asleep."

"Neither are you."

She lets out a breath that shakes. Then she starts talking.

"Jag was nine when our parents married. I was a baby, but I remember flashes of him in those early years. When our parents were still alive. I remember him hiding under the bed with me during their arguments, just to keep me company. And slipping extra dessert onto my plate when no one was looking. He was protective, even then."

I stroke her back, slow circles, silent encouragement.

"When we lost them, everything changed." She takes me through her life without stopping, from that first year on the streets to the night she ran after Jag in a wedding gown.

She tells me about the cardboard forts, tent villages, abandoned houses, and cold sidewalks they called home.

She tells me about the foster system, the bullies, abuse, molestations, and overall lack of adult supervision, and how Jag saved her from every bad situation with a promise in the bend of his pinky finger.

She tells me about the night she started her period and what happened after she told Jag her virginity had been taken from her.

She tells me about the deep, innocent love she had for him, and how it burned straight through her.

Then she tells me how he killed that love in a drug dealer's house, how he hurt her so profoundly their relationship never recovered.

I can picture him in those early years, in his late teens, early twenties, homeless, feral, ready to torch the world for her. I can guess why he fucked those women after she offered her too-young body to him. He knew it would end her inappropriate crush and end whatever temptations he was fighting.

Deep down, she knows this, too. She just hasn't been able to see past the excruciating devastation he inflicted.

"I thought he hated me and wanted to punish me." Her hand fists in my shirt.

wolfson

"You were fifteen, Bluebird. He screwed up how he handled it, like a typical twenty-year-old, idiot male. But rejecting you that night was the right thing, the only responsible choice, and he paid for it. Hell, he's still paying for it."

"I know that." Her breath strikes my collarbone, warm and shaking. "Doesn't excuse his behavior for the last seventeen years."

"Dead on, darling." I skate my fingers across her shoulders, tracing the faint scars in silent question.

"The marks are from that night. When I caught him with those women, I ran, shoved myself through a metal fence, and didn't have the supplies to mend the wounds correctly."

I keep my hand on her shoulder, but the scars don't need more words tonight. "We need to sleep."

She nods, exhausted enough that the motion barely registers.

"When we wake, I'll return to Jag and see if he read the journal." I yawn. "See if he's ready to build trust and let me help."

"I'm coming with you."

"No."

It's the same crossroads as the dock. Same tension crackling between us.

"You promised." She lifts her head, glaring.

Fuck. I did. Hours ago, amid the arguing and frustration, I told her if she stayed on the island, she could go next time.

"I'm going." She taps my lips. "But not to see him."

That stops me.

"I'd rather go to the garage." She settles into the pillow. "I need to put in my notice to quit. Finish the repairs that need my attention. Then I'll wait there."

I search her face, trying to find the angle I'm missing.

"I want to be close to you, Wolf. In case something goes sideways. If he pulls his usual shit, if you get triggered or shut down..." She presses her forehead to my chest. "I don't want to be an ocean away if you need me."

"This has nothing to do with me being tri-curious?"

"Tri-what?"

"Let me ask you something. If Jag was trustworthy—"

"He's not."

"If he'd shown up tonight as the man you loved before everything went to hell, if he'd begged your forgiveness and tossed all his secrets at your feet, would you have considered building a relationship with him? A *sexual* relationship?"

Her breath catches.

"A relationship that involved you and him and me," I say. "Would you have been interested in exploring something together?"

Silence.

Not cold or angry silence. She sinks into soundless introspection, her eyes shifting in the dark, up to my face, then away, then back again.

I don't move. I don't rush her. I wait, hand on her neck, pulse loud in my ears.

Finally, she exhales with an agonized, "Yes." Her expression creases, fraught with reluctant honesty. "Jag might've been the only person I would ever consider sharing you with. But hang on. Are you…? Would you share me with him? I mean, you're possessive and jealous. You were going to stab your brother just for walking in on us."

"I would never share you with anyone. But he already has your heart, whether you'll admit it or not. And I like him."

"You want to fuck him."

"I want to get to know him. There's more there, hidden under that rugged exterior, and I want to understand it."

"He isn't trustworthy, Wolf. He's cruel, manipulative, and ruthlessly violent. Tell me you'll remember that when you see him again."

"Yes, and then some."

Trust isn't a feeling. It's a structure. And Jag's trust is cracked straight through.

I pull her closer, fitting her hips against mine. Her breathing evens out against my chest, and eventually her weight sinks into me.

But my mind stays wide awake. Because now I know something I can't unknow.

Long ago, there was a version of Jag who might've fit into this life with us. And there's a future she could imagine, even now, if he hadn't turned his past into a graveyard.

After I get some sleep, I'll go to Jag with open hands, but I won't forget what she said.

Not everyone who wants to stay knows how.

PAM GODWIN
When I return to Sitka, I'll find out which man Jag really is.

wolfson
FIFTY

Sitka greets us with that fake-nice summer bullshit, sun out, air warm, like it didn't spend nine months trying to kill everyone.

Dove and I linger in the doorway of the mechanic shop while the security guys do their thing, radios chirping, eyes everywhere at once. They'll turn the garage inside out, lock it down, and make it solid enough that I can leave her here under their watch.

She braces a shoulder against the doorframe, smiling, as a group of people walk past us, their heads turned, openly staring at me.

Yeah, I've armored up today.

A black lace corset ties loosely under my cropped jacket, my scars peeking above the boning. A plaid kilt hangs low on my hips, cut for movement, not ceremony. I layered fishnet under it because Sitka summer is still Sitka.

My stompy combat boots look as loud and mean as my heavy black eyeliner, which flares out toward my cheeks in scalloped, Gothic streaks. I added the pearls at my throat mostly because I like how they confuse people who think they've already figured me out.

Today calls for extra of everything. Because if Jag Rath read my journal, he now knows my weaknesses. The only way to prepare for that is to own who I am.

"All clear, sir." Carl steps out of the garage. "Found this taped to the wall."

He hands me a scrap of cardboard that reads *Lunch* in thick marker.

"Guess Taaq and Chester took a late break." Dove pauses in the doorway. Not in. Not out.

Sunlight slashes across her face, catching on her septum, Medusa, and eyebrow piercings. Her hair hangs unbound, rippling around her in ocean-blue waves.

A sleeveless cherry-printed crop top knots at her ribs, and her high-waisted black shorts have enough stretch to squat under a chassis without flashing the universe.

She catches me staring and quirks a brow. "What?"

"Just appreciating my excellent taste in clothes and the woman who wears them."

"Pretty sure you bought these clothes for yourself."

"Pretty sure they're too small for me."

"That's not what I mean, and you know it." She crouches, grabbing her quad skates from the side where she always kicks them.

After she shoves them on and ties the laces, she continues to stall in the doorway.

I stall with her. Too close to leave. Too far to pretend I'm not stalling.

"You can just let Jag go, you know," she says.

"I know."

She takes me in from head to toe. The eyeliner. The kilt. The way my shoulders set like I'm bracing for impact instead of a conversation.

"You're wickedly intimidating." A corner of her mouth lifts. "He won't know what to do with you."

"No one does."

"I do." She hooks a finger in my corset and pulls me close.

Dear goddess of diesel fumes, I fucking love this woman.

She's strong without advertising it. Fierce without cruelty. Her quiet doesn't ask for permission. It just exists.

I don't want to leave her here. The thought digs into my gut and refuses to be polite.

"I'll be here." She straightens the pearls at my throat and

traces an exposed scar. "Only a few blocks away."

"I know. Still don't like it."

"Go." She presses a toe stop into the cement and nudges me backward. "Do the thing."

"Yeah." I keep backing up, eyes glued to her gorgeous face. "There's something I need to do first."

She stays where she is, framed by the open doorway, sunlight outlining her like heaven's trying to steal her back.

I keep walking backward, right into the street, and stop dead in the middle of it.

Arms out and boots planted, I yell, "Hey, everyone! I have an announcement!"

People flinch. Heads turn. A guy with a coffee freezes mid-stride. Two tourists look thrilled, like they just stumbled into local entertainment.

An older woman with grocery bags clocks me, makes the sign of the cross, and hurries away like I'm the anti-Christ.

"Ma'am!" I shout after her. "You're gonna want to hear this!"

She runs away like she absolutely does not want to hear it.

A couple of younger guys linger by the curb, grinning. One of them pulls out his phone.

"Everybody scoot closer." I wave them in. "This is a group experience. Don't be shy. I'm fragile but committed."

Dove covers her mouth, her eyes bright. Oh, no. Does she know what this is? She definitely knows.

I take a big breath. Too big. Then I bellow, "I love this woman!"

The harbor echoes it back.

"Her." I point at her hard in case there's any confusion. "Right there. In the doorway. With the skates."

A guy laughs. Someone claps once, unsure.

"I love her. I love her. I loooooove her!" I spin in a slow circle, addressing the street, the docks, the sky, the entire postal code. "I love her when she's quiet. I love her when she's mad. I love her when she's fixing engines and ignoring me on purpose. I love her all the time."

Dove laughs, full-bodied and unguarded, with pink cheeks and wet-honey eyes.

She pushes off the doorway on her skates, rolls forward, and cups her hands around her mouth. "I love you, too!"

People cheer. Someone whistles. The guy filming gives me a thumbs-up.

I bow, dramatic and unnecessary, then backpedal out of the road, grinning like an asshole with a pulse.

From the sidewalk across the street, I catch her gaze and blow her a kiss. She snatches it out of the air, licks it, and fires it back at me.

I stay there a second longer, watching her roll backward into the garage. The door yawns wider to take her in. The light shifts. She's inside, probably already reaching for a tool.

The guards move into place, two at the door, two flanking the lot. Exactly where they belong.

That's when I turn.

Extra eyeliner. Extra steel. Extra resolve. I head for the tattoo parlor, ready to face whatever Jag Rath thinks he has waiting for me.

A few blocks away, the front door gives way under my hand. Too easy. It should've been locked. The shop is closed today.

"Shit." I pull a knife from my boot and rush inside.

And slam to a stop.

My brain tries to process the mess on the floor.

The blood.

The bodies.

One by the front desk. One half-curled like he tried to crawl. Blood slicks across the concrete, dragged by boots that don't belong to the people left behind. Throats open. Stab wounds everywhere else.

My chest collapses.

"No." I step around them, moving deeper into the shop. "No, no, no."

Another body near the chairs. Another by the coffee machine. Eyes open.

I force myself to look at them, one by one, dread climbing higher with each heartbeat.

Please don't be him. Please don't be him.

My hands shake, and my airway pinches shut. Extra eyeliner feels like a joke as I grab wrists, check necks, and examine faces.

All four guards are dead, and they're still warm. Not cooling or stiff. Heat clings to skin, the blood fresh. Whatever happened here is breathing down my neck.

My eyes lift.

wolfson

The break room door stands open. Blood trails toward it. Or from it? Footprints overlap, in and out.

If Jag is in there…

My pulse roars in my ears as I step closer, every sense on high alert. I brace for anything. Another body, a final stand, Jag on the floor with his throat torn open.

I push the door fully open.

More blood.

A knocked-over table.

No Jag.

He isn't here, and neither is his duffel bag. The corner, where the bag sat only hours earlier, is empty.

He left.

And everyone between him and the exit paid for it.

Dove.

She flashes through my head like a siren, and my phone is in my hand before I realize it.

My thumb shakes against the screen as I swipe to call her security team. But before I connect, the screen flashes with an incoming call.

GI Joe Carl

"Carl." I sheathe the knife in my boot and head to the door. "Jag's gone. Guards are dead. Move Dove. Now! Get her to the yacht—"

"Sir," Carl snaps. "She already left."

"What?" I stumble onto the sidewalk.

"She said she didn't feel well and wanted to head back to the yacht to wait for you. That's why I'm calling. We initiated a location change and have eyes on her."

"The entire security team is with her?"

"Affirmative, sir. Did you say Mr. Rath is gone? And the guards—?"

"Rath is gone. Guards are dead." The phone bounces against my ear as I tear down the street. "I'm coming to you. Where exactly—?"

"Hold on." An explosion of wrong sounds blasts through the line. Wind. Shouting. Footsteps pounding.

My pulse skyrockets, and I pick up my pace.

"Shit! She's running." Carl barks commands at his team, panting. "She bolted. Took off through the harbor. She shook the two closest guys—"

"Why is she running?" I shout, sprinting down the street. "Where is she?"

The sidewalk blurs. The sky tilts. My boots slam pavement hard enough to rattle my teeth.

"Where is she?" I yell.

"Heading east through the docks," Carl wheezes. "Near the fish processors."

I cut corners, and people shout as I shove past them. Someone curses. Someone stumbles. I don't slow down. My lungs burn. My legs scream. I push harder.

"She's fast." Carl's footfalls pound through the phone. "Jesus, she's fast."

My chest locks up with fear so sharp it tries to fold me in half.

Why is she running? Something must've spooked her.

"Carl," I gasp. "If he gets anywhere near her—"

"We won't lose her." His voice cracks. "You hear me? We're not—"

I disconnect as the pier comes into view. Wood planks, rocking boats, rigging clattering like bones... I scan the throngs of people as the harbor clangs in my ears.

"Dove!" I yell into the crowd and the air and the universe like she might hear me through sheer force. "Dove!"

Then I see it.

A flash of blue a few docks down. Just a glimmer, just enough to hook my spine and yank.

"Dove!" I tear toward it, running faster than I ever have in my life. Faster than fear. Faster than thought. Faster than anything Jag Rath ever planned for.

My boots strike the planks, lungs shredding and vision tunneling as I scream her name.

"Dove! Stop!" As I close the distance, a speedboat slides in beside her, smooth and wrong, entirely out of place.

She keeps her back to me, and my panic goes feral.

"Dove!" I roar again. "Look at me!"

She doesn't.

What the hell is her problem?

The crowd shifts, giving me a quick glimpse of her feet. She switched her skates for sneakers. Plain white sneakers I've never seen before. And the flannel shirt draped over her? It hangs to her knees, swallowing her frame.

My stomach free-falls.

All of this feels wrong.

The boat nudges the dock, and she jumps without hesitation, landing on the seat beside a man I've never seen in my life. Nondescript. Forgettable. Built to disappear.

Who the fuck is that?

He cranks the throttle.

"No! Nooooo!" I hit the end of the dock as the boat surges forward, water exploding behind it.

I scream until my throat bleeds, and my voice fractures.

The wind whips her hard as they take off, and her blue hair lifts. Then it peels away, sails clean off her head, and spirals into the harbor.

A wig.

It hits the water and spreads, bright and false against the dark chop.

My heart stops as she turns to watch it sink. Then her eyes lift and find me.

Not Dove's eyes.

Similar features. Similar coloring. Same height and build, maybe. But wrong in every place that matters. Her hair is brown, and her gaze is empty of recognition, empty of anything at all.

Not Dove.

A decoy.

A distraction.

My blood turns ice-cold as the truth detonates in my chest.

Dove is still at the mechanic shop.

Alone.

Unprotected.

Dread curdles. Fear pummels. I spin on my heel and run.

"That wasn't her," Carl shouts from the entrance of the harbor.

No shit.

Two blocks ahead, the other three guards sprint hard, tearing back toward the mechanic shop with trained speed. They blow past people, past carts, past shouting voices, all of it blurring into noise in their wake.

I'm right behind or trying to be.

My phone's in my hand again, my thumb slamming the

screen.

"Come on, Dove. Pick up."

Ring. Ring. Ring.

"Pick up," I snarl under my breath, lungs ripping and legs on fire. "Pick up. Pick up."

It goes to voice mail.

Carl falls in beside me, matching my stride as he switches between his headset and radio, calling all units and dispatching teams to the tattoo parlor and the mechanic shop.

My world narrows to one thing.

Getting to her.

My lungs feel too small as I pump my arms and overdrive my legs, letting the pain turn into fuel. Anyone in my way gets flattened. Anyone near her when I arrive is dead. I will tear this town apart if I have to.

I don't think about the blood in the tattoo shop.

I don't think about Jag missing.

I think about her laugh, her kiss, and the way she rolled backward into that shop like nothing bad could touch her there.

If anyone has—

If anyone—

I bare my teeth and run.

Carl shouts into his mic, spitting coordinates and rerouting bodies. He glances at me once, sees my face, and doesn't try to slow me down.

I skid into the garage seconds after the security team, breath tearing out of my chest in ragged pulls.

"Clear!" someone shouts.

I blow past them and into the bays where she should be.

The shop is wrong in a way I recognize instantly. Too still. Tools laid out mid-thought. A creeper abandoned halfway under a lift.

Guards fan out, methodical, weapons up, checking corners, checking shadows, checking places that can't possibly hold her.

I already know.

My eyes go straight to the spot by the workbench where she dropped her bag.

It's still there.

But her skates aren't. They're not on the floor. Not tucked under the bench. Not kicked aside, where she always leaves them.

A guard shakes his head at Carl and holds out a phone. Dove's phone.

The garage tilts, and I have to plant my boots wider to stay upright. My hands curl into fists. My vision tunnels, and every nerve lights up. Then goes numb.

I replay it all at once. The doorway, the sunlight, and the kiss she caught and threw back. She told me to go, and I listened.

I should've stayed.

I should've known.

I should've—

The thoughts don't finish. They fracture, scatter, and burn.

Pain floods in and spreads everywhere, behind my eyes, in my throat, and down my spine. All the noise fades, the guards, the radios, and the city outside, leaving a hollowed-out space where she's supposed to be.

Carl comes up beside me, breathing hard. "We're canvassing the blocks. Cameras. Harbor feeds. Everyone's moving. Your family is inbound."

I nod once, because nodding is all I can manage.

Dove is gone.

wolfson
FIFTY-ONE

Sitka slams shut like a fist. Red and blue everywhere. Sirens slice the air. Radios bark codes. Cops flood the streets, and harbor patrols choke the docks.

None of it matters if Dove isn't safe.

I scan faces, lights, and shadows, looking for her where she can't possibly be.

Monty Strakh stands at the center of it all, calm in a terrifying way I've only seen once before. The night I met him at the doctor's dead-body dinner party.

Phone glued to his ear, Monty points, and people snap to attention around him. Private security. Federal favors. Maritime contacts. Money moving faster than the law ever can.

"I want the town shut down yesterday." He pauses, listening to the mayor on the phone. "You heard me. I want the floatplanes grounded. Ferries stalled. Coast Guard cutters idle in the water. All roads bottlenecked. Every possible exit becomes a barricade with a badge in front of it."

He's done this before. When Frankie vanished, he bent the world until it screamed.

He's doing it again.

But I can't stand still long enough to watch.

When Carl confirms the cameras were smashed and the footage wiped in both shops, that's my cue to go.

I take my motorcycle and tear through Sitka. Up the hills. Down by the water. Through neighborhoods where porch lights flick on, and faces appear behind curtains. I search alleys, doorways, and shadows that look like people until they don't.

Through it all, a familiar engine rumbles behind me, close enough to feel like a hand on my shoulder.

Leo.

Every turn I take, he takes. Each burst of speed he matches without crowding me. He's not chasing. He's shepherding, babysitting, making sure I come back from this ride in one piece, even if I hate him for it later.

As we rip along the waterfront, my throttle hand twitches, urging me faster, harder, anywhere but inside my head.

Every denim jacket turns my stomach. Every thirty-something woman makes my heart kick.

She's nowhere.

This town spans nearly three-thousand square miles. She could be anywhere.

And Jag…

Satan save me from my own stupidity. Jag said he was leaving Sitka today. He couldn't have been clearer about it.

He also said he wanted Dove to stay with me. He said it like a promise. Looked me in the eye when he said it.

What changed?

Did he read my journal? Did seeing the worst parts of me make him question my ability to protect Dove? I'm not that broken kid anymore. I survived. I learned. If he read all of it, he would know that, godsdammit.

I ride harder, faster, reckless enough that the bike shudders beneath me. Warm air knifes my lungs. My hands ache from gripping the bars too tightly. Leo stays with me, a constant pressure in my mirrors.

Did Jag kill the guards, peel out of there, and snatch Dove while I was on the pier? Did he plan the decoy before or after he sucked my thumb like a blow job? Was that always the move? Bait me, split my focus, take what matters, and disappear?

Dove told me he was manipulating me. She warned me, and I didn't listen.

I wanted to believe Jag would read my story and stay long enough to tell me his. I wanted to believe the best version of him was real.

Now I don't know what I believe.

I only know the streets keep coming up empty, and my chest is tearing itself apart from the inside. Every second stretches too long. Every minute without her ratchets my panic.

I circle back toward the harbor, engine screaming, eyes burning, brain stuck in a loop, replaying her smile, her kiss, and the way she told me to go.

My gut told me to stay. Why didn't I listen to it?

That thought doesn't leave. It claws.

I ride until my hands shake, my vision blurs, and the city pushes in from all sides, daring me to break.

Leo speeds up alongside me and points in the direction of the tattoo parlor.

Has there been news? Did they find something?

I crank a one-eighty and gun it back toward the shop with Leo glued to my flank.

The barricades come into view, a mayhem of metal, lights, and uniforms. No way to get close. I ditch the bike and take off on foot, knowing Leo will deal with it.

Monty waits for me at the door. That alone is wrong.

He steps closer, his expression ice-quiet. "There's another body."

My brain refuses it. I left before they finished cataloging the scene, but another body? How the hell did I miss that?

"Who?"

"Declan."

I stagger, and Monty reaches for me, pulling me against his chest.

Declan. Loud, coffee-drinking, conspiracy-weaving, always-talking, always-there Declan, who taught me how to use a tattoo machine and showed up every day.

Except today was his day off. He wasn't supposed to be here.

"How?" I grip the lapels of Monty's suit jacket, wrinkling the expensive fabric. "Where?"

"Stabbed before he entered the shop." Monty embraces me, cupping the back of my head. "He didn't make it inside. They found his body in the side alley."

The world goes red at the edges. I hear myself breathe like

it's someone else. Too fast. Too hard. My hands curl and uncurl, and something inside me tears loose.

Jag Rath.

Did he do this? Did he kill four guards and Declan? And rip Dove from my life?

It's always him, Wolf. It's what he does.

Her words drill into me, and my grief turns feral. It shreds into howling ribbons of fury, ripping from my throat.

I shove past Monty, my thoughts scattering as I race into the city, toward the night, toward whoever did this.

Jag? His enemies? His associates? I want names. I want faces. I want the sound of someone realizing they chose the wrong place and the wrong people.

"Wolf!" Leo bellows from somewhere behind me.

I run faster.

Declan is dead.

Dove is missing.

I don't care how long this takes or what it costs me. I *will* find her.

The docks, the alleys, the dead-end streets... I comb every inch of Sitka for hours.

Cigarette after cigarette burns down to my fingers as I replay every word Jag said. Every look Dove gave me. Every instinct I overruled because I wanted to believe in fairy-tale endings.

Rage boils up my spine, bending my frame under the pressurized coil and drawing me so tight my teeth ache from clenching.

I kick a trashcan into the side of a building and roar at the top of my lungs.

My fingers crack one by one as I flex them, testing how much force I can put behind a strike before bone answers bone. I punch a piling. The air. The brick. The violence needs somewhere to go until I can wrap my hands around a throat, paint the pavement with blood, and drink vodka from the skull of whoever did this.

I pace. I stop. I pace again. My boots grind glass into the concrete.

Where is she? Is she scared? Hurting? Fighting like hell to get back to me?

I shake out my hands, hard. Again. Again. My shoulders

burn from holding myself back. My breath comes too fast. Smoke swamps my lungs as I light another cigarette and let it burn down too close, too consumed by a dark place where all I see is death.

I'm back on that cliff. The place where I stop being strategic and start being terminal.

Haven't I learned anything?

Rage like this won't find Dove. It just makes more bodies.

I crush the cigarette under my heel and stand there until the red haze thins, the city comes back into focus, and my hands stop shaking.

My legs give out, and I sink to the ground, my back against an alley wall.

I'm not alone. Haven't been all night. Leo peels away from the shadows and lowers beside me, snaking an arm around my shoulders.

He doesn't speak, knowing I'm on the edge.

My jaw grinds. My chest hammers. The violence hasn't left. It waits behind my breastbone, pacing and snarling.

I force myself to sit there, picking at a rip in my fishnets, widening it without thinking.

My kilt is all twisted from the run, and when I rub my face, my hands come away black. Makeup streaks my fingers, and I stare at the mess, breathing slowly. Controlled. In. Out. Again.

Leo stays silent and solid at my side, letting me pull myself back together piece by piece. The fury still rattles my ribs, but it quiets enough for me to stand.

Leo rises with me. As I start to turn away, he catches my arm.

"Hey." He grips my face in both hands. "You're not alone."

"I know. I lucked out with the best least-favorite brother from another uncle."

"Don't get sappy on me." He rests his forehead against mine. "It'll ruin the moment."

"If I get any sap on you, that's on you for standing too close."

"I'm not going anywhere." He pulls me closer and tucks his nose into my hair, breathing me in and holding me steady.

He used to hold me like this in Hoss when the trembling wouldn't stop. When Denver's evil broke me. When sleep came in scraps and fear did most of the talking. Leo couldn't fix anything back then, but he stayed. He let me borrow his strength until I could find my own again.

wolfson

Same grip now. Same patience. He holds me until he feels the shift, until my weight settles back into my own legs, and I'm no longer leaning.

"Let's go find your girl." He releases me, trusting me to stay upright.

I turn back toward the street, back toward the hunt, back to the tattoo parlor with Leo on my heels.

The crime scene lights illuminate the entire block. Tape flutters. People murmur. Monty's presence sits heavy over everything, his power and reach unfurling in real time.

He's built for this kind of war. So am I, when I stop letting my heart drive.

I step inside, and everything in me shifts from feral to cold.

Monty stands near the back wall, issuing quiet directives. Leo sticks to my side, eyes tracking every corner. Kody's absence tells me he took Frankie back to the island. Good.

Carl relays updates into a headset. Jasper leans against a workbench, sleeves rolled, watching for threats. More Strakh guards swarm the property, some I don't recognize. New faces, clean lines, disciplined postures... Pros. Monty's pulling from deeper benches.

Wilson, the private investigator, is here, too, flanked by his own people. They claimed a table with laptops spread out on it.

The uniforms, radios, and clipped voices of Sitka PD crowd the perimeter, trying to look useful while staying out of Monty's way.

The bodies are gone. Photos have been taken, evidence logged. The forensics team finished their sweep and cleared out.

I cut straight to Monty.

When he clocks me, he pauses mid-sentence, his eyes sweeping over my busted knuckles, rigid posture, and smeared makeup. There's concern in the way he examines me. Real concern. He just doesn't let it show.

"You good?" he asks quietly.

"Focused." I set my jaw. "Catch me up on everything."

He nods and pivots us out of the traffic flow, shielding the conversation with his body.

"We found this." He reaches into a satchel and hands me the journal. "It was under the mattress on the cot."

"Under it? Like it was hidden there?"

"Yes."

I flip through the book, hunting for any sign Jag touched it. Dog-eared pages, notes in the margins, anything. But there's nothing. No fingerprints. No tells. It looks exactly the way I left it.

"If Jag didn't give a shit..." I pass it back. "Wouldn't he have left it out in the open?"

"Don't read intent where there's absence." He returns the book to his satchel. "Wilson's pulling cross-referenced feeds."

Beside us, the private investigator turns a laptop toward me, displaying harbor feeds, CCTV traffic videos, and private cams.

"No luck on the camera here or at the mechanic shop?" My pulse races.

"No. Those were destroyed and can't be recovered." Wilson switches to another screen. "We have plate hits pending, cell pings moving, and guard rotations mapped down to minutes."

"Is the city still locked down? All exits blocked?" I look at Monty, knowing he doesn't have that much power.

"Not the way it needs to be. I can't shut down Sitka like a private island, and I won't interfere with an active police investigation." He sighs. "But I'm leaning on permits, port authority cooperation, and private security checkpoints on the main arteries. Anything commercial or chartered is slowed, logged, and flagged. I have eyes on all of it."

"So civilian traffic still moves." My stomach sinks. "Commercial flights, public ferries, fishing vessels..."

"Yes." A muscle ticks in his jaw. "I can't stop the world, Wolf. But if someone tries to disappear from Sitka, they'll leave a trail. And we're watching it."

Wilson nods beside him. "We're correlating departures with your timelines."

"This is as tight as it gets." Monty meets my eyes. "Without crossing lines that don't come back clean."

I hear what he's not saying. He'll stay clean where it counts and dirty where it can't be traced. Every asset he owns will face outward, and anywhere the rules stop watching, he'll step over them. If someone sneezes in Sitka tonight, he'll know which direction it blows.

"Okay. How do I help?" I hold out my arms. "Tell me where you need me."

Wilson's people make room for me at the table and start assigning tasks, splitting teams, and cross-checking assumptions.

wolfson

Leo slides a coffee toward me and takes an empty chair, waiting for his assignment.

If Jag did this, we'll find the fracture point. If it's his enemies, we'll follow the blast radius. If this is something else entirely, it won't stay hidden long.

I'll personally make whoever did this answer for Declan, and I won't stop until Dove is back in my arms, alive and safe.

Whoever did this just activated every tool my family owns and every piece of restraint I have left.

Now we hunt.

wolfson
FIFTY-TWO

The hunt is nothing like the ones in Hoss. Hunting in the Arctic meant movement, cold air, cramping muscles, and tracks in the snow that told me when I was close and when it was over.

This hunt is the opposite.

It's staring at screens instead of the ground, waiting for information that never reveals its tracks, and sitting still until my bones ache. There's no scent, nothing tangible to chase. Just long, grinding days stacked on days with nothing to show for it except new folders, new maps, and new theories that collapse under their own logic.

I spend most of my time in Monty's den, a room built of power, dark wood, and screens lining the walls.

Monty doesn't leave my side, his presence steady and terrifyingly focused, pulling strings, burning through favors, and organizing alliances. Everything he did when Frankie was missing.

He's doing all the same shit for Dove.

Private bush planes scour Alaska. Coast Guard District 17 sweeps the shoreline. The ABI keeps every department talking, and private investigators fan out across the country, running facial recognition through public cameras, transit hubs, gas

wolfson

stations, grocery stores, anywhere Dove's face might appear.

Every morning starts the same. No sightings. No hits. No breakthroughs. No proof Dove Rath is alive or dead. No proof Jag Rath took her. No proof he didn't.

The Raths evaporated in open air. In daylight. Not a single camera in Sitka caught their exits. The few witnesses didn't see more than a blur.

Declan is dead. The guards are dead. All stabbed silently and up close.

I keep circling that part.

How did one man get the jump on four trained, armed guards?

How did he escape his room without alerting them?

Why kill Declan, an innocent bystander, who had nothing to do with any of this?

Every answer spawns worse questions.

And denial.

Logic lines Jag up dead center. Clean escape. Decoy. Timing too precise to be luck. When we lay it all out on a board, he's the only piece that fits without forcing it.

But my gut won't cooperate. As monstrous as Jag can be, he has rules.

In all of Dove's stories, Jag's violence had a line. He took out her abusers, molesters, and rapists. Not once did she tell me a story where he killed someone who didn't deserve it.

Declan doesn't fit. He was harmless and kind. He didn't hurt anyone. Didn't threaten anyone. He wasn't in Jag's way.

Jag doesn't kill innocent people.

Either everything I think I know about him is wrong, or an enemy grabbed both of them.

That thought scares me more than believing Jag did it.

My heartbeat hurts. Every thump feels personal. I lie awake listening to it, half-expecting it to give up before I do.

I can tell Monty's worried about me. Every time his eyes land on me, he chews the inside of his cheek as if my appearance makes him uneasy. Maybe it's the heavy eyeliner packed under my eyes. Or all the black layers I wear even when the house is warm. I want distance. I want to look like someone nobody should try to comfort.

Every night, when the den empties and Monty tells me to get

some rest, I don't.

I go to the guest house and pace until my feet hurt. I smoke until my throat feels raw. One after another, I light them and watch them burn, lost in my head.

Sometimes I play the sax.

The sound comes out wrong, too loud, or too thin. I don't care. I play until my fingers cramp, until my chest tightens, until the ache in my ribs syncs up with the noise. The notes wander. They don't resolve. They just exist and hurt.

Other times, I sit on the floor and draw.

Emo Disney stuff. Ruined princesses. Dark castles. Big-eyed characters with smeared makeup and crooked crowns. I don't sketch happily-ever-afters. I sketch aftermaths.

A week passes.

Seven days since Declan's murder.

Seven days since the decoy.

Seven days since Dove smiled like she was safe.

Rage comes in waves. So does despair. Sometimes they overlap, and I can't tell which one is steering. I snap at people. Then I go quiet for hours. I replay my last conversation with Jag until it loses shape.

He said he was leaving.

He said he was leaving Dove with me.

He was convincing on both counts.

I ricochet between blaming Jag and defending him like it's a full-time job.

Some days, I line him up in my head and pull the trigger without flinching. Other days, I tear the case apart trying to prove he couldn't have done it. Today is one of those days. Today, Jag doesn't feel like the villain.

Monty sits across from me in the den, quiet and patient, watching me spiral through the same arguments I had yesterday and the day before. He doesn't interrupt. He just lets it happen, recognizing the pattern because he's lived it.

"This is what it was like for you." I lean back on the couch. "When Frankie disappeared."

"Yeah." He reclines beside me, raking a hand through his perfect hair, disheveling it. "I didn't know if she left me or if someone took her. I ran both versions into the ground. Tore myself apart trying to make one of them stick."

I look at him, at the man who, despite all his money and

power, couldn't brute-force certainty out of the worst moment of his life.

"I didn't know which truth would hurt less." He releases a breath. "So I lived in both for a while."

"What stopped you?"

"My gut. Deep down, I knew Frankie wouldn't hurt me like that, no matter how much I deserved it. If she left on her own, she would've given me proof of life. Once I accepted that, I knew what I was dealing with."

Something in my chest shifts. Not relief. Not clarity. Just alignment.

I think about the pain in Jag's eyes when he said he had to see Dove one last time.

"It's easier to believe Jag took her." I drum my fingers on my thigh. "In that scenario, they're both alive and safe. Out of my reach, sure, but I know he would protect her with his life and never physically harm her."

"But?"

"But my gut tells me this isn't betrayal. Someone took them both."

Monty watches me land there and gives a slow nod. He knows the cost of that conclusion and what it means.

If someone took them—someone who kills innocent people—then Jag and Dove are somewhere bad.

Maybe being tortured.

Maybe already dead.

Grief rises without warning and punches me in the throat. My breath locks up then breaks apart. I try to swallow it down, clenching my jaw and sucking air through my nose. But the pain keeps coming, scrabbling its way up from somewhere too deep.

The first sob rips out, cracking my ribs. The next one erupts louder and wetter. My hands curl into fists on my thighs, nails digging in, trying to anchor myself, but I'm slipping, body shaking, and I lose it, right there in front of my father.

I hate it. Hate how weak and small I feel.

Until his arms envelop me, reminding me I'm safe with him.

He hugs me like it's the most natural thing in our lives, one hand at the back of my neck, the other around my shoulder, as if he can somehow bear part of it for me.

I lean into him, shaking and crying like the world just ended, because maybe it fucking has.

It takes a while to pull myself back together, to slow the sobs and breathe without breaking. When I finally lift my head, my nose is wet, and makeup streaks my face.

But he's not judging me. Not a hint of disappointment in his eyes. Just steady warmth.

"You're strong." He grips my shoulder and squeezes. "Stronger than I've ever been."

I blink at him, stunned.

Montgomery Strakh, the man who built a kingdom out of nothing, who clawed his way through grief and guilt and the ruins of our wrecked family, is calling me strong?

"Jag didn't do this." My throat seals around a lump. "He's violent, obsessive, and possessive as hell. But he didn't take Dove."

Monty nods, like he's been waiting for me to get here.

"Jag knows his enemies." He straightens and shuffles through the papers on the coffee table. "He would've been prepared for this, maybe even saw them coming."

"His computer lair." I wipe my face with my sleeve, heart squeezing painfully. "I asked him about it once, asked how he hacked private cameras and where he kept all his equipment. All he said was *blue princess*."

"Dove?"

"I guess? Knowing Jag, he would've installed more cameras, *hidden* cameras that feed into a hidden location."

"The team did a camera sweep in both shops and didn't find anything."

"Let's do another one." I stand. "Maybe they missed something."

An hour later, I stand in the tattoo shop, refusing to let myself think about what happened here.

Instead, I focus on the ceilings, corners, and angles Jag might've used.

Monty and Carl set up at the front counter, flanked by two of their best tech guys. Ex-NSA or some high-speed shit.

Theo, the tech with wire-frame glasses and zero personality, powers on his equipment as he explains RF spectrum analysis and frequency anomalies. The taller, meaner-looking tech, Ross, waves a sleek black scanner across the ceiling.

I leave them to their toys and run my hand along the

drywall, tracing the edges of the fresh panels Jag installed. He built this room just for me.

Or did he build it to hide recording equipment that no one would find?

"No standard camera signatures so far." Ross moves deeper into the shop.

"Considering we still haven't cracked Jag's firewall," Theo says, "I doubt any of our equipment will detect his."

"Jag doesn't use standard." Carl types on his laptop. "That means we're not looking for what's common. We're looking for what's off."

"Off how?" I ask.

"Wrong paint match. A seam that runs too clean. A screw that isn't factory issue." Carl looks up from his screen. "If there's a camera in here, it's probably watching us."

I hadn't considered that.

For half a second, I imagine finding the lens, staring straight into it, and telling him to bring her back.

Then the thought evaporates.

If there is a hidden camera, Jag isn't watching it.

Because he can't.

I skim my hands along every inch of the newly constructed walls three times before I feel it. A slight dip under my fingertips. Too smooth. Too intentional. My brows draw tight.

"Here." I rise on my toes and tap the spot. "Get a light on this."

Theo steps in with a penlight, sweeping the beam across the seam where the wall meets the ceiling.

There's a barely visible irregularity. A circle the size of a quarter that doesn't match the rest of the surface. Not paint. Not putty.

"What is it?" Monty appears at my side.

"Sheetrock flaw?" Carl inches closer.

"No. That's a cover. Look." Theo removes a small tool and cuts around the dimple. "Camera lens is behind it. Wireless."

"Hello, Satan's Ring cam." My heart pounds. "Can you trace it? Where does the feed go?"

Theo and Ross pull out more gear. Laptops open, signal intercepts, decrypt attempts... Nothing.

"This thing's locked down tighter than a bank vault." Ross

switches to a different computer. "Encrypted at a level I haven't seen outside black ops. No wonder it didn't trigger our equipment."

"We can't trace the feed." Theo's brow creases. "Wherever it's going, it's not a commercial endpoint. No pings. No reflection."

"Figure it out." Monty crosses his arms.

"It's not going to a cloud." Theo pauses. "It's going to a physical system. Closed loop. Somewhere nearby."

"Blue princess," I mutter under my breath.

They all look at me.

"That's what he called it." I shrug. "His setup. His lair. That's where the feed's going."

Carl nods. "Where—?"

"Hold up. There's a dead-end road..." Monty removes his phone, and his thumbs fly over the screen. "A couple of blocks from here." He angles the display toward us, showing a zoomed-in map. "Princess Way."

"There's a fucking street called Princess Way? And I'm just now hearing about it?" I'm already moving, heading toward the door.

Monty and Carl flank me as I cut through the streets. Following Monty's directions, I turn right, then left, and two blocks later, I stop at the entrance of a dead-end road.

Princess Way.

How many times have I passed this street? It's so unremarkable I never gave it a thought.

It consists of four beat-up houses that slump into waist-high grass. Old chairs and busted appliances rot on the porches, and mailboxes tilt at crooked angles.

One house is straight-up rotting, the windows smashed, and the front door hanging off the hinges. But it's the backyard that grabs me.

Tucked into the overgrowth, as if trying to disappear, sits a concrete shed.

Dead freight piles up around it. Cracked plastic bins, broken shelving, and splintered pallets lean against the ugly, unassuming cement-block walls with weathered, faded paint.

Blue paint.

A blue shed on Princess Way.

"That's it." My pulse spikes as I break into a run, boots

crunching through weeds and gravel.

I circle the shed, checking for tracks and clues. No windows. No vents. Just one steel door with a black keypad embedded beneath the handle. A solid, industrial thing. Too new for this building or this neighborhood.

Monty retraces my steps around the shed as Carl pulls on gloves and kneels to inspect the keypad.

"Blue princess." Monty picks at the chipped blue paint. "Do you think Jag left you this breadcrumb by accident?"

I crouch beside Carl and study the door and keypad. My mind spins through possibilities, traps, bait, and the million ways this could be a dead end. Or a setup.

But my gut doesn't scream danger. It hums.

"No." I straighten, wiping sweat from my brow. "Jag leaves rock trails for Dove. Coded breadcrumbs are literally his thing."

Monty nods. He already knew that. He just wanted to hear me say it.

Carl looks up from the keypad. "Then let's hope he left you the passcode, because this door will be impossible to open without it."

"Explain." A cold weight drops in my chest.

"This isn't consumer-grade." Carl taps the keypad with the back of his knuckle. "It's black-market, military-adjacent tech. I'll have Theo and Ross confirm, but I've seen something like this before. It's booby-trapped in a digital sense. Wrong code or too many attempts, and the lock bricks itself permanently. Power fries."

"So we get one shot." My stomach plummets.

"At best." Carl sighs. "Assuming the passcode isn't time-locked, location-locked, or biometric on top of it."

I have no idea what the passcode could be. Did Jag leave it somewhere I might find it? Or Dove...?

"The graves." My heart rate redoubles. "He leaves rocks under his parents' graves in Anaheim. Coded rocks for Dove. Holy fuck, that's it!"

Monty's already pulling out his phone, fingers moving fast.

"Wilson," he says in greeting, "I need the cemetery where David and Celeste Rath are buried. Anaheim, California. And I need someone you trust on-site within the hour." He glances at me, eyes asking for details.

"Tell them to look under a newly planted flower or tree." I start pacing.

When Jag killed Gavin, he was in California. He could've left a message then, especially if he intended to run.

Monty relays the information and ends the call. "Now we wait."

I lean against the shed wall, hands in my pockets, adrenaline surging.

"Even if we get inside…" Monty eyes me. "There's a possibility Jag erased the feed or cleared out the equipment."

"You don't need to manage my expectations, Dad. Disappointment is basically my side hustle. I've been eating that shit for breakfast since I could walk."

His eyes soften with regret. Whenever I mention my childhood, it reminds him he wasn't there for it. He stares at me like he wants to rewind time and beat the hell out of everyone who let me down.

Including himself.

"Come on." I head to the back stoop of the rotting house and light a cigarette.

Monty joins me, the porch groaning under our weight.

The shed looms in front of us. Carl paces nearby, speaking on the phone with Theo and Ross.

I can't stop staring at the keypad. Can't stop bouncing my leg. Can't stop thinking about Dove.

Monty rests his elbows on his knees, watching the sky shift above the trees. He doesn't try to fix this. Doesn't say it's going to be okay. I'm grateful for that.

Theo and Ross eventually show up, carrying all their gear.

One hour. Sixty minutes. A thousand years.

Then, finally, Monty's phone buzzes.

He grabs it quickly, stands, and answers without looking at the screen.

"Wilson." A pause. He listens. His shoulders shift. "Copy that. Send the photo." He hangs up and meets my eyes. "They found it."

"What's on it?" I lurch to my feet.

He hands me his phone.

A photo lights up the screen, showing a smooth white rock nestled in the dirt beside a young sapling. Written across its surface in thick black sharpie are six numbers.

wolfson

Blood thrashes in my ears as I cross the yard to the shed. I don't hesitate. Don't second-guess.

I punch in the code.

Each beep feels like a detonation. When I enter the last digit, the lock buzzes.

Click.

The door unseals with a hiss and cracks open.

I shove it wide.

Cool, recycled air hits my face. Inside, the hum is constant, alive, a soft electric heartbeat in the dark.

My pulse spikes, chest pounding as I step in slowly, eyes adjusting.

Stacks of towers line the back wall. Rows of monitors flicker to life as I cross the threshold. Feeds, windows, command lines, maybe a dozen active systems, all still running.

He left it all.

Relief hits me like a drug.

Then comes the drop.

If Jag orchestrated his and Dove's disappearance, none of this would still be here. He would've wiped it, burned it, or taken it with him.

But he didn't. He left it running. Which means this wasn't part of the plan.

If he intended to run, he never got the chance.

wolfson
FIFTY-THREE

I edge farther inside Jag's computer lair, squeezing between racks of servers and stepping over thick, veiny cables. The blinking lights and hum of processors vibrate with the power of an electronic brain.

The amount of tech in here? It's way beyond me.

I know enough to boot up a system and browse the Internet. This is something else. Black computer boxes stack two and three high, flashing with multicolor LEDs. I don't touch a damn thing.

Instead, I scan the monitors.

Most of them are live camera feeds of familiar streets and buildings. Every screen tracks a different piece of Sitka, following a clear path from the harbor to the mechanic shop.

One feed locks on the front door of the garage, a different angle than the busted camera Taaq had installed. That one died the day Dove disappeared. But this one is hidden.

The video is clear, streaming in full res and showing the mechanic shop open again.

Taaq is there, face pinched and hands busy under the hood of a car. Chester moves across the frame with a coil of hoses over one shoulder.

No Dove.

If she were there, she'd be everywhere.

I drag a chair in front of the screen and sit down hard. My hands shake, so I ball them into fists on my lap.

This camera shouldn't exist. Not from this angle. Not from that wall. Not even Taaq knows it's there.

"Is this video stream saving somewhere?" I point at the screen. "How do we see the footage of the day she disappeared?"

Theo and Ross push in, eyes wide as they take in Jag's systems.

"Jesus." Theo whistles under his breath. "This is a fortress. Looks like he built a government-grade network out of spare parts and paranoia."

Ross makes a beeline to the nearest tower, slipping on gloves as he surveys the setup.

Monty and Carl step back, letting the techs take over. I stay planted in front of the monitor, eyes fixed on that front-door feed as if she'll appear.

"Yeah, it's recording." Theo taps a few keys, leaning in and scanning fast. "Custom loop system on the shop camera and the one he installed on the street." He glances over his shoulder at Ross. "Encrypted video retention protocol. He's storing everything. Days, weeks, months of footage in compressed bursts."

"Can you access it?" My pulse races.

"Not easily." Ross scowls at the screen. "He layered this thing like a psychopath. We're talking multi-tier AES encryption, with AI-scrambled keys that rotate every sixty seconds. He basically turned a DVR into a CIA asset."

"But you can crack it?" I grind my molars.

"Give me twenty minutes and a Red Bull." Theo accepts the energy drink from Carl and cracks it open. "This guy is ten steps ahead of anything I've seen."

"He didn't just lock the system." Ross moves from one keyboard to the next, fingers flying. "If we mess up the decryption order, it'll overwrite the sector with garbage data."

"So don't fuck it up." My insides clench.

Somewhere, buried deep in this digital labyrinth, is the moment Dove vanished.

They settle into the controls, mumbling about Jag's code,

how it's obsessively written, beautifully structured, and elegant in the most terrifying way. They scroll through camera IDs, file logs, and encrypted directories labeled with nothing but symbols and rotating characters.

"This isn't hacking," Ross mutters. "It's breaking into someone's mind."

Thirty minutes later, Theo exhales a triumphant whoop.

"I got it!" His fingers hover over the keyboard. "This is the log for the mechanic shop, inside and on the street."

Everyone crowds in behind him as he pulls up the time stamp.

The footage rolls.

I see myself on the screen, standing out on the street, voice carrying as I shout *I love her* to the world.

Jag's camera angle is higher than the streetlight, angled just right. I look younger somehow. Hopeful and happy. Fucking stupid.

Monty's hand clamps onto my shoulder, and it stays there, anchoring me to the chair, as Theo fast-forwards.

The footage jumps. Skips over the blur of people dispersing. Over the moment I left. Over the empty street.

Then the decoy appears.

She slips around the corner of the building, casual, unhurried, right into the line of sight of the two guards stationed near the garage bays.

She looks like Dove, walks like her, same blue hair. With her head down, I can't see her face.

"She came from the back." Carl leans in, eyes narrowing. "She said she felt sick and went outside to puke. I didn't question it. Didn't think about how we never saw her come out of the building."

On the screen, the guards react immediately. One steps forward, radio already up, body language shifting into escort mode.

They route her fast. Away from the garage. Toward the harbor, efficient and professional.

Monty's grip tightens on my shoulder. I can't look away, knowing Dove was still inside that shop as her protection left.

The footage keeps rolling. Seconds tick by. Too many of them.

Then movement.

Dove appears in the doorway of the shop, wearing her skates.

That alone tells me everything. She didn't plan to go anywhere.

She rolls over the threshold, slow and reactive, her instinct screaming that something isn't right. Her posture changes, shoulders tensing, chin lifting, subtle, but I know her.

She looks down the street, where the guards went. The wrong direction.

Someone moves behind her.

He slips into frame as if he's been there the whole time, hiding outside the camera's edge. He's masked, average height, average build, wearing street clothes. Nothing remarkable about him.

My breath leaves me in a broken sound as he clamps a hand over her mouth.

She doesn't even get a second to fight. He lifts her and drags her backward, out of the camera's view. Gone in a blur of motion and blue hair.

"That's not Jag." I lurch forward, hands braced on the desk. "Jag's bigger. Taller. Broader through the shoulders."

"Whoever it is took her to the service road behind the shop." Carl scans the screen, his voice thick with guilt and failure. "There's a blind stretch there. No cameras. He must've known that."

Theo freezes the frame, zooming in on the empty edge where she disappeared.

"He probably had a car waiting," Carl says. "Engine running. In and out in under ten seconds."

Monty exhales through his nose.

"Which means while we were chasing the decoy through the harbor, Dove was already leaving town." I sit back, sick to my soul.

The room feels too small, the hum too loud. My heartbeat is everywhere, in my ears, my throat, my teeth.

"By the time the roads locked down, she was probably already outside city limits." Monty gives my shoulder another squeeze and lets go. "Could've been driven straight to a private airstrip or transferred to a boat offshore."

She was gone before we realized we fucked up.

I squeeze my eyes shut for half a second, just enough to survive it.

Jag didn't orchestrate this.

"Pull the log of the tattoo parlor." I meet Theo's gaze behind his glasses.

Theo nods and turns back to the wall of monitors, fingers flying across the keys. The screen flashes, loads a grid of feeds, and centers on one. The hidden camera from the tattoo shop.

Since Jag concealed it near the ceiling, the overhead angle shows every corner of the main room.

The time stamp rolls back to ten minutes before I walked in, when the Strakh guards were still alive.

Everyone quiets.

The screen goes black. Not dim or shadowed. Gone.

"What the fuck?" My heart pounds.

"The lights in the shop," Ross says. "Someone shut them off."

There isn't a drop of natural light or street bleed because the only window in the shop sits inside the room Jag built for me. Sealed off.

"Fuck!" I shove my hands in my hair, panic rising.

Theo hits a key, and the feed snaps to night vision.

Green washes over the screen, and my stomach drops.

The door opens, letting in a blast of blinding light and a rush of men dressed in black. In a blink, they're inside with the door shut, trapping the Strakh guards in the pitch-black.

Each of them wears low-profile goggles as they fan out, already knowing where everything is. No hesitation. No whispered orders.

The Strakh guards freeze, confused, hands out, blinking into nothing. They can't see a damn thing. They spin, backs to each other, trying to orientate, trying to figure out why the lights went out and who just entered the shop.

My throat closes as I count six goggled men. Military haircuts. Lean builds with zero wasted movement.

"Night vision goggles." Monty exhales sharply.

"Yes." Carl nods. "Lightweight tactical vests with holsters and blades mounted at their thighs. Coms in their ears. Matching gear, right down to the boots."

Each one knows exactly where he's going.

The guards don't.

It's a slaughter.

A hand clamps down. A blade flashes, and the first guard goes slack without a sound. Another drops near the counter, taken from the side before he can even turn his head.

Six against four.

Unfair doesn't begin to cover it.

The remaining guards reach for their guns, fingers scrabbling at holsters, but the men in goggles are already on them. One disarms. Another strikes low. A third steps in and finishes it.

No gunshots. No yelling. Just bodies folding to the floor in the quiet hum of night-vision static.

It's over in seconds.

I can't breathe.

They didn't come for a fight. They came to clear the room.

"These aren't street thugs or local muscle." Monty rubs his nape.

"This was funded and rehearsed," Carl says. "High-end gear. Military spec."

I'm going to be sick. The room spins, needles fill my gut, and pain grabs in my chest.

The feed keeps rolling.

Night vision holds steady as the green-hued bodies shift. The six attackers no longer move like predators. They sweep the room, checking pulses and confirming kills.

"They waited until you dropped Dove at the mechanic shop." Theo pauses the video and compares the time stamps. "See? They timed it to the second, attacking the tattoo parlor right as you were leaving the garage."

"They knew I would be distracted by what I found at the tattoo shop and moved in on Dove." I grind my molars. "Organized confusion."

Theo restarts the recording, and a moment later, Jag bursts into frame with a metal chair in his hands. Shirtless and barefoot, he wears sweatpants that hang lopsided on his hips.

"We put a lock on that break room door." Carl moves closer. "How did he get out?"

"He would've known something was wrong when the power shut off. Probably threw himself through that door." My breathing quickens. "And we took all his weapons."

Jag holds the chair like a weapon, his legs braced, head

cocked and listening, but the pitch-black gives him nothing.

My stomach buckles with dread.

One of the attackers tears the chair from his grip. Another tries to pin his arm. But Jag fights back, dropping the man with a brutal elbow to the throat. Then he spins and catches another in the face.

It's chaos. Six against one and still, *still*, they struggle to take him down.

I bend toward the screen, my hands white-knuckled on the desk.

"Jesus Christ," Carl mutters. "He's holding his own."

"No." My voice strangles. "He's losing."

They swarm him.

Blows land hard, driving the air from his lungs. His knees hit the ground, but he leaps back up, blood streaking his temple, one arm limp, dislocated or broken.

Still, he fights.

As he pivots, his foot hits something. *Someone.* One of the dead guards. His body jerks in recognition. He can't see, but he knows. I can tell by the way he drops, fast and desperate, hands feeling for a weapon in the dark.

He finds it, pulling a pistol off the guard's belt in one smooth motion.

When he raises the gun, it's not toward his attackers, but to his own temple.

My heart stops.

"I'll do it!" he bellows into the dark, his voice guttural and soaked in rage. "Swear to God, I'll fucking do it! You want me alive? Tell that cunt Adrian Crowe he should've come himself!"

"Adrian Crowe?" Monty stiffens. "The tech billionaire?"

I've heard of him, nothing more. He floats through headlines often enough to be a household name, one associated with politicians, royalty, elite social access, all the celebrated infamy of the untouchable upper crust.

How the hell does he know Jag Rath?

On the screen, the attackers freeze.

Even in night vision, I feel the hesitation. None of them expected that.

Jag doesn't shake or flinch. He holds the gun like it's a promise. Like his life is worth more to them than to himself.

I can't look away.

He's bleeding out, one arm dangling uselessly, barely able to stand, and still, he's the one in control.

For some reason, they need him breathing, and he knows it.

Until one of the men says, "We have Dove Rath."

Fire scorches my lungs and chars my airway.

"I don't believe you." Jag wildly casts his gaze around in the dark, his body broken in half a dozen places.

The lights come on.

He flinches, blinking hard, swaying, and disoriented. Blood drips from his mouth as he squints at them.

One of the attackers steps forward, holding a phone. Jag looks at the screen, and his face crumples.

I can't see what it shows, but I can guess.

He falls to his knees, drops the gun, and his agonized roar rips through the audio feed, savage and raw.

I feel his pain to the depths of my soul.

"Don't you hurt her!" He doubles over at the waist and releases an agonizing, bone-chilling sound. "Don't fucking touch her!"

Heat seethes through my throat and into my eyes. I blink rapidly, forcing it down. But the pressure bites back, burning, swelling, overwhelming. My fists clench so hard my knuckles crack as I try to keep the tears from spilling over.

Monty's breath grows shallow beside me, his body frozen like mine, as we watch a man we all feared become something else entirely.

"You want her alive?" The man pockets the phone. "Then come quietly."

Jag lowers his head, his jaw flexing like he's swallowing a sob. His whole posture slumps. Not in surrender. In devastation.

One of the attackers comes out of the break room with Jag's duffel bag. Another one enters the shop, wiping a bloody knife on his pants.

"Side alley's clear." The newcomer sheathes the blade. "Took down the shop employee. Dumped the body. We're done here. Move out."

Declan's killer.

Jag stays on his knees, silent and crushed.

His last act wasn't escape.

It was sacrifice.

wolfson
FIFTY-FOUR

I don't have faith. I have family, and my family doesn't solve problems politely.

Jag and Dove aren't coming back through warrants, missing-persons flyers, badges, or agencies. They'll be found the Strakh way, by breaking laws, spilling blood, and destroying everyone and everything in our path.

Perks of being born into the Russian mob.

The instant we watch Jag sacrifice himself on the camera feed, Monty makes the call.

The Ghost lives alone in the cabin we gave him in Hoss, the one soaked in ruined childhoods. Yeah. That one. We would burn it to the ground before ever choosing to live there again.

But for a retired Russian executioner? It's prime real estate. A secluded place to rot on his terms and be left alone.

No one outside our inner circle knows that cabin exists.

When Monty makes the call, he doesn't beg. Doesn't explain. He doesn't need to. Twenty-four hours later, a helicopter thunders in, rotors chopping the night apart. It lands on the island's helicopter pad, lights cutting through the dark.

I stand outside as it arrives, barely holding myself together. I haven't slept right in days. Every time I close my eyes, my brain

wolfson

fills in what might be happening to Jag and Dove.

Stress has been riding shotgun so long it's part of my spine now. I'm running on fumes and fury, hollowed out and overcharged. One wrong breath will either knock me flat or send me straight through a wall.

I just need to keep it together a little longer.

Monty hovers beside me as the helicopter door slides open. The Ghost steps out first.

Oliver Popov looks exactly as I remember him, his eyes dead-calm, and his coat tailored for a five-star dinner rather than murder. No hurry in his gait. No nerves. Just that same controlled stillness he exuded the night I met him in Hoss. The night we butchered the doctor.

Then a second man exits the helicopter.

He looks like he belongs in the background. Lean build, early thirties, shaved sides with dark hair on top. Plain black hoodie. Plain boots. No jewelry. No phone in his hands.

His eyes never stop moving. Not darting. More like counting exits, cameras, and heartbeats at the same time.

"This is Mikhail. Not his real name. Don't ask for it." Oliver meets my gaze.

I know that look. It says ethical lines will be erased and worse men than him will bleed before this is over.

Which is why Theo, Ross, and the rest of Monty's security team aren't here. Oliver only trusts his mobsters.

Like Mikhail. Best criminal hacker in the world, according to Oliver. I have my doubts. No one is better than Jag, according to Dove.

Mikhail nods at Monty. Then at me.

"You are Wolf," he says in a thick Russian accent. No question in it.

"Tell me you'll find them." I search his dark gaze. "Don't waste our time."

"You're emotional."

"I'm motivated." I curl my lips, baring my teeth.

"Good. That accelerates decisions."

I hope he's good enough to slip inside Jag's systems without breaking them. Good enough to find the trail Jag buried. Good enough to give us something to chase before time runs out.

Before the rotor wash settles, Mikhail is already walking,

carrying nothing but a single hard case.

We lead him to the guest house.

Jag's computer equipment scatters the living room and kitchen table. Servers, drives, monitors, and backups stacked on backups. Oliver ordered everything hauled here to prevent Jag's attackers from destroying it.

This gear isn't just hardware. It's the trail. It's how we figure out who snatched them and why.

Mikhail doesn't waste time. He unzips his case, pulls on gloves, and goes to work. No yanking cables or rushed reconnects. He photographs every port, labels nothing, and keeps it all in his head.

Thirty minutes later, Jag's systems hum back to life. Screens flare. Code loads. Cameras come online, and the guest house fills with the whir of computers thinking hard.

"How long?" I lean against the wall, arms crossed so tightly my shoulders ache. It's the only way to keep my hands from shaking.

Mikhail tilts his head, considering. "If they are still alive? Hours. If they are moving? Longer. If they think they can't be found?" A thin smile. "They are wrong."

Alive.

The word hits and keeps hitting. What does alive look like for them? Jag breathing somewhere in the dark? Dove fighting for her life? Both counting on me to show up a week ago?

I lock my jaw until it hurts. I don't let myself ask the questions scratching at my throat. Moved where? Hurt how bad? How much time have I already wasted?

Everything inside me is screaming. I keep my back to the wall, breathing shallow and controlled, when all I want to do is strap on every knife I own and start hunting.

Oliver stands beside Monty, hands clasped behind him, his demeanor radiating respect and old history, blood-deep and unspoken.

"Tell me everything." He turns to Monty and me.

We give him the rundown, the footage, the decoy, the blind spots, Jag on his knees, and the name Adrian Crowe.

Oliver listens without interrupting. When we're done, he exhales through his nose.

"Adrian Crowe." A curl of contempt touches his lips. "He recruits through retreats and talent programs. Targets underage girls, invites them into his exclusive world, and tells them they're chosen." His eyes flick to mine. "These girls are isolated. No family or anchors."

My jaw grinds. I feel it creeping up my spine, that familiar burn.

"He trades in psychological debt and dependency." Oliver frowns. "The illusion of consent."

Underage girls.

Children.

No consent there.

"He sells them." I swallow hard, the room tilting with the sick memories of my own childhood. "He traffics them."

"Yes. But he keeps his hands clean, hiding behind lawyers, donations, and compromised officials. His public image is armor, protecting what he really is. A trafficker. A collector of victims."

I see it then, all of it clicking into place so fast I feel nauseous.

Dove being dragged into white rooms and soft voices and hands that pretend they're helping. Dove being told she chose this. Dove being erased carefully, methodically, until no one knows where to look.

"That's why Jag surrendered." I push off the wall and pace. "He knew. He fucking knew what Crowe would do to her."

Monty's hand comes up, gripping my arm, hard and grounding and necessary.

I can barely breathe.

"This isn't ransom." Acid rises in my throat. "It's inventory. He intends to traffic her."

"No. It is more complicated." Mikhail doesn't look up. "I found a file on Crowe. Jag Rath has been stalking him for... Twenty years."

"What?" I shift closer and squint at the screen over Mikhail's shoulder, my pulse climbing.

Folders nest inside folders. Time-stamped photos. Crowe stepping out of private jets. Crowe laughing at galas. Crowe shaking hands with men who dominate headlines. Shipping manifests. Flight numbers. Guest lists.

Jag collected twenty years of this shit? That's not curiosity. It's obsession.

What's his infatuation with Adrian Crowe?

Mikhail scrolls sideways, pages down, and opens a directory. Jag's personal notes.

My chest constricts as I scan years' worth of records, bank accounts, surveillance, and history. Jag meticulously documented patterns, faces, and aliases, tracking Crowe like prey.

"Why?" I rub my neck. "Does he want the billionaire's money?"

"This is not about money." Mikhail flips through digital memos, scanning, searching.

"Then what?"

He leans closer to the screen and opens a file named *First Meeting with Adrian Crowe - California Tavern*. It's an audio file dated seventeen years ago.

Mikhail hits play.

Static. Old static. Sounds like a cheap recorder or a phone hidden in a pocket. Noise muffles in the background, glasses clinking and someone coughing off-mic. The recording is messy, handheld, and outdated.

A young, raspy male voice comes through. "Why are you following me, Crowe?"

"That's Jag." My pulse surges as I find Monty's eyes. "I'm certain it's him."

Seventeen years ago... That would make Jag twenty-three and Dove fifteen. I wonder if this meeting happened before or after the night she ran from him at the drug dealer's house?

A chair scrapes through the recording.

"I have a business proposal," Adrian Crowe says, his tone cold and incisive.

"Rot in hell." Jag makes a disgusted sound. "I know what you did to Celeste Rath."

Celeste.

Dove's mother.

My stomach drops.

Is Adrian Crowe connected to her murder?

The tavern noise swells, muddying Adrian's response. "Celeste isn't her real name, but you already know that."

"Yeah," Jag snaps. "I also know you found her through your talent agency, groomed her, flew her out, locked her on your island with your sick perversions and your cameras, and got her pregnant." A pause. "Then you sold her to one of your rich, child-raping friends."

Ice clinks. A slow exhale.

"Why would I sell a pregnant woman?" Adrian asks dryly.

"You didn't know she was pregnant. And she wasn't a woman." Rage seethes through Jag's voice. "She was fifteen. A goddamn child."

"Watch your mouth."

"You should've watched your paperwork. She ran, changed names, married my father at a legal, *consensual* age, and raised your kid without you finding her."

A chair creaks, and Adrian laughs. "Except I did find her, didn't I? I found all of you. Tell me, how's life on the streets?"

Something slams hard, and glass shatters. Jag's breathing turns rough and loud, all restraint gone, a deep animal sound grinding through clenched teeth. Then a violent scrape, table legs dragged, a body shoved forward, and the mic crackles.

"You're smarter than this," Adrian says, his voice closer now. "If you hurt me, my guards will kill you. Who will protect Dove then, hmm?"

Crowd noise spikes. Voices overlap, and Jag's fury cuts through it all. Ragged breaths, a strangled snarl, the sound of a man holding himself one second away from murder.

Then fabric rustles, and a final, brutal exhale.

"Accept my offer and work for me." Adrian's tone shifts, moving farther away. "She'll no longer need protection, and you'll have everything my friends have. Planes. Retreats. Women who don't say no. A real seat at the table."

My blood boils, and a vein throbs in my temple.

"I'll die first," Jag growls.

"That can be arranged." A smile floats through Adrian's voice.

"Stay away from her."

"I'm not interested in the girl. But if you walk away from my offer? I'll make her my only interest."

"If you touch her—"

Static spikes, and the audio ends.

"Holy fuck." I can't feel my legs. "Adrian Crowe is Dove's father."

"Yeah." Monty scowls. "He raped Dove's fifteen-year-old mother."

"When Dove was eight, he found them. That's when he killed David and Celeste. And Jag knew. All this time, he fucking knew who killed them and never told Dove."

He put himself directly in front of a monster, never stepped aside, and never accepted the offer.

Bees swarm my stomach as the pieces click into place. Jag and Dove on the run, always half-packed and ready to disappear. The way Jag hovered without hovering, following Dove from city to city, never leaving her unprotected, never telling her about her past.

His control wasn't about ownership. It was about distance from her raping sperm donor, a human sex trafficker who would see her as a business deal instead of a person.

Jag watched everything. Cameras where they didn't belong. Feeds no one else knew existed. He tracked patterns, who circled too close, who asked the wrong questions.

When he hacked, it wasn't about money and power. It was surveillance.

When he stalked, it wasn't desire. It was protection.

Even the way he curated her companions makes sense now. The boundaries, betrayals, and constant friction... He needed her angry enough to push back, sharp enough to run when she had to, smart enough to surround herself with loyal people, and mean enough to survive without him.

He didn't just guard her body. He guarded her origin. She didn't know who sired her. Didn't know who hunted her.

I bet she knows now.

My rib cage shrinks, crushing my lungs until every breath hurts. I press my tongue to the roof of my mouth and stare at the dead space on the screen where the truth finally showed itself.

"That is why Jag Rath watched him for twenty years." Mikhail closes the file. "He protects his stepsister."

Wet blotches invade my vision, and the floor sways beneath me.

Jag watched Crowe for twenty years, knowing this day might come. Knowing exactly what kind of monster would come for her.

"Dove's mother..." Mikhail skims through Jag's notes. "She appeared in Crowe's network thirty-three years ago. A retreat in California. She vanished six months later. New name. New town. No paper trail."

"She was sold." Fury floods my veins. "Does it show who bought her?"

"No. She ran. Must have escaped during transport to the buyer or wherever she was taken. Jag's note says Crowe searched for her for eight years. Quiet, paid searches."

"And now he has Dove." I drag in a breath that barely works.

Crowe has her, and Jag still stepped forward, dropped to his knees, and traded himself for... What? Does he have a plan? Is he buying time?

Rage rises in my chest, burning through grief, fear, and guilt until there's nothing left but purpose.

Crowe didn't just take Dove. He touched a line Jag guarded for decades.

And now?

Now it's my turn. I'll get them back.

"Can you find them?" I hover closer.

"Already started." Mikhail hunches over the keyboard, hood down and eyes sharp as the screens crawl with maps, data streams, and strings of characters that pull shell companies and commercial properties layered so deep they almost disappear.

"Crowe funds private acquisitions," Mikhail switches screens. "People. Tech. Talent. Real estate. Sometimes silence." His fingers pause. "He prefers assets that do not belong to governments."

"Jag is an asset Crowe wanted."

"Yes." He finally looks at me. "Dove Rath was leverage. Crowe did not take her to sell her. He took her to control Jag."

"So this is about Jag's hacking skills?" Monty stands off to the side, arms crossed. "Jag is that good?"

"I have seen cartel systems, state systems, and private intelligence systems." Mikhail brings up pages of logs. "This is better than all of them. I am not even inside yet. I am only touching the surface. He built layers inside layers. Traps that do not announce themselves. I make one wrong assumption, and it will eat itself."

"So he's better than you." My neck tenses.

"Yes. I can unravel some of his work, but I cannot build anything close to this. In my world, organizations kill each other to own a mind like his. Wars start over less. And now, he is in the hands of Adrian Crowe. That is very bad."

"Find them," I say quietly, my voice ironed by fury. "And I'll bring them home."

The room hums with machines, decisions lining up, and looming objections.

"No." Monty pivots to me. "This isn't a hunt in the Arctic, Wolf. You can't go in with guns half-cocked."

"Oh, I'm fully cocked and done waiting."

"Crowe isn't some back-alley criminal. He's insulated, connected, and powerful. I won't lose you after everything. I only just found you."

"This is why I'm here." Oliver steps in, calm and stern. "I will do the extraction."

My fists flex. "If you expect me to watch from the sidelines—"

"You're not risking your life." Monty thrusts a finger at me.

"Tell Jag that." I laugh, and it comes out ugly.

"You will not—"

"I already did. The second they took Jag and Dove."

He opens his mouth again, ready to pull rank or blood or both, and the door opens.

Frankie rushes in, breathless, hair damp from the drizzle outside. Her eyes sweep the room, land on me, and soften. Then she sees The Ghost.

"Oliver." Her voice cracks.

He turns, and his face changes. Not gentleness. Recognition. History.

Oliver Popov was Frankie and Monty's private chef for years on this island. He fed them while keeping his head down and his knives sharp. They didn't know then what he'd been before the aprons and menus.

When Dr. Howell abducted her, Oliver stopped pretending.

I wasn't here when he revealed himself as The Ghost, but I was present for the feral last stand, when he helped us escape the doctor.

Frankie crosses the room in three fast steps and throws her arms around him. He stiffens for a heartbeat then lets it happen, one hand coming up to steady her.

"I missed you." She presses her face into his shoulder.

"I missed your Eggs Benedict," Monty mutters.

That earns a small smile from Oliver. "I will make them now while Mikhail works."

"Please." Frankie releases him. "Before Monty burns the house down."

Oliver turns toward the door, already rolling up his sleeves. Monty and Frankie follow him, pulled by routine and comfort.

I stay where I am, eyes on the screens as Mikhail dives deeper, lines of code stacking and feeds flickering.

"You should eat." Monty lingers in the doorway.

"I can't." My stomach is a knot of acid and vicious anger.

With reluctance, he leaves. I grab my sketchbook and pull up a chair beside Mikhail.

Long into the night, Mikhail's fingers glide over the board, the keys clicking in soft bursts. He doesn't stretch or drink or look away from his task. Whatever zone he's in, it doesn't include time.

With my sketchbook open beside him, I don't draw princesses. I sketch outcomes, corridors, entry points, and blind corners. I rough out rescues like crime scenes in reverse.

If Jag and Dove are being held in a warehouse, there will be loading docks, forklifts, stacked containers, and snipers on catwalks.

If it's a cave, it will be single access, choke points, tunnels, condemning echoes, lights out, and close work.

If it's some underground lair, there will be security doors, biometric locks, cameras, vents, and service shafts.

Every version ends the same way.

Get in. Get them. Get out.

I don't draw revenge. I can't let myself plan Crowe's death. Jag has been watching that man for twenty years, tracking him, studying him, and waiting for an opening that never came.

He's been sitting on that incriminating audio file of Crowe for seventeen years and never leaked it to the press. Why? Because it would've endangered Dove?

If Jag couldn't topple Crowe with decades of prep, I'm not delusional enough to think I'll do it in one night.

This won't be a reckoning. It'll be a retrieval.

Mikhail exhales softly and shifts screens. Maps snap into place. Routes clarify. Data stops swimming and starts pointing.

My pencil stills.

Whatever he's seeing, it's real now.

"What do you have?" I close the sketchbook.

He turns a screen toward me.

Shipping routes? Air traffic logs? What am I looking at?

"They moved fast. Multiple boats, private planes, and vehicles." His fingers dance across the keys. "I have not identified Dove yet, but Jag is here." He hovers the cursor over a building in downtown Los Angeles.

The information lands in my chest and detonates.

"They split them up?" I ask.

"Possibly. Or they arrived separately. This will not be a clean extraction." He opens a digital blueprint. "Jag has been watching this nightclub for years."

"They're being held in a nightclub?"

"There is a kill room in the basement."

"What's a kill room?" My heart hammers.

"That is what Jag calls it in his notes."

"What's a fucking kill room, Mikhail?"

"A room where the killing happens."

"Why is there a fucking kill room in a fucking nightclub?" Panic swamps my bloodstream. "You think that's where they're holding Jag and Dove? Why the fuck would they be in a kill room, Mikhail?"

"Calm down." He squints at me. "Jag is useless to Crowe if he is dead, and he will not cooperate if Dove is harmed, yes?"

"Yeah. Okay. They're alive."

Saying it doesn't quiet the howling in my wrecked heart. Alive can mean anything. It can mean they're being brutalized and raped. Barely alive isn't the same as alive.

"His blueprints detail the layout." He zooms in on the diagram. "Guards at every entry point. Cameras at all angles. The best security money can buy. I do not see a way in, let alone a way out."

"I see a way." I grab my sketchbook and flip it open.

Pages of half-mad contingencies slide past, routes that assume luck, timing that assumes mercy. I don't stop on those. I skip to the last page, the one that will get me killed if I miscount a breath.

Spinning the book around, I shove it toward him.

Mikhail studies it, leaning in, eyes sharpening, and a slow grin spreads across his face. Teeth this time. Real ones.

"For this..." He taps the page. "You need The Ghost."

"Yeah, I do, deep and dirty." Anticipation heats my chest.

"Bombs away."

"It's suicide."

"I'm kind of known for that."

Mikhail's grin widens.

Monty's going to have feelings. Oh, well. He can yell later. I'm moving now.

wolfson
FIFTY-FIVE

The van smells like warm metal, coffee gone cold, and nerves that have been burning for two straight days.

We're parked a block from Adrian Crowe's nightclub. The building matches the description in Jag's notes with its black glass, concrete, and high-end security. A haven for predators hiding behind refinement and exclusivity.

Los Angeles pulses around us, traffic and bass and oblivious lives sliding past the curb.

Leo and Frankie stayed on the island, safe and furious, pretending they're not counting seconds. She hugged me before I left, while Leo spat all the reasons he hates my plan.

Add it to the pile.

The arguments started the moment I said the plan out loud. They didn't stop on the flight from Sitka to Los Angeles. Monty flew the jet himself, all red-faced and yelling fury.

Leo called my plan aggressively dumb. Kody called it batshit. All of them called it a closed-casket suicide run.

And here we are.

Inside the van, Monty sits in the driver's seat, hands strangling the wheel. Beside him, Kody glares out the windshield, lost to the violence in his head.

In the back, Mikhail hunches over a laptop, calm as a Russian mobster, and feeds live data into my skull through an undetectable earpiece.

Oliver moves around me, tightening the strap on my vest, like he's adjusting a tie before dinner.

"This will work," he says loud enough for Monty and Kody to hear.

"Fuck off, Oliver." Monty smacks the steering wheel. "The fact that you're going along with this bullshit, back-of-the-napkin plan makes me question your reputation."

"Firstly, it's a back-of-the-sketchbook plan." I uncap a sharpie and find my reflection in the rear window. "And secondly, you're going along with it, too."

"Uncheerfully," he grumbles.

"Sounds like you need to exfoliate. Something extra abrasive for those grumpy layers. Maybe concrete." I set the marker to my face and start drawing.

The plan is simple in the way bad ideas always are.

I'll walk through the front door of the nightclub and ask for Adrian Crowe. I'll make sure he understands that if Jag and Dove don't come out breathing, the building won't stay standing. And neither will I.

Because I have one of Oliver's homemade specials strapped to my chest.

The bomb sits flat against my breastbone under the vest. No wires hanging out or blinking lights.

It's a seamless design. No fumbling, second-guessing, or chance that someone can take it and use it against me. If it blows, it will be because I chose to hit the switch.

I don't plan to use it. That's the point. But every person who sees me has to believe I will. They need to believe I'm unstable enough to take myself out and everyone within reach, including the two people I'm here to collect. I need them to believe I don't give a fuck about Jag and Dove.

They can't see my attachment or smell my devotion. They can't even suspect it. They need to look at me and see a violent, unhinged mental patient, one that's scarier than them.

That belief will open doors.

In and out.

Easy peasy.

Finished with my face, I cap the sharpie and toss it toward the front.

Monty's eyes meet mine over his shoulder, and there's a whole argument sitting there. But it cuts off as he takes in my smile.

My Glasgow smile.

I didn't carve it into myself the way the myth goes. No blades or blood. I drew it instead, the heavy black ink dragging from the corners of my mouth toward my ears. A grin too wide to belong to anyone sane.

I've only worn it once before.

The last time Denver hurt me.

The night I made the devil's bargain.

That night, I didn't have language for what I felt. I had fear and rage and a need to look scarier and stronger than I was. The ink was a way to tell Denver I could still choose how my face told the story.

As Monty studies it now, he seems to understand. This isn't humor or bravado. It's me choosing sacrifice over self-preservation, crossing a line I can't uncross, accepting how the night might end for me, and doing it anyway.

Jag put himself between a predator and the woman we love. Dove is paying for blood she never asked for. If this is the price to pull them out, I won't hesitate.

It matters. It's the only thing that matters. Maybe it's the most important thing I'll ever do.

Monty stares at my face like he's memorizing it. Kody glances at him, and they exchange a look I recognize immediately.

Understanding. Not approval or permission. But an acknowledgment that the argument is over. This is happening with or without their help.

Thanks to the sharpie ink, my smile will hold until the end. My hands won't shake. Whatever's left of me locks into place, gut-deep and focused.

Jag and Dove have been missing for ten days. That ends tonight.

"Crowe is inside," Mikhail says into the earpiece. "VIP lounge."

Oliver checks one last connection and pats my shoulder.

Monty twists in the front seat to face me head-on.

"Don't." Kody grunts and grips Monty's shoulder.

Silence stretches, tight and brittle. Then Monty nods and reaches for me.

I go to him, awkwardly in the confined space, and let him envelop me in a hug.

"Bring them home." He rests his mouth against my temple. "And don't you dare touch that kill switch."

If Jag and Dove are dead, I'll probably blow up the whole damn building with me inside it. But I won't tell him that.

Stepping back, I straighten as much as the roof of the van will allow and hold out my arms.

"How's the fit?" I do a half-turn, side to side.

The black vest sits flat against my chest, balanced so it doesn't drag or shift when I move. The quick-release is built into the front seam, so I can peel it open with a flick of my finger when it's time to show them who and what they're dealing with.

Below it, the gauze-thin ivory skirt hangs to the floor and parts with each step, transparent enough to show the black sequin shorts underneath. My black boots are thigh-high, steel-toed, and heavy, made to kick doors and asses.

Around my neck, I wear a short chain, blackened silver, with a large anarchist circle-A, embedded with crystals. Oliver modified it, replacing one of the crystals with a camera lens.

Rings stack on every finger, the thick bands mismatched and worn. Enough steel to turn my hands into brass knuckles. One of them carries a hidden switch on the underside. Not a button anyone else could use. Just a private decision point built into the metal, waiting for me to flick it with my thumb.

That's the part Monty hates the most. He said if I wasn't planning to detonate the bomb, I didn't need a trigger. I reminded him that this is my circus, and his objections are noted and overruled.

At their silence, I look down at myself, then back up at them.

"Oh." I grin, feral and proud. "It's a look."

No one laughs. No one breathes.

Oliver shifts into my space and adjusts the necklace.

"Camera is on." Mikhail turns the laptop, showing a close-up angle of Oliver's necktie.

Everyone in the van will be watching and listening, right there with me every second.

"Look alive, my pretties." I roll my neck, feel the gear settle against my chest, feel how little room there is for hesitation. "You're about to find out where myths come from."

"We'll be with you the entire time." Oliver holds out a thin sliver of metal.

Small, lethally sharp, and easy to underestimate, the razor blade was my idea. I take it from him and tuck it where no one thinks to look. Inside my cheek.

When they search me, they won't find it.

The hard part is remembering not to clench my jaw or grind my molars. Sudden mouth movements would turn it from insurance into damage.

I roll my tongue, locate the cutting edge, and relax my face.

Whatever I am right now—a bomb, a bluff, a wolf, or a drag queen—I don't look like a terrorist who would walk into a club and end the night if he felt like it.

"Don't wait up, ladies." I open the door and hop onto the sidewalk.

The block feels longer than it is. Bass thumps through the pavement, and a line snakes from the entrance of the club, filled with glitter, cologne, too-white teeth, and socialites rehearsing fake versions of themselves.

I cut straight past them.

Someone mutters. Someone laughs. Someone reaches out like they might grab my arm and thinks better of it when they get a good look at me.

The bouncer clocks me two steps out. Big guy. Neck like a fridge. Earpiece coiled against his shaved hairline. He opens his mouth to order me back in line.

"Tell Adrian Crowe that Wolfson Strakh is here." I dip into an overdone curtsy, all show and no respect. "I've come to discuss Jag Rath, our shared problem."

That stops him cold.

I don't know which name does it. Jag's or mine. Or maybe it's the wide, theatrical smile I flash him like we're sharing a private joke he's not in on. His eyes travel over the skirt, the vest, and return to the smile I'm still holding like a googly-eyed crackpot.

He cringes and turns away, murmuring into his earpiece.

I wait.

The line behind me goes quiet, tension rippling as if the

crowd realized they're standing too close to a ticking time bomb. Figuratively, of course. No one can see my explosive device.

The bouncer listens. His jaw jumps. A pause stretches long enough to be interesting. Then he steps aside and jerks his chin toward the door.

Huh. That was anticlimactic. I thought there'd be some lip service, posturing, twerking, maybe a little strip tease, and a trip to the pavement. Guess tonight is full of surprises.

I blow the bouncer a kiss and step inside.

My very first nightclub.

I expect the movie version. Red-rope fantasy, velvet shadows, and bartenders flipping bottles.

None of that is here.

It's exactly what Crowe would build. Minimalist. Expensive. Black marble and gold accents. Soft lighting designed to flatter and conceal. Music engineered to vibrate bones without distorting thought. The air smells like citrus, smoke, and money.

Before I step out of the entryway, a security guard materializes.

"This way." His dead tone matches his dead eyes and boring suit.

I follow him past the main bar, past a second bar tucked behind a half-wall, and around the dance floor pulsing with beautiful, sweaty bodies.

We veer toward the back, away from the noise, into corridors where the lighting dims, and past doors that look decorative.

A biometric scanner flashes green without the guard breaking stride.

The VIP lounge waits on the other side, filled with plush seating, muted sound, and one-way glass looking out on the club like it's an exhibit. The people here aren't dancing. They're watching, talking low, and smiling like sharks.

Somewhere below this room, deeper still, Jag and Dove are waiting.

Adrian Crowe knows I'm here. He sits alone in the darkest corner of the lounge, a small pool of shadow carved out just for him. A table. One glass.

Half a dozen men in tailored suits stand guard around him, their arms close to their sides and jackets cut to hide intent, all of them armed.

My pulse races as I start toward him.

Until a straight arm snaps out across my chest, stopping me.

"Need to check you for weapons," my escort says.

"By all means, frisk me." Lifting my arms, palms out, I touch my tongue against the blade in my cheek. "Don't rush."

He does it quickly and professionally, head to shoulders, down my sides, hands firm and impersonal. He checks my waist, my thighs, my boots. Then his hand hits the vest.

Here we go.

"You need to open this." His forehead creases.

"You do it, sugar." I wink.

A flicker of irritation crosses his face, but duty wins. He fingers the seam, finds the release, and pulls.

The vest falls open.

"What the hell is that?" He reaches for his gun.

"A pacemaker." I flutter my lashes. "Very temperamental."

Weapons come up all at once, and the lounge starts to empty as security barks orders, and staff ushers out patrons.

My escort casts me a murderous glare.

"Whoopsie?" I widen my eyes an expression that promises nothing good.

wolfson
FIFTY-SIX

Across the VIP lounge, the bodyguards rush Adrian Crowe toward a private exit.

Hope in motion. Adorable. I almost admire the optimism.

I set two fingers in my mouth and release a loud whistle, drawing their attention.

"I'll level the place before you make it to that door." I hold up my hand and point to the small switch on the underside of my rings. "If you shoot me, the bomb blows. If you piss me off, the bomb blows. If Mr. Crowe doesn't return his ass to that chair, guess what?" I look at my sour-faced escort. "Tell them, baby doll."

"The bomb blows," he grumbles.

The weapons trained on me don't matter. Everyone in the room knows my weapon is bigger.

Crowe studies my face, my inked smile, and the open vest. He swallows and lowers himself back into the chair.

I clock the one man at the bar who doesn't move. He chews a toothpick like it owes him money. A wicked scar divides his face, and his eyes stay with me. No flinch. No rush. Just watching and measuring.

He takes his time standing, gives me a look that promises it won't be the last, and follows the others out. As he passes through the door, the creepy smile he flings over his shoulder rivals mine.

I shake it off and cross the room.

Every step pulls a dozen guns with me, muzzles tracking, fingers on triggers, and breaths held.

I don't rush. Rushing looks nervous.

At Crowe's table, I hook a chair with my boot, drag it out slow enough to be annoying, and sit with a heavy sigh.

Up close, he's exactly what the world pays for and consumes. Mid-sixties, physically fit in the curated way money buys, silver threaded neatly through dark hair. His smile is practiced, meant to reassure donors, clients, and anyone young enough to mistake charisma for kindness.

But his eyes won't settle. They dart to the vest, to my hands, to the exits that won't help him.

"The guns are making me twitchy." I wriggle my thumb over the switch near my palm, close enough to be suggestive.

A ripple moves through the guards.

Crowe lifts one hand, palm down.

They pull back a step. Then another. Still close. Still armed. But no longer breathing down my neck.

Better.

"Wow." I lean forward, elbows on the table, grin stretching psycho-wide. "I can't believe this is happening."

Crowe blinks.

"I mean... You," I gush, pitching it high and bright, all cracked enthusiasm. "I've never met a famous person. This is insane. Can we take a selfie? Because, you know, if there's no photo, it never happened."

"What?" He stares at me like I just tripped from borderline to completely off-the-rails.

"Shit." I pat my nonexistent pockets, frown, and sigh dramatically. "I don't have my phone. Typical. Every time something epic happens."

He watches me as if trying to determine if my insanity is real or strategic. Unease leaks through the polish. Not panic, but his calculating demeanor is definitely going fuzzy at the edges. He's used to owning rooms. And now? He knows the room no longer belongs to him.

"You made your point." His voice is smooth, honed to sell

retreats and nonconsent in the same breath. "Let's lower the theatrics."

"You first."

For a half second, the smile he's famous for wobbles.

Good. Now he's listening.

I lean in, letting the manic edge drain away. I'm done performing.

"Let's chat about Jag Rath." I drop the temperature in my tone, cold as a polar night. "You have him in a room under us. Concrete. No windows."

Crowe's eyes flick down, then back to me. Tiny tell. Not enough to give him away in court. But plenty for me.

"I'm not here to negotiate philosophy." I drum my ringed fingers on the table. "You're going to take me to him. I'm going to collect what I came for. Then I'll walk out the same door I came in. No sirens. No big boom."

I don't say her name. I won't.

Mikhail couldn't confirm she's in this building, and I'm not about to drag her into a room she might not be near. If Dove is here, Jag will tell me the second he sees my face. If she isn't, if she's somewhere else entirely, I'll probably make a bloody mess out of some throats.

Future-Wolf problems.

"You're making assumptions." Crowe studies me, the practiced calm back in place, but thinner now.

"I'm making a schedule." I smile again, this one meaner. "You can walk me down there, or I can start improvising with explosives. I'm leaving with Jag Rath, or we're all leaving in pieces. Your choice."

"Do you know why I let you into my club?"

"Because you thought I was an underage girl?"

He ignores the jab. "Because I know your family. The moment Jag Rath entangled himself with you, I had you investigated. Curiously, your name doesn't exist the way it should. No trail. No childhood or schooling. Nothing that explains you."

"I lived off-grid with a psychopath for twenty-four years."

If that surprises him, he doesn't show it. "How old are you?"

"Twenty-four. Too legal for you, honeybun."

He blinks once, the math catching up.

"If you did your homework, you'd know I lean hard into suicidal solutions." I recline in the chair, the bomb on full display. "Go ahead. Call my bluff."

I know how deranged I must look to him with my sequins, eyeliner, painted smile, and plan that ends in dismemberment.

"What do you want with Rath?" His gaze dips to the exposed scars on my chest.

"I was raised by a monster who preyed on kids and told us we were special."

His face empties.

"I recognize the type." I look him up and down. "You collect children, abuse them until you're bored, pass them on to your friends, and make a profit on their suffering." I fold my hands on the table, metal rings clinking together. "You took Jag because he's useful. A skill set like his will clean up your messes, erase your filthy tracks, and keep you out of prison."

Crowe opens his mouth.

"I'll kill him before I let you keep a weapon like that." I tip my head, inked smile holding. "If the only way to stop you is to turn this place into rubble, I'll pay that price. So choose. Give me the hacker and keep breathing. Or play your games and find out how serious I am."

My heart pounds in my throat, and I wonder if he notices. His terrible silence lasts too long, tightening my skin and sandblasting my lungs.

Then I see it, the moment it lands, the exact second his options finish rearranging themselves. The mask evaporates. The choices narrow, and he realizes there's no angle left where he keeps both his control and his survival.

"Follow me." He pushes his chair back.

Survival, it is.

The guards close in immediately, a tight ring of suits and steel. Crowe doesn't look at them. He turns stiffly and walks.

I rise and go with him.

We slip through a private exit behind velvet curtains, turn into a corridor, and open a door to the rear stairwell.

"Yay." I clap my hands. "Basement time."

Crowe leads. I follow. Guns move with us, never more than a breath away.

And that is how I get a free guided tour of Adrian Crowe's dungeon.

"Wolf." Oliver's voice cuts into my earpiece. "This could be a trap."

I almost laugh as the door closes behind us, sealing off the easy exit and any change of heart.

It all makes sense now. Crowe didn't let me into his club because he was curious. The instant I said Jag's name at the door, that made me a loose end he needed to erase.

Skip the foreplay. Welcome to the kill room.

He had a tidy ending in mind but didn't budget for the bomb. Rookie mistake.

I keep walking, down the stairs, and straight into the part where people disappear.

My nerves riot, and my heart sprints frantically. I don't let it show.

The underground tunnel echoes with our footsteps. Cameras stud the low ceiling at regular intervals, black lenses staring straight down. Fluorescent strips light the way. No signs on the bare concrete. No sounds of life.

No voices. No crying. No begging. Not even the echo of music bleeding from above.

I should be performing. I should be cracking maniacal jokes, flashing the inked grin, and playing the role of damaged goods. But my tongue is two sizes too big, and my throat is trying to swallow itself.

I don't know if Jag is missing body parts or broken beyond recognition. I don't know if Dove is here or already dead. I run through the worst versions in my head and force myself to accept them now, here, before they can knock me flat later.

Hope is crushing. Preparation isn't. I keep my face loose, breathing measured, and hands motionless while I brace myself for whatever waits at the end of this tunnel.

Crowe slows.

Ahead, a single steel door interrupts the corridor. One guard stands watch, rifle held at rest, eyes forward. He doesn't blink at my Glasgow smile, my skirt, or my open vest. He doesn't react to any of us.

Not until Crowe nods at him.

He pulls open the door and steps aside.

"Inside." My heart rate goes ballistic, but I keep my voice even. "All of you."

When Crowe hesitates, I lift my hand and wave the switch in his face.

"All the crows. Including their rapey daddy." I drop my voice to a stage whisper. "That's you."

The guards file inside, and Crowe follows. The room beyond smells like disinfectant, metal, and something I refuse to identify.

I step over the threshold last, close the door, and...

My heart stops.

The scene hits like an explosion in my chest.

Jag is on his knees against the far wall. Shackles bite into his wrists, his arms wrenched back and chained high enough to keep him from collapsing forward.

A brutal contraption forces his head upright. It straps to his face, leather cinched tight, and metal prongs prying his eyes open, refusing him the mercy of blinking.

He knows he's not alone, but he can't turn his neck. He can't see me by the door.

His bloodshot eyes leak red-tinged tears and fury. Dried blood cakes his throat and chest. New bruises bloom over old ones. Ten days' worth.

He's barely recognizable. Except for the pants. He wears the same gray sweatpants from the video of his capture.

My chest buckles, straining to release a roar. My lungs seize, breath hitching fast. Panic claws up my spine, wanting out through my throat.

I don't let it. I lock everything down, face blank, eyes flat. They can't see it. They cannot know.

"Wolf." Oliver's voice snaps through my earpiece. "I can hear your breathing. Slow it down. Now."

I stare at Jag's ruined face and tell myself to breathe like this is just another room, another problem, another monster I can handle. I'm still the one in control.

"Remember the mission." Oliver exhales. "Get Jag and Dove and get out."

Dove.

My vision tunnels.

"There's a screen," Oliver says. "I need you to show me what he's being forced to watch."

I already know.

The screen sits out of my line of sight, angled away from me, positioned perfectly so Jag can't escape it. I don't want to look. I don't want confirmation of the thing already tearing holes through my heart.

Because if they're using her as leverage, if Jag's still resisting, they're hurting her. Probably right now.

"Wolf," Oliver says, sharper this time. "Pull your shit together. I need eyes on that screen."

I can't feel my feet. They're disconnected from the rest of me as I force them forward, each step mechanical, completely detached from the body that's trying its damnedest to fold itself in half.

I move toward Jag. Toward the screen. Toward whatever they're using to break him. And I pray to the false God of miserable Earth that I'm wrong.

As I pass Crowe, I grip his arm and drag him with me, keeping him close enough to remind him why he's still alive.

When I step into Jag's view, I don't glance at him. I can't. Not yet. I don't trust myself to meet his eyes and keep my face vacant. One crack, and they'll see it. One twitch, and Crowe will call my bluff.

Instead, I turn my body toward the screen, angle the pendant at my throat, and let the tiny lens catch what I don't want to see.

Then I force myself to look.

The soundless feed is already rolling.

My brain skids, scrambles, and grabs fragments.

Dove.

Restrained to a bed.

Naked.

Gagged.

Body stretched like an X.

A man between her legs.

Hurting her the way Denver hurt me.

Thrusting.

Thrusting.

Thrusting.

The video, the room, everything smears into a hot, violent, blood-red blur.

It hurts.

It hurts in ways I've never hurt before.

Rage crashes in from every direction, molten and blinding. It feels like I'm swallowing glass and dying a thousand fiery deaths.

Anguish stabs behind my eyes, the unbearable pressure splitting my skull. Breathing becomes a conscious act, each inhale and exhale ripping me apart as I fight to keep the sounds from leaking out.

I don't blink or react. My posture stays loose. But the effort costs me. I clamp my teeth too hard, and the razor bites back.

Pain spikes inside my cheek. Copper washes across my tongue, and a warm trickle runs down my chin.

I relax my jaw, but it's already done.

"You're bleeding." Crowe stares at my mouth.

"Smile, Wolf," Oliver says in my ear. "Give them your worst, most crazed smile. Make them look away."

How? How can I smile with a fucking sob stuffed in my throat? Everything inside me is shaking violently, unraveling, coming apart at the seams.

My seams.

She's my seams. She's my fairy tale, my queen, my happily ever after and after and after...

And they're hurting her.

Raping her.

Every unsound, no-return, cliff-diving part of me wants to swipe my thumb and blow these ass pelicans into shits and bits.

But I won't.

I won't give up on Jag. I won't quit until Dove is free.

This isn't the end.

Make them look away.

I drag the corners of my mouth up by force alone, blood in my teeth, muscles screaming, and cheeks stretching where they don't want to go. I make it wide. Too wide. I make it wrong.

It's one of the hardest things I've ever done.

The room recoils from it, eyes sliding away and discomfort rippling with a shudder.

I hold the grin, jaw burning, blood slick and metallic.

New plan.

No retreat. No restraint. Tonight is the reckoning.

wolfson
FIFTY-SEVEN

My fingers clinch around Adrian Crowe's arm, a casual grip that pretends we're just two men watching doom-scroll bait.

I angle the necklace cam at the screen while maintaining the charisma of a nutjob.

Meanwhile, it feels like a rusted blade is sawing back and forth across my soul.

Doesn't matter if the video is live or recorded. The intent is the same. This is what they're forcing Jag to watch. For how long? Why are they trying to break him? Have they succeeded?

"What's the point?" I tilt my head, studying the screen like a critic. "You need the hacker. Why scramble his mind like this?"

"I require his cooperation." Crowe watches the video with a bored, proprietary calm that makes my teeth itch. "He's being stubborn, and the woman provides context."

"Wolf." In my ear, Mikhail cuts in. "I am analyzing the room she's in, and something is off. The shadows don't line up. Camera angle is lying."

Keeping my breath even and the necklace aimed where it needs to be, I turn my head to meet Jag's eyes for the first time.

They're red-rimmed and ruined, held open by the metal prongs that prevent him from blinking. His gaze bounces between me and the screen like a trapped animal, frantic, overworked, but still alive. No gag. No sound. Not a single plea.

I can't tell if that means he's broken or strong as fuck.

Ten days of this would shatter anyone. Ten days of being forced to watch the woman he loves being raped over and over? That would poison the inside of his skull. Yet he doesn't speak. Doesn't beg. Doesn't give Crowe the satisfaction.

Maybe he already cracked.

Or maybe he knows something he won't say in front of Crowe.

"If his brain is sludge, he's no use to me." I gesture at the guards. "Take that off his head."

No one moves.

"What? Do you need written instructions?" I lift my hand and wave the bomb switch. "Or do you need incentive?"

One of the guards steps forward and unfastens the contraption. Metal scrapes. Straps release. The device clatters to the floor, freeing Jag's eyes.

He blinks but doesn't look away from the screen.

My chest clenches, and I follow his gaze back to the feed.

It's fucking unbearable. Blistering pressure scorches through my skull and blooms behind my eyes. I ride it, breathe through it, and focus past the agony, the same way I focused past Denver's horrors.

The camera angles from above, looking down on the bed. The abuser between her legs repositions, shifting back enough to open the view and expose her naked body.

I scan without staring and catalog without reacting, looking for life-threatening damage.

Tangled blue hair, facial and nipple piercings, old scars on her shoulders. Nothing imperfect there. No visible signs of starvation, broken bones, or bleeding wounds. Her eyes squeeze shut, her lips stretched and cracked around the gag.

Unable to watch another second, I start to turn away until something catches my eye. Or doesn't catch it. Something's missing.

Her collarbone is bare.

No beauty mark. It's not there.

My pulse accelerates.

Where is it?

I keep searching while holding my expression like an

unspooled madman seeing a naked woman for the first time.

No beauty mark. No beauty mark. No fucking beauty mark.

I step away from Crowe, pretending boredom while drifting closer to the screen a half step at a time.

"She's a hot piece." With crazy eyes, I smile through the roar in my chest. "Twenty years too old for you, Crowe."

"Like I said." He grits his teeth. "She's motivation for him."

"Doesn't seem to be working."

Every muscle in my body vibrates to tear, crush, and castrate House of Crowe. Instead, I lean in to give the lens a better look. Just enough to feed the van the angle they need.

I search again.

No beauty mark.

I fake a yawn, lifting my hand to cover my mouth, and whisper into the mic, "Not her."

"Stand by," Mikhail says. "I am analyzing."

I drop my hand, keep my posture loose, my face neutral.

If that isn't Dove on the screen, where is she? Still in this building? Moved somewhere else? Another country?

Dead?

No.

I shove down that last thought hard and keep my smile crooked and wrong, playing the part while my brain scrabbles for footing. I need minutes. Seconds even. I need Mikhail to rip that feed apart and tell me where she is.

The guards shift, boots adjusting, weight redistributing, and fingers edging closer to triggers.

"Take him." Crowe's patience thins. "Grab the hacker and go."

"Settle down before you start molting." I wave a hand at Jag. "I'm evaluating the merchandise. If you broke his mind, that's just sloppy." I make a tutting sound. "He might not be worth the trouble of hauling him out of here."

I circle Jag like a compromised circus clown wired for disaster and savoring the moment.

Because I'm not leaving without her.

Until I know where she is, nobody in this room is going anywhere.

"He's a well-built man. Sexy if you're into muscles. I mean, who's not? And look at that. Legal age of consent." I give Crowe a pointed look and return to Jag, twirling my skirt. "Nice collarbones. I just love collarbones. My last pet had the sexiest little beauty mark right here."

I tap Jag's chest, precisely where Dove's mole is, knowing Mikhail is watching through the lens.

Jag's desolate gaze latches onto mine, and a flare of understanding flashes in the bloodshot depths. I step out of the way and watch him refocus on the screen, his eyes examining, probing, looking for a beauty mark that's not there.

Ducking under the chains stretched high on the wall, I move in close behind him.

The shackles rattle as his hands shift against my legs. I pause at his back and bend, draping my arms over his shoulders as if I belong there, just another cruelty he has to endure.

"Tell me." I nuzzle his ear, my voice lazy and theatrical. "Did they break you, kitten?"

For a heartbeat, there's nothing.

Then Jag breathes out a laugh as rough as sandpaper scraping bone. "Fuck you."

Hell's choir, I could weep. He's still in there.

I press my inked smile against his neck and direct my eyes to the video. "Found your blue princess."

He goes rigid, instantly understanding my meaning.

His computer lair.

Crowe studies our intimate position. To him, it sounds like I'm referencing the woman on the screen. Ownership. Leverage. All the ugly things he comprehends.

Mikhail's voice pipes into my ear. "I magnified the images. Ran comparisons. No beauty moles. And there are other discrepancies. Height, shoulder span, micro-ratios... The dimensions of the woman's body on the screen do not match the footage we have of Dove Rath."

My lungs unlock, and my head spins.

"The video is not real, Wolf," Mikhail confirms. "It is AI-generated. Deep fake. That is not Dove Rath."

My heart stops, restarts, and flies off the handle.

Fuck. Me. Gently. With a miracle. Relief slams into me so hard it almost drops me to my knees.

To conceal my surging, pounding shock, I bury my face in Jag's neck and breathe in his proof of life, inhaling the scents of blood, sweat, iron, and him.

For the room, I cackle like an anti-vaxxer in a tinfoil hat, bred for bad endings.

For Jag, I discreetly trace my thumb along his shackled wrist. His fingers curl, reaching, and I give them a quick caress.

He's mine, and I'm getting him the fuck out of here.

Slowly, shamelessly, I ease back, running my lips along his ear, my smile tipped to look like a cracked-open creeper.

I let my hair fall forward to curtain my face and hide the movement of my mouth as I whisper, "Deep fake. Not her."

Jag's breath catches.

I straighten, hands sliding off his shoulders, the smile holding as I turn away.

"I'll take him." I snap my fingers at the nearest guard. "Remove his shackles."

"She is not there," Mikhail says. "I hacked every camera, searched every room in the building. Get out of there."

Where is she?

Is Crowe holding her in another nightclub? Another city? Or was it all a bluff?

If he has her, why would he use a fake video to motivate Jag?

Was the video of her capture another deep fake?

Maybe Jag had her snatched and sent somewhere safe? But if that's the case, why did he surrender?

No. Up until two seconds ago, Jag believed that video of Dove was real.

The guard fumbles with Jag's restraints, metal clanging as the shackles fall free. Jag sways, barely catching himself. I keep half my attention on him, half on Crowe, half on the guards, half on the bomb. Too many halves and not enough time.

"I have a secret." I step toward Crowe.

"No." He recoils on instinct, hands lifting, shaking his head. "Stay back."

"Relax, sweetie." I stay with him, matching his retreat step for step. "You don't want Rath to hear this."

He glances toward Jag—chains falling, guards distracted—and loses his battle with curiosity. He stops.

I press closer and whisper for his ears only, "You don't have Dove Rath."

It's subtle, but I see it. The stutter in his breath. The twitch in his eye.

My pulse skids sideways and slams the red line.

"You want your daughter's secret hiding place?" I whisper. "Bob your head for yes."

For a long, heart-pounding second, he weighs it.

Could I actually know where she is? Of course, I could. I found Jag Rath, didn't I?

Would I actually give Crowe such a vital secret? Why not? I'm wearing a bomb in a nightclub. That makes me certifiable and unpredictable.

He knows if he gets his hands on Dove, he'll get Jag back. Where Dove goes, Jag follows.

So I'm not surprised when he nods his dumb head, reluctant and greedy despite himself.

And that's all the confirmation I need.

He doesn't have her.

Thank you, random violence of fate.

The universe tripped over its dick, fell in my favor, and I'm not wasting it.

This is the opportunity Jag wanted for decades.

I crook a finger, beckoning him closer. He hesitates, then bends in, drawn by the promise like every predator before him.

Clamping a hand on his shoulder, I dip my mouth to his neck. Carefully, I roll the razor blade with my tongue, slide it from my cheek, and bite it between my canines.

"This is for Celeste and David," I whisper past clenched teeth.

With my back to the room, the guards can only assume I'm running my lips across Crowe's throat. They don't know I'm slicing him ear to ear until he gurgles and spurts and makes a nasty, wet mess.

Blood drenches my face and chest before I can dodge it. The trajectory and reach of the projectile spray is fucking impressive. I'd love to watch it spew until the end, but the room is slowly losing its ever-loving shit.

"Please remain calm." I hold up the bomb switch. "Or we all die screaming."

Bodies surge, and guns fly up, like they didn't hear a word I said.

Fucking mall-cop energy.

The rent-a-cop behind me shouts, cut off mid-sound, as I spin and open his throat with the blade in my mouth.

wolfson

The taste of blood clogs my throat, making me gag. I spit the dental weapon into my hand, dance into the mob, and start slashing fingers, arms, bellies, faces, every inch of exposed flesh within reach.

"Congratulations." I slam my modified brass knuckles into an angry face. "You unlocked the bonus level."

Adrenaline detonates through me as I finish him off with the razor.

Sweat stings my eyes. Breath burns, and every nerve screams as I move faster.

Wounds open in flashes. Fabric darkens. Crimson splashes the concrete, and the air fills with the tang of blood and the grunts of effort, pain, and surprise.

Jag is a storm beside me.

The chain snaps taut between his hands, steel singing as he whips it up and around a man's throat. One hard pull, a sharp jerk, and the body drops.

He's done that before.

The next guard doesn't get his weapon up before Jag pivots and cracks the chain across the man's face.

He swings it again, using it as a shield, garrote, lasso, whatever presents itself. Metal and flesh tangle as he drives forward with brutal economy.

That's what ten days of restraint looks like when it breaks loose all at once.

His injuries don't slow him. They sharpen him. And I'm feverishly, inappropriately turned on.

"Focus!" Oliver shouts in my ear. "Get out of there!"

Fists smack flesh. Chains clang, and someone lunges. I dodge by inches and feel heat rush past my ribs.

Hands slip. Bodies collide. My razor sinks deep, again and again. The floor slicks underfoot. Someone stumbles. Someone doesn't get back up. Another crow stupidly aims his gun at me.

"Careful." I gesture at my open vest. "This outfit explodes if startled."

As the goon waffles, Jag steps behind him and snaps his neck.

Two more crows rush me, all bad timing and worse judgment.

"If I trip..." I smile at them. "We all redecorate."

My hands move on instinct, and I feel it through the rings, the wet crunch of steel meeting bone.

One of them staggers back, nose gone wrong and soundless shock splashed across his face.

The other hesitates long enough for regret to register. I love that half-second, the moment they realize my rings aren't decoration, and the skirt-wearing wacko is very, very good at this.

I pounce, knuckles heavy, breath hot, and heart kicking. There's no mercy here. No room for it. Only the need to end the threat before it ends us.

The rings bite. The razor slices. Faces fold, and one by one, the room empties of resistance.

The noise collapses into ragged breathing. The echo of movement fades. Silence creeps back in, thick and stunned, broken only by the drip of blood against concrete.

Every crow in the room lies unmoving on the floor.

Jag stands beside me, breathing hard, eyes wild but clear. Still upright. Still here.

I wipe gore from my face with the back of my hand, spit a mouthful of blood, and meet Jag's eyes.

His hands shake. His breath comes in sharp, uneven pulls, and his muscles appear locked as if the fight might start again. I know the feeling. My own pulse is crashing, heat draining fast, leaving a hollow tremor behind my ribs. Shock with teeth.

His gaze flicks to the body on the floor.

Adrian Crowe.

The pedophile kingpin he hunted for two decades.

The reason he and Dove lost their parents and lived on the streets.

No more.

"Where is she?" His wrecked, broken voice guts me almost as much as the question itself.

"She's not here. Surveillance confirmed she's not in this building."

The swollen lines in his face fracture. Not loud or dramatic. Just a hairline split where hope had been white-knuckled into place. His eyes return to me, and through the damage, behind the bruises and blood and ten days of hell, I see it.

Trust.

He's barely standing, held together by adrenaline and determination, a twitch away from buckling.

wolfson

There's so much I want to say. So much I need to say. But there's a van full of mobsters and mouth-breathers listening and watching. This isn't the moment to break.

"Move!" Oliver snaps in my ear. "Now. Sirens are inbound."

"We'll find her." I push into Jag's space, clasp his hand, and hook our pinkies together in a language he understands. "I swear it."

He stares down at our entwined fingers, his eyes stark and brows furrowed. Then his gaze lifts to mine, and he nods. That's all he's got. It's enough.

I turn us toward the door, my shoulder braced against his and my grip tight on his hand.

We hurry out of the kill room, out of the building, and away from the bodies, the blood, and the monster that tried to keep him.

wolfson
FIFTY-EIGHT

Jag keeps pace beside me, barefoot, shirtless, every inch of him streaked red. His body wobbles on sputtering adrenaline, each step costing him a world of pain. I would offer to carry him, but he would never permit it. So I keep him close enough to catch him if he tips.

We don't stop running until the stairs spit us out into the vacant nightclub. The lights pulse to nobody, the bass thudding like a dying heart.

A few guards hover near the exits, weapons lowered, eyes wide. No one wants to tackle the psycho in a skirt with a live bomb and a bloodied smile.

We burst through the door into humid air and neon glare.

Monty is there, hands catching Jag's shoulders, checking him for injuries, and finding too many. Kody flanks me, one hand on my back, the other on Jag, his eyes black and furious.

"Move." Monty herds us forward. "Now."

Sirens rise in the distance, swelling fast.

We half-jog, half-stagger down the block. Someone yanks the van door open, and we pile in. The sirens scream, and Monty slides behind the wheel. A second later, we're moving.

Jag drops to the floor with his back against the wall, legs

spread, head tipped forward.

He looks wrecked, face covered in stubble, skin blotched with bruises, hair standing in blood-soaked spikes. No less lethal.

"Where are you hurt?" I sink between his knees, hands already moving, scanning him by muscle memory and instinct.

"You came for me." He lifts his head and stares at me as if trying to decide if I'm real.

"I was in the neighborhood." A crooked grin pulls at my mouth despite everything.

His gaze darts around the van, at Monty, Kody, Mikhail's calm silhouette, and Oliver already moving toward my vest.

"You came…" His voice scrapes. "With the Russian mob."

"I saw what you did in the tattoo shop. The surrender." I meet his eyes. "I knew you didn't take her."

He doesn't soften. I'm not sure he knows how. But his expression eases, the smallest give, as his body stops arguing with reality.

The van makes a sharp turn, and I brace a hand on his shoulder, holding him in place.

Oliver crouches and starts stripping the vest off me, fingers quick and practiced. Wires disengage. Explosives disarm. The weight lifts.

"That was a real bomb?" Jag watches in disbelief. "It was live?"

"It would've made a helluva mess." I remove the earpiece and pass it to Oliver.

"Suicidal drama queen."

"That's me. But you'd already know that if you read my journal."

"I did."

"You did?"

"Every word." He lines up his glare with mine. "I started reading the second you left and finished it right before the power shut off. I tried to hide it under the mattress."

"We found it." My throat closes, and traitorous heat crawls behind my eyes.

I look away before it spills and scrub a hand down my crusty face.

He reaches for me, his fingers tracing blood and ink from the corner of my mouth, along my jaw, and back toward my ear, slow and knowing. The compassion in his swollen, amber eyes says he remembers what I wrote about the last time I wore the Glasgow smile.

He knows about the devil's bargain, the lifetime of abuse, the cliff, and the scalpel. He knows all my despicable secrets, and he doesn't look away.

The van lurches, a hard sideways sway, and we both move on instinct. Our hands find each other and clutch tight, bracing against the slide.

When the rocking eases, our grip loosens but doesn't break. Neither does our eye contact.

We hold each other's stare, close enough that I feel the warmth of his body, the proof that he's still breathing, still fighting. There's no rush in it. No claim. Just shared ground after an ugly battle.

Ten days.

That's how long they worked him. Beat him. Strapped him down, forced his eyes open, and made him watch Dove suffer on a loop.

By every rule I know, his brain should be soup. He should be curled in the fetal position, rocking, empty, gone somewhere I can't reach.

It hasn't hit him yet.

Shock is holding the line. Purpose is holding the line. Dove, being out there somewhere, is holding the line. He doesn't have room to fall apart because this isn't finished. Survival hasn't loosened its grip.

I see it in the way his eyes never stop moving, and how his jaw remains fixed despite the threat being gone.

He's functioning on borrowed time and unfinished business. His system hasn't caught up to what his body just escaped.

Maybe he won't break the way people expect. But I know this much. When we're alone, when the noise drops and the danger clears, the demons will come. In the quiet moments. In the dark. In ways neither of us can outrun.

I'll be there for it.

He continues to stare at me, never letting his gaze drift as if I might vanish. His focus isn't frantic. It's fierce and clinging, threaded with the heaviest, most pressing thought.

"Dove." A wet sheen veils his eyes, and he blinks. "I can't breathe. She's..."

"I know." My heart hurts. It fucking howls and thrashes and doesn't stop.

I press a hand against my chest, rubbing the stabbing pain as everything inside me tries to rupture right there.

But I don't let it. I can't. He needs me stitched up and sane. So I fight the urge to spiral. Fight the images. Fight the clock that's suddenly loud again. I don't know where she is, but panic won't help him. Panic won't find her.

"Mikhail." I twist toward him, where he hunches over a laptop. "Pull up the video of Dove's capture."

His fingers tap over the keyboard. Moments later, he swivels the screen toward us and hits play.

I shift to sit beside Jag and force myself to watch Dove's capture again.

"That's my camera. I hid it on the street outside the mechanic shop." Jag leans in, eyes locked. "That's not what they showed me when I surrendered. Their video had her dragged off the pier and thrown onto a boat."

"Another fake." Mikhail turns away with the laptop.

"How was she taken from your guards?" Jag stares at me. No accusation. He seems genuinely baffled.

"There was a decoy."

I walk through every detail of that vile day from the moment I left her in the shop. I describe the slaughter I found in the tattoo parlor, the decoy that ran from the security team, the realization that we fucked up, and Dove's disappearance without a trace.

"A decoy." Something ignites behind his eyes. Not panic. Realization.

"What?" I clasp his arm. "You know something."

"Show me the video again." He looks at Mikhail. "Pause on the man who took her."

"He was masked." Mikhail twists toward us, the video already cued up.

"Zoom in on his hands." Jag grips my thigh as he bends toward the screen. "There."

As the masked man snatches her, his sleeves inch up, revealing black gauze around his wrists, threaded neatly with thin white thread.

"Fucking hell." Jag's breathing goes ragged, heaving his chest, as he slumps back against the van.

"What?" Panic detonates, shooting shrapnel through my veins. "You recognize him."

"Yeah." He squeezes his eyes shut, and a single tear slips free.

That's all it takes. My control snaps, sending my hysteria from functional to feral.

"Who has her?" I shove my face in his and roar, "Where is she?"

He blinks, directs a pointed look at Mikhail, at Oliver in the front, and shakes his head.

A shut-mouth, don't-ask *no.*

But when he turns back to me and sees my expression, his stubborn armor slips.

The horror must be written all over me. His eyes go round, filling with something akin to affection or mercy. He opens his arms and pulls me in. His hands cup my jaw, and his thumbs rest against my cheeks.

"She's safe," he whispers.

"Safe?"

"I promise." He holds my gaze and lets me look as long as I need, laying it all out there for my inspection, for my doubt, for my fear.

I search his eyes and find only certainty.

Air flees my lungs in a violent rush. "Safe where?"

He glances at the van's occupants and looks back at me, apologetic but resolute.

I don't push. I think.

Whoever Jag is mixed up with isn't a name he'll drop casually. That narrows the field fast. If he won't say it in front of the Russians, they must not play well with whoever's holding her.

"He's retired." I gesture at Oliver, keeping my voice low.

Jag arches a brow, but it barely works given the swollen state of his face.

"Fine. Does that mean she's not a hostage?" I whisper. "She's a protected asset?"

He nods and lets his head rest against the wall like it weighs a ton. Spent. He rolls his face toward me, inches away from mine, watching me process.

He believes she's okay.

I see it in the way his shoulders finally loosen. In the tear he didn't mean to let escape. In the way his hands stop shaking. Most of all, I see it in the way he looks at me. Open, pleading, asking me to trust him with the one thing that matters.

I do.

I trust him because I know this about Jag Rath. He would carve out his heart before letting harm touch her. He would burn every bridge, sell every secret, and ruin himself without hesitation if that's what it took.

So if he says she's safe, she is.

We're not done. Not even close. The second we're alone, I'll demand the whole story. I'll want names, locations, motivations, and an idiot-proof backup plan that comes with vodka, eyeliner, and a spare apocalypse.

But for now, I wait, clinging to the one solid truth I have left.

We're coming for her together.

jag
FIFTY-NINE

The engines settle into a soothing thrum as the city drops away beneath us. Los Angeles shrinks. The Pacific stretches, and the air inside Monty's private jet smells like recycled oxygen and mobsters.

Fucking Russians. I don't trust them.

I don't trust Monty's island. I don't trust the plane, the sky, or the silence between the turbulence.

But I trust Wolf.

I still can't wrap my head around it.

Twenty years of tracking Adrian Crowe. Twenty years of building traps and watching him slip free every time. I mapped his money, his routes, his business deals, and those of his evil business partners. I stalked him through data, every second of every day, for two fucking decades.

And Wolf walked in and ended him in a single night. A bomb on his chest, a razor blade behind his inked smile, and no fucks to give.

I'd throttle him for it if I didn't want to grab his hair, shove a hand under his skirt, and assault his mouth until he comes in his hot sequined shorts.

He's beautiful in a way that makes my chest ache. Reckless

jag

in a way that begs for punishment. And he's mine, if the world would give us five uninterrupted minutes to say the things we're not saying.

I owe him my life.

I owe him Dove.

Sitting near the rear of the plane, I rest my hands on my lap because if I don't, they'll start searching for things to break.

The Restrepo cartel has my little bird.

They fucking took her.

That truth jolts in my head. Not relief. Not terror. But the extremes of both, braided into a live wire.

I need my computer equipment.

Wolf said they moved everything to the island before Crowe's people could destroy it. Servers, drives, redundancies stacked on redundancies. My work, my mind, all laid out in metal and code.

Except for my connection to the Restrepo cartel. Those files are buried so deep I built them to survive excavation, layers upon layers, the kind that would take Mikhail years to peel back, if he ever managed it at all.

But if he somehow corrupted or compromised my servers, I won't be able to contact the cartel.

I shut that thought down. I'll know soon enough.

Monty's in the cockpit, flying us back to Sitka. His co-pilot, Oliver, sits beside him. Kodiak sprawls near the front with Mikhail, pretending not to listen while listening to everything.

I track Wolf by feel, following his restless orbit through the cabin.

He stops in the doorway of the cockpit, a hand braced on the bulkhead, and speaks quietly with Monty.

From the moment we left the nightclub, Monty hasn't relaxed his jaw or released his breath. He wears the look of a father who knows his son keeps stepping into fires he can't follow. He's terrified of losing Wolf again.

Wolf lowers his brow to Monty's head and murmurs something that makes Monty's shoulders loosen a fraction. Whatever Wolf says, it's meant only for Monty, a quiet assurance from a son who knows precisely how much fear he leaves in his wake and is asking to be trusted anyway.

He checks Kody next, a quick scan, a wordless exchange of

eye contact I can't begin to decipher.

Then he's standing before me. Baptized by Adrian Crowe's jugular. Blood cakes his inked smile, clings to his jaw, and mats into his hairline.

The eyeliner didn't survive the night. It smudges his eyes into dark ruin and bleeds down his cheeks in inky trails that cut through drying red.

More gore splatters his ivory lace skirt that hangs obscenely over mean thigh-high boots. The rings and necklace are gone. The vest and bomb long gone. He's shirtless, his chest bludgeoned with more scars than I have the years, or the right, to count. Old lines. New ones. Wounds that healed clean. Others that didn't bother.

I've seen monsters up close. I hunted one for most of my life. Wolf isn't that.

He's aftermath. Drenched in blood that isn't his. Hair wild. Eyes chillingly ferocious. He's never looked more beautiful.

"You look like roadkill." He gives me a once-over and wrinkles his nose. "Come on."

He offers his hand, and I take it without hesitation.

At the rear, he pushes open the narrow bathroom door. The shower stall is barely more than a coffin with plumbing.

"You first." He glances at it, then at me, mouth twitching. "I'll help."

We both know it's impossible. There isn't room for the two of us to breathe, let alone move.

"Rain check." I brush my thumb along his bottom lip.

He grasps the hand I hold to his face, presses a kiss to my palm, and steps back.

The door seals. The hum of the engines dulls, replaced by the hiss of water. When it hits my skin, it hurts. Everything does.

The stream runs red immediately. Ten days of rust-dark filth and nightmares.

I brace my palms against the wall, forehead following, and take inventory.

Shoulder. Dislocated ten days ago and slammed back in without finesse. It's stiff, sore, but holding.

Wrist. Broken a month ago and still aches, but usable.

Ribs. Kicked by boots and bruised into a kaleidoscope of colors. Breathing is tight, but no stabbing pain. Nothing broken.

Face. Swollen, tender, jaw clicks when I open my mouth.

jag

Probably fine.

Eyes. The skin around them burns where the metal prongs dug in, tiny cuts I feel more than see. I rinse carefully, blinking through the sting.

The water clears, pink fading to nothing.

After I brush my teeth, I stand there longer than necessary, steam fogging the walls, grounding myself in the simple fact that I'm upright, unrestrained, and alone with my thoughts for the first time since Crowe's men took me.

Outside the door, I hear Wolf shift his stance. Waiting. Guarding.

When I shut off the water and reach for a towel, the door cracks. An arm shoves through, holding out clean clothes.

"I didn't see your duffel bag." Wolf meets my eyes through the opening, his brow creasing.

The same worried look he gave me that night, when he asked if the bag was all I had to my name.

"They took the duffel." I accept the clothes from him. "It was part of the setup to make it look like I killed your guards and skipped town."

"They killed Declan."

"I know." My stomach twists. "I'm so sorry, pup."

He looks away and waits while I dress. The lounge pants and plain tee fit perfectly. They must belong to Wolf. He and I are the same size. I pull the neckline to my nose and sniff. Delicious. Definitely Wolf.

While Wolf showers, I stretch out on the narrow sofa at the back of the plane, and my eyes drift closed despite myself.

I'm halfway under when the door slides open.

Wolf steps out in similar lounge wear, soft fabric clinging where it shouldn't. His black hair drips on his shoulders, the blood and makeup gone. Clean skin, except not entirely.

The sharpie lines remain, albeit faded and pink, as if he scrubbed them until his skin screamed.

"I can't..." He gestures helplessly at his face, holding a bottle of hand sanitizer. "If Frankie sees this..."

"Come here." I push myself up, making room for him on the couch between my legs.

He settles there, facing me, shoulders hunched. I take the bottle from his hand, soak the cloth, and bring it to his cheek.

"Frankie was there." I start slow, making small, careful circles. "The last time you drew this on."

He makes an uncomfortable sound in his throat.

"That's why you don't want her to see it?" I keep my touch light. "It'll traumatize her?"

"Yeah." His mouth flattens beneath my fingers, troubled and sad. "Like a breaking storm."

I work the sanitizer into the ink, watching the lines blur, lift, and surrender in streaks of gray and pink. His skin is already irritated, tender from over-cleaning.

I think about the life he survived. The isolation, starvation, kin punishment, molestation, and men who enjoyed breaking things. Loss layered on loss until pain became background noise. Worse than the hell Dove and I navigated, and ours was fucking brutal.

I'm glad he let me read the journal.

Without it, I don't think I could sit here like this. I'd still be guessing at his depths and angles instead of understanding the cost. It gives me the clarity I need to move forward with him, whatever forward ends up meaning.

The cloth darkens. The smile fades.

In Sitka, I'll get my equipment back. I'll contact Restrepo. I'll bargain, threaten, and trade favors I shouldn't owe.

I'll sell my soul to get Dove back.

Whatever is left of me when it's done, I'll give to her and Wolf.

I know what I am now. A hacker for the cartel, and they don't let go. I won't pretend I can escape, not without dragging hell behind me. That door is closed.

But if I let myself dream, just for a second, I would give Dove and Wolf the world. Not to own it. Not to stand in the middle of it. Just to be allowed to exist at the edges of their life together.

Eventually, the last of the ink disappears. I use a bottle of water to wipe away the harsh sting of sanitizer.

When I'm done, I tip his chin up with two fingers and look him over. "It's gone."

"Blue princess." He studies my face.

I hold his gaze, waiting for the questions.

"Were you leaving breadcrumbs for me on purpose?" His eyes sharpen despite the exhaustion. "Or was it a slip?"

"It was a clue. Insurance. One I didn't think you'd ever

jag

need."

He nods, absorbing that, then tilts his head. "What about the rock at the gravesite? The passcode?"

"That was for Dove. I left it the last time I went to California."

"When you killed Gavin."

Shock grips me, followed by a hard snap of defensiveness. I don't know why I bother feeling either. Wolf doesn't miss details. He devours them.

He's frighteningly smart.

And Dove? Yeah. She pieced it together, too.

"I'd do it again." I let the confession hover.

He watches me, seeing everything, and somehow still staying right where he is.

"You know all my secrets. I'm fully exposed." His mouth tips. "You have the advantage, because I don't know yours."

"Dove told you everything, I'm sure."

"Only what she knows. I want *your* story."

"There's too much to unpack." I lean back along the sofa, air leaving my lungs. "None of it happens with Russians on board."

"Then start with the past ten days." He softens his tone. "Tell me about the kill room."

The engine hum fills the space between us. I close my eyes for a second, seeing concrete and chains and torture that never turns off.

Then I open them and meet his patient gaze.

"All right." I shift on the couch and open my arms.

He moves in, careful at first. We adjust without speaking, twisting our too-big frames in the narrow space. I stretch along the seats with my back to the wall, and he settles on his side against my chest and between my legs. His head fits just right in the crook of my shoulder, and I rest my arm around him.

Dove is the only person I've ever held this way. That long-lost familiarity burrows inside my chest, old and warm and quietly devastating.

Christ, I miss her.

Closing my eyes, I let myself sink beneath the heat of Wolf's body. Then I tell him about the kill room.

I don't linger on the beatings. Those were crude and predictable. I move past them and go straight to the part that mattered.

"The screen never turned off. They unhooked the rig sometimes so it wouldn't damage my eyes. But when I closed them, she was still there. That was part of the torture. Let me think I escaped for a minute. Then find her again inside my head."

Wolf stays still, breathing steady, listening.

"I refused to cooperate." I run the backs of my fingers along his arm. "I told Crowe I'd do nothing until I saw her in person. Not on a feed or through a camera lens. Something felt wrong. I couldn't explain it, but my gut kept telling me the video wasn't right. How did you know it was a fake?"

"Mikhail said the shadows didn't line up. So I looked closer."

"That's when you noticed the missing beauty mark."

"One of my favorite parts of her." He smiles.

My chest flutters. Not with jealousy. With contentment.

"I couldn't see that detail from across the room. The distance was deliberate. No audio, either. Crowe wasn't taking any chances. He knew I was suspicious. Thought he could frighten me enough to override that instinct, and maybe, if he pushed hard enough, I'd do anything he asked." My hand tightens in the fabric of Wolf's shirt. "I was close. Closer than I want to admit. Maybe a day. Maybe only hours. I don't know how much longer I would've held."

"You held longer than I did. When Frankie killed Denver and sealed our fates, I didn't last a day before I broke and chose the cliff over starvation."

"That's not the same thing."

"You're right. Lasting ten days in a kill room? That's brave. Jumping off a cliff? That was weak."

The anger slams into me fast and unbidden.

"No." I tighten my arm around him and lean down, mouth close to his ear. "You don't get to say that."

He stiffens.

"It's unacceptable." I pull back enough to look at him. "You didn't fail. You survived. That isn't weakness."

"Jag..."

"You walked into a den I spent twenty years circling and took down the most protected predator on the planet in one night. You did what governments, vigilantes, and criminals like me couldn't do. You ended him. Completely."

jag

He lifts his head, eyes finding mine. The praise settles through him, and his body leans in without permission. His hands travel to my shoulders. Mine mold along his spine.

We hold each other's gaze.

There's too much in it. Respect, hunger, things neither of us are ready to say, and gravity that pulls and pulls until resisting takes monumental effort. The air between us ignites, charged with the impulse to close the final inch and claim the moment.

We don't.

Dove exists in this space with us, and loving her means not crossing lines that would hurt her. Whatever this is between Wolf and me, it will wait. Or it'll die unfinished.

I drop my forehead to his, a controlled retreat. He exhales, and the urge to kiss him hardens my stomach. He senses it, fights it, and returns to his position against my chest.

"Sometimes I forget how old you are." He traces a finger through the dusting of hair on my forearm. "You reminded me just now."

"How so?"

"Commanding as hell. Dangerously confident. Older and knows it. You're checking a lot of my boxes, kitten."

"Wolf..." Blood rushes south, and I groan with frustration. "Knock it off."

"Not until you tone down the dominating daddy energy."

"I'm not that much older than you."

"I'm twenty-four, and you're... Forty?"

"Yeah."

"Fun fact. You're ten years older than my oldest brother. That makes you older than everyone in my family except my old man." He snorts. "And holy shit, it's working for you."

"Moving on."

"You've been watching Adrian Crowe for twenty years."

"You've been digging through my encrypted files."

"How do you think I found you?"

"I know how you found me." I rest my lips on the top of his head. "And I'm grateful, Wolf. More than you know."

"How did you know Crowe was behind the murder of your parents?"

That's a history I can share, considering Mikhail probably already scraped it from my servers.

Pulling in a breath, I say the words I've never spoken out loud. "Celeste told me about Crowe before she died."

My throat dries, but the words keep coming.

"Celeste and my dad were together for six years. Never fought. Not once that I can remember. Until the last few months." I stare past the cabin window, back into that house. "Dove was eight. She hated the arguments and always hid under the bed when they started. I'd sit with her, make up games, and distract her until it was over. But one night, it went longer than usual. I heard them talking when I went to check on them. I didn't mean to listen. But I heard Celeste say someone was hunting them. She was scared. My dad was, too. She wanted all four of us to go into witness protection. Change names. Disappear."

Wolf shifts, listening with his whole body.

"My dad didn't believe the threat was that bad. He thought they could manage it, thought they had time. Celeste saw me around the corner, and she knew I'd heard."

"You were sixteen?"

"Yeah. Old enough to understand danger. Too young to control it. After everyone went to bed, she came into my room, woke me up, and told me the truth." My voice cracks. "About Adrian Crowe. That he got her pregnant, sold her to a rich man, and she escaped. She made me promise never to tell Dove. Never."

"Why?"

"She was terrified of him. She said if anything happened, I couldn't go to the police. Crowe owned badges in every city, and if I told the wrong person, he'd take Dove."

"She knew Dove was too young to hold that information." His jaw hardens. "One slip from an eight-year-old's mouth…"

"Exactly."

"So she put it on you. Made you carry it."

"She was the only mother I knew." I release a shuddery breath. "I loved her. So I promised to keep her secret, never go to the cops, and never tell Dove."

"Of course, you kept that promise, you loyal asshole. And that loyalty almost killed you. More than once. I'm pissed she put you in that position. You were fucking sixteen."

"Celeste was only six years older than me. Practically a kid herself."

"Does Dove know how young she was?"

"No. She doesn't remember." My chest constricts. "All those years in our cardboard forts and tents, moving from place to place, Dove never stopped asking about our parents. She wanted descriptions, stories, any scrap I would throw her. I was so afraid I would slip and reveal too much or say something she would piece together later. So I gave her nothing."

"You have to tell her."

"I know. I will."

"Wow. That explains... Way too much." He makes a humming sound. "So let me get this straight. Crowe sent a hitman to take out your whole family, but he didn't count on *you*, a sixteen-year-old kid, escaping with Dove."

"Dove wasn't part of the hit that night."

"She was supposed to be taken alive? To be trafficked? His own daughter?"

"Yeah. He hunted her for the next couple of years, but as I honed my hacking skills and Dove grew older, *I* became his target."

"And Dove was the leverage."

"Yes."

"You said she's safe." He eases back into me. "I'm taking you at your word and staking everything I am on it."

"She's safe."

Adrian Crowe is dead. House of Crowe will follow. But I'm not finished.

I don't want him gone. I want him exposed on the world stage. Him and every fixer, buyer, and polished monster who fed at his table. I want the money trails lit up, the shell companies cracked, and the quiet men who signed checks and looked away dragged into daylight where they can't hide behind titles or philanthropy.

I'll plan it properly, use the cartel, and hunt every Crowe associate, every predator who trafficked flesh through him, every coward who profited from silence.

Then I'll end them.

This isn't revenge anymore. It's cleanup.

But for now, I keep my arm around Wolf and let the past settle where it belongs, spoken but not forgiven.

Wolf's heavy frame grows even heavier against me, the

sharp edges of him softening as sleep takes hold. His head rests solid against my chest, his body slack with trust, every exhale slow and even.

I hold completely still, worried any sudden movement might wake him and break whatever fragile truce his nervous system just signed.

I've been alone a long time. Long enough that sharing space like this feels foreign and dangerous. My body remembers holding Dove this way, her tiny hands, the soft silk of her hair, and the adoring way she looked at me. That memory stings, but it doesn't hurt the way I expect.

Because this is different.

This is Wolf, choosing to rest against me without question.

The feeling settles into my circulation, quiet and earned. I didn't realize how starved I was for this simple thing, another human trusting me with their unconsciousness, their vulnerability.

I've never had a partner. No girlfriend. No boyfriend. Sex has always been a transaction, a source of income, leverage, or a role to play and discard. I know how to perform, and I know how to be a protector for Dove. I don't know how to belong to someone, how to be a *significant other*.

For the first time in my life, I don't feel like a solitary structure braced against collapse. With Wolf, I feel aligned, bonded, and fiercely aware of how much it means that he's at my side, breathing and safe.

So I stay awake, guarding his sleep the way I once guarded Dove's.

Midway through the flight, Kodiak comes back without a word. He lowers himself beside the sofa, careful as a mountain settling, and studies Wolf where he snoozes against me.

The look on Kodiak's face is pure love, vast and fathomless. The kind of love that survived things no one should. The journal graphically illustrated what they endured together. Years of hunger, cold, and abuse, with one another as their only constant. Seeing that history reflected in Kodiak's eyes reshapes things in my chest.

Then his gaze lifts to me.

He scrutinizes my arm around Wolf, the way I've angled my body to shield him from the aisle, and the calm soaked into Wolf's sleeping face.

jag

After a long, assessing perusal that measures intent and outcome, he gives a single, almost imperceptible nod.

Approval.

"I've never seen him like this," he whispers so softly it barely sounds like him. "Not once. Never saw peace on him. Never saw hope. Nothing even close to happy. Not until you and Dove stormed into his life."

Then he straightens, all bulk and gravity returning, and lumbers toward the front without looking back.

I relax into the couch, breathing in time with Wolf, as the plane carries us north through the dark, toward debts still due, promises not yet made, and the single most important priority. Taking back our little bird.

jag
SIXTY

The island greets us with damp air and lush darkness. The moment we arrive, Monty and Kodiak peel off, heading straight to bed. They earned it.

Wolf and I should do the same. But we can't. Sleep is a luxury for men who have their woman in bed beside them.

To my disappointment, the Russians stay. Crashing in the main house means proximity, eyes and ears everywhere, and I don't have the privacy I need to work.

I'm set up in the guest house before the engine heat fades from my bones. Laptop open. Secondary rig humming. Satellite uplink clean. Air-gapped backup live. I test every line, every handshake, every packet on the network.

The Russians were good. Which means I assume compromise until proven otherwise.

My wrist throbs as I type, and my shoulder screams when I reach too far. I welcome the pain. It keeps me focused.

"Sit still." Frankie flutters like a moth in scrubs, prodding at my arm.

"No." I bare my teeth.

She already stuck Wolf with needles to send samples off to a lab to test for bloodborne disease transmission. Then she flushed

jag

his mouth, made him spit until his jaw hurt, and checked his gums and tongue for cuts. All necessary, given the amount of foreign blood he swallowed.

"This is why it's not healing." She catches my wrist mid-keystroke and clicks her tongue. "And that shoulder you're pretending wasn't dislocated…"

"It's relocated."

"By whom? You? With a vengeance?"

I go back to the screen. She doesn't let go.

Murmurs drift from the couch behind me, Leonid's growly voice, and Wolf's louder, faster timbre, threading humor through horror as he catches Leonid up on the last few days.

I don't turn, but I hear what Wolf isn't saying. *Where's Dove? Who has her? How are we getting her back?*

He's giving me space to do what I'm good at, but his patience has limits.

"You need rest." Frankie releases my arm.

"Abort mission, Mama Bear," Wolf says. "The angry marshmallow won't rest until Dove's back."

My mouth curves despite myself.

"Neither will I." He rises from the couch and approaches the back of my chair.

Frankie drops a bottle of pills next to my keyboard and plants her hands on her hips. So much attitude for such a tiny woman.

"You." She fixes Wolf with a withering look. "Don't let him overdo it when you're… You know…" She makes a jerk-off gesture.

"When we're… What?" Wolf mimics her hand motion. "Buffing a breadstick? Starting a lawnmower? Slapping the bass?"

She sighs like she's tired of all of us. "When you're banging."

Heat coils between my legs, unwanted, unhelpful, entirely Wolf. I set my jaw and keep typing, my heartbeat loud in my ears.

"Solid advice." He nods. "I'll add it to the pile of bad ideas we're actively considering."

Frankie rolls her eyes and pivots toward Leonid. He's already striding toward her.

"Thank you." Wolf watches her, his fingers tucked in the

pockets of his lounge pants.

She turns back and closes the distance, taking Wolf's face in her hands.

"Thank you for not dying." She lifts on tiptoes and kisses his brow. "Now go get your girl back."

Leonid stops by the door like he's thinking about leaving something behind. He doesn't posture or threaten as his dual-colored eyes stare at me long enough to be awkward.

Whatever he sees must pass inspection, because he nods.

"You did what most wouldn't do. You surrendered your control when it counted." He pauses, considering. "You don't have to like how we live. You don't have to agree with it. But if you stand with us, you stand all the way. No half-steps. If you're all in, welcome to the family."

Frankie squeezes my arm on her way past, already planning my recovery, like I belong to her workload now. She gives Wolf a look that says behave and disappears with her Viking husband into the night.

The door shuts.

The last time I stepped onto this island, I was escorted off by armed men. And now? The treasured jewel of the Strakh family patched me up, and a man built like a saga welcomed me into his bloodline.

That kind of turn doesn't happen by accident.

Wolf's reflection flickers on the dark screen in front of me. He hasn't spoken or moved closer, but I know that look. He's inside my head.

"They saw the video of the attack at the tattoo parlor. All of it." His hands rest on my shoulders. "You didn't try to save yourself. You gave up everything for Dove without knowing the outcome." He bends closer, blanketing my back with his body heat. "If there's one thing my family respects, it's loyalty. You've been proving yours for over twenty years."

Acceptance. Belonging. That's what this strange elastic band is around my chest.

I didn't hack my way into this family. Didn't break into it or outmaneuver it.

I earned it.

A swallow sticks in my throat. My jaw aches, and my eyes burn to the point of pissing me off.

The Strakhs have claimed me, but my life is no longer my

own.

I made a deal with no escape. I'm dangerous, compromised, and hunted. But I'm not alone.

That changes everything.

I set my fingers on the keyboard. The screen resolves. A door opens in code. I lean in, pain forgotten, every sense narrowing to the thread that leads outward, off the island, across the dark, toward the only point that matters.

No more delaying. It's time to tell him.

"Two weeks ago, I made a painstaking decision." I twist in the chair and grip Wolf's wrist, pulling him to stand before me. "I traded my life in exchange for protection. Protection for you and Dove."

"Traded..." His eyes thin to deadly slits. "With whom?"

"The Restrepo cartel."

"I'm sorry... What?" His face turns violent-red. "You traded your life? To a cartel?"

"I need you to remain calm."

"I will do no such thing!" His snarl whips through the room. "Undo it, Jag. Undo it, right now. You have ten seconds to reverse the trade before I walk into traffic and make this weird, public, and deeply regrettable."

"Shut up and listen." I launch to my feet and grab his throat. Not hard. Just enough to get his attention. "This isn't about me. It's about getting Dove back."

"She's with the fucking Restrepo cartel!" His eyes bulge, and his breath seethes. "You told me she was safe!"

"Goddammit, she is!" I lower my voice and look him square in the eyes. "I'm getting her back, but this is delicate."

"How delicate?"

"They're paranoid. I'm calling them now, and I need you to be dead quiet. Okay?"

He blinks, presses his lips together, and nods.

"Okay." I blow out a breath and return to the chair.

No hesitation this time. Same burner. Same cradle. Same ritual. Set the token, enter the code, and don't breathe until the lights cycle and the line tunnels its way around the world.

It rings once.

Twice.

Then the click.

I put the call on speaker and give Wolf a warning look.

"*¿Otra vez?*" The voice is unmistakable. Calm, amused, and predatory in the way only men with nothing to fear can afford. "*El Vigilante* already spent his favor."

"You know why I'm calling."

"*Si*," Matias Restrepo says. "We have her."

Wolf goes rigid beside me, his body sharpening like a blade about to slip its sheath.

"I agreed to your terms." I force my hands to relax on the keyboard. "Those terms did not include taking her."

"We had two options," Matias says mildly. "Save the bird. Or save you. Did we make the wrong choice?"

"No. You didn't." I swallow the roar in my throat. "Return her to me, and I'll come to you freely and permanently."

Wolf's head snaps toward me, shaking hard, furious disagreement reddening his face.

I jab a finger at him and give him my stoniest expression.

Matias hums, thoughtful. "The terms have changed."

"What?" Blood drains from my cheeks. "How?"

"The wolf comes with you."

"No. That isn't—"

"We'll discuss in person. You *and* the wolf."

I feel Wolf vibrating beside me, every instinct screaming at him to intervene. But he doesn't. He trusts me. Or he's trying to.

Every instinct I have wants to push, threaten, bargain, anything that proves I'm still in control. I swallow all of it. I know better.

The *jefe* is waiting for the crack, waiting for me to bleed into the line. I don't give it to him. I don't argue, plead, or ask for mercy that doesn't exist.

I make one request. "Let me hear her voice."

"Send the Russians away." Matias exhales slowly. "Then we speak. Tomorrow night."

"Put her on the phone. I need to hear—"

The line goes dead.

"Fuck!" I hurl the cradle across the room. "Fuck! Fuck! Fuuuuck!"

I need her.

I need to see her. I need to hear her breathe, hear her say my name, curse me to hell, or tell me to stop controlling everything. Anything. This silence is killing me faster than Crowe ever could.

jag

The setback drops me like a collapsing floor.

Ten days in the kill room come rushing back, light that never dimmed, chains that never loosened, the screen that never shut off. And it keeps going. Years pile on. Decades. Running, planning, cutting pieces off myself to survive. All of it crashes into me, and I can't pull in enough air.

My chest caves in, and my hands claw uselessly at my shirt. Black rings the edges of my vision, and I make a sound I don't recognize. A raw, tortured sound. It wrenches out of me before I can stop it.

A sob. Loud. Ugly. Out of control.

I know I'm frightening Wolf. He crouches beside me, grabbing my shoulders, my face, my hair, shouting, demanding, and pleading, ready to fight the world for me. I don't want him to see this. I don't want anyone to see this.

But I can't shut it down.

Everything is everywhere. Fear, rage, grief, regret, there's no order or hierarchy as the vicious storm barrels through me. I double over, elbows on my knees, and forehead in my hands, unable to stop another sob shuddering out of me, broken and useless.

I've spent my entire life being the one in control, and now, I have none.

The spiral grows louder. Images of Dove, bound, raped, and screaming where I can't reach her—it's all I see.

Until a fist grips the back of my head. Fingers tighten in my hair. My neck is forced back, my lips opened without negotiation as Wolf's mouth attacks mine.

He doesn't ask. He doesn't tease.

He demands.

The kiss hauls me back from the edge by force, rough and unbending, all teeth and growl. It's an order delivered with a strong, combative tongue, lapping the air from my lungs and replacing the noise in my head with *Stay here. Feel me.*

I snarl into it and grab him back, one hand around his neck, the other catching his hip. I drag him onto my lap, and he straddles me like that was always his destination.

The kiss turns feral, licking and biting in a clash of mouths that edges toward fighting, both of us pouring everything we want into the connection.

Hunger thickens every breath, but it's secondary. This isn't about taking.

It's about anchoring.

The aggression bleeds off slowly, his mouth softening, and my grip loosening. We breathe into each other, foreheads brushing and lips still touching.

When he eases back, my pulse has slowed. The images have receded. The chaos in my head has been pushed into folders I can manage again.

I have my control back. And I know, with a clarity that cuts through everything else, that he gave it to me.

"Why did you do that?" I suck in a breath. "Why did you kiss me?"

"You were short-circuiting. I had no other choice." He drapes his forearms over my shoulders and sits back, relaxing his weight on my lap. "That's the story I'll tell Dove."

Her name sends a bolt of cold lightning through me.

He sees it. "You keep telling me she's safe, but after that call... Who the hell was that?"

"The kingpin of the Colombian cartel."

"You're fucking with me."

"Wish I were."

"Cool. Cool, cool, cool. Just casually chatting with He Who Shall Not Be Named near, around, or in front of the Russians. Tell me the part again where she's safe."

"I'll show you." I motion at the other kitchen chairs. "Pull up a seat."

"Not yet." He remains straddled on my lap, his arctic eyes scanning my face, taking a second assessment as if the breakdown a minute ago disqualifies me from making decisions for a while.

Fair.

"I know how this looks." I let out a breath and tip my head back. "But this isn't new."

His brow clenches.

"I cracked like that a few times." I squeeze his legs. "Usually after something happened to Dove. When a foster brother touched her or a boyfriend assaulted her. Every time someone hurt her. I handled it, ended the problem, and washed the blood off my hands. I had to be strong for her. But when she was safe and asleep, I went somewhere alone and fell apart. Sometimes I cried. Sometimes I put holes in walls. Sometimes I just sat in the corner and shook until it burned itself out. There was never anyone there to pull me back. I never had someone grab me and yank me out of my head like that. Definitely never had someone kiss me hard enough and mean enough to shut out the pain. So… Thank you."

"You never have to thank me for kissing you." Wolf's mouth curves, feral and soft all at once.

That almost pulls a laugh out of me.

"I'm okay now." I run my hands along his thighs, not asking him to move, just grounding us both. "We're getting her back. Just focus on that."

"You're so disgustingly in love with her." He pokes my chest.

"So are you."

"Madly." He dips his head and touches his lips against mine, chastely, sweetly, as if to prove not all his kisses are hard and mean.

Then he climbs off my lap and pulls up a chair. Back to business.

"Right." I crack my knuckles and turn toward the keyboard. "I'll show you why she's safe."

jag
SIXTY-ONE

Wolf makes the most colorful faces when he's thinking hard.

His mouth pulls to one side. His brows pinch, one higher than the other. He squints at the screen, lips parting. A second later, his jaw bounces, and his tongue presses against his cheek.

There it is, the *this is bullshit* look, followed by a slow blink.

I don't interrupt.

Muscles shift under his milk-white complexion, his skin nearly bare of hair, smooth in places that aren't scarred.

Thick black waves brush his shoulders, half-shadowing his face and making his eyes stand out even more. Ice blue eyes, lethal enough to cut out my heart.

Those lashes don't make sense on a man built like him. Neither does the mouth. Too pretty. Too expressive. Too dangerous in how easily it makes me hard as a rock.

I want him. Not abstractly or tactfully. I want to fuck his brains out. I want the heat of him beneath me, the friction, and the release that comes from collision.

The urge doesn't rush. It locks in. The same way it locked in when I no longer saw Dove as my little sister.

But this sexual tension that Wolf and I share? It's unlike anything I've felt. The pressure is ever-present and all-consuming. One wrong move will detonate the barrier between us and change the physics of the room.

Wanting Wolf isn't a thought I can argue with or a craving I can starve out. He's the moon in motion, recruiting my organs, engaging my nerves, and controlling every drop of blood in my body.

He doesn't chase. He alters the pull of the room just by existing in it. Currents shift. Gravity strengthens. Distances shorten, and I feel myself drawn, dragged closer by forces I don't command.

His nose wrinkles. He leans back, stares at the ceiling, and exhales through his teeth as if the information on the screen doesn't make sense.

It doesn't.

I gave him the profiles of all twenty-two members of the cartel's inner circle. Faces, aliases, timelines, lieutenants, spies, drug lords, and former sex slaves.

"What in the lord's sweaty balls am I looking at?" He scrolls, pauses, scrolls again, and shakes his head.

I know that face. I wore it myself years ago, staring at the same profiles, realizing the story I thought I knew was only half the truth and the dangerous half at that.

The further I dug into Restrepo and The Shadow Collection, the more the ground shifted under my feet. Every assumption I carried shattered.

Watching Wolf process it now is like seeing the moment a lock turns, confusion giving way to pattern, disbelief sharpening into understanding.

He finally looks over at me, eyes bright and unsettled, mouth caught between a grin and a scowl.

Yeah. That's the face he makes when the world just got bigger and meaner and a hell of a lot more complicated.

"This isn't right." He shoots me a confused glare. "Cartels don't do this. They run countries like dictators and rule through fear. They traffic people, slaughter families, and make gory examples out of disobedience."

"That reputation is cultivated."

"Cultivated?" He scoffs.

"Maintained. Aggressively." I point to a page of my notes that he's hovering over. "They keep the enemies at bay by letting the world believe they're exactly what the world expects. It keeps

jag

rivals cautious and governments predictable."

"These operations..." Wolf scrolls again, stops, and reads deeper. "They're not profit-driven."

"No. They're surgical."

"They're *hunting* human sex traffickers."

"Yep. Erasing them, one by one."

"That's not how the world works."

"It does for them." I sit back. "The Shadow Collection is the name everyone fears. But privately, they call themselves The Freedom Fighters."

"They're vigilantes." He blinks. "They're the good guys."

"Good? Not exactly. They're ruthless, bloodthirsty, avenging criminals. They'll do anything and kill anyone to protect their cause."

The words hang there while he reads on, cross-checking and confirming with his own instincts.

I see the moment it clicks. Not comfort or approval. Clarity. The world isn't simple. Monsters wear many faces, and sometimes the scariest mask keeps the real heroes hidden.

"Let me get this straight." Wolf slumps in the chair. "They play the villain so the villains don't see them coming."

"Exactly. If you're wondering why Matias Restrepo personally answered my call, it's because you don't ignore people who can tell the difference."

"This changes things."

"It doesn't. It explains them."

"No wonder you traded your life to them. They're hunting predators, killing them, and protecting girls who'd otherwise disappear. That's basically your whole résumé." He lifts both eyebrows, half-grin, half-disbelief. "Bet you couldn't sign up fast enough."

Anger ignites so fast it snaps my teeth together.

"This isn't a punchline." I slam my fist on the table.

He stills.

"I didn't want this. I fought it. For fucking years." I surge to my feet and shove my hands in my hair. "I tried every other path. Every angle. Every shadow route that didn't end with them. Then you came along, and I was suddenly out of excuses."

"You made the decision believing Dove would be safe with me. That she'd be protected."

"Yeah. I surrendered my life to the cartel with the conviction that I would *never* drag her or you into it."

"Oh, shit." Understanding flares in his eyes. "The night you sneaked onto the island, when you said goodbye..."

"Yeah. I'd just signed myself over."

"Fuck. You were really fucking leaving. Severing ties forever." He exhales, stunned. "You didn't want us anywhere near this."

"No, I fucking didn't. The consequences aren't theoretical. They're permanent." I tap the screen and meet his eyes. "Everything I'm showing you makes you a target. If they know you understand this, really understand it, you're exposed."

"So they treat their vigilante secret like contraband. Got it."

"I'm the only outsider who knows the true nature of their operation." My heart hammers. "And now you."

"Why does the Capo of Consequences want me to come with you?"

"He collects deadly skill sets."

"I kill bad family members. My mother. Dove's father. Is that my flex?"

"You took down Adrian Crowe with a hidden razor blade in your mouth."

"Sure did." He brushes imaginary dust off his shoulder.

"As much as I hate it, you're dragged into this, and I need you to be prepared. I want you to read the inner circle's histories, memorize their faces and aliases, and know their weaknesses. Because keeping you in the dark isn't protection. It'll just get you killed slower."

"I hear you." He refocuses on the screen, seeing the implications clearly now. "Say it again for my sanity. They won't hurt Dove?"

"They won't touch her. Most of them have been tortured by the worst monsters imaginable." I take control of the keyboard and pull up a diagram. "This is the org chart of the inner circle. Twenty-two trauma-bonded members, each with their own horror story."

jag

RESTREPO CARTEL - INNER CIRCLE
aliases: The Shadow Collection, The Freedom Fighters

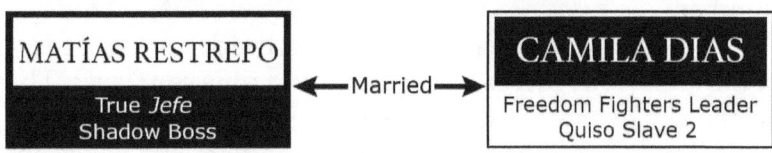

LEGACY POWER & BLOODLINES

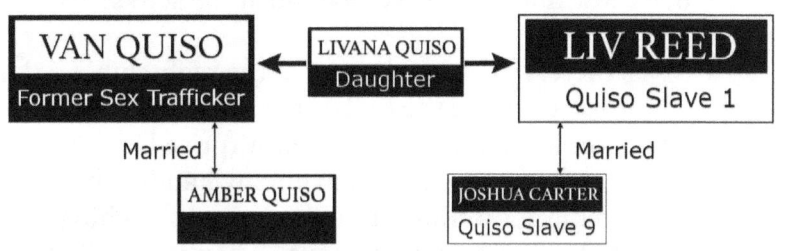

ENFORCEMENT

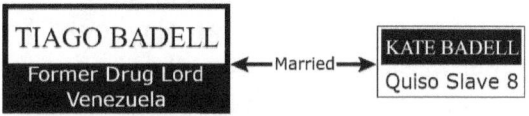

INTELLIGENCE / COUNTER-SURVEILLANCE

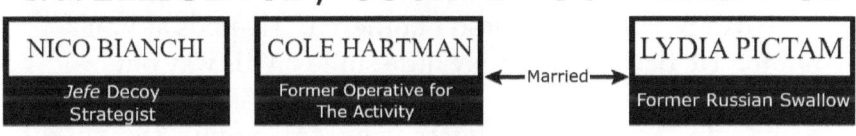

SPIES / UNDERCOVER OPS

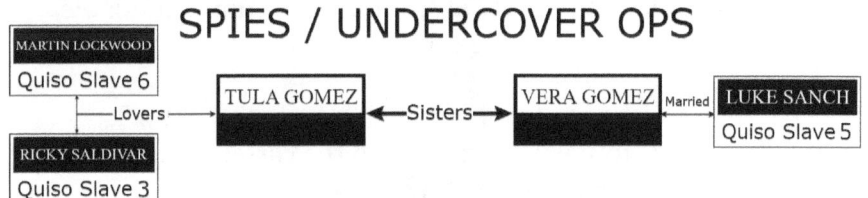

OPERATIVES

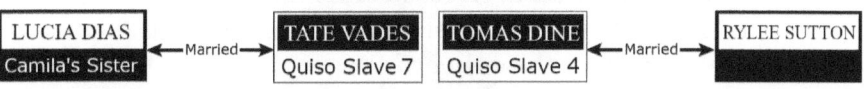

He scans the chart I painstakingly compiled over the years, his attention landing on the unexpected anomalies.

"What does this mean?" He points to the labels attached to nine of the members. "They all say *Quiso Slave,* followed by a number."

"Van Quiso is a former human sex trafficker. Over the span of his inglorious career in Texas, he had nine sex slaves. They're all active vigilantes in the cartel's inner circle."

I flip through the photos of each member and pause on Van Quiso's scarred face.

"Oh, I know him." He waves a hand at the screen.

"What?"

"He was there. In the VIP lounge at the nightclub. Looking all tall and scary, chewing the hell out of a toothpick." He narrows his eyes at me. "You don't look surprised."

"The cartel does *not* want me in enemy hands. They would've been there running surveillance and sketching a retrieval plan. A clean, patient retrieval. Then you walked in. Wearing a bomb."

Wolf lets out a quiet breath.

"You didn't follow a playbook," I say. "Didn't wait for permission, backup, or other options. You saw the problem and cut straight through it."

"I skipped a few steps."

"You showed them how it's done."

"Bad Boy Supreme wasn't bothered." He nods at Van's photo. "He flashed me a sexy little smile on his way out."

"I'm sure he did. He's a terrible flirt but also deeply devoted to his wife." I steeple my fingers against my mouth, thinking. "This is the play. We'll get Dove. That part's non-negotiable. After that, they'll try to bargain for you, but I'll secure your freedom."

"Yeah, that's a *no* from me. We're not splitting up."

"You want to stay with me? With the cartel?" I hold his gaze until the heat burns. "What about Dove?"

The silence is instant.

He opens his mouth, closes it, and looks away.

"You don't have an answer." I drop a hand on his thigh and squeeze. "And that's the answer."

His jaw works, his frustration loud.

"The Russians can't stay on the island." I turn back to the

keyboard.

"I'll handle it."

"Tomorrow, when I call Restrepo back, I'll line up our meeting and go from there. Until then, you need to sleep, eat, and study those profiles. In that order."

"And you?"

I don't look away from the screen. "I'll run through every contingency and plan accordingly."

"Do you like it?" He watches my hands move on the keyboard. "The hacking? The coding? All of it?"

"Yeah. I do." I stare at the streaming algorithms. "But I've always wanted to use it differently. For people who don't have power. The innocent ones who get taken and killed because no one's watching."

"You know… If you hadn't joined the cartel, that fake video of Dove would've been real. Crowe would've taken her. Not the cartel."

"I know."

"That's what you'll be doing with them. Bigger missions. Rescuing more girls like Dove."

"Yes."

"But to do that…" He sighs. "You have to give up Dove."

"And you." My chest hurts. "There's no way out of this."

"The ultimate sacrifice." He watches me carefully.

"That's the cost."

"We'll see." His eyes narrow. "Speaking of your special skills… How did you know what I did to the doctor? When we first met, you were very specific about the details."

"I bugged the tattoo parlor."

"Yeah, I found your camera in the new sheetrock."

"Before that. When I bought the place. I wired it so I could keep tabs on it while I lived in California." I lick my lips. "When you started working there six months ago, I watched. And listened. A lot."

"Pervert." His mouth twitches.

"One night, you were there late, working alone, and Monty came in. He tried to get you to talk about the doctor."

"I remember." He closes his eyes. "I told him I cut the bitch into pieces, and there was nothing left to discuss." He opens one eye and looks at me sideways. "You're such a creepy stalker."

"I'm efficient."

"Unhinged."

"Effective."

"You know that's not normal." He grins.

"You know you're not normal." I grin back.

"I'm aware."

"Normal doesn't keep people alive."

"You win." He yawns mid-breath, jaw stretching, exhaustion clinging to the creases in his beautiful face.

"That's it." I stand and power off the monitors. "Bedtime."

"Every part of me says *yes*."

We head upstairs, the house unnervingly quiet. At the landing, uncertainty plants my feet. I know this guest house, memorized its blind spots, entry points, and every room. Two bedrooms. One choice too many.

He doesn't give me time to decide.

Capturing my wrist, he steers me down the hall, opens his bedroom door, and gestures me inside.

"You've been alone for too damn long." He toes off his shoes. "You're not sleeping by yourself tonight."

Relief funnels through me, and a contained little thrill hums under my skin. I feel younger for it. Reckless in a way that doesn't end with bloodstains under my fingernails.

We shed our shirts and leave on our lounge pants, drawing a line neither of us pretends doesn't exist. My gaze catches anyway.

Wolf's chest, pale and quilted with scars, is devastating. It doesn't take away from his stunning perfection. It tells a story of strength and resilience, one I hope to hear more about someday.

I stare too long, and he notices.

"You know how it happened." He rubs his thumb over a raised, pink line near his hipbone.

"Your journal." I soften my eyes, relaying compassion and admiration the best way I know how.

"Will you tell me how you got yours?" He eases into my space and runs a palm over the stab wound beneath my rib cage.

"Before Adrian Crowe saw me as a weapon to use, he saw me as a loose end. He tried to kill me more times than I can count." I rest a hand over Wolf's on my scar. "This is the only time he got close enough to do it himself."

His eyes widen. "The night in the California tavern? Your

meeting with him?"

"You listened to the audio file."

"Yeah. You wouldn't take his offer." His jaw hardens. "So the cunt shanked you?"

"Got me good, but I survived."

And he didn't, thanks to Wolf.

"Come on." I shut off the lights, dropping the room into shadow.

We slide into bed and turn onto our sides, facing each other. Close enough to feel body warmth. Not near enough to touch. The space between us thrums, and neither of us moves.

"There's something I need to say." He inches toward me until his legs rest against mine. "I don't want commentary. Just... Hear me out."

I stay still.

"We both love Dove." He clears his throat. "And I love fairy tales."

I swallow, knowing where this is going.

"You know my family." He watches me in the dark. "Four people. Married. It works. It's my normal. A three-way situation isn't wild in my world. It's a plus-one plus-one. You plus Dove plus me. That's the math, if you're wondering where we're headed. The cartel notwithstanding."

"Dove hates me."

He tsks softly. "She hates what she thinks you are. When you tell her about Celeste's promise and every ugly choice and sacrifice you made to keep her alive, she's going to fall into your arms." A velvet whisper. "And your bed."

My pulse thuds as longing gathers low and fierce, a dangerous bloom. The images form, uninvited and vivid, the three of us tangled, kissing and sucking and fucking. My body reacts before my discipline can shut it down, quickening my breath and hardening my dick.

"This isn't a fate you can control." He brushes his fingers along my erection and pulls me flush against him. "It's going to happen."

I lie there in his arms, jaw locked and blood pumping, wishing, hoping, praying he's right.

"I did some online shopping." His voice is soft, the edges blunted by sleep. "You'll have clothes by tomorrow."

I stiffen. His fashion sense only works because it's him. On me, it would be absurd. I'm bracing for sequins, leotards, Hawaiian prints, things that require confidence I don't possess.

"Relax." He squeezes my ass, affectionate and infuriating. "I behaved."

"I don't believe you."

"I got you denim." He yawns. "The straight-leg variety that says *I pay taxes* and nothing else. Black jeans that look identical to the blue ones, you know, for when you want options without emotional risk. Plain crew-neck tees in all the aggressively normal colors. Henleys with buttons, but only a few. We're not animals. Socks in thrilling, electrifying beige. Work boots, stomp-approved. Boxer briefs, boner-approved. Dark hoodie with pockets for secrets, and so many more uninspiring pieces. You'll fit in just fine with all the other boring white people."

"You shouldn't have done that." My shoulders ease.

"Full disclosure. Dove is a way better shopping experience."

"I bet." I trail my fingers along his jaw, slow and grateful. "Thank you. I've been living out of a bag so long I forgot what it's like to have options."

"I know, darling." He closes his eyes, halfway gone. "I had my tattoo supplies sent to the island. Just in case."

The offer sits there, open-ended and waiting. I don't let myself imagine the unfinished ink lines finding their way home, but my pulse kicks up anyway.

Slowly, quietly, he drifts off to sleep. I catalog the small things because that's how my brain works. The cadence of his breathing, the warmth building between our fused bodies, and the feel of his soft cock against my thigh. I don't move. The promise alone is enough.

Two decades of sleeping with one eye open have taught me not to want this. Wanting makes mistakes. Wanting gives enemies a handle.

Tonight, wanting feels like permission.

I breathe in his wild wolf scent, energized and oddly calm, as I drift off, thinking about his plus-one plus-one fairy tale.

wolfson
SIXTY-TWO

The Ghost and Mikhail are already gone when I wake. One less thing to manage.

I'll send gift baskets to thank them for their service. Later.

Today has one priority. Learn the inner circle's innies and outies.

I start after breakfast and read until my eyes cross. Then I keep going.

Profiles stack on profiles. Faces blur until I force myself to slow down. I learn the rhythm of them, their habits, their tells, who trusts whom, and who sleeps with whom. I memorize tattoos and scars, the way mouths tilt when they lie. I build a mental lineup and walk it again. And again.

Nine of them were kidnapped and forced into sexual slavery.

Nine human beings broken under Van Quiso when he was at his worst. The details make my jaw ache. I wouldn't have believed redemption was possible if the file didn't trace the arc all the way back to Van's childhood. Neglect, coercion, and cruelty I know too well. The trauma doesn't excuse it. But it explains a lot.

This inner circle is a nightmare split down the middle, monsters on one side, and the people they hurt on the other, all bound together in a tribe that shouldn't work.

The world's worst criminals stand shoulder to shoulder with their victims. It makes my brain itch.

I scroll back to Van Quiso's photo. Scar down his face. Eyes like steel blades. A man who learned too late what his hands had become and chose to use them differently.

Against my better judgment, a grin creeps in.

I want to meet him.

Across the room, Jag is chained to his keyboard, the keys ticking and chair shifting. He shaved today and pulled on his new clothes with an inappropriate amount of appreciation in his eyes.

I haven't had time to explore that appreciation. We pass each other for water. Food appears and disappears untouched. We trade looks, not words.

Everything funnels toward the call.

The hours crowd in, dragging and pressing. The waiting gnaws. I feel it in my teeth, my hands, and the way my leg won't stop bouncing. By the time the sun sets, I've chewed a hole in my cheek.

Jag finally lifts his head. "Time."

I cross the room and sit beside him, letting our knees touch. My nerves light up the second I stop moving. My shoulders tense. My hands don't know where to land. My pulse keeps skipping even though nothing has happened yet.

Jag, meanwhile, might as well be made of stone. His face gives nothing away. No tension around his mouth. No tell in his eyes.

He reaches for equipment, swaps phones, flips a switch on a small box, types a string of nonsense, pauses, deletes, and starts again.

The laptop screen fractures into windows within windows, timers, hashes, and a map that isn't a map. Numbers roll and invert. Fucking witchcraft.

Then he waits exactly long enough for my skin to crawl.

I hook my fingers together to keep them from shaking and lean back in the chair, trying to match his stillness. It doesn't work. My leg starts up again.

Jag glances at me and sets a steady hand on my knee.

Then he presses a button.

The call begins. Not with a ring, but with silence. Thick,

waiting silence.

I hold my breath.

Then...

"Wolf?" Her voice cuts through the speaker, soft and real and alive.

I flatten a hand against the thunder in my chest, ordering my heart to calm down.

"I'm here, Bluebird." I lean toward the console, elbows on my knees, and meet Jag's molten amber gaze.

"Okay. Good." She exhales on the other end, a sound I desperately miss. "I was starting to worry you'd do something dramatic."

"Never." I give Jag an innocent look. "I'm all restraint and safety first."

He pinches the bridge of his nose.

"That's a lie." A smile teases her voice. "But listen to me. I'm safe. I'm healthy. I'm... Comfortable."

I glance sideways at Jag. He hasn't moved, but his jaw tightens.

"This place... It's not what you think. I'm not scared. Not hurt. No one's touched me."

"It's been eleven days." My lungs finally start working again.

"Yeah. I know. But they've kept me busy. There's a garage. Like, you wouldn't believe the cars. The food is crazy good. And the women?" She inhales. "They're terrifying in the best way. Badass doesn't cover it."

I close my eyes, picturing Liv Reed, Camila Dias, the Gomez sisters, and Lydia the former Russian operative... Yeah. Those women don't survive things. They go to war.

"Don't worry about me. I..." Her hesitation snaps my eyes open. "Is he there?"

Jag's expression fractures in a way I've never seen. Raw relief. Bottomless love. And regret. His sadness is so heavy it darkens everything else.

"Yeah. He's here." I find his hand on his thigh and lace our fingers together. "He can hear you."

"Oh." She pauses as if rearranging herself. "I don't know what's going on. Not all of it. Probably not even a sliver of it. But I know whatever this is, it involves you saving my life. Again. I have so many questions, but I was given very specific instructions about what I can and can't say on this line, so I'm trying not to screw that up."

"I'm coming for you." His voice breaks.

"I know. That's the one thing I've always been able to count on." She draws in a breath, and it comes out choppy. "I've had time to think, and after talking with some new friends, I've been able to look back, see things differently, and sort out pieces I couldn't line up before. But when I see you again, you better fucking be straight with me. About all of it."

"I will." He glances down at his hand and discreetly lifts his smallest finger. "I swear it."

"He's staring at his pinkie." I grip it and bring it to my mouth. "From here on out, we tell the truth."

She makes an un-Dove-like whimpering sound and coughs to cover it up.

"When you come for me..." Her voice wobbles. "I want you united. The way I know you want to be."

I clutch Jag's hand, and he stares back at me, stunned.

"What are you saying?" I tilt my head.

"Is he trustworthy?" she asks.

I remember our conversation the night before she was taken, when she admitted she could've shared me with Jag... If he were trustworthy.

"That's a stupidly easy *yes*. He's solid and proven all the way down." I take a breath. "There's so much you don't know yet. So many things we'll tell you when we see you."

"Yeah. I'm quickly realizing that the not-knowing part is the main issue." She sniffs. "But you trust him, and I trust you. So what you choose to do together won't hurt me. Just... Don't forget about me. Because I'm not stepping aside."

"Sweet Bird..." I laugh, breathless and wrecked, tears prickling behind my eyes. "There is no version of reality where there's an us without you. You're the whole point."

She smiles into the line. I can't hear it, but I know all her pauses.

"Do you have clothes? Shoes?" I ask.

"Yeah. The women here have been gracious. I have plenty to wear."

"Are you alone right now?"

"No. There's a terrifying, flesh-eating overlord standing over me, listening to every word while casually picking at a platter of dead puppies."

"*Despídete ya, chino*," Matias Restrepo growls in the background.

She giggles. Fucking giggles. The sound is so unexpected, I choke on my tongue. Jag and I lock eyes, wide and stunned, both of us frozen until she speaks again.

"He has a reputation to maintain," she whispers. Another giggle. Then... "I'm going to let you go before he pops a blood vessel. I love you. Both of you."

Jag clamps a hand over his mouth and squeezes his eyes shut, trying to hold himself together. The fearsome *Vigilante* is absolutely one breath away from tears.

Movement sounds on the line as a presence slides in and takes over the air.

"Tomorrow at dusk," the *jefe* says, clipped and unmistakably in charge. "Same as last time."

The call disconnects.

Jag lowers his hand, eyes damp and breath ragged. I stare at him, this brilliant, ruthless man undone by a giggle and three words of love, while my heart tries to beat itself out of my chest.

She's safe. Comfortably safe. We'll see her tomorrow, and until then...

What you choose to do together won't hurt me.

The strain that's been pulling between us for a month finally snaps.

We move at the same time and collide in a crash of mouths. Desperate and uncoordinated, the kiss seethes with hunger, relief, and everything we've been ignoring.

His hand flies to my hair. Mine fists in the waistband of his jeans. We consume each other with tongues and teeth, and the past eleven days drain out of me in a rush. Fear, pressure, the constant stab of *what if*, it all bleeds away beneath the unwavering assault of his lips.

His mouth dominates, and mine answers with equal fervor. We stumble, knock into furniture, and everything narrows to the rhythm of us breathing and grinding together.

The destination doesn't matter as long as it includes bare skin and something solid under us.

We stay fused as we stagger toward the stairs, hands grabbing and ripping fabric. Every step is clumsy and urgent.

Jeans, shirts, boxers, our discarded clothes mark our path until there are none left.

Midway up the stairs, he starts to reach for my cock and freezes. His eyes find mine as he struggles for breath.

"Don't stop." I trap him against the wall, grab his hand, and close his fingers around my aching shaft. "If I spiral, you'll pull me back."

"Wolf."

"Jag."

"We'll go slow." He twists his wrist in a long, unhurried stroke.

"Sweet hell." I rock my hips, pumping into his fist. "I give it thirty seconds."

My hands roam across the wide plane of his chest, over boulders of shoulders and bulges of biceps. I learn the shape and texture of his strong throat, pausing to feel his pulse kick under my fingers. His jaw flexes against my palm, muscle and tendon straining as we devour each other in a wet, obscene, open-mouth kiss.

He's all man, rock-hard and battle-tested, as he jerks me with a practiced hand. No wasted motion. Nothing held back.

I want him. I'm on fucking fire for him. But I don't know what that means.

Who will fuck whom? I've never done consensual anal. It's probably a trigger-heavy zone. I know he's bottomed, but that was when he was turning tricks on the street.

The Jag standing before me, with his broad-shouldered, well-endowed, very masculine, very naked body flexing under my questing hands, is not a bottom.

He drives me back a step, then another, his grip firm on my ass as he turns us on the stairs. The world tips. He lowers me to the steps and brackets me there with his muscle-packed weight, knocking the air from my lungs.

His breath fans hot against my face, his eyes swirling with fierce need. He's starving, and all his restraint is finally giving way.

His mouth leaves mine to trace a steamy path along my throat and collarbone, reverent and relentless. I feel his urgency in the heavy hardness pulsing against my hip. I grip him, running my fingers along his length as his attention travels lower, lower, until his dick pulls from my grasp.

wolfson

Shifting down a few steps, he settles between my legs and scatters hungry kisses along my inner thighs. When he reaches my balls, he stops.

"Who has put their mouth here?" He pets and nuzzles my cock, making me groan.

"Dove."

A smile twitches his cheek. "No one else?"

"No."

"I haven't done this in a long time."

"Then don't."

"I was never forced, pup. But I never wanted to do it. Not until now."

wolfson
SIXTY-THREE

Tingles ripple through me, scattering shockwaves across my skin, as Jag lowers his head.

His mouth stretches, and his tongue swirls, sliding over my crown like a jaguar lapping blood from a fresh kill.

"Fuck!" I gasp, legs opening and hips thrusting, moving of their own volition.

Then he puts his lips in motion, and holy mother, he sucks me. The force and pull of his mouth sends my ass off the stairs, but his hands clamp me back down.

His tongue lashes without mercy, and the delicious heat of his throat drives me insane. I can't hold still, can't catch my breath, can't stop the orgasm from slamming into me.

"Jag, I'm coming." I yank on his hair in urgent warning. "I'm fucking coming."

He doesn't relent. I thrash and groan and fuck his mouth until I'm spent.

I don't know what I expected from the notorious hacker, but I didn't think he'd devour me so completely.

"Damn." He leans back, licking his lips. "That's the first time I ever enjoyed that."

"Did I even last thirty seconds?"

"Not even close." He smirks.

"I'm so turned on right now."

"Ready to go again?" He slaps my cock and watches it thicken. "Already? Now I feel old."

"Are you usually one and done?"

"Yeah. Sex was always a job. A means to an end."

"Not anymore."

"No." His hand cups the back of my head. "Not anymore." He pulls me in for a languorous kiss.

Without breaking apart, we rise and stumble up the stairs, groping each other's cocks. Slowly, clumsily, we make it to the bedroom, bumping into the wall with stops and starts and ceaseless kissing and touching.

I push him toward the bed, fraught with nerves and desire. "My turn to suck you."

"No." He braces his feet, unmoving. "Your journal... He forced himself down your throat."

"That's the past. I want the future."

I need him to impale me on his cock and fuck me until I forget. I want his filthy commands in my ear as he fills me with hot come and sweet memories.

"I'm not going to fuck you. Not your throat. Not your ass." He reaches between us and palms my erection. "Not tonight."

"I hate that for you. Try again."

"Don't be a brat. We'll try something safe tonight." He grips himself with his free hand and strokes us in tandem. "Something new for both of us."

"I'm listening." I cling to his shoulders as fresh need spikes fast, driving my hips and working myself in his grip.

"Do you have lube?" He kisses my lips, my neck, his hand never slowing between my legs.

"Bathroom."

We separate long enough to cross the room and file into the en suite. I perch on the edge of the counter and glance at his tattoo.

Jaguar claws curl protectively around a feathered heart, fully healed. The composition, the restraint, the promise of what's coming... I love how good it looks.

My gaze lifts to his. "I want to finish it."

"Yes, with my hands on you."

We share a moment of eye contact, panting, muscles tense, ready to tear each other apart. The release he gave me feels like a preview, just enough to light every nerve on fire.

He finds the lube in the first drawer he opens.

"Is this yours?" He squirts a generous glob into his palm.

"It's a throwback to when Frankie shared this place with the pillow humpers."

He rubs his palms together and greases up my cock.

His divine mastery of my anatomy, the speed at which his hands work me into a lather, and the promise glinting in his heavy-lidded eyes... Damn it all. This is torture.

"Sweet suffering balls." My legs shake, and my head falls back on my shoulders. "You're a dick-whispering wizard."

"And you're my—"

"Does that sentence end in *magic wand?*"

"Maybe." He traps a smile between his front teeth.

"Cute. How about I do the jokes, and you do—" I shudder in the cruel squeeze of his fist. "*That.*"

"Let's switch places."

He doesn't release my cock as we circle each other, trading ground and pressing closer. He stops at the sink, turns his back to me, and drags his hands down his inner thighs, rubbing the remainder of the lube into his skin.

Thrown by what he's doing, I stare at the twin dimples above his sculpted ass.

The set of his shoulders, the lubrication along the inside of his legs, and the way he doesn't look back to check if I'm following...

It's an invitation.

But for what exactly?

Charged and buzzing, I press into the space he's offering. "What are the rules of engagement here?"

"Keep your dick out of my ass. Neither of us is ready for that." His chiseled glutes clench as he stands rod straight. "Everything else is up for grabs."

"Everything?" I reach around and grab the thick base of his erection, making him groan.

I slot my body behind his, my chest snug against his back. Since we're the same height and similar build, my chin fits easily on his shoulder.

In the mirror, our reflections line up, two silhouettes sharing one shape, edges matching where they meet. The alignment makes it easy to fit my dick into the tight, lubricated crease between his powerful thighs.

Then it dawns on me.

"This is the safe thing you want to try." I give an experimental thrust, testing the friction.

"Fuck yeah," he breathes.

"You've never done this?" I lock an arm around his chest and kick my hips, grinding into it.

"Never." He strengthens his spine, crosses his legs at the ankles, and squeezes my dick with his adductor muscles. "Pound away, Wolf."

The warm, lubed-up pocket beneath his taint is so fucking narrow. I slam my hips faster and harder, my arm restraining him against me as I bear down on him. I jerk him with my free hand, and his breathing goes wild.

"You're almost as tight as your sister," I rasp in his ear.

He releases a guttural groan and reaches a hand back to claw at my flexing butt. His other hand curls around my fist on his dick and shows me the pressure and pace he wants.

"Feels so fucking good." My muscles shake with the need to come. "What do you get out of this?"

"The perineum..." He gasps, shaking violently as his body surges into our combined fists. "It's a nerve-rich pleasure center." Another strangled gasp. "Massive orgasmic potential."

"What do we call this? Screwing the gooch? Tapping the taint? Grinding the grundle?"

"The slow burn."

I'm burning, all right. Sweat beads my forehead, and volcanic pressure builds in my balls.

"Please, tell me you're close." I meet his eyes in the mirror.

"Waiting for you." He jerks our hands faster on his dick and hisses past clenched teeth.

He's fucking magnificent. The power in his physique, the hunger in his eyes, and the brutal girth of him in my fist.

"Mine." I hold his stare in the mirror and sink my teeth into the curve of his neck, breaking skin.

We fall over the edge together, bucking, groaning, spurting onto the floor, and coming undone. Pleasure tunnels through me, wave after wave, liquefying my legs and starving the room of air.

The musky, intoxicating scent of our sex chases my inhales as I collapse against his back, exhausted and sated.

When I can finally breathe again, I lift my head and find him staring at his neck in the mirror.

A bloody bruise rises there, darkening fast and spreading under the skin like a storm finding shape. It imprints him quietly, a bloom of color that says, *Mine*.

The day you tattooed me, you said something that stuck." He traces a finger around the bite mark. "You said when this tug of war turns on me…"

"You would already have my teeth in your throat." I rest my chin on his shoulder. "Regrets?"

"With you? None."

"Tomorrow." I kiss the hinge of his jaw. "We'll get her back. Then you can face your regrets with her and stop punishing yourself without her."

His shoulders stay rigid, and his hand curls on the counter. He wants the same future I want, but he doesn't know how to believe in it.

He'll catch up.

We shower off our mess, shut off the lights, and fall into bed, foregoing clothes. I curl on my side and fit myself against him, head tucked into his chest. I don't ask. I just follow my instincts and go where my body decides it belongs.

It feels bold and brave, my way of claiming intimacy with this hard-edged, seemingly untouchable man. But he doesn't flinch. Instead, he sinks his fingers into my hair and combs through the wet strands.

"You didn't spiral." His nails scrape my scalp. "What's up with those triggers?"

"You didn't make it weird this time."

"I didn't make it weird the first time."

"You had a fever, no working hands, a creaky cot, bad breath—"

"Now you're being a dick."

"Yeah." I sigh. "I don't know why it didn't set me off this time. My triggers don't follow rules. Just like me."

"What did you do after your last panic attack?"

"I wrote the journal. Ironic, huh? My reaction to you prompted me to put my story into words for the first time." My eyes close. "Then I let Dove read it."

"And after?"

"I stopped hiding. I let my family see the scars and read what I survived. It changed how I see myself in the wreckage."

"Maybe that's why the panic didn't sneak in this time. You emptied what you were carrying instead of letting it pile up. Gave the fear fewer places to hide."

"Maybe."

"Tell me something." He adjusts beneath me, getting comfortable. "Something about your life in the Arctic that isn't in the journal."

I think for a second and reach for a day I've never put on paper or said out loud.

"After I killed my mother for abusing Leo, Denver had to leave on a final supply run before the long winter. Leo sneaked me into a shipping crate before it was loaded onto the bush plane. I was eight."

Jag's fingers slow in my hair.

"The dumb animal was hellbent on my escape and gave me precise instructions. When the plane lands, sneak away. Find help. Don't think about him or Kody or Hoss ever again." I loosen a breath. "I waited in that box for hours, felt it get dragged onto the plane, and heard Leo tell Denver I'd run off into the hills because I couldn't handle what I'd done to my mother. But when the engine kicked on, I knew what would happen. Denver would return to Hoss, find me gone for good, and hurt my brothers until someone broke."

I shift, remembering the cold fear, the terrible choice.

"You didn't go." Jag strokes a supportive hand along my spine.

"I jumped out before Denver took off and told him everything. I blamed it all on Leo. Said he put me in the box and told me how to escape."

"Were you afraid he'd punish Leo for that?"

"Yeah, but not the way you think. I knew Denver would punish him by hurting me. Kin punishment." I stare at the dark. "He heated a knife in the fire, held me down, and pressed it across my chest. Leo screamed louder than I did. I hated that part."

"Goddammit, Wolf." Jag's breath hitches as he hauls me

closer.

"You can't see the burn mark anymore. It's buried under everything else. But I feel it sometimes and remember the choice I made. A choice I never regretted."

"You think I'll put you in a proverbial box and send you away from the cartel?"

"You'll try. I'll respond. Act surprised later if you want."

"You don't know what you're signing up for."

"That ship sailed. I already signed on the line. Paperwork's done. Let me draw you a picture."

I tell him everything from the second I walked into the tattoo parlor and saw the carnage. I tell him how the fear hit, then the panic, then the helpless fury, how I flipped between blaming him and grieving him, and how I tore through Sitka, street by street, dock by dock, screaming their names. I tell him how I cracked, how I couldn't breathe, couldn't eat, couldn't sleep, and how my world imploded. Then it shattered again when I found his computer equipment, the videos, all the reasons I strapped on a bomb and pulled him out of hell.

"I know the cost, Jag, because I already paid it."

"I'm sorry." He bows his head to my shoulder, breath stuttering, grief heavy in his voice. "So damn sorry."

I don't want his apology. I want his commitment.

love
SIXTY-FOUR

Rotors chop the wet air as a shape breaks through the green ceiling of the rainforest. I stand at the edge of the helipad, my bare toes curling against the painted ring and my stomach writhing with nerves.

Humidity slicks my skin, damp and sticky, heavy with the promise of rain. I'm standing in the steamy bowels of a jungle, so sweat is a given.

Twelve days. That's how long I've been inside the cartel's citadel.

From the pad, the fortress looks unreal. White marble and glass rise out of endless green. Bulletproof panes wrap the exterior. Cameras dot the eaves. Motion sensors click in places I can't see.

Nothing here is decorative. Iris scanners, hidden shutters, war rooms... This isn't a home pretending to be safe. It's safety pretending to be a home. A vault wearing silk gloves.

And somehow, it hasn't been terrible.

That thought still surprises me.

The cartel is terrifying the way storms are terrifying. Vast, organized, and indifferent to anything in their path. But the twenty-two in the inner circle? They're something else.

love

Dangerous, yes. Also watchful, protective, and affectionate in a silent-but-deadly way.

They're a family that has meals together. Laughter that comes fast and loud. Arguments that end with hands on shoulders and knives put away.

They took me in without asking me to cower or pretend. They made room and made me feel safe.

Safe.

Not a word I expected to associate with a cartel. They've kept their secrets from me, but I've put together enough to see the truth. They're far more complex than the villains they want the world to believe they are.

If I'm honest, really honest, I like it here. A lot.

The only thing missing is Wolf. And Jag's constant vigilance.

The helicopter drops lower, and the wind whips my hair loose from its braid. The pad vibrates under my feet, and my nerves skitter, excitement and relief tangling in my chest. My heart thunders as the skids kiss the concrete and the engine begins to wind down.

The doors swing open.

Jag steps out first, all lean muscle and dark violence, his eyes mapping exits and angles before landing on me.

I shiver beneath the familiar, over-protective inquisition of his gaze as he scans me head to toe.

Wolf hops down next, bright as a flare, holding a bottle of vodka. One of Kody's special reserves, no doubt.

Black eyeliner rings his arctic blue eyes. Denim cut-offs ride low on his hips, and a black leather corset cinches him tight. Over it, a sheer white lace robe floats and snaps in the rotor wash, brushing against daisy-printed rain boots that have no business being that cute on a cartel helipad.

He scans the pad, one quick pass, and his eyes lock on me.

The smile is instant.

It lifts his cheeks and tunnels straight through my ribs, electrocuting and melting everything inside me.

The mob boss Matias breezes past me, his long-legged strides eating up the distance to the helicopter. I dart forward, but he reaches Wolf and Jag first, grips Jag's offered handshake, and stops short when he clocks the bottle in Wolf's fist.

"Vodka." Wolf lifts it in a lazy salute.

"We drink tequila here." Matias accepts the gift with an arched brow.

"Not after this."

Laughter ripples through the men nearby. Even the air seems to lighten.

Wolf passes Matias off to Jag with a flick of his wrist and turns back to me like there was never any other destination.

I cross the pad in a run, and he meets me halfway, arms opening wide. I barely have time to breathe before his hands catch my hips and lift me off the ground. I laugh a girlish sound that turns into a squeal, as he spins us, the world blurring into white stone and green jungle.

He smacks his lips all over my face, covering my cheeks, my temples, and the corners of my mouth, no aim, no restraint, just pure joy poured out in kisses.

"I missed you." He slows to a stop and lowers my feet to the ground. "From rifles and wedding gowns to tiny pancakes and beyond, I love you."

"I love *you*, my darling wolf." I fist my fingers in the lace at his shoulders, inhaling his Alaskan scents of vodka, leather, and smoke, the familiar wildness of him untying me at the seams.

His mouth fuses to mine, and it's a starburst of fire and light, a breath that feels like apology, and a compass needle spinning past directions that no longer feel like home. My heart knows the way, and it will forever and always point me back to him, back to the only north my body knows.

The urgency and ache of days spent apart spark between our lips. Breaths of longing stack onto heartbeats of absence. My arms wrap around his neck, and my legs lock around his waist, every muscle and tendon claiming him.

The kiss deepens, consuming my air and giving me his in return. The noise of the citadel drops away, the helicopter, the guards, and the cartel with its dangerous secrets all gone. There's only this. The press of his mouth, the way he holds me with the intent to keep me, and the way my chest finally stops hurting.

When we break apart, our foreheads touch, both of us panting and smiling like lovesick weirdos.

For the first time since I arrived, the place feels complete.

"Let me look at you." I untangle us and step back, taking in his outfit. "Love the look. It's giving... *Safe in your own skin and dangerous to anyone who underestimates you.*"

love

"Checks out. Also..." He nudges the ground with a daisy-printed rain boot. "The forecast called for rain."

"I fucking love you."

"Keep saying it. It'll never get old." His lips quirk. "Speaking of old..."

I follow his gaze over my shoulder and land unerringly on Jag.

Our eyes meet and hold.

He stays back, parking himself a few steps from the helicopter, shoulders drawn in, and hands shoved deep into his pockets. Guilt sits in the hard lines of his face. Relief, too. And other things I can't name because there's so much I don't know.

Too many questions crowd my throat. Too many years of redacted truths and fill-in-the-blanks. The cartel told me nothing, only that everything Jag has done, every choice, every cruelty, was done for me.

I don't know what that means yet. But whatever it is, it took its toll on our relationship.

"He let you believe the worst in him," Wolf says quietly. "Worked really hard to keep his best parts hidden."

"Why?"

"That's between you and him. He has some groveling to do, but when that's done, hear him out, okay?"

"Okay." My pulse quickens.

"Go on. Talk to him. Kiss and make up. But when you're ready to fuck, I want to be there. To watch." He waggles his eyebrows and backs away. "For now, I'm going to mingle and make some *sicarios* uncomfortable."

"Fearless."

"Nah. Just too stubborn to flinch." He spins on his heel and strolls straight into the citadel, arms spread wide, like he's greeting old friends. "Hello, darlings. Who's in charge of hospitality? I'm thirsty and emotionally available."

"What are the odds he'll get us killed?"

I jolt at the sound of Jag's voice right behind me. His breath stirs my hair, too near, too quiet, making my heart tick too fast.

Pushing back my shoulders, I turn to face him.

His gaze tracks Wolf for a half-second before lowering to me. "These people aren't his friends."

"They will be when he's finished with them."

His mouth tilts, and a nod follows.

A cloud of feelings and thoughts piles up in his expression as his eyes rake over me. I see him trying to sort through it, testing sentences in his head and discarding them, his face twitching with the effort to find the right words instead of the wrong ones.

At last, he exhales and meets my stare. "I'm so fucking sorry."

"I don't know what you're apologizing for. The things I know about? Or the things I don't?"

"All of it."

"The night before the cartel took me, you came to the island to say goodbye. Is that because you joined them and agreed to move here?"

"Yes."

"You did it for me? Because someone bad was coming for us? An enemy you and the cartel both want stopped?"

"Yes."

"Are you...?" My breath rushes out as I look him over. "Are you okay? Safe?"

"Yes."

"And you'll be safe here now? In this fortress? Behind your keyboard?"

"Yes."

"That's the extent of what I've pieced together. Everything else is muffled secrets and pressed lips. I'm so fucking sick of living in the dark." I rub my face in frustration. "Will I ever get the entire truth?"

"Yes."

"Say something else, dammit! Something more than *yes*. Tell me where you've been, what you had for breakfast, how many people you killed today." I wave my hands around and let them drop to my sides. "I don't know. Give me something. Anything."

"You look... Good." The compliment scrapes out of him as if he might trigger an explosive argument. Then he straightens and tries again. "You look beautiful."

Well, this is awkward.

I finger the messy blue braid slung over my shoulder, twisting and tucking the loose ends back into the knot.

His gaze tracks the motion, and I wonder if he's thinking about fixing it, unraveling the tangled mess, and starting over. He was always better at that than I was.

love

Out of habit, I glance at his hands and search his fingernails for blood, finding none.

We stand there, hovering too close and not close enough, stranded outside the roles we understand. We know how to be brother and sister, protector and ward, stalker and prey, and enemies with shared baggage.

But this? None of our familiar roles fit in this strange, uneasy space, and neither of us knows how to navigate it.

This could be a new beginning for us. A do-over. A second chance. But only if he opens his mouth and gives me more than one-word answers.

"Jag—"

"I don't want to do this here." His eyes flick past me, clocking every lens tucked into corners and ceilings. "Not in front of cameras." He drags a hand down his face. Then he stands taller and squares his shoulders as if trying to compose himself. "I'm working very hard not to come apart."

"Why? What's wrong?"

"You undo me." His whisper breaks like a confession he hates needing. "You always have, and—" He paces a half-step and turns back. "I need to take a shower and wash the flight off me. Come with me. Please. I can't stand the idea of you leaving my sight right now. After I clean up, I'll tell you everything you want to know."

If that will help him find his footing, I'm all for it.

"Follow me." I turn toward the doors Wolf disappeared through and start walking.

"I'll be honest." He strolls along beside me, eyes darting everywhere. "I expected to find you confined in a soundproof room. You've had free run of this place the entire time?"

"Of course. It's not like I'm sitting in on their meetings."

"This is worrisome." He trails me down a long marble hallway. "If you know too much—"

"I don't know their secrets, but I've gotten to know the inner circle. Some more than others." A smile tugs at my mouth. "I have my favorites."

"Who?"

"Luke and I bonded—"

"Don't finish that sentence."

I narrow my eyes. "We bonded over his hypercar collection."

"He's a deadly..." He glances at a camera. "Man."

"He's married."

"I know."

"I adore his wife Vera."

"Also deadly. She's an underground MMA fighter. I'm talking *fight to the death*."

"Yeah, she's been teaching me self-defense."

"Oh." He blinks.

"Do you know what they call you around here?"

"*El Vigilante.*"

"The Watchman." I nod. "I've heard them whisper other names, too. The Shadow With A Million Cameras. The Hunter Who Never Blinks. My personal favorite is *El Que Ya Sabe.*"

"The One Who Already Knows."

"You've heard these."

"Most of them."

"You've made quite an impression on these people."

"Attention has a price. This one comes with a lifetime contract and no exit clause."

I have so many questions, but I'll hold them until we're alone.

The corridor spills us into the citadel's main artery, a massive atrium with white marble everywhere and floor-to-ceiling windows that offer cinematic views of a jungle so deep it could swallow entire governments. Or in this case, a sprawling cartel fortress.

I hear Wolf before I see him.

"Wait, you're Ricky, and you're Martin, right? All right, be honest. Everybody knows that 'Livin' La Vida Loca' is your go-to song when you're fucking."

I round the corner as Martin flips off Wolf, and Ricky groans.

"Also, I was told you share your woman." Wolf scratches his jaw. "Which means I'm gonna need tips. Strictly academic. How do you decide on positions? Do you draw straws? Rock-paper-scissors? Hypothetically, do you rehearse? Or is it all improv?" He holds up his fist. "Poly kings. Teach me your ways."

They bump him without hesitation.

Jag stiffens beside me, his protective instinct roaring to life. I barely have time to enjoy that before Matias appears at Jag's side.

"A word." He strides away, expecting Jag to follow.

love

"Stay here." He trails Matias into the shadow of a column, keeping me in his line of sight.

I can't hear what Matias says as he gestures and grips Jag's shoulder. Jag nods once, looks away, and nods again. Then he's back at my side, expression shuttered but resolved.

"What did he say?" I stare at Matias's back as he strides out of the room.

"He's giving me a couple of days to focus on you and figure out what we're going to do."

"You mean, what *I* am going to do. Because you can't follow me back to Alaska. This is your life now, right?"

He nods.

"Will they let Wolf and me leave?" I whisper. "Now that we've seen the inside of their citadel?"

"You've only seen what they allowed you to see. For all my intel, I couldn't dig up the schematics of this place. Couldn't even pin down a general location. It's buried deep, deliberately unreachable, as hidden and impossible to find as Wolf's cabin in Hoss."

"You read his journal." A flutter lifts my chest.

"Yeah. The night he left it with me."

I let that sink in as men in dark clothes stream past us, their arms stacked with luggage. Bag after bag after bag. Hard cases, garment bags, duffels, the procession doesn't stop.

"Did Wolf bring the whole island with him?"

"We had words about it." Jag makes an amused sound, cutting through the strain.

"Words?" I glance at him.

"He said while I've been living out of a bag, he's been living out of a rich daddy."

"He's ridiculous."

"He brought his tattoo gear with plans to scar the cartel. Optimistically and artistically. His words."

I snort, watching another tower of cases roll by. "Did you at least bring your computers?"

"No electronics. Cartel rule. They took our phones, too. Wolf complained. Loudly."

"Of course, he did."

Across the atrium, he moves from person to person, making friends and sending the entire room into laughter.

Then he sees Frizz.

One look at the man's stitched mouth, and Wolf grins like he found his people.

"You're a whole vibe." He looks Frizz up and down and lets out a low whistle. "We should absolutely be best friends."

"We can't leave him unsupervised." Jag rubs his brow.

"Probably not."

As if Wolf can hear us, he holds up a finger to his audience and peels away. The room bends around him as he floats toward us, unbothered, luminous, entirely himself.

I missed him so fucking much. He closes the distance, and I feel it everywhere, that mystical force that always pulls me into his orbit.

"Bring it in." Without waiting, he wraps his arms around us and brings himself in. "How's it going?"

"It's going." I flick the pearls at his throat. "How's it going with you?"

"I'm working the room, living my best life. What I need to see more of is you two working each other."

"What does that even mean?" Jag's forehead creases.

"Don't ask me. This is *your* sexy party. Figure it out."

"I'm going to show Jag our room." I motion toward the hall. "He wants to shower."

"Yeah. Do that." Wolf points an unwavering glare at Jag. "You'll tell her everything, including the deep fake and eye prongs and how that made you feel."

"Deep fake and... What now?" I look between them.

Jag sighs. "Wolf—"

"No omissions. Lay it all out there, take the time, fight it out, and fuck it dry." He takes Jag's face in his hands and plants a kiss on his lips. Then he turns to me and does the same. "I don't want to see either of you until you've hashed it out so hard that you can't keep your hands off each other. I'll be here when you're ready for that part."

With that, he spins away and saunters back to his new friends.

Jag and I exchange a halting moment of eye contact, and in that space, a nascent bond forms without either of us reaching for it. There's no challenge or regret in the sudden, unfamiliar connection. Only understanding.

As I struggle to put my thoughts into words, he does it for

love

me.

"Whatever else we are to each other now, we are aligned here. In him. In loving Wolf without apology or rivalry. In wanting his joy more than our own certainty."

"Yeah." My throat closes. I couldn't have said it better myself. "So... You love him."

"I never had a choice."

"Me, neither. He's impossible not to love."

"He's our way back to each other, Little Bird. He already carried us halfway. The rest is on us." His eyes turn to burnished ice, his features hardening in that familiar, commanding, bossy-stepbrother look that expects compliance. "We're not going back to the way things were."

"No?" My skin heats. "Where are we going?"

"Take us to our room."

jag
SIXTY-FIVE

I follow Dove through the cartel's stronghold, every nerve attuned to her presence and the danger around her.

My mind builds maps, exits, and choke points in the corridors and rooms we pass. I mark the places where walls can slide open, panels can drop, and cameras can pivot, searching for seams undetected by the untrained eye.

But I keep losing track of all of that because she's in front of me.

She navigates this viper nest like she belongs here, her hair braided down her back, and her luscious ass swaying in tiny black shorts, all easy confidence, undaunted by her surroundings.

Her bare feet pad across white marble, her toes and fingers painted the same blue as her hair. Being this close to her, watching her without a camera lens, fucks with my concentration.

The braid is slowly coming loose. A strand slips free, then another. My fingers twitch to fix it for her. I was good at that once.

I pry my gaze away before she realizes how fucking hungry I am for her.

jag

The domestic scents of citrus polish and bleach ride the air. Beneath it lurks the undertow of violence, metallic and faint, the coppered shadow of what happens when debts are collected, and mercy isn't on the menu.

I track the cameras in the ceilings, the motion sensors out of range, and the armed men positioned in every direction. This place is a machine, built to keep danger outside and control inside, while tucking its teeth behind a smile.

She glances back at me, braid shifting and unraveling, the blue strands catching the light.

How many times have I imagined locking her inside a fortress like this and making her stand in front of floor-to-ceiling glass to watch the world shrink into safety? The thought surfaces with the ache of possibility.

She would be protected here the way the inner circle protects its own, guarded around the clock, and folded into the family.

But she would never be allowed to leave this life.

A marble cage.

That's precisely why I can't make it hers.

"This is us." She pauses at the entrance of a private suite and leans into the retinal scanner.

I need to break into that device and change the security so that only the three of us can enter. But it can wait.

Dove comes first.

The double doors swing open, and I follow her into a massive space with a bedroom and en suite bathroom at one end and a sitting room and kitchenette at the other. Splashes of blue and gold textiles break up the monotony of white marble.

The bed dominates my field of view, wide enough for three bodies without negotiation, dressed in layered linens that look too expensive to touch.

I don't admire it. I clear it.

My eyes go straight to corners, ceilings, and shadows, looking for places to hide electronics. No visible cameras. No obvious recording devices. Nothing jumps out on a first pass.

The balcony doors open to a citrus grove and the rainforest beyond it.

In the walk-in closet, Wolf's luggage lines up along the wall, ready to fill shelves and drawers. My single bag sits among the others.

I know Wolf packed an entire closet for me. And for her. Clothes chosen with intention and the assumption of time. Not days. Not weeks.

A while.

Maybe forever.

I cross the suite in long strides, opening doors and testing echoes. The bathroom is outrageous. My largest apartment would've fit into one corner of it.

This is more space than I would ever need. More luxury than I could ever give her.

I don't have a life outside of protecting Dove. I've never considered marriage, children, or settling down with someone else. I wouldn't know how to hold those things without breaking them.

Maybe that's why no one has ever loved me. Not the way my little bird did all those years ago.

And now there's Wolf. And the possibility of Dove choosing me again. Maybe this isn't love by anyone else's definition, but it feels like it is. It frightens me as much as it thrills me, making my head spin and knocking my balance off center.

"I didn't request this." I pause at the foot of the bed, staring at the promise of it. "There were no discussions about sleeping arrangements."

"I know." She sits on the corner of the mattress. "Matias told me how it would be."

"And how is that exactly?"

"He has you locked in. He wants Wolf for some reason, and he made it clear that I'm part of the equation. I have to stay for it all to work."

"Fuck that." My neck tenses. "I won't allow you to be caged by him or this place or anyone. Nobody decides your future except you. If and when you're ready to leave, I'll make it happen. Understand?"

"Go shower, Jag." She stares at her hands on her lap. "Then we'll talk."

"Stay in this room." I leave her there and strip in the bathroom.

In the shower, I let the hot spray pound my skin as my thoughts start to unravel.

Deep down, I know they aren't going back to Alaska.

jag

Wolf is already mentally and emotionally committed to me and Dove and a life with the cartel.

And the moment I tell Dove about the promise I made to her mother and the twenty years I sacrificed to keep her alive, it will upend everything she stands on.

She'll need time to process it. Then she'll forgive me. And she'll want to stay.

Every instinct I have tells me to take that choice away from her, to lie to her and let her hate me if that's what sends her running from this place and its teeth.

That's how I've always handled things. I decide for her, absorb the damage, and move us forward, whether she understands or not. That was the job when she was a kid.

But she isn't anymore.

She's not my ward. She's not the little sister who trusted me because she had no alternative. She's a woman who deserves the truth, even if it drags her deeper into the cartel.

And it isn't just her and me against the world anymore. There's Wolf.

A vote already cast. A third axis I'll never control. A future already bending around him.

I scrub my hands over my face and down my chest, trying to wash off the instinct to manipulate instead of protect. I have to relearn where my authority ends.

Shutting off the water, I step out, reach for a towel, and freeze.

Dove sits cross-legged on the vanity, watching me with unreadable eyes. I was so buried in my thoughts that I didn't even hear her sneak in.

"Before we dive into the topic of you and me…" Her gaze lowers down my naked body, lingers on my thigh tattoo, pauses on my hardening cock, and skitters back to my gaze. "I want to address my concerns about Wolf."

"Go ahead." I wipe the towel across my skin.

"You read his journal and probably know about his last panic attack."

"I know I triggered a full-blown breakdown that started on the pier and ended in a freezing shower."

"Okay." She nods as if checking off a box. "Good. I don't know if you and Wolf have already… If you're, uh…"

"If we're fucking? No. We've been taking it slow. Lots of kissing, touching, and coming." I drop my voice to a purr. "I've had him in my mouth."

"Oh." A flush reddens her neck. "He enjoys it, then? Being with you?"

"No question."

"So... That answers that." She straightens, bracing her hands behind her on the vanity. "He likes men and women."

"He's attracted to you and me. That's all that matters."

"When you take the next step, please be careful with him." She studies me, searching for any hint that I don't understand what she's asking. "He was abused by men, and I don't know how he'll handle sex with a man or what that means for you and him. I assume you'll be the... One in control?"

"The top?"

"I guess?"

I spot a pile of folded clothes on the table beside me and lift a brow in question.

She nods and watches me dress beneath the veil of her lashes, her gaze clinging to my tattoo.

"This is weird." She pulls in a breath.

"Which part?" I drag on briefs, jeans, and an *aggressively normal* white shirt.

"All of it. Talking about sex, watching you dress, making plans for the future... You *know* this is weird for us."

"It is. But it's necessary."

"I don't know much about your sexual history." She exhales, shoulders loosening a fraction. "Only what I saw when I was younger. The things you did for money, the women in Cracker's house, and the friends and boyfriends I found you in bed with, all of that was bad. Traumatic."

"I'm sorry." I erase the distance and step into her space. "I'll spend the rest of my life atoning for the pain I inflicted. And yeah, I sold my body for the first five years we lived on the streets. That was the last time I bottomed for anyone."

She looks up, meeting my eyes head-on. There's no judgment there. She stares at me with concern and sadness, sparking a strange, new honesty between us.

"With Wolf..." She chews the inside of her cheek. "When you top him, it can't feel like ownership or pressure. He needs choice. Safety."

jag

"I understand that." And I do. More than she knows. "I appreciate you telling me. This—" I gesture between us. "This is vital. The talking and honesty. Instead of circling old land mines, we're clearing new ground together. Without the yelling and wall punching parts."

Her mouth curves into a small, uncertain smile. "If we're going to do this, whatever this is, we can't pretend the land mines don't exist."

"Agreed."

"When you left Alaska, what did Wolf tell his family?"

"He didn't dramatize it. He told them to be patient with his absence. Promised he'd be careful. He warned them it could be months before they hear from him." I pause, choosing the truth carefully. "He told them this is his life now and that he needs their support."

"Are they freaking out?" She swallows.

"They're worried. But they see him." I rest a knuckle under her chin, lifting it. "Wolf's happy. That's what they want more than anything else."

She sits back and fidgets with her unruly braid, her fingers worrying at it as lines form between her eyes. She looks unsettled, out of place, and painfully, irresistibly beautiful.

I want her with every breath in my body, and it's taking considerable concentration to keep my dick from responding.

"May I?" I nod at her hair.

The look she gives me burns bright and unguarded, illuminating her stunning face. She nods eagerly, letting a glimmer of eight-year-old Dove shine through.

I lift her down from the vanity, set her on her feet, and lead her to the bed. We fall into our customary positions as she sits between my knees, her back to my chest.

With patient hands, I untangle and smooth her soft hair, unable to stop myself from lifting the strands to my nose.

A rush of long-lost fragrances fills my lungs. Clean soap, California sunshine, and warm Dove skin. The scents unleash an avalanche of memories, drowning me in pinkie promises, pockets of stolen peanuts, open windows, and a Trail Cat named Little Jag.

My chest caves in, and stabbing heat pricks the backs of my eyes.

"You're smelling my hair."

"I'm reminiscing." I let the strands fall to her back and steady myself.

"Yeah." She rests her hands on my knees, where they bracket hers. "Me, too."

"Ask me the question you always asked back then." I take a breath, bracing for it. "The one you never let go."

She stills, her fingers biting into my legs. "Will you tell me about our parents?"

"Yeah. I will." I part her hair into two neat sections, my hands surprisingly steady. "Celeste had gentle eyes and long blond hair. Whenever she sang, my skin pebbled in happy goosebumps. Her smile was her best feature. It went all the way to her soul, reflecting her bottomless kindness. That kindness made her even more beautiful. You look just like her. And she was… She was young, Dove. Only fifteen-years-old when she got pregnant with you."

"What?" Her voice strangles. "How?"

And so I tell her.

jag
SIXTY-SIX

The motion of braiding Dove's hair used to calm me. But I'm no longer staring at the back of my little sister's head.

A woman sits between my legs. The one and only woman I've been jerking it to for years.

My desire for her grows layers as I lift a section of hair to my nose and sniff.

Fuck. I need to focus.

I thread the silky blue strands, passing them over and under each other, my hands remembering what they've always known.

As I sink into the old rhythm, I come clean about her childhood.

"Adrian Crowe," Dove says slowly as if testing the name on her tongue. "He's my father."

"Only in DNA."

"Why didn't you tell me?"

"I promised Celeste that I wouldn't. She depended on me to keep you away from it, to keep you safe."

I tell her about the vow I made to her mother and how it ruled every decision for the next twenty years. No police, no confessions, no telling anyone. I don't frame it as sacrifice. I don't soften it. I make sure she understands exactly how it unfolded and why I never broke the promise I made to Celeste.

"Why tell me now?" she asks numbly, not moving, barely breathing.

"Adrian Crowe is dead."

"Oh." Her hand spasms on my leg. "That's where you've been for the past twelve days."

"Yes."

I finish the braids down her back, giving her time to absorb, dissect, and reshape her unforgivable childhood.

Any minute, she'll spin around and throw a barrage of questions at me. I'm ready for it. Ready to tell her everything she wants to know. Then I'll tell her about Wolf's role in Crowe's death.

At last, she twists to face me, her eyes glistening with tears that haven't fallen. Her face doesn't crumple. Her mouth doesn't move. She just stares, her eyes darting between mine, perhaps looking at me through a new lens.

Her hands lift, and she places them on my face. Slowly, deliberately, her fingers trail around my eyes, down the bridge of my nose, scraping through the rough shadow along my jaw, and tracing the shape of my lips. Inspecting. Revising. Redrawing my features. Redrawing the man in front of her, adjusting angles, updating truths, and fitting the past to what's sitting here now.

When she's done, her chin trembles. Her eyes soften, and a small whimper escapes her.

Then she's on me, hands in my hair, and mouth crashing into mine, lips parting, tongue chasing, demanding and spectacularly fierce.

She climbs onto my lap in a fluid motion, knees sliding around my hips, thighs straddling, crowding me back on the bed as if proximity is the answer. She kisses with her whole body, no restraint or uncertainty.

Just like Dove to make the first move and choose physical contact over words to express her feelings.

For a heartbeat, I'm stunned by it. Then I take control.

I meet her heat and ignite it, one hand firm at her waist, the other supporting her neck as I angle her head where I want it. I deepen the kiss, diving into her mouth and guiding the rhythm until urgency turns into wild abandon.

Our mouths fit together the way they were meant to, passionately locked, tongues tangled, teeth clashing, and lips

jag

feasting. I claim the pace, feed her what she needs, and my hungry little bird bites and whimpers and goes wild in my arms.

Her hands grab at my neck, my shoulders, holding on. I hold her right back, anchoring her where she is, where we are, letting the kiss say what neither of us can manage yet.

Everything led here. Every cardboard fort. Every drop of blood I washed down the drain. Every line of code and bargain made. All of it brought us to this moment—her trust, my hands, and the truth finally between us.

The need for air forces us to ease apart. Breathing hard, foreheads touching, we stare into each other's eyes.

I want more. She does, too. It's written all over her mouth, her hands, and the electricity sparking between us.

There's still too much left unsaid.

My attention drops to her wrist. Two hair ties. Familiar. They used to live on *my* wrist.

I hook a finger under them and slide them free. Then I start tying off the ends of her braids, lifting one, then the other, where they drape over her chest.

As I twist the bands to secure them, the backs of my fingers brush against her nipples, teasing her piercings. I do it again, letting my knuckles graze the sensitive buds and watching her reaction.

She swallows, eyes darkening, and pupils blown wide. Desire rolls off her in waves.

My cock thickens painfully, pressing against my zipper as I draw out the task, caressing the shape of her breast, and testing her resolve. She doesn't look away. Doesn't tell me to stop.

"I want to see your beauty mark." My balls tighten.

"My... Beauty mark?"

"Your sweet little mole." I rest a finger over its hiding spot on her collarbone beneath the shirt. "Show it to me."

"Why?"

"Because I told you to."

"Bossy. I thought we weren't going back to the way things were."

"I'm playing with your nipples while fixing your braids. *That* is where we're going. Now take off your shirt."

She gulps, shivers, and slowly removes her top. My attention homes in on the tiny dark mark at her collarbone.

Exactly as I remembered it.

I lean in and set my mouth there, a reverent press of lips, lingering, worshiping. She answers with a breathy sigh that goes straight to my cock.

Without breaking contact, I guide her onto her back and stretch over her. Braced on my elbows, I swirl my tongue around the beauty mark, licking, kissing, and drawing it into my mouth. Then I firm my lips and suck hard, harder, pulling blood to the surface until her pulse answers and color rises to meet me.

She releases a quiet moan, and I hold the suction long enough to leave proof behind for Wolf.

When I lean back, a dark bloom encircles her mole. Wolf will see it, and he'll know. Her beauty mark was instrumental in keeping me from breaking at the end. Wolf used it to pull me back from a false reality where she was brutally raped on a loop for ten days.

I brush my thumb against the love bite, watching her smile at the tenderness I left behind.

That smile... I can't stop myself from devouring it. Shifting my weight, I take her mouth, and everything else falls away.

I kiss her with all the longing and desperation I've been storing for years. Goddamn, I hunger for her, my heart's blood, my precious Dove.

The intensity climbs fast, burning from fiercely focused to rabid and out of control. I taste the metal at her lip and drag my tongue over the piercing, the sight of it driving me insane.

She answers with equal passion, matching me with clawing nails and heaving breaths. We roll across the bed, legs tangling, hands roaming, grabbing at clothes and hair.

My little bird is a wild animal. Nothing tentative about her. No brakes. Just need answering need.

My mouth leaves hers to chart a path lower, skimming skin and mapping her hourglass shape. My fingers follow, tracing curves and dips and pulling sounds from her that test the limits of my restraint.

I take my time sucking her pierced tits, then lower, lower, until my lips settle at the waistband of her shorts, thumbs hooked in the fabric.

"Just need a taste. Then we'll resume our conversation."

"Yes. Please, Jag." She writhes beneath my hungry smile.

With a flick of a finger, I release the button and strip off her shorts and underwear in one motion.

Her hand falls between her legs, her eyes wide and searching as she watches me down the length of her flawlessly nude body.

"Show me your pussy, Dove."

"Oh, God." She moans. "Words I never thought I'd hear you say."

"Let me see the cunt I'm dying to devour."

"Fuck, Jag." She removes her hand and covers her face.

"Watch." I slap her clit, making her yelp. "Eyes on me."

She lowers her arms to the mattress, fingers curling into the quilt.

"I'm going to make you very, very wet." I drag my nose along the blond strip of hair on her mound, inhaling deeply. "You'll be so messy when I'm done, you'll ruin this expensive bedding."

"Don't care." She grinds her hips in the air, seeking my mouth.

I give it to her. Lips, tongue, and hands... I give it all to her, burying my face and sinking my fingers into her tight, wet sheath.

Holy fuck, I'm eating Dove's pussy.

I've seen her naked. I've watched her have sex through my cameras, calling it vigilance when it was actually punishment.

Year after year, I followed her from one lover to the next, punishing myself, forcing myself to remember my place. Guardian, protector, oath keeper. Never a participant. Not even a taste.

I told myself it was necessary, that it was discipline, and wanting her was a failure I could manage if I bled quietly. And I bled with every man she took to her bed, dying a slow death, over and over and over.

That ends now. She's with me the way I dreamed, and I finally, *finally*, know her taste.

Rich, honeyed sweetness spills out of her, washing over my tongue and shaking the foundation of my world.

This is real. It's fucking happening. I'm tongue-deep inside my little bird, lapping up her arousal, sucking on her clit, and edging her toward release.

She grabs my hair and fucks my mouth, chasing that hot, shimmering pleasure. No more prolonging. We've both waited long enough.

I shove a finger inside her, curling it just right, and stroke the spot that sends her tumbling.

The sounds of her growling, groaning, screaming pleasure make me harder than I've ever been. As her inner muscles spasm around my finger, I grind my aching dick into the mattress, seeking relief and finding none.

Christ, I need to fuck her. But I can't until I've revealed every truth I've kept from her.

As she catches her breath, I slowly crawl up her trembling body. My hands follow the sinuous curves of her sides, outlining her hips and cradling her ribs. My fingers slot into the grooves between bones as if her rib cage was made for my grip.

I hold her close as my lips reunite with her love-bitten beauty mark. Then I fall into the lush heat of her mouth, deep and consuming, letting the kiss claim me as fully as I claim her.

There's no end to this obsession. I love her madly, shamelessly, and could spend the remainder of my life with her mouth against mine, floating and buzzing in this blissful fantasy.

But I owe her answers.

"Dove..." I slow the kiss, despite her sounds of protest. "Sweetheart..." I ease back, cupping her face. "We need to talk. And if we stay in this room, I'll have come dripping from your lips, your cunt, and your sweet little asshole."

A moan vibrates in her throat as she lowers her gaze to the chub tenting my jeans.

"Don't even think about it." I grab her discarded clothes and help her pull them back on.

Once we put ourselves together, I follow her to the door.

"Is there a place where we can talk?" I glance up at the ceiling, looking for cameras. "The walls out there have eyes and ears."

"I know a place." She fits her hand in mine, just like she did all those years ago, and leads me outside to the citrus grove.

Jungle heat hangs low beneath a sky layered with thick, silver clouds. The fragrance of sweet orange blossoms saturates the air. Green leaves gleam dark and waxy, and fruit glows like small suns against the shade.

I follow her to a stone bench set at the center, worn smooth by years of quiet use.

"Matias grew this grove for Camila." She smiles up at the canopy of fruit-bearing trees. "Long before she was his."

jag

"Matias would argue that Camila has always belonged to him."

"Is that true for you? Have I always been yours?"

"Yes, Little Dove. Say it again."

"I've always been yours, Jag."

My dick hardens, ready to thrust that promise deep inside her body.

Her eyes glimmer, and she pivots toward the citadel.

"Second floor." She points upward, indicating a balcony tucked into white and glass. "That's us."

We sit side by side on the bench. I shift closer until our shoulders meet, until her thigh rests against mine.

Our hands find each other, fingers threading together, settling on my lap and taking me back to another time, to all the other benches that cradled us in the dark at night.

"All right." I draw a slow breath and tip my head toward her. "Ask what you need to ask. Or I can start back when it was just us and the streets."

"Tell me about *you*, Jag. I want to know about the man you worked so hard to keep hidden."

wolfson
SIXTY-SEVEN

Pulse humming and shoulders loose, I stroll into the private suite with my new ride-or-die bestie at my side.

Frizz shuts the door behind us, and I scan the bougie space I'll be sharing with Jag and Dove.

They're not here.

Absence leaves a trace, and yeah, Jag and Dove left one. My eyes go straight to the bed.

Whatever happened, the mattress lost the fight. Sheets twisted, pillows flung, the quilt dragged halfway to the floor... If I press my nose to it, will I smell the climax of their reconciliation workout?

One can only hope.

Beside me, Frizz waggles his eyebrows, his lips twitching behind the stitches.

"Stepsiblings." I clap him on the back. "They're a whole genre of filthy."

He folds in half, shaking with silent laughter.

This guy. He laughs at all my jokes.

When he straightens, he wipes his eyes and jabs a thumb toward the door.

"Yeah. Go on." I wave him off. "Don't forget. Tattoo session at ten."

He gives me a thumbs-up and slips out.

Unhooking my corset, I let it fall to the floor. Then I explore the suite, opening drawers, evaluating space, and emptying the luggage.

I hang what needs hanging, fold the rest, and line up shoes. I packed enough clothes for Jag and Dove to accommodate every mood swing, identity shift, and wardrobe crisis.

Honestly, what would they do without me?

The sun slides down the glass windows, turning everything honey-gold. Outside, the jungle presses close, hovering like a dark, patient thing, beckoning me.

I grab my smokes and step onto the balcony.

The view drops away, the whole compound laid out beneath me.

When we flew in, they blindfolded me. Protocol. But I can picture the route, how long the helicopter banked, how the air changed, how my ears popped with altitude and distance. We're deep in the rainforest. No roads, no civilization, no walking out alive.

Remote doesn't scare me. Isolation and I have history. We've had long talks.

This place feels as off-the-map as Hoss.

Instead of freaking out about that, I find comfort in it.

Down below, men in black move with purpose, crossing paths, turning corners, rifles carried at ease, not brandished.

I light up and lean on the rail, smoke curling into the damp air.

The thing I don't expect is how *not* lonely this place feels. There's noise under the quiet, footsteps on marble, laughter around every corner, and camaraderie everywhere. The walls pulse with life.

And the inner circle? I grin to myself. They're a pack of emotionally-damaged cupcakes with hidden knives and murderous tendencies.

I take a drag and let myself think the thought all the way through. I like them. All the ones I've met so far. I like that I can joke about my childhood trauma and no one flinches, rushes to smooth it over, or asks if I'm okay. I say uncomfortable shit, and they nod like, *Yeah, been there. Done that.*

For me, that's home.

I follow the balcony around the corner and stare out over the citrus grove below, the trees heavy with green and gold. A clearing opens at the center, and there they are.

Jag and Dove sit on a bench, their heads tipped together, in their own little world. Jag grips her hands and says something that makes her spring to her feet.

Uh oh.

She starts pacing, fingers yanking at her braids, voice climbing, arms cutting the air. I don't catch every word, just the loudest ones.

"He wore a fucking bomb?" Her eyes snap up.

Straight to me.

That's my cue to back away. So naturally, I step forward and curtsy.

I don't need 20/20 vision to see the look she spears me. I feel it grab me by the balls.

Jag slides along the bench and pulls her down to his lap. He cups her face, thumbs brushing her cheeks. She's crying too hard for a kiss, so he captures her nape and brings their foreheads together.

"You would make a terrible spy," says a gravelly male voice behind me.

I spin and come face-to-face with Van Quiso.

Impossible to mistake him with that toothpick parked between his lips. Or the scar cutting from his eye to his mouth, wrecking the symmetry of his face and somehow sharpening everything else.

When I saw him in the nightclub, I didn't know who he was.

Now that I've memorized his dossier, I understand exactly why his presence makes my blood run cold.

Hands clasped behind him and boots braced apart, he radiates a dominant posture, one that says he owns this view, this moment, maybe the whole damned kingdom.

Legacy King of The Freedom Fighters.

Former human sex trafficker.

His nine victims now stand shoulder to shoulder with him in the inner circle.

And I am wildly, inappropriately gobsmacked. Not in an approval way. In a staring-at-a-volcano way. I don't want to go near him. I also don't want to look away.

"Hi." I crush out the cigarette. "Do you prefer a high-five, a bent knee, or should I just scream and throw myself off the balcony?"

One dark eyebrow lifts. "You're different."

"Never heard that before."

"We like different around here." He flicks the toothpick from one side of his mouth to the other as his gaze sweeps over my shirtless, scarred chest. "You'll fit in just fine."

"Cool." I glance past him, then back. "How did you get in here?"

"I wanted to see if Jag hacked the security and changed the locks yet." He crosses muscled arms. "He hasn't."

"Jag's been busy."

His gaze drifts over my shoulder, and I follow it to the clearing where Jag holds Dove on his lap.

I step into Van's line of sight, blocking it.

He hums quietly, thoughtful.

"I stopped by for two reasons." He removes the toothpick, spins it between his fingers, and returns it to his mouth. "First, I want a tattoo."

My brain short-circuits.

A tattoo.

On Van Quiso.

Of all the things I expected to come out of his mouth, that wasn't even on the list. The idea of putting my needles anywhere near that scarred, people-eating myth of a man sends a wicked thrill through me.

"Yeah." I play it cool. "My schedule's pretty packed."

"Everyone's talking. People lining up, figuring out what they want from the resident artist."

Resident artist?

Love that for me.

He steps closer, making sure I'm aware of him in a very biological way. "You'll do me first."

"Actually, Frizz is first."

He glares at me with silver eyes that don't hurry. The pause stretches long enough for my guts to reconsider all my life choices.

"Fine." He shrugs. "You'll do me after Frizz."

"I'm not cheap. It's going to cost you an arm and a leg."

Another glare. My insides shrivel.

"But for you?" I lift a finger, adjusting. "Just the arm. Maybe a toe."

The corner of his mouth tips into an almost smile.

"The last thing." He drops his voice to a velvet rumble. "I like how you handled Crowe. The bomb. The razor blade."

My heart skips.

"I was running surveillance at the nightclub that night. Had a dozen operatives on standby, a mole buried behind enemy lines, and we were still days, maybe weeks out from making a clean grab for Jag." His eyes bore into mine. "You made us all look slow."

"I get impatient when people I love are taken from me."

"You thought outside the box, kid. And you didn't flinch. We need a mind like yours on the team."

"You offering me a job?"

"I'm offering you a life. Right here. At the table. With Jag."

"What about Dove?"

"She's already in. Making friends, getting grease under her nails while working on Luke's cars, rolling through the halls on her skates, and painting her toes with the ladies. She's not going anywhere."

I feel the *yes* line up in my chest, but I don't say it. Not without Jag and Dove weighing in.

"I mean..." I motion between us, the grove, the citadel, the general state of my existence. "That's a hell of a pitch. Let me... Sit with the vibe. Consult the council. Scream into a pillow. I'll circle back."

"You do that."

"Leave him alone, Van."

I turn toward the musical voice, and *Holy Mother of all,* Liv Reed steps out of the shadows.

Long black hair spills down her back in glossy sheets. Her black mini dress leaves little to the imagination, the arrangement of straps looking edgy and severe without trying.

She's the incarnate of Kate Beckinsale, Death Dealer of the Underworld, and Elvira, Mistress of the Dark.

Hard to believe she was Van's first slave.

Dominatrix energy blasts from her, shaking my legs with the urge to kneel for her and press my lips to her stilettos.

And the scar on her face? Same line. Same angle. An exact

mirror of Van's.

"Pay up." She holds out a palm to Van.

He exhales through his nose and reaches into his pocket. A Colombian paper bill appears. The big one. He stabs it with his toothpick and holds it out like an offering.

"Gross." She pinches it by the corner and finally looks at me.

I'm openly staring.

"We had a bet." She stuffs the money between her breasts. "On how long it would take your boy to hack the security system. I knew it wouldn't be today. He's too busy being in love."

Van grunts, accepting the loss.

My skin itches with nerves and restlessness. I reach for my smokes, and her eyes narrow the second the flame flares.

"Are you the smoke police?" I take a drag.

"Hardly." She gives a feminine snort. Then continues to glare.

"Want one?" I hold out the pack.

She accepts it without hesitation.

My hands shake as I strike the lighter again, cupping the flame for her. I hate that she notices.

She leans in, inhales, and tips her head back through a long, slow exhale like she's been waiting years for it. Her shoulders loosen. Her spine eases. The entire jungle sighs with her.

Then she pins me with a stare that could peel paint off steel. "If you tell my husband I smoke, I'll crush your precious little jewels under my boot."

My balls recoil into my body, running for cover.

I can't tell her I've memorized the portfolio for every member of the inner circle. So I slap on my dumbest face.

"Which one is he?" I tilt my head, squinting a little. "Tall, dark, and handsome? Big, bronze, and scary?"

"Don't fuck with me, boy." She steps into my space, leans in, and exhales a slow, intimidating stream of smoke.

Her dark eyes imprison mine, daring me to shrink.

I don't move. Don't cough. I blink through the haze and let it wash over me, because flinching would be a mistake.

"Your poker face isn't bad." She straightens and returns to the railing. "But no one wears a mask as well as I do."

"She's not wrong," Van says unhelpfully.

"My husband…" She prompts, waiting for me to fess up.

"Joshua Carter." I wipe my palms on my shorts. "Retired linebacker with pale green eyes and black hair."

"He will *not* find out about this." She waves the cigarette. "Your secret. Buried. Unmarked grave."

Van chuckles and ruffles my hair.

Then something wild happens.

They pull up chairs. Casual. Like this is a patio in the suburbs and not the nerve center of a criminal mythos.

Liv crosses her legs, stiletto hooked on the rung, cigarette balanced just so. Van pours tequila. Time loosens its grip. And we... Hang out.

They gossip about inner-circle nonsense, who's having the most sex, who's pretending not to care, which spouse grovels the most, which one never uses the gym, which Gomez sister can kick Van's ass. Liv razzes Van about leaving toothpicks everywhere. Van fires back about her reorganizing the kitchen like it's a crime scene.

They argue like siblings.

It's bizarre. Deeply so. These two share a history born of horror, captivity, and coercion. Things that should never lead to a shared life, let alone a shared daughter. Yet here they are, sniping and smirking and passing tequila like normal people who forgot to be notorious criminals.

The topic of Dove comes up, of course. Her love of vintage engines and her interest in fixing Van's 1965 Mustang. Van says Luke's cars run better after she touches them. Liv grins like she's already claimed her.

I laugh more than I expect to. I relax more than I plan to.

Beneath the bloodlust and carnage, they're just people. Scarred, disturbing, kinky, freaky people who bicker, keep secrets, and love fiercely.

There's another layer there, too. The thing they don't talk about. The real work. The hunting of monsters worse than themselves.

The conversation remains friendly, deliberately harmless, and carefully clean. It'll stay that way until I choose to sit at the real table.

Until then, we talk about tattoos and marriages and who owes who money. And I realize I'm no longer bracing for the drop. I'm just there, enjoying it.

wolfson
SIXTY-EIGHT

I must've fallen asleep.

As I wake on the bed, the mattress dips with movement. My eyes open to Jag hovering above me.

Braced on hands and knees, he cages me with masculine heat and hooded amber eyes.

I melt.

His gorgeous face... He looks different. The sculpted angles remain, the danger simmering beneath the granite, but the constant tension that lives behind his eyes is missing. The creases have smoothed out, replaced with... Dare I say? Happiness.

"So..." I blink up at him, half-dreaming. "How is the fauxcest progressing?"

"The faux... What?"

"Family role play, brother on sister, everybody pretending they're biologically related. I'll be the creepy uncle."

"I do *not* want to see your porn searches."

"Don't need porn when I have the real thing." I clasp the thickening cock hanging between his spread legs and search the room for Dove.

Panic jolts fast when I don't see her. As I start to push up, Jag drops more of his weight, trapping me to the bed.

"She's showering." He nods at the bathroom. "Right there."

I sag beneath him, breathing again. "How did she handle the honesty grenade?"

"She needs time to process. There were a lot of questions. More will come. But..." He lowers his head and nuzzles my cheek with his nose. "The important things are out in the open."

He smells citrusy and earthy, calm scents I'm not used to associating with him.

"Is she ready for a 69 train?" I palm his firm buttocks, pulling him closer. "Doggy deluxe? Double penetration?"

"Jesus."

"Jesus can find his own threesome. Where are we at on ours?"

His sharp exhale of laughter warms my lips. Then he lifts his head, sobering.

"We haven't talked about the future." He brushes my hair out of my eyes. "But she supports this thing between you and me."

"*This* thing?" I grind my erection against his, holding us tightly together with my hands on his ass.

"Yeah. This..." His breath falters. "And more."

I tug him down, and he comes willingly, giving me all his weight. My arms hook around him, and his mouth falls upon mine.

He kisses me slowly. Not hungry or rough. This is patient Jag, honest and devoted. He's here. He's staying, and for once, nothing is on fire, and no one is hunting Dove.

I kiss him back, taking my time, letting the low voltage curl through my toes and gather between our fused hips. Our heads tilt to deepen the connection, not chasing anything.

My lips move with unspoken questions, and every answer he gives pulls me closer, his tongue licking mine and his body grinding with promise.

We both sense her at the same time and ease apart, our gazes swinging toward the bathroom.

Dove lingers in the doorway, wrapped in a towel, clutching a small bottle of something. Wet hair clings to her bare shoulders in blue ribbons, dripping water down her collarbones and over her...

"Is that a hickey?" I squint at her beauty mark.

"Thank me later." Jag lifts, sliding to my side and making room for her. "Come here, Little Bird."

"I'd rather watch." She pads across the room and sets a bottle of lube beside us.

Her shoulders droop, posture soft with fatigue that runs deeper than physical exertion. Her warm-honey eyes fixate on us, not sad or frightened. But heavy. Weighed down by ugly truths and rewritten memories.

She looks emotionally exhausted and off-balance, holding the knot of the towel against her like it's the only thing keeping her upright.

"Hey." I rise on an elbow. "We should sleep."

Her head snaps as if I startled her. She shakes it, small but firm, stepping closer.

"Please, don't stop." She glances between us. "I want to see you two together. As an outsider."

"Dove." Jag sets his jaw. "You're not—"

"That's all I can handle right now. We talked about this."

I understand what she's asking.

She's been angry with Jag for seventeen years. Even though he has now begged for forgiveness and laid every ugly truth at her feet, there are still miles between what they were and what they want to be. She's not going to leap from guardian and ward, brother and sister, and enemies with history, straight into lovers and call it healed.

Jag's already there. He crossed that line years ago in his head and heart. But Dove hasn't. Not yet. She needs room to move at her own pace, to choose him without feeling shoved or cornered by time or expectation.

But she doesn't want to be shut out or pushed to the sidelines while her insides are rearranging. She wants to witness stability in our fragile threesome and experience the pleasure of watching us fuck instead of being inside the storm of it. She wants participation without the pressure.

Jag gets it. He looks at me, and our gazes tangle, refusing to separate. His dick thickens against my hip, and I curl my hand around it, giving him a teasing stroke.

"Remove your clothes." He smacks my thigh and climbs off the bed.

Grabbing a chair, he sets it close, right beside me. Then he turns to Dove.

"One request." He rests a hand over hers on the towel. "Take this off. Let us look at you while you're looking at us."

She nods, staring up at him with so much trust in her eyes. He earned that, and I'm stupidly happy for him.

He pulls the towel free, lets it fall from her body, and spreads it over the seat of the chair.

She stands there naked, unguarded, and so fucking arresting that my heart seizes. Jag lets himself look, too, hungrily, brazenly, cock straining his jeans, and a groan vibrating in his chest.

He's seen her naked more times than I have, but always through a camera lens. This must feel surreal to him. To both of them.

Taking her hand, he guides her to the chair and positions her on the towel as if to protect her from invisible dirt.

While he does that, I shed my clothes and leave them where they fall, settling back on the bed with my hands braced behind me.

My pulse thrashes in my ears, and blood pounds in my saluting dick. I don't know how the mechanics of this will work or how I'll respond. I just know that I trust him.

He pulls off his clothes, revealing a physique carved in bold, vascular lines. Broad shoulders, shredded torso, washboard stomach, and a long, thick cock, all strength and endurance, built for stamina.

"Trust me?" He snags the bottle of lube and squirts it onto his palm.

"Yeah. Fully."

He kneels on the bed, grips my dick with his lubed hand, and collars my throat with the other. Then he holds me there, staring into my eyes and jerking me with ruthless strokes.

Within seconds, my stomach clenches, and my balls tighten with an overpowering need to come. He edges me right up to the cusp and stops.

I open my mouth to complain and shut it when I see his expression.

Slowly, he releases me, drags his pinkie along mine, and hooks our fingers together. Then he looks at Dove as if asking permission.

She sits with her knees bent against her chest, her features creasing, half-anger, half-ache, one-hundred-percent beautiful as she glares at the tiny connection between our fingers.

"Dove, what's wrong?" Jag watches her closely. "Use your words."

"I'm thinking about our cardboard forts, when it was just you and me, when that…" She nods at our linked pinkies. "That was mine. I claimed that." Her voice cracks. "Why are you sharing it with him?"

The room falls still.

"It's still yours." He twitches his finger against mine.

"So is this." I touch the scar under his ribs with my free hand, tracing the familiar edge. "It's yours."

Tears hover in her eyes, unshed and confused.

"You don't want to share him with me?" I lower my hand.

"I do. Of course, I do. It's not that. It's just… The memories were all I had left of him, the only connection I had for so long, and I've fiercely guarded every fragment, every piece of Jag that I lost. I know you're not trying to steal that from me. My jealousy doesn't make sense, especially since we're all naked, and you two are about to have sex. I don't want to be territorial or difficult or whatever this is."

Jag shifts to go to her.

"Stay." She lifts a hand. "Please, stay right there."

He freezes, looking conflicted and torn.

I feel the pull in him, the instinct to fix, to gather her up and make it stop hurting, but he swallows it for her.

"You're not wrong for guarding that." I hold her gaze. "You survived on those memories."

She squeezes her arms tighter around her knees.

"I'm not trying to reach back there and take anything." I tilt my head. "What I am is here now, with both of you. You don't have to stop feeling what you're feeling. You don't have to be cool or evolved or generous about it. You're allowed to be messy and protective."

"I'm not going anywhere." Jag lowers his chin, regarding her from beneath hooded eyes. "Not from you. Not from us. This isn't a trade, and you will never be replaced."

"I know." She pulls a breath through her nose.

"Do you want us to stop?" He nods at our entwined pinkies, our erections, everything implied.

She shakes her head fast. Too fast.

"Do you want to join us?" His voice drops, careful again.

Another head shake.

"Tell us what you want," I say. "Not what scares you."

"I want you to keep going." She rests her chin on her knees. "I need to feel my way through this."

"Keep going?" Jag flips me over, sets me on my knees, and presses my face into the mattress. "Like this?"

"Yes." Her eyes lift, searching, wanting, her breath quickening.

"Keep your eyes on us." With a hand on my nape and the other closing around my cock, he bends over me and starts jerking me again. "Watch us, Dove. See what it is. See what it isn't."

"You're meant to be together." Desire thickens her voice. "So fucking beautiful. Don't stop."

"Holy fuck." I claw at the bedding, rocking my hips. "Listen to her, Jag. Don't stop. I need to come."

"Don't you dare." He presses in behind me and drags his hot, steel length along the cleft of my ass. "I'm going to feel so good inside you." His grip on my dick tightens, kicking the air from my lungs. "You'll beg me to fuck you, day and night."

If he triggers me, it'll suck big ones. But after writing the journal and reliving it with Dove, the demons have been unusually quiet. Maybe we slew them.

Dove digs her feet into the seat's edge, her heavy-lidded eyes tracking Jag's stroking fist as her hand slips between her legs.

Sexy little voyeur.

Draped over my back, Jag nips along my shoulder and ruts against my backside, the length of him rubbing against the underside of my balls. My hips kick, answering his thrusts, and he chases it, fucking me without penetration.

It's maddening and cruel. Fucking hell, why do I want him to fuck me so badly? I know what that feels like, the pain and helplessness. Yet somehow, I know it won't be anything like that with him.

"Fuck me, you fucker." I grind back against him, throbbing and leaking in the vise-like grip of his fist. "Do it."

"Too soon for begging, pup." The hand on my nape caresses down my spine, trying and failing to calm me.

"Then kiss me."

wolfson

His hands fly to my waist and flip me to my back.

Panting, I stare up at him, at this rough-hewn beast of a man carved by a vindictive god and dropped onto my lap. His brown hair spikes in every direction, wrecked in the best way, and his chest heaves, flexing with each breath, restraint ready to unleash.

He shifts forward. The bed dips, and his solid weight settles where my greedy hunger lengthens and throbs.

His throat flexes as he lowers his chest to mine and pauses. His bedroom eyes wander to Dove, and his pupils expand, dark and molten.

Before I can follow his gaze, he turns back and destroys me with his mouth.

The kiss steals my air, my control, and my very last brain cell. He's a windstorm of aggression and masculinity, all challenge and domination, lips dragging and teeth scraping, stretching my jaw past the point of pain.

He tongue-fucks my mouth, showing me how thoroughly he intends to fuck me with his cock. I open for him, taking everything he gives me and claiming him right back.

Too soon, he rips himself away and lifts on his knees, his dick angry and engorged, drooling precome down the veiny length.

Reaching for the lube, he squirts a generous glob onto my tip and slathers it down to my nuts.

Shouldn't he be greasing himself? He's on top. He *is* a top.

"What are you doing?" I grip his hand, where it wraps around my base.

An infuriating curl plucks at his lips as he angles my dick beneath him and slowly lowers onto it.

My breath stops. My back arches, and my hands claw at his thighs.

That initial push past his tight ring of muscle... I choke. Then I groan. Then I release a howling roar of pleasure.

Dammit to hell, he's tight. Too tight. I can't fucking breathe. I'm on the brink of passing out.

"Hold still." He grits his teeth, sinking lower, impaling himself deeper.

"Jag... Fuck." I thicken inside him, pulsing and jumping, unable to control my reaction. "I'm hurting you."

"You're not. It's..." He fists his dick, seats himself to the root, and groans long and deep. "Goddamn, Wolf. I feel you in my fucking ribs."

A whimper sounds beside us, and we both turn our heads.

Dove's legs have fallen open, stopped only by the arms of the chair. She frantically rubs her soaked cunt with one hand, the fingers of her other caught between her teeth. Her tits bounce with the rapid bursts of her breath, and her eyes glaze with lust.

"That's the hottest thing I've ever seen." Unable to look away, Jag blindly reaches for my nipple and tweaks it as ruthlessly as he beats his cock.

By the grace of slapping gonads, I'm about to be feral.

I bite down on a hiss and clench every muscle in the world's greatest effort to stave off premature ejaculation.

Then Jag rolls his hips.

Merciless gods.

His abs ripple, pulling him into a sensual motion. He puts his back into it, surging forward and grinding down, arms flexing as he clasps his fingers behind his neck, elbows bent outward like wings.

He rides me like that, letting me watch the flex and play of his muscles and the straining bob of his cock, giving me the most erotic lap dance in existence. Nipples drawn tight, sweat slicking his skin, he's a masterpiece of brawn and shadow.

And his eye contact? It's fucking electric.

He sets a wicked tempo, bearing down and squeezing his ass with each thrust. Lift, tighten, sink, grind. Over and over, the motion hits. The friction sparks. I'm barely hanging on.

His cock nods against his abs. So I grab it with both hands and work him into a panting, growling, rutting animal. His thighs tense against my sides, power coiling, his control unfurling. He shifts, breath breaking and chin dropping as his hands clamp onto my wrists to slow my strokes.

Then a third pair of hands is there. Smaller. Softer.

Dove's face comes into view above me, close enough to feel her breath before her mouth covers mine. She kisses me hard, and I kiss her back, my arms coming up to hold her for just one more greedy moment.

She pulls away, attention turning, and crawls toward Jag.

His movements slow to a stop as he captures her neck and hauls her to his mouth. He consumes her lips savagely, groaning into the kiss, thrusting his hips, digging hard, and driving me deeper inside him.

When they break apart, I surge up between them. Moving on instinct, I grip his ass, lift him, and drop him to his back.

He lands on the mattress, eyes locked on mine. With my cock rammed deep, it's a vulnerable position, one I never imagined putting him in.

"Is this okay?" I reach out and trace his beautiful, seductive mouth.

"Yes, until you're shaking." He bites my finger.

"Until we're all shaking." I brace my hands on the backs of his thighs and spread him open.

Then I look at Dove.

Her smile comes fast and breathless, her pupils swallowing her honey eyes.

She leans over Jag's face, wraps a hand around his erection, and kisses him until he's panting against her mouth. I rock forward, pistoning into him, and quickly catch a rhythm that will send us both spiraling.

After a moment, Dove changes positions, turning to put her face where her hand is. She lowers her head, studies Jag's dick, and draws him into her mouth.

His entire body stiffens beneath me, his ass muscles clamping viciously around my invasion.

"Holy fuck, Jag." My thrusts grow erratic as I pump and grind with abandon. "I'm going to come."

"Sit on my face, Dove." He swats her butt. Then slaps it again impatiently. "Now."

She swings her backside around, straddles his head, and pushes her pussy against his mouth.

A vibrating hum escapes her lips, half-muffled by the cock slamming into her throat.

We don't last long.

I drive into him mercilessly while he thrusts into her mouth and devours her cunt, making all my 69-train dreams come true.

My fingers tangle in her hair, flexing and releasing, as heaven edges closer and closer.

Jag cups her ass, spreading her open for his plunging tongue as she works his cock with lips and fists.

Drawing him to the back of her throat, she scoops her

fingers under his balls and runs her knuckles along the top of my shaft, setting me off.

"I'm coming." I slam into him, growling and jerking.

He's growling, too, right against her cunt. She follows us, swallowing him through her moans and writhing on his chest.

The sloppy wet sounds of our orgasms settle through the room as we slow our bodies and collapse in a boneless pile.

"I need a second after that." Jag drapes a leg over mine and an arm across Dove's chest.

"That was insane." She rests a hand on his forearm, trying to catch her breath.

"I felt that everywhere." I roll into Jag's side and pinch his nipple. "Pretty sure I got you pregnant."

"You're obnoxious." He wheezes through a laugh.

"I'm your favorite fella." I drop my chest onto his and dig a knuckle into his ribs. "Say it."

"I love you."

We both freeze as the words leave him, our gazes intertwined and searching.

I clap a hand over his mouth and put my face in his. "You can't take it back."

He pries my fingers away and releases a labored breath. "I love you, Wolfson Strakh."

"That's convenient, because I'm utterly in love with you. It's a healthy obsession. Yours. Not mine."

We both look at Dove.

Propped on an elbow, she presses her fingers to her mouth as her eyes fill with shiny, happy tears.

"I love you, Little Bird." Jag strokes her thigh.

"Yes. We all love one another. Group hug." I gather them into my arms and tackle them to the bed in a shower of kisses and laughter.

love

SIXTY-NINE

We clean up in the bathroom, and I take longer than needed, lingering at the vanity, hands braced on the marble.

Sounds of movement drift from the other room, the bed creaking as the guys settle back in. Deep voices. Sated murmurs. Familiar rhythms.

Jag and Wolf.

They're devastating together. Heartbreakingly divine in their love for each other. Captivating and utterly torrid in the way their bodies fit and move together. I can't unsee it. I never want to let it go.

And Jag? He's everything I idolized as a child. Every myth I told myself about him is true. Guardian, superhero, protector, family... He's all those things and more. More human. More resilient. More damaged and real.

I still haven't recovered from the shocking, mind-blowing intimacy.

He ate my pussy.

Twice.

Jag, my stepbrother, the man I've been fantasizing about for seventeen years, shoved his tongue up inside me and made me come.

The truth lands in pieces, struggling to stick. Reality far exceeds every version I dreamed, every safe fantasy, every impossible hope. The real Jag isn't cleaner or easier. He's filthy, messy, and beautifully, disarmingly complicated.

What he did for me when we had nothing, what he endured so I could eat, breathe, and go to school, it cuts even deeper now that I understand it.

I was a nightmare. An angry brat with a chip on her shoulder and an inappropriate infatuation with her stepbrother. I made everything harder on him without meaning to, without knowing what he was carrying.

I didn't know any of it. Not a damn thing about Adrian Crowe or my mother or the promise Jag made to her. I need to give myself grace for that ignorance. I was a kid.

But guilt doesn't listen to reason. It festers and bleeds inside me. I want to rewind and redo every moment where I failed him.

I can't.

So I breathe and accept that this reckoning in my heart will take time. Love doesn't erase the past. It asks me to sit with the consequences and learn how to live differently going forward.

In the mirror, I meet my own eyes and push my shoulders back.

This isn't something to rush.

The best part? I don't have to sort through it alone.

I scoop Jag's discarded shirt off the floor, the one he wore on the flight here. It smells like him and travel and the familiarity of home, making my chest ache.

As a child, I didn't always have a roof over my head. But I was never homeless. Not until I lost the warmth of his arms around me.

Tears burn behind my eyes as I pull the shirt over my head. The hem slips past my thighs, settling on me the way his shirts always did.

When I was fifteen, I made a promise to myself and never spent another night with Jag Rath. It hardened me when I needed to learn how to be independent. It protected my heart when he rescued me from harm. It did its job.

Now it's time to let it go.

I leave the bathroom and cross the room toward the bed, toward the love and promise waiting there.

Jag and Wolf sprawl on their backs, heads on pillows, and

sheets tangled around their legs. They're both naked, their cocks lying limp across their stomachs, languid and assuaged.

Wolf's fingers relax on Jag's dick, his thumb absently stroking the soft, fat length. Jag's head rests on his bent arm behind him, his eyes half-mast, reflecting his lazy pleasure. His other hand traces the scars on Wolf's chest, wordlessly acknowledging them.

They watch me approach the bed with rapt attention. Two pairs of eyes. Arctic wolf blue. Molten jaguar amber. All predatory focus.

Wolf slips his hand from Jag and shifts, opening a space between them. A pocket made just for me.

I set a knee on the bed.

"Stop." He points at me. "You're violating the dress code. No shirts allowed. Or clothes, in general."

Heat flushes my skin, and a soft laugh escapes me. I tug off the shirt and crawl into the space they made for me.

Wolf crowds in, his chest flush against my back. I curl forward into Jag, and his arms close around me, protective and familiar, just like I remember.

Home. My body recognizes him immediately, my breath falling into an easy, relaxed rhythm.

But it isn't the same safety I knew as a child. Wolf's presence at my back changes the energy and geometry. And Jag's embrace? There's intention there now. Desire. Hardness. A swelling between our hips.

He wants me. I want him. And we're both viscerally aware of that want.

Jag's fingers find the small mark at my collarbone, and I reach for the old scar beneath his ribs, tracing it with the same quiet respect. We both know what those places cost. We both know why they matter.

Wolf drapes an arm over our hips and regales us with stories about his day. Joy spills out of him as he talks about the people he met, the tattoo appointments stacking up, the visit from Van Quiso and Liv Reed, and how a casual hello turned into secret cigarettes, plans, tequila, and gossip.

Only Wolf can walk into a brood of vipers and come out with a client list, a job offer, and a new best friend.

I laugh. Jag groans, and underneath the amusement, we're

all thinking it.

How do we hold onto this? How do we secure a future that looks and feels like this moment right here?

Three messy souls. One perfect braid. Threaded together with bloodstained fingers.

Jag's future is fixed. So Wolf and I will bend and weave ourselves around him. Our place is wherever he is.

But tonight isn't for maps or decisions. Nothing heavy. Nothing that demands answers.

Wolf keeps talking. I keep smiling. Jag keeps making noises like he's suffering. He isn't.

We breathe together, three scarred bodies in perfect alignment, as the stories taper off and sleep finds us where we are.

jag
SEVENTY

Three nights later, I wake from an erotic dream, hard as a rock and leaking from the tip. My fucking balls are soaked.

A wet dream? Am I fourteen again?

My eyes open to total darkness. I hold still, trying not to breathe too loudly.

Dove stirs beside me, and I turn my neck to find her watching me.

Her face rests close to mine on the pillow, hair mussed, mouth soft with sleep. Her gaze sinks into mine, pupils wide and dark with arousal. Then she looks down.

I follow her line of sight, squinting as the room resolves in pieces. Sheets pushed low. Legs spread. Hers and mine.

Wolf moves between us with hands, lips, and tongue. He licks her pussy while jerking me and sucks my cock while fingering her, back and forth, smiling and moaning.

Holy fuck, it feels so fucking good.

He's never taken me in his mouth.

Yet there he is, his chiseled lips wrapped around my dick, and his throat working as he takes me to the root and swallows.

"Goddammit, Wolf!" My back bows, and my hand fumbles for Dove's, lacing our fingers.

He and I have been fooling around for three days. No sex since the night he fucked my ass.

I set that pace on purpose. Guiding him a step at a time. Watching his tells. Keeping it slow so his body stays with his mind. So far, nothing has set him off like the first time we were together.

But if I left it to him, he would charge full-speed ahead, wearing a grin and a live bomb, consequences be damned.

That recklessness is part of what I love about him. But it could flip an unknown trigger and send him into a full breakdown.

He pulls his mouth off me with a wet slurp and buries his face in Dove's cunt.

She's the other reason I slowed us down. She's still sorting through some corrosive thoughts and misplaced guilt. We talk about it. I push back where I can, reminding her what belongs to her and what never did. But that's a crossing only she can make. I can't drag her over it.

The need to fuck her is killing me slowly. My dick wants in her so badly I can taste it. But I've waited years. I can handle a few more days.

I squeeze her hand as she writhes and thrashes on Wolf's tongue. He's mastered the art of cunnilingus, pulling sounds from her I've never heard her make. When she comes, he leaves her breathless and turns back to me.

My cock hits his throat, pulsing and dripping as he sucks me like a pro.

I don't know how many times this act was forced on him as a child, but he gives no indication of those memories sneaking in. They remain buried as he torments my balls and devours every inch of me.

Dove rests her head on my shoulder and watches him carefully, searching for signs of distress.

Her vigilance gives me leave to sink into the hot pleasure of his mouth. The familiar grip of his hands, the delicious suction of his lips, and the slippery swirl of his tongue are my undoing.

My insides clench. My fingers tighten on Dove's, and my hips thrust, chasing, reaching...

"Coming! Fuck, Wolf! I'm fucking coming!" I explode in his mouth, roaring, shaking, and jerking uncontrollably.

Black spots blotch my vision as my cock kicks, spurting and

knocking against his throat.

He swallows it all and sits back, grinning like a gorgeous fiend.

"You cured me." He falls to the mattress beside us. "Medicine never tasted so good."

"That's not how it works." I nudge him with a boneless leg. "You don't need a cure, pup."

"You're right." He kisses my hip and crawls to his spot behind Dove. "I just needed the throat goat and the belle of the balls."

"I'm afraid to ask who is whom." She snuggles into my arms, pressing a drowsy smile against my chest.

"Labels are flexible. I appreciate you both equally for your specialized talents." He tucks in closer behind her, his hand reaching across her to rest on my hip. "I'm inclusive like that."

My chest loosens, the air finally moving all the way in and out of my lungs without catching. This is the space I didn't know how to name. The shape I spent my entire life trying and failing to survive without.

I needed this. *Them.* Not as an idea. Not as a fantasy. As this. Affection and acceptance and shared breath. They're proof that the world can hold more than vigilance and duty.

"I love you," I say quietly, because anything louder would fracture the moment. I touch my mouth to Dove's hair, my hand settling on Wolf's neck. "Both of you."

They remain still, listening as I break open.

"I spent my whole life clenching and bracing." The words drag from places I don't usually expose. "Waiting. Guarding. Holding the line. But with you, I don't have to do that. You don't just stand with me. You fill the emptiness. I carried this void, and *fuck*, it ached so badly. But not anymore. You complete my life. Not by fixing it. By sharing it. God, it's just... I can finally breathe now."

"I get it. Not the same way. But close enough." Wolf shifts, twining his legs around ours. "I thought I had to choose sides. Women or men. Straight or gay. But those choices don't fit me. Being with you two... That fits. You both helped me realize there were never walls to begin with."

Dove presses her forehead to my chest, her arm snaking around my waist.

"Before you," Wolf says, "my life didn't feel like mine. My body, my fear, my future, even my desire felt dangerous." He swallows. "When I started wanting without panic, wanting freely, wanting both of you, it felt… Right. Fated. And the best part? Loving you didn't fracture me. It put me together."

I relish the relief in his voice. The wonder. The quiet joy of not having to justify himself to anyone in the room. He doesn't frame his bi-awakening as a revelation so much as a homecoming. His desire no longer feels fenced in or scary. It's simply his.

"This, being here, being seen, there's no judgment." He looks at me, then Dove. "No rules about who I'm allowed to be. My sexuality isn't caged. It's free and mine, and I get to share it with you."

I take that in, the steadiness of it, the courage it took him to get here. Pride lifts my chest. But more than that, I'm filled with reverence.

"I'm so happy for you." Dove rolls to her back between us, meeting each of our gazes in turn. "For both of you. Watching you find yourselves like this, without fear or apology, it's everything I ever wanted for you." A small smile curves her mouth. "I get to love you both exactly as you are. That makes me feel so fucking lucky."

"I love you, too." I draw them closer, my hand firm at Wolf's nape, anchoring us all in the quiet that follows.

This honesty is the thing I didn't know I was allowed to want. Hearing them say it, I know it's real. Three breaths syncing without effort. Three lives aligned, not by force or necessity, but by choice.

We're here. We're enough. For the first time I can remember, nothing inside me is on guard.

And that's how we fall asleep. In a tangle of limbs and a growing trust that holds.

love

SEVENTY-ONE

My roller skates hum against polished concrete as I carve lazy loops around Luke's hypercars.

This space is big enough to swallow Monty's garage with room left over for echoes. Everything gleams with glass, steel, and chrome, orderly to the point of obsession.

I drift past a wall of tools, snag what I need without stopping, and coast back to the red lady that owns my attention.

Luke's 1956 Porsche Speedster sits where he parked it when he moved his collection here years ago. I'm obsessed with this car for the same reason I'm obsessed with anything vintage and mechanical. It tells me the truth when I listen. It rewards precision, punishes carelessness, and *my God*, the rumble, the electricity, the sexy power.

All it needs is a tune-up. I roll close, drop into a crouch, and set to work, losing myself in the rhythm of hands and thought.

A week ago, Jag and Wolf arrived in a storm of testosterone and truth bombs. A week of recalibration and sleeping soundly in the arms of two men.

Jag disappears into meetings most days, deep in the inner machinery of the cartel, sliding into his cybercriminal skin. He spends the rest of his time with me, checking in without hovering, present without crowding. It's a careful balance, and he's good at it.

Wolf took Van's job offer the way Wolf takes anything, headfirst and smiling like a weirdo. He sits in on cartel meetings, planning the demise of every monster that preyed on the victims of House of Crowe. But the majority of his time is spent tattooing cartel guards, service staff, and the inner circle, filling his calendar with names, skin, and stories.

And me? I skate. I make things run right. I fix what was neglected. I remind myself that I'm allowed to be happy.

I'm torquing a bolt when I sense Jag behind me.

It's always been like that. A change in the air. A shift that makes my spine straighten and my breath hitch. I don't look up right away. I know he'll wait.

His footsteps stop a few feet away. When I glance up, he's leaning against a workbench, sleeves rolled, and shirt unbuttoned at the collar. Always so heart-stoppingly gorgeous. But the look in his amber eyes is different today. Not cautious. Not rushed. Finished with something.

He watches me for an endless moment, gaze hard and assessing. Not the way he watches rooms and cameras. This is him when he's done pretending patience is a virtue.

I straighten, roll closer, and rest a hip against the Speedster. "Long day?"

"Long enough." He pushes off the bench and steps into my space, towering over me. His eyes don't wander. They lock with mine and stay. "Tonight."

That's it. One word. No explanation.

My stomach drops in the best possible way. Heat slides low and deep, gathering and swirling. I know what he wants, and he's done waiting for me to finish punishing myself.

Extending his hands between us, he pinches strong fingers around the barbells in my nipples. With that grip, he tugs me to him.

My breath leaves me as the skates roll forward, bumping his boots. My mouth tips upward, and he plunders it. Hot breath. Sinful tongue. His lips raid in sucking pulls.

A moment later, he releases me, pivots on his heel, and leaves without another word.

I stand there, hands still, pulse hammering, the hum of the garage suddenly too bright.

love

A shiver creeps up. Then it's everywhere, tightening my skin and rattling my bones as every nerve ending stretches to chase him.

Images invade, memories of Wolf's hands, Jag's mouth, their cocks rubbing together, muscles flexing, and hips thrusting.

Fuck!

I force myself back into motion. Tools clink. The 356 Speedster comes back to life. I let myself feel good at this. Let myself feel wanted without bargaining for it.

Until my concentration fractures again. I can still think, still move, but everything routes back to my body. The tingling in my belly sharpens, insistent, turning every breath into need. I'm aware of how I'm standing, how my shorts rub against my pussy, and how my nipples harden against my shirt.

When I finish the Speedster, I circle the Mustang. Van's 1965 GT Fastback sits in the corner, darker, meaner, all muscle. I glide around it, palm brushing the curve of the fender as I think about what I'll need to bring it back into proper shape. The plan helps. Focus helps.

But underneath it all, the anticipation simmers.

It follows me like a low current as the day toils on. I skate until my calves burn, and my shirt sticks to my back. I eat without tasting much. I keep busy so I don't tumble into my head and stay there.

Every so often, I catch myself smiling for no reason.

Wolf breezes through at one point, ink smudged on his fingers, telling me a story about a client who cried then laughed then booked another session. Holding his saxophone case, he says offhandedly that there were requests to hear him play. Then he kisses my lips and saunters off, buzzing with bright energy.

I watch him go, affection warming my chest.

Jag doesn't return to the garage. That feels deliberate.

At the end of the day, I finish what I'm doing, wipe my hands, and unlace my skates. I don't rush. I don't stall. I leave the garage and stride to our suite, my nerves tuning tight. But it isn't fear. It's readiness.

They're on the balcony when I come in, two tall silhouettes locked in an embrace and kissing in the dark. I don't interrupt.

I slip into the bathroom and let the shower take the day off me, warm water chasing away grease and grit and the sticky arousal that's been dripping between my legs since Jag's visit.

When I step back into the bedroom, I don't bother with clothes.

Jag stands near the bed, and Wolf sits on the edge, both wearing tight briefs and nothing else.

They watch me approach, their expressions unreadable.

Meanwhile, I unravel with every step I erase between us. The fire inside me isn't just hunger. Affection dances in the blaze along with the certainty that I'm wanted exactly as I am.

My pulse lifts. My smile comes easy. I cross the room feeling happier and hornier than I've ever been. Love does this to me. It makes me giddy and wanton.

"We need your consent, Dovey." Wolf reaches for my hand.

"You have it."

"You don't even know what you're consenting to." Jag shifts his weight, subtly adjusting the bulge in his briefs.

"I'm consenting to sex with both of you, for now and forever, in all the positions. Anal, DP, every hole, two in one hole... If it fits, I want it." I glance between them. "Keeping up with the libidos of two virile men may prove challenging. But that's the beauty in having boyfriends who are boyfriends. You can fuck each other ten times a day and still keep me satisfied. Right?"

"Hell's balls." Wolf grips himself and lets out a deep, guttural groan.

"Pull it together." Jag swats him on the back of the head. "Or you won't last the night."

"Right." Wolf composes himself and stands, bending his knees until his eyes are level with mine. "Jag's going to fuck you. I'll be right here. But when he's inside you, it's just you and him."

"You guys have this all planned out?"

"Yes, with our dicks in our hands." He kisses me, climbs to the top of the bed, and sits with his back against the headboard.

"Tonight, we leave the past behind." Jag folds his arms over his bare chest, drawing my attention to all the defined ridges decorating his abdomen. "Look at me, Dove."

"I'm looking." At the muscular masterpiece on display before me.

"My eyes."

Wolf chews on his smile, staring at Jag's body, too.

I meet Jag's stern gaze.

"Tonight, you'll find nothing here but the future. A future

love

that includes the three of us, living together, fucking together, and making decisions together." He searches my eyes. "Any hesitation?"

"Been hesitating for seventeen years, Jag. No more running or waiting. I'm not your ward or your little sister or a promise you made when you were sixteen. I want you to fuck me and spend your life with me because I'm the woman you fell in love with and decided to keep."

"Fuck, I love you. Never letting you go." He grabs my face and kisses me fiercely.

I rise on tiptoes and meet his passion until we're both gasping for air. He sucks on my Medusa piercing and forces himself to calm, his mouth softening without losing the edge. He draws it out, a slow provocation, lips skimming and tongue pressing in until my balance tips, and I'm leaning into him, melting.

Kissing him is never just lips. It's the cut of his jaw as it tightens, the line of his neck as he angles closer, the sweep of his hungry tongue, all the masculine angles that pull me in.

Once I'm wobbly and breathless, he scoops me up. My arms go slack around his neck, sensation taking over everything else.

The room blurs as he sets me on the bed, my pulse galloping and every muscle in my body vibrating and clenching.

He removes his underwear and stands near my feet, dragging his gaze over my shivering flesh.

"Be a good little bird and spread your legs." He takes himself in hand, stroking lazily.

I curl my fingers in the sheets above my head and open my knees as far as they'll go.

"Holy fuck." His fist moves faster on his dick, his forearms flexing in an erotic show of sculpted, veiny contours. "You're so goddamn sexy. I love when you're naked."

"Keep looking at me like that, and I'll come before you touch me."

"Can't stop looking. I want to kiss every inch of you, but I've waited years for this." He crawls between my legs and lowers himself over me. "Not waiting another fucking second to be inside you."

Heat and strength radiate from him as his body covers me like a slab of hot granite. He braces his weight on an elbow and reaches between us, angling his cock against my opening.

The feel of his broad head right there, sliding through my wetness, pushing against my entrance, and ready to breach my body... It makes everything else fall quiet while need and urgency tear through me.

"I can't wait to feel you around me." He lowers his forehead to mine and presses in, giving me the tip.

"Oh, God. This is happening." I adjust my grip on his shoulders, shaking uncontrollably. "Please, Jag. I can feel your dick throbbing. Give it to me."

"I want you to look me in the eyes while I'm inside you." He leans in, fusing our connection with his gaze.

Then he thrusts, impaling me to the root.

"Fuck. Dove... Fuck." A choking sound breaks from him as he rocks forward and back, changes the angle, and grinds down. "Goddammit. Feels so fucking good."

I can't respond. Can't push breath past my lips. I can only stare into the black abyss of his blown pupils as he rolls his hips and fucks me hard.

He's done things I can't fully measure. He's killed for me. Sold his body for me. But seeing him like this? Feeling him moving between my legs? This is the Jag I've been dying to meet. This man is achingly human, stripped down to feeling, and unmoored by love.

"You look unbelievably sexy when you're balls-deep inside me." I dart my tongue along the seam of his parted lips.

He gathers my thighs around his waist, lifts my ass, and hauls my body tighter to his. Then he lowers his mouth to mine.

"I love you." He breathes the oath against my lips.

His next thrust drives home the point. He fucks me and kisses me, and I open to all of it, my mouth full of his tongue and my pussy stuffed with his cock.

My nails scratch down his back, fingers tracing lines I know by heart, as my body answers the pull between us.

Sex with Jag is exquisite beyond words, heavy with history, shimmering with promise, and overwhelmingly beautiful as it all finally lands at once.

"I love to hear you moan while I'm fucking you." He groans against my mouth.

"Fuck me harder, and you can hear me moan while I come."

And so he does. He kicks up the tempo and unleashes his

power, ramming, stabbing, and rubbing me right there.

"Right there. Right there. Oh, God. Don't stop." Pinned beneath two-hundred pounds of shredded muscle, I fall into his bedroom eyes and let go. "I'm coming, Jag! Fucking coming all over you."

The tendons in his neck go taut. His hips stutter, and his breath grows erratic. I swear the amber in his eyes completely disappears as he opens his mouth and roars.

We come together, bucking and moaning, my chest and legs burning, trembling and twitching in the shimmer of orgasmic bliss.

His weight sinks into me, his breath hot and fast against my neck. Even as he softens inside me, his hips continue to languidly thrust.

"Wolf." He kisses my neck, giving no sign of pulling away. "How hard are you?"

"Is that a real question?" Wolf's face appears above mine, his hair falling forward, blue eyes gleaming with lust.

He gives me a sexy as fuck smile, leans down, and kisses me. Upside down. All lips and confidence.

Jag sits back, and Wolf moves toward him, crawling down my body from my head to where I'm joined with Jag. Wolf sets his mouth there, licking the clamp of my pussy around Jag's impaled cock.

Jag and I moan at the same time. I clutch Wolf's thighs, where they straddle my head and draw his heavy ball sack into my mouth. He growls between my legs and reaches down to angle his dick against my lips.

I take it, sucking him deep and swirling my tongue. We stay like that, pleasuring each other with our mouths and fingers.

Jag is semi-hard as he slides out and shoves himself between Wolf's lips. Wolf licks him clean, slurping and smacking as he restlessly fucks my throat.

When Jag eases back, Wolf turns his attention to my pussy. Then we take full advantage of the 69 position, riding each other's faces. He gags me with his unapologetic thrusts as his tongue lashes and curls inside me.

Before I can come, he swings around, seats himself between my legs, and pushes inside my cunt. Then he fucks me.

His spine rolls. His hips flex, and his pecs contract and

stretch his scars, as he drives deeper and harder. He feels so good I might cry.

Jag moves in beside us and kisses me, then Wolf, then the three of us are kissing one another, taking turns and tangling our tongues together. Three mouths, fusing and consuming in a union of love.

Pushing up on a vascular arm, Jag cups Wolf's neck and angles his head to deepen the kiss. Their jaws stretch open, and their tongues rub and slide together, rough and unmistakably masculine, making Wolf pound harder between my legs.

Beneath Jag's dominance, Wolf is pure heat and surrender, his lips parting under the slant of Jag's mouth, his chest rising hard as he snatches air in the brief pauses between kisses.

Watching them together, seeing how Jag sets the pace and how Wolf yields to it, turns me on like nothing else, lighting every cell in my body on fire.

"Are you ready to go again, old man?" Wolf growls against Jag's lips.

Jag sits back, his cock hard as steel, throwing an impressive shadow against the rippled expanse of his abs.

In answer to Wolf, he grabs the lube and rubs it along his length.

"He's going to fuck us." Wolf draws a finger down my chest and tweaks each of my nipples. "Can you handle that, Bluebird?"

"Can you?"

"Yes, with your pussy squeezing around me." He groans, stroking deep. "Fucking hell, you're tight."

Jag kneels behind Wolf and trails a hand down the length of his spine.

"Double penetration." He finds my eyes over Wolf's shoulder. "This is a first for all of us."

That surprises me. And thrills me to no end.

Bending over Wolf's back, he works his fingers inside me, fitting them alongside Wolf's dick. Then he replaces his hand with something much larger.

The stretch, the burn, the absolute feeling of fullness... *Oh, my God.* They're in me. Both of them. Inside me.

It takes effort to swallow. My skin prickles with a feverish chill, perspiration beading across my chest and down my spine.

I'm breathless, nailed to the mattress by two huge cocks, and *fuck me...* Why does it feel so perfect?

love

"Dove?" Jag gives a small, testing thrust. "You okay?"

"Never been better. Just..." I squirm beneath their panting bodies. "Please, fuck me."

Jag shifts, presses in tight against Wolf, eases back, and shoves forward, stroking, rocking, rutting into me and taking Wolf with him.

Their dicks move together, rubbing in and out, dragging along nerves and pleasure centers I didn't know I had. The friction, the pressure, it's too much. Too good.

"I'm going to come. Jag, Wolf, I'm... Coming!" It hits me sideways, blasting through my body in sizzling sparks.

I feel it in my toes, my veins, and the roots of my hair.

"That's it." Jag fucks me through it while licking and kissing Wolf's neck. "Such a good little bird."

As my body liquefies beneath them, Jag pulls out and adjusts his angle higher, pressing against Wolf's entrance.

I can't see behind Wolf, but I feel him inside me, his cock pulsing and jumping in anticipation of Jag's thrust.

Reaching up, I take Wolf's face in my hands and force his eyes on me.

"Look at me." My thumbs brush across his flushed cheeks. "Stay with me. Don't look away."

"I'm *in* you, darling." He grinds his hips against mine. "Not going anywhere."

"Nice and easy." Jag places a reverent kiss on Wolf's spine.

Then, with a slow crunch of his abs, he curls his pelvis forward and sinks into Wolf.

Wolf's mouth hangs open on a strangled breath. He grips the sheets above my head, chokes on a low, pleasure-soaked groan, and stares into my eyes.

I watch him, holding him to me, with me. When he starts breathing again, a smile pulls on his mouth, all teeth and wicked delight.

Then we move together, building a rhythm. Our rhythm. Three bodies, three hearts, chasing our forever.

wolfson
SEVENTY-TWO

It's never felt like this. Never felt like my balls are going to explode from sublime, unholy, all-consuming rapture.

The pressure doesn't hurt. It drowns me in ecstasy. Jag's cock feels enormous, sliding and swelling inside me. I feel every ridge, every pulse in his thick, exquisite length.

"I can't fucking wait for you to come in me." I push against him, taking him to the root, and thrust forward, sinking into my darling Dove.

The best of both worlds. I don't want it to end. But I'm close. Too fucking close.

"Wolf." Jag reaches around and caresses my scars, pausing to tweak each of my nipples. "Talk to me."

"Living the dream, Jag. Now be a good kitty, and fuck me as hard as you can."

Jag rests a hand low on Dove's belly, feeling me thrust inside her as he thrusts into me.

"I love hearing the sound of your bodies slapping together." Dove holds my face in her hands, her eyes creased in concentration.

Staving off her orgasm? Or watching me for signs of distress?

With her beneath me and Jag in my ass, I think about the

last time I was in this position.

Last year.

The devil's bargain.

But as I stare down at Dove, I don't see Frankie and her tears. And as Jag ruts inside me, I don't feel Denver's violation.

I can think about the abuse without reliving it.

Progress.

Maybe Frankie was on to something. Writing about my demons forced me to confront them. It gave me control over my past. And my future.

I choose this. I want it. Because I love Jag and Dove.

"Come, Little Dove." I circle a finger around her clit, rolling it the way she likes it. "Come on my cock."

She tenses, trembles, and unravels with a scream that jiggles her tits and widens her eyes.

Spasms ignite in her pussy, fisting around me mercilessly. *Oh, Shit,* I'm going to join her. I can't… I can't…

Jag pulls out, flips me over, and slams into me again, with his hand on my dick and his eyes locked on mine.

"With me." He jerks me and fucks me, and we chase it, finishing together in a grunting, shaking, spurting explosion.

When we collapse, it's with groaning laughter and tangled limbs.

"I have an abundance of come left." I slap a limp hand across Dove's ass, making her moan. "Who's ready?"

"You're going to kill me." Jag face-plants into the bedding, out of breath.

"Please, don't tell me you're too old for all this." I gesture at my sweaty body.

"Give me a minute," he grumbles. "Or an hour."

"We'll be in the shower while you wait for your Viagra to kick in." I lunge for Dove and haul her up, draping her listless body over my shoulder.

She bursts into laughter, the sound chasing us as I head for the bathroom.

We don't make it through a proper cleaning before I'm fucking her against the wall. During our second attempt to wash, Jag finally joins us.

She and I wash him thoroughly. Then we suck him together. My new favorite thing.

He busts a nut so fast, we barely have time to catch his load in our mouths.

After the shower, he sits us down in the kitchenette and makes us drink water and eat the leftovers in the fridge.

Then it's on.

We christen every surface of the suite. Oral, anal, spitroast, ride and blow, and DP in all her holes. We take breathers. We take power naps. But all three of us stay connected and involved long into the night.

Eventually, the sun breaks the horizon, and Dove can't stop yawning. She sits on my lap, my cock at rest inside her, with Jag's cheek pressed to her inner thigh.

He sprawls between our legs, eyes closed. I'm certain he's asleep until his sharp exhale brushes against my balls.

"Dinner meeting tomorrow night." He kisses Dove's clit, then lower, where she and I are joined. "Everyone at the table."

"You mean tonight." I gesture at the window and the first rays of light.

"Tonight. All twenty-two members of the inner circle will be in attendance."

"And you'll be there?" Dove rakes her fingers through his hair.

"Yes. I'll be there with my plus-one plus-one and my nonnegotiable demands about our future together."

jag

SEVENTY-THREE

"You're certain about this?" My heart gallops as I look at Dove first. "If you have regrets later—"

"No regrets." She steps toward me, her heels adding four-inches to her height as she grips my jaw and pierces me with her gilded stare. "No hesitation."

We stand in the entryway of our suite, minutes from heading to the dinner meeting. I wear a fitted suit, black and serviceable, uninspiring enough to disappear into a crowd. Fabric and obligation pulls where they shouldn't, pinching at my collar.

I'm not nervous. Just ready to go so we can get back.

Back to our room.

Back to our bed.

"That dress belongs on the floor." I give her a slow perusal.

"Excuse me?" She anchors her fists on her hips.

The cocktail dress outlines every gorgeous curve of her figure, the corset bodice fitted to push her tits up and out. The neckline frames the beauty mark at her collarbone, drawing the eye to all that cleavage.

"When I rip it from your body and carry you to the bed, you'll understand." I arch a brow.

A pretty flush colors her cheeks.

jag

The top half of her hair pulls into two buns, crowned with black beads. The rest spills over her shoulders in ombré ripples of blue and green. Her legs are bare, unapologetically so, set off by strappy black heels.

"You look lethal." My dick hardens. "Devastatingly beautiful."

She looks like she belongs exactly where she is.

"Thank you." She dips into a curtsy.

I turn to Wolf. "What about you?"

"As my family would say, I'm all in." He drapes an arm over Dove's shoulders and strikes a pose.

He wears a similar suit to mine, the tailored cuts made unruly by the man inside it.

A fishnet top sits under the jacket, where a proper shirt would be, skin and scars visible beneath the weave. A pearl necklace rests at his throat, and matching earrings dangle from his ears.

He styled his skater-long hair to sweep across his brow instead of in his eyes. Rings crowd his fingers, and heavy eyeliner sharpens the effect, making his blue eyes impossible to ignore.

"You clean up." I meet his gaze.

"I know." He grins.

I think about the room he'll walk into wearing that suit. The men who will underestimate him because he looks beautiful. The ones who will clock the intelligence behind the style and hesitate. Wolf has always understood optics. Tonight, he's weaponized them.

We spent the day in bed together, sunlight shifting across the room while we talked about what staying here actually means for them.

Before Wolf and I arrived in Colombia, Dove had already told Matias she would remain if Wolf did. I know that now. I also know I won't let that be the only condition on the table.

I have demands.

Tonight, I intend to make them clear.

I open the door and step into the corridor. Wolf falls in at my right, Dove between us. We link hands without discussion. It steadies the pace and keeps us aligned as we move through the citadel.

Three people choosing the same direction.

jag

The walk to the dining hall takes ten minutes. By the time we arrive, the room is already coming alive. Chairs slide back. Quiet discussions taper off. One by one, the rest of the twenty-two filters in.

Matias takes his place at the head of the table, Camila on his right and Van on his left.

Camila motions at me then the chair beside her. I take the offered seat with Wolf at my side and Dove next to him.

Conversation fills the table as plates arrive in an endless procession of appetizers. Crisped *arepas* topped with warm *hogao*. Bowls of *ajiaco* broth, fragrant with *guascas*.

I'm slowly learning the food, but there are a few things I don't recognize as the hiss of hot plates meets wood.

The aromas of corn, citrus, and slow-cooked meats circulate the room, threaded with the clink of cutlery and the murmurs of easy camaraderie. Family updates are shared, jokes traded, and a few dry comments draw laughter. I answer where appropriate and nod where it's expected.

Wolf charms without trying, asking a question here, offering an offensive punchline there. Dove listens, eyes moving, absorbing the dynamics with the same attention she gives an engine.

Matias rises.

The room quiets with him, chairs easing back, and conversations tapering into stillness. He lifts his glass and looks down the length of the table, expression composed and satisfied.

"Welcome home." He smiles warmly. "It's rare to have us all in one place. We're usually scattered across the globe, most of you on reconnaissance or undercover operations, dangerous work that keeps us moving. But for this..." He tips his drink in my direction. "For *El Vigilante*, you all came back."

"It's called FOMO." Camila laughs.

A ripple of assent moves around the table. Glasses lift.

"And you..." Matias turns fully toward me. "You have done this. Your presence gathered the circle. For that, you have my thanks. Our thanks." He lifts his glass higher. "*Salud.*"

"*Salud*," the table answers, voices overlapping and glasses meeting with ringing clinks.

I take a sip, let the moment settle, and set down my glass.

When I clear my throat, it's soft but deliberate. Heads turn.

The room yields again.

"Thank you for the hospitality. For the welcome. For the food." I incline my head to Camila, then Matias. "It's been... Thorough."

A few smiles flicker. I don't return them.

"There's something we need to discuss before the next course." I square my shoulders. "A demand. Two of them, actually."

"This should be interesting." Van reclines, waggling a toothpick between his lips.

Matias lifts a hand, the motion casual but carrying weight.

"*Hable con todos.*" He flicks his fingers outward, indicating the table. "Speak."

"All right." I turn my body toward the circle and let my gaze travel, meeting eyes and measuring attention. "Wolf accepted your job offer, but I have limits. His involvement will be solely in an intelligence capacity. He'll provide analysis, strategy, and ideas." I clamp a hand on his jogging knee beneath the table, calming him. "He will not be deployed as a spy. He will not be an operative. He will not be placed in the field or anywhere that requires a weapon."

I squeeze his knee, a quiet warning, and feel the argument coil in him anyway. When we talked this through earlier, he said this condition wasn't necessary, that he could handle himself.

Dove and I didn't budge.

In our democracy of three, he lost that vote.

"He stays here." I keep my hand on his leg, reminding him to remain quiet. "At the table. In rooms like this. Where minds are used instead of bodies."

"What I'm hearing is..." Van grins around the toothpick. "No more wearable surprises?"

"No bombs. No bullets. No danger. Wolf stays out of the line of fire." I set my forearms on the table and harden my voice. "I agreed to give you my life for one reason only. The protection of Wolf and Dove."

"The terms changed." Matias sips from his glass, watching me over the rim. "When your Wolf arrived wearing a bomb, he demonstrated capabilities that align with our needs."

"He is *not* collateral!" I slam a fist onto the table, rattling the dishes. "He's not leverage or incentive or a fucking clause in a contract. Everything else is negotiable. *That* is not."

jag

The room goes quiet, eyes shifting, calculating, but not objecting.

Matias studies Wolf, assessing posture and expression, marking Wolf's stillness, which reads as confidence rather than compliance. Then his gaze returns to me.

"I'll agree," he says at last. "With conditions."

Here we go.

"I'm listening."

"Wolf answers to the table." He tips his glass at the inner circle. "Not to you alone. When we ask for his mind, we get it. Fully."

"That was always implied."

"And we want the Russians." His eyes cut to Wolf. "In the nightclub, you wore devices no one detected, cameras and other hidden communications that allowed the Russians to see and hear everything. And the explosive... It was invisible enough to sneak inside." He tilts his head. "The Ghost built all that?"

"Yep. With two of these." Wolf lifts both hands, fingers splayed and wriggling, irreverent as fuck. "DIY."

Murmurs move around the table.

"You want the Russians?" I look at Matias. "I thought you didn't trust them?"

"I had to be sure, and now I know." His dark eyes glint. "The Ghost and his associates don't traffic humans. That makes them amenable to our cause. Persuadable. Useful. We want them to help us."

"The Ghost is retired." Wolf shrugs.

"Then you have your first assignment, Wolfson Strakh. Make him unretired."

"Sure." He coughs. "Totally doable. No problem." He nods, shifting. "I'm on it."

"This is where the second demand comes in." I turn back to the table. "We want time in Alaska. The three of us. Time with our family there."

"How much time?" Matias asks.

"Half the year." I steady my breathing. "Fifty percent here, fifty percent there."

"Your home is *here*." He sets his jaw.

I grit my teeth. I knew this would be the hard one.

A chair shifts at the far end of the table. Tiago Badell leans back, arm draped over his wife's lap. Former kingpin of Venezuela, still holding himself like the crown never left.

"Kate and I spend most of the year in Eritrea." Tiago lifts a brow at Matias.

"*Siempre haces lo que te da la gana.*" Matias scowls.

"*Porque soy mi propio jefe.*" Tiago shrugs, a lazy roll of one shoulder.

A few quiet sounds ripple down the table. I really need to learn Spanish. Like yesterday.

"*Algún día esa boca te va a costar caro.*" Matias leans forward, arms angrily braced on his knees.

"Stop flirting." Tiago laughs. "I might get the wrong idea."

The room settles again, tension redistributed.

"Just going to pile on here." Across the table, Cole Hartman winks at me and turns to Matias. "Lydia and I spend our summers in Russia and winters in Ireland. It's never been an issue."

Beside him, Joshua Carter leans toward his wife. "Liv and I live in Texas during football season." He looks straight at Matias. "Be reasonable, *jefe.*"

Silence follows. Not empty or hostile. Evaluative.

Matias's expression tightens with irritation. He doesn't like being boxed in by his own circle. He likes it even less when they're right.

What I've learned about these people is simple. Family comes first, their loved ones outrank everything else, and every voice at the table carries weight.

I stay still, hands relaxed, eyes on the shadow boss.

"*¿Alguna otra opinión?*" Matias asks the room.

No one speaks.

He holds the silence for a moment, sipping from his glass. When he sets it down, his smile is already in place.

"It's settled." He looks directly at me. "You may come and go as you want. Use our helicopters. Our planes. Be present for all required meetings." His tone sharpens. "But your home base is here. With The Freedom Fighters. *¿Comprende?*"

I nod. Beside me, Wolf and Dove nod, too.

"*Bueno.*" Matias leans in. "One more thing."

I wait.

"Every time you return to Colombia…" He flicks his eyes to Wolf. "You will bring Strakh Vodka."

jag

"Knew it." Wolf grins.

"Understood." I incline my head, hiding my smile.

The table exhales and drifts back into conversations about travel windows, aircraft maintenance, and the perfect heat level in the sauce. Plates shift. Glasses refill. The machine resumes its hum.

I rest an arm along the back of Wolf's chair and let my fingers trail over the nape of his neck. He stills under the touch without looking at me, a subtle acknowledgment that stirs so many things in my chest.

Dove leans across Wolf and reaches for me. I catch her hand easily.

"I'm happy, Jag," she whispers for only our circle of three. "Are you... Happy?"

"Yes."

"Promise?"

"I swear it." I hook our pinkies together and lift them to my lips.

Then I offer our intertwined fingers to Wolf.

He cradles both our hands in his palms, dips his head, and kisses our fingers with a seriousness that silences me.

When he looks up, the three of us hold one another's eyes over the small bridge of skin and promise.

The moment loosens, and we separate to eat.

I turn back to my plate and find Camila watching me from my other side, her expression unreadable.

"Welcome to the family." She lifts her glass, her finger tapping against the stem. "I told you in our first meeting that I'd been watching you, studying the jobs you refuse and the people you protect."

"I remember."

"You turned down every contract tied to human trafficking. Every operation that involved harming people who couldn't fight back. That told me everything." Her nostrils pulse with a slow inhale. "You belong here. In the circle." Her gaze moves to Wolf and Dove. "So do they. You were never going to survive without them." Her eyes return to me. "Without them, you would've never been able to breathe."

Realization slams into me with sudden, alarming clarity.

This wasn't coincidence or convenience. It was design.

Bringing Dove here, drawing Wolf in, folding them into the family so completely that leaving would never be a consideration. Because I would always choose them.

My jaw locks down on a smile. "You set me up."

She lifts her glass to her mouth and takes an unhurried sip with a glimmer dancing in her eyes.

love
SEVENTY-FOUR

One year later

The Strakh island pulses with ordinary miracles.

The couch faces the wide windows, ocean light slanting in while the TV murmurs news about falling markets and border disputes. None of it reaches us.

I watch Wolf instead.

He holds his little sister in the crook of his arm. She's four months old and already controlling every man in the room. He nuzzles her nose with his, makes ridiculous snorting sounds, and whispers nonsense like it's classified information.

Her red hair declares allegiance to Frankie, but as she studies Wolf with a serious little face, her brows pinch in a severe expression that's pure Monty.

Whenever she throws a fit, she clenches her tiny fists. That's all Leo.

But right now she's calm, issuing small, satisfied grunts that are unmistakably Kody.

We were all here for her arrival. Frankie's husbands argued over names for weeks leading up to the birth. So Frankie solved it herself.

Kaya.

After Kody's mother. After Monty's childhood friend. The name stuck the second she said it.

Jag stands behind the couch with Monty, both of them half-turned toward the TV screen, deep into talks about global politics, fiscal consequences, or whatever boring shit they call relaxing. Jag is in his element, a hacktivist at heart. Monty counters a point. Jag nods and pushes back. It's a friendly chess match, all restraint and respect.

Frankie and I share the loveseat. She has that post-baby glow that's more about relief than sleep. She tells me about her return to the hospital after maternity leave and how much she needed to be a nurse again.

Monty slid easily into his new role as a stay-at-home father, taking the night shifts and controlling diaper changes and feeding schedules. Frankie talks about it like it's normal.

It is now.

I tell her about the car Wolf surprised me with last week. Another vintage beauty, rescued and ready to restore. He buys me a car for every occasion. Birthdays, anniversaries, holidays. Once, because I had a sinus infection.

My collection is obscene at this point, rivaling Luke's, and it makes me laugh every time I step into the garage. I love the cars, sure. But I love the way Wolf watches me work on them more.

Across the room, he pries his eyes off Kaya and looks up at me, giving me a blinding, proud, big-brother smile.

He's taken his art to the next level, past skill, past reputation, and into something that feels inevitable. Everyone at the citadel wears his work on their skin. Jag and I included.

He finished Jag's leg sleeve last month. It's a mural of places and moments, and at its center is the face of a blue-eyed Arctic wolf, its muzzle breaking through the surface of an icy river, in a rise of ink and smoke.

Mine is smaller, tucked high on my thigh. Wolf designed it exactly to my specifications. A circle formed by three figures in motion. A jaguar in mid-prowl. A wolf curved opposite it. At the center, a dove in flight.

I also have a Trail Cat on my arm, with a black shirt and red boots. Jag pets it every time he sees it.

Wolf has been working on himself, too. His scars keep him from touching his chest, so he inked upward and outward,

love

shading his throat, arms, and shoulders in symbols and fragments of his life. Not the bad parts. The good ones. Places. People. Moments that made him feel safe and alive. His ink is a record of joy, layered and intentional, growing as he does.

Jag glances over at me mid-sentence, checking in with a look that says, *You good?* I nod. Wolf grins and returns his attention to Kaya.

This is us now. No scrambling. No apologies. No waiting for the other shoe. We fit. We choose each other daily, without bargains or fear.

I'm deliriously happy. With Jag's protective love. With Wolf's feral devotion. With the life we built and keep choosing to live.

The broadcast in the background stutters, and a banner flashes across the TV screen.

Breaking News.

The living room shifts. Sound sharpens. My breath catches before I know why.

The anchor's voice turns grave as footage rolls through emails, voice recordings, and red strings connecting names I already know by heart.

Adrian Crowe's buried files and financial records have finally been dragged into the light. Decades of money trails. Front charities. Private jets. Offshore accounts.

Amid the flashing of videos and interviews are the words that fist my throat and pull me to my feet. Trafficking, underage girls, bought, moved, silenced...

Clips cut fast. A famous face, handcuffed and defeated. Another one, older and powerful, being rushed into a car. A Supreme Court justice, jaw clenched. A Hollywood legend, hiding his face. And the big one, the former U.S. president, surrounded by agents, his expression pale and furious.

I don't gasp. I already knew every monster's name.

The U.S. government has been trying to indict these powerful men for decades. And a criminal syndicate brought them down in twelve months.

That is vigilante justice.

Then the reporter says the one name I've been waiting for. The man who bought my mother from Adrian Crowe.

My vision blurs, and my chest caves in.

Jag found him months ago. He and Wolf went after him with single-minded focus and deadly patience, peeling apart his multibillion-dollar software empire piece by piece. Contracts voided. Boards turned. Allies gone. Billions of dollars rerouted to offshore accounts controlled by the cartel.

Now the truth is pouring out on live television, and there he is, dragged forward, wrists bound, eyes wild.

Exposed.

Finished.

The tears come, hot and relentless. I fold in on myself, and Jag is there instantly, arms around me, holding me as my legs give out and relief crashes in.

Wolf moves just as fast, passing Kaya to Leo before kneeling before me, kissing my cheeks, my forehead, my mouth. His own eyes shine, tears streaking down his face.

On the screen, the reporter mentions the ongoing speculation that Adrian Crowe was assassinated by an unknown terrorist group. The perpetrator remains at large.

Wolf looks at me. Then at Jag.

For one breathless second, we all stare at one another.

Then we break, laughing and crying at once, the sound torn out of us, ugly and free and impossible to stop.

The baby fusses somewhere behind us. The TV shuts off. The world finally shifts its weight.

I cling to them both, shaking, lighter than I've ever been.

It's over.

It's really fucking over.

wolfson
SEVENTY-FIVE

I sit on the edge of Frankie's bed and watch Kaya sleep.

She sprawls on her back, tiny fist curled, and mouth slack in perfect peace. I'm in love beyond words.

Today's my last day on the island before heading back to Colombia. I'll be back next month, but a month feels huge when she's this small. She'll grow and change and do something new I won't see.

The thought tightens my chest in a way I don't love.

Frankie stands at the window with her glass, bourbon catching the light and dark Amarena cherries bouncing along the bottom. She stares out at the ocean the way she often does, her mind somewhere else.

The image lines up too neatly with the details she wrote in her journal. The night she waited for Monty. The night Denver took her.

"Would you change anything?" I ask quietly.

"No. Nothing." She turns from the window, green eyes cloudless. Then a smile. "Everything brought us here. Full circle. Isn't it beautiful?"

Beautiful? Hmm. I never imagined a life where I worked for a cartel. Not once.

But that's not how I see this.

I was born in hell, raised there, hurt there, trapped inside it for twenty-three years with a devil who starved, raped, and broke me in places so dark I stopped hoping for daylight.

This path with the cartel? It isn't corruption.

It's redemption. Deliverance. Repossession of a stolen life. And justice for so many others.

I'm a vigilante. That part is obvious now. I move through the underworld, slaying monsters like the one who stole my childhood.

There will always be more Denver Strakhs. More Rhett Howells. More Adrian Crowes. The names change. The damage doesn't.

I don't pick the cities or the countries stamped on my passport. I don't kick in doors or spill blood in alleyways. Jag made damn sure of that.

But I'm traveling the world with him, sitting in surveillance vans and hotel rooms full of screens and murmuring voices, watching patterns tighten, lies unravel, and traps slam shut.

Dove travels with us, too. Always at our sides. Happy and safe.

But I'm not a saint.

When we're in Colombia, I let my inner wolf out. A wolf built in the Arctic Circle.

Cold taught me patience. Hunger taught me precision. Survival taught me how to play with blood. I know weapons. I know how fear sounds when it runs out of places to hide. That makes me useful in rooms where monsters finally have to answer for what they've done.

When the cartel needs information pulled from a human trafficker, I step in. I let my knives do the work and my animal nature sink into their bones.

In those moments, I don't see the prisoners.

I see the doctor.

I see Denver.

I see every night I suffered in pain.

And when I walk out of the torture room, Jag and Dove are always there. My hands are steady. My heart is clear, and the world is safer than it was before.

I love this life. The purpose. The rebellion. The savage annihilation of sexual predators and the systems that protect them. The way every day asks something of me and gives something back. It's an adventure shaped by survival and stubborn joy. It's more than I ever let myself want.

My life makes sense now.

With Dove and Jag.

With The Freedom Fighters.

I came full circle the long way around.

From victim to vigilante.

From prey to hunter.

From discarded to wanted.

From alone to ours.

From nothing to *this*.

"Yeah." I return Frankie's smile. "It's fucking beautiful."

I still go to therapy. That part doesn't stop just because my life finally fits.

Sometimes it's just me and the couch and the slow work of learning how to breathe through memories that still have teeth. Sometimes Dove comes with me. Sometimes Jag does. Sometimes all three of us sit together, laying our histories out on the table.

Sometimes, when I'm tired or caught off guard, a panic spike will sneak up on me. But they're smaller now. Shorter. Nothing like that day in the shower.

Talking helps. Dove, Jag, and I discuss our childhoods like adults. No competition. No minimizing. Just truth.

Jag talks about the streets and the things he did to keep Dove alive. Dove talks about guilt and anger and about learning to forgive a younger version of herself. I talk about Hoss and the cliff and the long road back into my skin.

We don't fix each other. We hold space. We check in. We laugh when things get heavy and stop when they need stopping.

Healing isn't loud. It's consistent. It's choosing to stay. It's waking up and realizing the night didn't take anything from us.

I still have scars. I always will. But they don't run the show anymore.

I do.

"You know…" Frankie's cheeks rise, dimpling with mischief. "I just saw Jag and Dove heading toward the dock. Definitely up to something."

"Don't do it. Don't—"

She makes a jerk-off gesture.

At my deadpan stare, she pushes her tongue into her cheek in a blow job motion.

"They're up to... What?" I mimic her tongue movement and squint at her. "Chewing tobacco? Practicing whale calls? Brushing their molars?"

She snorts through a laugh. "What am I going to do without you?"

"Oh, my little red wary berry." I walk toward her, open my arms, and gather her up. "You're going to enjoy the blessed silence for approximately twelve minutes before you miss me terribly and cry into your pillow." I kiss her cheek. "But don't worry. I'm extremely hard to get rid of."

"Fine. Go." She pushes me, grinning adorably. "Get out of here."

I wriggle my fingers at her and leave with a lingering look at Kaya's sleeping form.

Outside, I welcome the mild breeze. Summer in Colombia is thick and heavy, pressing in from every side. Sitka's summer is quieter. Lighter. It smells like salt and pine and cold water.

I stroll toward the dock as the sun slides into the ocean in a wash of gold and blue.

And there she is.

I bought a yacht.

Not just any yacht.

A floating Magic Kingdom.

Towers, turrets, and elaborate railings crank the castle-on-the-water vibes to eleven. A three-person throne sits on the upper deck. One of my favorite places to ride Jag's cock while Dove rides mine.

The figurehead on the bow features an ornate carving of a bare-breasted woman with wings for arms, stretched forward as if gliding over the sea. She does her job, protecting the crew, appeasing the sea gods, and turning me on every time I see her.

Her name shines in gold letters painted along the hull.

Blue Princess.

I love this ridiculous, beautiful thing. I love that I get to share it with them.

When we're in Alaska, we sleep on the yacht. Sometimes, we drift along the coastline and wake up to mountains. Or we follow the water south, all the way to the mainland.

I step onto the deck already grinning, my sandals flopping as the Blue Princess rocks beneath me. I'm ready to see my people, to steal a kiss, crack a joke, and rub dicks with Jag, hopefully while we're inside our woman.

I find them at the railing on the upper deck, silhouetted against the gloaming sky.

The view is spectacular, golden red bleeding into dark blue and catching the water on fire. Jag and Dove don't seem to notice, their attention rapt on each other.

He stands behind her, his face buried in her neck, and their bodies moving as one. Her skater dress is hiked to her tits, baring all her flawless skin for Jag's hands, as his cock slams inside her with zero apologies.

His shorts sag around his ankles, a testament to urgency and poor planning.

I hang back and watch. Because honestly? They're the best view in Alaska.

Jag is all force and intention, a man who chooses with his whole body. Dove is motion and attraction, gravity wrapped in skin. Together, they're my center of mass, the balance point of my existence.

I love them the way storms love coastlines, by shaping them, testing them, and returning again and again until the ground knows my name.

My love for them isn't soft. It's primal and permanent. It punctures with needles and leaves eternal marks. It says *Stay* and *Mine* and *Here* in the same breath.

Watching them pries me open. Radiance floods in. Calm locks into place, and I stand there grinning like I've cracked the code to the universe.

They're my northern lights.

My Arctic Circle.

My proof that happily-ever-afters exist.

He grips her chin and turns her head, capturing her lips in a savage kiss. Her hips buck helplessly as he drives her against the railing, rutting and groaning and devouring her mouth with a talented tongue.

His other hand works between her legs, parting her pussy for his relentless thrusts, fingers stroking her clit, and making her wild.

I'm so fucking hard it hurts.

"You better get over here before she comes." Jag lifts his head and finds my eyes.

"The question is..." I stroll toward them as if I don't have a pitched tent in my pants. "Which ass do I want tonight?"

Jag rarely bottoms. Like never. If I pushed for it, he would bend. But I prefer him topping. He's so fucking good at it.

"Mine." Dove moans. "Please, Wolf. Fuck my ass while he's inside my pussy."

That's her favorite.

"Grab the lube." Jag pivots, impaling her on his cock while his fingers spread her open for my eyes.

My pace quickens. I snag the lube from the cabinet on my way and shed my shorts before I reach them.

The rest of my clothes follow. Then lube. Then my hands are on her, skimming along her thighs, where they wrap around his waist. I cup her backside, grease her tiny back hole, and caress her cunt where it stretches around his thrusts.

"I love you," I say to them.

They exchange a glance, a flush of shared knowing, and turn to me, their faces warmed by the sinking sun.

"We love you," they answer together.

Their eyes glow, honey and amber blended into one quiet moment, and the world holds still long enough for me to know I'm exactly where I'm meant to be.

When I sink inside her ass, we all moan together.

The waning sunlight dances along our joined bodies, throwing shadows across his flexing muscles and catching the sheen of sweat on her skin.

We fuck against the railing with my back to the edge, rocking and kissing and chasing that blissful drop.

I angle backward over the rail with Jag and Dove in my arms and the world waiting below. When I dip too far, they twist and reach for me at the same time, hands grabbing and scrambling to pull me to safety.

"This is it." I straighten and kiss Dove, then Jag, laughing through it because my chest can't hold this much joy quietly. "This is my fairy tale."

Their grips tighten, and I know with complete certainty that they have me.

Forever after.

wolfson

They'll never let me fall.

Thank you for walking the edge of the world with these feral Alaskan men.

Do you want to read the origin story of
The Freedom Fighters?
It begins with Cole Hartman in the Tangled Lies trilogy, an angsty, epic love triangle.

Meet the The Freedom Fighters in the Deliver Series, a gritty, erotic, dark romance, where the main characters are murderers, kidnappers, human traffickers, and cartel.
Forget your comfort zones—this world isn't pretty.
But it's oh-so kinky and twisty.

RECOMMENDED READING ORDER
Tangled Lies Trilogy
One is a Promise
Two is a Lie
Three is a War

Deliver Series
Deliver (#1)
Vanquish (#2)
Disclaim (#3)
Devastate (#4)
Take (#5)
Manipulate (#6)
Unshackle (#7)
Dominate (#8)
Complicate (#9)

OTHER BOOKS BY PAM GODWIN

DARK COWBOY ROMANCE
TRAILS OF SIN
Knotted #1
Buckled #2
Booted #3

DARK PARANORMAL ROMANCE
TRILOGY OF EVE
Heart of Eve
Dead of Eve #1
Blood of Eve #2
Dawn of Eve #3

DARK HISTORICAL PIRATE ROMANCE
King of Libertines
Sea of Ruin

STUDENT-TEACHER / PRIEST
Lessons In Sin

STUDENT-TEACHER ROMANCE
Dark Notes

ROCK-STAR DARK ROMANCE
Beneath the Burn

BILLIONAIRE REVENGE
Dirty Ties

OLDER WOMAN/YOUNGER MAN
Incentive

New York Times, *Wall Street Journal*, and *USA Today* bestselling author, Pam Godwin, lives in the Midwest with her husband, cats, retired greyhounds, and an old, foul-mouthed parrot. She traveled the world for seven years, attended three universities, married the vocalist of her favorite rock band, and retired from her quantitative analyst career in 2014 to write full-time.

Her interests veer toward the unconventional: bourbon, full-body tattoos, and tragic villains. Equally peculiar are her aversions to sleeping, eating meat, and dolls with blinking eyes.

EMAIL: pamgodwinauthor@gmail.com

www.ingramcontent.com/pod-product-compliance
Lightning Source LLC
LaVergne TN
LVHW040034080526
838202LV00045B/3336